PRAISE FOR *NEW YORK TIMES*
BESTSELLING AUTHOR
JAMES LEE BURKE
AND HIS DAVE ROBICHEAUX NOVELS

"Burke's dialogue sounds true as a tape recording; his
writing about action is strong and economical. . . .
Burke is a prose stylist to be reckoned with."
—*Los Angeles Times Book Review*

"BURKE FLIES MILES ABOVE MOST
CONTEMPORARY CRIME NOVELISTS."
—*The Orlando Sentinel*

"Among writers in the genre, only Tony Hillerman's
novels about the Navajo tribal police match Burke's
ability to write evocatively about the natural
world. . . . It's hard to imagine readers not bolting
it down like a steaming plate of crawfish étouffée."
—*Entertainment Weekly*

"BURKE WRITES PROSE THAT HAS A
PRONOUNCED STREAK OF POETRY IN IT."
—*The New York Times*

"James Lee Burke isn't simply a crime writer—he's
the Graham Greene of the bayou."
—New York *Daily News*

"IF YOU HAVEN'T ALREADY DISCOVERED
BURKE'S NOVELS, FIND ONE!"
—*Chicago Tribune*

Please turn the page for more extraordinary acclaim. . . .

SUNSET LIMITED

JAMES LEE BURKE

A DELL BOOK

Published by
Dell Publishing
a division of
Bantam Doubleday Dell Publishing Group, Inc.
1540 Broadway
New York, New York 10036

ISBN: 0-440-29561-0

Reprinted by arrangement with Doubleday

Printed in the United States of America

November 1998

10 9 8 7 6 5 4 3 2

OPM

FOR BILL AND SUSAN NELSON

I would like to thank the following attorneys for all the legal information they have provided me in the writing of my books over the years: my son James L. Burke, Jr., and my daughter Alafair Burke and my cousins Dracos Burke and Porteus Burke.

I would also like once again to thank my wife Pearl, my editor Patricia Mulcahy, and my agent Philip Spitzer for the many years they have been on board.

I'd also like to thank my daughters Pamela McDavid and Andree Walsh, from whom I ask advice on virtually everything.

ONE

I HAD SEEN A DAWN like this one only twice in my life: once in Vietnam, after a Bouncing Betty had risen from the earth on a night trail and twisted its tentacles of light around my thighs, and years earlier outside of Franklin, Louisiana, when my father and I discovered the body of a labor organizer who had been crucified with sixteen-penny nails, ankle and wrist, against a barn wall.

Just before the sun broke above the Gulf's rim, the wind, which had blown the waves with ropes of foam all night, suddenly died and the sky became as white and brightly grained as polished bone, as though all color had been bled out of the air, and the gulls that had swooped and glided over my wake lifted into the haze and the swells flattened into an undulating sheet of liquid tin dimpled by the leathery backs of stingrays.

The eastern horizon was strung with rain clouds and the sun should have risen out of the water like a mist-shrouded egg yolk, but it didn't. Its red light mushroomed along the horizon, then rose into the sky in a cross, burning in the center, as though fire were trying to take the shape of a man, and the water turned the heavy dark color of blood.

Maybe the strange light at dawn was only coincidence and had nothing to do with the return to New Iberia of Megan Flynn, who, like a sin we had concealed in the confessional, vexed our conscience, or worse, rekindled our envy.

But I knew in my heart it was not coincidence, no more so than the fact that the man crucified against the barn wall was Megan's father and that Megan herself was waiting for me at my dock and bait shop, fifteen miles south of New Iberia, when Clete Purcel, my old Homicide partner from the First District in New Orleans, and I cut the engines on my cabin cruiser and floated through the hyacinths on our wake, the mud billowing in clouds that were as bright as yellow paint under the stern.

It was sprinkling now, and she wore an orange silk shirt and khaki slacks and sandals, her funny straw hat spotted with rain, her hair dark red against the gloom of the day, her face glowing with a smile that was like a thorn in the heart.

Clete stood by the gunnel and looked at her and puckered his mouth. "Wow," he said under his breath.

SHE WAS ONE OF those rare women gifted with eyes that could linger briefly on yours and make you feel, rightly or wrongly, you were genuinely invited into the mystery of her life.

"I've seen her somewhere," Clete said as he prepared to climb out on the bow.

"Last week's *Newsweek* magazine," I said.

"That's it. She won a Pulitzer Prize or something. There was a picture of her hanging out of a slick," he said. His gum snapped in his jaw.

She had been on the cover, wearing camouflage pants and a T-shirt, with dog tags around her neck, the downdraft of the British helicopter whipping her hair and flattening her clothes against her body, the strap of her camera laced around one wrist, while, below, Serbian armor burned in columns of red and black smoke.

But I remembered another Megan, too: the in-your-face orphan of years ago, who, with her brother, would run away from foster homes in Louisiana and Colorado, until they were old enough to finally disappear into that wandering army of fruit pickers and wheat harvesters whom their father, an unrepentant IWW radical, had spent a lifetime trying to organize.

I stepped off the bow onto the dock and walked toward my truck to back the trailer down the ramp. I didn't mean to be impolite. I admired the Flynns, but you paid a price for their friendship and proximity to the vessel of social anger their lives had become.

"Not glad to see me, Streak?" she said.

"Always glad. How you doin', Megan?"

She looked over my shoulder at Clete Purcel, who had pulled the port side of the boat flush into the rubber tires on my dock and was unloading the cooler and rods out of the stern. Clete's thick arms and fire-hydrant neck were peeling and red with fresh sunburn. When he stooped over with the cooler, his tropical shirt split across his back. He grinned at us and shrugged his shoulders.

"That one had to come out of the Irish Channel," she said.

"You're not a fisher, Meg. You out here on business?"

"You know who Cool Breeze Broussard is?" she asked.

"A house creep and general thief."

"He says your parish lockup is a toilet. He says your jailer is a sadist."

"We lost the old jailer. I've been on leave. I don't know much about the new guy."

"Cool Breeze says inmates are gagged and handcuffed to a detention chair. They have to sit in their own excrement. The U.S. Department of Justice believes him."

"Jails are bad places. Talk to the sheriff, Megan. I'm off the clock."

"Typical New Iberia. Bullshit over humanity."

"See you around," I said, and walked to my truck. Rain was pinging in large, cold drops on the tin roof of the bait shop.

"Cool Breeze said you were stand-up. He's in lockdown now because he dimed the jailer. I'll tell him you were off the clock," she said.

"This town didn't kill your father."

"No, they just put me and my brother in an orphanage where we polished floors with our knees. Tell your Irish friend he's beautiful. Come out to the house and visit us, Streak," she said, and walked across the dirt road to where she had parked her car under the trees in my drive.

Up on the dock, Clete poured the crushed ice and canned drinks and speckled trout out of the cooler. The trout looked stiff and cold on the board planks.

"You ever hear anything about prisoners being

gagged and cuffed to chairs in the Iberia Parish Prison?" I asked.

"That's what that was about? Maybe she ought to check out what those guys did to get in there."

"She said you were beautiful."

"She did?" He looked down the road where her car was disappearing under the canopy of oaks that grew along the bayou. Then he cracked a Budweiser and flipped me a can of diet Dr Pepper. The scar over his left eyebrow flattened against his skull when he grinned.

THE TURNKEY HAD BEEN a brig chaser in the Marine Corps and still wore his hair buzzed into the scalp and shaved in a razor-neat line on the back of his neck. His body was lean and braided with muscle, his walk as measured and erect as if he were on a parade ground. He unlocked the cell at the far end of the corridor, hooked up Willie Cool Breeze Broussard in waist and leg manacles, and escorted him with one hand to the door of the interview room, where I waited.

"Think he's going to run on you, Top?" I said.

"He runs at the mouth, that's what he does."

The turnkey closed the door behind us. Cool Breeze looked like two hundred pounds of soft black chocolate poured inside jailhouse denims. His head was bald, lacquered with wax, shiny as horn, his eyes drooping at the corners like a prizefighter's. It was hard to believe he was a second-story man and four-time loser.

"If they're jamming you up, Cool Breeze, it's not on your sheet," I said.

"What you call Isolation?"

"The screw says you asked for lockdown."

His wrists were immobilized by the cuffs attached to the chain around his waist. He shifted in his chair and looked sideways at the door.

"I was on Camp J up at Angola. It's worse in here. A hack made a kid blow him at gunpoint," he said.

"I don't want to offend you, Breeze, but this isn't your style."

"What ain't?"

"You're not one to rat out anybody, not even a bad screw."

His eyes shifted back and forth inside his face. He rubbed his nose on his shoulder.

"I'm down on this VCR beef. A truckload of them. What makes it double bad is I boosted the load from a Giacano warehouse in Lake Charles. I need to get some distance between me and my problems, maybe like in the Islands, know what I saying?"

"Sounds reasonable."

"No, you don't get it. The Giacanos are tied into some guys in New York City making dubs of movies, maybe a hundred t'ousand of them a week. So they buy lots of VCRs, cut-rate prices, Cool Breeze Midnight Supply Service, you wit' me?"

"You've been selling the Giacanos their own equipment? You're establishing new standards, Breeze."

He smiled slightly, but the peculiar downward slope of his eyes gave his expression a melancholy cast, like a bloodhound's. He shook his head.

"You still don't see it, Robicheaux. None of these guys are that smart. They started making dubs of them kung fu movies from Hong Kong. The money behind them kung fus comes from some very bad guys. You heard of the Triads?"

"We're talking about China White?"

"That's how it gets washed, my man."

I took out my business card and wrote my home number and the number of the bait shop on the back. I leaned across the table and slipped it in his shirt pocket.

"Watch your butt in here, Breeze, particularly that ex-jarhead."

"Meet the jailer. It's easy to catch him after five. He like to work late, when they ain't no visitors around."

MEGAN'S BROTHER CISCO OWNED a home up Bayou Teche, just south of Loreauville. It was built in the style of the West Indies, one story and rambling, shaded by oaks, with a wide, elevated gallery, green, ventilated window shutters, and fern baskets hanging from the eaves. Cisco and his friends, movie people like himself, came and went with the seasons, shooting ducks in the wetlands, fishing for tarpon and speckled trout in the Gulf. Their attitudes were those of people who used geographical areas and social cultures as play-grounds and nothing more. Their glittering lawn par-ties, which we saw only from the road through the myrtle bushes and azalea and banana trees that fringed his property, were the stuff of legend in our small sugar-cane town along the Teche.

I had never understood Cisco. He was tough, like his sister, and he had the same good looks they had both inherited from their father, but when his reddish-brown eyes settled on yours, he seemed to search inside your skin for something he wanted, perhaps coveted, yet couldn't define. Then the moment would pass and his attention would wander away like a balloon on the breeze.

He had dug irrigation ditches and worked the fruit orchards in the San Joaquin and had ended up in Hollywood as a road-wise, city-library-educated street kid who was dumbfounded when he discovered his handsome face and seminal prowess could earn him access to a movie lot, first as an extra, then as a stuntman.

It wasn't long before he realized he was not only braver than the actors whose deeds he performed but that he was more intelligent than most of them as well. He co-wrote scripts for five years, formed an independent production group with two Vietnam combat veterans, and put together a low-budget film on the lives of migrant farmworkers that won prizes in France and Italy.

His next film opened in theaters all over the United States.

Now Cisco had an office on Sunset Boulevard, a home in Pacific Palisades, and membership in that magic world where bougainvillea and ocean sun were just the token symbols of the health and riches that southern California could bestow on its own.

It was late Sunday evening when I turned off the state road and drove up the gravel lane toward his veranda. His lawn was blue-green with St. Augustine grass and smelled of chemical fertilizer and the water sprinklers twirling between the oak and pine trees. I could see him working out on a pair of parallel bars in the side yard, his bare arms and shoulders cording with muscle and vein, his skin painted with the sun's late red light through the cypresses on the bayou.

As always, Cisco was courteous and hospitable, but

in a way that made you feel his behavior was learned rather than natural, a barrier rather than an invitation.

"Megan? No, she had to fly to New Orleans. Can I help you with something?" he said. Before I could answer, he said, "Come on inside. I need something cold. How do you guys live here in the summer?"

All the furniture in the living room was white, the floor covered with straw mats, blond, wood-bladed ceiling fans turning overhead. He stood shirtless and barefooted at a wet bar and filled a tall glass with crushed ice and collins mix and cherries. The hair on his stomach looked like flattened strands of red wire above the beltline of his yellow slacks.

"It was about an inmate in the parish prison, a guy named Cool Breeze Broussard," I said.

He drank from his glass, his eyes empty. "You want me to tell her something?" he asked.

"Maybe this guy was mistreated at the jail, but I think his real problem is with some mobbed-up dudes in New Orleans. Anyway, she can give me a call."

"Cool Breeze Broussard. That's quite a name."

"It might end up in one of your movies, huh?"

"You can't ever tell," he replied, and smiled.

On one wall were framed still shots from Cisco's films, and on a side wall photographs that were all milestones in Megan's career: a ragged ditch strewn with the bodies of civilians in Guatemala, African children whose emaciated faces were crawling with blowflies, French Legionnaires pinned down behind sandbags while mortar rounds geysered dirt above their heads.

But, oddly, the color photograph that had launched her career and had made *Life* magazine was located at the bottom corner of the collection. It had been shot in the opening of a storm drain that bled into the Mississippi just as an enormous black man, in New Orleans City Prison denims strung with sewage, had burst out of the darkness into the fresh air, his hands raised toward the sun, as though he were trying to pay tribute to its energy and power. But a round from a sharpshooter's rifle had torn through his throat, exiting in a bloody mist, twisting his mouth open like that of a man experiencing orgasm.

A second framed photograph showed five uniformed cops looking down at the body, which seemed shrunken and without personality in death. A smiling crew-cropped man in civilian clothes was staring directly at the camera in the foreground, a red apple with a white hunk bitten out of it cupped in his palm.

"What are you thinking about?" Cisco asked.

"Seems like an inconspicuous place to put these," I said.

"The guy paid some hard dues. For Megan and me, both," he said.

"Both?"

"I was her assistant on that shot, inside the pipe when those cops decided he'd make good dog food. Look, you think Hollywood's the only meat market out there? The cops got citations. The black guy got to rape a sixteen-year-old white girl before he went out. I get to hang his picture on the wall of a seven-hundred-thousand-dollar house. The only person who didn't get a trade-off was the high school girl."

"I see. Well, I guess I'd better be going."

Through the French doors I saw a man of about

fifty walk down the veranda in khaki shorts and slippers with his shirt unbuttoned on his concave chest. He sat down in a reclining chair with a magazine and lit a cigar.

"That's Billy Holtzner. You want to meet him?" Cisco said.

"Who?"

"When the Pope visited the studio about seven years ago, Billy asked him if he had a script. Wait here a minute."

I tried to stop him but it was too late. The rudeness of his having to ask permission for me to be introduced seemed to elude him. I saw him bend down toward the man named Holtzner and speak in a low voice, while Holtzner puffed on his cigar and looked at nothing. Then Cisco raised up and came back inside, turning up his palms awkwardly at his sides, his eyes askance with embarrassment.

"Billy's head is all tied up with a project right now. He's kind of intense when he's in preproduction." He tried to laugh.

"You're looking solid, Cisco."

"Orange juice and wheat germ and three-mile runs along the surf. It's the only life."

"Tell Megan I'm sorry I missed her."

"I apologize about Billy. He's a good guy. He's just eccentric."

"You know anything about movie dubs?"

"Yeah, they cost the industry a lot of money. That's got something to do with this guy Broussard?"

"You got me."

When I walked out the front door the man in the

reclining chair had turned off the bug light and was smoking his cigar reflectively, one knee crossed over the other. I could feel his eyes on me, taking my measure. I nodded at him, but he didn't respond. The ash of his cigar glowed like a hot coal in the shadows.

TWO

THE JAILER, ALEX GUIDRY, LIVED outside of town on a ten-acre horse farm devoid of trees or shade. The sun's heat pooled in the tin roofs of his outbuildings, and grit and desiccated manure blew out of his horse lots. His oblong 1960s red-brick house, its central-air-conditioning units roaring outside a back window twenty-four hours a day, looked like a utilitarian fortress constructed for no other purpose than to repel the elements.

His family had worked for a sugar mill down toward New Orleans, and his wife's father used to sell Negro burial insurance, but I knew little else about him. He was one of those aging, well-preserved men with whom you associate a golf photo on the local sports page, membership in a self-congratulatory civic club, a charitable drive that is of no consequence.

Or was there something else, a vague and ugly story years back? I couldn't remember.

Sunday afternoon I parked my pickup truck by his stable and walked past a chain-link dog pen to the riding ring. The dog pen exploded with the barking of two German shepherds who caromed off the fencing, their teeth bared, their paws skittering the feces that lay baked on the hot concrete pad.

Alex Guidry cantered a black gelding in a circle, his booted calves fitted with English spurs. The gelding's neck and sides were iridescent with sweat. Guidry sawed the bit back in the gelding's mouth.

"What is it?" he said.

"I'm Dave Robicheaux. I called earlier."

He wore tan riding pants and a form-fitting white polo shirt. He dismounted and wiped the sweat off his face with a towel and threw it to a black man who had come out of the stable to take the horse.

"You want to know if this guy Broussard was in the detention chair? The answer is no," he said.

"He says you've put other inmates in there. For days."

"Then he's lying."

"You have a detention chair, though, don't you?"

"For inmates who are out of control, who don't respond to Isolation."

"You gag them?"

"No."

I rubbed the back of my neck and looked at the dog pen. The water bowl was turned over and flies boiled in the door of the small doghouse that gave the only relief from the sun.

"You've got a lot of room here. You can't let your dogs run?" I said. I tried to smile.

"Anything else, Mr. Robicheaux?"

"Yeah. Nothing better happen to Cool Breeze while he's in your custody."

"I'll keep that in mind, sir. Close the gate on your way out, please."

I got back in my truck and drove down the shell road toward the cattle guard. A half dozen Red Angus grazed in Guidry's pasture, while snowy egrets perched on their backs.

Then I remembered. It was ten or eleven years back, and Alex Guidry had been charged with shooting a neighbor's dog. Guidry had claimed the dog had attacked one of his calves and eaten its entrails, but the neighbor told another story, that Guidry had baited a steel trap for the animal and had killed it out of sheer meanness.

I looked into the rearview mirror and saw him watching me from the end of the shell drive, his legs slightly spread, a leather riding crop hanging from his wrist.

MONDAY MORNING I RETURNED to work at the Iberia Parish Sheriff's Department and took my mail out of my pigeonhole and tapped on the sheriff's office.

He tilted back in his swivel chair and smiled when he saw me. His jowls were flecked with tiny blue and red veins that looked like fresh ink on a map when his temper flared. He had shaved too close and there was a piece of bloody tissue paper stuck in the cleft in his chin. Unconsciously he kept stuffing his shirt down over his paunch into his gunbelt.

"You mind if I come back to work a week early?" I asked.

"This have anything to do with Cool Breeze Broussard's complaint to the Justice Department?"

"I went out to Alex Guidry's place yesterday. How'd we end up with a guy like that as our jailer?"

"It's not a job people line up for," the sheriff said. He scratched his forehead. "You've got an FBI agent in your office right now, some gal named Adrien Glazier. You know her?"

"Nope. How'd she know I was going to be here?"

"She called your house first. Your wife told her. Anyway, I'm glad you're back. I want this bullshit at the jail cleared up. We just got a very weird case that was thrown in our face from St. Mary Parish."

He opened a manila folder and put on his glasses and peered down at the fax sheets in his fingers. This is the story he told me.

THREE MONTHS AGO, UNDER a moon haloed with a rain ring and sky filled with dust blowing out of the sugarcane fields, a seventeen-year-old black girl named Sunshine Labiche claimed two white boys forced her car off a dirt road into a ditch. They dragged her from behind the wheel, walked her by each arm into a cane field, then took turns raping and sodomizing her.

The next morning she identified both boys from a book of mug shots. They were brothers, from St. Mary Parish, but four months earlier they had been arrested for a convenience store holdup in New Iberia and had been released for lack of evidence.

This time they should have gone down.

They didn't.

Both had alibis, and the girl admitted she had been smoking rock with her boyfriend before she was raped. She dropped the charges.

Late Saturday afternoon an unmarked car came to the farmhouse of the two brothers over in St. Mary Parish. The father, who was bedridden in the front room, watched the visitors, unbeknown to them, through a crack in the blinds. The driver of the car wore a green uniform, like sheriff's deputies in Iberia Parish, and sunglasses and stayed behind the wheel, while a second man, in civilian clothes and a Panama hat, went to the gallery and explained to the two brothers they only had to clear up a couple of questions in New Iberia, then they would be driven back home.

"It ain't gonna take five minutes. We know you boys didn't have to come all the way over to Iberia Parish just to change your luck," he said.

The brothers were not cuffed; in fact, they were allowed to take a twelve-pack of beer with them to drink in the back seat.

A half hour later, just at sunset, a student from USL, who was camped out in the Atchafalaya swamp, looked through the flooded willow and gum trees that surrounded his houseboat and saw a car stop on the levee. Two older men and two boys got out. One of the older men wore a uniform. They all held cans of beer in their hands; all of them urinated off the levee into the cattails.

Then the two boys, dressed in jeans and Clorox-stained print shirts with the sleeves cut off at the armpits, realized something was wrong. They turned and stared stupidly at their companions, who had stepped backward up the levee and were now holding pistols in their hands.

The boys tried to argue, holding their palms outward, as though they were pushing back an invisible adversary. Their arms were olive with suntan, scrolled with reformatory tattoos, their hair spiked in points with butch wax. The man in uniform raised his gun and shouted an unintelligible order at them, motioning at the ground. When the boys did not respond, the second armed man, who wore a Panama hat, turned them toward the water with his hand, almost gently, inserted his shoe against the calf of one, then the other, pushing them to their knees, as though he were arranging manikins in a show window. Then he rejoined the man in uniform up the bank. One of the boys kept looking back fearfully over his shoulder. The other was weeping uncontrollably, his chin tilted upward, his arms stiff at his sides, his eyes tightly shut.

The men with guns were silhouetted against a molten red sun that had sunk across the top of the levee. Just as a flock of ducks flapped across the sun, the gunmen clasped their weapons with both hands and started shooting. But because of the fading light, or perhaps the nature of their deed, their aim was bad.

Both victims tried to rise from their knees, their bodies convulsing simultaneously from the impact of the rounds.

The witness said, "Their guns just kept popping. It looked like somebody was blowing chunks out of a watermelon."

After it was over, smoke drifted out over the water and the shooter in the Panama hat took close-up flash pictures with a Polaroid camera.

"THE WITNESS USED A pair of binoculars. He says the guy in the green uniform had our department patch on his sleeve," the sheriff said.

"White rogue cops avenging the rape of a black girl?"

"Look, get that FBI agent out of here, will you?"

He looked at the question in my face.

"She's got a broom up her ass." He rubbed his fingers across his mouth. "Did I say that? I'm going to go back to the laundry business. A bad day used to be washing somebody's golf socks," he said.

I LOOKED THROUGH MY office window at the FBI agent named Adrien Glazier. She sat with her legs crossed, her back to me, in a powder-blue suit and white blouse, writing on a legal pad. Her handwriting was filled with severe slants and slashes, with points in the letters that reminded me of incisor teeth.

When I opened the door she looked at me with ice-blue eyes that could have been taken out of a Viking's face.

"I visited William Broussard last night. He seems to think you're going to get him out of the parish prison," she said.

"Cool Breeze? He knows better than that."

"Does he?"

I waited. Her hair was ash-blond, wispy and broken on the ends, her face big-boned and adversarial. She was one of those you instinctively know have a carefully nursed reservoir of anger they draw upon as needed, in the same way others make use of daily prayer. My stare broke.

"Sorry. Is that a question?" I said.

"You don't have any business indicating to this man you can make deals for him," she said.

I sat down behind my desk and glanced out the

window, wishing I could escape back into the coolness of the morning, the streets that were sprinkled with rain, the palm fronds lifting and clattering in the wind.

I picked up a stray paper clip and dropped it in my desk drawer and closed the drawer. Her eyes never left my face or relented in their accusation.

"What if the prosecutor's office does cut him loose? What's it to you?" I said.

"You're interfering in a federal investigation. Evidently you have a reputation for it."

"I think the truth is you want his *cojones* in a vise. You'll arrange some slack for him after he rats out some guys you can't make a case against."

She uncrossed her legs and leaned forward. She cocked her elbow on my desk and let one finger droop forward at my face.

"Megan Flynn is an opportunistic bitch. What she didn't get on her back, she got through posing as the Joan of Arc of oppressed people. You let her and her brother jerk your pud, then you're dumber than the people in my office say you are," she said.

"This has to be a put-on."

She pulled a manila folder out from under her legal pad and dropped it on my desk blotter.

"Those photos are of a guy named Swede Boxleiter. They were taken in the yard at the Colorado state pen in Canon City. What they don't show is the murder he committed in broad daylight with a camera following him around the yard. That's how good he is," she said.

His head and face were like those of a misshaped Marxist intellectual, the yellow hair close-cropped on the scalp, the forehead and brainpan too large, the cheeks tapering away to a mouth that was so small it looked obscene. He wore granny glasses on a chiseled nose, and a rotted and torn weight lifter's shirt on a torso that rippled with cartilage.

The shots had been taken from an upper story or guard tower with a zoom lens. They showed him moving through the clusters of convicts in the yard, faces turning toward him the way bait fish reflect light when a barracuda swims toward their perimeter. A fat man was leaning against the far wall, one hand squeezed on his scrotum, while he told a story to a half circle of his fellow inmates. His lips were twisted with a word he was forming, purple from a lollypop he had been eating. The man named Swede Boxleiter passed an inmate who held a tape-wrapped ribbon of silver behind his back. After Swede Boxleiter had walked by, the man whose palm seemed to have caught the sun like a heliograph now had his hands stuffed in his pockets.

The second-to-last photo showed a crowd at the wall like early men gathered on the rim of a pit to witness the death throes and communal roasting of an impaled mammoth.

Then the yard was empty, except for the fat man, the gash across his windpipe bubbling with saliva and blood, the tape-wrapped shank discarded in the red soup on his chest.

"Boxleiter is buddies with Cisco Flynn. They were in the same state home in Denver. Maybe you'll get to meet him. He got out three days ago," she said.

"Ms. Glazier, I'd like to—"

"It's Special Agent Glazier."

"Right. I'd like to talk with you, but . . . Look, why not let us take care of our own problems?"

"What a laugh." She stood up and gazed down at me. "Here it is. Hong Kong is going to become the property of Mainland China soon. There're some people we want to put out of business before we have to deal with Beijing to get at them. Got the big picture?"

"Not really. You know how it is out here in the provinces, swatting mosquitoes, arresting people for stealing hog manure, that sort of thing."

She laughed to herself and dropped her card on my desk, then walked out of my office and left the door open as though she would not touch anything in our department unless it was absolutely necessary.

AT NOON I DROVE down the dirt road by the bayou toward my dock and bait shop. Through the oak trees that lined the shoulder I could see the wide gallery and purple-streaked tin roof of my house up the slope. It had rained again during the morning, and the cypress planks in the walls were stained the color of dark tea, the hanging baskets of impatiens blowing strings of water in the wind. My adopted daughter Alafair, whom I had pulled from a submerged plane wreck out on the salt when she was a little girl, sat in her pirogue on the far side of the bayou, fly-casting a popping bug into the shallows.

I walked down on the dock and leaned against the railing. I could smell the salty odor of humus and schooled-up fish and trapped water out in the swamp. Alafair's skin was bladed with the shadows of a willow tree, her hair tied up on her head with a blue bandanna, her hair so black it seemed to fill with lights when she brushed it. She had been born in a primitive village in El Salvador, her family the target of death squads because they had sold a case of Pepsi-Cola to the rebels. Now she was almost sixteen, her Spanish and early childhood all but forgotten. But sometimes at night she cried out in her sleep and would have to be shaken from dreams filled with the marching boots of soldiers, peasants with their thumbs wired together behind them, the dry ratcheting sound of a bolt being pulled back on an automatic weapon.

"Wrong time of day and too much rain," I said.

"Oh, yeah?" she said.

She lifted the fly rod into the air, whipping the popping bug over her head, then laying it on the edge of the lily pads. She flicked her wrist so the bug popped audibly in the water, then a goggle-eye perch rose like a green-and-gold bubble out of the silt and broke the surface, its dorsal fin hard and spiked and shiny in the sunlight, the hook and feathered balsa-wood lure protruding from the side of its mouth.

Alafair held the fly rod up as it quivered and arched toward the water, retrieving the line with her left hand, guiding the goggle-eye between the islands of floating hyacinths, until she could lift it wet and flopping into the bottom of the pirogue.

"Not bad," I said.

"You had another week off. Why'd you go back to work?" she said.

"Long story. See you inside."

"No, wait," she said, and set her rod down in the pirogue and paddled across the bayou to the concrete boat ramp. She stepped out into the water with a stringer of catfish and perch wrapped around her wrist, and climbed the wood steps onto the dock. In the last two years all the baby fat had melted off her body, and her face and figure had taken on the appearance of a mature woman's. When she worked with me in the bait shop, most of our male customers made a point of focusing their attention everywhere in the room except on Alafair.

"A lady named Ms. Flynn was here. Bootsie told me what happened to her father. You found him, Dave?" she said.

"My dad and I did."

"He was crucified?"

"It happened a long time ago, Alf."

"The people who did it never got caught? That's sickening."

"Maybe they took their own fall down the road. They all do, one way or another."

"It's not enough." Her face seemed heated, pinched, as though by an old memory.

"You want some help cleaning those fish?" I asked.

Her eyes looked at me again, then cleared. "What would you do if I said yeah?" she asked. She swung the stringer so it touched the end of my polished loafer.

"MEGAN WANTS ME TO get her inside the jail to take pictures?" I said to Bootsie in the kitchen.

"She seems to think you're a pretty influential guy," she replied.

Bootsie was bent over the sink, scrubbing the burnt grease off a stove tray, her strong arms swollen with her work; her polo shirt had pulled up over her jeans, exposing the soft taper of her hips. She had the most beautiful hair I had ever seen in a woman. It was the color of honey, with caramel swirls in it, and its thickness and the way she wore it up on her head seemed to make the skin of her face even more pink and lovely.

"Is there anything else I can arrange? An audience with the Pope?" I said.

She turned from the drainboard and dried her hands on a towel.

"That woman's after something else. I just don't know what it is," she said.

"The Flynns are complicated people."

"They have a way of finding war zones to play in. Don't let her take you over the hurdles, Streak."

I hit her on the rump with the palm of my hand. She wadded up the dish towel and threw it past my head.

We ate lunch on the redwood table under the mimosa tree in the back yard. Beyond the duck pond at the back of our property my neighbor's sugarcane was tall and green and marbled with the shadows of clouds. The bamboo and periwinkles that grew along our coulee rippled in the wind, and I could smell rain and electricity in the south.

"What's in that brown envelope you brought home?" Bootsie asked.

"Pictures of a mainline sociopath in the Colorado pen."

"Why bring them home?"

"I've seen the guy. I'm sure of it. But I can't remember where."

"Around here?"

"No. Somewhere else. The top of his head looks like a yellow cake but he has no jaws. An obnoxious FBI agent told me he's pals with Cisco Flynn."

"A head like a yellow cake? A mainline con? Friends with Cisco Flynn?"

"Yeah."

"Wonderful."

That night I dreamed of the man named Swede Boxleiter. He was crouched on his haunches in the darkened exercise yard of a prison, smoking a cigarette, his granny glasses glinting in the humid glow of lights on the guard towers. The predawn hours were cool and filled with the smells of sage, water coursing over boulders in a canyon riverbed, pine needles layered on the forest floor. A wet, red dust hung in the air, and the moon seemed to rise through it, above the mountain's rim, like ivory skeined with dyed thread.

But the man named Swede Boxleiter was not one to concern himself with the details of the alpine environment he found himself in. The measure of his life and himself was the reflection he saw in the eyes of others, the fear that twitched in their faces, the unbearable tension he could create in a cell or at a dining table simply by not speaking.

He didn't need a punk or prune-o or the narcissistic pleasure of clanking iron in the yard or even masturbation for release from the energies that, unsatiated, could cause him to wake in the middle of the night and sit in a square of moonlight as though he were on an airless plateau that echoed with the cries of animals. Sometimes he smiled to himself and fantasized about telling the prison psychologist what he really felt inside, the pleasure that climbed through the tendons in his arm when he clasped a shank that had been ground from a piece of angle iron on an emery wheel in the shop, the intimacy of that last moment when he looked into the eyes of the hit. The dam that seemed to break in his loins was like water splitting the bottom of a paper bag.

But prison shrinks were not people you confided in, at least if you were put together like Swede Boxleiter and ever wanted to make the street again.

In my dream he rose from his crouched position, reached up and touched the moon, as though to despoil it, but instead wiped away the red skein from one corner with his fingertip and exposed a brilliant white cup of light.

I sat up in bed, the window fan spinning its shadows on my skin, and remembered where I had seen him.

EARLY THE NEXT MORNING I went to the city library on East Main Street and dug out the old *Life* magazine in which Megan's photos of a black rapist's death inside a storm drain had launched her career. Opposite the full-page shot of the black man reaching out futilely for the sunlight was the group photo of five uniformed cops staring down at his body. In the foreground was Swede Boxleiter, holding a Red Delicious apple with a white divot bitten out of it, his smile a thin worm of private pleasure stitched across his face.

BUT I WASN'T GOING to take on the Flynns' problems, I told myself, or worry about a genetic misfit in the Colorado pen.

I was still telling myself that late that night when Mout' Broussard, New Iberia's legendary shoeshine man and Cool Breeze's father, called the bait shop and told me his son had just escaped from the parish prison.

THREE

CAJUNS OFTEN HAVE TROUBLE WITH the *th* sound in English, and as a result they drop the *h* or pronounce the *t* as a *d*. Hence, the town's collectively owned shoeshine man, Mouth Broussard, was always referred to as Mout'. For decades he operated his shoeshine stand under the colonnade in front of the old Frederic Hotel, a wonderful two-story stucco building with Italian marble columns inside, a ballroom, a saloon with a railed mahogany bar, potted palms and slot and racehorse machines in the lobby, and an elevator that looked like a polished brass birdcage.

Mout' was built like a haystack and never worked without a cigar stub in the corner of his mouth. He wore an oversized gray smock, the pockets stuffed with brushes and buffing rags ribbed with black and oxblood stains. The drawers under the two elevated chairs on the stand were loaded with bottles of liquid polish, cans of wax and saddle soap, toothbrushes and steel dental picks he used to clean the welts and stitches around the edges of the shoe. He could pop his buffing rags with a speed and rhythm that never failed to command a silent respect from everyone who watched.

Mout' caught all the traffic walking from the Southern Pacific passenger station to the hotel, shined all the shoes that were set out in the corridors at night, and guaranteed you could see your face in the buffed point of your shoe or boot or your money would be returned. He shined the shoes of the entire cast of the 1929 film production of *Evangeline;* he shined the shoes of Harry James's orchestra and of U.S. Senator Huey Long just before Long was assassinated.

"Where is Cool Breeze now, Mout'?" I said into the phone.

"You t'ink I'm gonna tell you that?"

"Then why'd you call?"

"Cool Breeze say they gonna kill him."

"Who is?"

"That white man run the jail. He sent a nigger try to joog him in the ear with a wire."

"I'll be over in the morning."

"The morning? Why, t'ank you, suh."

"Breeze went down his own road a long time ago, Mout'."

He didn't reply. I could feel the late-summer heat and the closeness of the air under the electric light.

"Mout'?" I said.

"You right. But it don't make none of it easier. No suh, it surely don't."

At sunrise the next morning I drove down East Main, under the canopy of live oaks that spanned the street, past City Hall and the library and the stone grotto and statue of Christ's mother, which had once been the site of George Washington Cable's home, and the sidewalks cracked by tree roots and the blue-green lawns filled with hydrangeas and hibiscus and philodendron and the thick stand of bamboo that framed the yard of the 1831 plantation manor called The Shadows, and finally into the business district. Then I was on the west side of town, on back streets with open ditches, railroad tracks that dissected yards and pavement, and narrow paintless houses, in rows like bad teeth, that had been cribs when nineteenth-century trainmen used to drink bucket beer from the saloon with the prostitutes and leave their red lanterns on the gallery steps when they went inside.

Mout' was behind his house, flinging birdseed at the pigeons that showered down from the telephone wires into his yard. He walked bent sideways at the waist, his eyes blue with cataracts, one cheek marbled pink and white by a strange skin disease that afflicts people of color; but his sloped shoulders were as wide as a bull's and his upper arms like chunks of sewer pipe.

"It was a bad time for Breeze to run, Mout'. The prosecutor's office might have cut him loose," I said.

He mopped his face with a blue filling-station rag and slid the bag of birdseed off his shoulder and sat down heavily in an old barber's chair with an umbrella mounted on it. He picked up a fruit jar filled with coffee and hot milk from the ground and drank from it. His wide mouth seemed to cup around the bottom of the opening like a catfish's.

"He gone to church wit' me and his mother when he was a li'l boy," he said. "He played ball in the park, he carried the newspaper, he set pins in the bowling alley next to white boys and didn't have no trouble. It was New Orleans done it. He lived with his mother in the projects. Decided he wasn't gonna be no shoeshine man, have white folks tipping their cigar ashes down on his head, that's what he tole me."

Mout' scratched the top of his head and made a sound like air leaving a tire.

"You did the best you could. Maybe it'll turn around for him someday," I said.

"They gonna shoot him now, ain't they?" he said.

"No. Nobody wants that, Mout'."

"That jailer, Alex Guidry? He use to come down here when he was in collitch. Black girls was three dollars over on Hopkins. Then he'd come around the shoeshine stand when they was black men around, pick out some fella and keep looking in his face, not letting go, no, peeling the skin right off the bone, till the man dropped his head and kept his eyes on the sidewalk. That's the way it was back then. Now y'all done hired the same fella to run the jail."

Then he described his son's last day in the parish prison.

THE TURNKEY WHO HAD been a brig chaser in the Marine Corps walked down the corridor of the Isolation unit and opened up the cast-iron door to Cool Breeze's cell. He bounced a baton off a leather lanyard that was looped around his wrist.

"Mr. Alex says you going back into Main Pop. That is, if you want," he said.

"I ain't got no objection."

"It must be your birthday."

"How's that?" Cool Breeze said.

"You'll figure it out."

"I'll figure it out, huh?"

"You wonder why you people are in here? When you think an echo is a sign of smarts?"

The turnkey walked him through a series of barred doors that slid back and forth on hydraulically operated steel arms, ordered him to strip and shower, then handed him an orange jumpsuit and locked him in a holding cell.

"They gonna put Mr. Alex on suspension. But he's doing you right before he goes out. So that's why I say it must be your birthday," the turnkey said. He bounced the baton on its lanyard and winked. "When he's gone, I'm gonna be jailer. You might study on the implications."

At four that afternoon Alex Guidry stopped in front of Cool Breeze's cell. He wore a seersucker suit and red tie and shined black cowboy boots. His Stetson hung from his fingers against his pant leg.

"You want to work scrub-down detail and do sweep-up in the shop?" he asked.

"I can do that."

"You gonna make trouble?"

"Ain't my style, suh."

"You can tell any damn lie you want when you get out of here. But if I'm being unfair to you, you tell me to my face right now," he said.

"People see what they need to."

Alex Guidry turned his palm up and looked at it and picked at a callus with his thumb. He started to speak, then shook his head in disgust and walked down the corridor, the leather soles of his boots clicking on the floor.

Cool Breeze spent the next day scrubbing stone walls and sidewalks with a wire brush and Ajax, and at five o'clock reported to the maintenance shop to begin sweep-up. He used a long broom to push steel filings, sawdust, and wood chips into tidy piles that he shoveled onto a dustpan and dumped into a trash bin. Behind him a mulatto whose golden skin was spotted with freckles the size of dimes was cutting a design out of a piece of plywood on a jigsaw, the teeth ripping a sound out of the wood like an electrified scream.

Cool Breeze paid no attention to him, until he heard the plywood disengage from the saw. He turned his head out of curiosity just as the mulatto balled his fist and tried to jam a piece of coat-hanger wire, sharpened to a point like an ice pick and driven vertically through the wood handle off a lawn-mower starter rope, through the center of Cool Breeze's ear and into his brain.

The wire point laid open Cool Breeze's cheek from the jawbone to the corner of his mouth.

He locked his attacker's forearm in both his hands, spun with him in circles, then walked the two of them toward the saw that hummed with an oily light.

"Don't make me do it, nigger," he said.

But his attacker would not give up his weapon, and Cool Breeze drove first the coat hanger, then the balled fist and the wood plug gripped inside the palm into the saw blade, so that bone and metal and fingernails and wood splinters all showered into his face at once.

He hid inside the barrel of a cement mixer, where by all odds he should have died. He felt the truck slow at the gate, heard the guards talking outside while they walked the length of the truck with mirrors they held under the frame.

"We got one out on the ground. You ain't got him in your barrel, have you?" a guard said.

"We sure as hell can find out," the truck driver said.

Gears and cogs clanged into place, then the truck vibrated and shook and giant steel blades began turning inside the barrel's blackness, lifting curtains of wet cement into the air like cake dough.

"Get out of here, will you? For some reason that thing puts me in mind of my wife in the bathroom," the guard said.

Two hours later, on a parish road project south of town, Cool Breeze climbed from inside the cement mixer and lumbered into a cane field like a man wearing a lead suit, his lacerated cheek bleeding like a flag, the cane leaves edged with the sun's last red light.

"I DON'T BELIEVE IT, Mout'," I said.

"Man ain't tried to joog him?"

"That the jailer set it up. He's already going on suspension. He'd be the first person everyone suspected."

" 'Cause he done it."

"Where's Breeze?"

Mout' slipped his sack of birdseed over his shoulder and begin flinging handfuls into the air again. The pigeons swirled about his waxed bald head like snowflakes.

MY PARTNER WAS DETECTIVE Helen Soileau. She wore slacks and men's shirts to work, seldom smiled or put on makeup, and faced you with one foot cocked at an angle behind the other, in the same way a martial artist strikes a defensive posture. Her face was lumpy, her eyes unrelenting when they fixed on you, and her blond hair seemed molded to her head like a plastic wig. She leaned on my office windowsill with both arms and watched a trusty gardener edging the sidewalk. She wore a nine-millimeter automatic in a hand-tooled black holster and a pair of handcuffs stuck through the back of her gunbelt.

"I met Miss Pisspot of 1962 at the jail this morning," she said.

"Who?"

"That FBI agent, what's her name, Glazier. She thinks we set up Cool Breeze Broussard to get clipped in our own jail."

"What's your take on it?"

"The mulatto's a pipehead. He says he thought Breeze was somebody else, a guy who wanted to kill him because he banged the guy's little sister."

"You buy it?" I asked.

"A guy who wears earrings through his nipples? Yeah, it's possible. Do me a favor, will you?" she said.

"What's up?"

Her eyes tried to look casual. "Lila Terrebonne is sloshed at the country club. The skipper wants me to drive her back to Jeanerette."

"No, thanks."

"I could never relate to Lila. I don't know what it is. Maybe it's because she threw up in my lap once. I'm talking about your AA buddy here."

"She didn't call me for help, Helen. If she had, it'd be different."

"If she starts her shit with me, she's going into the

drunk tank. I don't care if her grandfather was a U.S. senator or not."

She went out to the parking lot. I sat behind my desk for a moment, then pinged a paper clip in the wastebasket and flagged down her cruiser before she got to the street.

LILA HAD A POINTED face and milky green eyes and yellow hair that was bleached the color of white gold by the sun. She was lighthearted about her profligate life, undaunted by hangovers or trysts with married men, laughing in a husky voice in nightclubs about the compulsions that every two or three years placed her in a hospital or treatment center. She would dry out and by order of the court attend AA meetings for a few weeks, working a crossword puzzle in the newspaper while others talked of the razor wire wrapped around their souls, or staring out the window with a benign expression that showed no trace of desire, remorse, impatience, or resignation, just temporary abeyance, like a person waiting for the hands on an invisible clock to reach an appointed time.

From her adolescent years to the present, I did not remember a time in her life when she was not the subject of rumor or scandal. She was sent off by her parents to the Sorbonne, where she failed her examinations and returned to attend USL with blue-collar kids who could not even afford to go to LSU in Baton Rouge. The night of her senior prom, members of the football team glued her photograph on the rubber machine in Provost's Bar.

When Helen and I entered the clubhouse she was by herself at a back table, her head wreathed in smoke from her ashtray, her unfilled glass at the ends of her fingertips. The other tables were filled with golfers and bridge players, their eyes careful never to light on Lila and the pitiful attempt at dignity she tried to impose on her situation. The white barman and the young black waiter who circulated among the tables had long since refused to look in her direction or hear her order for another drink. When someone opened the front door, the glare of sunlight struck her face like a slap.

"You want to take a ride, Lila?" I said.

"Oh, Dave, how are you? They didn't call you again, did they?"

"We were in the neighborhood. I'm going to get a membership here one day."

"The same day you join the Republican Party. You're such a riot. Would you help me up? I think I twisted my ankle," she said.

She slipped her arm in mine and walked with me through the tables, then stopped at the bar and took two ten-dollar bills from her purse. She put them carefully on the bar top.

"Nate, this is for you and that nice young black man. It's always a pleasure to see you all again," she said.

"Come back, Miss Lila. Anytime," the barman said, his eyes shifting off her face.

Outside, she breathed the wind and sunshine as though she had just entered a different biosphere. She blinked and swallowed and made a muted noise like she had a toothache.

"Please drive me out on the highway and drop me wherever people break furniture and throw bottles through glass windows," she said.

"How about home, instead?" I asked.

"Dave, you are a total drag."

"Better appreciate who your friends are, ma'am," Helen said.

"Do I know you?" Lila said.

"Yeah, I had the honor of cleaning up your—"

"Helen, let's get Miss Lila home and head back for the office."

"Oh, by all means. Yes, indeedy," Helen said.

WE DROVE SOUTH ALONG Bayou Teche toward Jeanerette, where Lila lived in a plantation home whose bricks had been dug from clay pits and baked in a kiln by slaves in the year 1791. During the Depression her grandfather, a U.S. senator, used dollar-a-day labor to move the home brick by brick on flatboats up the bayou from its original site on the Chitimacha Indian Reservation. Today, it was surrounded by a fourteen-acre lawn, live oak and palm trees, a sky-blue swimming pool, tennis courts, gazebos hung with orange passion vine, two stucco guest cottages, a flagstone patio and fountain, and gardens that bloomed with Mexicali roses.

But we were about to witness a bizarre spectacle when we turned onto the property and drove through the tunnel of oaks toward the front portico, the kind of rare event that leaves you sickened and ashamed for your fellow human beings. A movie set consisting of paintless shacks and a general store with a wide gallery set up on cinder blocks, put together from weathered cypress and rusted tin roofs and Jax beer and Hadacol signs to look like the quarters on a 1940s corporation farm, had been constructed on the lawn, a dirt road laid out and sprinkled with hoses in front of the galleries. Perhaps two dozen people milled around on the set, unorganized, mostly at loose ends, their bodies shiny with sweat. Sitting in the shade of a live oak tree by a table stacked with catered food was the director, Billy Holtzner, and next to him, cool and relaxed in yellow slacks and white silk shirt, was his friend and business partner, Cisco Flynn.

"Have you ever seen three monkeys try to fuck a football? I'd like to eighty-six the whole bunch but my father has a yen for a certain item. It tends to come in pink panties," Lila said from the back seat.

"We'll drop you at the porch, Lila. As far as I'm concerned, your car broke down and we gave you a lift home," I said.

"Oh, stop it. Both of you get down and have something to eat," she said. Her face had cleared in the way a storm can blow out of a sky and leave it empty of clouds and full of carrion birds. I saw her tongue touch her bottom lip.

"Do you need assistance getting inside?" Helen said.

"Assistance? That's a lovely word. No, right here will do just fine. My, hasn't this all been pleasant?" Lila said, and got out and sent a black gardener into the house for a shaker of martinis.

Helen started to shift into reverse, then stopped, dumbfounded, at what we realized was taking place under the live oak tree.

Billy Holtzner had summoned all his people around him. He wore khaki shorts with flap pockets and Roman sandals with lavender socks and a crisp print shirt with the sleeves folded in neat cuffs on his flaccid arms.

Except for the grizzled line of beard that grew along his jawline and chin, his body seemed to have no hair, as though it had been shaved with a woman's razor. His workmen and actors and grips and writers and camera people and female assistants stood with wide grins on their faces, some hiding their fear, others rising on the balls of their feet to get a better look, while he singled out one individual, then another, saying, "Have you been a good boy? We've been hearing certain rumors again. Come on now, don't be shy. You know where you have to put it."

Then a grown man, someone who probably had a wife or girlfriend or children or who had fought in a war or who at one time had believed his life was worthy of respect and love, inserted his nose between Billy Holtzner's index and ring fingers and let him twist it back and forth.

"That wasn't so bad, was it? Oh, oh, I see somebody trying to sneak off there. Oh, *Johnny* . . ." Holtzner said.

"These guys are out of a special basement, aren't they?" Helen said.

Cisco Flynn walked toward the cruiser, his face good-natured, his eyes earnest with explanation.

"Have a good life, Cisco," I said out the window, then to Helen, "Hit it."

"You don't got to me tell me, boss man," she replied, her head looking back over her shoulder as she steered, the dark green shadows of oak leaves cascading over the windshield.

FOUR

THAT NIGHT THE MOON WAS yellow above the swamp. I walked down to the dock to help Batist, the black man who worked for me, fold up the Cinzano umbrellas on our spool tables and close up the bait shop. There was a rain ring around the moon, and I pulled back the awning that covered the dock, then went inside just as the phone rang on the counter.

"Mout' called me. His son wants to come in," the voice said.

"Stay out of police business, Megan."

"Do I frighten you? Is that the problem here?"

"No, I suspect the problem is use."

"Try this: he's fifteen miles out in the Atchafalaya Basin and snakebit. That's not metaphor. He stuck his arm in a nest of them. Why don't you deliver a message through Mout' and tell him just to go fuck himself?"

After I hung up I flicked off the outside flood lamps. Under the moon's yellow light the dead trees in the swamp looked like twists of paper and wax that could burst into flame with the touch of a single match.

• • •

AT DAWN THE WIND was out of the south, moist and warm and checkered with rain, when I headed the cabin cruiser across a long, flat bay bordered on both sides by flooded cypress trees that turned to green lace when the wind bent their branches. Cranes rose out of the trees against a pink sky, and to the south storm clouds were piled over the Gulf and the air smelled like salt water and brass drying in the sun. Megan stood next to the wheel, a thermos cup full of coffee in her hand. Her straw hat, which had a round dome and a purple band on it, was crushed over her eyes. To get my attention, she clasped my wrist with her thumb and forefinger.

"The inlet past that oil platform. There's a rag tied in a bush," she said.

"I can see it, Megan," I replied. Out of the corner of my eye I saw her face jerk toward me.

"I shouldn't speak or I shouldn't touch? Which is it?" she said.

I eased back the throttle and let the boat rise on its wake and drift into a cove that was overgrown by a leafy canopy and threaded with air vines and dimpled in the shallows with cypress knees. The bow scraped, then snugged tight on a sandspit.

"In answer to your question, I was out at your brother's movie set yesterday. I've decided to stay away from the world of the Big Score. No offense meant," I said.

"I've always wondered what bank guards think all day. Just standing there, eight hours, staring at nothing. I think you've pulled it off, you know, gotten inside their heads."

I picked up the first-aid kit and dropped off the bow and walked through the shallows toward a beached houseboat that had rotted into the soft texture of moldy cardboard.

I heard her splash into the water behind me.

"Gee, I hope I can be a swinging dick in the next life," she said.

THE HOUSEBOAT FLOOR WAS tilted on top of the crushed and rusted oil drums on which it had once floated. Cool Breeze sat in the corner, dressed in clothes off a wash line, the wound in his cut face stitched with thread and needle, his left arm swollen like a black balloon full of water.

I heard Megan's camera start clicking behind me.

"Why didn't you call the Feds, Breeze?" I asked.

"That woman FBI agent wants me in front of a grand jury. She say I gonna stay in the system, too, till they done wit' me."

I looked at the electrical cord he had used for a tourniquet, the proud flesh that had turned the color of fish scale around the fang marks, the drainage that had left viscous green tailings on his shirt. "I tell you what, I'll dress those wounds, hang your arm in a sling, then we'll get a breath of fresh air," I said.

"You cut that cord loose, the poison gonna hit my heart."

"You're working on gangrene now, partner."

I saw him swallow. The whites of his eyes looked painted with iodine.

"You're jail-wise, Breeze. You knew the Feds would take you over the hurdles. Why'd you want to stick it to Alex Guidry?"

This is the story he told me while I used a rubber suction cup to draw a mixture of venom and infection from his forearm. As I listened on one knee, kneading the puncture wounds, feeling the pain in his body flicker like a candle flame under his skin, I could only wonder again at the white race's naïveté in always sending forth our worst members as our emissaries.

TWENTY YEARS AGO, DOWN the Teche, he owned a dirt-road store knocked together from scrap boards, tin stripped off a condemned rice mill, and Montgomery Ward brick that had dried out and crusted and pulled loose from the joists like a scab. He also had a pretty young wife named Ida, who cooked in a cafe and picked tabasco peppers on a corporate farm. After a day in the field her hands swelled as though they had been stung by bumblebees and she had to soak them in milk to relieve the burning in her skin.

On a winter afternoon two white men pulled up on the bib of oyster shell that served as a parking lot in front of the gallery, and the older man, who had jowls like a bulldog's and smoked a cigar in the center of his mouth, asked for a quart of moonshine.

"Don't tell me you ain't got it, boy. I know the man from Miss'sippi sells it to you."

"I got Jax on ice. I got warm beer, too. I can sell you soda pop. I ain't got no whiskey."

"That a fact? I'm gonna walk back out the door, then come back in. One of them jars you got in that box behind the motor oil better be on the counter or I'm gonna redecorate your store."

Cool Breeze shook his head.

"I know who y'all are. I done paid already. Why y'all giving me this truck?" he said.

The younger white man opened the screen door and came inside the store. His name was Alex Guidry, and he wore a corduroy suit and cowboy hat and western boots, with pointed, mirror-bright toes. The older man picked up a paper bag of deep-fried cracklings from the counter. The grease in the cracklings made dark stains in the paper. He threw the bag to the younger man and said to Cool Breeze, "You on parole for check writing now. That liquor will get you a double nickel. Your woman yonder, what's her name, Ida? She's a cook, ain't she?"

THE MAN WITH BULLDOG jowls was named Harpo Delahoussey, and he ran a ramshackle nightclub for redbones (people who are part French, black, and Indian) by a rendering plant on an oxbow off the Atchafalaya River. When the incinerators were fired up at the plant, the smoke from the stacks filled the nearby woods and dirt roads with a stench like hair and chicken entrails burned in a skillet. The clapboard nightclub didn't lock its doors from Friday afternoon until late Sunday night; the parking lot (layered with thousands of flattened beer cans) became a maze of gas-guzzlers and pickup trucks; and the club's windows rattled and shook with the reverberations of rub board and thimbles, accordion, drums, dancing feet, and electric guitars whose feedback screeched like fingernails on slate.

At the back, in a small kitchen, Ida Broussard sliced potatoes for french fries while caldrons of red beans and rice and robin gumbo boiled on the stove, a bandanna knotted across her forehead to keep the sweat out of her eyes.

But Cool Breeze secretly knew, even though he tried to deny it to himself, that Harpo Delahoussey had not blackmailed him simply to acquire a cook, or even to reinforce that old lesson that every coin pressed into your palm for shining shoes, cutting cane, chopping cotton, scouring ovens, dipping out grease traps, scrubbing commodes, cleaning dead rats from under a house, was dispensed by the hand of a white person in the same way that oxygen could be arbitrarily measured out to a dying hospital patient.

One night she wouldn't speak when he picked her up, sitting against the far door of the pickup truck, her shoulders rounded, her face dull with a fatigue that sleep never took away.

"He ain't touched you, huh?" Cool Breeze said.

"Why you care? You brung me to the club, ain't you?"

"He said the rendering plant gonna shut down soon. That mean he won't be needing no more cook. What you gonna do if I'm in Angola?"

"I tole you not to bring that whiskey in the store. Not to listen to that white man from Miss'sippi sold it to you. Tole you, Willie."

Then she looked out the window so he could not see her face. She wore a rayon blouse that had green and orange lights in it, and her back was shaking under the cloth, and he could hear her breath seizing in her throat, like hiccups she couldn't control.

HE TRIED TO GET permission from his parole officer to move back to New Orleans.

Permission denied.

He caught Ida inhaling cocaine off a broken mirror behind the house. She drank fortified wine in the morning, out of a green bottle with a screw cap that made her eyes lustrous and frightening. She refused to help out at the store. In bed she was unresponsive, dry when he entered her, and finally not available at all. She tied a perforated dime on a string around her ankle, then one around her belly so that it hung just below her navel.

"Gris-gris is old people's superstition," Cool Breeze said.

"I had a dream. A white snake, thick as your wrist, it bit a hole in a melon and crawled inside and ate all the meat out."

"We gonna run away."

"Mr. Harpo gonna be there. Your PO gonna be there. State of Lou'sana gonna be there."

He put his hand under the dime that rested on her lower stomach and ripped it loose. Her mouth parted soundlessly when the string razored burns along her skin.

The next week he walked in on her when she was naked in front of the mirror. A thin gold chain was fastened around her hips.

"Where you get that?" he asked.

She brushed her hair and didn't answer. Her breasts looked as swollen and full as eggplants.

"You ain't got to cook at the club no more. What they gonna do? Hurt us more than they already have?" he said.

She took a new dress off a hanger and worked it

over her head. It was red and sewn with colored glass beads like an Indian woman might wear.

"Where you got money for that?" he asked.

"Mine to know, yours to find out," she replied. She fastened a hoop earring to her lobe with both hands, smiling at him while she did it.

He began shaking her by the shoulders, her head whipping like a doll's on her neck, her eyelids closed, her lipsticked mouth open in a way that made his phallus thicken in his jeans. He flung her against the bedroom wall, so hard he heard her bones knock into the wood, then ran from the house and down the dirt road, through a tunnel of darkened trees, his brogans exploding through the shell of ice on the chuckholes.

IN THE MORNING HE tried to make it up to her. He warmed boudin and fixed cush-cush and coffee and hot milk, and set it all out on the table and called her into the kitchen. The dishes she didn't smash on the wall she threw into the back yard.

He drove his pickup truck through the bright coldness of the morning, the dust from his tires drifting out onto the dead hyacinths and the cattails that had winter-killed in the bayou, and found Harpo Delahoussey at the filling station he owned in town, playing dominoes with three other white men at a table by a gas stove that hissed with blue flame. Delahoussey wore a fedora, and a gold badge on the pocket of his white shirt. None of the men at the table looked up from their game. The stove filled the room with a drowsy, controlled warmth and the smell of shaving cream and aftershave lotion and testosterone.

"My wife ain't gonna be working at the club no more," Cool Breeze said.

"Okay," Delahoussey said, his eyes concentrated on the row of dominoes in front of him.

The room seemed to scream with silence.

"Mr. Harpo, maybe you ain't understood me," Cool Breeze said.

"He heard you, boy. Now go on about your business," one of the other men said.

A moment later, by the door of his truck, Cool Breeze looked back through the window. Even though he was outside, an oak tree swelling with wind above his head, and the four domino players were in a small room beyond a glass, he felt it was he who was somehow on display, in a cage, naked, small, an object of ridicule and contempt.

Then it hit him: *He's old. An old man like that, one piece of black jelly roll just the same as another. So who give her the dress and wrap the gold chain around her stomach?*

He wiped his forehead on the sleeve of his canvas coat. His ears roared with sound and his heart thundered in his chest.

HE WOKE IN THE middle of the night and put on an overcoat and sat under a bare lightbulb in the kitchen, poking at the ashes in the wood stove, wadding up paper and feeding sticks into the flame that wouldn't catch, the cold climbing off the linoleum through his socks and into his ankles, his confused thoughts wrapped around his face like a net.

What was it that tormented him? Why was it he couldn't give it words, deal with it in the light of day, push it out in front of him, even kill it if he had to?

His breath fogged the air. Static electricity crackled in the sleeves of his overcoat and leaped off his fingertips when he touched the stove.

He wanted to blame Harpo Delahoussey. He remembered the story his daddy, Mout', had told him of the black man from Abbeville who broke off a butcher knife in the chest of a white overseer he caught doing it with his wife against a tree, then had spit in the face of his executioner before he was gagged and hooded with a black cloth and electrocuted.

He wondered if he could ever possess the courage of a man like that.

But he knew Delahoussey was not the true source of the anger and discontent that made his face break a sweat and his palms ring as though they had been beaten with boards.

He had accepted his role as cuckold, had even transported his wife to the site of her violation by a white man (and later, from Ida's mother, he would discover the exact nature of what Harpo Delahoussey did to her), because his victimization had justified a lifetime of resentment toward those who had forced his father to live gratefully on tips while their cigar ashes spilled down on his shoulders.

Except his wife had now become a willing participant. Last night she had ironed her jeans and shirt and laid them out on the bed, put perfume in her bathwater, washed and dried her hair and rouged her cheekbones to accentuate the angular beauty of her face. Her skin had seemed to glow when she dried herself in front of the mirror, a tune humming in her throat. He tried to confront her, force the issue, but her eyes were veiled with secret expectations and private meaning that made him ball his hands into fists. When he refused to drive her to the nightclub, she called a cab.

The fire wouldn't catch. An acrid smoke, as yellow as rope, laced with a stench of rags or chemically treated wood, billowed into his face. He opened all the windows, and frost speckled on the wallpaper and kitchen table. In the morning, the house smelled like a smoldering garbage dump.

She dressed in a robe, closed the windows, opened the air lock in the stove by holding a burning newspaper inside the draft, then began preparing breakfast for herself at the drainboard. He sat at the table and stared at her back stupidly, hoping she would reach into the cabinet, pull down a bowl or cup for him, indicate in some way they were still the people they once were.

"He tole me, you shake me again, you going away, Willie," she said.

"Who say that?"

She walked out of the room and didn't answer.

"Who?" he called after her.

IT WAS THE LETTER that did it.

Or the letter that he didn't read in its entirety, at least not until later.

He had driven the truck back from the store, turned into his yard, and seen her behind the house, pulling her undergarments, jeans, work shirts, socks, and dresses, her whole wardrobe, off the wash line.

A letter written with a pencil stub on a sheet of lined paper, torn from a notebook, lay on the coffee table in the living room.

He could hear his breath rising and falling in his

mouth when he picked it up, his huge hand squeezing involuntarily on the bottom of the childlike scrawl.

Dear Willie,

You wanted to know who the man was I been sleeping with. I am telling you his name not out of meaness but because you will find out anyway and I dont want you to go back to prison. Alex Guidry was good to me when you were willing to turn me over to Mr. Harpo because of some moonshine whisky. You cant know what it is like to have that old man put his hand on you and tell you to come into the shed with him and make you do the things I had to do. Alex wouldnt let Mr. Harpo bother me any more and I slept with him because I wanted to and—

He crumpled up the paper in his palm and flung it into the corner. In his mind's eye he saw Alex Guidry's fish camp, Guidry's corduroy suit and western hat hung on deer antlers, and Guidry himself mounted between Ida's legs, his muscled buttocks thrusting his phallus into her, her fingers and ankles biting for purchase into his white skin.

Cool Breeze hurled the back screen open and attacked her in the yard. He slapped her face and knocked her into the dust, then picked her up and shook her and shoved her backward onto the wood steps. When she tried to straighten her body with the heels of her hands, pushing herself away from him simultaneously, he saw the smear of blood on her mouth and the terror in her eyes, and realized, for the first time in his life, the murderous potential and level of self-hatred that had always dwelled inside him.

He tore down the wash line and kicked over the

basket that was draped with her clothes. The leafless branches of the pecan tree overhead exploded with the cawing of crows. He didn't hear the truck engine start in the front and did not realize she was gone, that he was alone in the yard with his rage, until he saw the truck speeding into the distance, the detritus of the sugarcane harvest spinning in its vacuum.

TWO DUCK HUNTERS FOUND her body at dawn, in a bay off the Atchafalaya River. Her fingers were coated with ice and extended just above the water's surface, the current silvering across the tips. A ship's anchor chain, one with links as big as bricks, was coiled around her torso like a fat serpent. The hunters tied a Budweiser carton to her wrist to mark the spot for the sheriff's department.

A week later Cool Breeze found the crumpled paper he had flung in the corner. He spread it flat on the table and began reading where he had left off before he had burst into the back yard and struck her across the face.

I slept with him because I wanted to and because I was so mad at you and hurt over what you did to the wife that has always loved you.

But Alex Guidry dont want a blak girl in his life, at least not on the street in the day lite. I know that now and I dont care and I tole him that. I will leave if you want me to and not blame you for it. I just want to say I am sorry for treating you so bad but it was like you had thrown me away forever.

Your wife,

Ida Broussard

• • •

COOL BREEZE LAY ON a row of air cushions inside the cabin cruiser, his arm in a sling, his face sweating. When he had finished speaking, Megan looked at me sadly, her eyes prescient with the knowledge that a man's best explanation for his life can be one that will never satisfy him or anybody else.

"Y'all ain't gonna say nothing?" he asked.

"Let go of it, partner," I said.

"The Man always got the answer," he replied.

"Your daddy is an honest and decent person. If you're still ashamed of him because he shined shoes, yeah, I think that's a problem, Breeze," I said.

"*Dave . . .*" Megan said.

"Give it a break, Megan," I said.

"No . . . Behind us. The G sent us an escort," she said.

I turned and looked back through the hatch at our wake. Coming hard right up the trough was a large powerboat, its enamel-white bow painted with the blue-and-red insignia of the United States Coast Guard. A helicopter dipped out of the sky behind the Coast Guard boat, yawing, its downdraft hammering the water.

I entered a channel that led to the boat ramp where my truck and boat trailer were parked. The helicopter swept past us and landed in the shell parking area below the levee. The right-hand door opened and the FBI agent named Adrien Glazier stepped out and walked toward us while the helicopter's blades were still spinning.

I waded through the shallows onto the concrete ramp.

"You're out of your jurisdiction, so I'm going to save you a lot of paperwork," she said.

"Oh?"

"We're taking Mr. William Broussard into our custody. Interstate transportation of stolen property. You want to argue about it, we can talk about interference with a federal law officer in the performance of her duty."

Then I saw her eyes focus over my shoulder on Megan, who stood on the bow of my boat, her hair blowing under her straw hat.

"You take one picture out here and I'll have you in handcuffs," Adrien Glazier said.

"Broussard's been snakebit. He needs to be in a hospital," I said.

But she wasn't listening. She and Megan stared at each other with the bright and intimate recognition of old adversaries who might have come aborning from another time.

FIVE

THE NEXT DAY AT LUNCHTIME Clete Purcel picked me up at the office in the chartreuse Cadillac convertible that he had bought from a member of the Giacano crime family in New Orleans, a third-generation miscreant by the name of Stevie Gee who decided to spot-weld a leak in the gas tank but got drunk first and forgot to fill the tank with water before he fired up the welding machine. The scorch marks had faded now and looked like smoky gray tentacles on the back fenders.

The back seat was loaded with fishing rods, a tackle box that was three feet long, an ice chest, air cushions, crushed beer cans, life preservers, crab traps, a hoop net that had been ground up in a boat propeller, and a tangled trot line whose hooks were ringed with dried smelt.

Clete wore baggy white pants without a shirt and a powder-blue porkpie hat, and his skin looked bronzed and oily in the sun. He had been the best cop I ever knew until his career went south, literally, all the way to

Central America, because of marriage trouble, pills, booze, hookers, indebtedness to shylocks, and finally a murder warrant that his fellow officers barely missed serving on him at the New Orleans airport.

I went inside Victor's on Main Street for a take-out order, then we crossed the drawbridge over Bayou Teche and drove past the live oaks on the lawn of the gray and boarded-up buildings that used to be Mount Carmel Academy, then through the residential section into City Park. We sat at a picnic table under a tree, not far from the swimming pool, where children were cannonballing off the diving board. The sun had gone behind the clouds and rain rings appeared soundlessly on the bayou's surface, like bream rising to feed.

"That execution in St. Mary Parish . . . the two brothers who got clipped after they raped the black girl? How bad you want the perps?" he said.

"What do you think?"

"I see it as another parish's grief. As a couple of guys who got what they had coming."

"The shooters had one of our uniforms."

He set down the pork-chop sandwich he was eating and scratched the scar that ran through his left eyebrow.

"I'm still running down skips for Nig Rosewater and Wee Willie Bimstine. Nig went bail for a couple of chippies who work a regular Murphy game in the Quarter. They're both junkies, runny noses, scabs on their thighs, mainlining six and seven balloons a day, sound familiar, scared shitless of detoxing in City Prison, except they're even more scared of their pimp, who's the guy they have to give up if they're going to beat the Murphy beef.

"So they ask Nig if they should go to the prosecutor's office with this story they got off a couple of johns who acted like over-the-hill cops. These guys were talking to each other about capping some brothers out in the Basin. One of the chippies asks if they're talking about black guys. One duffer laughs and says, 'No, just some boys who should have kept practicing on colored girls and left white bread alone.' "

"Where are these guys out of?"

"They said San Antone. But johns usually lie."

"What else do the girls know?"

"They're airheads, Dave. The intellectual one reads the shopping guide on the toilet. Besides, they're not interested in dealing anymore. Their pimp decided to plea out, so they're off the hook."

"Write down their names, will you?"

He took a piece of folded paper from his pants pocket, with the names of the two women and their addresses already written on it, and set it on the plank table. He started eating again, his green eyes smiling at nothing.

"Old lesson from the First District, big mon. When somebody wastes a couple of shit bags . . ." He realized I wasn't listening, that my gaze was focused over his shoulder on the swimming pool. He turned and stared through the tree trunks, his gaze roving across the swimmers in the pool, the parents who were walking their children by the hand to an instruction class a female lifeguard was putting together in the shallow end. Then his eyes focused on a man who stood between the wire enclosure and the bathhouse.

The man had a peroxided flattop, a large cranium, like a person with water on the brain, cheekbones that tapered in an inverted triangle to his chin, a small mouth full of teeth. He wore white shoes and pale orange slacks and a beige shirt with the short sleeves rolled in neat cuffs and the collar turned up on the neck. He pumped a blue rubber ball in his right palm.

"You know that dude?" Clete said.

"His name's Swede Boxleiter."

"A graduate?"

"Canon City, Colorado. The FBI showed me some photos of a yard job he did on a guy."

"What's he doing around here?"

Boxleiter wore shades instead of the granny glasses I had seen in the photos. But there was no doubt about the object of his attention. The children taking swim lessons were lined up along the edge of the pool, their swimsuits clinging wetly to their bodies. Boxleiter snapped the rubber ball off the pavement, ricocheting it against the bathhouse wall, retrieving it back into his palm as though it were attached to a magic string.

"Excuse me a minute," I said to Clete.

I walked through the oaks to the pool. The air smelled of leaves and chlorine and the rain that was sprinkling on the heated cement. I stood two feet behind Boxleiter, who hung on to the wire mesh of the fence with one hand while the other kneaded the rubber ball. The green veins in his forearm were pumped with blood. He chewed gum, and a lump of cartilage expanded and contracted against the bright slickness of his jaw.

He felt my eyes on the back of his neck.

"You want something?" he asked.

"We thought we'd welcome you to town. Have you drop by the department. Maybe meet the sheriff."

He grinned at the corner of his mouth.

"You think you seen me somewhere?"

I continued to stare into his face, not speaking. He removed his shades, his eyes askance.

"Soooo, what kind of gig are we trying to build here?" he asked.

"I don't like the way you look at children."

"I'm looking at a swimming pool. But I'll move."

"We nail you on a short-eyes here, we'll flag your jacket and put you in lockdown with some interesting company. This is Louisiana, Swede."

He rolled the rubber ball down the back of his forearm, off his elbow, and caught it in his palm, all in one motion. Then he rolled it back and forth across the top of his fingers, the gum snapping in his jaw all the while.

"I went out max time. You got no handle. I got a job, too. In the movies. I'm not shitting you on that," he said.

"Watch your language, please."

"My language? Wow, I love this town already." Then his face tilted, disconcerted, his breath drawing through his nose like an animal catching a scent. "Why's Blimpo staring at me like that?"

I turned and saw Clete Purcel standing behind me. He grinned and took out his comb and ran it through his sandy hair with both hands. The skin under his arms was pink with sunburn.

"You think I got a weight problem?" he asked.

"No. 'Cause I don't know you. I don't know what kind of problem you got."

"Then why'd you call me Blimpo?"

"So maybe I didn't mean anything by it."

"I think you did."

But Boxleiter turned his back on us, his attention fixed on the deep end of the pool, his right hand opening and closing on the blue rubber ball. The wind blew lines in his peroxided hair, and his scalp had the dead gray color of putty. His lips moved silently.

"What'd you say?" Clete asked. When Boxleiter didn't reply, Clete fitted his hand under Boxleiter's arm and turned him away from the fence. "You said, 'Blow me, Fatso'?"

Boxleiter slipped the ball in his pocket and looked out into the trees, his hands on his hips.

"It's a nice day. I'm gonna buy me a sno'ball. I love the spearmint sno'balls they sell in this park. You guys want one?" he said.

We watched him walk away through the trees, the leaves crunching under his feet like pecan shells, toward a cold drink stand and ice machine a black man had set up under a candy-striped umbrella.

"Like the boy says, he doesn't come with handles," Clete said.

THAT AFTERNOON THE SHERIFF called me into his office. He was watering his window plants with a hand-painted teakettle, smoking his pipe at the same time. His body was slatted with light through the blinds, and beyond the blinds I could see the whitewashed crypts in the old Catholic cemetery.

"I got a call from Alex Guidry. You reported him to the Humane Society?" he said.

"He keeps his dogs penned on a filthy concrete slab without shade."

"He claims you're harassing him."

"What did the Humane Society say?"

"They gave him a warning and told him they'd be back. Watch your back with this character, Dave."

"That's it?"

"No. The other problem is your calls to the FBI in New Orleans. They're off our backs for a while. Why stir them up?"

"Cool Breeze should be in our custody. We're letting the Feds twist him to avoid a civil suit over the abuse of prisoners in our jail."

"He's a four-time loser, Dave. He's not a victim. He fed a guy into an electric saw."

"I don't think it's right."

"Tell that to people when we have to pass a parish sales tax to pay off a class action suit, particularly one that will make a bunch of convicts rich. I take that back. Tell it to that female FBI agent. She was here while you were out to lunch. I really enjoyed the half hour I spent listening to her."

"Adrien Glazier was here?"

IT WAS FRIDAY, AND when I drove home that evening I should have been beginning a fine weekend. Instead, she was waiting for me on the dock, a cardboard satchel balanced on the railing under her hand. I parked the car in the drive and walked down to meet her. She looked hot in her pink suit, her ice-blue eyes filmed from the heat or the dust on the road.

"You've got Breeze in lockdown and everybody around here scared. What else do you want, Ms. Glazier?"

"It's Special Agent Gla—"

"Yeah, I know."

"You and Megan Flynn are taking this to the media, aren't you?"

"No. At least I'm not."

"Then why do both of you keep calling the Bureau?"

"Because I'm being denied access to a prisoner who escaped from our jail, that's why."

She stared hard into my face, as though searching for the right dials, her back teeth grinding softly, then said, "I want you to look at a few more photos."

"No."

"What's the matter, you don't want to see the wreckage your gal leaves in her wake?"

She pulled the elastic cord loose from the cardboard satchel and spilled half the contents on a spool table. She lifted up a glossy eight-by-ten black-and-white photo of Megan addressing a crowd of Latin peasants from the bed of a produce truck. Megan was leaning forward, her small hands balled into fists, her mouth wide with her oration.

"Here's another picture taken a few days later. If you look closely, you'll recognize some of the dead people in the ditch. They were in the crowd that listened to Megan Flynn. Where was she when this happened? At the Hilton in Mexico City."

"You really hate her, don't you?"

I heard her take a breath, like a person who has stepped into fouled air.

"No, I don't hate her, sir. I hate what she does. Other people die so she can feel good about herself," she said.

I sifted through the photos and news clippings with my fingers. I picked up one that had been taken from the *Denver Post* and glued on a piece of cardboard backing. Adrien Glazier was two inches away from my skin. I could smell perspiration and body powder in her clothes. The news article was about thirteen-year-old Megan Flynn winning first prize in the *Post*'s essay contest. The photo showed her sitting in a chair, her hands folded demurely in her lap, her essay medal worn proudly on her chest.

"Not bad for a kid in a state orphanage. I guess that's the Megan I always remember. Maybe that's why I still think of her as one of the most admirable people I've ever known. Thanks for coming by," I said, and walked up the slope through the oak and pecan trees on my lawn, and on into my lighted house, where my daughter and wife waited supper for me.

MONDAY MORNING HELEN SOILEAU came into my office and sat on the corner of my desk.

"I was wrong about two things," she said.

"Oh?"

"The mulatto who tried to do Cool Breeze, the guy with the earring through his nipple? I said maybe I bought his story, he thought Breeze was somebody else? I checked the visitors' sheet. A lawyer for the Giacano family visited him the day before."

"You're sure?"

"Whiplash Wineburger. You ever meet him?"

"Whiplash represents other clients, too."

"Pro bono for a mulatto who works in a rice mill?"

"Why would the Giacanos want to do an inside hit on a guy like Cool Breeze Broussard?"

She raised her eyebrows and shrugged.

"Maybe the Feds are squeezing Breeze to bring

pressure on the Giacanos," I said, in answer to my own question.

"To make them cooperate in an investigation of the Triads?"

"Why not?"

"The other thing I was going to tell you? Last night Lila Terrebonne went into that new zydeco dump on the parish line. She got into it with the bartender, then pulled a .25 automatic on the bouncer. A couple of uniforms were the first guys to respond. They got her purse from her with the gun in it without any problem. Then one of them brushed against her and she went ape shit.

"Dave, I put my arm around her and walked her out the back door, into the parking lot, with nobody else around, and she cried like a kid in my arms . . . You following me?"

"Yeah, I think so," I said.

"I don't know who did it, but I know what's been done to her," she said. She stood up, flexed her back, and inverted the flats of her hands inside the back of her gunbelt. The skin was tight around her mouth, her eyes charged with light. My gaze shifted off her face.

"When I was a young woman and finally told people what my father did to me, nobody believed it," she said. " 'Your dad was a great guy,' they said. 'Your dad was a wonderful parent.' "

"Where is she now?"

"Iberia General. Nobody's pressing charges. I think her old man already greased the owner of the bar."

"You're a good cop, Helen."

"Better get her some help. The guy who'll pay the

bill won't be the one who did it to her. Too bad it works out that way, huh?"

"What do I know?" I said.

Her eyes held on mine. She had killed two perps in the line of duty. I think she took no joy in that fact. But neither did she regret what she had done nor did she grieve over the repressed anger that had rescinded any equivocation she might have had before she shot them. She winked at me and went back to her office.

SIX

WITH REGULARITY POLITICIANS TALK about what they call the war against drugs. I have the sense few of them know anything about it. But the person who suffers the attrition for the drug trade is real, with the same soft marmalade-like system of lungs and heart and viscera inherited from a fish as the rest of us.

In this case her name was Ruby Gravano and she lived in a low-rent hotel on St. Charles Avenue in New Orleans, between Lee Circle and Canal, not far from the French Quarter. The narrow front entrance was framed by bare lightbulbs, like the entrance to a 1920s movie theater. But quaint similarities ended there. The interior was superheated and breathless, unlighted except for the glare from the airshaft at the end of the hallways. For some reason the walls had been painted firehouse red with black trim, and now, in the semi-darkness, they had the dirty glow of a dying furnace.

Ruby Gravano sat in a stuffed chair surrounded by the litter of her life: splayed tabloid magazines, pizza cartons, used Kleenex, a coffee cup with a dead roach inside, a half-constructed model of a spaceship that had been stuck back in the box and stepped on.

Ruby Gravano's hair was long and black and made her thin face and body look fuller than they were. She wore shorts that were too big for her and exposed her underwear, and foundation on her thighs and forearms, and false fingernails and false eyelashes and a bruise like a fresh tattoo on her left cheek.

"Dave won't jam you up on this, Ruby. We just want a string that'll lead back to these two guys. They're bad dudes, not the kind you want in your life, not the kind you want other girls to get mixed up with. You can help a lot of people here," Clete said.

"We did them in a motel on Airline Highway. They had a pickup truck with a shell on it. Full of guns and camping gear and shit. They smelled like mosquito repellent. They always wore their hats. I've seen hogs eat with better table manners. They're johns. What else you want to know?" she said.

"Why'd you think they might be cops?" I asked.

"Who else carries mug shots around?"

"Beg your pardon?" I said.

"The guy I did, he was undressing and he finds these two mug shots in his shirt pocket. So he burns them in an ashtray and that's when his friend says something about capping two brothers."

"Wait a minute. You were all in the same room?" Clete said.

"They didn't want to pay for two rooms. Besides, they wanted to trade off. Connie does splits, but I wouldn't go along. One of those creeps is sickening enough. Why don't you bug Connie about this stuff?"

"Because she blew town," Clete said.

She sniffed and wiped her nose with her wrist. "Look, I'm not feeling too good. Y'all got what you need?" she said.

"Did they use a credit card to pay for the room?" I asked.

"It's a trick pad. My manager pays the owner. Look, believe it or not, I got another life besides this shit. How about it?"

She tried to look boldly into my face, but her eyes broke and she picked up the crushed model of a spaceship from its box on the floor and held it in her lap and studied it resentfully.

"Who hit you, Ruby?" I asked.

"A guy."

"You have a kid?"

"A little boy. He's nine. I bought him this, but it got rough in here last night."

"These cops, duffers, whatever they were, they had to have names," I said.

"Not real ones."

"What do you mean?"

"The one who burned the pictures, the other guy called him Harpo. I go, 'Like that guy in old TV movies who's a dummy and is always honking a horn?' The guy called Harpo goes, 'That's right, darlin', and right now I'm gonna honk *your* horn.'"

She tried to fit the plastic parts of the model back together. Her right cheek was pinched while she tried to focus, and the bruise on it knotted together like a cluster of blue grapes. "I can't fix this. I should have put it up in the closet. He's coming over with my aunt," she said. She pushed hard on a plastic part and it slid sharply across the back of her hand.

"How old a man was Harpo?" I asked.

"Like sixty, when they start acting like they're your father and Robert Redford at the same time. He has hair all over his back . . . I got to go to the bathroom. I'm gonna be in there a while. Look, you want to stay, maybe you can fix this. It's been a deeply fucked-up day."

"Where'd you buy it?" I asked.

"K&B's. Or maybe at the Jackson Brewery, you know, that mall that used to be the Jax brewery . . . No, I'm pretty sure it wasn't the Brewery." She bit a hangnail.

Clete and I drove to a K&B drugstore up St. Charles. It was raining, and the wind blew the mist out of the trees that arched over the streetcar tracks. The green-and-purple neon on the drugstore looked like scrolled candy in the rain.

"Harpo was the name of the cop who took Cool Breeze Broussard's wife away from him," I said.

"That was twenty years ago. It can't be the same guy, can it?"

"No, it's unlikely."

"I think all these people deserve each other, Streak."

"So why are we buying a toy for Ruby Gravano's son?"

"I seldom take my own advice. Sound like anybody else you know, big mon?"

ON WEDNESDAY I DROVE a cruiser down the old bayou road toward Jeanerette and Lila Terrebonne's home. As I neared the enormous lawn and the oak-lined driveway, I saw the production crew at work on the set that had been constructed to look like the quarters on a corporation farm, and I kept driving south, toward Franklin and the place where my father and I had discovered a crucifixion.

Why?

Maybe because the past is never really dead, at least not as long as you deny its existence. Maybe because I knew that somehow the death of Cisco and Megan Flynn's father was about to come back into our lives.

The barn was still there, two hundred yards from the Teche, hemmed in by banana trees and blackberry bushes. The roof was cratered with a huge hole, the walls leaning in on themselves, the red paint nothing more than thin strips that hadn't yet been weathered away by wind and sun.

I walked through the blackberry bushes to the north side of the barn. The nail holes were sealed over with dust from the cane fields and water expansion in the wood, but I could still feel their edges with the tips of my fingers and, in my mind's eye, see the outline of the man whose tormented face and broken body and blood-creased brow greeted my father and me on that fiery dawn in 1956.

No grass grew around the area where Jack Flynn died. (But there was no sunlight there, I told myself, only green flies buzzing in the shade, and the earth was hardpan and probably poisoned by herbicides that had been spilled on the ground.) Wild rain trees, bursting with bloodred flowers, stood in the field, and the blackberries on the bushes were fat and moist with their own juices when I touched them. I wondered at the degree of innocence that allowed us to think of Golgotha as an incident trapped inside history. I wiped the sweat off

my face with a handkerchief and unbuttoned my shirt
and stepped out of the shade into the wind, but it
brought no relief from the heat.

I drove back up the bayou to the Terrebonne home
and turned into the brick drive and parked by the carriage house. Lila was ebullient, her milky green eyes
free of any remorse or memory of pulling a gun in a bar
and being handcuffed to a bed in Iberia General Hospital. But like all people who are driven by a self-centered
fear, she talked constantly, controlling the environment
around her with words, filling in any silent space that
might allow someone to ask the wrong question.

Her father, Archer Terrebonne, was another matter.
He had the same eyes as his daughter, and the same
white-gold hair, but there was no lack of confidence in
either his laconic speech or the way he folded his arms
across his narrow chest while he held a glass of shaved
ice and bourbon and sliced oranges. In fact, his money
gave him the kind of confidence that overrode any unpleasant reflection he might see in a mirror or the eyes
of others. When you dealt with Archer Terrebonne,
you simply accepted the fact that his gaze was too direct
and personal, his skin too pale for the season, his mouth
too red, his presence too close, as though there were a
chemical defect in his physiology that he wore as an
ornament and imposed upon others.

We stood under an awning on the back terrace.
The sunlight was blinding on the surface of the swimming pool. In the distance a black groundskeeper was
using an air blower to scud leaves off the tennis courts.

"You won't come inside?" Archer said. He glanced
at his watch, then looked at a bird in a tree. The ring
finger of his left hand was missing, sawed off neatly at

the palm, so that the empty space looked like a missing key on a piano.

"Thanks, anyway. I just wanted to see that Lila was all right."

"Really? Well, that was good of you."

I noticed his use of the past tense, as though my visit had already ended.

"There're no charges, but messing with guns in barrooms usually has another conclusion," I said.

"We've already covered this territory with other people, sir," he said.

"I don't think quite enough," I said.

"Is that right?" he replied.

Our eyes locked on each other's.

"Dave's just being an old friend, Daddy," Lila said.

"I'm sure he is. Let me walk you to your cruiser, Mr. Robicheaux."

"*Daddy,* I mean it, Dave's always worrying about his AA friends," she said.

"You're not in that organization. So he doesn't need to worry, does he?"

I felt his hand cup me lightly on the arm. But I said goodbye to Lila and didn't resist. I walked with him around the shady side of the house, past a garden planted with mint and heart-shaped caladiums.

"Is there something you want to tell me, sir?" he asked. He took a swallow from his bourbon glass and I could feel the coldness of the ice on his breath.

"A female detective saved your daughter from a re-sisting arrest charge," I said.

"Yes?"

"She thinks Lila has been sexually molested or violated in some way."

His right eye twitched at the corner, as though an insect had momentarily flown into his vision.

"I'm sure y'all have many theories about human behavior that most of us wouldn't understand. We appreciate your good intentions. However, I see no need for you to come back," he said.

"Don't count on it, sir."

He wagged his finger back and forth, then walked casually toward the rear of the house, sipping his drink as though I had never been there.

THE SUN WAS WHITE in the sky and the brick drive was dappled with light as bright as gold foil. Through the cruiser's front window I saw Cisco Flynn walk toward me from a trailer, his palms raised for me to stop.

He leaned down on the window.

"Take a walk with me. I got to keep my eye on this next scene," he said.

"Got to go, Cisco."

"It's about Swede Boxleiter."

I turned off the ignition and walked with him to a canvas awning that was suspended over a worktable and a half dozen chairs. Next to the awning was a trailer whose air-conditioning unit dripped with moisture like a block of ice.

"Swede's trying to straighten out. I think he's going to make it this time. But if he's ever a problem, give me a call," Cisco said.

"He's a mainline recidivist, Cisco. Why are you hooked up with him?"

"When we were in the state home? I would have been anybody's chops if it hadn't been for Swede."

"The Feds say he kills people."

"The Feds say my sister is a Communist."

The door to the trailer opened and a woman stepped out on the small porch. But before she could close the door behind her, a voice shouted out, "God-damnit, I didn't say you could leave. Now, you listen, hon. I don't know if the problem is because your brains are between your legs or because you think you've got a cute twat, but the next time I tell that pissant to rewrite a scene, you'd better not open your mouth. Now you get the fuck back to work and don't you ever contradict me in front of other people again."

Even in the sunlight her face looked refrigerated, bloodless, the lines twisted out of shape with the humiliation that Billy Holtzner bathed her with. He shot an ugly look at Cisco and me, then slammed the door.

I turned to go.

"There's a lot of stress on a set, Dave. We're three million over budget already. That's other people's money we're talking about. They get mad about it," Cisco said.

"I remember that first film you made. The one about the migrant farmworkers. It was sure a fine movie."

"Yeah, a lot of college professors and 1960s left-overs dug it in a big way."

"The guy in that trailer is a shithead."

"Aren't we all?"

"Your old man wasn't."

I got into the cruiser and drove through the corridor of trees to the bayou road. In the rearview mirror Cisco Flynn looked like a miniature man trapped inside an elongated box.

• • •

THAT NIGHT, AS BOOTSIE and I prepared to go to bed, dry lightning flickered behind the clouds and the pecan tree outside the window was stiffening in the wind.

"Why do you think Jack Flynn was killed?" Bootsie asked.

"Working people around here made thirty-five cents an hour back then. He didn't have a hard time finding an audience."

"Who do you think did it?"

"Everyone said it came from the outside. Just like during the Civil Rights era. We always blamed our problems on the outside."

She turned out the light and we lay down on top of the sheets. Her skin felt cool and warm at the same time, the way sunlight does in the fall.

"The Flynns are trouble, Dave."

"Maybe."

"No, no maybe about it. Jack Flynn might have been a good man. But I always heard he didn't become a radical until his family got wiped out in the Depression."

"He fought in the Lincoln Brigade. He was at the battle of Madrid."

"Good night," she said.

She turned toward the far wall. When I spread my hand on her back I could feel her breath rise and fall in her lungs. She looked at me over her shoulder, then rolled over and fit herself inside my arms.

"Dave?" she said.

"Yes?"

"Trust me on this. Megan needs you for some reason she's not telling you about. If she can't get to you directly, she'll go through Clete."

"That's hard to believe."

"He called tonight and asked if I knew where she was. She'd left a message on his answering machine."

"Megan Flynn and Clete Purcel?"

I WOKE AT SUNRISE the next morning and drove through the leafy shadows on East Main and then five miles up the old highway to Spanish Lake. I was troubled not only by Bootsie's words but also by my own misgivings about the Flynns. Why was Megan so interested in the plight of Cool Breeze Broussard? There was enough injustice in the world without coming back to New Iberia to find it. And why would her brother Cisco front points for an obvious psychopath like Swede Boxleiter?

I parked my truck on a side road and poured a cup of coffee from my thermos. Through the pines I could see the sun glimmering on the water and the tips of the flooded grass waving in the shallows. The area around the lake had been the site of a failed Spanish colony in the 1790s. In 1836 two Irish immigrants who had survived the Goliad Massacre during the Texas Revolution, Devon Flynn and William Burke, cleared and drained the acreage along the lake and built farmhouses out of cypress trees that were rooted in the water like boulders. Later the train stop there became known as Burke's Station.

Megan and Cisco's ancestor had been one of those Texas soldiers who had surrendered to the Mexican army with the expectation of boarding a prison ship bound for New Orleans, and instead had been marched down a road on Palm Sunday and told by their Mexican captors to kneel in front of the firing squads that were forming into position from two directions. Over 350 men and boys were shot, bayoneted, and clubbed to death. Many of the survivors owed their lives to a prostitute who ran from one Mexican officer to the next, begging for the lives of the Texans. Her name and fate were lost to history, but those who escaped into the woods that day called her the Angel of Goliad.

I wondered if Cisco ever thought about his ancestor's story as material for a film.

The old Flynn house still stood by the lake, but it was covered by a white-brick veneer now and the old gallery had been replaced by a circular stone porch with white pillars. But probably most important to Megan and Cisco was the simple fact that it and its terraced gardens and gnarled live oaks and lakeside gazebo and boathouse all belonged to someone else.

Their father was bombed by the Luftwaffe and shot at by the Japanese on Guadalcanal and murdered in Louisiana. Were they bitter, did they bear us a level of resentment we could only guess at? Did they bring their success back here like a beast on a chain? I didn't want to answer my own question.

The wind ruffled the lake and the longleaf pine boughs above my truck. I glanced in the rearview mirror and saw the sheriff's cruiser pull in behind me. He opened my passenger door and got inside.

"How'd you know I was out here?" I asked.

"A state trooper saw you and wondered what you were doing."

"I got up a little early today."

"That's the old Flynn place, isn't it?"

"We used to dig for Confederate artifacts here. Camp Pratt was right back in those trees."

"The Flynns bother me, too, Dave. I don't like Cisco bringing this Boxleiter character into our midst. Why don't both of them stay in Colorado?"

"That's what we did to Megan and Cisco the first time. Let a friend of their dad dump them in Colorado."

"You'd better define your feelings about that pair. I got Boxleiter's sheet. What kind of person would bring a man like that into his community?"

"We did some serious damage to those kids, Sheriff."

"We? You know what your problem is, Dave? You're just like Jack Flynn."

"Excuse me?"

"You don't like rich people. You think we're in a class war. Not everybody with money is a sonofabitch."

He blew out his breath, then the heat went out of his face. He took his pipe from his shirt pocket and clicked it on the window jamb.

"Helen said you think Boxleiter might be a pedophile," he said.

"Yeah, if I had to bet, I'd say he's a real candidate."

"Pick him up."

"What for?"

"Think of something. Take Helen with you. She can be very creative."

Idle words that I would try to erase from my memory later.

SEVEN

I DROVE BACK TOWARD THE office. As I approached the old Catholic cemetery, I saw a black man with sloping shoulders cross the street in front of me and walk toward Main. I stared at him, dumbfounded. One cheek was bandaged, and his right arm was stiff at his side, as though it pained him.

I pulled abreast of him and said, "I can't believe it."

"Believe what?" Cool Breeze said. He walked bent forward, like he was just about to arrive somewhere. The whitewashed crypts behind him were beaded with moisture the size of quarters.

"You're supposed to be in federal custody."

"They cut me loose."

"Cut you loose? Just like that?"

"I'm going up to Victor's to eat breakfast."

"Get in."

"I don't mean you no disrespect, but I ain't gonna have no more to do with po-licemens for a while."

"You staying with Mout'?"

But he crossed the street and didn't answer.

• • •

AT THE OFFICE I called Adrien Glazier in New Orleans.

"What's your game with Cool Breeze Broussard?" I asked.

"Game?"

"He's back in New Iberia. I just saw him."

"We took his deposition. We don't see any point in keeping him in custody," she replied.

I could feel my words binding in my throat.

"What's in y'all's minds? You've burned this guy."

"Burned him?"

"You made him rat out the Giacanos. Do you know what they do to people who snitch them off?"

"Then why don't you put him in custody yourself, Mr. Robicheaux?"

"Because the prosecutor's office dropped charges against him."

"Really? So the same people who complain when we investigate their jail want us to clean up a local mess for them?"

"Don't do this."

"Should we tell Mr. Broussard his friend Mr. Robicheaux would like to see him locked up again? Or will you do that for us?" she said, and hung up.

Helen opened my door and came inside. She studied my face curiously.

"You ready to boogie?" she asked.

SWEDE BOXLEITER HAD TOLD me he had a job in the movies, and that's where we started. Over in St. Mary Parish, on the front lawn of Lila Terrebonne.

But we didn't get far. After we had parked the

cruiser, we were stopped halfway to the set by a couple of off-duty St. Mary Parish sheriff's deputies with American flags sewn to their sleeves.

"Y'all putting us in an embarrassing situation," the older man said.

"You see that dude there, the one with the tool belt on? His name's Boxleiter. He just finished a five bit in Colorado," I said.

"You got a warrant?"

"Nope."

"Mr. Holtzner don't want nobody on the set ain't got bidness here. That's the way it is."

"Oh yeah? Try this. Either you take the marshmallows out of your mouth or I'll go down to your boss's office and have your ass stuffed in a tree shredder," Helen said.

"Say what you want. You ain't getting on this set," he said.

Just then, Cisco Flynn opened the door of a trailer and stepped out on the short wood porch.

"What's the problem, Dave?" he asked.

"Boxleiter."

"Come in," he said, making cupping motions with his upturned hands, as though he were directing an aircraft on a landing strip.

Helen and I walked toward the open door. Behind him I could see Billy Holtzner combing his hair. His eyes were pale and watery, his lips thick, his face hard-planed like gray rubber molded against bone.

"Dave, we want a good relationship with everybody in the area. If Swede's done something wrong, I want to know about it. Come inside, meet Billy. Let's talk a minute," Cisco said.

But Billy Holtzner's attention had shifted to a woman who was brushing her teeth in a lavatory with the door open.

"Margot, you look just like you do when I come in your mouth," he said.

"Adios," I said, walking away from the trailer with Helen.

Cisco caught up with us and waved away the two security guards.

"What'd Swede do?" he asked.

"Better question: What's he got on you?" I said.

"What have I done that you insult me like this?"

"Mr. Flynn, Boxleiter was hanging around small children at the city pool. Save the bullshit for your local groupies," Helen said.

"All right, I'll talk to him. Let's don't have a scene," Cisco said.

"Just stay out of the way," she said.

Boxleiter was on one knee, stripped to the waist, tightening a socket wrench on a power terminal. His Levi's were powdered with dust, and black power lines spidered out from him in all directions. His torso glistened whitely with sweat, his skin rippling with sinew each time he pumped the wrench. He used his hand to mop the sweat out of one shaved armpit, then wiped his hand on his jeans.

"I want you to put your shirt on and take a ride with us," I said.

He looked up at us, smiling, squinting into the sun. "You don't have a warrant. If you did, you'd have already told me," he said.

"It's a social invitation. One you really don't want to turn down," Helen said.

He studied her, amused. Dust swirled out of the dirt street that had been spread on the set. The sky was cloudless, the air moist and as tangible as flame against the skin. Boxleiter rose to his feet. People on the set had stopped work and were watching now.

"I got a union book. I'm like anybody else here. I don't have to go anywhere," he said.

"Suit yourself. We'll catch you later," I said.

"I get it. You'll roust me when I get home tonight. It don't bother me. Long as it's legal," he said.

Helen's cheeks were flushed, the back of her neck damp in the heat. I touched her wrist and nodded toward the cruiser. Just as she turned to go with me, I saw Boxleiter draw one stiff finger up his rib cage, collecting a thick dollop of sweat. He flicked it at her back.

Her hand went to her cheek, her face darkening with surprise and insult, like a person in a crowd who cannot believe the nature of an injury she has just received.

"You're under arrest for assaulting a police officer. Put your hands behind you," she said.

He grinned and scratched at an insect bite high up on his shoulder.

"Is there something wrong with the words I use? Turn around," she said.

He shook his head sadly. "I got witnesses. I ain't done anything."

"You want to add 'resisting' to it?" she said.

"Whoa, mama. Take your hands off me . . . Hey, enough's enough . . . Buddy, yeah, you, guy with the mustache, you get this dyke off me."

She grabbed him by the shoulders and put her shoe

behind his knee. Then he brought his elbow into her breast, hard, raking it across her as he turned.

She slipped a blackjack from her pants pocket and raised it over her shoulder and swung it down on his collarbone. It was weighted with lead, elongated like a darning sock, the spring handle wrapped with leather. The blow made his shoulder drop as though the tendons had been severed at the neck.

But he flailed at her just the same, trying to grab her around the waist. She whipped the blackjack across his head, again and again, splitting his scalp, wetting the leather cover on the blackjack each time she swung.

I tried to push him to the ground, out of harm's way, but another problem was in the making. The two off-duty sheriff's deputies were pulling their weapons.

I tore my .45 from my belt holster and aimed into their faces.

"Freeze! It's over! . . . Take your hand off that piece! Do it! Do it! Do it!"

I saw the confusion and the alarm fix in their eyes, their bodies stiffening. Then the moment died in their faces. "That's it . . . Now, move the crowd back. That's all you've got to do . . . That's right," I said, my words like wet glass in my throat.

Swede Boxleiter moaned and rolled in the dirt among the power cables, his fingers laced in his hair. Both my hands were still squeezed tight on the .45's grips, my forearms shining with sweat.

The faces of the onlookers were stunned, stupefied. Billy Holtzner pushed his way through the crowd, turned in a circle, his eyebrows climbing on his forehead, and said, "I got to tell you to get back to work?" Then he walked back toward his trailer, blowing his nose on a Kleenex, flicking his eyes sideways briefly as though looking at a minor irritant.

I was left staring into the self-amused gaze of Archer Terrebonne. Lila stood behind him, her mouth open, her face as white as cake flour. The backs of my legs were still trembling.

"Do y'all specialize in being public fools, Mr. Robicheaux?" he asked. He touched at the corner of his mouth, his three-fingered hand like that of an impaired amphibian.

THE SHERIFF PACED IN his office. He pulled up the blinds, then lowered them again. He kept clearing his throat, as though there were an infection in it.

"This isn't a sheriff's department. I'm the supervisor of a mental institution," he said.

He took the top off his teakettle, looked inside it, and set the top down again.

"You know how many faxes I've gotten already on this? The St. Mary sheriff told me not to put my foot in his parish again. That sonofabitch actually threatened me," he said.

"Maybe we should have played it differently, but Boxleiter didn't give us a lot of selection," I said.

"Outside our jurisdiction."

"We told him he wasn't under arrest. There was no misunderstanding about that," I said.

"I should have used their people to take him down," Helen said.

"Ah, a breakthrough in thought. But I'm suspending you just the same, at least until I get an IA finding," the sheriff said.

"He threw sweat on her. He hit her in the chest with his elbow. He got off light," I said.

"A guy with twenty-eight stitches in his head?"

"You told us to pick him up, skipper. That guy would be a loaded gun anyplace we tried to take him down. You know it, too," I said.

He crimped his lips together and breathed through his nose.

"I'm madder than hell about this," he said.

The room was silent, the air-conditioning almost frigid. The sunlight through the slatted blinds was eye-watering.

"All right, forget the suspension and IA stuff. See me before you go into St. Mary Parish again. In the meantime, you find out why Cisco Flynn thinks he can bring his pet sewer rats into Iberia Parish . . . Helen, you depersonalize your attitude toward the perps, if that's possible."

"The sewer rats?" I said.

He filled his pipe bowl from a leather pouch and didn't bother to look up until we were out of the room.

THAT EVENING CLETE PURCEL parked his Cadillac convertible under the shade trees in front of my house and walked down to the bait shop. He wore a summer suit and a lavender shirt with a white tie. He went to the cooler and opened a bottle of strawberry soda.

"What, I look funny or something?" he said.

"You look sharp."

He drank out of the pop bottle and watched a boat out on the bayou.

"I'll treat y'all to dinner at the Patio in Loreauville," he said.

"I'd better work."

He nodded, then looked at the newscast on the television set that sat above the counter.

"Thought I'd ask," he said.

"Who you going to dinner with?"

"Megan Flynn."

"Another time."

He sat down at the counter and drank from his soda. He drew a finger through a wet ring on the wood.

"I'm only supposed to go out with strippers and junkies?" he said.

"Did I say anything?"

"You hide your feelings like a cat in a spin dryer."

"So she's stand-up. But why's she back in New Iberia? We're Paris on the Teche?"

"She was born here. Her brother has a house here."

"Yeah, he's carrying weight for a psychopath, too. Why you think that is, Clete? Because Cisco likes to rehabilitate shank artists?"

"I hear Helen beat the shit out of Boxleiter with a slapjack. Maybe he's got the message and he'll get out of town."

I mopped down the counter and tossed the rag on top of a case of empty beer bottles.

"You won't change your mind?" he said.

"Come back tomorrow. We'll entertain the bass."

He made a clicking sound with his mouth and walked out the door and into the twilight.

•   •   •

AFTER SUPPER I DROVE over to Mout' Broussard's house on the west side of town. Cool Breeze came out on the gallery and sat down on the swing. He had removed the bandage from his cheek, and the wound he had gotten at the jail looked like a long piece of pink string inset in his skin.

"Doctor said I ain't gonna have no scar."

"You going to hang around town?" I asked.

"Ain't got no pressing bidness nowheres else."

"They used you, Breeze."

"I got Alex Guidry fired, ain't I?"

"Does it make you feel better?"

He looked at his hands. They were wide, big-boned, lustrous with callus.

"What you want here?" he asked.

"The old man who made your wife cook for him, Harpo Delahoussey? Did he have a son?"

"What people done tole you over in St. Mary Parish?"

"They say he didn't."

He shook his head noncommittally.

"You don't remember?" I said.

"I don't care. It ain't my bidness."

"A guy named Harpo may have executed a couple of kids out in the Basin," I said.

"Those dagos in New Orleans? You know what they do to a black man snitch them off? I'm suppose to worry about some guy blowing away some po'-white trash raped a black girl?"

"When those men took away your wife twenty years ago, you couldn't do anything about it. Same kind of guys are still out there, Breeze. They function only because we allow them to."

"I promised Mout' to go crabbing with him in the morning. I best be getting my sleep," he said.

But when I got into my truck and looked back at him, he was still in the swing, staring at his hands, his massive shoulders slumped like a bag of crushed rock.

IT WAS HOT AND dry Friday night, with a threat of rain that never came. Out over the Gulf, the clouds would vein and pulse with lightning, then the thunder would ripple across the wetlands with a sound like damp cardboard tearing. In the middle of the night I put my hands inside Bootsie's nightgown and felt her body's heat against my palms, like the warmth in a lampshade. Her eyes opened and looked into mine, then she touched my hardness with her fingertips, her hand gradually rounding itself, her mouth on my cheek, then on my lips. She rolled on her back, her hand never leaving me, and waited for me to enter her.

She came before I did, both of her hands pushing hard into the small of my back, her knees gathered around my thighs, then she came a second time, with me, her stomach rolling under me, her voice muted and moist in my ear.

She went into the bathroom and I heard the water running. She walked toward me out of the light, touching her face with a towel, then lay on top of the sheet and put her head on my chest. The ends of her hair were wet and the spinning blades of the window fan made shadows on her skin.

"What's worrying you?" she asked.

"Nothing."

She kicked me in the calf.

"Clete Purcel. I think he's going to be hurt," I said.

"Advice about love and money. Give it to anyone except friends."

"You're right. You were about Megan, too. I'd thought better of her."

She ran her fingernails through my hair and rested one ankle across mine.

SUNDAY MORNING I WOKE at dawn and went down to the bait shop to help Batist open up. I was never sure of his age, but he had been a teenager during World War II when he had worked for Mr. Antoine, one of Louisiana's last surviving Confederate veterans, at Mr. Antoine's blacksmith shop in a big red barn out on West Main. Mr. Antoine had willed Batist a plot of land and a small cypress home on the bayou, and over the years Batist had truck farmed there, augmented his income by trapping and fishing with my father, buried two wives, and raised five children, all of whom graduated from high school. He was illiterate and sometimes contentious, and had never traveled farther from home than New Orleans in one direction and Lake Charles in the other, but I never knew a more loyal or decent person.

We started the fire in the barbecue pit, which was fashioned from a split oil drum with handles and hinges welded on it, laid out our chickens and sausage links on the grill for our midday customers, and closed down the lid to let the meat smoke for at least three hours.

Batist wore a pair of bell-bottomed dungarees and a white T-shirt with the sleeves razored off. His upper arms bunched like cantaloupes when he moved a spool table to hose down the dock under it.

"I forgot to tell you. That fella Cool Breeze was by here last night," he said.

"What did he want?"

"I ain't ax him."

I expected him to say more but he didn't. He didn't like people of color who had jail records, primarily because he believed they were used by whites as an excuse to treat all black people unfairly.

"Does he want me to call him?" I asked.

"I know that story about his wife, Dave. Maybe it wasn't all his fault, but he sat by while them white men ruined that po' girl. I feel sorry for him, me, but when a man got a grief like that against hisself, there ain't nothing you can do for him."

I looked up Mout's name in the telephone book and dialed the number. While the phone rang Batist lit a cigar and opened the screen on the window and flicked the match into the water.

"No one home," I said after I hung up.

"I ain't gonna say no more."

He drew in on his cigar, his face turned into the breeze that blew through the screen.

BOOTSIE AND ALAFAIR AND I went to Mass, then I dropped them off at home and drove to Cisco Flynn's house on the Loreauville road. He answered the door in a terry-cloth bathrobe that he wore over a pair of scarlet gym shorts.

"Too early?" I said.

"No, I was about to do a workout. Come in," he

said, opening the door wide. "Look, if you're here to apologize about that stuff on the set—"

"I'm not."

"Oh."

"The sheriff wants to know why the city of New Iberia is hosting a mainline con like your friend Boxleiter."

We were in the living room now, by the collection of photographs that had made Megan famous.

"You were never in a state home, Dave. How would you like to be seven years old and forced to get up out of bed in the middle of the night and suck somebody's cock? Think you could handle that?"

"I think your friend is a depraved and violent man."

"He's violent? Y'all put him in the hospital over a drop of sweat."

Through the French doors I could see two dark-skinned people sitting at a glass table under a tree in the back yard. The man was big, slightly overweight, with a space between his front teeth and a ponytail that hung between his shoulder blades. The woman wore shorts and a tank top and had brownish-red hair that reminded me of tumbleweed. They were pouring orange juice into glasses from a clear pitcher. A yellow candle stub was melted to the table.

"Something bothered me the last time I was here. These photos that were in *Life* magazine? Y'all caught the kill from inside the drainpipe, just as the bullet hit the black guy in the neck?"

"That's right."

"What were you doing in the pipe? How'd you know the guy was coming out at that particular place?"

"We made an arrangement to meet him, that's all."

"How'd the cops know he was going to be there?"

"I told you. He raped a high school girl. They had an all-points out on him."

"Somehow that doesn't hang together for me," I said.

"You think we set it up? We were *inside* the pipe. Bullets were ricocheting and sparking all around us. What's the use? I've got some guests. Is there anything else?"

"Guests?"

"Billy Holtzner's daughter and her boyfriend."

I looked out the French doors again. I saw a glassy reflection between the fingers of the man's right hand.

"Introduce me."

"It's Sunday. They're just getting up."

"Yeah, I can see."

"Hey, wait a minute."

But I opened the French doors and stepped outside. The man with the ponytail, who looked Malaysian or Indonesian, cupped the candle stub melted to the table, popping the waxy base loose, and held it behind his thigh. Holtzner's daughter had eyes that didn't fit her fried hair. They were a soapy blue, mindless, as devoid of reason as a drowsy cat's when small creatures run across its vision.

A flat, partially zippered leather case rested on a metal chair between her and her boyfriend.

"How y'all doing?" I asked.

Their smiles were self-indulgent rather than warm, their faces suffused by a chemical pleasure that was working in their skin like flame inside tallow. The woman lowered her wrist into her lap and the sunlight fell like a spray of yellow coins on the small red swelling inside her forearm.

"The officer from the set," the man said.

"It is," the woman said, leaning sideways in her chair to see behind me. "Is that blond lady here? The one with the blackjack. I mean that guy's head. Yuck."

"We're not in trouble, are we?" the man said. He smiled. The gap in his front teeth was large enough to insert a kitchen match in.

"You from the U.K.?" I said.

"Just the accent. I travel on a French passport," he said, smiling. He removed a pair of dark glasses from his shirt pocket and put them on.

"Y'all need any medical attention here?"

"No, not today, I don't think," the man said.

"Sure? Because I can run y'all down to Iberia General. It's no trouble."

"That's very kind of you, but we'll pass," the man said.

"What's he talking about?" the woman said.

"Being helpful, that sort of thing, welcoming us to the neighborhood," the man said.

"Hospital?" She scratched her back by rubbing it against her chair. "Did anybody ever tell you you look like Johnny Wadd?"

"Not really."

"He died of AIDS. He was very underrated as an artist. Because he did porno, if that's what you want to call it." Then her face went out of focus, as though her own words had presented a question inside herself.

"Dave, can I see you?" Cisco said softly behind me.

I left Billy Holtzner's daughter and the man with the ponytail without saying goodbye. But they never noticed, their heads bent toward each other as they laughed over a private joke.

Cisco walked with me through the shade trees to my truck. He had slipped on a golf shirt with his gym shorts, and he kept pulling the cloth away from the dampness of his skin.

"I don't have choices about what people around me do sometimes," he said.

"Choose not to have them here, Cisco."

"I work in a bowl of piranhas. You think Billy Holtzner is off the wall? He twists noses. I can introduce you to people who blow heads."

"I didn't have probable cause on your friends. But they shouldn't take too much for granted."

"How many cops on a pad have you covered for? How many times have you seen a guy popped and a throw-down put on his body?"

"See you, Cisco."

"What am I supposed to feel, Dave? Like I just got visited by St. Francis of Assisi? In your ear."

I walked to my truck and didn't look back at him. I heard the woman braying loudly in the back yard.

WHEN I WENT DOWN to the bait shop to open up Monday morning, Cool Breeze Broussard was waiting for me at a spool table, the Cinzano umbrella ruffling over his head. The early sun was dark red through the trunks of the cypresses.

"It gonna be another hot one," he said.

"What's the haps, Breeze?"

"I got to talk . . . No, out here. I like to talk in the open space . . . How much of what I tell you other people got to learn about?"

"That depends."

He made a pained face and looked at the redness of the sun through the trees.

"I went to New Orleans Saturday. A guy up Magazine, Jimmy Fig, Tommy Figorelli's brother, the guy the Giacanos sawed up and hung in pieces from a ceiling fan? I figured Jimmy didn't have no love for the Giacanos 'cause of his brother, and, besides, me and Jimmy was in the Block together at Angola, see. So I t'ought he was the right man to sell me a cold piece," Cool Breeze said.

"You're buying unregistered guns?" I said.

"You want to hear me or not? . . . So he go, 'Willie, in your line of work, you don't need no cold piece.'

"I go, 'This ain't for work. I got in bad wit' some local guys, maybe you heard. But I ain't got no money right now, so I need you to front me the piece.'

"He say, 'You feeling some heat from somewhere, Breeze?' And he say it wit' this smart-ass grin on his face.

"I say, 'Yeah, wit' the same dudes who freeze-wrapped your brother's parts in his own butcher shop. I hear they drank eggnog while he was spinning round over their heads.'

"He say, 'Well, my brother had some sexual problems that got him into trouble. But it ain't Italians you got to worry about. The word is some peckerwoods got a contract to do a black blabbermouth in New Iberia. I just didn't know who it was.'

"I say, 'Blabbermouth, huh?'

"He go, 'You was ripping off the Giacanos and selling their own VCRs back to them? Then you snitch

them off and come to New Orleans figuring somebody's gonna front you a piece? Breeze, nothing racial
meant, but you people ought to stick to pimping and
dealing rock.' "

"Who are these peckerwoods?" I asked.

"When I tole you the story about me and Ida,
about how she wrapped that chain round her t'roat and
drowned herself, I left somet'ing out."

"Oh?"

"A year after Ida died, I was working at the Terrebonne cannery, putting up sweet potatoes. Harpo Delahoussey run the security there for Mr. Terrebonne.
We come to the end of the season and the cannery shut
down, just like it do every winter, and everybody got
laid off. So we went on down to the unemployment
office and filed for unemployment insurance. Shouldn't
have been no problem.

"Except three weeks go by and the state sends us a
notice we ain't qualified for no checks 'cause we cannery workers, and 'cause the cannery ain't open, we
ain't available to work.

"I went on down to see Mr. Terrebonne, but I
never got past Harpo Delahoussey. He's sitting there at
a big desk wit' his foot in the wastebasket, sticking a
po'boy sandwich in his mout'. He go, 'It's been explained to you, Willie. Now, you don't want wait
round here till next season, you go on down to New
Orleans, get you a job, try to stay out of trouble for a
while. But don't you come round here bothering Mr.
Terrebonne. He been good to y'all.'

" 'Bout a week later they was a big fire at the cannery. You could smell sweet potatoes burning all the
way down to Morgan City. Harpo Delahoussey jumped

out a second-story window wit' his clothes on fire. He'da died if he hadn't landed in a mud puddle."

"You set it?"

"Harpo Delahoussey had a nephew wit' his name. He use to be a city po-liceman in Franklin. Everybody called him Li'l Harpo."

"You think this is one of the peckerwoods?"

"Why else I'm telling you all this? Look, I ain't running no more."

"I think you're living inside your head too much, Breeze. The Giacanos use mechanics out of Miami or Houston."

"Jimmy Fig tole me I was a dumb nigger ought to be pimping and selling crack. What you saying ain't no different. I feel bad I come here."

He got up and walked down the dock toward his truck. He passed two white fishermen who were just arriving, their rods and tackle boxes gripped solidly in their hands. They walked around him, then glanced over their shoulders at his back.

"That boy looks like his old lady just cut him off," one of them said to me, grinning.

"We're not open yet," I said, and went inside the bait shop and latched the screen behind me.

EIGHT

YOU READ THE JACKET ON a man like Swede Boxleiter and dismiss him as one of those genetically defective creatures for whom psychologists don't have explanations and let it go at that.

Then he does or says something that doesn't fit the pattern, and you go home from work with boards in your head.

Early Monday morning I called Cisco Flynn's home number and got his answering service. An hour later he returned my call.

"Why do you want Swede's address? Leave him alone," he said.

"He's blackmailing you, isn't he?"

"I remember now. You fought Golden Gloves. Too many shots to the head, Dave."

"Maybe Helen Soileau and I should drop by the set again and talk to him there."

BOXLEITER LIVED IN A triplex built of green cinder blocks outside St. Martinville. When I turned into his drive he was throwing a golf ball against the cement steps on the side of the building, ricocheting it off two surfaces before he retrieved it out of the air again, his hand as fast as a snake's head, *click-click, click-click, click-click*. He wore blue Everlast boxing trunks and a gauzy see-through black shirt and white high-top gym shoes and leather gloves without fingers and a white bill cap that covered his shaved and stitched head like an inverted cook pan. He glanced at me over his shoulder, then began throwing the ball again.

"The Man," he said. The back yard had no grass and lay in deep shade, and beyond the tree trunks the bayou shimmered in the sunlight.

"I thought we'd hear from you," I said.

"How's that?"

"Civil suit, brutality charges, that kind of stuff."

"Can't ever tell."

"Give the golf game a break a minute, will you?"

His eyes smiled at nothing, then he flipped the ball out into the yard and waited, his sunken cheeks and small mouth like those of a curious fish.

"I couldn't figure the hold you had on Cisco," I said. "But it's that photo that began Megan's career, the one of the black man getting nailed in the storm drain, isn't it? You told the cops where he was coming out. Her big break was based on a fraud that cost a guy his life."

He cleaned an ear with his little finger, his eyes as empty of thought as glass.

"Cisco is my friend. I wouldn't hurt him for any reason in the world. Somebody try to hurt him, I'll cut them into steaks."

"Is that right?"

"You want to play some handball?"

"Handball?"

"Yeah, against the garage."

"No, I—"

"Tell the dyke I got no beef. I just didn't like the roust in front of all them people."

"Tell the dyke? You're an unusual man, Swede."

"I heard about you. You were in Vietnam. Anything on my sheet you probably did in spades."

Then, as though I were no longer there, he did a handstand in the yard and walked on stiffened arms through the shade, the bottoms of his gym shoes extended out like the shoulders of a man with no head.

CLETE PURCEL SAT IN the bow of the outboard and drained the foam out of a long-necked bottle of beer. He cast his Rapala between two willow trees and retrieved it back toward him, the sides of the lure flashing just below the surface. The sun was low on the western horizon and the canopy overhead was lit with fire, the water motionless, the mosquitoes starting to form in clouds over the islands of algae that extended out from the flooded cypress trunks.

A bass rose from the silt, thick-backed, the black-green dorsal fin glistening when it broke the water, and knocked the Rapala into the air without taking the treble hook. Clete set his rod on the bow and slapped the back of his neck and looked at the bloody smear on his palm.

"So this guy Cool Breeze is telling you a couple of crackers got the whack on him? One of them is maybe the guy who did these two brothers out in the Atchafalaya Basin?" he said.

"Yeah, that's about it."

"But you don't buy it?"

"When did the Giacanos start using over-the-hill peckerwoods for button men?"

"I wouldn't mark it off, mon. This greaseball in Igor's was complaining to me about how the Giacano family is falling apart, how they've lost their self-respect and they're running low-rent action like porno joints and dope in the projects. I say, 'Yeah, it's a shame. The world's really going to hell,' and he says, 'You telling me, Purcel? It's so bad we got a serious problem with somebody, we got to outsource.'"

"I say, 'Outsource?'"

"He goes, 'Yeah, niggers from the Desire, Vietnamese lice-heads, crackers who spit Red Man in Styrofoam cups at the dinner table.'"

"It's the Dixie Mafia, Dave. There's a nest of them over on the Mississippi coast."

I drew the paddle through the water and let the boat glide into a cove that was freckled with sunlight. I cast a popping bug with yellow feathers and red eyes on the edge of the hyacinths. A solitary blue heron lifted on extended wings out of the grass and flew through an opening in the trees, dimpling the water with its feet.

"But you didn't bring me out here to talk about wiseguy bullshit, did you?" Clete said.

I watched a cottonmouth extend its body out of the water, curling around a low branch on a flooded willow, then pull itself completely into the leaves.

"I don't know how to say it," I said.

"I'll clear it up for both of us. I like her. Maybe we got something going. That rubs you the wrong way?"

"A guy gets involved, he doesn't see things straight sometimes," I said.

" 'Involved,' like in the sack? You're asking me if I'm in the sack with Megan?"

"You're my friend. You carried me down a fire escape when that kid opened up on us with a .22. Something stinks about the Flynn family."

Clete's face was turned into the shadows. The back of his neck was the color of Mercurochrome.

"On my best day I kick in some poor bastard's door for Nig Rosewater. Last week a greaseball tried to hire me to collect the vig for a couple of his shylocks. Megan's talking about getting me on as head of security with a movie company. You think that's bad?"

I looked at the water and the trapped air bubbles that chained to the surface out of the silt. I heard Clete's weight turn on the vinyl cushion under him.

"Say it, Dave. Any broad outside of a T&A joint must have an angle if she'd get involved with your podjo. I'm not sensitive. But lay off Megan."

I disconnected the sections of my fly rod and set them in the bottom of the boat. When I lifted the outboard and yanked the starter rope, the dry propeller whined like a chain saw through the darkening swamp. I didn't speak again until we were at the dock. The air was hot, as though it had been baked on a sheet of tin, the current yellow and dead in the bayou, the lavender sky thick with birds.

Up on the dock, Clete peeled off his shirt and stuck his head under a water faucet. The skin across his shoulders was dry and scaling.

"Come on up for dinner," I said.

"I think I'm going back to New Orleans tonight."

He took his billfold out of his back pocket and removed a five-dollar bill and pushed it into a crack in the railing. "I owe for the beer and gas," he said, and walked with his spinning rod and big tackle box to his car, his love handles aching with fresh sunburn.

THE NEXT NIGHT, UNDER a full moon, two men wearing hats drove a pickup truck down a levee in Vermilion Parish. On either side of them marshlands and saw grass seemed to flow like a wide green river into the Gulf. The two men stopped their truck on the levee and crossed a plank walkway that oozed sand and water under their combined weight. They passed a pirogue that was tied to the walkway, then stepped on ground that was like sponge under their western boots. Ahead, inside the fish camp, someone walked across the glare of a Coleman lantern and made a shadow on the window. Mout' Broussard's dog raised its head under the shack, then padded out into the open air on its leash, its nose lifted into the wind.

NINE

MOUT' STOOD IN THE DOORWAY of the shack and looked at the two white men. Both were tall and wore hats that shadowed their faces. The dog, a yellow-and-black mongrel with scars on its ears, growled and showed its teeth.

"Shut up, Rafe!" Mout' said.

"Where's Willie Broussard at?" one of the men said. The flesh in his throat was distended and rose-colored, and gray whiskers grew on his chin.

"He gone up the levee to the sto'. Coming right back. Wit' some friends to play bouree. What you gentlemens want?" Mout' said.

"Your truck's right yonder. What'd he drive in?" the second man said. He wore a clear plastic raincoat and his right arm held something behind his thigh.

"A friend carried him up there."

"We stopped there for a soda. It was locked up. Where's your outboard, old man?" the man with whiskers said.

"Ain't got no outboa'd."

"There's the gas can yonder. There's the cut in the cattails where it was tied. Your boy running a trot line?"

"What y'all want to bother him for? He ain't done you nothing."

"You don't mind if we come inside, do you?" the man in the raincoat said. When he stepped forward, the dog lunged at his ankle. He kicked his boot sideways and caught the dog in the mouth, then pulled the screen and latch out of the doorjamb.

"You stand over in the corner and stay out of the way," the man with whiskers said.

The man in the raincoat lifted the Coleman lantern by the bail and walked into the back yard with it. He came back in and shook his head.

The man with whiskers bit off a corner on a to-bacco plug and worked it into his jaw. He picked up an empty coffee can out of a trash sack and spit in it.

"I told you we should have come in the a.m. You wake them up and do business," the man in the rain-coat said.

"Turn off the lantern and move the truck."

"I say mark it off. I don't like guessing who's com-ing through a door."

The man with whiskers looked at him meaning-fully.

"It's your rodeo," the man in the raincoat said, and went back out the front door.

The wind blew through the screens into the room. Outside, the moonlight glittered like silver on the water in the saw grass.

"Lie down on the floor where I can watch you. Here, take this pillow," the man with whiskers said.

"Don't hurt my boy, suh."

"Don't talk no more. Don't look at my face either."

"What's I gonna do? You here to kill my boy."

"You don't know that. Maybe we just want to talk to him . . . Don't look at my face."

"I ain't lying on no flo'. I ain't gonna sit by while y'all kill my boy. What y'all t'ink I am?"

"An old man, just like I'm getting to be. You can have something to eat or put your head down on the table and take a nap. But don't mix in it. You understand that? You mix in it, we gonna forget you're an old nigra don't nobody pay any mind to."

The man in the raincoat came back through the door, a sawed-off over-and-under shotgun in his right hand.

"I'm burning up. The wind feels like it come off a desert," he said, and took off his coat and wiped his face with a handkerchief. "What was the old man talking about?"

"He thinks the stock market might take a slide."

"Ask him if there's any stray pussy in the neighborhood."

The man with whiskers on his chin leaned over and spit tobacco juice into the coffee can. He wiped his lips with his thumb.

"Bring his dog in here," he said.

"What for?"

"Because a dog skulking and whimpering around the door might indicate somebody kicked it."

"I hadn't thought about that. They always say you're a thinking man, Harpo."

The man with the whiskers spit in the can again and looked hard at him.

The man who had worn the raincoat dragged the dog skittering through the door on its leash, then tried to haul it into the air. But the dog's back feet found purchase on the floor and its teeth tore into the man's hand.

"Oh, shit!" he yelled out, and pushed both his hands between his thighs.

"Get that damn dog under control, old man, or I'm gonna shoot both of you," the man with whiskers said.

"Yes, suh. He ain't gonna be no trouble. I promise," Mout' said.

"You all right?" the man with whiskers asked his friend.

His friend didn't answer. He opened an ice chest and found a bottle of wine and poured it on the wound. His hand was strung with blood, his fingers shaking as though numb with cold. He tied his handkerchief around the wound, pulling it tight with his teeth, and sat down in a wood chair facing the door, the shotgun across his knees.

"This better come out right," he said.

MOUT' SAT IN THE corner, on the floor, his dog between his thighs. He could hear mullet splash out in the saw grass, the drone of a distant boat engine, dry thunder booming over the Gulf. He wanted it to rain, but he didn't know why. Maybe if it rained, no, stormed, with lightning all over the sky, Cool Breeze would take shelter and not try to come back that night. Or if it was thundering real bad, the two white men wouldn't hear Cool Breeze's outboard, hear him lifting the crab traps out of the aluminum bottom, hefting up the bucket loaded with catfish he'd unhooked from the trot line.

"I got to go to the bat'room," he said.

But neither of the white men acknowledged him.

"I got to make water," he said.

The man with whiskers stood up from his chair and straightened his back.

"Come on, old man," he said, and let Mout' walk ahead of him out the back door.

"Maybe you a good man, suh. Maybe you just ain't giving yourself credit for being a good man," Mout' said.

"Go ahead and piss."

"I ain't never give no trouble to white people. Anybody round New Iberia tell you that. Same wit' my boy. He worked hard at the bowling alley. He had him a li'l sto'. He tried to stay out of trouble but wouldn't nobody let him."

Then Mout' felt his caution, his lifetime of deference and obsequiousness and pretense slipping away from him. "He had him a wife, her name was Ida, the sweetest black girl in Franklin, but a white man said she was gonna cook for him, just like that, or her husband was gonna go to the penitentiary. Then he took her out in the shed and made her get down on her knees and do what he want. She t'rowed up and begged him not to make her do it again, and every t'ree or fo' nights he walked her out in the shed and she tole herself it's gonna be over soon, he gonna get tired of me and then me and Cool Breeze gonna be left alone, and when he got finished wit' her and made her hate herself and hate my boy, too, another white man come along and give her presents and took her to his bed and tole her t'ings to tell Cool Breeze so he'd know he wasn't nothing but a nigger and a nigger's wife is a white man's jelly roll whenever he want it."

"Shake it off and zip up your pants," the man with whiskers said.

"You cain't get my boy fair. He'll cut yo' ass."

"You better shut up, old man."

"White trash wit' a gun and a big truck. Seen y'all all my life. Got to shove niggers round or you don't know who you are."

The man with whiskers pushed Mout' toward the shack, surprised at the power and breadth of muscle in Mout's back.

"I might have underestimated you. Don't take that as good news," he said.

MOUT' WOKE JUST BEFORE first light. The dog lay in his lap, its coat stiff with mud. The two white men sat in chairs facing the front door, their shoulders slightly rounded, their chins dropping to their chests. The man with the shotgun opened his eyes suddenly, as though waking from a dream.

"Wake up," he said.

"What is it?"

"Nothing. That's the point. I don't want to drive out of here in sunlight."

The man with whiskers rubbed the sleep out of his face.

"Bring the truck up," he said.

The man with the shotgun looked in Mout's direction, as if asking a question.

"I'll think about it," the man with whiskers said.

"It's mighty loose, Harpo."

"Every time I say something, you got a remark to make."

The man with the shotgun rewrapped the bloody handkerchief on his hand. He rose from the chair and threw the shotgun to his friend. "You can use my raincoat if you decide to do business," he said, and went out into the dawn.

Mout' waited in the silence.

"What do you think we ought to do about you?" the man with whiskers asked.

"Don't matter what happen here. One day the devil gonna come for y'all, take you where you belong."

"You got diarrhea of the mouth."

"My boy better than both y'all. He outsmarted you. He know y'all here. He out there now. Cool Breeze gonna come after you, Mr. White Trash."

"Stand up, you old fart."

Mout' pushed himself to his feet, his back against the plank wall. He could feel his thighs quivering, his bladder betraying him. Outside, the sun had risen into a line of storm clouds that looked like the brow of an angry man.

The man with whiskers held the shotgun against his hip and fired one barrel into Mout's dog, blowing it like a bag of broken sticks and torn skin into the corner.

"Get a cat. They're a lot smarter animals," he said, and went out the door and crossed the board walkway to the levee where his friend sat on the fender of their pickup truck, smoking a cigarette.

TEN

'COOL BREEZE RUN OUT OF gas. That's why he didn't come back to the camp," Mout' said.

It was Wednesday afternoon, and Helen and I sat with Mout' in his small living room, listening to his story.

"What'd the Vermilion Parish deputies say?" Helen asked.

"Man wrote on his clipboa'd. Said it was too bad about my dog. Said I could get another one at the shelter. I ax him, 'What about them two men?' He said it didn't make no sense they come into my camp to kill a dog. I said, 'Yeah, it don't make no sense 'cause you wasn't listening to the rest of it.' "

"Where's Cool Breeze, Mout'?"

"Gone."

"Where?"

"To borrow money."

"Come on, Mout'," I said.

"To buy a gun. Cool Breeze full of hate, Mr. Dave.

Cool Breeze don't show it, but he don't forgive. What bother me is the one he don't forgive most is himself."

BACK AT MY OFFICE, I called Special Agent Adrien Glazier at the FBI office in New Orleans.

"Two white men, one with the first name of Harpo, tried to clip Willie Broussard at a fish camp in Vermilion Parish," I said.

"When was this?"

"Last night."

"Is there a federal crime involved here?"

"Not that I know of. Maybe crossing a state line to commit a felony."

"You have evidence of that?"

"No."

"Then why are you calling, Mr. Robicheaux?"

"His life's in jeopardy."

"We're not unaware of the risk he's incurred as a federal witness. But I'm busy right now. I'll have to call you back," she said.

"You're busy?"

The line went dead.

A UNIFORMED DEPUTY PICKED up Cool Breeze in front of a pawnshop on the south side of New Iberia and brought him into my office.

"Why the cuffs?" I said.

"Ask him what he called me when I told him to get in the cruiser," the deputy replied.

"Take them off, please."

"By all means. Glad to be of service. You want anything else?" the deputy said, and turned a tiny key in the lock on the cuffs.

"Thanks for bringing him in."

"Oh, yeah, anytime. I always had aspirations to be a bus driver," he said, and went out the door, his eyes flat.

"Who you think is on your side, Breeze?" I said.

"Me."

"I see. Your daddy says you're going to get even. How you going to do that? You know who these guys are, where they live?"

He was sitting in the chair in front of my desk now, looking out the window, his eyes downturned at the corners.

"Did you hear me?" I said.

"You know how come one of them had a raincoat on?" he said.

"He didn't want the splatter on his clothes."

"You know why they left my daddy alive?"

I didn't reply. His gaze was still focused out the window. His hands looked like black starfish on his thighs.

"Long as Mout's alive, I'll probably be staying at his house," he said. "Mout' don't mean no more to them than a piece of nutria meat tied in a crab trap."

"You didn't answer my question."

"Them two men who killed the white boys out in the Basin? They ain't did that in St. Mary Parish without permission. Not to no white boys, they didn't. And it sure didn't have nothing to do with any black girl they raped in New Iberia."

"What are you saying?"

"Them boys was killed 'cause of something they done right there in St. Mary."

"So you think the same guys are trying to do you,

and you're going to find them by causing some trouble over in St. Mary Parish? Sounds like a bad plan, Breeze."

His eyes fastened on mine for the first time, his anger unmasked. "I ain't said that. I was telling you how it work round here. Blind hog can find an ear of corn if you t'row it on the ground. But you tell white folks grief comes down from the man wit' the money, they ain't gonna hear that. You done wit' me now, suh?"

LATE THAT SAME AFTERNOON, an elderly priest named Father James Mulcahy called me from St. Peter's Church in town. He used to have a parish made up of poor and black people in the Irish Channel, and had even known Clete Purcel when Clete was a boy, but he had been transferred by the Orleans diocese to New Iberia, where he did little more than say Mass and occasionally hear confessions.

"There's a lady here. I thought she came for reconciliation. But I'm not even sure she's Catholic," he said.

"I don't understand, Father."

"She seems confused, I think in need of counseling. I've done all I can for her."

"You want me to talk to her?"

"I suspect so. She won't leave."

"Who is she?"

"Her name is Lila Terrebonne. She says she lives in Jeanerette."

Helen Soileau got in a cruiser with me and we drove to St. Peter's. The late sun shone through the stained glass and suffused the interior of the church with a peculiar gold-and-blue light. Lila Terrebonne sat in a pew by the confessional boxes, immobile, her hands in her lap, her eyes as unseeing as a blind person's. An enormous replication of Christ on the cross hung on the adjacent wall.

At the vestibule door Father Mulcahy placed his hand on my arm. He was a frail man, his bones as weightless as a bird's inside his skin.

"This lady carries a deep injury. The nature of her problem is complex, but be assured it's of the kind that destroys people," he said.

"She's an alcoholic, Father. Is that what we're talking about here?" Helen said.

"What she told me wasn't in a sacramental situation, but I shouldn't say any more," he replied.

I walked up the aisle and sat in the pew behind Lila.

"You ever have a guy try to pick you up in church before?" I asked.

She turned and stared at me, her face cut by a column of sunshine. The powder and down on her cheeks glowed as though illuminated by klieg lights. Her milky green eyes were wide with expectation that seemed to have no source.

"I was just thinking about you," she said.

"I bet."

"We're all going to die, Dave."

"You're right. But probably not today. Let's take a ride."

"It's strange I'd end up sitting here under the Crucifixion. Do you know the Hanged Man in the Tarot?"

"Sure," I said.

"That's the death card."

"No, it's St. Sebastian, a Roman soldier who was martyred for his faith. It represents self-sacrifice," I said.

"The priest wouldn't give me absolution. I'm sure I was baptized Catholic before I was baptized Protestant. My mother was a Catholic," she said.

Helen stood at the end of Lila's pew, chewing gum, her thumbs hooked in her gunbelt. She rested three fingers on Lila's shoulders.

"How about taking us to dinner?" she said.

AN HOUR LATER WE crossed the parish line into St. Mary. The air was mauve-colored, the bayou dimpled with the feeding of bream, the wind hot and smelling of tar from the highway. We drove up the brick-paved drive of the Terrebonne home. Lila's father stood on the portico, a cigar in his hand, his shoulder propped against a brick pillar.

I pulled the cruiser to a stop and started to get out.

"Stay here, Dave. I'm going to take Lila to the door," Helen said.

"That isn't necessary. I'm feeling much better now. I shouldn't have had a drink with that medication. It always makes me a bit otherworldly," Lila said.

"Your father doesn't like us, Lila. If he wants to say something, he should have the chance," Helen said.

But evidently Archer Terrebonne was not up to confronting Helen Soileau that evening. He took a puff from his cigar, then walked inside and closed the heavy door audibly behind him.

The portico and brick parking area were deep in shadow now, the gold and scarlet four-o'clock flowers in full bloom. Helen walked toward the portico with her arm around Lila's shoulders, then watched her go in the house and close the door. Helen continued to look at the door, working the gum in her jaw, the flat of one hand pushed down in the back of her gunbelt.

She opened the passenger door and got in.

"I'd say leapers and vodka," I said.

"No odor, fried terminals. Yeah, that sounds right. Great combo for a coronary," she replied.

I turned around in front of the house and drove toward the service road and the bridge over the bayou. Helen kept looking over the seat through the rear window.

"I wanted to kick her old man's ass. With a baton, broken teeth and bones, a real job," she said. "Not good, huh, bwana?"

"He's one of those guys who inspire thoughts like that. I wouldn't worry about it."

"I had him made for a child molester. I was wrong. That woman's been raped, Dave."

ELEVEN

THE NEXT MORNING I CALLED Clete Purcel in New Orleans, signed out of the office for the day, and drove across the elevated highway that spanned the chain of bays in the Atchafalaya Basin, across the Mississippi bridge at Baton Rouge, then down through pasture country and the long green corridor through impassable woods that tapered into palmettos and flooded cypress on the north side of Lake Pontchartrain. Then I was at the French Quarter exit, with the sudden and real urban concern of having to park anywhere near the Iberville Welfare Project.

I left my truck off Decatur, two blocks from the Cafe du Monde, and crossed Jackson Square into the shade of Pirates Alley between the lichen-stained garden of the Cathedral and the tiny bookstore that had once been the home of William Faulkner. Then I walked on down St. Ann, in sunlight again, to a tan stucco building with an arched entrance and a courtyard and a grilled balcony upstairs that dripped bougainvillea, where Clete Purcel kept his private investigative agency and sometimes lived.

"You want to take down Jimmy Fig? How hard?" he said.

"We don't have to bounce him off the furniture, if that's what you mean."

Clete wore a pressed seersucker suit with a tie, and his hair had just been barbered and parted on the side and combed straight down on his head so that it looked like a little boy's.

"Jimmy Figorelli is a low-rent sleaze. Why waste time on a shit bag?" he said.

"It's been a slow week."

He looked at me with the flat, clear-eyed pause that always indicated his unbelief in what I was saying. Through the heavy bubbled yellow glass in his doors, I saw Megan Flynn walk down the stairs in blue jeans and a T-shirt and carry a box through the breezeway to a U-Haul trailer on the street.

"She's helping me move," Clete said.

"Move where?"

"A little cottage between New Iberia and Jeanerette. I'm going to head security at that movie set."

"Are you crazy? That director or producer or whatever he is, Billy Holtzner, is the residue you pour out of spittoons."

"I ran security for Sally Dio at Lake Tahoe. I think I can handle it."

"Wait till you meet Holtzner's daughter and boyfriend. They're hypes, or at least she is. Come on, Clete. You were the best cop I ever knew."

Clete turned his ring on his finger. It was made of

gold and silver and embossed with the globe and anchor of the U.S. Marine Corps.

"Yeah, 'was' the best cop. I got to change and help Megan. Then we'll check out Jimmy Fig. I think we're firing in the well, though," he said.

After he had gone upstairs I looked out the back window at the courtyard, the dry wishing well that was cracked and never retained water, the clusters of untrimmed banana trees, Clete's rust-powdered barbells that he religiously pumped and curled, usually half full of booze, every afternoon. I didn't hear Megan open the door to the breezeway behind me.

"What'd you say to get him upset?" she asked. She was perspiring from her work and her T-shirt was damp and shaped against her breasts. She stood in front of the air-conditioning unit and lifted the hair off the back of her neck.

"I think you're sticking tacks in his head," I said.

"Where the hell you get off talking to me like that?"

"Your brother's friends are scum."

"Two-thirds of the world is. Grow up."

"Boxleiter and I had a talk. The death photo of the black guy in the drainpipe was a setup."

"You're full of shit, Dave."

We stared at each other in the refrigerated coolness of the room, almost slit-eyed with antagonism. Her eyes had a reddish-brown cast in them like fire inside amber glass.

"I think I'll wait outside," I said.

"You know what homoeroticism is? Guys who aren't quite gay but who've got a yen they never deal with?" she said.

"You'd better not hurt him."

"Oh, yeah?" she said, and stepped toward me, her hands shoved in her back pockets like a baseball manager getting in an umpire's face. Her neck was sweaty and ringed with dirt and her upper lip was beaded with moisture. "I'm not going to take your bullshit, Dave. You go fuck yourself." Then her face, which was heart-shaped and tender to look at and burning with anger at the same time, seemed to go out of focus. *"Hurt* him? My father was nailed alive to a board wall. You lecture me on hurting people? Don't you feel just a little bit embarrassed, you self-righteous sonofabitch?"

I walked outside into the sunshine. Sweat was running out of my hair; the backdraft of a passing sanitation truck enveloped me with dust and the smell of decaying food. I wiped my forehead on my sleeve and was repelled by my own odor.

CLETE AND I DROVE out of the Quarter, crossed Canal, and headed up Magazine in his convertible. He had left the top down while the car had been parked on the street and the seats and metal surfaces were like the touch of a clothes iron. He drove with his left hand, his right clenched around a can of beer wrapped in a paper sack.

"You want to forget it?" I asked.

"No, you want to see the guy, we see the guy."

"I heard Jimmy Fig wasn't a bad kid before he was at Khe Sanh."

"Yeah, I heard that story. He got wounded and hooked on morphine. Makes great street talk. I'll tell you another story. He was the wheelman on a jewelry store job in Memphis. It should have been an easy in-

and-out, smash-and-grab deal, except the guys with him decided they didn't want witnesses, so they executed an eighty-year-old Jew who had survived Bergen-Belsen."

"I apologize to you and Megan for what I said back there."

"I've got hypertension, chronic obesity, and my own rap sheet at NOPD. What do guys like us care about stuff like that?"

He pressed his aviator glasses against his nose, hiding his eyes. Sweat leaked out of his porkpie hat and glistened on his flexed jaw.

JIMMY FIGORELLI RAN A sandwich shop and cab stand on Magazine just below Audubon Park. He was a tall, kinetic, wired man, with luminous black eyes and black hair that grew in layers on his body.

He was chopping green onions in an apron and never missed a beat when we entered the front door and stood under the bladed ceiling fan that turned overhead.

"You want to know who put a hit on Cool Breeze Broussard? You come to my place of business and ask me a question like that, like you need the weather report or something?" He laughed to himself and raked the chopped onions off the chopping board onto a sheet of wax paper and started slicing a boned roast into strips.

"The guy doesn't deserve what's coming down on him, Jimmy. Maybe you can help set it right," I said.

"The guys you're interested in don't fax me their day-to-day operations," he replied.

Clete kept lifting his shirt up from his shoulders with his fingers.

"I got a terrible sunburn, Jimmy. I want to be back in the air-conditioning with a vodka and tonic, not listening to a shuck that might cause a less patient person to come around behind that counter," Clete said.

Jimmy Figorelli scratched an eyebrow, took off his apron and picked up a broom and began sweeping up green sawdust from around an ancient Coca-Cola cooler that sweated with coldness.

"What I heard is the clip went to some guys already got it in for Broussard. It's nigger trouble, Purcel. What else can I tell you? *Semper fi,*" he said.

"I heard you were in the First Cav at Khe Sanh," I said.

"Yeah, I was on a Jolly Green that took a RPG through the door. You know what I think all that's worth?"

"You paid dues lowlifes don't. Why not act like it?" I said.

"I got a Purple Heart with a *V* for valor. If I ever find it while I'm cleaning out my garage, I'll send it to you," he said.

I could hear Clete breathing beside me, almost feel the oily heat his skin gave off.

"You know what they say about the First Cav patch, Jimmy. 'The horse they couldn't ride, the line they couldn't cross, the color that speaks for itself,'" Clete said.

"Yeah, well, kiss my ass, you Irish prick, and get out of my store."

"Let's go," I said to Clete.

He stared at me, his face flushed, the skin drawn

back against the eye sockets. Then he followed me outside, where we stood under an oak and watched one of Jimmy Fig's cabs pick up a young black woman who carried a red lacquered purse and wore a tank top and a miniskirt and white fishnet stockings.

"You didn't like what I said?" Clete asked.

"Why get on the guy's outfit? It's not your way."

"You got a point. Let me correct that."

He walked back inside, his hands at his sides, balled into fists as big as hams.

"Hey, Jimmy, I didn't mean anything about the First Cav. I just can't take the way you chop onions. It irritates the hell out of me," he said.

Then he drove his right fist, lifting his shoulder and all his weight into the blow, right into Jimmy Figorelli's face.

Jimmy held on to the side of the Coca-Cola box, his hand trembling uncontrollably on his mouth, his eyes dilated with shock, his fingers shining with blood and bits of teeth.

THREE DAYS LATER IT began to rain, and it rained through the Labor Day weekend and into the following week. The bayou by the dock rose above the cattails and into the canebrake, my rental boats filled with water, and moccasins crawled into our yard. On Saturday night, during a downpour, Father James Mulcahy knocked on our front door.

He carried an umbrella and wore a Roman collar and a rain-flecked gray suit and a gray fedora. When he stepped inside he tried not to breathe into my face.

"I'm sorry for coming out without calling first," he said.

"We're glad you dropped by. Can I offer you something?" I said.

He touched at his mouth and sat down in a stuffed chair. The rain was blowing against the gallery, and the tin roof of the bait shop quivered with light whenever thunder was about to roll across the swamp.

"Would you like a drink, sir?" I asked.

"No, no, that wouldn't be good. Coffee's fine. I have to tell you about something, Mr. Robicheaux. It bothers me deeply," he said.

His hands were liver-spotted, ridged with blue veins, the skin as thin as parchment on the bones. Bootsie brought coffee and sugar and hot milk on a tray from the kitchen. When the priest lifted the cup to his mouth his eyes seemed to look through the steam at nothing, then he said, "Do you believe in evil, Mr. Robicheaux? I don't mean the wicked deeds we sometimes do in a weak moment. I mean evil in the darkest theological sense."

"I'm not sure, Father. I've seen enough of it in people not to look for a source outside of ourselves."

"I was a chaplain in Thailand during the Vietnam War. I knew a young soldier who participated in a massacre. You might have seen the pictures. The most unforgettable was of a little boy holding his grandmother's skirts in terror while she begged for their lives. I spent many hours with that young soldier, but I could never remove the evil that lived in his dreams."

"I don't understand how—" I began.

He raised his hand. "Listen to me," he said. "There was another man, a civilian profiteer who lived on the air base. His corporation made incendiary bombs. I told

him the story of the young soldier who had machine-
gunned whole families in a ditch. The profiteer's re-
joinder was to tell me about a strafing gun his company
had patented. In thirty seconds it could tear the sod out
of an entire football field. In that moment I think that
man's eyes were the conduit into the abyss."

Bootsie's face wore no expression, but I saw her
look at me, then back at the priest.

"Please have dinner with us," she said.

"Oh, I've intruded enough. I really haven't made
my point either. Last night in the middle of the storm a
truck stopped outside the rectory. I thought it was a
parishioner. When I opened the door a man in a slouch
hat and raincoat was standing there. I've never felt the
presence of evil so strongly in my life. I was convinced
he was there to kill me. I think he would have done it if
the housekeeper and Father Lemoyne hadn't walked up
behind me.

"He pointed his arm at me and said, 'Don't you
break the seal.' Then he got back in his truck and drove
away with the lights off."

"You mean divulge the content of a confession?" I
asked.

"He was talking about the Terrebonne woman. I'm
sure of it. But what she told me wasn't under the seal,"
he replied.

"You want to tell me about Lila, Father?" I said.

"No, it wouldn't be proper. A confidence is a confidence. Also, she wasn't entirely coherent and I might
do her a great disservice," he said. But his face clouded,
and it was obvious his own words did little to reassure
him.

"This man in the truck, Father? If his name is Harpo, we want to be very careful of him," I said.

"His eyes," the priest said.

"Sir?"

"They were like the profiteer's. Without moral light. A man like that speaking of the confessional seal. It offends something in me in a way I can't describe."

"Have dinner with us," I said.

"Yes, that's very kind of you. Your home seems to have a great warmth to it. From outside it truly looked like a haven in the storm. Could I have that drink after all?"

He sat at the table with a glass of cream sherry, his eyes abstract, feigning attention, like those of people who realize that momentary refuge and the sharing of fear with others will not relieve them of the fact that death may indeed have taken up residence inside them.

MONDAY MORNING I DROVE down Bayou Teche through Jeanerette into the little town of Franklin and talked to the chief of police. He was a very light mulatto in his early forties who wore sideburns and a gold ring in his ear and a lacquered-brim cap on the back of his head.

"A man name of Harpo? There used to be a Harpo Delahoussey. He was a sheriff's deputy, did security at the Terrebonne cannery," the police chief said.

"That's not the one. This guy was maybe his nephew. He was a Franklin police officer. People called him Little Harpo," I said.

He fiddled with a pencil and gazed out the window. It was still raining, and a black man rode a bicycle down the sidewalk, his body framed against the smoky neon of a bar across the street.

"When I was a kid there was a cop round here name of H. Q. Scruggs." He wet his lips. "When he come into the quarters we knew to call him Mr. H.Q. Not Officer. That wasn't enough for this gentleman. But I remember white folks calling him Harpo sometimes. As I recall, he'd been a guard up at Angola, too. If you want to talk about him, I'll give you the name and address of a man might hep you."

"You don't care to talk about him?"

He laid the pencil flat on his desk blotter. "I don't like to even remember him. Fortunately today I don't have to," he said.

CLEM MADDUX SAT ON his gallery, smoking a cigarette, in a swayback deer-hide chair lined with a quilt for extra padding. One of his legs was amputated at the torso, the other above the knee. His girth was huge, his stomach pressing in staggered layers against the oversized ink-dark blue jeans he wore. His skin was as pink and unblemished as a baby's, but around his neck goiters hung from his flesh like a necklace of duck's eggs.

"You staring at me, Mr. Robicheaux?" he asked.

"No, sir."

"It's Buerger's Disease. Smoking worsens it. But I got diabetes and cancer of the prostate, too. I got diseases that'll outlive the one that kills me," he said, then laughed and wiped spittle off his lips with his wrist.

"You were a gun bull at Angola with Harpo Scruggs?"

"No, I was head of farm machinery. I didn't carry

a weapon. Harpo was a tower guard, then a shotgun guard on horseback. That must have been forty years ago."

"What kind of hack was he?"

"Piss-poor in my opinion. How far back you go?"

"You talking about the Red Hat gang and the men buried under the levee?"

"There was this old fart used to come off a corn-whiskey drunk meaner than a razor in your shoe. He'd single out a boy from his gang and tell him to start running. Harpo asked to get in on it."

"Asked to kill someone?"

"It was a colored boy from Laurel Hill. He'd sassed the field boss at morning count. When the food truck come out to the levee at noon, Harpo pulled the colored boy out of the line and told him he wasn't eating no lunch till he finished sawing a stump out of the river bottom. Harpo walked him off into some gum trees by the water, then I seen the boy starting off on his own, looking back uncertain-like while Harpo was telling him something. Then I heard it, *pow, pow,* both barrels. Double-ought bucks, from not more than eight or ten feet."

Maddux tossed his cigarette over the railing into the flower bed.

"What happened to Scruggs?" I asked.

"He done a little of this, a little of that, I guess."

"That's a little vague, cap."

"He road-ganged in Texas a while, then bought into a couple of whorehouses. What do you care any-way? The sonofabitch is probably squatting on the coals."

"He's squatting—"

"He got burned up with a Mexican chippy in Juárez fifteen years ago. Wasn't nothing left of him except a bag of ash and some teeth. Damn, son, y'all ought to update and get you some computers."

TWELVE

TWO DAYS LATER I SAT at my desk, sifting through the Gypsy fortune-telling deck called the Tarot. I had bought the deck at a store in Lafayette, but the instruction book that accompanied it dealt more with the meaning of the cards than with the origins of their iconography. Regardless, it would be impossible for anyone educated in a traditional Catholic school not to recognize the historical associations of the imagery in the Hanged Man.

The phone on my desk buzzed.

"Clete Purcel and Megan Flynn just pulled up," the sheriff said.

"Yeah?"

"Get him out of here."

"Skipper—"

He hung up.

A moment later Clete tapped on my glass and opened the door, then paused and looked back down the hall, his face perplexed.

"What happened, the john overflow in the waiting room again?" he said.

"Why's that?"

"A pall is hanging over the place every time I walk in. What do those guys do for kicks, watch snuff films? In fact, I asked the dispatcher that. Definitely no sense of humor."

He sat down and looked around my office, grinned at me for no reason, straightened his back, flexed his arms, bounced his palms up and down on the chair.

"Megan's with you?" I said.

"How'd you know that?"

"Uh, I think the sheriff saw y'all from his window."

"The sheriff? I get it. He told you to roll out the welcome wagon." His eyes roved merrily over my face. "How about we treat you to lunch at Lagniappe Too?"

"I'm buried."

"Megan gave you her drill instructor impersonation the other day?"

"It's very convincing."

He beat out a staccato with his hands on the chair arms.

"Will you stop that and tell me what's on your mind?" I said.

"This cat Billy Holtzner. I've seen him somewhere. Like from Vietnam."

"Holtzner?"

"So we had nasty little marshmallows over there, too. Anyway, I go, 'Were you in the Crotch?' He says, 'The Crotch?' I say, 'Yeah, the Marine Corps. Were you around Da Nang?' What kind of answer do I get?

He sucks his teeth and goes back to his clipboard like I'm not there."

He waited for me to speak. When I didn't he said, *"What?"*

"I hate to see you mixed up with them."

"See you later, Streak."

"I'm coming with you," I said, and stuck the Hanged Man in my shirt pocket.

WE ATE LUNCH AT Lagniappe Too, just down from The Shadows. Megan sat by the window with her hat on. Her hair was curved on her cheeks, and her mouth looked small and red when she took a piece of food off her fork. The light through the window seemed to frame her silhouette against the green wall of bamboo that grew in front of The Shadows. She saw me staring at her.

"Is something troubling you, Dave?" she asked.

"You know Lila Terrebonne?"

"The senator's granddaughter?"

"She comes to our attention on occasion. The other day we had to pick her up at the church, sitting by herself under a crucifix. Out of nowhere she asked me about the Hanged Man in the Tarot."

I slipped the card out of my shirt pocket and placed it on the tablecloth by Megan's plate.

"Why tell me?" she said.

"Does it mean something to you?"

I saw Clete lower his fork into his plate, felt his eyes fix on the side of my face.

"A man hanging upside down from a tree. The tree forms a cross," Megan said.

"The figure becomes Peter the Apostle, as well as

Christ and St. Sebastian. Sebastian was tied to a tree and shot with darts by his fellow Roman soldiers. Peter asked to be executed upside down. You notice, the figure makes a cross with his legs in the act of dying?" I said.

Megan had stopped eating. Her cheeks were freckled with discoloration, as though an invisible pool of frigid air had burned her face.

"What is this, Dave?" Clete said.

"Maybe nothing," I said.

"Just lunch conversation?" he said.

"The Terrebonnes have had their thumbs in lots of pies," I said.

"Will you excuse me, please?" Megan said.

She walked between the tables to the rest room, her purse under her arm, her funny straw hat crimped across the back of her red hair.

"What the hell's the matter with you?" Clete said.

THAT EVENING I DROVE to Red Lerille's Health & Racquet Club in Lafayette and worked out with free weights and on the Hammer-Strength machines, then ran two miles on the second-story track that overlooked the basketball courts.

I hung my towel around my neck and did leg stretches on the handrail. Down below, some men were playing a pickup basketball game, thudding into one another clumsily, slapping one another's shoulders when they made a shot. But an Indonesian or Malaysian man at the end of the court, where the speed and heavy bags were hung, was involved in a much more intense and solitary activity. He wore sweats and tight red leather gloves, the kind with a metal dowel across the palm, and he ripped his fists into the heavy bag and sent it spinning on the chain, then speared it with his feet, hard enough to almost knock down a kid who was walking by.

He grinned at the boy by way of apology, then moved over to the speed bag and began whacking it against the rebound board, without rhythm or timing, slashing it for the effect alone.

"You were at Cisco's house. You're Mr. Robicheaux," a woman's voice said behind me.

It was Billy Holtzner's daughter. But her soapy blue eyes were focused now, actually pleasant, like a person who has stepped out of one identity into another.

"You remember me?" she asked.

"Sure."

"We didn't introduce ourselves the other day. I'm Geraldine Holtzner. The boxer down there is Anthony. He's an accountant for the studio. I'm sorry for our rudeness."

"You weren't rude."

"I know you don't like my father. Not many people do. We're not problem visitors here. If you have one, it's Cisco Flynn," she said.

"Cisco?"

"He owes my father a lot of money. Cisco thinks he can avoid his responsibilities by bringing a person like Swede Boxleiter around."

She gripped the handrail and extended one leg at a time behind her. Her wild, brownish-red hair shimmered with perspiration.

"You let that guy down there shoot you up?" I asked.

"I'm all right today. Sometimes I just have a bad

day. You're a funny guy for a cop. You ever have a screen test?"

"Why not get rid of the problem altogether?"

But she wasn't listening now. "This area is full of violent people. It's the South. It lives in the woodwork down here. This black man who's coming after the Terrebonnes, why don't you do something about him?" she said.

"Which black man? Are you talking about Cool Breeze Broussard?"

"Which? Yeah, that's a good question. You know the story about the murdered slave woman, the children who were poisoned? If I had stuff like that in my family, I'd jump off a cliff. No wonder Lila Terrebonne's a drunk."

"It was nice seeing you," I said.

"Gee, why don't you just say fuck you and turn your back on people?"

Her skin was the color of milk that has browned in a pan, her blue eyes dancing in her face. She wiped her hair and throat with a towel and threw it at me.

"That kick-boxing stuff Anthony's doing? He learned it from me," she said.

Then she raised her face up into mine, her lips slightly parted, speckled with saliva, her eyes filled with anticipation and need.

ON THE WAY BACK home I stopped in the New Iberia city library and looked up a late-nineteenth-century reminiscence written about our area by a New England lady named Abigail Dowling, a nurse who came here during a yellow fever epidemic and was radicalized not by slavery itself and the misery it visited upon the black race but by what she called its dehumanizing effects on the white.

One of the families about which she wrote in detail was the Terrebonnes of St. Mary Parish.

Before the Civil War, Elijah Terrebonne had been a business partner in the slave trade with Nathan Bedford Forrest and later had ridden at Forrest's side during the battle of Brice's Crossing, where a minié shattered his arm and took him out of the war. But Elijah had also been below the bluffs at Fort Pillow when black troops who begged on their knees were executed at point-blank range in retaliation for a sixty-mile scorched-earth sweep by Federal troops into northern Mississippi.

"He was of diminutive stature, with a hard, compact body. He sat his horse with the rigidity of a clothes pin," Abigail Dowling wrote in her journal. "His countenance was handsome, certainly, of a rosy hue, and it exuded a martial light when he talked of the War. In consideration of his physical stature I tried to overlook his imperious manner. In spite of his propensity for miscegenation, he loved his wife and their twin girls and was unduly possessive about them, perhaps in part because of his own romantic misdeeds.

"Unfortunately for the poor black souls on his plantation, the lamps of charity and pity did not burn brightly in his heart. I have been told General Forrest tried to stop the slaughter of negro soldiers below the bluffs. I believe Elijah Terrebonne had no such redemptive memory for himself. I believe the fits of anger that made him draw human blood with a horse whip had their origins in the faces of dead black men who journeyed nightly to Elijah's bedside, vainly begging mercy from one who had murdered his soul."

The miscegenation mentioned by Abigail Dowling involved a buxom slave woman named Lavonia, whose husband, Big Walter, had been killed by a falling tree. Periodically Elijah Terrebonne rode to the edge of the fields and called her away from her work, in view of the other slaves and the white overseer, and walked her ahead of his horse into the woods, where he copulated with her in an unused sweet potato cellar. Later, he heard that the overseer had been talking freely in the saloon, joking with a drink in his hand at the fireplace, stoking the buried resentment and latent contempt of other landless whites about the lust of his employer. Elijah laid open his face with a quirt and adjusted his situation by moving Lavonia up to the main house as a cook and a wet nurse for his children.

But when he returned from Brice's Crossing, with pieces of bone still working their way out of the surgeon's incision in his arm, the Teche country was occupied, his house and barns looted, the orchards and fields reduced to soot blowing in the wind. The only meat on the plantation consisted of seven smoked hams Lavonia had buried in the woods before the Federal flotilla had come up the Teche.

The Terrebonnes made coffee out of acorns and ate the same meager rations as the blacks. Some of the freed males on the plantation went to work on shares; others followed the Yankee soldiers marching north into the Red River campaign. When the food ran out, Lavonia was among a group of women and elderly folk who were assembled in front of their cabins by Elijah Terrebonne and then told they would have to leave.

She went to Elijah's wife.

Abigail Dowling wrote in the journal, "It was a

wretched sight, this stout field woman without a husband, with no concept of historical events or geography, about to be cast out in a ruined land filled with night riders and drunken soldiers. Her simple entreaty could not have described her plight more adequately: 'I'se got fo' children, Missy. What's we gonna go? What's I gonna feed them with?' "

Mrs. Terrebonne granted her a one-month reprieve, either to find a husband or to receive help from the Freedmen's Bureau.

The journal continued: "But Lavonia was a sad and ignorant creature who thought guile could overcome the hardness of heart in her former masters. She put cyanide in the family's food, believing they would become ill and dependent upon her for their daily care.

"Both of the Terrebonne girls died. Elijah would have never known the cause of their deaths, except for the careless words of Lavonia's youngest child, who came to him, the worst choice among men, to seek solace. The child blurted out, 'My mama been crying, Mas'er. She got poison in a bottle under her bed. She say the devil give it to her and made her hurt somebody with it. I think she gonna take it herself.'

"By firelight Elijah dug up the coffins of his children from the wet clay and unwound the wrappings from their bodies. Their skin was covered with pustules the color and shape of pearls. He pressed his hand on their chests and breathed the air trapped in their lungs and swore it smelled of almonds.

"His rage and madness could be heard all the way across the fields to the quarters. Lavonia tried to hide with her children in the swamp, but to no avail. Her own people found her, and in fear of Elijah's wrath, they hanged her with a man's belt from a persimmon tree."

WHAT DID IT ALL mean? Why did Geraldine Holtzner allude to the story at Red's Gym in Lafayette? I didn't know. But in the morning Megan Flynn telephoned me at the dock. Clete Purcel had been booked on a DWI and a black man had started a fire on the movie set in the Terrebonnes' front yard.

She wanted to talk.

"Talk? Clete's in the bag and you want to talk?" I said.

"I've done something terribly wrong. I'm just down the road. Will it bother you if I come by?"

"Yes, it will."

"Dave?"

"What?"

Then her voice broke.

THIRTEEN

MEGAN SAT AT A BACK table in the bait shop with a cup of coffee and waited for me while I rang up the bill on two fishermen who had just finished eating at the counter. Her hat rested by her elbow and her hair blew in the wind from the fan, but there was a twisted light in her eyes, as though she could not concentrate on anything outside her skin.

I sat down across from her.

"Y'all had a fight?" I asked.

"It was over the black man who started the fire," she said.

"That doesn't make any sense," I said.

"It's Cool Breeze Broussard. It has to be. He was going to set fire to the main house but something scared him off. So he poured gasoline under a trailer on the set."

"Why should you and Clete fight over that?"

"I helped get Cool Breeze out of jail. I knew about all his trouble in St. Mary Parish and his wife's suicide and his problems with the Terrebonne family. I wanted

the story. I pushed everything else out of my mind
. . . Maybe I planted some ideas in him about re-
venge."

"You still haven't told me why y'all fought."

"Clete said people who set fires deserve to be human candles themselves. He started talking about some
marines he saw trapped inside a burning tank."

"Breeze has always had his own mind about things.
He's not easily influenced, Megan."

"Swede will kill him. He'll kill anybody he thinks
is trying to hurt Cisco."

"That's it, huh? You think you're responsible for
getting a black man into it with a psychopath?"

"Yes. And he's not a psychopath. You've got this
guy all wrong."

"How about getting Clete into the middle of it?
You think that might be a problem, too?"

"I feel very attached—"

"Cut it out, Megan."

"I have a deep—"

"He was available and you made him your point
man. Except he doesn't have any idea of what's going
on."

Her eyes drifted onto mine, then they began to
film. I heard Batist come inside the shop, then go back
out.

"Why'd you want to put him on that movie set?" I
said.

"My brother. He's mixed up with bad people in
the Orient. I think the Terrebonnes are in it, too."

"What do you know about the Terrebonnes?"

"My father hated them."

A customer came in and picked a package of Red

Man off the wire rack and left the money on the register. Megan straightened her back and touched at one eye with her finger.

"I called the St. Mary Sheriff's Department. Clete will be arraigned at ten," I said.

"You don't hold me in very high regard, do you?"

"You just made a mistake. Now you've owned up to it. I think you're a good person, Meg."

"What do I do about Clete?"

"My father used to say never treat a brave man as less."

"I wish Cisco and I had never come back here."

But you always do, I thought. *Because of a body arched into wood planks, its blood pooling in the dust, its crusted wounds picked by chickens.*

"What did you say?" she asked.

"Nothing. I didn't say anything."

"I'm going. I'll be at Cisco's house for a spell."

She put a half dollar on the counter for the coffee and walked out the screen door. Then, just before she reached her automobile, she turned and looked back at me. She held her straw hat in her fingers, by her thigh, and with her other hand she brushed her hair back on her head, her face lifted into the sunlight.

Batist flung a bucket full of water across one of the spool tables.

"When they make cow eyes at you, it ain't 'cause they want to go to church, no," he said.

"What?"

"Her daddy got killed when she was li'l. She always coming round to talk to a man older than herself. Like they ain't no other man in New Iberia. You got to go to collitch to figure it out?" he said.

• • •

TWO HOURS LATER HELEN and I drove over to Mout' Broussard's house on the west side of town. A black four-door sedan with tinted windows and a phone antenna was parked in the dirt driveway, the back door open. Inside, we could see a man in a dark suit, wearing aviator glasses, unlocking the handcuffs on Cool Breeze Broussard.

Helen and I walked toward the car as Adrien Glazier and two male FBI agents got out with Cool Breeze.

"What's happenin', Breeze?" I said.

"They give me a ride to my daddy's," he replied.

"Your business here needs to wait, Mr. Robicheaux," Adrien Glazier said.

Out of the corner of my eye I saw one of the male agents touch Cool Breeze on the arm with one finger and point for him to wait on the gallery.

"What are you going to do with him?" I asked Adrien Glazier.

"Nothing."

"Breeze is operating out of his depth. You know that. Why are you leaving the guy out there?" I said.

"Has he complained to you? Who appointed you his special oversight person?" she replied.

"You ever hear of a guy named Harpo Scruggs?" I asked.

"No."

"I think he's got the contract on Breeze. Except he's supposed to be dead."

"Then you've got something to work on. In the meantime, we'll handle things here. Thanks for dropping by," the man who had uncuffed Cool Breeze said.

He was olive-skinned, his dark blond hair cut short, his opaque demeanor one that allowed him to be arrogant without ever being accountable.

Helen stepped toward him, her feet slightly spread.

"Reality check, you pompous fuck, this is our jurisdiction. We go where we want. You try to run us off an investigation, you're going to be picking up the soap in our jail tonight," she said.

"She's the one busted up Boxleiter," the other male agent said, his elbow hooked over the top of the driver's door, a smile at the edge of his mouth.

"Yes?" she said.

"Impressive . . . Mean shit," he said.

"We're gone," Adrien Glazier said.

"Run this guy Scruggs. He was a gun bull at Angola. Maybe he's hooked up with the Dixie Mafia," I said.

"A dead man? *Right,"* she said, then got in her car with her two colleagues and drove away.

Helen stared after them, her hands on her hips.

"Broussard's the bait tied down under the tree stand, isn't he?" she said.

"That's the way I'd read it," I said.

Cool Breeze watched us from the swing on the gallery. His brogans were caked with mud and he spun a cloth cap on the tip of his index finger.

I sat down on the wood steps and looked out at the street.

"Where's Mout'?" I asked.

"Staying at his sister's."

"You're playing other people's game," I said.

"They gonna know when I'm in town."

"Bad way to think, podna."

I heard the swing creak behind me, then his brogans scuffing the boards under him as the swing moved back and forth. A young woman carrying a bag of groceries walked past the house and the sound of the swing stopped.

"My dead wife Ida, I hear her in my sleep sometimes. Talking to me from under the water, wit' that icy chain wrapped round her. I want to lift her up, out of the silt, pick the ice out of her mout' and eyes. But the chain just too heavy. I pull and pull and my arms is like lead, and all the time they ain't no air getting down to her. You ever have a dream like that?" he said.

I turned and looked at him, my ears ringing, my face suddenly cold.

"I t'ought so. You blame me for what I do?" he said.

THAT AFTERNOON I MADE telephone calls to Juárez, Mexico, and to the sheriff's departments in three counties along the Tex-Mex border. No one had any information about Harpo Scruggs or his death. Then an FBI agent in El Paso referred me to a retired Texas Ranger by the name of Lester Cobb. His accent was deep down in his breathing passages, like heated air breaking through the top of oatmeal.

"You knew him?" I said into the receiver.

"At a distance. Which was as close as I wanted to get."

"Why's that?"

"He was a pimp. He run Mexican girls up from Chihuahua."

"How'd he die?"

"They say he was in a hot pillow joint acrost the

river. A girl put one in his ear, then set fire to the place and done herself."

"They say?"

"He was wanted down there. Why would he go back into Juárez to get laid? That story never did quite wash for me."

"If he's alive, where would I look for him?"

"Cockfights, cathouses, pigeon shoots. He's the meanest bucket of shit with a badge I ever run acrost . . . Mr. Robicheaux?"

"Yes, sir?"

"I hope he's dead. He rope-drug a Mexican behind his Jeep, out through the rocks and cactus. You get in a situation with him . . . Oh, hell, I'm too damn old to tell another lawman his business."

IT RAINED THAT EVENING, and from my lighted gallery I watched it fall on the trees and the dock and the tin roof of the bait shop and on the wide, yellow, dimpled surface of the bayou itself.

I could not shake the images of Cool Breeze's recurring dream from my mind. I stepped out into the rain and cut a half dozen roses from the bushes in the front garden and walked down the slope with them to the end of the dock.

Batist had pulled the tarp out on the guy wires and turned on the string of electric lights. I stood at the railing, watching the current drift southward toward West Cote Blanche Bay and eventually the Gulf, where many years ago my father's drilling rig had punched into an early pay sand, blowing the casing out of the hole. When the gas ignited, a black-red inferno ballooned up through the tower, all the way to the monkey board where my father worked as a derrick man. The heat was so great the steel spars burned and collapsed like matchsticks.

He and my murdered wife Annie and the dead men from my platoon used to speak to me through the rain. I found saloons by the water, always by the water, where I could trap and control light and all meaning inside three inches of Beam, with a Jax on the side, while the rain ran down the windows and rippled the walls with neon shadows that had no color.

Now, Annie and my father and dead soldiers no longer called me up on the phone. But I never underestimated the power of the rain or the potential of the dead, or denied them their presence in the world.

And for that reason I dropped the roses into the water and watched them float toward the south, the green leaves beaded with water as bright as crystal, the petals as darkly red as a woman's mouth turned toward you on the pillow for the final time.

ON THE WAY BACK up to the house I saw Clete Purcel's chartreuse Cadillac come down the dirt road and turn into the drive. The windows were streaked with mud, the convertible top as ragged as a layer of chicken feathers. He rolled down the window and grinned, in the same way that a mask grins.

"Got a minute?" he said.

I opened the passenger door and sat in the cracked leather seat beside him.

"You doing okay, Cletus?" I asked.

"Sure. Thanks for calling the bondsman." He rubbed his face. "Megan came by?"

"Yeah. Early this morning." I kept my eyes focused

on the rain blowing out of the trees onto my lighted gallery.

"She told you we were quits?"

"Not exactly."

"I got no bad feelings about it. That's how it shakes out sometimes." He widened his eyes. "I need to take a shower and get some sleep. I'll be okay with some sleep."

"Come in and eat with us."

"I'm keeping the security gig at the set. If you see this guy Broussard, tell him not to set any more fires . . . Don't look at me like that, Streak. The trailer he burned had propane tanks on it. What if somebody had been in there?"

"He thinks the Terrebonnes are trying to have him killed."

"I hope they work it out. In the meantime, tell him to keep his ass off the set."

"You don't want to eat?"

"No. I'm not feeling too good." He looked out into the shadows and the water dripping out of the trees. "I got in over my head. It's my fault. I'm not used to this crap."

"She's got strong feelings for you, Clete."

"Yeah, my temp loves her cat. See you tomorrow, Dave."

I watched him back out into the road, then shift into low, his big head bent forward over the wheel, his expression as meaningless as a jack-o'-lantern's.

AFTER BOOTSIE AND ALAFAIR and I ate dinner, I drove up the Loreauville road to Cisco Flynn's house. When no one answered the bell, I walked the length of the gallery, past the baskets of hanging ferns, and looked through the side yard. In back, inside a screened pavilion, Cisco and Megan were eating steaks at a linen-covered table with Swede Boxleiter. I walked across the grass toward the yellow circle of light made by an outside bug lamp. Their faces were warm, animated with their conversation, their movements automatic when one or the other wanted a dish passed or his silver wine goblet refilled. My loafer cracked a small twig.

"Sorry to interrupt," I said.

"Is that you, Dave? Join us. We have plenty," Cisco said.

"I wanted to see Megan a minute. I'll wait out in my truck," I said.

The three of them were looking out into the darkness, the tossed salad and pink slices of steak on their plates like part of a nineteenth-century French still life. In that instant I knew that whatever differences defined them today, the three of them were held together by a mutual experience that an outsider would never understand. Then Boxleiter broke the moment by picking up a decanter and pouring wine into his goblet, spilling it like drops of blood on the linen.

Ten minutes later Megan found me in the front yard.

"This morning you told me I had Boxleiter all wrong," I said.

"That's right. He's not what he seems."

"He's a criminal."

"To some."

"I saw pictures of the dude he shanked in the Canon City pen."

"Probably courtesy of Adrien Glazier. By the way, the guy you think he did? He was in the Mexican Mafia. He had Swede's cell partner drowned in a toilet . . . This is why you came out here?"

"No, I wanted to tell you I'm going to leave y'all alone. Y'all take your own fall, Megan."

"Who asked you to intercede on our behalf anyway? You're still pissed off about Clete, aren't you?" she said.

I walked across the lawn toward my truck. The wind was loud in the trees and made shadows on the grass. She caught up with me just as I opened the door to the truck.

"The problem is you don't understand your own thinking," she said. "You were raised in the church. You see my father's death as St. Sebastian's martyrdom or something. You believe in forgiving people for what's not yours to forgive. I'd like to take their eyes out."

"Their eyes. Who is *their,* Megan?"

"Every hypocrite in this—" She stopped, stepping back as though retreating from her own words.

"Ah, we finally got to it," I said.

I got in the truck and closed the door. I could hear her heated breathing in the dark, see her chest rise and fall against her shirt. Swede Boxleiter walked out of the side yard into the glow of light from the front gallery, an empty plate in one hand, a meat fork in the other.

FOURTEEN

THE TALL MAN WHO WORE yellow-tinted glasses and cowboy boots and a weathered, smoke-colored Stetson made a mistake. While the clerk in a Lafayette pawnshop and gun store bagged up two boxes of .22 magnum shells for him, the man in the Stetson happened to notice a bolt-action military rifle up on the rack.

"That's an Italian 6.5 Carcano, ain't it? Hand it down here and I'll show you something," he said.

He wrapped the leather sling over his left arm, opened the bolt, and inserted his thumb in the chamber to make sure the gun was not loaded.

"This is the same kind Oswald used. Now, here's the mathematics. The shooter up in that book building had to get off three shots in five and a half seconds. You got a stopwatch?" he said.

"No," the clerk said.

"Here, look at my wristwatch. Now, I'm gonna dry-fire it three times. Remember, I ain't even aiming and Oswald was up six stories, shooting at a moving target."

"That's not good for the firing pin," the clerk said.

"It ain't gonna hurt it. It's a piece of shit anyway, ain't it?"

"I wish you wouldn't do that, sir."

The man in the Stetson set the rifle back on the glass counter and pinched his thumb and two fingers inside his Red Man pouch and put the tobacco in his jaw. The clerk's eyes broke when he tried to return the man's stare.

"You ought to develop a historical curiosity. Then maybe you wouldn't have to work the rest of your life at some little pissant job," the man said, and picked up his sack and started for the front door.

The clerk, out of shame and embarrassment, said to the man's back, "How come you know so much about Dallas?"

"I was there, boy. That's a fact. The puff of smoke on the grassy knoll?" He winked at the clerk and went out.

The clerk stood at the window, his face tingling, feeling belittled, searching in his mind for words he could fling out the door but knowing he would not have the courage to do so. He watched the man in the Stetson drive down the street to an upholstery store in a red pickup truck with Texas plates. The clerk wrote down the tag number and called the sheriff's department.

ON FRIDAY MORNING FATHER James Mulcahy rose just before dawn, fixed two sandwiches and a thermos of coffee in the rectory kitchen, and drove to Hen-

derson Swamp, outside of the little town of Breaux
Bridge, where a parishioner had given him the use of a
motorized houseboat.

He drove along the hard-packed dirt track atop the
levee, above the long expanse of bays and channels and
flooded cypress and willows that comprised the swamp.
He parked at the bottom of the levee, walked across a
board plank to the houseboat, released the mooring
ropes, and floated out from the willows into the current
before he started the engine.

The clouds in the eastern sky were pink and gray,
and the wind lifted the moss on the dead cypress
trunks. Inside the cabin, he steered the houseboat along
the main channel, until he saw a cove back in the trees
where the bream were popping the surface along the
edge of the hyacinths. When he turned into the cove
and cut the engine, he heard an outboard coming hard
down the main channel, the throttle full out, the noise
like a chain saw splitting the serenity of the morning.
The driver of the outboard did not slow his boat to
prevent his wake from washing into the cove and disturbing the water for another fisherman.

Father Mulcahy sat in a canvas chair on the deck
and swung the bobber from his bamboo pole into the
hyacinths. Behind him, he heard the outboard turning
in a circle, heading toward him again. He propped his
pole on the rail, put down the sandwich he had just
unwrapped from its wax paper, and walked to the other
side of the deck.

The man in the outboard killed his engine and
floated in to the cove, the hyacinths clustering against
the bow. He wore yellow-tinted glasses, and he reached
down in the bottom of his boat and fitted on a smoke-

colored Stetson that was sweat-stained across the base of the crown. When he smiled his dentures were stiff in his mouth, the flesh of his throat red like a cock's comb. He must have been sixty-five, but he was tall, his back straight, his eyes keen with purpose.

"I'm fixing to run out of gas. Can you spare me a half gallon?" he said.

"Maybe your high speed has something to do with it," Father Mulcahy said.

"I'll go along with that." Then he reached out for an iron cleat on the houseboat as though he had already been given permission to board. Behind the seat was a paper bag stapled across the top and a one-gallon tin gas can.

"I know you," Father Mulcahy said.

"Not from around here you don't. I'm just a visitor, not having no luck with the fish."

"I've heard your voice."

The man stood up in his boat and grabbed the handrail and lowered his face so the brim of his hat shielded it from view.

"I have no gas to give you. It's all in the tank," Father Mulcahy said.

"I got a siphon. Right here in this bag. A can, too."

The man in the outboard put one cowboy boot on the edge of the deck and stepped over the rail, drawing a long leg behind him. He stood in front of the priest, his head tilted slightly as though he were examining a quarry he had placed under a glass jar.

"Show me where your tank's at. Back around this side?" he said, indicating the lee side of the cabin, away from the view of anyone passing on the channel.

"Yes," the priest said. "But there's a lock on it. It's on the ignition key."

"Let's get it, then, Reverend," the man said.

"You know I'm a minister?" Father Mulcahy said.

The man did not reply. He had not shaved that morning, and there were gray whiskers among the red and blue veins in his cheeks. His smile was twisted, one eye squinted behind the lens of his glasses, as though he were arbitrarily defining the situation in his own mind.

"You came to the rectory . . . In the rain," the priest said.

"Could be. But I need you to hep me with this chore. That's our number one job here."

The man draped his arm across the priest's shoulders and walked him inside the cabin. He smelled of deodorant and chewing tobacco, and in spite of his age his arm was thick and meaty, the crook of it like a yoke on the back of the priest's neck.

"Your soul will be forfeit," the priest said, because he could think of no other words to use.

"Yeah, I heard that one before. Usually when a preacher was trying to get me to write a check. The funny thing is, the preacher never wanted Jesus's name on the check."

Then the man in the hat pulled apart the staples on the paper bag he had carried on board and took out a velvet curtain rope and a roll of tape and a plastic bag. He began tying a loop in the end of the rope, concentrating on his work as though it were an interesting, minor task in an ordinary day.

The priest turned away from him, toward the window and the sun breaking through the flooded cypress, his head lowered, his fingers pinched on his eyelids.

The parishioner's sixteen-gauge pump shotgun was propped just to the left of the console. Father Mulcahy picked it up and leveled the barrel at the chest of the man in the Stetson hat and clicked off the safety.

"Get off this boat," he said.

"You didn't pump a shell into it. There probably ain't nothing in the chamber," the man said.

"That could be true. Would you like to find out?"

"You're a feisty old rooster, ain't you?"

"You sicken me, sir."

The man in yellow-tinted glasses reached in his shirt pocket with his thumb and two fingers and filled his jaw with tobacco.

"Piss on you," he said, and opened the cabin door to go back outside.

"Leave the bag," the priest said.

FIFTEEN

THE PRIEST CALLED THE SHERIFF'S office in St. Martin Parish, where his encounter with the man in the Stetson had taken place, then contacted me when he got back to New Iberia. The sheriff and I interviewed him together at the rectory.

"The bag had a velvet cord and a plastic sack and a roll of tape in it?" the sheriff said.

"That's right. I left it all with the sheriff in St. Martinville," Father Mulcahy said. His eyes were flat, as though discussing his thoughts would only add to the level of degradation he felt.

"You know why he's after you, don't you, Father?" I said.

"Yes, I believe I do."

"You know what he was going to do, too. It would have probably been written off as a heart attack. There would have been no rope burns, nothing to indicate any force or violence," I said.

"You don't have to tell me that, sir," he replied.

"It's time to talk about Lila Terrebonne," I said.

"It's her prerogative to talk with you as much as she wishes. But not mine," he said.

"Hubris isn't a virtue, Father," I said.

His face flared. "Probably not. But I'll be damned if I'll be altered by a sonofabitch like the man who climbed on my boat."

"That's one way of looking at it. Here's my card if you want to put a net over this guy," I said.

When we left, rain that looked like lavender horse tails was falling across the sun. The sheriff drove the cruiser with the window down and ashes blew from his pipe onto his shirt. He slapped at them angrily.

"I want that guy in the hat on a respirator," he said.

"We don't have a crime on that houseboat, skipper. It's not even in our jurisdiction."

"The intended victim is. That's enough. He's a vulnerable old man. Remember when you lived through your first combat and thought you had magic? A dangerous time."

A half hour later a state trooper pulled over a red pickup truck with a Texas tag on the Iberia–St. Martin Parish line.

THE SHERIFF AND I stood outside the holding cell and looked at the man seated on the wood bench against the back wall. His western-cut pants were ironed with sharp creases, the hard points of his ox-blood cowboy boots buffed to a smooth glaze like melted plastic. He played with his Stetson on his index finger.

The sheriff held the man's driver's license cupped in his palm. He studied the photograph on it, then the man's face.

"You're Harpo Scruggs?" the sheriff asked.

"I was when I got up this morning."

"You're from New Mexico?"

"Deming. I got a chili pepper farm there. The truck's a rental, if that's what's on your mind."

"You're supposed to be dead," the sheriff said.

"You talking about that fire down in Juárez? Yeah, I heard about that. But it wasn't me."

His accent was peckerwood, the Acadian inflections, if they had ever existed, weaned out of it.

"You terrorize elderly clergymen, do you?" I said.

"I asked the man for a can of gas. He pointed a shotgun at me."

"You mind going into a lineup?" the sheriff asked.

Harpo Scruggs looked at his fingernails.

"Yeah, I do. What's the charge?" he said.

"We'll find one," the sheriff said.

"I don't think y'all got a popcorn fart in a windstorm," he said.

He was right. We called Mout' Broussard's home and got no answer. Neither could we find the USL student who had witnessed the execution of the two brothers out in the Atchafalaya Basin. The father of the two brothers was drunk and contradictory about what he had seen and heard when his sons were lured out of the house.

It was 8 P.M. The sheriff sat in his swivel chair and tapped his fingers on his jawbone.

"Call Juárez, Mexico, and see if they've still got a warrant," he said.

"I already did. It was like having a conversation with impaired people in a bowling alley."

"Sometimes I hate this job," he said, and picked up a key ring off his desk blotter.

Ten minutes later the sheriff and I watched Harpo Scruggs walk into the parking lot a free man. He wore a shirt with purple and red flowers on it, and it swelled with the breeze and made his frame look even larger than it was. He fitted on his hat and slanted the brim over his eyes, took a small bag of cookies from his pocket and bit into one of them gingerly with his false teeth. He lifted his face into the breeze and looked with expectation at the sunset.

"See if you can get Lila Terrebonne in my office tomorrow morning," the sheriff said.

Harpo Scruggs's truck drove up the street toward the cemetery. A moment later Helen Soileau's unmarked car pulled into the traffic behind him.

THAT NIGHT BOOTSIE AND I fixed ham and onion sandwiches and dirty rice and iced tea at the drainboard and ate on the breakfast table. Through the hallway I could see the moss in the oak trees glowing against the lights on the dock.

"You look tired," Bootsie said.

"Not really."

"Who's this man Scruggs working for?"

"The New Orleans Mob. The Dixie Mafia. Who knows?"

"The Mob letting one of their own kill a priest?"

"You should have been a cop, Boots."

"There's something you're not saying."

"I keep feeling all this stuff goes back to Jack Flynn's murder."

"The Flynns again." She rose from the table and

put her plate in the sink and looked through the window into the darkness at the foot of our property. "Why always the Flynns?" she said.

I didn't have an adequate answer, not even for myself when I lay next to Bootsie later in the darkness, the window fan drawing the night air across our bed. Jack Flynn had fought at the battle of Madrid and at Alligator Creek on Guadalcanal; he was not one to be easily undone by company goons hired to break a farmworkers' strike. But the killers had kidnapped him out of a hotel room in Morgan City, beaten him with chains, impaled his broken body with nails as a lesson in terror to any poor white or black person who thought he could relieve his plight by joining a union. To this day not one suspect had been in custody, not one participant had spoken carelessly in a bar or brothel.

The Klan always prided itself on its secrecy, the arcane and clandestine nature of its rituals, the loyalty of its members to one another. But someone always came forward, out of either guilt or avarice, and told of the crimes they committed in groups, under cover of darkness, against their unarmed and defenseless victims.

But Jack Flynn's murderers had probably not only been protected, they had been more afraid of the people they served than Louisiana or federal law.

Jack Flynn's death was at the center of our current problems because we had never dealt with our past, I thought. And in not doing so, we had allowed his crucifixion to become a collective act.

I propped myself up on the mattress with one elbow and touched Bootsie's hair. She was sound asleep and did not wake. Her eyelids looked like rose petals in the moon's glow.

• • •

EARLY SATURDAY MORNING I turned into the Terrebonne grounds and drove down the oak-lined drive toward the house. The movie set was empty, except for a bored security guard and Swede Boxleiter, who was crouched atop a plank building, firing a nail gun into the tin roof.

I stood under the portico of the main house and rang the chimes. The day had already turned warm, but it was cool in the shade and the air smelled of damp brick and four-o'clock flowers and the mint that grew under the water faucets. Archer Terrebonne answered the door in yellow-and-white tennis clothes, a moist towel draped around his neck.

"Lila's not available right now, Mr. Robicheaux," he said.

"I'd very much like to talk to her, sir."

"She's showering. Then we're going to a brunch. Would you like to leave a message?"

"The sheriff would appreciate her coming to his office to talk about her conversation with Father James Mulcahy."

"Y'all do business in an extraordinary fashion. Her discussions with a minister are the subject of a legal inquiry?"

"This man was almost killed because he's too honorable to divulge something your daughter told him."

"Good day, Mr. Robicheaux," Terrebonne said, and closed the door in my face.

I drove back through the corridor of trees, my face tight with anger. I started to turn out onto the service road, then stopped the truck and walked out to the movie set.

"How's it hangin', Swede?" I said.

He fired the nail gun through the tin roof into a joist and pursed his mouth into an inquisitive cone.

"Where's Clete Purcel?" I asked.

"Gone for the day. You look like somebody pissed in your underwear."

"You know the layout of this property?"

"I run power cables all over it."

"Where's the family cemetery?"

"Back in those trees."

He pointed at an oak grove and a group of white-washed brick crypts with an iron fence around it. The grass within the fence was freshly mowed and clipped at the base of the bricks.

"You know of another burial area?" I asked.

"Way in back, a spot full of briars and palmettos. Holtzner says that's where the slaves were planted. Got to watch out for it so the local blacks don't get their ovaries fired up. What's the gig, man? Let me in on it."

I walked to the iron fence around the Terrebonne cemetery. The marble tablet that sealed the opening to the patriarch's crypt was cracked across the face from settlement of the bricks into the softness of the soil, but I could still make out the eroded, moss-stained calligraphy scrolled by a stone mason's chisel: *Elijah Boethius Terrebonne, 1831–1878, soldier for Jefferson Davis, loving father and husband, now brother to the Lord.*

Next to Elijah's crypt was a much smaller one in which his twin girls were entombed. A clutch of wild-flowers, tied at the stems with a rubber band, was propped against its face. There were no other flowers in the cemetery.

I walked toward the back of the Terrebonne estate,

along the edge of a coulee that marked the property line, beyond the movie set and trailers and sky-blue swimming pool and guest cottages and tennis courts to a woods that was deep in shade, layered with leaves, the tree branches wrapped with morning glory vines and cobweb.

The woods sloped toward a stagnant pond. Among the palmettos were faint depressions, leaf-strewn, sometimes dotted with mushrooms. Was the slave woman Lavonia, who had poisoned Elijah's daughters, buried here? Was the pool of black water, dimpled by dragonflies, part of the swamp she had tried to hide in before she was lynched by her own people?

Why did the story of the exploited and murdered slave woman hang in my mind like a dream that hovers on the edge of sleep?

I heard a footstep in the leaves behind me.

"I didn't mean to give you a start," Lila said.

"Oh, hi, Lila. I bet you put the wildflowers on the graves of the children."

"How did you know?"

"Did your father tell you why I was here?"

"No . . . He . . . We don't always communicate very well."

"A guy named Harpo Scruggs tried to kill Father Mulcahy."

The blood drained out of her face.

"We think it's because of something you told him," I said.

When she tried to speak, her words were broken, as though she could not form a sentence without using one that had already been spoken by someone else. "I told the priest? That's what you're saying?"

"He's taking your weight. Scruggs was going to suffocate him with a plastic bag."

"Oh, Dave—" she said, her eyes watering. Then she ran toward the house, her palms raised in the air like a young girl.

WE HAD JUST RETURNED from Mass on Sunday morning when the phone rang in the kitchen. It was Clete.

"I'm at a restaurant in Lafayette with Holtzner and his daughter and her boyfriend," he said.

"What are you doing in Lafayette?"

"Holtzner's living here now. He's on the outs with Cisco. They want to come by," he said.

"What for?"

"To make some kind of rental offer on your dock."

"Not interested."

"Holtzner wants to make his pitch anyway. Dave, the guy's my meal ticket. How about it?"

An hour later Clete rolled up to the dock in his convertible, with Holtzner beside him and the daughter and boyfriend following in a Lincoln. The four of them strolled down the dock and sat at a spool table under a Cinzano umbrella.

"Ask the waiter to bring everybody a cold beer," Holtzner said.

"We don't have waiters. You need to get it yourself," I said, standing in the sunlight.

"I got it," Clete said, and went inside the shop.

"We'll pay you a month's lease but we'll be shooting for only two or three days," Anthony, the boyfriend, said. He wore black glasses, and when he smiled the gap in his front teeth gave his face the imbecilic look of a Halloween pumpkin.

"Thanks anyway," I said.

"*Thanks?* That's it?" Holtzner said.

"He thinks we're California nihilists here to do a culture fuck on the Garden of Eden," Geraldine, the daughter, said to no one.

"You got the perfect place here for this particular scene. Geri's right, you think we're some kind of disease?" Holtzner said.

"You might try up at Henderson Swamp," I said.

Clete came back out of the bait shop screen carrying a round tray with four sweating long-neck bottles on it. He set them one by one on the spool table, his expression meaningless.

"Talk to him," Holtzner said to him.

"I don't mess with Streak's head," Clete said.

"I hear you got Cisco's father on the brain," Holtzner said to me. "His father's death doesn't impress me. My grandfather organized the first garment workers' local on the Lower East Side. They stuck his hands in a stamp press. Irish cops broke up his wake with clubs, took the ice off his body and put it in their beer. They pissed in my grandmother's sink."

"You have to excuse me. I need to get back to work," I said, and walked toward the bait shop. I could hear the wind ruffling the umbrella in the silence, then Anthony was at my side, grinning, his clothes pungent with a smell like burning sage.

"Don't go off in a snit, nose out of joint, that sort of thing," he said.

"I think you have a problem," I said.

"We're talking about chemical dependencies now, are we?"

"No, you're hard of hearing. No offense meant," I said, and went inside the shop and busied myself in back until all of them were gone except Clete, who remained at the table, sipping from his beer bottle.

"Why's Holtzner want to get close to you?" he asked.

"You got me."

"I remembered where I'd seen him. He was promoting USO shows in Nam. Except he was also mixed up with some PX guys who were selling stuff on the black market. It was a big scandal. Holtzner was kicked out of Nam. That's like being kicked out of Hell . . . You just going to sit there and not say anything?"

"Yeah, don't get caught driving with beer on your breath."

Clete pushed his glasses up on his head and drank from his bottle, one eye squinted shut.

THAT NIGHT, IN A Lafayette apartment building on a tree-and-fern-covered embankment that overlooked the river, the accountant named Anthony mounted the staircase to the second-story landing and walked through a brick passageway toward his door. The underwater lights were on in the swimming pool, and blue strings of smoke from barbecue grills floated through the palm and banana fronds that shadowed the terrace. Anthony carried a grocery sack filled with items from a delicatessen, probably obscuring his vision, as evidently he never saw the figure that waited for him behind a potted orange tree.

The knife must have struck as fast as a snake's head, in the neck, under the heart, through the breastbone, because the coroner said Anthony was probably dead before the jar of pickled calf brains in his sack shattered on the floor.

SIXTEEN

HELEN SOILEAU AND I MET Ruby Gravano and
her nine-year-old boy at the Amtrak station in Lafayette
Monday afternoon. The boy was a strange-looking
child, with his mother's narrow face and black hair but
with eyes that were set unnaturally far apart, as though
they had been pasted on the skin. She held the boy,
whose name was Nick, by one hand and her suitcase by
the other.

"Is this gonna take long? Because I'm not feeling
real good right now," she said.

"There's a female deputy in that cruiser over there,
Ruby. She's going to take Nick for some ice cream,
then we'll finish with business and take y'all to a bed-
and-breakfast in New Iberia. Tomorrow you'll be back
on your way," I said.

"Did you get the money bumped up? Houston's a
lot more expensive than New Orleans. My mother said
I can stay a week free, but then I got to pay her rent,"
she said.

"Three hundred is all we could do," I said.

Her forehead wrinkled. Then she said, "I don't feel too comfortable standing out here. I don't know how I got talked into this." She looked up and down the platform and fumbled in her bag for a pair of dark glasses.

"You wanted a clean slate in Houston. You were talking about a treatment program. Your idea, not ours, Ruby," Helen said.

The little boy's head rotated like a gourd on a stem as he watched the disappearing train, the people walking to their cars with their luggage, a track crew repairing a switch.

"He's autistic. This is all new to him. Don't look at him like that. I hate this shit," Ruby said, and pulled on the boy's hand as though she were about to leave us, then stopped when she realized she had no place to go except our unmarked vehicle, and in reality she didn't even know where that was.

We put Nick in the cruiser with the woman deputy, then drove to Four Corners and parked across the street from a sprawling red-and-white motel that looked like a refurbished eighteenth-century Spanish fortress.

"How do you know he's in the room?" Ruby said.

"One of our people has been watching him. In five minutes he's going to get a phone call. Somebody's going to tell him smoke is coming out of his truck. All you have to do is look through the binoculars and tell us if that's the john you tricked on Airline Highway," I said.

"You really got a nice way of saying it," she replied.

"Ruby, cut the crap. The guy in that room tried to kill a priest Friday morning. What do you think he'll do to you if he remembers he showed you mug shots of two guys he capped out in the Basin?" Helen said.

Ruby lowered her chin and bit her lip. Her long hair made a screen around her narrow face.

"It's not fair," she said.

"What?" I asked.

"Connie picked those guys up. But she doesn't get stuck with any of it. You got a candy bar or something? I feel sick. They wouldn't turn down the air-conditioning on the train."

She sniffed deep in her nose, then wiped her nostrils hard with a Kleenex, pushing her face out of shape.

Helen looked through the front window at one of our people in a phone booth on the corner.

"It's going down, Ruby. Pick up the binoculars," she said.

Ruby held the binoculars to her eyes and stared at the door to the room rented by Harpo Scruggs. Then she shifted them to an adjacent area in the parking lot. Her lips parted slightly on her teeth.

"What's going on?" she said.

"Nothing. What are you talking about?" I said.

"That's not the guy with the mug shots. I don't know that guy's name. We didn't ball him either," she said.

"Take the oatmeal out of your mouth," Helen said.

I removed the binoculars from her hands and placed them to my eyes.

"The guy out there in the parking lot. He came to the diner where the guy named Harpo and the other john were eating with us. He talks like a coon-ass. They went outside together, then he drove off," she said.

"You never told us this," I said.

"Why should I? You were asking about johns."

I put the binoculars back to my eyes and watched Alex Guidry, the fired Iberia Parish jailer who had cuckolded Cool Breeze Broussard, knock on empty space just as Harpo Scruggs ripped open the door and charged outside, barefoot and in his undershirt and western-cut trousers, expecting to see a burning truck.

LATER THE SAME AFTERNOON, when the sheriff was in my office, two Lafayette homicide detectives walked in and told us they were picking up Cool Breeze Broussard. They were both dressed in sport clothes, their muscles swollen with steroids. One of them, whose name was Daigle, lit a cigarette and kept searching with his eyes for an ashtray to put the burnt match in.

"Y'all want to go out to his house with us?" he asked, and dropped the match in the wastebasket.

"I don't," I said.

He studied me. "You got some kind of objection, something not getting said here?" he asked.

"I don't see how you make Broussard for this guy's, what's his name, Anthony Pollock's murder," I replied.

"He's got a hard-on for the Terrebonne family. There's a good possibility he started the fire on their movie set. He's a four-time loser. He shanked a guy on Camp J. He mangled a guy on an electric saw in your own jail. You want me to go on?" Daigle said.

"You've got the wrong guy," I said.

"Well, fuck me," he said.

"Don't use that language in here, sir," the sheriff said.

"What?" Daigle said.

"The victim was an addict. He had overseas involvements. He didn't have any connection with Cool Breeze. I think you guys have found an easy dartboard," I said.

"We made up all that stuff on Broussard's sheet?" the other detective said.

"The victim was stabbed in the throat, heart, and kidney and was dead before he hit the floor. It sounds like a professional yard job," I said.

"A yard job?" Daigle said.

"Talk to a guy by the name of Swede Boxleiter. He's on lend-lease from Canon City," I said.

"Swede who?" Daigle said, taking a puff off his cigarette with three fingers crimped on the paper.

The sheriff scratched his eyebrow.

"Get out of here," he said to the detectives.

A FEW MINUTES LATER the sheriff and I watched through the window as they got into their car.

"At least Pollock had the decency to get himself killed in Lafayette Parish," the sheriff said. "What's the status on Harpo Scruggs?"

"Helen said a chippy came to his room in a taxi. She's still in there."

"What's Alex Guidry's tie-in to this guy?"

"It has something to do with the Terrebonnes. Everything in St. Mary Parish does. That's where they're both from."

"Bring him in."

"What for?"

"Tell him he's cruel to animals. Tell him his golf game stinks. Tell him I'm just in a real pissed-off mood."

• • •

TUESDAY MORNING HELEN AND I drove down Main, then crossed the iron drawbridge close by the New Iberia Country Club.

"You don't think this will tip our surveillance on Harpo Scruggs?" she said.

"Not if we do it right."

"When those two brothers were executed out in the Basin? One of the shooters had on a department uniform. It could have come from Guidry."

"Maybe Guidry was in it," I said.

"Nope, he stays behind the lines. He makes the system work for him."

"You know him outside the job?" I asked.

"He arrested my maid out on a highway at night when he was a deputy in St. Mary Parish. She's never told anyone what he did to her."

Helen and I parked the cruiser in front of the country club and walked past the swimming pool, then under a spreading oak to a practice green where Alex Guidry was putting with a woman and another man. He wore light brown slacks and two-tone golf shoes and a maroon polo shirt; his mahogany tan and thick salt-and-pepper hair gave him the look of a man in the prime of his life. He registered our presence in the corner of his eye but never lost his concentration. He bent his knees slightly and tapped the ball with a plop into the cup.

"The sheriff has invited you to come down to the department," I said.

"No, thank you," he said.

"We need your help with a friend of yours. It won't take long," Helen said.

The red flag on the golf pin popped in the wind. Leaves drifted out of the pecan trees and live oaks along the fairway and scudded across the freshly mowed grass.

"I'll give it some thought and ring y'all later on it," he said, and started to reach down to retrieve his ball from the cup.

Helen put her hand on his shoulder.

"Not a time to be a wise-ass, sir," she said.

Guidry's golf companions looked away into the distance, their eyes fixed on the dazzling blue stretch of sky above the tree line.

Fifteen minutes later we sat down in a windowless interview room. In the back seat of the cruiser he had been silent, morose, his face dark with anger when he looked at us. I saw the sheriff at the end of the hall just before I closed the door to the room.

"Y'all got some damn nerve," Guidry said.

"Someone told us you're buds with an ex-Angola gun bull by the name of Harpo Scruggs," I said.

"I know him. So what?" he replied.

"You see him recently?" Helen asked. She wore slacks and sat with one haunch on the corner of the desk.

"No."

"Sure?" I said.

"He's the nephew of a lawman I worked with twenty years ago. We grew up in the same town."

"You didn't answer me," I said.

"I don't have to."

"The lawman you worked with was Harpo Delahoussey. Y'all put the squeeze on Cool Breeze Broussard over some moonshine whiskey. That's not all you did either," I said.

His eyes looked steadily into mine, heated, searching for the implied meaning in my words.

"Harpo Scruggs tried to kill a priest Friday morning," Helen said.

"Arrest him, then."

"How do you know we haven't?" I asked.

"I don't. It's none of my business. I was fired from my job, thanks to your friend Willie Broussard," he said.

"Everyone else told us Scruggs was dead. But you know he's alive. Why's that?" Helen said.

He leaned back in the chair and rubbed his mouth, saying something in disgust against his hand at the same time.

"Say that again," Helen said.

"I said you damn queer, you leave me alone," he replied.

I placed my hand on top of Helen's before she could rise from the table. "You were in the sack with Cool Breeze's wife. I think you contributed to her suicide and helped ruin her husband's life. Does it give you any sense of shame at all, sir?" I said.

"It's called changing your luck. You're notorious for it, so lose the attitude, fucko," Helen said.

"I tell you what, when you're dead from AIDS or some other disease you people pass around, I'm going to dig up your grave and piss in your mouth," he said to her.

Helen stood up and massaged the back of her neck. "Dave, would you leave me and Mr. Guidry alone a minute?" she said.

• • •

BUT WHATEVER SHE DID or said after I left the room, it didn't work. Guidry walked past the dispatcher, used the phone to call a friend for a ride, and calmly sipped from a can of Coca-Cola until a yellow Cadillac with tinted windows pulled to the curb in front.

Helen and I watched him get in on the passenger side, roll down the window, and toss the empty can on our lawn.

"What bwana say now?" Helen said.

"Time to use local resources."

THAT EVENING CLETE PICKED me up in his convertible in front of the house and we headed up the road toward St. Martinville.

"You call Swede Boxleiter a 'local resource'?" he said.

"Why not?"

"That's like calling shit a bathroom ornament."

"You want to go or not?"

"The guy's got electrodes in his temples. Even Holtzner walks around him. Are you listening?"

"You think he did the number on this accountant, Anthony Pollock?"

He thought about it. The wind blew a crooked part in his sandy hair.

"*Could* he do it? In a blink. Did he have motive? You got me, 'cause I don't know what these dudes are up to," he said. "Megan told me something about Cisco having a fine career ahead of him, then taking money from some guys in the Orient."

"Have you seen her?"

He turned his face toward me. It was flat and red in

the sun's last light, his green eyes as bold as a slap. He looked at the road again.

"We're friends. I mean, she's got her own life. We're different kinds of people, you know. I'm cool about it." He inserted a Lucky Strike in his mouth.

"Clete, I'm—"

He pulled the cigarette off his lip without lighting it and threw it into the wind.

"What'd the Dodgers do last night?" he said.

WE PULLED INTO THE driveway of the cinder-block triplex where Swede Boxleiter lived and found him in back, stripped to the waist, shooting marbles with a slingshot at the squirrels in a pecan tree.

He pointed his finger at me.

"I got a bone to pick with you," he said.

"Oh?"

"Two Lafayette homicide roaches just left here. They said you told them to question me."

"Really?" I said.

"They threw me up against the car in front of my landlord. One guy kicked me in both ankles. He put his hand in my crotch with little kids watching."

"Dave was trying to clear you as a suspect. These guys probably got the wrong signal, Swede," Clete said.

He pulled back the leather pouch on the slingshot, nests of veins popping in his neck, and fired a scarlet marble into the pecan limbs.

"I want to run a historical situation by you. Then you tell me what's wrong with the story," I said.

"What's the game?" he asked.

"No game. You're con-wise. You see stuff other people don't. This is just for fun, okay?"

He held the handle of the slingshot and whipped the leather pouch and lengths of rubber tubing in a circle, watching them gain speed.

"A plantation owner is in the sack with one of his slave women. He goes off to the Civil War, comes back home, finds his place trashed by the Yankees, and all his slaves set free. There's not enough food for everybody, so he tells the slave woman she has to leave. You with me?"

"Makes sense, yeah," Swede said.

"The slave woman puts poison in the food of the plantation owner's children, thinking they'll only get sick and she'll be asked to care for them. Except they die. The other black people on the plantation are terrified. So they hang the slave woman before they're all punished," I said.

Swede stopped twirling the slingshot. "It's bullshit," he said.

"Why?" I asked.

"You said the blacks were already freed. Why are they gonna commit a murder for the white dude and end up hung by Yankees themselves? The white guy, the one getting his stick dipped, he did her."

"You're a beaut, Swede," I said.

"This is some kind of grift, right?"

"Here's what it is," Clete said. "Dave thinks you're getting set up. You know how it works sometimes. The locals can't clear a case and they look around for a guy with a heavy sheet."

"We've got a shooter or two on the loose, Swede," I said. "Some guys smoked two white boys out in the Basin, then tried to clip a black guy by the name of Willie Broussard. I hate to see you go down for it."

"I can see you'd be broke up," he said.

"Ever hear of a dude named Harpo Scruggs?" I asked.

"No."

"Too bad. You might have to take his weight. See you around. Thanks for the help with that historical story," I said.

Clete and I walked back to the convertible. The air felt warm and moist, and the sky was purple above the sugarcane across the road. Out of the corner of my eye I saw Swede watching us from the middle of the drive, stretching the rubber tubes on his slingshot, his face jigsawed with thought.

WE STOPPED AT A filling station for gas down the road. The owner had turned on the outside lights and the oak tree that grew next to the building was filled with black-green shadows against the sky. Clete walked across the street and bought a sno'ball from a small wooden stand and ate it while I put in the gas.

"What was that plantation story about?" he asked.

"I had the same problem with it as Boxleiter. Except it's been bothering me because it reminded me of the story Cool Breeze told me about his wife's suicide."

"You lost me, big mon," Clete said.

"She was found in freezing water with an anchor chain wrapped around her. When they want to leave a lot of guilt behind, they use shotguns or go off rooftops."

"I'd leave it alone, Dave."

"Breeze has lived for twenty years with her death on his conscience."

"There's another script, too. Maybe he did her,"

Clete said. He bit into his sno'ball and held his eyes on mine.

EARLY THE NEXT MORNING Batist telephoned the house from the dock.

"There's a man down here want to see you, Dave," he said.

"What's he look like?"

"Like somebody stuck his jaws in a vise and busted all the bones. That ain't the half of it. While I'm mopping off the tables, he walks round on his hands."

I finished my coffee and walked down the slope through the trees. The air was cool and gray with the mist off the water, and molded pecan husks broke under my shoes.

"What's up, Swede?" I said.

He sat at a spool table, eating a chili dog with a fork from a paper plate.

"You asked about this guy Harpo Scruggs. He's an old fart, works out of New Mexico and Trinidad, Colorado. He freelances, but if he's doing a job around here, the juice is coming out of New Orleans."

"Yeah?"

"Something else. If Scruggs tried to clip a guy and blew it but he's still hanging around, it means he's working for Ricky the Mouse."

"Ricky Scarlotti?"

"There's two things you don't do with Ricky. You don't blow hits and you don't ever call him the Mouse. You know the story about the horn player?"

"Yes."

"That's his style."

"Would he have a priest killed?"

"That don't sound right."

"You ever have your IQ tested, Swede?"

"No, people who bone you five days a week don't give IQ tests."

"You're quite a guy anyway. You shank Anthony Pollock?"

"I was playing chess with Cisco. Check it out, my man. And don't send any more cops to my place. Believe it or not, I don't like some polyester geek getting his hand on my crank."

He rolled up his dirty paper plate and napkin, dropped them in a trash barrel, and walked down the dock to his car, snapping his fingers as though he were listening to a private radio broadcast.

RICKY SCARLOTTI WASN'T HARD to find. I went to the office, called NOPD, then the flower shop he owned at Carrollton and St. Charles.

"You want to chat up Ricky the Mouse with me?" I asked Helen.

"I don't think I'd go near that guy without a full-body condom on," she replied.

"Suit yourself. I'll be back this afternoon."

"Hang on. Let me get my purse."

We signed out an unmarked car and drove across the Atchafalaya Basin and crossed the Mississippi at Baton Rouge and turned south for New Orleans.

"So you're just gonna drop this Harpo Scruggs stuff in his lap?" Helen said.

"You bet. If Ricky thinks someone snitched him off, we'll know about it in a hurry."

"That story about the jazz musician true?" she said.

"I think it is. He just didn't get tagged with it."

The name of the musician is forgotten now, except among those in the 1950s who had believed his talent was the greatest since Bix Beiderbecke's. The melancholy sound of his horn hypnotized audiences at open-air concerts on West Venice beach. His dark hair and eyes and pale skin, the fatal beauty that lived in his face, that was like a white rose opening to black light, made women turn and stare at him on the street. His rendition of "My Funny Valentine" took you into a consideration about mutability and death that left you numb.

But he was a junky and jammed up with LAPD, and when he gave up the names of his suppliers, he had no idea that he was about to deal with Ricky Scarlotti.

Ricky had run a casino in Las Vegas, then a race track in Tijuana, before the Chicago Commission moved him to Los Angeles. Ricky didn't believe in simply killing people. He created living object lessons. He sent two black men to the musician's apartment in Malibu, where they pulled his teeth with pliers and mutilated his mouth. Later, the musician became a pharmaceutical derelict, went to prison in Germany, and died a suicide.

Helen and I drove through the Garden District, past the columned nineteenth-century homes shadowed by oaks whose root systems humped under sidewalks and cracked them upward like baked clay, past the iron green-painted streetcars with red-bordered windows clanging on the neutral ground, past Loyola University and Audubon Park, then to the levee where St. Charles ended and Ricky kept the restaurant, bookstore, and flower shop that supposedly brought him his income.

His second-story office was carpeted with a snow-white rug and filled with glass artworks and polished steel-and-glass furniture. A huge picture window gave onto the river and an enormous palm tree that brushed with the wind against the side of the building.

Ricky's beige pinstripe suit coat hung on the back of his chair. He wore a soft white shirt with a plum-colored tie and suspenders, and even though he was nearing sixty, his large frame still had the powerful muscle structure of a much younger man.

But it was the shape of his head and the appearance of his face that drew your attention. His ears were too large, cupped outward, the face unnaturally rotund, the eyes pouched with permanent dark bags, the eyebrows half-mooned, the black hair like a carefully scissored pelt glued to the skull.

"It's been a long time, Robicheaux. You still off the bottle?" he said.

"We're hearing some stuff that's probably all gas, Ricky. You know a mechanic, a freelancer, by the name of Harpo Scruggs?" I said.

"A guy fixes cars?" he said, and grinned.

"He's supposed to be a serious button man out of New Mexico," I said.

"Who's she? I've seen you around New Orleans someplace, right?" He was looking at Helen now.

"I was a patrolwoman here years ago. I still go to the Jazz and Heritage Festival in the spring. You like jazz?" Helen said.

"No."

"You ought to check it out. Wynton Marsalis is there. Great horn man. You don't like cornet?" she said.

"What is this, Robicheaux?"

"I told you, Ricky. Harpo Scruggs. He tried to kill

Willie Broussard, then a priest. My boss is seriously pissed off."

"Tell him that makes two of us, 'cause I don't like out-of-town cops 'fronting me in my own office. I particularly don't like no bride of Frankenstein making an implication about a rumor that was put to rest a long time ago."

"Nobody has shown you any personal disrespect here, Ricky. You need to show the same courtesy to others," I said.

"That's all right. I'll wait outside," Helen said, then paused by the door. She let her eyes drift onto Ricky Scarlotti's face. "Say, come on over to New Iberia sometime. I've got a calico cat that just won't believe you."

She winked, then closed the door behind her.

"I don't provoke no more, Robicheaux. Look, I know about you and Purcel visiting Jimmy Figorelli. What kind of behavior is that? Purcel smashes the guy in the mouth for no reason. Now you're laying off some hillbilly *cafone* on me."

"I didn't say he was a hillbilly."

"I've heard of him. But I don't put out contracts on priests. What d'you think I am?"

"A vicious, sadistic piece of shit, Ricky."

He opened his desk drawer and removed a stick of gum and peeled it and placed it in his mouth. Then he brushed at the tip of one nostril with his knuckle, huffing air out of his breathing passage. He pushed a button on his desk and turned his back on me and stared out the picture window at the river until I had left the room.

•   •   •

THAT EVENING I DROVE to the city library on East Main. The spreading oaks on the lawn were filled with birds and I could hear the clumps of bamboo rattling in the wind, and fireflies were lighting in the dusk out on the bayou. I went inside the library and found the hardback collection of Megan's photography that had been published three years ago by a New York publishing house.

What could I learn from it? Maybe nothing. Maybe I only wanted to put off seeing her that evening, which I knew I had to do, even though I knew I was breaking an AA tenet by injecting myself into other people's relationships. But you don't let a friend like Clete Purcel swing in the gibbet.

The photographs in her collection were stunning. Her great talent was her ability to isolate the humanity and suffering of individuals who lived in our midst but who nevertheless remained invisible to most passersby. Native Americans on reservations, migrant farmworkers, mentally impaired people who sought heat from steam grates, they looked at the camera with the hollow eyes of Holocaust victims and made the viewer wonder what country or era the photograph had been taken in, because surely it could not have been our own.

Then I turned a page and looked at a black-and-white photo taken on a reservation in South Dakota. It showed four FBI agents in windbreakers taking two Indian men into custody. The Indians were on their knees, their fingers laced behind their heads. An AR-15 rifle lay in the dust by an automobile whose windows and doors were perforated with bullet holes.

The cutline said the men were members of the American Indian Movement. No explanation was given for their arrest. One of the agents was a woman whose face was turned angrily toward the camera. The face was that of the New Orleans agent Adrien Glazier.

I drove out to Cisco's place on the Loreauville road and parked by the gallery. No one answered the bell, and I walked down by the bayou and saw her writing a letter under the light in the gazebo, the late sun burning like a flare beyond the willow trees across the water. She didn't see or hear me, and in her solitude she seemed to possess all the self-contained and tranquil beauty of a woman who had never let the authority of another define her.

Her horn-rimmed glasses gave her a studious look that her careless and eccentric dress belied. I felt guilty watching her without her knowledge, but in that moment I also realized what it was that attracted men to her.

She was one of those women we instinctively know are braver and more resilient than we are, more long-suffering and more willing to be broken for the sake of principle. You wanted to feel tender toward Megan, but you knew your feelings were vain and presumptuous. She had a lion's heart and did not need a protector.

"Oh, Dave. I didn't hear you come up on me," she said, removing her glasses.

"I was down at the library looking at your work. Who were those Indians Adrien Glazier was taking down?"

"One of them supposedly murdered two FBI agents. Amnesty International thinks he's innocent."

"There were some other photos in there you took of Mexican children in a ruined church around Trinidad, Colorado."

"Those were migrant kids whose folks had run off. The church was built by John D. Rockefeller after his goons murdered the families of striking miners up the road at Ludlow."

"I mention it because Swede Boxleiter told me a hit man named Harpo Scruggs had a ranch around there."

"He should know. He and Cisco were placed in a foster home in Trinidad. The husband was a pederast. He raped Swede until he bled inside. Swede took it so the guy wouldn't start on Cisco next."

I sat down on the top step of the gazebo and tossed a pebble into the bayou.

"Clete's my longtime friend, Megan. He says he needs this security job with Cisco's company. I don't think that's why he's staying here," I said.

She started to speak but gave it up.

"Even though he says otherwise, I don't think he understands the nature of y'all's relationship," I said.

"Is he drinking?"

"Not now, but he will."

She rested her cheek on her hand and gazed at the bayou.

"What I did was rotten," she said. "I wake up every morning and feel like a bloody sod. I just wish I could undo it."

"Talk to him again."

"You want Cisco and me out of his life. That's the real agenda, isn't it?"

"The best cop New Orleans ever had has become a grunt for Billy Holtzner."

"He can walk out of that situation anytime he wants. How about my brother? Anthony Pollock worked for some nasty people in Hong Kong. Who do you think they're going to blame for his death?"

"To tell you the truth, it's a long way from Bayou Teche. I don't really care."

She folded her letter and put away her pen and walked up the green bank toward the house, her silhouette surrounded by the tracings of fireflies.

CISCO FILMED LATE THAT night and did not return home until after 2 A.M. The intruders came sometime between midnight and then. They were big, heavy men, booted, sure of themselves and unrelenting in their purpose. They churned and destroyed the flower beds, where they disabled the alarm system, and slipped a looped wire through a window jamb and released the catch from inside. Each went through the opening with one muscular thrust, because hardly any dirt was scuffed into the bricks below the jamb.

They knew where she slept, and unlike the men who admired Megan for her strength, these men despised her for it. Their hands fell upon her in her sleep, wrenched her from the bed, bound her eyes, hurled her through the door and out onto the patio and down the slope to the bayou. When she pulled at the tape on her eyes, they slapped her to her knees.

But while they forced her face into the water, none of them saw the small memo recorder attached to a key ring she held clenched in her palm. Even while her mouth and nostrils filled with mud and her lungs burned for air as though acid had been poured in them, she tried to keep her finger pressed on the "record" button.

Then she felt the bayou grow as warm as blood around her neck just as a veined, yellow bubble burst in the center of her mind, and she knew she was safe from the hands and fists and booted feet of the men who had always lived on the edge of her camera's lens.

SEVENTEEN

THE TAPE ON THE SMALL recorder had only a twenty-second capacity. Most of the voices were muffled and inaudible, but there were words, whole sentences, sawed out of the darkness that portrayed Megan's tormenters better than any photograph could:

"Hold her, damnit! This is one bitch been asking for it a long time. You cain't get her head down, get out of the way."

"She's bucking. When they buck, they're fixing to go under. Better pull her up unless we're going all the way."

"Let her get a breath, then give it to her again. Ain't nothing like the power of memory to make a good woman, son."

It was 2:30 A.M. now and the ambulance had already left with Megan for Iberia General. The light from the flashers on our parked cruisers was like a blue, white, and red net on the trees and the bayou's surface and the back of the house. Cisco paced back and forth on the lawn, his eyes large, his face dilated in the glare.

Behind him I could see the sheriff squatted under the open window with a flashlight, peeling back the ruined flowers with one hand.

"You know who did it, don't you?" I said to Cisco.

"If I did, I'd have a gun down somebody's mouth," he replied.

"Give the swinging dick act a break, Cisco."

"I can't tell you who, I can only tell you why. It's payback for Anthony."

"Walk down to the water with me," I said, and cupped one hand on his elbow.

We went down the slope to the bayou, where the mudbank had been imprinted at the water's edge by Megan's bare knees and sliced by heavy boots that had fought for purchase while she struggled with at least three men. An oak tree sheltered us from the view of the sheriff and the uniformed deputies in the yard.

"Don't you lie to me. With these guys payback means dead. They want something. What is it?" I said.

"Billy Holtzner embezzled three-quarters of a million out of the budget by working a scam on our insurance coverage. But he put it on me. Anthony worked for the money people in Hong Kong. He believed what Billy told him. He started twisting my dials and ended up with big leaks in his arteries."

"Swede?"

"We were playing chess for a lot of the evening. I don't know if he did it or not. Swede's protective. Anthony was a prick."

"Protective? The victim was a prick? Great attitude."

"It's complicated. There's a lot of big finance involved. You're not going to understand it." He saw the look on my face. "I'm in wrong with some bad guys. The studio's going to file bankruptcy. They want to gut my picture and inflate its value on paper to liquidate their debts."

The current in the bayou was dead, hazed over with insects, and there was no air under the trees. He wiped his face with his hand.

"I'm telling the truth, Dave. I didn't think they'd go after Megan. Maybe there's something else involved. About my father, maybe. I don't understand it all either . . . Where you going?" he said.

"To find Clete Purcel."

"What for?"

"To talk to him before he hears about this from someone else."

"You coming to the hospital?" he asked, his fingers opened in front of him as though the words of another could be caught and held as physical guarantees.

IT WAS STILL DARK when I parked my truck by the stucco cottage Clete had rented outside Jeanerette. I pushed back the seat and slept through a rain shower and did not wake until dawn. When I woke, the rain had stopped and the air was heavy with mist, and I saw Clete at his mailbox in a robe, the *Morning Advocate* under his arm, staring curiously at my truck. I got out and walked toward him.

"What's wrong?" he said, lines breaking across his brow.

I told him of everything that happened at Cisco's house and of Megan's status at Iberia General. He listened and didn't speak. His face had the contained, heated intensity of a stainless-steel pan that had been left on a burner.

Then he said, "She's going to make it?"

"You bet."

"Come inside. I already have coffee on the stove." He turned away from me and pushed at his nose with his thumb.

"What are you going to do, Clete?"

"Go up to the hospital. What do you think?"

"You know what I mean."

"I'll fix eggs and sausage for both of us. You look like you got up out of a coffin."

Inside his kitchen I said, "Are you going to answer me?"

"I already heard about you and Helen visiting Ricky Scar. He's behind this shit, isn't he?"

"Where'd you hear about Scarlotti?"

"Nig Rosewater. He said Ricky went berserk after you left his office. What'd y'all do to jack him up like that?"

"Don't worry about it. You stay out of New Orleans."

He poured coffee in two cups and put a cinnamon roll in his mouth and looked out the window at the sun in the pine trees.

"Did you hear me?" I said.

"I got enough to do right here. I caught Swede Boxleiter in the Terrebonne cemetery last night. I think he was prizing bricks out of a crypt."

"What for?"

"Maybe he's a ghoul. You know what for. You planted all that Civil War stuff in his head. I'd love to tell Archer Terrebonne an ex-con meltdown is digging up his ancestors' bones."

But there was no humor in his face, only a tic at the corner of one eye. He went into the other room and called Iberia General, then came back in the kitchen, his eyes filled with private thoughts, and began beating eggs in a big pink bowl.

"Clete?"

"The Big Sleazy's not your turf anymore, Streak. Why don't you worry about how this guy Scruggs got off his leash? I thought y'all had him under surveillance."

"He lost the stakeout at the motel."

"You know the best way to deal with that dude? A big fat one between the eyes and a throw-down on the corpse."

"You might have your butt in our jail, if that's what it takes," I said.

He poured hot milk into my coffee cup. "Not even the perps believe that stuff anymore. You want to go to the hospital with me?" he said.

"You got it."

"The nurse said she asked for me. How about that? How about that Megan Flynn?"

I looked at the back of his thick neck and huge shoulders as he made breakfast and thought of warning NOPD before he arrived in New Orleans. But I knew that would only give his old enemies in the New Orleans Police Department a basis to do him even greater harm than Ricky Scarlotti might.

We drove back up the tree-lined highway to New Iberia in a corridor of rain.

•   •   •

AT IBERIA GENERAL I sat in the waiting room while Clete went in to see Megan first. Five minutes after we arrived I saw Lila Terrebonne walk down the hall with a spray of carnations wrapped in green tissue paper. She didn't see me. She paused at the open door to Megan's room, her eyelids blinking, her back stiff with apprehension. Then she turned and started hurriedly toward the elevator.

I caught her before she got on.

"You're not going to say hello?" I asked.

I could smell the bourbon on her breath, the cigarette smoke in her hair and clothes.

"Give these to Megan for me. I'll come back another time," she said.

"How'd you know she was here?"

"It was on the radio . . . Dave, get on the elevator with me." When the elevator door closed, she said, "I've got to get some help. I've had it."

"Help with what?"

"Booze, craziness . . . Something that happened to me, something I've never told anybody about except my father and the priest at St. Peter's."

"Why don't we sit in my pickup?" I said.

WHAT FOLLOWS IS MY reconstruction of the story she told me while the rain slid down the truck's windows and a willow tree by the bayou blew in the wind like a woman's hair.

She met the two brothers in a bar outside Morgan City. They were shooting pool, stretching across the table to make difficult shots, their sleeveless arms wrapped with green-and-red tattoos. They wore earrings and beards that were trimmed in neat lines along the jawbone, jeans that were so tight their genitalia were cupped to the smooth shape of a woman's palm. They sent a drink to her table, and one to an old man at the bar, and one to an oil-field roughneck who had used up his tab. But they made no overture toward her.

She watched them across the top of her gin ricky, the tawdry grace of their movements around the pool table, the lack of attention they showed anything except the skill of their game, the shots they speared into leather side pockets like junior high school kids.

Then one of them noticed her watching. He proffered the cue stick to her, smiling. She rose from her chair, her skin warm with gin, and wrapped her fingers around the cue's thickness, smiling back into the young man's face, seeing him glance away shyly, his cheeks color around the edges of his beard.

They played nine ball. Her father had taught her how to play billiards when she was a young girl. She could walk a cue ball down the rail, put reverse English on it and not leave an opponent an open shot, make a soft bank shot and drop the money balls—the one and the six and the nine—into the pocket with a tap that was no more than a whisper.

The two brothers shook their heads in dismay. She bought them each a bottle of beer and a gin ricky for herself. She played another game and beat them again. She noticed they didn't use profanity in her presence, that they stopped speaking in mid-sentence if she wished to interrupt, that they grinned boyishly and looked away if she let her eyes linger more than a few seconds on theirs.

They told her they built board roads for an oil company, they had been in the reformatory after their mother had deserted the family, they had been in the Gulf War, in a tank, one that'd had its treads blown off by an Iraqi artillery shell. She knew they were lying, but she didn't care. She felt a sense of sexual power and control that made her nipples hard, her eyes warm with toleration and acceptance.

When she walked to the ladies' room, the backs of her thighs taut with her high heels, she could see her reflection in the bar mirror and she knew that every man in the room was looking at the movement of her hips, the upward angle of her chin, the grace in her carriage that their own women would never possess.

The brothers did not try to pick her up. In fact, when the bar started to close, their conversation turned to the transmission on their truck, a stuck gear they couldn't free, their worry they could not make it the two miles to their father's fish camp. Rain streamed down the neon-lighted window in front.

She offered to follow them home. When they accepted, she experienced a strange taste in her throat, like copper pennies, like the wearing off of alcohol and the beginnings of a different kind of chemical reality. She looked at the faces of the brothers, the grins that looked incised in clay, and started to reconsider.

Then the bartender beckoned to her.

"Lady, taxicabs run all night. A phone call's a quarter. If they ain't got it, they can use mine free," he said.

"There's no problem. But thanks very much just the same. Thank you, truly. You're very nice," she replied, and hung her purse from her shoulder and let one of the brothers hold a newspaper over her head while they ran for her automobile.

They did it to her in an open-air tractor shed by a

green field of sugarcane in the middle of an electric storm. One held her wrists while the other brother climbed between her legs on top of a worktable. After he came his body went limp and his head fell on her breast. His mouth was wet and she could feel it leaving a pattern on her blouse. Then he rose from her and put on his blue jeans and lit a cigarette before clasping her wrists so his brother, who simply unzipped his jeans without taking them off, could mount her.

When she thought it was over, when she believed there was nothing else they could take from her, she sat up on the worktable with her clothes crumpled in her lap. Then she watched one brother shake his head and extend his soiled hand toward her face, covering it like a surgeon's assistant pressing an ether mask on a patient, forcing her back down on the table, then turning her over, his hand shifting to the back of her neck, crushing her mouth into the wood planks.

She saw a bolt of lightning explode in the fork of a hardwood tree, saw it split the wood apart and tear the grain right through the heart of the trunk. Deep in her mind she thought she remembered a green felt pool table and a boyish figure shoving a cue like a spear through his bridged fingers.

LILA'S FACE WAS TURNED slightly toward the passenger window when she finished her story.

"Your father had them killed?" I said.

"I didn't say that. Not at all."

"It's what happened, though, isn't it?"

"Maybe I had them killed. It's what they deserved. I'm glad they're dead."

"I think it's all right to feel that way," I said.

"What are you going to do with what I've told you?"

"Take you home or to a treatment center in Lafayette."

"I don't want to go into treatment again. If I can't do it with meetings and working the program, I can't do it at all."

"Why don't we go to a meeting after work? Then you go every day for ninety days."

"I feel like everything inside me is coming to an end. I can't describe it."

"It's called 'a world destruction fantasy.' It's bad stuff. Your heart races, you can't breathe, you feel like a piano wire is wrapped around your forehead. Psychologists say we remember the birth experience."

She pressed the heel of her hand to her forehead, then cracked the window as though my words had drawn the oxygen out of the air.

"Lila, I've got to ask you something else. Why were you talking about a Hanged Man?"

"I don't remember that. Not at all. That's in the Tarot, isn't it? I don't know anything about that."

"I see."

Her skin had gone white under her caked makeup, her eyelashes stiff and black and wide around her milky green eyes.

I WALKED THROUGH THE rain into the hospital and rode up in the elevator with Lila's tissue-wrapped spray of carnations in my hand. Helen Soileau was in the waiting room.

"You get anything?" I asked.

"Not much. She says she thinks there were three

guys. They sounded like hicks. One guy was running things," she replied.

"That's got to be Harpo Scruggs."

"I think we're going about this the wrong way. Cut off the head and the body dies."

"Where's the head?"

"Beats me," she said.

"Where's Purcel?"

"He's still in there."

I walked to the open door, then turned away. Clete was sitting on the side of Megan's bed, leaning down toward her face, his big arms and shoulders forming a tent over her. Her right hand rested on the back of his neck. Her fingers stroked his uncut hair.

THE SKY CLEARED THAT night, and Alafair and Bootsie and I cooked out in the back yard. I had told the sheriff about my conversation with Lila Terrebonne, but his response was predictable. We had established possible motivation for the execution of the two brothers. But that was all we had done. There was no evidence to link Archer Terrebonne, Lila's father, to the homicide. Second, the murders still remained outside our jurisdiction and our only vested interest in solving them was the fact that one of the shooters wore an Iberia Parish deputy sheriff's uniform.

I went with Lila to an AA meeting that night, then returned home.

"Clete called. He's in New Orleans. He said for you not to worry. What'd he mean?" Bootsie said.

EIGHTEEN

RICKY SCARLOTTI ATE BREAKFAST THE next morning with two of his men in his restaurant by St. Charles and Carrollton. It was a fine morning, smelling of the wet sidewalks and the breeze off the river. The fronds of the palm trees on the neutral ground were pale green and lifting in the wind against a ceramic-blue sky; the streetcar was loading with passengers by the levee, the conductor's bell clanging. No one seemed to take notice of a chartreuse Cadillac convertible that turned off St. Charles and parked in front of the flower shop, nor of the man in the powder-blue porkpie hat and seersucker pants and Hawaiian shirt who sat behind the steering wheel with a huge plastic seal-top coffee mug in his hand.

The man in the porkpie hat inserted a dime in the parking meter and looked with interest at the display of flowers an elderly woman was setting out on the sidewalk under a canvas awning. He talked a moment with the woman, then entered the restaurant and stopped by

the hot bar and wrapped a cold cloth around the handle
of a heavy cast-iron skillet filled with chipped beef.
He made his way unobtrusively between the checker-
cloth-covered tables toward the rear of the restaurant,
where Ricky Scarlotti had just patted his mouth with a
napkin and had touched the wrist of one of the men at
his side and nodded in the direction of the approaching
figure in the porkpie hat.

The man at Ricky Scarlotti's side had platinum hair
and a chemical tan. He put down his fork and got to his
feet and stood flat-footed like a sentinel in front of
Ricky Scarlotti's table. His name was Benny Grogan
and he had been a professional wrestler before he had
become a male escort for a notorious and rich Garden
District homosexual. NOPD believed he had also been
the backup shooter on at least two hits for the Calucci
brothers.

"I hope you're here for the brunch, Purcel," he
said.

"Not your gig, Benny. Get off the clock," Clete
said.

"Come on, make an appointment. Don't do this.
Hey, you deaf?" Then Benny Grogan reached out and
hooked his fingers on the back of Clete's shirt collar as
Clete brushed past him.

Clete flung the chipped beef into Benny Grogan's
face. It was scalding hot and it matted his skin like a
papier-mâché mask with slits for the eyes. Benny's
mouth was wide with shock and pain and an unintelligible sound that rose out of his chest like fingernails
grating on a blackboard. Then Clete whipped the bottom of the skillet with both hands across the side of

Benny's head, and backswung it into the face of the man who was trying to rise from his chair on the other side of Ricky Scarlotti, the cast-iron cusp ringing against bone, bursting the nose, knocking him backward on the floor.

Ricky Scarlotti was on his feet now, his mouth twisted, his finger raised at Clete. But he never got the chance to speak.

"I brought you some of your own, Ricky," Clete said.

He jammed a pair of vise grips into Ricky Scarlotti's scrotum and locked down the handles. Ricky Scarlotti's hands grabbed impotently at Clete's wrists while his head reared toward the ceiling.

Clete began backing toward the front door, pulling Ricky Scarlotti with him.

"Work with me on this. You can do it, Mouse. That a boy. Step lively now. Coming through here, gangway for the Mouse!" Clete said, pushing chairs and tables out of the way with his buttocks.

Out on the street he unhooked Scarlotti from the vise grips and bounced him off the side of a parked car, then slapped his face with his open hand, once, twice, then a third time, so hard the inside of Scarlotti's mouth bled.

"I'm not carrying, Mouse. Free shot," Clete said, his hands palm up at his sides now.

But Scarlotti was paralyzed, his mouth hanging open, his lips like red Jell-O. Clete grabbed him by his collar and the back of his belt and flung him to the sidewalk, then picked him up, pushed him forward, and flung him down again, over and over, working his way down the sidewalk, clattering garbage cans along the cement. People stared from automobiles, the street-car, and door fronts but no one intervened. Then, like a man who knows his rage can never be satiated, Clete lost it. He drove Scarlotti's head into a parking meter, smashing it repeatedly against the metal and glass. A woman across the street screamed hysterically and people began blowing car horns. Clete spun Scarlotti around by his bloodied shirtfront and threw him across a laddered display of flowers under the canvas awning.

"Tell these people why this is happening, Ricky. Tell them how you had a guy's teeth torn out, how you had a woman blindfolded and beaten and held underwater," Clete said, advancing toward him, his shoes crunching through the scattered potting soil.

Scarlotti dragged himself backward, his nose bleeding from both nostrils. But the elderly woman who had set the flowers out on the walk ran from the restaurant door and knelt beside him with her arms stretched across his chest, as though she were preventing him from rising. She screamed in Italian at Clete, her eyes serpentine and liquid.

Benny Grogan, the ex-wrestler, touched Clete on the elbow. Pieces of chipped beef still clung to his platinum hair. He held a ball-peen hammer in his hand, but he tossed it onto a sack of peat moss. For some reason, the elderly woman stopped screaming, as though a curtain had descended on a stage.

"You see a percentage in this, Purcel?" Benny Grogan said.

Clete looked at the elderly woman squatted by her son.

"You should go to church today, burn a candle, Mouse," he said.

He got in his convertible and drove to the corner, his tailpipe billowing white smoke, and turned down a shady side street toward St. Charles. He took his seal-top coffee mug off the dashboard and drank from it.

NINETEEN

IT WAS EARLY SATURDAY MORNING and Clete was changing a tire in my drive while he talked, spinning a lug wrench on a nut, his love handles wedging over his belt.

"So I took River Road and barrel-assed across the Huey Long and said goodbye to New Orleans for a while," he said. He squinted up at me and waited. "What?" he said.

"Scarlotti is a small player in this, Clete," I said.

"That's why you and Helen were pounding on his cage?" He got to his feet and threw his tools in the trunk. "I've got to get some new tires. I blew one coming off the bridge. What d'you mean, small player? That pisses me off, Dave."

"I think he and the Giacano family put the hit on Cool Breeze because he ratted them out to the Feds. But if you wanted to get even for Megan, you probably beat up on the wrong guy."

"The greaseballs are taking orders, even though they've run the action in New Orleans for a hundred years? Man, I learn something every day. Did you read that article in the *Star* about Hitler hiding out in Israel?"

His face was serious a moment, then he stuck an unlit cigarette in his mouth and the smile came back in his eyes and he twirled his porkpie hat on his finger while he looked at me, then at the sunrise behind the flooded cypresses.

I HELPED BATIST AT the bait shop, then drove to Cool Breeze's house on the west side of town and was told by a neighbor he was out at Mout's flower farm.

Mout' and a Hmong family from Laos farmed three acres of zinnias and chrysanthemums in the middle of a sugarcane plantation on the St. Martinville road, and each fall, when football season began, they cut and dug wagonloads of flowers that they sold to florists in Baton Rouge and New Orleans. I drove across a cattle guard and down a white shale road until I saw a row of poplars that was planted as a windbreak and Cool Breeze hoeing weeds out in the sunlight while his father sat in the shade reading a newspaper by a card table with a pitcher of lemonade on it.

I parked my truck and walked down the rows of chrysanthemums. The wind was blowing and the field rippled with streaks of brown and gold and purple color.

"I never figured you to take up farming, Breeze," I said.

"I give up on some t'ings. So my father made this li'l job for me, that's all," he said.

"Beg your pardon?"

"Getting even wit' people, t'ings like that. I ain't giving nobody reason to put me back in jail."

"You know what an exhumation order is?" I asked.

As with many people of color, he treated questions from white men as traps and didn't indicate an answer one way or another. He stooped over and jerked a weed and its root system out of the soil.

"I want to have a pathologist examine your wife's remains. I don't believe she committed suicide," I said.

He stopped work and rested his hands on the hoe handle. His hands looked like gnarled rocks around the wood. Then he put one hand inside the top of his shirt and rubbed his skin, his eyes never leaving mine.

"Say again?"

"I checked with the coroner's office in St. Mary Parish. No autopsy was done on Ida's body. It simply went down as a suicide."

"What you telling me?"

"I don't think she took her life."

"Didn't nobody have reason to kill her. Unless you saying I . . . Wait a minute, you trying to—"

"You're not a killer, Breeze. You're just a guy who got used by some very bad white people."

He started working the hoe between the plants again, his breath coming hard in his chest, his brow creased like an old leather glove. The wind was cool blowing across the field, but drops of sweat as big as marbles slid off his neck. He stopped his work again and faced me, his eyes wet.

"What we got to do to get this here order you talking about?" he asked.

•   •   •

WHEN I GOT HOME a peculiar event was taking place. Alafair and three of her friends were in the front yard, watching a man with a flattop haircut stand erect on an oak limb, then topple into space, grab a second limb and hang from it by his knees.

I parked my pickup and walked across the yard while Boxleiter's eyes, upside down, followed me. He bent his torso upward, flipped his legs in the air, and did a half-somersault so that he hit the ground on the balls of his feet.

"Alafair, would you guys head on up to the house and tell Bootsie I'll be there in a minute?" I said.

"She's on the gallery. Tell her yourself," Alafair said.

"*Alf . . .*" I said.

She rolled her eyes as though the moment was more than her patience could endure, then she and her friends walked through the shade toward the house.

"Swede, it's better you bring business to my office," I said.

"I couldn't sleep last night. I always sleep, I mean dead, like stone. But not last night. There's some heavy shit coming down, man. It's a feeling I get. I'm never wrong."

"Like what?"

"This ain't no ordinary grift." He fanned his hand at the air, as though sweeping away cobweb. "I never had trouble handling the action. You draw lines, you explain the rules, guys don't listen, they keep coming at you, you unzip their package. But that ain't gonna work on this one." He blotted the perspiration off his face with the back of his forearm.

"Sorry. You're not making much sense, Swede."

"I don't got illusions about how guys like me end up. But Cisco and Megan ain't like me. I was sleeping in the Dismas House in St. Louis after I finished my first bit. They came and got me. They see somebody jammed up, people getting pushed around, they make those people's problem their problem. They get that from their old man. That's why these local cocksuckers nailed him to a wall."

"You're going have to watch your language around my home, partner," I said.

His hand shot out and knotted my shirt in a ball.

"You're like every cop I ever knew. You don't listen. I can't stop what's going on."

I grabbed his wrist and thrust it away from me. He opened and closed his hands impotently.

"I hate guys like you," he said.

"Oh?"

"You go to church with your family, but you got no idea what life is like for two-thirds of the human race."

"I'm going inside now, Swede. Don't come around here anymore."

"What'd I do, use bad language again?"

"You cut up Anthony Pollock. I can't prove it, and it didn't happen in our jurisdiction, but you're an iceman."

"If I did it in a uniform, you'd be introducing me at the Kiwanis Club. I hear you adopted your kid and treated her real good. That's a righteous deed, man. But the rest of your routine is comedy. A guy with your brains ought to be above it."

He walked down the slope to the dirt road and his parked car. When he was out of the shade he stopped and turned around. His granny glasses were like ground diamonds in the sunlight.

"How many people did it take to crucify Megan and Cisco's old man and cover it up for almost forty years? I'm an iceman? Watch out one of your neighbors don't tack you up with a nail gun," he yelled up the slope while two fishermen unhitching a boat trailer stared at him openmouthed.

I RAKED AND BURNED leaves that afternoon and tried not to think about Swede Boxleiter. But in his impaired way he had put his thumb on a truth about human behavior that eludes people who are considered normal. I remembered a story of years ago about a fourteen-year-old boy from Chicago who was visiting relatives in a small Mississippi town not far from the Pearl River. One afternoon he whistled at a white woman on the street. Nothing was said to him, but that night two Klansmen kidnapped him from the home of his relatives, shot and killed him, and wrapped his body in a net of bricks and wire and sank it in the river.

Everyone in town knew who had done it. Two local lawyers, respectable men not associated with the Klan, volunteered to defend the killers. The jury took twenty minutes to set them free. The foreman said the verdict took that long because the jury had stopped deliberations to send out for soda pop.

It's a story out of another era, one marked by shame and collective fear, but its point is not about racial injustice but instead the fate of those who bear Cain's mark.

A year after the boy's death a reporter from a national magazine visited the town by the Pearl River to learn the fate of the killers. At first they had been avoided, passed by on the street, treated at grocery or hardware counters as though they had no first or last names, then their businesses failed—one owned a filling station, the other a fertilizer yard—and their debts were called. Both men left town, and when asked their whereabouts old neighbors would only shake their heads as though the killers were part of a vague and decaying memory.

The town that had been complicit in the murder ostracized those who had committed it. But no one had been ostracized in St. Mary Parish. Why? What was the difference in the accounts of the black teenager's murder and Jack Flynn's, both of which seemed collective in nature?

Answer: The killers in Mississippi were white trash and economically dispensable.

SUNDAY AFTERNOON I FOUND Archer Terrebonne on his side patio, disassembling a spinning reel on a glass table top. He wore slippers and white slacks and a purple shirt that was embroidered with his initials on the pocket. Overhead, two palm trees with trunks that were as gray and smooth as elephant hide creaked against a hard-blue sky. Terrebonne glanced up at me, then resumed his concentration, but not in an unpleasant way.

"Sorry to bother you on Sunday, but I suspect you're quite busy during the week," I said.

"It's no bother. Pull up a chair. I wanted to thank you for the help you gave my daughter."

You didn't do wide end runs around Archer Terrebonne.

"It's wonderful to see her fresh and bright in the morning, unharried by all the difficulties she's had, all the nights in hospitals and calls from policemen," he said.

"I have a problem, Mr. Terrebonne. A man named Harpo Scruggs is running all over our turf and we can't get a net over him."

"Scruggs? Oh yes, quite a character. I thought he was dead."

"His uncle was a guy named Harpo Delahoussey. He did security work at y'all's cannery, the one that burned."

"Yes, I remember."

"We think Harpo Scruggs tried to kill a black man named Willie Broussard and almost drowned Jack Flynn's daughter."

He set down the tiny screwdriver and the exposed brass mechanisms of the spinning reel. The tips of his delicate fingers were bright with machine oil. The wind blew his white-gold hair on his forehead.

"But you use the father's name, not the daughter's. What inference should I gather from that, sir? My family has a certain degree of wealth and hence we should feel guilt over Jack Flynn's death?"

"Why do you think he was killed?"

"That's your province, Mr. Robicheaux, not mine. But I don't think Jack Flynn was a proletarian idealist. I think he was a resentful, envious troublemaker who couldn't get over the fact his family lost their money through their own mismanagement. Castle Irish don't do well when their diet is changed to boiled cabbage."

"He fought Franco's fascists in Spain. That's a peculiar way to show envy."

"What's your purpose here?"

"Your daughter is haunted by something in the past she can't tell anybody about. It's connected to the Hanged Man in the Tarot. I wonder if it's Jack Flynn's death that bothers her."

He curled the tips of his fingers against his palm, as though trying to rub the machinist's oil off them, looking at them idly.

"She killed her cousin when she was fifteen. Or at least that's what she's convinced herself," he said. He saw my expression change, my lips start to form a word. "We had a cabin in Durango at the foot of a mountain. They found the key to my gun case and started shooting across a snowfield. The avalanche buried her cousin in an arroyo. When they dug her out the next day, her body was frozen upright in the shape of a cross."

"I didn't know that, sir."

"You do now. I'm going in to eat directly. Would you care to join us?"

When I walked to my truck I felt like a man who had made an obscene remark in the midst of a polite gathering. I sat behind the steering wheel and stared at the front of the Terrebonne home. It was encased in shadow now, the curtains drawn on all the windows. What historical secrets, what private unhappiness did it hold? I wondered if I would ever know. The late sun hung like a shattered red flame in the pine trees.

TWENTY

I REMEMBER A CHRISTMAS DAWN five years after I came home from Vietnam. I greeted it in an all-night bar built of slat wood, the floor raised off the dirt with cinder blocks. I walked down the wood steps into a deserted parking area, my face numb with alcohol, and stood in the silence and looked at a solitary live oak hung with Spanish moss, the cattle acreage that was gray with winter, the hollow dome of sky that possessed no color at all, and suddenly I felt the vastness of the world and all the promise it could hold for those who were still its children and had not severed their ties with the rest of the human family.

Monday morning I visited Megan at her brother's house and saw a look in her eyes that I suspected had been in mine on that Christmas morning years ago.

Had her attackers held her underwater a few seconds more, her body would have conceded what her will would not: Her lungs and mouth and nose would have tried to draw oxygen out of water and her chest and throat would have filled with cement. In that moment she knew the heartbreaking twilight-infused beauty that the earth can offer, that we waste as easily as we tear pages from a calendar, but neither would she ever forget or forgive the fact that her reprieve came from the same hands that did Indian burns on her skin and twisted her face down into the silt.

She was living in the guest cottage at the back of Cisco's house, and the French doors were open and the four-o'clocks planted as borders around the trees were dull red in the shade.

"What's that?" she said.

I lay a paper sack and the hard-edged metal objects inside it on her breakfast table.

"A nine-millimeter Beretta. I've made arrangements for somebody to give you instruction at the firing range," I said.

She slipped the pistol and the unattached magazine out of the sack and pulled back the slide and looked at the empty chamber. She flipped the butterfly safety back and forth.

"You have peculiar attitudes for a policeman," she said.

"When they deal the play, you take it to them with fire tongs," I said.

She put the pistol back in the sack and stepped out on the brick patio and looked at the bayou with her hands in the back pockets of her baggy khaki pants.

"I'll be all right after a while. I've been through worse," she said.

I stepped outside with her. "No, you haven't," I said.

"Excuse me?"

"It only gets so bad. You go to the edge, then you

join a special club. A psychologist once told me only about three percent of the human family belongs to it."

"I think I'll pass on the honor."

"Why'd you come back?"

"I see my father in my sleep."

"You want the gun?"

"Yes."

I nodded and turned to go.

"Wait." She took her eyeglass case out of her shirt pocket and stepped close to me. There was a dark scrape at the corner of her eye, like dirty rouge rubbed into the grain. "Just stand there. You don't have to do anything," she said, and put her arms around me and her head on my chest and pressed her stomach flat against me. She wore doeskin moccasins and I could feel the instep of her foot on my ankle.

The top of her head moved under my chin and against my throat and the wetness of her eyes was like an unpracticed kiss streaked on my skin.

RODNEY LOUDERMILK HAD LIVED two weeks on the eighth floor of the old hotel that was not two blocks from the Alamo. The elevator was slow and throbbed in the shaft, the halls smelled bad, the fire escapes leaked rust down the brick sides of the building. But there was a bar and grill downstairs and the view from his window was magnificent. The sky was blue and salmon-colored in the evening, the San Antonio River lighted by sidewalk restaurants and gondolas that passed under the bridges, and he could see the pinkish stone front of the old mission where he often passed himself off as a tour guide and led college girls through the porticoed walkways that were hung with grape-vines.

He was blind in one eye from a childhood accident with a BB gun. He wore sideburns and snap-button cowboy shirts with his Montgomery Ward suits. He had been down only once, in Sugarland, on a nickel-and-dime burglary beef that had gone sour because his fall partner, a black man, had dropped a crowbar off the roof through the top of a greenhouse.

But Rodney had learned his lesson: Stay off of roofs and don't try to turn watermelon pickers into successful house creeps.

The three-bit on Sugarland Farm hadn't been a wash either. He had picked up a new gig, one that had some dignity to it, that paid better, that didn't require dealing with fences who took him off at fifteen cents on the dollar. One week off the farm and he did his first hit. It was much easier than he thought. The target was a rancher outside Victoria, a loudmouth fat shit who drove a Cadillac with longhorns for a hood orna-ment and who kept blubbering, "I'll give you money, boy. You name the price. Look, my wife's gonna be back from the store. Don't hurt her, okay . . . ," then had started to tremble and messed himself like a child.

"That goes to show you, money don't put no lead in your pencil," Rodney was fond of telling his friends.

He also said the fat man was so dumb he never guessed his wife had put up the money for the hit. But Rodney let him keep his illusions. Why not? Business was business. You didn't personalize it, even though the guy was a born mark.

Their grief was their own, he said. They owed money, they stole it, they cheated on their wives. People sought justice in different ways. The state did it with a gurney and a needle, behind a viewing glass, while people watched like they were at an X-rated movie. Man, *that* was sick.

Rodney showered in the small tin stall and put on a fresh long-sleeve shirt, one that covered the tattooed chain of blue stars around his left wrist, then looked at his four suits in the closet and chose one that rippled with light like a sheet of buffed tin. He slipped on a new pair of black cowboy boots and fitted a white cowboy hat on his head, pulling the brim at an angle over his blind eye.

All you had to do was stand at the entrance to the Alamo and people came up and asked you questions. Clothes didn't make the person. Clothes *were* the person, he told people. You ever see a gun bull mounted on horseback without a hat and shades? You ever see a construction boss on a job without a clipboard and hard hat and a pocketful of ballpoints? You ever see a hooker that *ain't* made up to look like your own personal pinball machine?

Rodney conducted tours, gave directions around the city, walked tourists to their hotels so they wouldn't be mugged by what he called "local undesirables we're fixing to get rid of."

A buddy, a guy he'd celled with at Sugarland, asked him what he got out of it.

"Nothing. That's the point, boy. They got nothing I want."

Which wasn't true. But how did you explain to a pipehead that walking normals around, making them apprehensive one moment, relieving their fears another, watching them hang on his words about the cremation of the Texan dead on the banks of the river (an account he had memorized from a brochure) gave him a rush like a freight train loaded with Colombian pink roaring through the center of his head?

Or popping a cap on a slobbering fat man who thought he could bribe Rodney Loudermilk.

It was dusk when Rodney came back from showing two elderly nuns where Davy Crockett had been either bayoneted to death or captured against the barracks wall and later tortured. They both had seemed a little pale at the details he used to describe the event. In fact, they had the ingratitude to tell him they didn't need an escort back to their hotel, like he had BO or something. Oh, well. He had more important things on his mind. Like this deal over in Louisiana. He'd told his buddy, the pipehead, he didn't get into a new career so he could go back to strong-arm and B&E bullshit. That whole scene on the bayou had made him depressed in ways he couldn't explain, like somebody had stolen something from him.

She hadn't been afraid. When they're afraid, it proves they got it coming. When they're not afraid, it's like they're spitting in your face. Yeah, that was it. You can't pop them unless they're afraid, or they take part of you with them. Now he was renting space in his head to a hide (that's what he called women) he shouldn't even be thinking about. He had given her power, and he wanted to go back and correct the images that had left him confused and irritable and not the person he was when he gave guided tours in his western clothes.

He looked at the slip of paper he had made a note on when this crazy deal started. It read: *Meet H.S. in New Iberia. Educate a commonist?* A commonist? Republicans live in rich houses, not commonists. Any dumb shit knows that. Why had he gotten into this? He crumpled up the note in his palm and bounced it off the rim of the wastebasket and called the grill for a steak and baked potato, heavy on the cream and melted butter, and a green salad and a bottle of champale.

It was dusk and a purple haze hung on the rooftops when a man stepped out of a hallway window onto a fire escape, then eased one foot out on a ledge and worked his way across the brick side of the building, oblivious to the stares of two winos down in the alley eight floors below. When the ledge ended, he paused for only a moment, then with the agility of a cat, he hopped across empty space onto another ledge and entered another window.

Rodney Loudermilk had just forked a piece of steak into his mouth when the visitor seized him from behind and dragged him out of his chair, locking arms and wrists under Rodney's rib cage, lifting him into the air and simultaneously carrying him to the window, whose curtains swelled with the evening breeze. Rodney probably tried to scream and strike out with the fork that was in his hand, but a piece of meat was lodged like a stone in his throat and the arms of his visitor seemed to be cracking his ribs like sticks.

Then there was a rush of air and noise and he was out above the city, among clouds and rooftops and faces inside windows that blurred past him. He concentrated his vision on the dusky purple stretch of sky that was racing away from him, just like things had always raced away from him. It was funny how one gig led to another, then in seconds the rounded, cast-iron, lug-bolted dome of an ancient fire hydrant rose out of the cement and came at your head faster than a BB traveling toward the eye.

THE ACCOUNT OF RODNEY Loudermilk's death was given us over the phone by a San Antonio homicide investigator named Cecil Hardin, who had found the crumpled piece of notepaper by the wastebasket in Loudermilk's hotel room. He also read us the statements he had taken from the two witnesses in the alley and played a taped recording of an interview with Loudermilk's pipehead friend.

"You got any idea who H.S. is?" Hardin asked.

"We've had trouble around here with an ex-cop by the name of Harpo Scruggs," I said.

"You think he's connected to Loudermilk's death?" he asked.

"The killer was an aerialist? My vote would go to another local, Swede Boxleiter. He's a suspect in a murder in Lafayette Parish."

"What are y'all running over there, a school for criminals? Forget I said that. Spell the name, please." Then he said, "What's the deal on this guy Boxleiter?"

"He's a psychopath with loyalties," I said.

"You a comedian, sir?"

I DROVE UP THE Loreauville road to Cisco's house. Megan was reading a book in a rocking chair on the gallery.

"Do you know where Swede was on Sunday?" I asked.

"He was here, at least in the morning. Why?"

"Just a little research. Does the name Rodney Loudermilk mean anything to you?"

"No. Who is he?"

"A guy with sideburns, blind in one eye?"

She shook her head.

"Did you tell Swede anything about your attackers, how they looked, what they said?"

"Nothing I didn't tell you. I was asleep when they broke in. They wound tape around my eyes."

I scratched the back of my neck. "Maybe Swede's not our man."

"I don't know what you're talking about, Dave."

"Sunday evening somebody canceled out a contract killer in a San Antonio hotel. He was probably one of the men who broke into your house."

She closed the book in her lap and looked out into the yard. "I told Swede about the blue stars on a man's wrist," she said.

"What?"

"One of them had a string of stars tattooed on his wrist. I told that to one of your deputies. He wrote it down."

"If he did, the sheriff and I never saw it."

"What difference does it make?"

"The guy in San Antonio, he was thrown out an eighth-floor window by somebody who knows how to leap across window ledges. He had a chain of blue stars tattooed around his left wrist."

She tried to hide the knowledge in her eyes. She took her glasses off and put them back on again.

"Swede was here that morning. He ate breakfast with us. I mean, everything about him was normal," she said, then turned her face toward me.

"Normal? You're talking about Boxleiter? Good try, Meg."

• • •

HELEN AND I DROVE to the movie set on the Terrebonne lawn.

"Sunday? I was at Cisco's. Then I was home. Then I went to a movie," Swede said. He dropped down from the back of a flatbed truck, his tool belt clattering on his hips. His gaze went up and down Helen's body. "We're not getting into that blackjack routine again, are we?"

"Which movie?" I asked.

"Sense and Sensibility. Ask at the theater. The guy'll remember me 'cause he says I plugged up the toilet."

"Sounds good to me. What about you, Helen?" I said.

"Yeah, I always figured him for a fan of British novels," she said.

"What am I supposed to have done?"

"Tossed a guy out a window in San Antonio. His head hit a fire hydrant at a hundred twenty miles per. Big mess," I said.

"Yeah? Who is this fucking guy I supposedly killed?"

"Would you try not to use profanity?" I said.

"Sorry. I forgot, Louisiana is an open-air church. I got a question for you. Why is it guys like me are always getting rousted whenever some barf bag gets marched off with the Hallelujah Chorus? Does Ricky the Mouse do time? Is Harpo Scruggs sitting in your jail? Of course not. You turned him loose. If guys like me weren't around, you'd be out of a job." He pulled a screwdriver from his belt and began tapping it across his palm, rolling his eyes, chewing gum, rotating his head on his neck. "Is this over? I got to get to work."

"We might turn out to be your best friends, Swede," I said.

"Yeah, shit goes great with frozen yogurt, too," he said, and walked away from us, his bare triangular back arched forward like that of a man in search of an adversary.

"You going to let him slide like that?" Helen said.

"Sometimes the meltdowns have their point of view."

"Just coincidence he stops up a toilet in a theater on the day he needs an alibi?"

"Let's go to the airport."

BUT IF SWEDE TOOK a plane to San Antonio or rented one, we could find no record of it.

That night the air was thick and close and smelled of chrysanthemums and gas, then the sky filled with lightning and swirls of black rain that turned to hail and clattered and bounced like mothballs on the tin roof of the bait shop.

Two days later I drove to St. Mary Parish with Cool Breeze Broussard to watch the exhumation of his wife's body from a graveyard that was being eaten daily by the Atchafalaya River.

AT ONE TIME THE graveyard had sat on dry ground, fringed by persimmon and gum trees, but almost twenty years ago the Atchafalaya had broken a levee and channeled an oxbow through the woods, flooding the grave sites, then had left behind a swampy knob of sediment strung with river trash. One side of the graveyard dipped toward the river, and each year the water cut more deeply under the bank, so that the top layer hung like the edge of a mushroom over the current.

Most of the framed and spiked name tags that served as markers had been knocked down or stepped on and broken by hunters. The dime-store vases and the jelly glasses used for flower jars lay embedded in sediment. The graduation and wedding and birth pictures wrapped in plastic had been washed off the graves on which they had been originally placed and were now spotted with mud, curled and yellowed by the sun so that the faces on them were not only anonymous but stared incongruously out of situations that seemed to have never existed.

The forensic pathologist and a St. Mary Parish deputy and the two black men hired as diggers and the backhoe operator waited.

"You know which one it is?" I asked Cool Breeze.

"That one yonder, wit' the pipe cross. I welded it myself. The shaft goes down t'ree feet," he said.

The serrated teeth on the bucket of the backhoe bit into the soft earth and lifted a huge divot of loam and roots and emerald-colored grass from the top of the grave. Cool Breeze's shoulder brushed against mine, and I could feel the rigidity and muted power in his body, like the tremolo that rises from the boiler room of a ship.

"We can wait on the levee until they're finished," I said.

"I got to look," he said.

"Beg your pardon?"

"Cain't have nobody saying later that ain't her."

"Breeze, she's been in the ground a long time."

"Don't matter. I'll know. What you t'ink I am anyway? Other men can look at my wife, but I'm scared to do it myself?"

"I think you're a brave man," I said.

He turned his head and looked at the side of my face.

The backhoe was bright yellow against the islands of willow trees between the graveyard and the main portion of the river. The loam in the grave turned to mud as the bucket on the backhoe dipped closer to the coffin. The day was blue-gold and warm and flowers still bloomed on the levee, but the air smelled of humus, of tree roots torn out of wet soil, of leaves that have gone acidic and brown in dead water. At five feet the two black diggers climbed into the hole with spades and began sculpting the coffin's shape, pouring water from a two-gallon can on the edges, wiping the surface and corners slick with rags.

They worked a canvas tarp and wood planks under it, then ran ropes tied to chains under the tarp, and we all lifted. The coffin came free more easily than I had expected, rocking almost weightlessly in the bottom of the canvas loop, a missing panel in one side blossoming with muddy fabric.

"Open it up," Cool Breeze said.

The pathologist looked at me. He wore red suspenders and a straw hat and had a stomach like a small pillow pushed under his belt. I nodded, and one of the diggers prized the lid loose with a blade screwdriver.

I had seen exhumations before. The view of mortality they present to the living is not easily dismissed. Sometimes the coffin fills with hair, the nails, particularly on the bare feet, grow into claws, the face puckers into a gray apple, the burial clothes contain odors that cause people to retch.

That is not what happened to Ida Broussard.

Her white dress had turned brown, like cheesecloth dipped in tea, but her skin had the smooth texture and color of an eggplant and her hair was shiny and black on her shoulders and there was no distortion in her expression.

Cool Breeze's hand reached out and touched her cheek. Then he walked away from us, without speaking, and stood on the edge of the graveyard and looked out at the river so we could not see his face.

"How do you explain it?" I said to the pathologist.

"An oil company buried some storage tanks around here in the 1930s. Maybe some chemical seepage got in the coffin," he replied.

He looked back into my eyes. Then he spoke again. "Sometimes I think they wait to tell us something. There's no need for you to pass on my observation."

TWENTY-ONE

FRIDAY EVENING BOOTSIE AND I dropped Alafair at the show in Lafayette, then ate dinner at a restaurant on the Vermilion River. But as soon as Alafair was not with us, Bootsie became introspective, almost formal when she spoke, her eyes lingering on objects without seeing them.

"What is it?" I said outside the restaurant.

"I'm just tired," she replied.

"Maybe we should have stayed home."

"Maybe we should have."

After Alafair went to bed, we were alone in the kitchen. The moon was up and the trees outside were full of shadows when the wind blew.

"Whatever it is, just say it, Boots."

"She was at the dock today. She said she couldn't find you at your office. She didn't bother to come up to the house. Of course, she's probably just shy."

"She?"

"You know who. She finds any excuse she can to come out here. She said she wanted to thank you for the shooting lessons you arranged for her. You didn't want to give them to her yourself?"

"Those guys almost killed her. They might pull it off the next time."

"Maybe it's her own fault."

"That's a rough thing to say, Boots."

"She hides behind adversity and uses it to manipulate other people."

"I'll ask her not to come here again."

"Not on my account, please."

"I give up," I said, and went out into the yard.

The cane in my neighbor's field was green and dented with channels like rivers when the wind blew, and beyond his tree line I could see lightning fork without sound out of the sky. Through the kitchen window I heard Bootsie clattering dishes into the dishwasher. She slammed the washer door shut, the cups and silverware rattling in the rack. I heard the washer start to hum, then her shadow went past the window and disappeared from view and the overhead light went off and the kitchen and the yard were dark.

WE WANTED HARPO SCRUGGS. But we had nothing to charge him with. He knew it, too. He called the dock on Sunday afternoon.

"I want to meet, talk this thing out, bring it to an end," he said.

"It's not a seller's market, Scruggs."

"What you got is your dick in your hand. I can clean the barn for you. There's an old nigra runs a barbecue joint next to a motel on State Road 70 north of Morgan City. Nine o'clock," he said, and hung up.

I went outside the bait shop and hosed down a

rental boat a fisherman had just returned, then went back inside without chaining it up and called Helen Soileau at her home.

"You want to do backup on a meet with Harpo Scruggs?" I said.

"Make him come in."

"We don't have enough to charge him."

"There's still the college kid, the witness who saw the two brothers executed in the Basin."

"His family says he's on a walking tour of Tibet."

"He killed Mout's dog. Vermilion Parish can charge him with endangering."

"Mout' says he never got a good look at the guy's face."

"Dave, we need to work this guy. He doesn't bring the Feds into it, he doesn't plead out. We fit his head in a steel vise."

"So take a ride with me. I want you to bring a scoped rifle."

She was silent a moment. Then she said, "Tell the old man."

THE BARBECUE PLACE WAS a rambling, tin-roofed red building, with white trim and screen porches, set back in a grove of pines. Next door was a cinder-block motel that had been painted purple and fringed with Christmas lights that never came down. Through the screen on a side porch I saw Harpo Scruggs standing at the bar, a booted foot on the rail, his tall frame bent forward, his Stetson at an angle on his freshly barbered head. He wore a long-sleeve blue shirt with pink polka dots and an Indian-stitched belt and gray western slacks that flowed like water over the crook in his knee. He tilted back a shot glass of whiskey and sipped from a glass of beer.

I stood by a plank table at the edge of the clearing so he could see me. He put an unlit cigarette in his mouth and opened the screen door and lit the cigarette with a Zippo as he walked toward me.

"You got anybody with you?" he asked.

"You see anyone?"

He sat down at the plank table and smoked his cigarette, his elbows on the wood. The clouds above the pines were black and maroon in the sun's afterglow. He tipped his ashes carefully over the edge of the table so they wouldn't blow back on his shirt.

"I heard about a man got throwed out a window. I think one of two men done it. Swede Boxleiter or that bucket of whale sperm got hisself kicked off the New Orleans police force," he said.

"Clete Purcel?"

"If that's his name. You can tell them I didn't have nothing to do with hurting that woman."

"Tell them yourself."

"All this trouble we been having? It can end in one of two ways. That black boy, Broussard, don't testify against the dagos in New Orleans and some people gets paid back the money they're owed.

"The other way it ends is I get complete immunity as a government witness, all my real estate is sold and the proceeds are put in bearer bonds. Not one dollar of it gets touched by the IRS. Then I retire down in Guatemala. Y'all decide."

"Who the hell do you think you are?" I said.

A black man brought a bottle of Dixie beer on a

metal tray to the table. Scruggs tipped him a quarter and wiped the lip of the bottle with his palm.

"I'm the man got something you want, son. Or you wouldn't be sitting here," he replied.

"You took money from Ricky Scarlotti, then fucked up everything you touched. Now you've got both the Mob and a crazoid like Boxleiter on your case," I said.

He drank out of the beer and looked into the pine trees, sucking his false teeth, his expression flat. But I saw the muted change in his eyes, the way heat glows when the wind puffs ash off a coal.

"You ain't so different from me," he said. "You want to bring them rich people down. I can smell it in you, boy. A poor man's got hate in his glands. It don't wash out. That's why nigras stink the way they do."

"You've caused a lot of trouble and pain for people around here. So we've decided in your case it should be a two-way street. I'd hoped you'd provoke a situation here."

"You got a hideaway on your ankle?"

"My partner has your face in the crosshairs of a scoped .30-06. She'd looked forward to this evening with great anticipation, sir. Enjoy your beer. We'll catch you down the road."

I walked out to the parking lot and waited for Helen to pull my truck around from the other side of the motel. I didn't look behind me, but I could feel his eyes on my back, watching. When Helen drew to a stop in front of me, the scoped, bolt-action rifle on the gun rack, the dust drifting off the tires, she cocked one finger like a pistol and aimed it out the window at Harpo Scruggs.

• • •

TUESDAY MORNING THE SHERIFF called me into his office.

"I just got the surveillance report on Scruggs," he said. "He took the Amtrak to Houston, spent the night in a Mexican hot pillow joint, then flew to Trinidad, Colorado."

"He'll be back."

"I think I finally figured out something about wars. A few people start them and the rest of us fight them. I'm talking about all these people who use our area for a bidet. I think this state is becoming a mental asylum, I really do." Something outside the window caught his attention. "Ah, my morning wouldn't be complete without it. Cisco Flynn just walked in the front door."

FIVE MINUTES LATER CISCO sat down in front of my desk.

"You got anything on these guys who attacked Megan?" he asked.

"Yeah. One of them is dead."

"Did you clear Swede on that deal?"

"You mean did I check out his alibi? He created a memorable moment at the theater. Water flowed out of the men's room into the lobby. At about five in the afternoon."

"From what I understand, that should put him home free."

"It might."

I watched his face. His reddish-brown eyes smiled at nothing.

"Megan felt bad that maybe she made a suspect out of Swede," he said.

"You can pretend otherwise, but he's a dangerous man, Cisco."

"How about the cowboy who went out the window? Would you call him a dangerous man?"

I didn't answer. We stared at each other across the desk. Then his eyes broke.

"Good seeing you, Dave. Thanks for giving Megan the gun," he said.

I watched silently as he opened the office door and went out into the hall.

I propped my forehead on my fingers and stared at the empty green surface of my desk blotter. Why hadn't I seen it? I had even used the term "aerialist" to the San Antonio homicide investigator.

I went out the side door of the building and caught Cisco at his car. The day was beautiful, and his suntanned face looked gold and handsome in the cool light.

"You called the dead man a cowboy," I said.

He grinned, bemused. "What's the big deal?" he said.

"Who said anything about how the guy was dressed?"

"I mean 'cowboy' like 'hit man.' That's what contract killers are called, aren't they?"

"You and Boxleiter worked this scam together, didn't you?"

He laughed and shook his head and got in his car and drove out of the lot, then waved from the window just before he disappeared in the traffic.

THE FORENSIC PATHOLOGIST CALLED me that afternoon.

"I can give it to you over the phone or talk in person. I'd rather do it in person," he said.

"Why's that?"

"Because autopsies can tell us things about human behavior I don't like to know about," he replied.

An hour later I walked into his office.

"Let's go outside and sit under the trees. You'll have to excuse my mood. My own work depresses the hell out of me sometimes," he said.

We sat in metal chairs behind the white-painted brick building that housed his office. The hard-packed earth stayed in shade almost year-round and was green with mold and sloped down to a ragged patch of bamboo on the bayou. Out in the sunlight an empty pirogue that had pulled loose from its mooring turned aimlessly in the current.

"There're abrasions on the back of her head and scrape marks on her shoulder, like trauma from a fall rather than a direct blow," he said. "Of course, you're more interested in cause of death."

"I'm interested in all of it."

"I mean, the abrasions on her skin could have been unrelated to her death. Didn't you say her husband knocked her around before she fled the home?"

"Yes."

"I found evidence of water in the lungs. It's a bit complicated, but there's no question about its presence at the time she died."

"So she was alive when she went into the marsh?"

"Hear me out. The water came out of a tap, not a swamp or marsh or brackish bay, not unless the latter contains the same chemicals you find in a city water supply."

"A faucet?"

"But that's not what killed her." He wore an immaculate white shirt, and his red suspenders hung loosely on his concave chest. He snuffed down in his nose and fixed his glasses. "It was heart failure, maybe brought on by suffocation."

"I'm not putting it together, Clois."

"You were in Vietnam. What'd the South Vietnamese do when they got their hands on the Vietcong?"

"Water poured on a towel?"

"I think in this case we're talking about a wet towel held down on the face. Maybe she fell, then somebody finished the job. But I'm in a speculative area now."

The image he had called up out of memory was not one I wanted to think about. I looked at the fractured light on the bayou, a garden blooming with blue and pink hydrangeas on the far bank. But he wasn't finished.

"She was pregnant. Maybe two months. Does that mean anything?" he said.

"Yeah, it sure does."

"You don't look too good."

"It's a bad story, Doc."

"They all are."

TWENTY-TWO

THAT EVENING CLETE PARKED HIS convertible by the dock and hefted an ice chest up on his shoulder and carried it to a fish-cleaning table by one of the water faucets I had mounted at intervals on a water line that ran the length of the dock's handrail. He poured the ice and at least two dozen sac-a-lait out on the table, put on a pair of cloth gardener's gloves, and started scaling the sac-a-lait with a spoon and splitting open their stomachs and half-mooning the heads at the gills.

"You catch fish somewhere else and clean them at my dock?" I said.

"I hate to tell you this, the fishing's a lot better at Henderson. How about I take y'all to the Patio for dinner tonight?"

"Things aren't real cool at the house right now."

He kept his eyes flat, his face neutral. He washed the spooned fish scales off the board plank. I told him about the autopsy on Ida Broussard.

When I finished he said, "You like graveyard stories? How about this? I caught Swede Boxleiter going out of the Terrebonne cemetery last night. He'd used a trowel to take the bricks out of the crypt and pry open the casket. He took the rings from the corpse's fingers, and a pair of riding spurs and a silver picture frame that Archer Terrebonne says held a photo of some little girls a slave poisoned.

"I cuffed Boxleiter to a car bumper and went up to the house and told Terrebonne a ghoul had been in his family crypt. That guy must have Freon in his veins. He didn't say a word. He went down there with a light and lifted the bricks back out and dragged the casket out on the ground and straightened the bones and rags inside and put the stolen stuff back on the corpse, didn't blink an eye. He didn't even look at Boxleiter, like Boxleiter was an insect sitting under a glass jar."

"What'd you do with Boxleiter?"

"Fired him this morning."

"*You* fired him?"

"Billy Holtzner tends to delegate authority in some situations. He promised me a two-hundred-buck bonus, then hid in his trailer while I walked Boxleiter off the set. Have you told this Broussard guy his wife was murdered?"

"He's not home."

"Dave, I'll say it again. Don't let him come around the set to square a beef, okay?"

"He's not a bad guy, Clete."

"Yeah, they've got a lot of that kind on Camp J."

EARLY THE NEXT MORNING I sat with Cool Breeze on the gallery of his father's house and told him, in detail, of the pathologist's findings. He had been pushing the swing at an angle with one foot, then he stopped and scratched his hand and looked out at the street.

"The blow on the back of her head and the marks on her shoulders, could you have done that?" I said.

"I pushed her down on the steps. But her head didn't hit nothing but the screen."

"Was the baby yours?"

"Two months? No, we wasn't . . . It couldn't be my baby."

"You know where she went after she left your house, don't you?" I said.

"I do now."

"You stay away from Alex Guidry. I want your promise on that, Breeze."

He pulled on his fingers and stared at the street.

"I talked with Harpo Scruggs Sunday night," I said. "He's making noise about your testifying against the Giacanos and Ricky Scarlotti."

"Why ain't you got him in jail?"

"Sooner or later, they all go down."

"Ex-cop, ex-prison guard, man killed niggers in Angola for fun? They go down when God call 'em. What you done about Ida, it ain't lost on me. T'ank you."

Then he went back in the house.

I ATE LUNCH AT home that day. But Bootsie didn't sit at the kitchen table with me. Behind me, I heard her cleaning the drainboard, putting dishes in the cabinets, straightening canned goods in the cupboard.

"Boots, in all truth, I don't believe Megan Flynn

has any romantic interest in an over-the-hill small-town homicide cop," I said.

"Really?"

"When I was a kid, my father was often drunk or in jail and my mother was having affairs with various men. I was alone a lot of the time, and for some reason I didn't understand I was attracted to people who had something wrong with them. There was a big, fat alcoholic nun I always liked, and a half-blind ex-convict who swept out Provost's Bar, and a hooker on Railroad Avenue who used to pay me a dollar to bring a bucket of beer to her crib."

"So?"

"A kid from a screwed-up home sees himself in the faces of excoriated people."

"You're telling me you're Megan Flynn's pet bête noire?"

"No, I'm just a drunk."

I heard her moving about in the silence, then she paused behind my chair and let the tips of her fingers rest in my hair.

"Dave, it's all right to call yourself that at meetings. But you're not a drunk to me. And she'd better not ever call you one either."

I felt her fingers trail off my neck, then she was gone from the room.

TWO DAYS LATER HELEN and I took the department boat out on a wide bay off the Atchafalaya River where Cisco Flynn was filming a simulated plane crash. We let the bow of the boat scrape up onto a willow island, then walked out on a platform that the production company had built on pilings over the water. Cisco was talking to three other men, his eyes barely noting our presence.

"No, tell him to do it again," he said. "The plane's got to come in lower, right out of the sun, right across those trees. I'll do it with him if necessary. When the plane blows smoke, I want it to bleed into that red sun. Okay, everybody cool?"

It was impressive to watch him. Cisco used authority in a way that made others feel they shared in it. He was one of their own, obviously egalitarian in his attitudes, but he could take others across a line they wouldn't cross by themselves.

He turned to me and Helen.

"Watch the magic of Hollywood at work," he said. "This scene is going to take four days and a quarter of a million dollars to shoot. The plane comes in blowing black smoke, then we film a model crashing in a pond. We've got a tail section mounted on a mechanical arm that draws the wreckage underwater like a sinking plane, then we do the rescue dive in the LSU swimming pool. It edits down to two minutes of screen time. What d'you think about that?"

"I ran you through the National Crime Information Center. You and Swede Boxleiter took down a liquor store when you were seventeen," I said.

"Boy, the miracle of computers," he said. He glanced out at a boat that was moored in the center of the bay. It was the kind used for swamp tours, wide across the beam, domed with green Plexiglas, its white hull gleaming.

"Where were you Sunday evening, Cisco?" I said.

"Rented a pontoon plane and took a ride out on the Gulf."

"I have to pass on relevant information about you to a homicide investigator in San Antonio."

"So why tell me about it?"

"I try to do things in the daylight, at least when it involves people I used to trust."

"He's saying you're being treated better than you deserve," Helen said.

"The guy who soared on gilded wings out the hotel window? I think the Jersey Bounce was too easy. You saying I did it? Who cares?" Cisco replied.

"Rough words," I said.

"Yeah?" He picked up a pair of field glasses from a table and tossed them at me. "Check out the guys who are on that boat. That's reality out there. I wish it would go away, but I'm stuck with it. So give me a break on the wiseacre remarks."

I focused the glasses through an open window on a linen-covered table where Billy Holtzner and his daughter and two Asian men were eating.

"The two Chinese are the bean counters. When the arithmetic doesn't come out right, they count the numbers a second time on your fingers. Except your fingers aren't on your hands anymore," he said.

"I'd get into a new line of work," I said.

"Dave, I respect you and I don't want you to take this wrong. But don't bother me again without a warrant and in the meantime kiss my royal ass," Cisco said.

"You only try to get men to kiss your ass?" Helen said.

He walked away from us, both of his hands held in the air, as though surrendering to an irrational world, just as a twin-engine amphibian roared across the swamp at treetop level, a pipe in the stern blowing curds of black smoke across the sun.

THAT EVENING I JOGGED to the drawbridge on the dirt road while heat lightning veined the clouds and fireflies glowed and faded like wet matches above the bayou's surface. Then I did three sets each of push-ups, barbell curls, dead lifts, and military presses in the back yard, showered, and went to bed early.

On the edge of sleep I heard rain in the trees and Bootsie undressing in the bathroom, then I felt her weight next to me on the bed. She turned on her side so that her stomach and breasts were pressed against me, and put one leg across mine and her hand on my chest.

"You're drawn to people who have problems. My problem is I don't like other women making overtures to my husband," she said.

"I think that's a problem I can live with," I replied.

She raised her knee and hit me with it. Then her hand touched me and she lifted her nightgown and sat on my thighs and leaned over me and looked into my face.

Outside the window, I could see the hard, thick contours of an oak limb, wrapped with moonlight, glistening with rain.

THE NEXT DAY WAS Saturday. At false dawn I woke from a dream that lingered behind my eyes like cobweb. The dream was about Megan Flynn, and although I knew it did not signify unfaithfulness, it disturbed me just as badly, like a vapor that congeals around the heart.

In the dream she stood on a stretch of yellow hardpan, a treeless purple mountain at her back. The sky was brass, glowing with heat and dust. She walked toward me in her funny hat, her khaki clothes printed with dust, a tasseled red shawl draped around her shoulders.

But the red around her shoulders was not cloth. The wound in her throat had drained her face of blood, drenching her shirt, tasseling the ends of her fingers.

I went down to the dock and soaked a towel in the melted ice at the bottom of the cooler and held it to my eyes.

It was just a dream, I told myself. But the feeling that went with it, that was like toxin injected into the muscle tissue, wouldn't go away. I had known it in Vietnam, when I knew someone's death was at hand, mine or someone for whom I was responsible, and it had taken everything in me to climb aboard a slick that was headed up-country, trying to hide the fear in my eyes, the dryness in my mouth, the rancid odor that rose from my armpits.

But that had been the war. Since then I'd had the dream and the feelings that went with it only once—in my own house, the night my wife Annie was murdered.

TWENTY YEARS AGO ALEX Guidry had owned a steel-gray two-story frame house outside Franklin, with a staircase on the side and a second-floor screened porch where he slept in the hot months. Or at least this is what the current owner, an elderly man named Plo Castile, told me. His skin was amber, wizened, as hairless as a manikin's, and his eyes had the blue rheumy tint of oysters.

"I bought this property fo'teen years ago from Mr.

Alex. He give me a good price, 'cause I already owned the house next do','' he said. "He slept right out yonder on that porch, at least when it wasn't cold, 'cause he rented rooms sometimes to oil-field people."

The yard was neat, with two palm trees in it, and flowers were planted around the latticework at the base of the main house and in a garden by a paintless barn and around a stucco building with a tin roof elevated above the walls.

"Is that a washhouse?" I said.

"Yes, suh, he had a couple of maids done laundry for them oil-field people. Mr. Alex was a good bidnessman."

"You remember a black woman named Ida Broussard, Mr. Plo?"

He nodded. "Her husband was the one been in Angola. He run a li'l sto'." His eyes looked at a cane field beyond the barbed-wire fence.

"She come around here?"

He took a package of tobacco and cigarette papers out of his shirt pocket. "Been a long time, suh."

"You seem like an honest man. I believe Ida Broussard was murdered. Did she come around here?"

He made a sound, as though a slight irritation had flared in his throat.

"Suh, you mean they was a murder here, that's what you saying?" But he already knew the answer, and his eyes looked into space and he forgot what he was doing with the package of tobacco and cigarette papers. He shook his head sadly. "I wish you ain't come here wit' this. I seen a fight. Yeah, they ain't no denying that. I seen it."

"A fight?"

"It was dark. I was working in my garage. She drove a truck into the yard and gone up the back stairs. I could tell it was Ida Broussard 'cause Mr. Alex had the floodlight on. But, see, it was cold wet'er then and he wasn't sleeping on the porch, so she started banging on the do' and yelling he better come out.

"I seen only one light go on. All them oil-field renters was gone, they was working seven-and-seven offshore back then. I didn't want to hear no kind of trouble like that. I didn't want my wife to hear it either. So I went in my house and turned on the TV.

"But the fighting stopped, and I seen the inside light go out, then the floodlight, too. I t'ought: Well, he ain't married, white people, colored people, they been doing t'ings together at night they don't do in the day for a long time now, it ain't my bidness. Later on, I seen her truck go down the road."

"You never told anyone this?"

"No, suh. I didn't have no reason to."

"After she was found dead in the swamp?"

"He was a policeman. You t'ink them other policemen didn't know he was carrying on wit' a colored woman, they had to wait for me to tell them about it?"

"Can I see the washhouse?"

The inside was cool and dank and smelled of cement and water. Duckboards covered the floor, and a tin washtub sat under a water spigot that extended from a vertical pipe in one wall. I placed my palm against the roughness of the stucco and wondered if Ida Broussard's cries or strangled breath had been absorbed into the dampness of these same walls.

"I boil crabs out here now and do the washing in my machine," Mr. Plo said.

"Are those wood stairs out there the same ones that were on the building twenty years ago?" I asked.

"I painted them. But they're the same."

"I'd like to take some slivers of wood from them, if you don't mind."

"What for?"

"If you see Alex Guidry, you can tell him I was here. You can also tell him I took evidence from your staircase. Mr. Plo, I appreciate your honesty. I think you're a good man."

He walked across his yard toward the front door, his face harried with his own thoughts, as wrinkled as a turtle's foot. Then he stopped and turned around.

"Her husband, the one run the li'l sto'? What happened to him?" he asked.

"He went back to prison," I answered.

Mr. Plo crimped his mouth and opened his screen door and went inside his house.

FROM HIS KITCHEN WINDOW Swede Boxleiter could see the bayou through the pecan trees in the yard. It was a perfect evening. A boy was fishing in a green pirogue with a bamboo pole among the lily pads and cattails; the air smelled like rain and flowers; somebody was barbecuing steak on a shady lawn. It was too bad Blimpo nailed him coming out of the graveyard. He liked being with Cisco and Megan again, knocking down good money on a movie set, working out every day, eating seafood and fixing tropical health drinks in the blender. Louisiana had its moments.

Maybe it was time to shake it. His union card was gold in Hollywood. Besides, in California nobody got in your face because you might be a little singed around the edges. Weirded out, your arms stenciled with tracks, a rap sheet you could wallpaper the White House with? That was the bio for guys who wrote six-figure scripts. But he'd let Cisco call the shot. The problem was, the juice was just too big on this one. Taking down punks like Rodney Loudermilk or that accountant Anthony Whatever wasn't going to get anybody out of Shitsville.

He loaded the blender with fresh strawberries, bananas, two raw eggs, a peeled orange, and a can of frozen fruit cocktail, and flicked on the switch. Why was that guy from the power company still messing around outside?

"Hey, you! I told you, disconnect me again, your next job is gonna be on the trash truck!" Swede said.

"That's my day job already," the utility man replied.

They sure didn't have any shortage of wise-asses around here, Swede thought. How about Blimpo in his porkpie hat hooking him to a car bumper and going up to the Terrebonne house and bringing this guy back down to the crypt, like Swede's the pervert, a dog on a chain, not this fuck Terrebonne crawling around on his hands and knees, smoothing out the bones and rags in the casket, like he's packing up a rat's nest to mail it somewhere.

"What are you doing with my slingshot?" Swede said through the window.

"I stepped on it. I'm sorry," the utility man said.

"Put it down and get out of here."

But instead the utility man walked beyond Swede's vision to the door and knocked.

Swede went into the living room, shirtless and barefoot, and ripped open the door.

"It's been a bad week. I don't need no more trouble. I pay my bill through the super, so just pack up your shit and—" he said.

Then they were inside, three of them, and over their shoulders he saw a neighbor painting a steak with sauce on a grill and he wanted to yell out, to send just one indicator of his situation into the waning light, but the door closed quickly behind the men, then the kitchen window, too, and he knew if he could only change two seconds of his life, revise the moment between his conversation with the utility man at the window and the knock on the door, none of this would be happening, that's what two seconds could mean.

One of them turned on the TV, increasing the volume to an almost deafening level, then slightly lowering it. Were the three men smiling now, as though all four of them were involved in a mutually shameful act? He couldn't tell. He stared at the muzzle of the .25 automatic.

Man, in the bowl, big time, he thought.

But a fellow's got to try.

His shank had a four-inch blade, with a bone-and-brass handle, a brand called Bear Hunter, a real collector's item Cisco had given him. Swede pulled it from his right pocket, ticking the blade's point against the denim fabric, opening the blade automatically as he swung wildly at a man's throat.

It was a clean cut, right across the top of the chest, slinging blood in a diagonal line across the wall. Swede tried to get the second man with the backswing, perhaps even felt the knife arc into sinew and bone, but a sound like a Chinese firecracker popped inside his head, then he was falling into a black well where he should have been able to lie unmolested, looking up at the circle of peering faces far above him only if he wanted.

But they rolled him inside a rug and carried him to a place where he knew he did not want to go. He'd screwed up, no denying it, and they'd unzipped his package. But it should have been over. Why were they doing this? They were lifting him again now, out of a car trunk, over the top of the bumper, carrying him across grass, through a fence gate that creaked on a hinge, unrolling him now in the dirt, under a sky bursting with stars.

One of his eyes didn't work and the other was filmed with blood. But he felt their hands raising him up, molding him to a cruciform design that was foreign to his life, that should not have been his, stretching out his arms against wood. He remembered pictures from a Sunday school teacher's book, a dust-blown hill and a darkening sky and helmeted soldiers whose faces were set with purpose, whose fists clutched spikes and hammers, whose cloaks were the color of their work.

Hadn't a woman been there in the pictures, too, one who pressed a cloth against a condemned man's face? Would she do that for him, too? He wondered these things as he turned his head to the side and heard steel ring on steel and saw his hand convulse as though it belonged to someone else.

TWENTY-THREE

HELEN AND I WALKED THROUGH the clumps of banana trees and blackberry bushes to the north side of the barn, where a group of St. Mary Parish plainclothes investigators and uniformed sheriff's deputies and ambulance attendants stood in a shaded area, one that droned with iridescent green flies, looking down at the collapsed and impaled form of Swede Boxleiter. Swede's chest was pitched forward against the nails that held his wrists, his face hidden in shadow, his knees twisted in the dust. Out in the sunlight, the flowers on the rain trees were as bright as arterial blood among the leaves.

"It looks like we got joint jurisdiction on this one," a plainclothes cop said. His name was Thurston Meaux and he had a blond mustache and wore a tweed sports coat with a starched denim shirt and a striped tie. "After the photographer gets here, we'll take him down and send y'all everything we have."

"Was he alive when they nailed him up?" I asked.

"The coroner has to wait on the autopsy. Y'all say he took the head wound in his apartment?" he said.

"That's what it looks like," I replied.

"You found brass?"

"One casing. A .25."

"Why would somebody shoot a guy in Iberia Parish, then nail him to a barn wall in St. Mary?" Meaux said.

"Another guy died here in the same way forty years ago," I said.

"This is where that happened?"

"I think it's a message to someone," I said.

"We already ran this guy. He was a thief and a killer, a suspect in two open homicide cases. I don't see big complexities here."

"If that's the way you're going to play it, you won't get anywhere."

"Come on, Robicheaux. A guy like that is a walking target for half the earth. Where you going?"

Helen and I walked back to our cruiser and drove through the weeds, away from the barn and between two water oaks whose leaves were starting to fall, then back out on the state road.

"I don't get it. What message?" Helen said, driving with one hand, her badge holder still hanging from her shirt pocket.

"If it was just a payback killing, the shooters would have left his body in the apartment. When we met Harpo Scruggs at the barbecue place? He said something about hating rich people. I think he killed Swede and deliberately tied Swede's murder to Jack Flynn's to get even with somebody."

She thought about it.

"Scruggs took the Amtrak to Houston, then flew back to Colorado," she said.

"So he came back. That's the way he operates. He kills people over long distances."

She looked over at me, her eyes studying my expression.

"But something else is bothering you, isn't it?" she said.

"Whoever killed Swede hung him up on the right side of where Jack Flynn died."

She shook a half-formed thought out of her face.

"I like working with you, Streak, but I'm not taking any walks inside your head," she said.

ALEX GUIDRY WAS FURIOUS. He came through the front door of the sheriff's department at eight o'clock Monday morning, not slowing down at the information desk or pausing long enough to knock before entering my office.

"You're getting Ida Broussard's case reopened?" he said.

"You thought there was a statute of limitations on murder?" I replied.

"You took splinters out of my old house and gave them to the St. Mary Parish sheriff's office?" he said incredulously.

"That about sums it up."

"What's this crap about me suffocating her to death?"

I paper-clipped a sheaf of time sheets together and stuck them in a drawer.

"A witness puts you with Ida Broussard right before her death. A forensic pathologist says she was mur-

dered, that water from a tap was forced down her nose
and mouth. If you don't like what you're hearing, Mr.
Guidry, I suggest you find a lawyer," I said.

"What'd I ever do to you?"

"Sullied our reputation in Iberia Parish. You're a
bad cop. You bring discredit on everyone who carries a
badge."

"You better get your own lawyer, you sonofabitch.
I'm going to twist a two-by-four up your ass," he said.

I picked up my phone and punched the dispatcher's
extension.

"Wally, there's a man in my office who needs an
escort to his automobile," I said.

Guidry pointed one stiffened finger at me, without
speaking, then strode angrily down the hallway. A few
minutes later Helen came into my office and sat on the
edge of my desk.

"I just saw our ex-jailer in the parking lot. Somebody must have spit on his toast this morning. He
couldn't get his car door open and he ended up breaking off his key in the lock."

"Really?" I said.

Her eyes crinkled at the corners.

FOUR HOURS LATER OUR fingerprint man
called. The shell casing found on the carpet of Swede
Boxleiter's apartment was clean and the apartment contained no identifiable prints other than the victim's.
That same afternoon the sheriff called Helen and me
into his office.

"I just got off the phone with the sheriff's department in Trinidad, Colorado. Get this. They don't

know anything about Harpo Scruggs, except he owns a ranch outside of town," he said.

"Is he there now?" Helen said.

"That's what I asked. This liaison character says, 'Why you interested in him?' So I say, 'Oh, we think he might be torturing and killing people in our area, that sort of thing.'" The sheriff picked up his leather tobacco pouch and flipped it back and forth in his fingers.

"Scruggs is a pro. He does his dirty work a long way from home," I said.

"Yeah, he also crosses state lines to do it. I'm going to call that FBI woman in New Orleans. In the meantime, I want y'all to go to Trinidad and get anything you can on this guy."

"Our travel budget is pretty thin, skipper," I said.

"I already talked to the Parish Council. They feel the same way I do. You keep crows out of a cornfield by tying a few dead ones on your fence wire. That's a metaphor."

EARLY THE NEXT MORNING our plane made a wide circle over the Texas panhandle, then we dropped through clouds that were pooled with fire in the sunrise and came in over biscuit-colored hills dotted with juniper and pine and pinyon trees and landed at a small windblown airport outside Raton, New Mexico.

The country to the south was as flat as a skillet, hazed with dust in the early light, the monotony of the landscape broken by an occasional mesa. But immediately north of Raton the land lifted into dry, pinyon-covered, steep-sided hills that rose higher and higher into a mountainous plateau where the old mining town of Trinidad, once home to the Earps and Doc Holliday, had bloomed in the nineteenth century.

We rented a car and drove up Raton Pass through canyons that were still deep in shadow, the sage on the hillsides silvered with dew. On the left, high up on a grade, I saw a roofless church, with a façade like that of a Spanish mission, among the ruins and slag heaps of an abandoned mining community.

"That church was in one of Megan's photographs. She said it was built by John D. Rockefeller as a PR effort after the Ludlow massacre," I said.

Helen drove with one hand on the steering wheel. She looked over at me with feigned interest in her eyes.

"Yeah?" she said, chewing gum.

I started to say something about the children and women who were suffocated in a cellar under a burning tent when the Colorado militia broke a miners' strike at Ludlow in 1914.

"Go on with your story," she said.

"Nothing."

"You know history, Streak. But it's still the good guys against the shit bags. We're the good guys."

She put her other hand on the wheel and looked at me and grinned, her mouth chewing, her bare upper arms round and tight against the short sleeves of her shirt.

We reached the top of the grade and came out into a wide valley, with big mountains in the west and the old brick and quarried rock buildings of Trinidad off to the right, on streets that climbed into the hills. The town was still partially in shadow, the wooded crests of the hills glowing like splinters of black-green glass against the early sun.

We checked in with the sheriff's department and were assigned an elderly plainclothes detective named John Nash as an escort out to Harpo Scruggs's ranch. He sat in the back seat of our rental car, a short-brim Stetson cocked on the side of his head, a pleasant look on his face as he watched the landscape go by.

"Scruggs never came to y'all's attention, huh?" I said.

"Can't say that he did," he replied.

"Just an ordinary guy in the community?"

"If he's what you say, I guess we should have taken better note of him." His face was sun-browned, his eyes as blue as a butane flame, webbed with tiny lines at the corners when he smiled. He looked back out the window.

"This definitely seems like a laid-back place, yessiree," Helen said, her eyes glancing sideways at me. She turned off the state highway onto a dirt road that wound through an arroyo layered with exposed rock.

"What do you plan to do with this fellow?" John Nash said.

"You had a shooting around here in a while?" Helen said.

John Nash smiled to himself and stared out the window again. Then he said, "That's it yonder, set back against that hill. It's a real nice spot here. Not a soul around. A Mexican drug smuggler pulled a gun on me down by that creek once. I killed him deader than hell."

Helen and I both turned around and looked at John Nash as though for the first time.

Harpo Scruggs's ranch was rail-fenced and covered with sage, bordered on the far side by low hills and a creek that was lined with aspens. The house was gin-gerbread late Victorian, gabled and paintless, sur-rounded on four sides by a handrailed gallery. We could see a tall figure splitting firewood on a stump by the barn. Our tires thumped across the cattle guard. John Nash leaned forward with his arms on the back of my seat.

"Mr. Robicheaux, you're not hoping for our friend out there to do something rash, are you?" he said.

"You're an interesting man, Mr. Nash," I said.

"I get told that a lot," he replied.

We stopped the car on the edge of the dirt yard and got out. The air smelled like wet sage and wood smoke and manure and horses when there's frost on their coats and they steam in the sun. Scruggs paused in his work and stared at us from under the flop brim of an Australian bush hat. Then he stood another chunk of firewood on its edge and split it in half.

We walked toward him through the side yard. Cof-fee cans planted with violets and pansies were placed at even intervals along the edge of the gallery. For some reason John Nash separated himself from us and stepped up on the gallery and propped his hands on the rail and watched us as though he were a spectator.

"Nice place," I said to Scruggs.

"Who's that man up on my gallery?" he said.

"My boss man's brought the Feds into it, Scruggs. Crossing state lines. Big mistake," I said.

"Here's the rest of it. Ricky Scar is seriously pissed because a poor-white-trash peckerwood took his money and then smeared shit all over southwest Louisi-ana," Helen said.

"Plus you tied a current homicide to one that was committed forty years ago," I said.

"The real mystery is why the Mob would hire a used-up old fart who thinks bedding hookers will stop his johnson from dribbling in the toilet bowl three times a night. That Mexican hot pillow joint you visited in Houston? The girl said she wanted to scrub herself down with peroxide," Helen said. When Scruggs stared at her, she nodded affirmatively, her face dramatically sincere.

Scruggs leaned the handle of his ax against the stump and bit a small chew off a plug of tobacco, his shoulders and long back held erect inside his sun-faded shirt. He turned his face away and spit in the dirt, then rubbed his nose with the back of his wrist.

"You born in New Iberia, Robicheaux?" he asked.

"That's right."

"You think with what I know of past events, bodies buried in the levee at Angola, troublesome people killed in St. Mary Parish, I'm going down in a state court?"

"Times have changed, Scruggs," I said.

He hefted the ax in one hand and began splitting a chunk of wood into long white strips for kindling, his lips glazed with a brown residue from the tobacco in his jaw. Then he said, "If y'all going down to Deming to hurt my name there, it won't do you no good. I've lived a good life in the West. It ain't never been dirtied by nigra trouble and rich people that thinks they can make white men into nigras, too."

"You were one of the men who killed Jack Flynn, weren't you?" I said.

"I'm fixing to butcher a hog, then I got a lady

friend coming out to visit. I'd like for y'all to be gone
before she gets here. By the way, that man up on the
gallery ain't no federal agent."

"We'll be around, Scruggs. I guarantee it," I said.

"Yeah, you will. Just like a tumblebug rolling shit
balls."

We started toward the car. Behind me I heard his ax
blade splitting a piece of pine with a loud snap, then
John Nash called out from the gallery, "Mr. Scruggs,
where's that fellow used to sell you cordwood, do your
fence work and such, the one looks like he's got clap on
his face?"

"He don't work for me no more," Scruggs said.

"I bet he don't. Being as he's in a clinic down in
Raton with an infected knife wound," John Nash said.

IN THE BACK SEAT of the car Nash took a notebook from his shirt pocket and folded back several
pages.

"His name's Jubal Breedlove. We think he killed a
trucker about six years ago over some dope but we
couldn't prove it. I put him in jail a couple of times on
drunk charges. Otherwise, his sheet's not remarkable,"
he said.

"You found this guy on your own?" I said.

"I started calling hospitals when you first contacted
us. Wait till you see his face. People tend to remember it."

"Can you get on the cell phone and make sure
Breedlove isn't allowed any phone calls in the next few
minutes?" I said.

"I did that early this morning."

"You're a pretty good cop, Mr. Nash."

He grinned, then his eyes focused out the window on a snowshoe rabbit that was hopping through grass by an irrigation ditch. "By the way, I told you only what was on his sheet. About twenty years ago a family camping back in the hills was killed in their tents. The man done it was after the daughter. When I ran Jubal Breedlove in on a drunk charge, I found the girl's high school picture in his billfold."

Less than an hour later we were at the clinic in Raton. Jubal Breedlove lay in a narrow bed in a semi-private room that was divided by a collapsible partition. His face was tentacled with a huge purple-and-strawberry birthmark, so that his eyes looked squeezed inside a mask. Helen picked up his chart from the foot of the bed and read it.

"Boxleiter put some boom-boom in your bam-bam, didn't he?" she said.

"What?" he said.

"Swede slung your blood all over the apartment. He might as well have written your name on the wall," I said.

"Swede who? I was robbed and stabbed behind a bar in Clayton," he said.

"That's why you waited until the wound was infected before you got treatment," I said.

"I was drunk for three days. I didn't know what planet I was on," he replied. His hair was curly, the color of metal shavings. He tried to concentrate his vision on me and Helen, but his eyes kept shifting to John Nash.

"Harpo wouldn't let you get medical help down in Louisiana, would he? You going to take the bounce for a guy like that?" I asked.

"I want a lawyer in here," he said.

"No, you don't," Nash said, and fitted his hand on Breedlove's jaws and gingerly moved his head back and forth on the pillow, as though examining the function of Breedlove's neck. "Remember me?"

"No."

He moved his hand down on Breedlove's chest, flattening it on the panels of gauze that were taped across Breedlove's knife wound.

"Mr. Nash," I said.

"Remember the girl in the tent? I sure do." John Nash felt the dressing on Breedlove's chest with his fingertips, then worked the heel of his hand in a slow circle, his eyes fixed on Breedlove's. Breedlove's mouth opened as though his lower lip had been jerked downward on a wire, and involuntarily his hands grabbed at Nash's wrist.

"Don't be touching me, boy. That'll get you in a lot of trouble," Nash said.

"Mr. Nash, we need to talk outside a minute," I said.

"That's not necessary," he replied, and gathered a handful of Kleenex from a box on the nightstand and wiped his palm with it. "Because everything is going to be just fine here. Why, look, the man's eyes glisten with repentance already."

WE HAD ONE SUSPECT in Trinidad, Colorado, now a second one in New Mexico. I didn't want to think about the amount of paperwork and the bureaucratic legal problems that might lie ahead of us. After we dropped John Nash off at the sheriff's office, we ate lunch in a cafe by the highway. Through the window we could see a storm moving into the mountains and dust lifting out of the trees in a canyon and flattening on the hardpan.

"What are you thinking about?" Helen asked.

"We need to get Breedlove into custody and extradite him back to Louisiana," I said.

"Fat chance, huh?"

"I can't see it happening right now."

"Maybe John Nash will have another interview with him."

"That guy can cost us the case, Helen."

"He didn't seem worried. I had the feeling Breedlove knows better than to file complaints about local procedure." When I didn't reply, she said, "Wyatt Earp and his brothers used to operate around here?"

"After the shoot-out at the O.K. Corral they hunted down some other members of the Clanton gang and blew them into rags. I think this was one of the places on their route."

"I wonder what kind of salary range they have here," she said.

I paid the check and got a receipt for our expense account.

"That story Archer Terrebonne told me about Lila and her cousin firing a gun across a snowfield, about starting an avalanche?" I said.

"Yeah, you told me," Helen said.

"You feel like driving to Durango?"

WE HEADED UP THROUGH Walsenburg, then drove west into the mountains and a rainstorm that turned to snow when we approached Wolf Creek Pass. The juniper and pinyon trees and cinnamon-colored

country of the southern Colorado plateau were behind
us now, and on each side of the highway the slopes
were thick with spruce and fir and pine that glistened
with snow that began melting as soon as it touched the
canopy.

At the top of Wolf Creek we pulled into a rest stop
and drank coffee from a thermos and looked out on the
descending crests of the mountains. The air was cold
and gray and smelled like pine needles and wet boulders
in a streambed and ice when you chop it out of a wood
bucket in the morning.

"Dave, I don't want to be a pill . . ." Helen began.

"About what?"

"It seems like I remember a story years ago about
that avalanche, I mean about Lila's cousin being buried
in it and suffocating or freezing to death," she said.

"Go on."

"I mean, who's to say the girl wasn't frozen in the
shape of a cross? That kind of stuff isn't in an old newspaper article. Maybe we're getting inside our heads too
much on this one."

I couldn't argue with her.

When we got to the newspaper office in Durango
it wasn't hard to find the story about the avalanche back
in 1967. It had been featured on the first page, with
interviews of the rescuers and photographs of the slide,
the lopsided two-story log house, a barn splintered into
kindling, cattle whose horns and hooves and ice-
crusted bellies protruded from the snow like disem-
bodied images in a cubist painting. Lila had survived
because the slide had pushed her into a creekbed whose
overhang formed itself into an ice cave where she hud-

dled for two days until a deputy sheriff poked an iron pike through the top and blinded her with sunlight.

But the cousin died under ten feet of snow. The article made no mention about the condition of the body or its posture in death.

"It was a good try and a great drive over," Helen said.

"Maybe we can find some of the guys who were on the search and rescue team," I said.

"Let it go, Dave."

I let out my breath and rose from the chair I had been sitting in. My eyes burned and my palms still felt numb from involuntarily tightening my hands on the steering wheel during the drive over Wolf Creek Pass. Outside, the sun was shining on the nineteenth-century brick buildings along the street and I could see the thickly timbered, dark green slopes of the mountains rising up sharply in the background.

I started to close the large bound volume of 1967 newspapers in front of me. Then, like the gambler who can't leave the table as long as there is one chip left to play, I glanced again at a color photograph of the rescuers on a back page. The men stood in a row, tools in their hands, wearing heavy mackinaws and canvas overalls and stocking caps and cowboy hats with scarves tied around their ears. The snowfield was sunlit, dazzling, the mountains blue-green against a cloudless sky. The men were unsmiling, their clothes flattened against their bodies in the wind, their faces pinched with cold. I read the cutline below the photograph.

"Where you going?" Helen said.

I went into the editorial room and returned with a magnifying glass.

"Look at the man on the far right," I said. "Look at his shoulders, the way he holds himself."

She took the magnifying glass from my hand and stared through it, moving the depth of focus up and down, then concentrating on the face of a tall man in a wide-brim cowboy hat. Then she read the cutline.

"It says 'H. Q. Skaggs.' The reporter misspelled it. It's Harpo Scruggs," she said.

"Archer Terrebonne acted like he knew him only at a distance. I think he called him 'quite a character,' or something like that."

"Why would they have him at their cabin in Colorado? The Terrebonnes don't let people like Scruggs use their indoor plumbing," she said. She stared at me blankly, then said, as though putting her thoughts on index cards, "He did scut work for them? He's had something on them? Scruggs could be blackmailing Archer Terrebonne?"

"They're joined at the hip."

"Is there a Xerox machine out there?" she asked.

TWENTY-FOUR

WE GOT BACK TO NEW Iberia late the next day. I went to the office before going home, but the sheriff had already gone. In my mailbox he had left a note that read: "Let's talk tomorrow about Scruggs and the Feds."

That evening Bootsie and Alafair and I went to a restaurant, then I worked late at the dock with Batist. The moon was up and the water in the bayou looked yellow and high, swirling with mud, between the deep shadows of the cypress and willow trees along the banks.

I heard a car coming too fast on the dirt road, then saw Clete Purcel's convertible stop in front of the boat ramp, a plume of dust drifting across the canvas top. But rather than park by the ramp, he cut his lights and backed into my drive, so that the car tag was not visible from the road.

I went back into the bait shop and poured a cup of coffee. He walked down the dock, looking back over his shoulder, his print shirt hanging out of his slacks. He grinned broadly when he came through the door.

"Beautiful night. I thought I might get up early in the morning and do some fishing," he said.

"The weather's right," I said.

"How was Colorado?" he asked, then opened the screen door and looked back outside.

I started to pour him a cup of coffee, but he reached in the cooler and twisted the top off a beer and drank it at the end of the counter so he could see the far end of the dock.

"You mind if I sleep here tonight? I don't feel like driving back to Jeanerette," he said.

"What have you done, Clete?"

He ticked the center of his forehead with one fingernail and looked into space.

"A couple of state troopers almost got me by Spanish Lake. I'm not supposed to be driving except for business purposes," he said.

"Why would they be after you?"

"This movie gig is creeping me out. I went up to Ralph & Kacoo's in Baton Rouge," he said. "All right, here it is. But I didn't start it. I was eating oysters on the half-shell and having a draft at the bar when Benny Grogan comes up to me—you know, Ricky the Mouse's bodyguard, the one with platinum hair, the wrestler and part-time bone smoker.

"He touches me on the arm, then steps away like I'm going to swing on him or something. He says, 'We got a problem, Purcel. Ricky's stinking drunk in a back room.'

"I say, 'No, *we* don't got a problem. You got a problem.'

"He goes, 'Look, he's got some upscale gash in
there he's trying to impress, so everything's gonna be
cool. Long as maybe you go somewhere else. I'll pay
your tab. Here's a hundred bucks. You're our guest
somewhere else tonight.'

"I say, 'Benny, you want to wear food on your face
again, just put your hand on my arm one more time.'

"He shrugs his shoulders and walks off and I
thought that'd be the end of it. I was going to leave
anyway, right after I took a leak. So I'm in the men's
room, and they've got this big trough filled with ice in
it, and of course people have been pissing in it all night,
and I'm unzipping my pants and reading the newspaper
that's under a glass up on the wall and I hear the door
bang open behind me and some guy walking like the
deck is tilting under his feet.

"He goes, 'I got something for you, Purcel. They
say it hits your guts like an iron hook.'

"I'm not kidding you, Dave, I didn't think Ricky
Scar could make my heart seize up, but that's what
happened when I looked at what was in his hand. You
ever see the current thread between the prongs on a
stun gun? I go, 'Dumb move, Ricky. I was just leaving.
I consider our troubles over.'

"He goes, 'I'm gonna enjoy this.'

"Just then this biker pushes open the door and
brushes by Ricky like this is your normal, everyday
rest-room situation. When Ricky turned his head I
nailed him. It was a beaut, Dave, right in the eye. The
stun gun went sailing under the stalls and Ricky fell
backward in the trough. This plumber's helper was in
the corner, one of these big, industrial-strength jobs for
blowing out major toilet blockage. I jammed it over

Ricky's face and shoved him down in the ice and held him under till I thought he might be more reasonable, but he kept kicking and flailing and frothing at the mouth and I couldn't let go.

"The biker says, 'The dude try to cop your stick or something?'

"I go, 'Find a guy named Benny Grogan in the back rooms. Tell him Clete needs some help. He'll give you fifty bucks.'

"The biker goes, 'Benny Grogan gives head, not money. You're on your own, Jack.'

"That's when Benny comes through the door and sticks a .38 behind my ear. He says, 'Get out of town, Purcel. Next time, your brains are coming out your nose.'

"I didn't argue, mon. I almost made the front door when I hear the Mouse come roaring out of the can and charge down the hallway at me, streaming ice and piss and toilet paper that was stuck all over his feet.

"Except a bunch of people in a side dining room fling open this oak door, it must be three inches thick with wrought iron over this thick yellow glass panel in it, and they slam it right into the Mouse's face, you could hear the metal actually ding off his skull.

"So while Ricky's rolling around on the carpet, I eased on outside and decided to cruise very copacetically out of Baton Rouge and leave the greaseballs alone for a while."

"Why were state troopers after you? Why were you out by Spanish Lake instead of on the four-lane?"

His eyes clicked sideways, as though he were seriously researching the question.

"Ummm, I kept thinking about begging off from

the Mouse when he put his stun gun on snap, crackle, and pop. So out there in the parking lot were about eight or nine chopped-down Harleys. They belonged to the same bunch the Gypsy Jokers threatened to kill for wearing their colors. I still had all my repo tools in the trunk, so I found the Mouse's car and slim-jim-med the door and fired it up. Then I propped a board against the gas pedal, pointed it right into the middle of the Harleys, and dropped it into low.

"I cruised around for five minutes, then did a drive-by and watched it all from across the street. The bikers were climbing around on Ricky's car like land crabs, kicking windows out, slashing the seats and tires, tearing the wires out of the engine. It was perfect, Dave. When the cops got there, it was even better. The cops were throwing bikers in a van, Ricky was scream-ing in the parking lot, his broad trying to calm him down, Ricky swinging her around by her arm like she was a stuffed doll, people coming out every door in the restaurant like the place was on fire. Benny Grogan got sapped across the head with a baton. Anyway, it'll all cool down in a day or so. Say, you got any of those sandwiches left?"

"I just can't believe you," I said.

"What'd I do? I just wanted to eat some oysters and have a little peace and quiet."

"Clete, one day you'll create a mess you won't get out of. They're going to kill you."

"Scarlotti is a punk and a rodent and belongs under a sewer grate. Hey, the Bobbsey Twins from Homicide spit in their mouths and laugh it off, right? Quit worry-ing. It's only rock 'n' roll."

His eyes were green and bright above the beer bottle while he drank, his face flushed and dilated with his own heat.

JUST AFTER EIGHT THE next morning the sheriff came into my office. He stood at the window and propped his hands on the sill. His sleeves were rolled to his elbows, his forearms thick and covered with hair.

"I talked with that FBI woman, Glazier, about Harpo Scruggs. She's a challenge to whatever degree of civility I normally possess," he said.

"What'd she say?"

"She turned to an ice cube. That's what bothers me. He's supposed to be mixed up with the Dixie Mafia, but there's nothing in the NCIC computer on him. Why this general lack of interest?"

"Up until now his victims have been low profile, people nobody cared about," I said.

"That woman hates Megan Flynn. Why's it so personal with her?"

We looked at each other. "Guilt?" I said.

"Over what?"

"Good question."

I walked down to Helen's office, then we both signed out for New Orleans.

WE DROVE TO NEW Orleans and parked off Carondelet and walked over to the Mobil Building on Poydras Street. When we sat down in her office, she rose from her chair and opened the blinds, as though wishing to create an extra dimension in the room. Then she sat back down in a swivel chair and crossed her legs, her shoulders erect inside her gray suit, her ice-blue eyes fixed on something out in the hallway. But when I turned around, no one was there.

Then I saw it in her face, the dryness at the corner of the mouth, the skin that twitched slightly below the eye, the chin lifted as though to remove a tension in the throat.

"We thought y'all might want to help bring down this guy Scruggs. He's going back and forth across state lines like a Ping-Pong ball," I said.

"If you don't have enough grounds for a warrant, why should we?" she said.

"Every cop who worked with him says he was dirty. Maybe he even murdered convicts in Angola. But there's no sheet on him anywhere," I said.

"You're saying somehow that's our fault?"

"No, we're thinking Protected Witness Program or paid federal informant," Helen said.

"Where do you get your information? You people think—" she began.

"Scruggs is the kind of guy who would flirt around the edges of the Klan. Back in the fifties you had guys like that on the payroll," I said.

"You're talking about events of four decades ago," Adrien Glazier said.

"What if he was one of the men who murdered Jack Flynn? What if he committed that murder while he was in the employ of the government?" I said.

"You're not going to interrogate me in my own office, Mr. Robicheaux."

We stared mutely at each other, her eyes watching the recognition grow in mine.

"That's it, isn't it? You *know* Scruggs killed Megan

Flynn's father. You've known it all along. That's why you bear her all this resentment."

"You'll either leave now or I'll have you removed from the building," she said.

"Here's a Kleenex. Your eyes look a little wet, ma'am. I can relate to your situation. I used to work for the NOPD and had to lie and cover up for male bozos all the time," Helen said.

WE DROVE INTO THE Quarter and had beignets and coffee and hot milk at the Cafe du Monde. While Helen bought some pralines for her nephew, I walked across the street into Jackson Square, past the sidewalk artists who had set up their easels along the piked fence that surrounded the park, past the front of St. Louis Cathedral where a string band was playing, and over to a small bookstore on Toulouse.

Everyone in AA knows that his survival as a wet drunk was due partly to the fact that most people fear the insane and leave them alone. But those who are cursed with the gift of Cassandra often have the same fate imposed upon them. Gus Vitelli was a slight, bony Sicilian ex-horse trainer and professional bouree player whose left leg had been withered by polio and who had probably read almost every book in the New Orleans library system. He was obsessed with what he called "untold history," and his bookstore was filled with material on conspiracies of every kind.

He told anyone who would listen that the main players in the assassinations of both John Kennedy and Martin Luther King came from the New Orleans area. Some of the names he offered were those of Italian gangsters. But if the Mob was bothered by his accusations, they didn't show it. Gus Vitelli had long ago been dismissed in New Orleans as a crank.

The problem was that Gus was a reasonable and intelligent man. At least in my view.

He was wearing a T-shirt that exclaimed "I Know Jack Shit," and wrote prices on used books while I told him the story about the murder of Jack Flynn and the possible involvement of an FBI informant.

"It wouldn't surprise me that it got covered up. Hoover wasn't any friend of pinkos and veterans of the Lincoln Brigade," he said. He walked to a display table and began arranging a pile of paperback books, his left leg seeming to collapse and then spring tight again with each step. "I got a CIA manual here that was written to teach the Honduran army how to torture people. Look at the publication date, 1983. You think people are gonna believe that?" He flipped the manual at me.

"Gus, have you heard anything about a hit on a black guy named Willie Broussard?"

"Something involving the Giacanos or Ricky Scarlotti?"

"You got it."

"Nothing about a hit. But the word is Ricky Scar's sweating ball bearings 'cause he might have to give up some Asian guys. The truth is, I'm not interested. People like Ricky give all Italians a bad name. My great-grandfather sold bananas and pies out of a wagon. He raised thirteen kids like that. He got hung from a streetlamp in 1890 when the police commissioner was killed."

I thanked him for his time and started to leave.

"The guy who was crucified against the barn wall?" he said. "The reason people don't buy conspir-

acy theories is they think 'conspiracy' means everybody's on the same program. That's not how it works.
Everybody's got a different program. They just all want
the same guy dead. Socrates was a gadfly, but I bet he
took time out to screw somebody's wife."

I HAD WORRIED THAT Cool Breeze Broussard
might go after Alex Guidry. But I had not thought
about his father.

Mout' and two of his Hmong business partners
bounced their stake truck loaded with cut flowers into
the parking lot of the New Iberia Country Club.
Mout' climbed down from the cab and asked the golf
pro where he could find Alex Guidry. It was windy and
bright, and Mout' wore a suit coat and a small rainbow-
colored umbrella that clamped on his head like an elevated hat.

He began walking down the fairway, his haystack
body bent forward, his brogans rising and falling as
though he were stepping over plowed rows in a field, a
cigar stub in the side of his mouth, his face expressionless.

He passed a weeping willow that was turning gold
with the season, and a sycamore whose leaves looked
like flame, then stopped at a polite distance from the
green and waited until Alex Guidry and his three
friends had putted into the cup.

"Mr. Guidry, suh?" Mout' said.

Guidry glanced at him, then turned his back and
studied the next fairway.

"Mr. Guidry, I got to talk wit' you about my boy,"
Mout' said.

Guidry pulled his golf cart off the far slope of the

green. But his friends had not moved and were looking at his back now.

"Mr. Guidry, I know you got power round here. But my boy ain't coming after you. Suh, please don't walk away," Mout' said.

"Does somebody have a cell phone?" Guidry asked his friends.

"Alex, we can go over here and have a smoke," one of them said.

"I didn't join this club to have an old nigger follow me around the golf course," Guidry replied.

"Suh, my boy blamed himself twenty years for Ida's death. I just want you to talk wit' me for five minutes. I apologize to these gentlemen here," Mout' said.

Guidry began walking toward the next tee, his golf cart rattling behind him.

For the next hour Mout' followed him, perspiration leaking out of the leather brace that held his umbrella hat in place, the sun lighting the pink-and-white discoloration that afflicted one side of his face.

Finally Guidry sliced a ball into the rough, speared his club angrily into his golf bag, walked to the clubhouse, and went into the bar.

It took Mout' twenty minutes to cover the same amount of ground and he was sweating and breathing heavily when he came inside the bar. He stood in the center of the room, amid the felt-covered card tables and click of poker chips and muted conversation, and removed his umbrella hat and fixed his blue, cataract-frosted eyes on Guidry's face.

Guidry kept signaling the manager with one finger.

"Mr. Robicheaux say you held a wet towel over Ida's nose and mout' and made her heart stop. He gonna prove it, so that mean my boy don't have to do nothing, he ain't no threat to you," Mout' said.

"Somebody get this guy out of here," Guidry said.

"I'm going, suh. You can tell these people here anyt'ing you want. But I knowed you when you was buying black girls for t'ree dol'ars over on Hopkins. So you ain't had to go after Ida. You ain't had to take my boy's wife, suh."

The room was totally quiet. Alex Guidry's face burned like a red lamp. Mout' Broussard walked back outside, his body bent forward at the middle, his expression as blank as the grated door on a woodstove.

TWENTY-FIVE

LATE FRIDAY AFTERNOON I RECEIVED a call from John Nash in Trinidad.

"Our friend Jubal Breedlove checked out of the clinic in Raton and is nowhere to be found," he said.

"Did he hook up with Scruggs?" I asked.

"It's my feeling he probably did."

The line was silent.

"Why do you feel that, Mr. Nash?" I asked.

"His car's at his house. His clothes seem undisturbed. He didn't make a withdrawal from his bank account. What does that suggest to you, Mr. Robicheaux?"

"Breedlove's under a pile of rock?"

"Didn't Vikings put a dog at the foot of a dead warrior?" he asked.

"Excuse me?"

"I was thinking about the family he murdered in the campground. The father put up a terrific fight to protect his daughter. I hope Breedlove's under a pile of rock by that campground."

• • •

AFTER WORK I HAD to go after a boat a drunk smashed into a stump and left with a wrenched propeller on a sandbar. I tilted the engine's housing into the stern of the boat and was about to slide the hull back into the water when I saw why the drunk had waded through the shallows to dry land and walked back to his car: the aluminum bottom had a gash in it like a twisted smile.

I wedged a float cushion into the leak so I could pull the boat across the bayou into the reeds and return with a boat trailer to pick it up. Behind me I heard an outboard come around the corner and then slow when the man in the stern saw me standing among the flooded willows.

"I hope you don't mind my coming out here. The Afro-American man said it would be all right," Billy Holtzner said.

"You're talking about Batist?"

"Yes, I think that's his name. He seems like a good fellow."

He cut his engine and let his boat scrape up on the sandbar. When he walked forward the boat rocked under him and he automatically stooped over to grab the gunnels. He grinned foolishly.

"I'm not very good at boats," he said.

My experience has been that the physical and emotional transformation that eventually comes aborning in every bully never takes but one form. The catalyst is fear and its effects are like a flame on candle wax. The sneer around the mouth and the contempt and disdain in the eyes melt away and are replaced by a self-effacing smile, a confession of an inconsequential weakness, and a saccharine affectation of goodwill in the voice. The disingenuousness is like oil exuded from the skin; there's an actual stink in the clothes.

"What can I do for you?" I said.

He stood on the sandbar in rolled denim shorts and tennis shoes without socks and a thick white shirt sewn with a half dozen pockets. He looked back down the bayou, listening to the drone of an outboard engine, his soft face pink in the sunset.

"Some men might try to hurt my daughter," he said.

"I think your concern is for yourself, Mr. Holtzner."

When he swallowed, his mouth made an audible click.

"They've told me I either pay them money I don't have or they'll hurt Geri. These men take off heads. I mean that literally," he said.

"Come down to my office and make a report."

"What if they find out?" he asked.

I had turned to chain the damaged hull to the back of my outboard. I straightened up and looked into his face. The air itself seemed fouled by his words, his self-revelation hanging in the dead space between us like a dirty flag. His eyes went away from me.

"You can call me during office hours. Whatever you tell me will be treated confidentially," I said.

He sat down in his boat and began pushing it awkwardly off the sandbar by shoving a paddle into the mud.

"Did we meet somewhere before?" he asked.

"No. Why?"

"Your hostility. You don't hide it well."

He tried to crank his engine, then gave it up and drifted with the current toward the dock, his shoulders bent, the hands that had twisted noses splayed on his flaccid thighs, his chest indented as though it had been stuck with a small cannonball.

I DIDN'T LIKE BILLY Holtzner or the group he represented. But in truth some of my feelings had nothing to do with his or their behavior.

In the summer of 1946 my father was in the Lafayette Parish Prison for punching out a policeman who tried to cuff him in Antlers Pool Room. That was the same summer my mother met a corporal from Fort Polk named Hank Clausson.

"He was at Omaha Beach, Davy. That's when our people was fighting Hitler and run the Nazis out of Europe. He got all kind of medals he gonna show you," she said.

Hank was lean and tall, his face sun-browned, his uniform always starched and pressed and his shoes and brass shined. I didn't know he was sleeping over until I walked in on him in the bathroom one morning and caught him shaving in his underwear. The back of his right shoulder was welted with a terrible red scar, as though someone had dug at the flesh with a spoon. He shook his safety razor in the stoppered lavatory water and drew another swath under his chin.

"You need to get in here?" he asked.

"No," I said.

"That's where a German stuck a bayonet in me. That was so kids like you didn't end up in an oven," he said, and crimped his lips together and scraped the razor under one nostril.

He put a single drop of hair tonic on his palms and rubbed them together, then rubbed the oil into his scalp and drew his comb back through his short-cropped hair, his knees bending slightly so he could see his face fully in the mirror.

Hank took my mother and me to the beer garden and bowling alley out on the end of East Main. We sat at a plank table in a grove of oak trees that were painted white around the trunks and hung with speakers that played recorded dance music. My mother wore a blue skirt that was too small for her and a white blouse and a pillbox hat with an organdy veil pinned up on top. She was heavy-breasted and thick-bodied, and her sexuality and her innocence about it seemed to burst from her clothes when she jitterbugged, or, even a moment later, slow-danced with Hank, her face hot and breathless, while his fingers slipped down the small of her back and kneaded her rump.

"Hank's in a union for stagehands in the movie business, Davy. Maybe we going out to Hollywood and start a new life there," she said.

The loudspeakers in the trees were playing "One O'Clock Jump," and through the windows in the bar I could see couples jitterbugging, spinning, flinging each other back and forth. Hank tipped his bottle of Jax beer to his lips and took a light sip, his eyes focused on nothing. But when a blond woman in a flowered dress and purple hat walked across his gaze, I saw his eyes touch on her body like a feather, then go empty again.

"But maybe you gonna have to stay with your aunt just a little while," my mother said. "Then I'm gonna send for you. You gonna ride the Sunset Limited to Hollywood, you."

My mother went inside the bowling alley to use the rest room. The trees were glowing with the white flood lamps mounted on the branches, the air roaring with the music of Benny Goodman's orchestra. The blond woman in the flowered dress and purple hat walked to our table, a small glass of beer in one hand. The butt of her cigarette was thick with lipstick.

"How's the war hero?" she said.

He took another sip from his bottle of Jax and picked up a package of Lucky Strikes from the table and removed a cigarette gingerly by the tip and placed it in his mouth, never looking at the woman.

"My phone number's the same as it was last week. I hope nothing's been hard in your life," she said.

"Maybe I'll call you sometime," he replied.

"No need to call. You can come whenever you want," she said. When she grinned there was a red smear on her teeth.

"I'll keep it in mind," he said.

She winked and walked away, the cleft in her buttocks visible through the thinness of her dress. Hank opened a penknife and began cleaning his nails.

"You got something to say?" he asked me.

"No, sir."

"That woman there is a whore. You know what a whore is, Davy?"

"No." There was a glaze of starch on his khaki thigh. I could smell an odor like heat and soap and sweat that came from inside his shirt.

"It means she's not fit to sit down with your mother," he said. "So I don't want you talking about what you just heard. If you do, you'd best be gone when I come over."

Three days later my aunt and I stood on the platform at the train station and watched my mother and Hank climb aboard the Sunset Limited. They disappeared through the vestibule, then she came back and hugged me one more time.

"Davy, it ain't gonna be long. They got the ocean out there and movie stars and palm trees everywhere. You gonna love it, you," she said. Then Hank pulled her hand, and the two of them went into the observation car, their faces opaque now, like people totally removed from anything recognizable in their lives. Behind my mother's head I could see mural paintings of mesas and flaming sunsets.

But she didn't send for me, nor did she write or call. Three months later a priest telephoned collect from Indio, California, and asked my father if he could wire money for my mother's bus ticket back to New Iberia.

For years I dreamed of moonscape and skeletal trees along a railroad bed where white wolves with red mouths lived among the branches. When the Sunset Limited screamed down the track, the wolves did not run. They ate their young. I never discussed the dream with anyone.

TWENTY-SIX

A PSYCHOLOGIST WOULD PROBABLY agree
that unless a person is a sociopath, stuffed guilt can fill
him with a level of neurotic anxiety that is like waiting
for a headsman in a cloth hood to appear at the prison
door.

I didn't know if Alex Guidry was a sociopath or
not, but on Monday Helen and I began tightening a
couple of dials on his head.

We parked the cruiser at the entrance to his home
and watched him walk from his bunkerlike brick house
to the garage and open the garage door, simultaneously
looking in our direction. He drove down the long shell
drive to the parish road and slowed by the cruiser, rolling down his window on its electric motor. But Helen
and I continued talking to each other as though he
were not there. Then we made a U-turn and followed
him to the finance company his wife's family owned in
town, his eyes watching us in the rearview mirror.

Decades back the wife's father had made his way
through the plantation quarters every Saturday morn-

ing, collecting the half-dollar payments on burial poli-
cies that people of color would give up food, even
prostitute themselves, in order to maintain. The caskets
they were buried in were made out of plywood and
cardboard and crepe paper, wrapped in dyed cheesecloth and draped with huge satin bows. The plots were
in Jim Crow cemeteries and the headstones had all the
dignity of Hallmark cards. But as gaudy and cheap and
sad as it all was, the spaded hole in the ground and the
plastic flowers and the satin ribbons that decorated the
piled dirt did not mark the entrance to the next world
but the only level of accomplishment the dead could
achieve in this one.

The Negro burial insurance business had passed
into history and the plantation quarters were deserted,
but the same people came with regularity to the finance
company owned by the wife's family and signed papers
they could not read and made incremental loan payments for years without ever reducing the principal. A
pawnshop stood next door, also owned by the wife's
family. Unlike most businesspeople, Guidry and his in-
laws prospered most during economic recession.

We parked behind his car and watched him pause
on the sidewalk and stare at us, then go inside.

A moment later a brown Honda, driven by a tall
man in a gray suit, pulled to the curb, on the wrong
side of the street, and parked bumper to bumper in
front of Guidry's car. The driver, who was a DEA
agent named Minos Dautrieve, got out and met us on
the sidewalk in front of the finance company's glass
doors. His crew-cut blond hair was flecked with white
threads now, but he still had the same tall, angular good
looks that sports photographers had loved when he

played forward for LSU and was nicknamed "Dr. Dunkenstein" after he sailed through the air and slammed the ball so hard through the rim he shattered the backboard like hard candy.

"How's the fishing?" he said.

"They've got your name on every fin," I said.

"I'll probably come out this evening. How you doin', Helen?"

"Just fine. Lovely day, isn't it?" she replied.

"Do we have our friend's attention?" he asked, his back to the glass doors.

"Yep," I said.

He took a notebook out of his pocket and studied the first page of it.

"Well, I have to pick up a couple of things for my wife, then meet her and her mother in Lafayette. We'll see you-all," he said. He put the notebook back in his pocket, then walked to the front doors of the finance company, cupped his hands around his eyes to shield them from the sun, and peered through the tinted glass.

After he had driven away, Alex Guidry came out on the sidewalk.

"What are you people doing?" he said.

"You're an ex-cop. Guess," Helen said.

"That man's a federal agent of some kind," Guidry said.

"The guy who just left? He's an ex-jock. He was all-American honorable mention at LSU. That's a fact," I said.

"What is this?" he said.

"You're in the shithouse, Mr. Guidry. That's what it is," Helen said.

"This is harassment and I won't put up with it," he said.

"You're naive, sir. You're the subject of a murder investigation. You're also tied in with Harpo Scruggs. Scruggs has asked for immunity. You know where that leaves his friends? I'd get a parachute," I said.

"Fuck you," he said, and went back inside.

But his shirtsleeve caught on the door handle. When he pulled at it he ripped the cloth and hit a matronly white woman between the shoulder blades with his elbow.

TWO HOURS LATER GUIDRY called the office.

"Scruggs is getting immunity for what?" he asked.

"I didn't say he was 'getting' anything."

I could hear him breathing against the receiver.

"First guy in line doesn't do the Big Sleep," I said.

"Same answer. Do your worst. At least I didn't flush my career down the bowl because I couldn't keep a bottle out of my mouth," he said.

"Ida Broussard was carrying your baby when you killed her, Mr. Guidry."

He slammed down the phone.

THREE DAYS LATER, IN the cool of the evening, Lila Terrebonne and Geraldine Holtzner came down the dirt road in Clete Purcel's chartreuse Cadillac, the top down, and pulled into the drive. Alafair and I were raking leaves and burning them on the edge of the road. The leaves were damp and black, and the smoke from the fire twisted upward into the trees in thick yellow curds and smelled like marijuana burning in a wet field. Both Lila and Geraldine seemed delighted with the pink-gray loveliness of the evening, with our activity in the yard, with themselves, with the universe.

"What are you guys up to?" I said.

"We're going to a meeting. You want to tag along?" Geraldine said from behind the wheel.

"It's a thought. What are you doing with Clete's car?" I said.

"Mine broke down. He lent me his," Geraldine said. "I went back to Narcotics Anonymous, in case you're wondering. But I go to AA sometimes, too."

Lila was smiling, a wistful, unfocused beam in her eye. "Hop in, good-looking," she said.

"Did y'all make a stop before you got here?" I asked.

"Dave, I bet you urinated on radiators in elementary school," Lila said.

"I might see y'all up there later. Y'all be careful about Clete's tires. The air is starting to show through," I said.

"This is a lovely car. You drive it and suddenly it's 1965. What a wonderful time that was, just before everything started to change," she said.

"Who could argue, Lila?" I said.

Unless you were black or spent '65 in Vietnam, I thought as they drove away.

THE AA MEETING THAT evening was held in the upstairs rooms of an old brick church out on West Main. The Confederates had used the church for a hospital while they tried to hold back the Federals on the Teche south of town; then, after the town had been occupied and looted and the courthouse torched, the Federals inverted half the pews and filled them with hay for their horses. But most of the people in the upper rooms this evening cared little about the history of the building. The subject of the meeting was the Fifth Step of AA recovery, which amounts to owning up, or confessing, to one's past.

There are moments in Fifth Step meetings that cause the listeners to drop their eyes to the floor, to lose all expression in their faces, to clench their hands in their laps and wince inwardly at the knowledge that the barroom they had entered long ago had only one exit, and it opened on moral insanity.

Lila Terrebonne normally listened and did not speak at meetings. Tonight was different. She sat stiffly on a chair by the window, a tree silhouetted by a fiery sunset behind her head. The skin of her face had the polished, ceramic quality of someone who has just come out of a windstorm. Her hands were hooked together like those of an opera singer.

"I think I've had a breakthrough with my therapist," she said. "I've always had this peculiar sensation, this sense of guilt, I mean, a fixation I guess with crucifixes." She laughed self-deprecatingly, her eyes lowered, her eyelashes as stiff as wire. "It's because of something I saw as a child. But it didn't have anything to do with me, right? I mean, it's not part of the program to take somebody else's inventory. All I have to do is worry about what I've done. As people say, clean up my side of the street. Who am I to judge, particularly if I'm not in the historical context of others?"

No one had any idea of what she was talking about. She rambled on, alluding to her therapist, using terms most blue-collar people in the room had no understanding of.

"It's called psychoneurotic anxiety. It made me drink. Now I think most of that is behind me," she said. "Anyway, I didn't leave my panties anywhere today. That's all I have."

After the meeting I caught her by Clete's car. The oak tree overhead was filled with fireflies, and there was a heavy, wet smell in the air like sewer gas.

"Lila, I've never spoken like this to another AA member before, but what you said in there was total bullshit," I said.

She fixed her eyes on mine and blinked her eyelashes coyly and said nothing.

"I think you're stoned, too," I said.

"I have a prescription. It makes me a little funny sometimes. Now stop beating up on me," she said, and fixed my collar with one hand.

"You know who murdered Jack Flynn. You know who executed the two brothers in the swamp. You can't conceal knowledge like that from the law and expect to have any serenity."

"Marry me in our next incarnation," she said, and pinched my stomach. Then she made a sensual sound and said, "Not bad, big stuff."

She got in the passenger seat and looked at herself in her compact mirror and waited for Geraldine Holtzner to get behind the wheel. Then the two of them cruised down a brick-paved side street, laughing, the wind blowing their hair, like teenage girls who had escaped into a more innocent, uncomplicated time.

TWO DAYS PASSED, THEN I received another phone call from Alex Guidry, this time at the dock. His voice was dry, the receiver held close to his mouth.

"What kind of deal can I get?" he said.

"That depends on how far you can roll over."

"I'm not doing time."

"Don't bet on it."

"You're not worried about a dead black woman or a couple of shit bags who got themselves killed out in the Basin. You want the people who nailed up Jack Flynn."

"Give me a number. I'll call you back," I said.

"Call me back?"

"Yeah, I'm busy right now. I've already reached my quotient for jerk-off behavior today."

"I can give you Harpo Scruggs tied hand and foot on a barbecue spit," he said.

I could hear him breathing through his nose, like a cat's whisker scraping across the perforations. Then I realized the source of his fear.

"You've talked to Scruggs, haven't you?" I said. "You called him about his receiving immunity. Which means he knows you're in communication with us. You dropped the dime on yourself . . . Hello?"

"He's back. I saw him this morning," he said.

"You're imagining things."

"He's got an inoperable brain tumor. The guy's walking death. That's his edge."

"Better come in, Mr. Guidry."

"I don't give a deposition until he's in custody. I want the sheriff's guarantee on that."

"You won't get it."

"One day I'm going to make you suffer. I promise it." He eased the phone down into the cradle.

•   •   •

ON MONDAY, ADRIEN GLAZIER knocked on my office door. She was dressed in blue jeans and hiking shoes and a denim shirt, and she carried a brown cloth shoulder bag scrolled with Mexican embroidery. The ends of her ash-blond hair looked like they had been brushed until they crawled with static electricity, then had been sprayed into place.

"We can't find Willie Broussard," she said.

"Did you try his father's fish camp?"

"Why do you think I'm dressed like this?"

"Cool Breeze doesn't report in to me, Ms. Glazier."

"Can I sit down?"

Her eyes met mine and lingered for a moment, and I realized her tone and manner had changed, like heat surrendering at the end of a burning day.

"An informant tells us some people in Hong Kong have sent two guys to Louisiana to clip off a troublesome hangnail or two," she said. "I don't know if the target is Willie Broussard or Ricky Scarlotti or a couple of movie producers. Maybe it's all of the above."

"My first choice would be Scarlotti. He's the only person who has reason to give up some of their heroin connections."

"If they kill Willie Broussard, they take the squeeze off Scarlotti. Anyway, I'm telling you what we know."

I started to bring up the subject of Harpo Scruggs again and the possibility of his having worked for the government, but I let it go.

She dropped a folder on my desk. Clipped to two xeroxed Mexico City police memorandums was a grainy eight-by-ten photograph that had been taken in an open-air fruit market. The man in the photo stood at a stall, sucking a raw oyster out of its shell.

"His name is Rubén Esteban. He's one of the men we think Hong Kong has sent here."

"He looks like a dwarf."

"He is. He worked for the Argentine Junta. Supposedly he interrogated prisoners by chewing off their genitals."

"What?"

"The Triads always ruled through terror. The people they hire create living studies in torture and mutilation. Call Amnesty International in Chicago and see what they have to say about Esteban."

I picked up the photo and looked at it again. "Where's the material on the other guy?" I asked.

"We don't know who he is. Mr. Robicheaux, I'm sorry for having given you a bad time in some of our earlier conversations."

"I'll survive," I said, and tried to smile.

"My father was killed in Korea while people like Jack Flynn were working for the Communist Party."

"Flynn wasn't a Red. He was a Wobbly."

"You could fool me. He was lucky a House committee didn't have him shipped to Russia."

Then she realized she had said too much, that she had admitted looking at his file, that she was probably committed forever to being the advocate for people whose deeds were indefensible.

"You ever sit down and talk with Megan? Maybe y'all are on the same side," I said.

"You're too personal, sir."

I raised my hands by way of apology.

She smiled slightly, then hung her bag from her

shoulder and walked out of the office, her eyes already assuming new purpose, as though she were burning away all the antithetical thoughts that were like a thumbtack in her brow.

AT EIGHT-THIRTY THAT NIGHT Bootsie and I were washing the dishes in the kitchen when the phone rang on the counter.

"This is what you've done, asshole. My reputation's ruined. My job is gone. My wife has left me. You want to hear more?" the voice said.

"Guidry?" I said.

"There's a rumor going around I'm the father of a halfwit mulatto I sold to a cathouse in Morgan City. The guy who told me that said he heard it from your buddy Clete Purcel."

"Either you're in a bar or you've become irrational. Either way, don't call my home again."

"Here it is. I'll give you the evidence on Flynn's murder. I said *evidence,* not just information. I'll give you the shooters who did the two brothers, I'll give you the guys who almost drowned Megan Flynn, I'll give you the guy who's been writing the checks. What's on your end of the table?"

"The Iberia prosecutor will go along with aiding and abetting. We'll work with St. Mary Parish. It's a good deal. You'd better grab it."

He was quiet a long time. Outside, the heat lightning looked like silver plate through the trees.

"Are you there?" I said.

"Scruggs threatened to kill me. You got to bring this guy in."

"Give us the handle to do it."

"It was under your feet the whole time and you never saw it, you arrogant shithead."

I waited silently. The receiver felt warm and moist in my hand.

"Go to the barn where Flynn died. I'll be there in forty-five minutes. Leave the muff diver at home," he said.

"You don't make the rules, Guidry. Another thing, call her that again and I'm going to break your wagon."

I hung up, then dialed Helen's home number.

"You don't want to check in with the St. Mary sheriff's office first?" she said.

"They'll get in the way. Are you cool on this?" I said.

"What do you mean?"

"We take Guidry down clean. No scratches on the freight."

"The guy who said he'd dig up my grave and piss in my mouth? To tell you the truth, I wouldn't touch him with a baton. But maybe you'd better get somebody else for backup, bwana."

"I'll meet you at the end of East Main in twenty minutes," I said.

I went into the bedroom and took my holstered 1911 model U.S. Army .45 from the dresser drawer and clipped it onto my belt. I wiped my palms on my khakis unconsciously. Through the screen window the oak and pecan trees seemed to tremble in the heat lightning that leaped between the clouds.

"Streak?" Bootsie said.

"Yes?"

"I overheard your conversation. Don't worry about Helen. It's you that man despises," she said.

• • •

HELEN AND I DROVE down the two-lane through Jeanerette, then turned off on an oak-lined service road that led past the barn with the cratered roof and sagging walls where Jack Flynn died. The moon had gone behind a bank of storm clouds, and the landscape was dark, the blackberry bushes in the pasture humped against the lights of a house across the bayou. The leaves of the oaks along the road flickered with lightning, and I could smell rain and dust in the air.

"Guidry's going to do time, isn't he?" Helen said.

"Some anyway."

"I partnered with a New Orleans uniform who got sent up to Angola. First week down a Big Stripe cut his face. He had himself put in lockdown and every morning the black boys would spit on him when they went to breakfast."

"Yeah?"

"I was just wondering how many graduates of the parish prison will be in Guidry's cell house."

Helen turned the cruiser off the road and drove past the water oaks through the weeds and around the side of the barn. The wind was up now and the banana trees rattled and swayed against the barn. In the headlights we could see clusters of red flowers in the rain trees and dust swirling off the ground.

"Where is he?" Helen said. But before I could speak she pointed at two pale lines of crushed grass where a car had been driven out in the pasture. Then she said, "I got a bad feeling, Streak."

"Take it easy," I said.

"What if Scruggs is behind this? He's been killing people for forty years. I don't plan to walk blindfolded into the Big Exit." She cut the lights and unsnapped the strap on her nine-millimeter Beretta.

"Let's walk the field. You go to the left, I go to the right . . . Helen?"

"What?"

"Forget it. Scruggs and Guidry are both pieces of shit. If you feel in jeopardy, take them off at the neck."

We got out of the cruiser and walked thirty yards apart through the field, our weapons drawn. Then the moon broke behind the edge of a cloud and we could see the bumper and front fender of an automobile that was parked close behind a blackberry thicket. I circled to the right of the thicket, toward the rear of the automobile, then I saw the tinted windows and buffed, soft-yellow exterior of Alex Guidry's Cadillac. The driver's door was partly open and a leg in gray pants and a laced black shoe was extended into the grass. I clicked on the flashlight in my left hand.

"Put both hands out the window and keep them there," I said.

But there was no response.

"Mr. Guidry, you will put your hands out the window, or you will be in danger of being shot. Do you hear me?" I said.

Helen moved past a rain tree and was now at an angle to the front of the Cadillac, her Beretta pointed with two hands straight in front of her.

Guidry rose from the leather seat, pulling himself erect by hooking his arm over the open window. But in his right hand I saw the nickel-plated surfaces of a revolver.

"Throw it away!" I shouted. "Now! Don't think about it! Guidry, throw the piece away!"

Then lightning cracked across the sky, and out of the corner of his vision he saw Helen take up a shooter's position against the trunk of the rain tree. Maybe he was trying to hold the revolver up in the air and step free of the car, beyond the open door, so she could see him fully, but he stumbled out into the field, his right arm pressed against the wound in his side and the white shirt that was sodden with blood.

But to Helen, looking into the glare of my flashlight, Guidry had become an armed silhouette.

I yelled or think I yelled, *He's already hit,* but it was too late. She fired twice, *pop, pop,* the barrel streaking the darkness. The first round hit him high in the chest, the second in the mouth.

But Guidry's night in Gethsemane was not over. He stumbled toward the barn, his lower face like a piece of burst fruit, and swung his pistol back in Helen's direction and let off one shot that whined away across the bayou and made a sound like a hammer striking wood.

She began firing as fast as her finger could pull the trigger, the ejected shells pinging off the trunk of the rain tree, until I came behind her and fitted my hands on both her muscular arms.

"He's down. It's over," I said.

"No, he's still there. He let off another round. I saw the flash," she said, her eyes wild, the tendons in her arms jumping as though she were cold.

"No, Helen."

She swallowed, breathing hard through her mouth, and wiped the sweat off her nose with her shoulder, never releasing the two-handed grip on the Beretta. I shined the light out across the grass onto the north side of the barn.

"Oh, shit," she said, almost like a plea.

"Call it in," I said.

"Dave, he's lying in the same, I mean like, his arms are out like—"

"Get on the radio. That's all you have to do. Don't regret anything that happened here tonight. He dealt the play a long time ago."

"Dave, he's on the left side of where Flynn died. I can't take this stuff. I didn't know the guy was hit. Why didn't you yell at me?"

"I did. I think I did. Maybe I didn't. He should have thrown away the piece."

We stood there like that, in the blowing wind and dust and the raindrops that struck our faces like marbles, the vault of sky above us exploding with sound.

TWENTY-SEVEN

THE ARGENTINE DWARF WHO CALLED himself Rubén Esteban could not have been more unfortunate in his choice of a hotel.

Years ago in Lafayette, twenty miles from New Iberia, a severely retarded, truncated man named Chatlin Ardoin had made his living as a newspaper carrier who delivered newspapers to downtown businesses or sold them to train passengers at the Southern Pacific depot. His voice was like clotted rust in a sewer pipe; his arms and legs were stubs on his torso; his face had the expression of baked corn bread under his formless hat. Street kids from the north side baited him; an adman, the nephew of the newspaper's publisher, delighted in calling him Castro, driving him into an emotional rage.

The two-story clapboard hotel around the corner from the newspaper contained a bar downstairs where newsmen drank after their deadline. It was also full of hookers who worked the trade through the late afternoon and evening, except on Fridays, when the owner, whose name was Norma Jean, served free boiled shrimp for family people in the neighborhood. Every afternoon Chatlin brought Norma Jean a free newspaper, and every afternoon she gave him a frosted schooner of draft beer and a hard-boiled egg. He sat at the end of the bar under the air-conditioning unit, his canvas bag of rolled newspapers piled on the stool next to him, and peeled and ate the egg and drank the beer and stared at the soap operas on the TV with an intensity that made some believe he comprehended far more of the world than his appearance indicated. Norma Jean was thoroughly corrupt and allowed her girls no latitude when it came to pleasing their customers, but like most uneducated and primitive people, she intuitively felt, without finding words for the idea, that the retarded and insane were placed on earth to be cared for by those whose souls might otherwise be forfeit.

A beer and a hard-boiled egg wasn't a bad price for holding on to a bit of your humanity.

Fifteen years ago, during a hurricane, Chatlin was run over by a truck on the highway. The newspaper office was moved; the Southern Pacific depot across from the hotel was demolished and replaced by a post office; and Norma Jean's quasi-brothel became an ordinary hotel with a dark, cheerless bar for late-night drinkers.

Ordinary until Rubén Esteban checked into the hotel, then came down to the bar at midnight, the hard surfaces of his face glowing like corn bread under the neon. Esteban climbed on top of a stool, his Panama hat wobbling on his head. Norma Jean took one look at him and began screaming that Chatlin Ardoin had escaped from the grave.

Early Wednesday morning Helen and I were at the Lafayette Parish Jail. It was raining hard outside and the corridors were streaked with wet footprints. The homicide detective named Daigle took us up in the elevator. His face was scarred indistinctly and had the rounded, puffed quality of a steroid user's, his black hair clipped short across the top of his forehead. His collar was too tight for him and he kept pulling at it with two fingers, as though he had a rash.

"You smoked a guy and you're not on the desk?" he said to Helen.

"The guy already had a hole in him," I said. "He also shot at a police officer. He also happened to put a round through someone's bedroom wall."

"Convenient," Daigle said.

Helen looked at me.

"What's Esteban charged with?" I asked.

"Disturbing the peace, resisting. Somebody accidentally knocked him off the barstool when Norma Jean started yelling about dead people. The dwarf got off the floor and went for the guy's crotch. The uniform would have cut him loose, except he remembered y'all's bulletin. He said getting cuffs on him was like trying to pick up a scorpion," Daigle said. "What's the deal on him, again?"

"He sexually mutilated political prisoners for the Argentine Junta. They were buds with the Gipper," I said.

"The what?" he said.

Rubén Esteban sat on a wood bench by himself in the back of a holding cell, his Panama hat just touching the tops of his jug ears. His face was triangular in shape, dull yellow in hue, the eyes set at an oblique angle to his nose.

"What are you doing around here, podna?" I said.

"I'm a chef. I come here to study the food," he answered. His voice sounded metallic, as though it came out of a resonator in his throat.

"You have three different passports," I said.

"That's for my cousins. We're a—how you call it? —we're a team. We cook all over the world," Esteban said.

"We know who you are. Stay out of Iberia Parish," Helen said.

"Why?" he asked.

"We have an ordinance against people who are short and ugly," she replied.

His face was wooden, impossible to read, the eyes hazing over under the brim of his hat. He touched an incisor tooth and looked at the saliva on the ball of his finger.

"Governments have protected you in the past. That won't happen here. Am I getting through to you, Mr. Esteban?" I said.

"Me cago en la puta de tu madre," he answered, his eyes focused on the backs of his square, thick hands, his mouth curling back in neither a sneer nor a grimace but a disfigurement like the expression in a corpse's face when the lips wrinkle away from the teeth.

"What'd he say?" Daigle asked.

"He probably doesn't have a lot of sentiment about Mother's Day," I said.

"That's not all he don't have. He's got a tube in his pants. No penis," Daigle said, and started giggling.

Outside, it was still raining hard when Helen and I got in our cruiser.

"What'd Daigle do before he was a cop?" Helen asked.

"Bill collector and barroom bouncer, I think."

"I would have never guessed," she said.

Rubén Esteban paid his fine that afternoon and was released.

THAT NIGHT I SAT in the small office that I had fashioned out of a storage room in the back of the bait shop. Spread on my desk were xeroxed copies of the investigator's report on the shooting and death of Alex Guidry, the coroner's report, and the crime scene photos taken in front of the barn. The coroner stated that Guidry had already been hit in the rib cage with a round from a .357 magnum before Helen had ever discharged her weapon. Also, the internal damage was massive and probably would have proved fatal even if Helen had not peppered him with her nine-millimeter.

One photo showed the bloody interior of Guidry's Cadillac and a bullet hole in the stereo system and another in the far door, including a blood splatter on the leather door panel, indicating the original shooter had fired at least twice and the fatal round had hit Guidry while he was seated in the car.

Another photo showed tire tracks in the grass that were not the Cadillac's.

Two rounds had been discharged from Guidry's .38, one at Helen, the other probably at the unknown assailant.

The photo of Guidry, like most crime scene photography, was stark in its black and white contrasts. His back lay propped against the barn wall, his spine curving against the wood and the earth. His hands and lower legs were sheathed in blood, his shattered mouth hanging open, narrowing his face like a tormented figure in a Goya painting.

The flood lamps were on outside the bait shop, and the rain was blowing in sheets on the bayou. The water had overflowed the banks, and the branches of the willows were trailing in the current. The body of a dead possum floated by under the window, its stomach yellow and swollen in the electric glare, the claws of feeding blue-point crabs affixed to its fur. I kept thinking of Guidry's words to me in our last telephone conversation: *It was under your feet the whole time and you never saw it.*

What was under my feet? Where? By the barn? Out in the field where Guidry was hit with the .357?

Then I saw Megan Flynn's automobile park by the boat ramp and Megan run down the dock toward the bait shop with an umbrella over her head.

She came inside, breathless, shaking water out of her hair. Unconsciously, I looked up the slope through the trees at the lighted gallery and living room of my house.

"Wet night to be out," I said.

She sat down at the counter and blotted her face with a paper napkin.

"I got a call from Adrien Glazier. She told me about this guy Rubén Esteban," she said.

Not bad, Adrien, I thought.

"This guy's record is for real, Dave. I heard about him when I covered the Falklands War," she said.

"He was in custody on a misdemeanor in Lafayette

this morning. He doesn't blend into the wallpaper easily."

"We should feel better? Why do you think the Triads sent a walking horror show here?"

Megan wasn't one to whom you gave facile assurances.

"We don't know who his partner is. While we're watching Esteban, the other guy's peddling an ice-cream cart down Main Street," I said.

"Thank you," she said, and dried the back of her neck with another napkin. Her skin seemed paler, her mouth and her hair a darker shade of red under the overhead light. I glanced away from her eyes.

"You and Cisco want a cruiser to park by your house?" I asked.

"I have a bad feeling about Clete. I can't shake it," she said.

"Clete?" I said.

"Geri Holtzner is driving his car all around town. Look, nobody is going to hurt Billy Holtzner. You don't kill the people who owe you money. You hurt the people around them. These guys put bombs in people's automobiles."

"I'll talk to him about it."

"I already have. He doesn't listen. I hate myself for involving him in this," she said.

"I left my Roman collar up at the house, Meg."

"I forgot. Swinging dicks talk in deep voices and never apologize for their mistakes."

"Why do you turn every situation into an adversarial one?" I asked.

She raised her chin and tilted her head slightly. Her

mouth reminded me of a red flower turning toward light.

Bootsie opened the screen door and came in holding a raincoat over her head.

"Oh, excuse me. I didn't mean to walk into the middle of something," she said. She shook her raincoat and wiped the water off it with her hand. "My, what a mess I'm making."

THE NEXT AFTERNOON WE executed a search warrant on the property where Alex Guidry was shot. The sky was braided with thick gray and metallic-blue clouds, and the air smelled like rain and wood pulp and smoke from a trash fire.

Thurston Meaux, the St. Mary Parish plainclothes, came out of the barn with a rake in his hand.

"I found two used rubbers, four pop bottles, a horseshoe, and a dead snake. That any help to y'all?" he said.

"Pretty clever," I said.

"Maybe Alex Guidry was just setting you up, podna. Maybe you're lucky somebody popped him first. Maybe there was never anything here," Meaux said.

"Tell me, Thurston, why is it nobody wants to talk about the murder of Jack Flynn?"

"It was a different time. My grandfather did some things in the Klan, up in nort' Louisiana. He's an old man now. It's gonna change the past to punish him now?"

I started to reply but instead just walked away. It was easy for me to be righteous at the expense of another. The real problem was I didn't have any idea what we were looking for. The yellow crime scene tape formed a triangle from the barn to the spot where Guidry's Cadillac had been parked. Inside the triangle we found old shotgun and .22 shells, pig bones, a plowshare that groundwater had turned into rusty lace, the stone base of a mule-operated cane grinder overgrown with morning glory vine. A deputy sheriff swung his metal detector over a desiccated oak stump and got a hot reading. We splintered the stump apart and found a fan-shaped ax head, one that had been hand-forged, in the heart of the wood.

At four o'clock the uniformed deputies left. The sun came out and I watched Thurston Meaux sit down on a crate in the lee of the barn and eat a sandwich, let the wax paper blow away in the wind, then pull the tab on a soda can and drop it in the dirt.

"You're contaminating the crime scene," I said.

"Wrong," he replied.

"Oh?"

"Because we're not wasting any more time on this bullshit. You've got some kind of obsession, Robicheaux." He brushed the crumbs off his clothes and walked to his automobile.

Helen didn't say anything for a long time. Then she lifted a strand of hair out of her eye and said, "Dave, we've walked every inch of the field and raked all the ground inside and around the barn. You want to start over again, that's okay with me, but—"

"Guidry said, 'It was under your feet, you arrogant shithead.' Whatever he was talking about, it's physical, maybe something we walked over, something he could pick up and stick in my face."

"We can bring in a Cat and move some serious dirt."

"No, we might destroy whatever is here."

She let out her breath, then began scraping a long divot with a mattock around the edges of the hardpan.

"You're a loyal friend, Helen," I said.

"Bwana has the keys to the cruiser," she said.

I stood in front of the barn wall and stared at the weathered wood, the strips of red paint that were flaking like fingernail polish, the dust-sealed nail holes where Jack Flynn's wrists had been impaled. Whatever evidence was here had been left by Harpo Scruggs, not Alex Guidry, I thought. It was something Scruggs knew about, had deliberately left in place, had even told Guidry about. But why?

To implicate someone else. Just as he had crucified Swede Boxleiter in this spot to tie Boxleiter's death to Flynn's.

"Helen, if there's anything here, it's right by where Jack Flynn died," I said.

She rested the mattock by her foot and wiped a smear of mud off her face with her sleeve.

"If you say so," she said.

"Long day, huh?"

"I had a dream last night. Like I was being pulled back into history, into stuff I don't want to have anything to do with."

"You told me yourself, we're the good guys."

"When I kept shooting at Guidry? He was already done. I just couldn't stop. I convinced myself I saw another flash from his weapon. But I knew better."

"He got what he deserved."

"Yeah? Well, why do I feel the way I do?"

"Because you still have your humanity. It's because you're the best."

"I want to make this case and lock the file on it. I mean it, Dave."

She put down her mattock and the two of us began piercing the hardpan with garden forks, working backward from the barn wall, turning up the dirt from six inches below the surface. The subsoil was black and shiny, oozing with water and white worms. Then I saw a coppery glint and a smooth glass surface wedge out of the mud while Helen was prizing her fork against a tangle of roots.

"Hold it," I said.

"What is it?"

"A jar. Don't move the fork."

I reached down and lifted a quart-size preserve jar out of the mud and water. The top was sealed with both rubber and a metal cap. I squatted down and dipped water out of the hole and rinsed the mud off the glass.

"An envelope and a newspaper clipping? What's Scruggs doing, burying a time capsule?" Helen said.

We walked to the cruiser and wiped the jar clean with paper towels, then set it on the hood and unscrewed the cap. I lifted the newspaper clipping out with two fingers and spread it on the hood. The person who had cut it out of the *Times-Picayune* had carefully included the strip at the top of the page which gave the date, August 8, 1956. The headline on the story read: "Union Organizer Found Crucified."

Helen turned the jar upside down and pulled the envelope out of the opening. The glue on the flap was still sealed. I slipped my pocketknife in the corner of the flap and sliced a neat line across the top of the envelope and shook three black-and-white photos out on the hood.

Jack Flynn was still alive in two of them. In one, he was on his hands and knees while men in black hoods with slits for eyes swung blurred chains on his back; in the other, a fist clutched his hair, pulling his head erect so the camera could photograph his destroyed face. But in the third photo his ordeal had come to an end. His head lay on his shoulder; his eyes were rolled into his head, his impaled arms stretched out on the wood of the barn wall. Three men in cloth hoods were looking back at the camera, one pointing at Flynn as though indicating a lesson to the viewer.

"This doesn't give us squat," Helen said.

"The man in the middle. Look at the ring finger on his left hand. It's gone, cut off at the palm," I said.

"You know him?"

"It's Archer Terrebonne. His family didn't just order the murder. He helped do it."

"Dave, there's no face to go with the hand. It's not a felony to have a missing finger. Look at me. A step at a time and all that jazz, right? You listening, Streak?"

TWENTY-EIGHT

IT WAS AN HOUR LATER. Terrebonne had not been at his home, but a maid had told us where to find him. I parked the cruiser under the oaks in front of the restaurant up the highway and cut the engine. The water dripping out of the trees steamed on the hood.

"Dave, don't do this," Helen said.

"He's in Iberia Parish now. I'm not going to have these pictures lost in a St. Mary Parish evidence locker."

"We get them copied, then do it by the numbers."

"He'll skate."

"You know a lot of rich guys working soybeans in Angola? That's the way it is."

"Not this time."

I went inside the foyer, where people waited in leather chairs for an available table. I opened my badge on the maître d'.

"Archer Terrebonne is here with a party," I said.

The maître d's eyes locked on mine, then shifted to Helen, who stood behind me.

"Is there a problem?" he asked.

"Not yet," I said.

"I see. Follow me, please."

We walked through the main dining room to a long table at the rear, where Terrebonne was seated with a dozen other people. The waiters had just taken away their shrimp cocktails and were now serving the gumbo off of a linen-covered cart.

Terrebonne wiped his mouth with a napkin, then waited for a woman in a robin's-egg-blue suit to stop talking before he shifted his eyes to me.

"What burning issue do you bring us tonight, Mr. Robicheaux?" he asked.

"Harpo Scruggs pissed in your shoe," I said.

"Sir, would you not—" the maître d' began.

"You did your job. Beat it," Helen said.

I lay the three photographs down on the tablecloth.

"That's you in the middle, Mr. Terrebonne. You chain-whipped Jack Flynn and hammered nails through his wrists and ankles, then let your daughter carry your guilt. You truly turn my stomach, sir," I said.

"And you're way beyond anything I'll tolerate," he said.

"Get up," I said.

"What?"

"Better do what he says," Helen said behind me.

Terrebonne turned to a silver-haired man on his right. "John, would you call the mayor's home, please?" he said.

"You're under arrest, Mr. Terrebonne. The mayor's not going to help you," I said.

"I'm not going anywhere with you, sir. You put your hand on my person again and I'll sue you for battery," he said, then calmly began talking to the woman in a robin's-egg-blue suit on his left.

Maybe it was the long day, or the fact the photos had allowed me to actually see the ordeal of Jack Flynn, one that time had made an abstraction, or maybe I simply possessed a long-buried animus toward Archer Terrebonne and the imperious and self-satisfied arrogance that he and his kind represented. But long ago I had learned that anger, my old enemy, had many catalysts and they all led ultimately to one consequence, an eruption of torn red-and-black color behind the eyes, an alcoholic blackout without booze, then an adrenaline surge that left me trembling, out of control, and possessed of a destructive capability that later filled me with shame.

I grabbed him by the back of his belt and hoisted him out of the chair, pushed him facedown on the table, into his food, and cuffed his wrists behind him, hard, ratcheting the curved steel tongues deep into the locks, crimping the veins like green string. Then I walked him ahead of me, out the foyer, into the parking area, pushing past a group of people who stared at us openmouthed. Terrebonne tried to speak, but I got the back door of the cruiser open and shoved him inside, cutting his scalp on the jamb.

When I slammed the door I turned around and was looking into the face of the woman in the robin's-egg-blue suit.

"You manhandle a sixty-three-year-old man like that? My, you must be proud. I'm so pleased we have policemen of your stature protecting us from ourselves," she said.

•   •   •

THE SHERIFF CALLED ME into his office early the next morning. He rubbed the balls of his fingers back and forth on his forehead, as though the skin were burned, and looked at a spot six inches in front of his face.

"I don't know where to begin," he said.

"Terrebonne was kicked loose?"

"Two hours after you put him in the cage. I've had calls from a judge, three state legislators, and a U.S. congressman. You locked him in the cage with a drag queen and a drunk with vomit all over his clothes?"

"I didn't notice."

"I bet. He says he's going to sue."

"Let him. He's obstructed and lied in the course of a murder investigation. He's dirty from the jump, skipper. Put that photo and his daughter in front of a grand jury and see what happens."

"You're really out to burn his grits, aren't you?"

"You don't think he deserves it?" I said.

"The homicide was in St. Mary Parish. Dave, this guy had to have stitches in his head. Do you know what his lawyers are going to do with that?"

"We've been going after the wrong guys. Cut off the snake's head and the body dies," I said.

"I called my insurance agent about an umbrella policy this morning, you know, the kind that protects you against losing your house and everything you own. I'll give you his number."

"Terrebonne skates?"

The sheriff picked up a pink memo slip in the fingers of each hand and let them flutter back to his ink blotter.

"You've figured it out," he said.

• • •

LATE THAT AFTERNOON, JUST as the sun dipped over the trees, Cisco Flynn walked down the dock where I was cleaning the barbecue pit, and sat on the railing and watched me work.

"Megan thinks she caused some trouble between you and your wife," he said.

"She's right," I said.

"She's sorry about it."

"Look, Cisco, I'm kind of tired of y'all's explanations about various things. What's the expression, 'Get a life'?"

"That guy who got thrown out the hotel window in San Antonio? Swede did it, but I helped set up the transportation and the alibi at the movie theater."

"Why tell me?"

"He's dead, but he was a good guy. I'm not laying off something I did on a friend."

"You got problems with your conscience about the hotel flyer, go to San Antone and turn yourself in."

"What's with you, man?"

"Archer Terrebonne, the guy who has money in your picture, killed your father. Come down to the office and check out the photos. I made copies before I turned the originals over to St. Mary Parish. The downside of the story is I can't touch him."

His face looked empty, insentient, as though he were winded, his lips moving without sound. He blinked and swallowed. "Archer Terrebonne? No, there's something wrong. He's been a guest in my home. What are you saying?" he said.

I went inside the bait shop and didn't come back out until he was gone.

• • •

THAT NIGHT THE MOON was down and leaves were blowing in the darkness outside, rattling against the trunks of the oak and pecan trees. When I went into the bedroom the light was off and Bootsie was sitting in front of her dresser in her panties and a T-shirt, looking out the window into the darkness.

"You eighty-sixed Cisco?" she said.

"Not exactly. I just didn't feel like talking to him anymore."

"Was this over Megan?"

"When she comes out here, we have trouble," I said.

The breeze ginned the blades in the window fan and I could hear leaves blowing against the screen.

"It's not her fault, it's mine," Bootsie said.

"Beg your pardon?"

"You take on other people's burdens, Dave. It's just the way you are. That's why you're the man I married."

I put my hand on her shoulder. She looked at our reflection in the dresser mirror and stood up, still facing the mirror. I slipped my arms around her waist, under her breasts, and put my face in her hair. Her body felt muscular and hard against mine. I moved my hand down her stomach, and she arched her head back against mine and clasped the back of my neck. Her stiffening breasts, the smoothness of her stomach and the taper of her hips, the hardness of her thighs, the tendons in her back, the power in her upper arms, when I embraced all these things with touch and mind and eye, it was like watching myself become one with an alabaster figure who had been infused with the veined warmth of a new rose.

Then I was between her thighs on top of the sheet and I could hear a sound in my head like wind in a conch shell and feel her press me deeper inside, as though both of us were drawing deeper into a cave beneath the sea, and I knew that concerns over winged chariots and mutability and death should have no place among the quick, even when autumn thudded softly against the window screen.

IN VIETNAM I HAD anxieties about toe-poppers and booby-trapped 105 duds that made the skin tighten around my temples and the blood veins dilate in my brain, so that during my waking hours I constantly experienced an unrelieved pressure band along one side of my head, just as though I were wearing a hat. But the visitor who stayed on in my nightmares, long after the war, was a pajama-clad sapper by the name of Bedcheck Charlie.

Bedcheck Charlie could cross rice paddies without denting the water, cut crawl paths through concertina wire, or tunnel under claymores if he had to. He had beaten the French with resolve and a shovel rather than a gun. But there was no question about what he could do with a bolt-action rifle stripped off a dead German or Sudanese Legionnaire. He waited for the flare of a Zippo held to a cigarette or the tiny blue flame from a heat tab flattening on the bottom of a C-rat can, then he squeezed off from three hundred yards out and left a wound shaped like a keyhole in a man's face.

But I doubt if Ricky Scarlotti ever gave much thought to Vietnamese sappers. Certainly his mind was focused on other concerns Saturday morning when he sat outside the riding club where he played polo sometimes, sipping from a glass of burgundy, dipping bread in olive oil and eating it, punching his new girlfriend, Angela, in the ribs whenever he made a point. Things were going to work out. He'd gotten that hillbilly, Harpo Scruggs, back on the job. Scruggs would clip that snitch in New Iberia, the boon, what was his name, the one ripping off the Mob's own VCRs and selling them back to them, Broussard was his name, clip him once and for all and take the weight off Ricky so he could tell that female FBI agent to shove her Triad bullshit up her nose with chopsticks.

In fact, he and Angela and the two bodyguards had tickets for the early flight to Miami Sunday morning. Tomorrow he'd be sitting on the beach behind the Doral Hotel, with a tropical drink in his hand, maybe go out to the trotters or the dog track later, hey, take a deep-sea charter and catch a marlin and get it mounted. Then call up some guys in Hallandale who he'd pay for each minute they had that fat shit Purcel begging on videotape. Ricky licked his lips when he thought about it.

A sno'ball truck drove down the winding two-lane road through the park that bordered the riding club. Ricky took off his pilot's glasses and wiped them with a Kleenex, then put them back on again. What's a sno'ball truck doing in the park when no kids are around? he thought. The sno'ball truck pulled into the oak trees and the driver got out and watched the ducks on the pond, then disappeared around the far side of the truck.

"Go see what that guy's doing," Ricky said to one of his bodyguards.

"He's lying in the shade, taking a nap," the body-guard replied.

"Tell him this ain't Wino Row, go take his naps somewhere else," Ricky said.

The bodyguard walked across the road, into the trees, and spoke to the man on the ground. The man sat up and yawned, looked in Ricky's direction while the bodyguard talked, then started his truck and drove away.

"Who was he?" Ricky asked the bodyguard.

"A guy sells sno'balls."

"Who *was* he?"

"He didn't give me his fucking name, Ricky. You want I should go after him?"

"Forget it. We're out of drinks here. Get the waiter back."

An hour later Ricky's eyes were red with alcohol, his skin glazed with sweat from riding his horse hard in the sun. An ancient green milk truck, with magnetized letters on the side, drove down the two-lane road through the park, exited on the boulevard, then made a second pass through the park and stopped in the trees by the duck pond.

Benny Grogan, the other bodyguard, got up from Ricky's table. He wore a straw hat with a multicolored band on his platinum hair.

"Where you going?" Ricky said.

"To check the guy out."

"He's a knife grinder. I seen that truck all over the neighborhood," Ricky said.

"I thought you didn't want nobody hanging around, Ricky," Benny said.

"He's a midget. How's he reach the pedals? Bring the car around. Angela, you up for a shower?" Ricky said.

The milk truck was parked deep in the shade of the live oaks. The rear doors opened, flapping back on their hinges, and revealed a prone man in a yellow T-shirt and dark blue jeans. His long body was stretched out behind a sandbag, the sling of the scoped rifle twisted around his left forearm, the right side of his face notched into the rifle's stock.

When he squeezed off, the rifle recoiled hard against his shoulder and a flash leaped off the muzzle, like an electrical short, but there was no report.

The bullet tore through the center of Ricky's throat. A purple stream of burgundy flowed from both corners of his mouth, then he began to make coughing sounds, like a man who can neither swallow nor expel a chicken bone, while blood spigoted from his wound and spiderwebbed his chest and white polo pants. His eyes stared impotently into his new girlfriend's face. She pushed herself away from the table, her hands held out in front of her, her knees close together, like someone who did not want to be splashed by a passing car.

The shooter slammed the back doors of the milk truck and the driver drove the truck through the trees and over the curb onto the boulevard. Benny Grogan ran down the street after it, his .38 held in the air, automobiles veering to each side of him, their horns blaring.

•   •   •

IT WAS MONDAY WHEN Adrien Glazier gave me all the details of Scarlotti's death over the phone.

"NOPD found the truck out by Lake Pontchartrain. It was clean," she said.

"You got anything on the shooter?"

"Nothing. It looks like we've lost our biggest potential witness against the boys from Hong Kong," she said.

"I'm afraid people in New Orleans won't mourn that fact," I said.

"You can't tell. Greaseball wakes are quite an event. Anyway, we'll be there."

"Tell the band to play 'My Funny Valentine,' " I said.

TWENTY-NINE

THAT EVENING I DROVE DOWN to Clete's cottage outside Jeanerette. He was washing his car in the side yard, rubbing a soapy sponge over the hood.

"I think I'm going to get it restored, drive it around like a classic instead of a junk heap," he said. He wore a pair of rubber boots and oversized swimming trunks, and the hair on his stomach was wet and plastered to his skin.

"Megan thinks the guys who did Ricky Scar might try to hurt Holtzner by going through his daughter. She thinks you shouldn't let her drive your car around," I said.

"When those guys want to pop somebody, they don't do it with car bombs. It's one on one, like Ricky Scar got it."

"Have you ever listened to me once in your life about anything?"

"On the perfecta that time at Hialeah. I lost three hundred bucks."

"Archer Terrebonne killed Cisco Flynn's father. I told Cisco that."

"Yeah, I know. He says he doesn't believe you." Clete moved the sponge slowly back and forth on the car hood, his thoughts sealed behind his face, the water from the garden hose sluicing down on his legs.

"What's bothering you?" I asked.

"Terrebonne's a major investor in Cisco's film. If Cisco walks out, his career's a skid mark on the bowl. I just thought he might have more guts. I bet a lot of wrong horses."

He threw the bucket of soapy water into a drainage ditch. The sun looked like a smoldering fire through the pine trees.

"You want to tell me what's really bothering you?" I said.

"I thought Megan and me might put it back together. That's why I scrambled Ricky Scar's eggs, to look like big shit, that simple, mon. Megan's life is international, I mean, all this local stuff is an asterisk in her career." He blew his breath out. "I got to stop drinking. I've got a buzz like a bad neon sign in my head."

"Let's put a line in the water," I said.

"Dave, those pictures Harpo Scruggs buried in the ground? That dude's got backup material somewhere. Something that can put a thumb in Terrebonne's eye."

"Yeah, but I can't find Scruggs. The guy's a master at going in and out of the woodwork," I said.

"Remember what that retired Texas Ranger in El Paso told you? About looking for him in cathouses and at pigeon shoots and dogfights?"

His skin was pink in the fading light, the hair on his shoulders ruffling in the breeze.

"Dogfights? No, it was something else," I said.

THE COCKFIGHTS WERE HELD in St. Landry Parish, in a huge, rambling wood-frame nightclub, painted bright yellow and set back against a stand of green hardwoods. The shell parking lot could accommodate hundreds of automobiles and pickup trucks, and the patrons (blue-collar people, college students, lawyers, professional gamblers) who came to watch the birds blind and kill each other with metal spurs and slashers did so with glad, seemingly innocent hearts.

The pit was railed, enclosed with chicken wire, the dirt hard-packed and sprinkled with sawdust. The rail, which afforded the best view, was always occupied by the gamblers, who passed thousands of dollars in wagers from hand to hand, with neither elation nor resentment, as though the matter of exchanging currency were impersonal and separate from the blood sport taking place below.

It was all legal. In Louisiana fighting cocks are classified as fowl and hence are not protected by the laws that govern the treatment of most animals. In the glow of the scrolled neon on the lacquered yellow pine walls, under the layers of floating cigarette smoke, in the roar of noise that rattled windows, you could smell the raw odor of blood and feces and testosterone and dried sweat and exhaled alcohol that I suspect was very close to the mix of odors that rose on a hot day from the Roman arena.

Clete and I sat at the end of the bar. The bartender, who was a Korean War veteran named Harold who wore black slacks and a short-sleeve white shirt and combed his few strands of black hair across his pate, served Clete a vodka collins and me a Dr Pepper in a glass filled with cracked ice. Harold leaned down toward me and put a napkin under my glass.

"Maybe he's just late. He's always been in by seven-thirty," he said.

"Don't worry about it, Harold," I said.

"We gonna have a public situation here?" he said.

"Not a chance," Clete said.

We didn't have long to wait. Harpo Scruggs came in the side door from the parking lot and walked to the rail around the cockpit. He wore navy blue western-cut pants with his cowboy boots and hat, and a silver shirt that tucked into his Indian-bead belt as tightly as tin. He made a bet with a well-known cockfighter from Lafayette, a man who when younger was both a pimp and a famous barroom dancer.

The cocks rose into the air, their slashers tearing feathers and blood from each other's bodies, while the crowd's roar lifted to the ceiling. A few minutes later one of the cocks was dead and Scruggs gently pulled a sheaf of hundred-dollar bills from between the fingers of the ex-pimp he had made his wager with.

"I think I'm experiencing Delayed Stress Syndrome. There was a place just like this in Saigon. The bar girls were VC whores," Clete said.

"Has he made us?" I asked.

"I think so. He doesn't rattle easy, does he? Oh-oh, here he comes."

Scruggs put one hand on the bar, his foot on the brass rail, not three feet from us.

"Has that worm talked to you yet?" he said to Harold.

"He's waiting right here for you," Harold said, and lifted a brown bottle of mescal from under the bar and set it before Scruggs, with a shot glass and a saucer of chicken wings and a bottle of Tabasco.

Scruggs took a twenty-dollar bill from a hand-tooled wallet and inserted it under the saucer, then poured into the glass and drank from it. His eyes never looked directly as us but registered our presence in the same flat, lidless fashion an iguana's might.

"You got a lot of brass," I said to him.

"Not really. Since I don't think your bunch could drink piss out of a boot with the instructions printed on the heel," he replied. He unscrewed the cork in the mescal bottle with a squeak and tipped another shot into his glass.

"Some out-of-town hitters popped Ricky Scar. That means you're out of the contract on Willie Broussard and you get to keep the front money," I said.

"I'm an old man. I'm buying quarter horses to take back to Deming. Why don't y'all leave me be?" he said.

"You use vinegar?" Clete said.

This time Scruggs looked directly at him. "Say again."

"You must have got it on your clothes. When you scrubbed the gunpowder residue off after you smoked Alex Guidry. Those .357s leave powder residue like you dipped your hand in pig shit," Clete said.

Scruggs laughed to himself and lit a cigarette and smoked it, his back straight, his eyes focused on his reflection in the bar mirror. A man came up to him, made a bet, and walked away.

"We found the photos you buried in the jar. We want the rest of it," I said.

"I got no need to trade. Not now."

"We'll make the case on you eventually. I hear you've got a carrot growing in your brain. How'd you like to spend your last days in the jail ward at Charity?" I said.

He emptied the mescal bottle and shook the worm out of the bottom into the neck. It was thick, whitish green, its skin hard and leathery. He gathered it into his lips and sucked it into his mouth. "Is it true the nurse's aides at Charity give blow jobs for five dollars?" he asked.

Clete and I walked out into the parking lot. The air was cool and smelled of the fields and rain, and across the road the sugarcane was bending in the wind. I nodded to Helen Soileau and a St. Landry Parish plainclothes who sat in an unmarked car.

An hour later Helen called me at the bait shop, where I was helping Batist clean up while Clete ate a piece of pie at the counter. Scruggs had rented a house in the little town of Broussard.

"Why's he still hanging around here?" I asked Clete.

"A greedy piece of shit like that? He's going to put a soda straw in Archer Terrebonne's jugular."

ON WEDNESDAY AFTERNOON I left the office early and worked in the yard with Alafair. The sun was gold in the trees, and red leaves drifted out of the branches onto the bayou. We turned on the soak hoses in the flower beds and spaded out the St. Augustine grass that had grown through the brick border, and the air, which was unseasonably cool, smelled of summer, like cut lawns and freshly turned soil and water from a garden hose, rather than autumn and shortening days.

Lila Terrebonne parked a black Oldsmobile with darkly tinted windows by the boat ramp and rolled down the driver's window and waved. Someone whom I couldn't see clearly sat next to her. The trunk was open and filled with cardboard boxes of chrysanthemums. She got out of the Oldsmobile and crossed the road and walked into the pecan trees, where Alafair and I were raking up pecan husks and leaves that had gone black with water.

Lila wore a pale blue dress and white pumps and a domed straw hat, one almost like Megan's. For the first time in years her eyes looked clear, untroubled, even happy.

"I'm having a party tomorrow night. Want to come?" she said.

"I'd better pass, Lila."

"I did a Fifth Step, you know, cleaning house. With an ex-hooker, can you believe it? It took three hours. I think she wanted a drink when it was over."

"That's great. I'm happy for you."

Lila looked at Alafair and waited, as though an unstated expectation among us had not been met.

"Oh, excuse me. I think I'll go inside. Talk on the phone. Order some drugs," Alafair said.

"You don't need to go, Alf," I said.

"Bye-bye," she said, jittering her fingers at us.

"I've made peace with my father, Dave," Lila said, watching Alafair walk up the steps of the gallery. Then: "Do you think your daughter should talk to adults like that?"

"If she feels like it."

Her eyes wandered through the trees, her long lashes blinking like black wire. "Well, anyway, my father's in the car. He'd like to shake hands," she said.

"You've brought your—"

"Dave, I've forgiven him for the mistakes he made years ago. Jack Flynn was in the Communist Party. His friends were union terrorists. Didn't you do things in war you regretted?"

"You've forgiven him? Goodbye, Lila."

"No, he's been good enough to come out here. You're going to be good enough to face him."

I propped my rake against a tree trunk and picked up two vinyl bags of leaves and pecan husks and carried them out to the road. I hoped that somehow Lila would simply drive away with her father. Instead, he got out of the Oldsmobile and approached me, wearing white trousers and a blue sports coat with brass buttons.

"I'm willing to shake hands and start over again, Mr. Robicheaux. I do this out of gratitude for the help you've given my daughter. She has enormous respect for you," he said.

He extended his hand. It was manicured and small, the candy-striped French cuff lying neatly across the wrist. It did not look like a hand that possessed the strength to whip a chain across a man's back and sunder his bones with nails.

"I'm offering you my hand, sir," he said.

I dropped the two leaf bags on the roadside and wiped my palms on my khakis, then stepped back into the shade, away from Terrebonne.

"Scruggs is blackmailing you. You need me, or

someone like me, to pop a cap on him and get him out of your life. That's not going to happen," I said.

He tapped his right hand gingerly on his cheek, as though he had a toothache.

"I tried. Truly I have. Now, I'll leave you alone, sir," he said.

"You and your family pretend to gentility, Mr. Terrebonne. But your ancestor murdered black soldiers under the bluffs at Fort Pillow and caused the deaths of his twin daughters. You and your father brought grief to black people like Willie Broussard and his wife and killed anyone who threatened your power. None of you are what you seem."

He stood in the center of the road, not moving when a car passed, the dust swirling around him, his face looking at words that seemed to be marching by in front of his eyes.

"I congratulate you on your sobriety, Mr. Robicheaux. I suspect for a man such as yourself it was a very difficult accomplishment," he said, and walked back to the Oldsmobile and got inside and waited for his daughter.

I turned around and almost collided into Lila.

"I can't believe what you just did. How dare you?" she said.

"Don't you understand what your father has participated in? He crucified a living human being. Wake up, Lila. He's the definition of evil."

She struck me across the face.

I stood in the road, with the ashes of leaves blowing around me, and watched their car disappear down the long tunnel of oaks.

"I hate her," Alafair said behind me.

"Don't give them power, Alf," I replied.

But I felt a great sorrow. Inside all of Lila's alcoholic madness she had always seen the truth about her father's iniquity. Now, the restoration of light and the gift of sobriety in her life had somehow made her morally blind.

I put my arm on Alafair's shoulder, and the two of us walked into the house.

THIRTY

CISCO FLYNN WAS IN MY office the next morning. He sat in a chair in front of my desk, his hands opening and closing on his thighs.

"Out at the dock, when I told you to look at the photos? I was angry," I said, holding the duplicates of the three photographs from the buried jar.

"Just give them to me, would you?" he said.

I handed the photographs across the desk to him. He looked at them slowly, one by one, his face never changing expression. But I saw a twitch in his cheek under one eye. He lay the photos back on the desk and straightened himself in the chair.

His voice was dry when he spoke. "You're sure that's Terrebonne, the dude with the missing finger?"

"Every road we take leads to his front door," I said.

"This guy Scruggs was there, too?"

"Put it in the bank."

He stared out the window at the fronds of a palm tree swelling in the wind.

"I understand he's back in the area," Cisco said.

"Don't have the wrong kind of thoughts, partner."

"I always thought the worst people I ever met were in Hollywood. But they're right here."

"Evil doesn't have a zip code, Cisco."

He picked up the photos and looked at them again. Then he set them down and propped his elbows on my desk and rested his forehead on his fingers. I thought he was going to speak, then I realized he was weeping.

AT NOON, WHEN I was on my way to lunch, Helen caught up with me in the parking lot.

"Hang on, Streak. I just got a call from some woman named Jessie Rideau. She says she was in the hotel in Morgan City the night Jack Flynn was kidnapped," she said.

"Why's she calling us now?"

We both got in my truck. I started the engine. Helen looked straight ahead, as though trying to rethink a problem she couldn't quite define.

"She says she and another woman were prostitutes who worked out of the bar downstairs. She says Harpo Scruggs made the other woman, someone named Lavern Viator, hide a lockbox for him."

"A lockbox? Where's the Viator woman?"

"She joined a cult in Texas and asked Rideau to keep the lockbox. Rideau thinks Scruggs killed her. Now he wants the box."

"Why doesn't she give it to him?"

"She's afraid he'll kill her after he gets it."

"Tell her to come in."

"She doesn't trust us either."

I parked the truck in front of the cafeteria on Main

Street. The drawbridge was up on Bayou Teche and a shrimp boat was passing through the pilings.

"Let's talk about it inside," I said.

"I can't eat. Before Rideau got panicky and hung up on me, she said the killers were shooting craps in the room next to Jack Flynn. They waited till he was by himself, then dragged him down a back stairs and tied him to a post on a dock and whipped him with chains. She said that's all that was supposed to happen. Except Scruggs told the others the night was just beginning. He made the Viator woman come with them. She held Jack Flynn's head in a towel so the blood wouldn't get on the seat."

Helen pressed at her temple with two fingers.

"What is it?" I said.

"Rideau said you can see Flynn's face on the towel. Isn't that some bullshit? She said there're chains and a hammer and handcuffs in the box, too. I got to boogie, boss man. The next time this broad calls, I'm transferring her to your extension," she said.

I SPENT THE REST of the day with the paperwork that my file drawer seemed to procreate from the time I closed it in the afternoon until I opened it in the morning. The paperwork all concerned the Pool, that comic Greek chorus of miscreants who are always in the wings, upstaging our most tragic moments, flatulent, burping, snickering, catcalling at the audience. It has been my long-held belief as a police officer that Hamlet and Ophelia might command our respect and admiration, but Sir Toby Belch and his minions usually consume most of our energies.

Here are just a few random case file entries in the lives of Pool members during a one-month period.

A pipehead tries to smoke Drāno crystals in a hookah. After he recovers from destroying several thousand brain cells in his head, he dials 911 and dimes his dealer for selling him bad dope.

A man steals a blank headstone from a funeral home, engraves his mother's name on it, and places it in his back yard. When confronted with the theft, he explains that his wife poured his mother's ashes down the sink and the man wished to put a marker over the septic tank where his mother now resides.

A woman who has fought with her common-law husband for ten years reports that her TV remote control triggered the electronically operated door on the garage and crushed his skull.

Two cousins break into the back of a liquor store, then can't start their car. They flee on foot, then report their car as stolen. It's a good plan. Except they don't bother to change their shoes. The liquor store's floor had been freshly painted and the cousins track the paint all over our floors when they file their stolen car report.

THAT EVENING CLETE AND I filled a bait bucket with shiners and took my outboard to Henderson Swamp and fished for sac-a-lait. The sun was dull red in the west, molten and misshaped as though it were dissolving in its own heat among the strips of lavender cloud that clung to the horizon. We crossed a wide bay, then let the boat drift in the lee of an island that was heavily wooded with willow and cypress trees. The mosquitoes were thick in the shadows of the trees, and you could see bream feeding among the lily pads and smell an odor like fish roe in the water.

I looked across the bay at the levee, where there was a paintless, tin-roofed house that had not been there three weeks ago.

"Where'd that come from?" I said.

"Billy Holtzner just built it. It's part of the movie," Clete said.

"You're kidding. That guy's like a disease spreading itself across the state."

"Check it out."

I reached into the rucksack where I had packed our sandwiches and a thermos of coffee and my World War II Japanese field glasses. I adjusted the focus on the glasses and saw Billy Holtzner and his daughter talking with a half dozen people on the gallery of the house.

"Aren't you supposed to be out there with them?" I asked Clete.

"They work what they call a twelve-hour turn-around. Anyway, I go off the clock at five. Then he's got some other guys to boss around. They'll be out there to one or two in the morning. Dave, I'm going to do my job, but I think that guy's dead meat."

"Why?"

"You remember guys in Nam you knew were going to get it? Walking fuckups who stunk of fear and were always trying to hang on to you? Holtzner's got that same stink on him. It's on his breath, in his clothes, I don't even like looking at him."

A few drops of rain dimpled the water, then the sac-a-lait started biting. Unlike bream or bass, they would take the shiner straight down, pulling the bobber with a steady tension into the water's darkness. They would fight hard, pumping away from the boat, until they broke the surface, when they would turn on their side and give it up.

We layered them with crushed ice in the cooler, then I took our ham-and-onion sandwiches and coffee thermos out of the rucksack and lay them on the cooler's top. In the distance, by the newly constructed movie set, I saw two figures get on an airboat and roar across the bay toward us.

The noise of the engine and fan was deafening, the wake a long, flat depression that swirled with mud. The pilot cut the engine and let the airboat float into the lee of the island. Billy Holtzner sat next to him, a blue baseball cap on his head. He was smiling.

"You guys on the job?" he said.

"No. We're just fishing," I said.

"Get out of here," he said, still smiling.

"We fish this spot a lot, Billy. We're both off the clock," Clete said.

"Oh," Holtzner said, his smile dying.

"Everything copacetic?" Clete said.

"Sure," Holtzner said. "Want to come up and watch us shoot a couple of scenes?"

"We're heading back in a few minutes. Thanks just the same," I said.

"Sure. My daughter's with me," he said, as though there were a logical connection between her presence and his invitation. "I mean, maybe we'll have a late-night dinner later."

Neither Clete nor I responded. Holtzner touched the boat pilot on the arm, and the two of them roared back across the bay, their backdraft showering the water's surface with willow leaves.

"How do you read that?" I said.

"The guy's on his own, probably for the first time in his life. It must be rough to wake up one morning and realize you're a gutless shit who doesn't deserve his family," Clete said, then bit into his sandwich.

THE NEXT DAY TWO uniformed city cops and I had to arrest a parolee from Alabama by the swimming pool at City Park. Even with cuffs on, he spit on one cop and kicked the other one in the groin. I pushed him against the side of the cruiser and tried to hold him until I could get the back door open, then the cop who had been spit on Maced him and sprayed me at the same time.

I spent the next ten minutes rinsing my face and hair in the lavatory inside the recreation building. When I came back outside, wiping the water off my neck with a paper towel, the parolee and the city cops were on their way to the jail and Adrien Glazier was standing by my pickup truck. Out on the drive, among the oak trees, I saw a dark blue waxed car with two men in suits and shades standing by it. Leaves were swirling in eddies around their car.

"The sheriff told us you were here. How's that stuff feel?" she said.

"Like somebody holding a match to your skin."

"We just got a report from Interpol on the dwarf. He's enjoying himself on the Italian Riviera."

"Glad to hear it," I said.

"So maybe the shooter who did Ricky Scar left with him."

"You believe that?" I asked.

"No. Take a walk with me."

She didn't wait for a reply. She turned and began walking slowly through the trees toward the bayou and the picnic tables that were set under tin sheds by the waterside.

"What's going on, Ms. Glazier?" I said.

"Call me Adrien." She rested her rump against a picnic table and folded her arms across her chest. "Did Cisco Flynn confess his involvement in a homicide to you?"

"Excuse me?"

"The guy who got chucked out a hotel window in San Antonio? I understand his head hit a fire hydrant. Did Cisco come seeking absolution at your bait shop?"

"My memory's not as good as it used to be. Y'all have a tap on his phone or a bug in his house?"

"We're giving you a free pass on this one. That's because I acted like a pisspot for a while," she said.

"It's because you know Harpo Scruggs was a federal snitch when he helped crucify Jack Flynn."

"You should come work for us. I never have any real laughs these days."

She walked off through the trees toward the two male agents who waited for her, her hips undulating slightly. I caught up with her.

"What have you got on the dwarf's partner?" I asked.

"Nothing. Watch your ass, Mr. Robicheaux," she replied.

"Call me Dave."

"Not a chance," she said. Then she grinned and made a clicking goodbye sound in her jaw.

•   •   •

THAT NIGHT I WATCHED the ten o'clock news before going to bed. I looked disinterestedly at some footage about a State Police traffic check, taken outside Jeanerette, until I saw Clete Purcel on the screen, showing his license to a trooper, then being escorted to a cruiser.

Back in the stew pot, I thought, probably for violating the spirit of his restricted permit, which allowed him to drive only for business purposes.

But that was Clete, always in trouble, always out of sync with the rest of the world. I knew the trooper was doing his job and Clete had earned his night in the bag, but I had to pause and wonder at the illusionary cell glue that made us feel safe about the society we lived in.

Archer Terrebonne, who would murder in order to break unions, financed a movie about the travail and privation of plantation workers in the 1940s. The production company helped launder money from the sale of China white. The FBI protected sociopaths like Harpo Scruggs and let his victims pay the tab. Harpo Scruggs worked for the state of Louisiana and murdered prisoners in Angola. The vested interest of government and criminals and respectable people was often the same.

In my scrapbook I had an inscribed photograph that Clete had given me when we were both in uniform at NOPD. It had been taken by an Associated Press photographer at night on a Swift Boat in Vietnam, somewhere up the Mekong, in the middle of a firefight. Clete was behind a pair of twin fifties, wearing a steel pot and a flack vest with no shirt, his youthful face lighted by a flare, tracers floating away into the darkness like segmented neon.

I could almost hear him singing, "I got a freaky old lady name of Cocaine Katie."

I thought about calling the jail in Jeanerette, but I knew he would be back on the street in the morning, nothing learned, deeper in debt to a bondsman, trying to sweep the snakes and spiders back in their baskets with vodka and grapefruit juice.

He made me think of my father, Aldous, whom people in the oil field always called Big Al Robicheaux, as though it were one name. It took seven Lafayette cops in Antlers Pool Room to put him in jail. The fight wrecked the pool room from one end to the other. They hit him with batons, broke chairs on his shoulders and back, and finally got his mother to talk him into submission so they didn't have to kill him.

But jails and poverty and baton-swinging cops never broke his spirit. It took my mother's infidelities to do that. The Amtrak still ran on the old Southern Pacific roadbed that had carried my mother out to Hollywood in 1946, made up of the same cars from the original Sunset Limited she had ridden in, perhaps with the same desert scenes painted on the walls. Sometimes when I would see the Amtrak crossing through winter fields of burned cane stubble, I would wonder what my mother felt when she stepped down on the platform at Union Station in Los Angeles, her pillbox hat slanted on her head, her purse clenched in her small hand. Did she believe the shining air and the orange trees and the blue outline of the San Gabriel Mountains had been created especially for her, to be discovered in exactly this moment, in a train station that echoed like a cathedral? Did she walk into the green roll of the Pacific and feel the water balloon her dress out from her thighs and fill her with a sexual pleasure that no man ever gave her?

What's the point?

Hitler and George Orwell already said it. History books are written by and about the Terrebonnes of this world, not jarheads up the Mekong or people who die in oil-well blowouts or illiterate Cajun women who believe the locomotive whistle on the Sunset Limited calls for them.

THIRTY-ONE

ADRIEN GLAZIER CALLED Monday morning from New Orleans.

"You remember a hooker by the name of Ruby Gravano?" she asked.

"She gave us the first solid lead on Harpo Scruggs. She had an autistic son named Nick," I said.

"That's the one."

"We put her on the train to Houston. She was getting out of the life."

"Her career change must have been short-lived. She was selling out of her pants again Saturday night. We think she tricked the shooter in the Ricky Scar gig. Unlucky girl."

"What happened?"

"Her pimp is a peckerwood named Beeler Grissum. Know him?"

"Yeah, he's a Murphy artist who works the Quarter and Airline Highway."

"He worked the wrong dude this time. He and Ruby Gravano tried to set up the outraged-boyfriend skit. The john broke Grissum's neck with a karate kick. Ruby told NOPD she'd seen the john a week or so ago with a dwarf. So they thought maybe he was the shooter on the Scarlotti hit and they called us."

"Who's the john?"

"All she could say was he has a Canadian passport, blond or gold hair, and a green-and-red scorpion tattooed on his left shoulder. We'll send the composite through, but it looks generic—egg-shaped head, elongated eyes, sideburns, fedora with a feather in it. I'm starting to think all these guys had the same mother."

"Where's Ruby now?"

"At Charity."

"What'd he do to her?"

"You don't want to know."

A FEW MINUTES LATER the composite came through the fax machine and I took it out to Cisco Flynn's place on the Loreauville road. When no one answered the door, I walked around the side of the house toward the patio in back. I could hear the voices of both Cisco and Billy Holtzner, arguing furiously.

"You got a taste, then you put your whole face in the trough. Now you swim for the shore with the rats," Holtzner said.

"You ripped them off, Billy. I'm not taking the fall," Cisco said.

"This fine house, this fantasy you got about being a southern gentleman, where you think it all comes from? You made your money off of me."

"So I'm supposed to give it back because you burned the wrong guys? That's the way they do business in the garment district?"

Then I heard their feet shuffling, a piece of iron furniture scrape on brick, a slap, like a hand hitting a body, and Cisco's voice saying, "Don't embarrass yourself on top of it, Billy."

A moment later Holtzner came around the back corner of the house, walking fast, his face heated, his stare twisted with his own thoughts. I held up the composite drawing in front of him.

"You know this guy?" I asked.

"No."

"The FBI thinks he's a contract assassin."

Holtzner's eyes were dilated, red along the rims, his skin filmed with an iridescent shine, a faint body odor emanating from his clothes, like a man who feels he's about to slide down a razor blade.

"So you bring it out to Cisco Flynn's house? Who you think is the target for these assholes?" he said.

"I see. You are."

"You got me made for a coward. It doesn't bother me. I don't care what happens to me anymore. But my daughter never harmed anybody except herself. All pinhead back there has to do is mortgage his house and we can make a down payment on our debt. I'm talking about my daughter's life here. Am I getting through to you?"

"You have a very unpleasant way of talking to people, Mr. Holtzner," I said.

"Go fuck yourself," he said, and walked across the lawn to his automobile, which he had parked under a shade tree.

I followed him and propped both my hands on the edge of his open window just as he turned the ignition.

He looked up abruptly into my face. His leaded eyelids made me think of a frog's.

"Your daughter's been threatened? Explicitly?" I said.

"Explicitly? I can always spot a thinker," he said. He dropped the car into reverse and spun two black tracks across the grass to the driveway.

I went back up on the gallery and knocked again. But Megan came to the door instead of Cisco. She stepped outside without inviting me in, a brown paper bag in her hand.

"I'm returning your pistol," she said.

"I think you should hang on to it for a while."

"Why'd you show Cisco those photos of my father?"

"He came to my office. He asked to see them."

"Take the gun. It's unloaded," she said. She pushed the bag into my hands.

"You're worried he might go after Archer Terrebonne?"

"You shouldn't have shown him those photos. Sometimes you're unaware of the influence you have over others, Dave."

"I tell you what. I'm going to get all the distance I can between me and you and Cisco. How's that?"

She stepped closer to me, her face tilted up into mine. I could feel her breath on my skin. For a moment I thought she was being flirtatious, deliberately confrontational. Then I saw the moisture in her eyes.

"You've never read the weather right with me. Not on anything. It's not Cisco who might do something to Archer Terrebonne," she said. She continued to stare

into my face. There were broken veins in the whites of
her eyes, like pieces of red thread.

THAT EVENING I SAW Clete's chartreuse convertible coming down the dirt road toward the dock, with
Geraldine Holtzner behind the wheel, almost unrecognizable in a scarf and dark glasses, and Clete padding along behind the car, in scarlet trunks, rotted
T-shirt, and tennis shoes that looked like pancakes on
his feet.

Geraldine Holtzner braked to a stop by the boat
ramp and Clete opened the passenger door and took a
bottle of diet Pepsi out of the cooler and wiped the ice
off with his palm. He breathed through his mouth,
sweat streaming out of his hair and down his chest.

"You trying to have a heart attack?" I said.

"I haven't had a drink or a cigarette in two days. I
feel great. You want some fried chicken?" he said.

"They pulled your license altogether?" I said.

"Big time," he said.

"Clete—" I said.

"So beautiful women drive me around now. Right,
Geri?"

She didn't respond. Instead, she stared at me from
behind her dark glasses, her mouth pursed into a button. "Why are you so hard on my father?" she said.

I looked at Clete, then down the road, in the shadows, where a man in a ribbed undershirt was taking a
fishing rod and tackle box out of his car trunk.

"I'd better get back to work," I said.

"I'll take a shower in the back of the bait shop and
we'll go to a movie or something. How about it,
Geri?" Clete said.

"Why not?" she said.

"I'd better pass," I said.

"I've got a case of 12-Step PMS today, you know, piss, moan, and snivel. Don't be a sorehead," Geraldine said.

"Come back later. We'll take a boat ride," I said.

"I can't figure what Megan sees in you," Geraldine said.

I went back down the dock to the bait shop, then turned and watched Clete padding along behind the convertible, like a trained bear, the dust puffing around his dirty tennis shoes.

A FEW MINUTES LATER I walked up to the house and ate supper in the kitchen with Alafair and Bootsie. The phone rang on the counter. I picked it up.

"Dave, this probably don't mean nothing, but a man was axing about Clete right after you went up to eat," Batist said.

"Which man?"

"He was fishing on the bank, then he come in the shop and bought a candy bar and started talking French. Then he ax in English who own that convertible that was going down the road. I tole him the only convertible I seen out there was for Clete Purcel. Then he ax if the woman driving it wasn't in the movies.

"I tole him I couldn't see through walls, no, so I didn't have no idea who was driving it. He give me a dol'ar tip and gone back out and drove away in a blue car."

"What kind of French did he speak?" I asked.

"I didn't t'ink about it. It didn't sound no different from us."

"I'll mention it to Clete. But don't worry about it."

"One other t'ing. He only had an undershirt on. He had a red-and-green tattoo on his shoulder. It look like a, what you call them t'ings, they got them down in Mexico, it ain't a crawfish, it's a—"

"Scorpion?" I said.

I CALLED CLETE AT his cottage outside Jeanerette.

"The Scarlotti shooter may be following you. Watch for a blond guy, maybe a French Canadian—" I began.

"Guy with a tattoo on his shoulder, driving a blue Ford?" Clete said.

"That's the guy."

"Geri and I stopped at a convenience store and I saw him do a U-turn down the street and park in some trees. I strolled on down toward a pay phone, but he knew I'd made him."

"You get his tag number?" I asked.

"No, there was mud on it."

"Can you get hold of Holtzner?"

"If I have to. The guy's wiring is starting to spark. I smelled crack in his trailer today."

"Where's Geraldine?"

"Where's any hype? In her own universe. That broad's crazy, Dave. After I told her we were being followed by the guy with the tattoo, she accused me of setting her up. Every woman I meet is either unattainable or nuts . . . Anyway, I'll try to find Holtzner for you."

An hour later he called me back.

"Holtzner just fired me," he said.

"Why?"

"I got him on his cell phone and told him the Canadian dude was in town. He went into a rage. He asked me why I didn't take down this guy when I had the chance. I go, 'Take down, like cap the guy?'

"He goes, 'What, an ex-cop kicked off the police force for killing a federal witness has got qualms?'

"I say, 'Yeah, as a matter of fact I do.'

"He goes, 'Then sign your own paychecks, Rhino Boy.'

"*Rhino Boy?* How'd I ever get mixed up with these guys, Dave?"

"Lots of people ask themselves that question," I said.

THE EX-PROSTITUTE NAMED JESSIE Rideau, who claimed to have been present when Jack Flynn was kidnapped, called Helen Soileau's extension the next day. Helen had the call transferred to my office.

"Come talk to us, Ms. Rideau," I said.

"You giving out free coffee in lockup?" she said.

"We want to put Harpo Scruggs away. You help us, we help you."

"Gee, where I heard that before?" I could hear her breath flattening on the receiver, as though she were trying to blow the heat out of a burn. "You ain't gonna say nothing?"

"I'll meet you somewhere else."

"St. Peter's Cemetery in ten minutes."

"How will I recognize you?" I asked.

"I'm the one that's not dead."

I parked my truck behind the cathedral and walked over to the old cemetery, which was filled with brick-

and-plaster crypts that had settled at broken angles into the earth. She sat on the seat of her paint-blistered gas-guzzler, the door open, her feet splayed on the curb, her head hanging out in the sunlight as I approached her. She had coppery hair that looked like it had been waved with an iron, and brown skin and freckles like a spray of dull pennies on her face and neck. Her shoulders were wide, her breasts like watermelons inside her blue cotton shirt, her turquoise eyes fastened on me, as though she had no means of defending herself against the world once it escaped her vision.

"Ms. Rideau?"

She didn't reply. A fire truck passed and she never took her eyes off my face.

"Give us a formal statement on Scruggs, enough to get a warrant for his arrest. That's when your problems start to end," I said.

"I need money to go out West, somewhere he cain't find me," she said.

"We don't run a flea market. If you conceal evidence in a criminal investigation, you become an accomplice after the fact. You ever do time?"

"You a real charmer."

I looked at my watch.

"Maybe I'd better go," I said.

"Harpo Scruggs gonna kill me. I had that box hid all them years for him. Now he gonna kill me over it. That's what y'all ain't hearing."

"Why does he want the lockbox now?" I asked.

"Him and me run a house toget'er. Fo' years ago I found out he killed Lavern Viator in Texas. Lavern was the other girl that was in Morgan City when they beat that man wit' chains. So I moved the box to a different place, one he ain't t'ought about."

"Let's try to be honest here, Jessie. Did you move it because you knew he was blackmailing someone with it and you thought it was valuable?"

Raindrops were falling out of the sunlight. There were blue tattoos of hearts and dice inside Jessie Rideau's forearms. She stared at the crypts in the cemetery, her eyes recessed, her face like that of a person who knows she will never have any value to anyone other than use.

"I gonna be wit' them dead people soon," she said.

"Where'd you do time?"

"A year in St. John the Baptist. Two years in St. Gabriel."

"Let us help you."

"Too late." She pulled the car door shut and started the engine. The exhaust pipe and muffler were rusted out, and smoke billowed from under the car frame.

"Why does he want the lockbox now?" I said.

She shot me the finger and gunned the car out into the street, the roar of her engine reverberating through the crypts.

THERE ARE DAYS THAT are different. They may look the same to everyone else, but on certain mornings you wake and know with absolute certainty you've been chosen as a participant in a historical script, for reasons unknown to you, and your best efforts will not change what has already been written.

On Wednesday the false dawn was bone-white, just like it had been the day Megan came back to New Iberia, the air brittle, the wood timbers in our house aching with cold. Then hailstones clattered on the tin roof and through the trees and rolled down the slope onto the dirt road. When the sun broke above the horizon the clouds in the eastern sky trembled with a glow like the reflection of a distant forest fire. When I walked down to the dock, the air was still cold, crisscrossed with the flight of robins, more than I had seen in years. I started cleaning the congealed ash from the barbecue pit, then rinsed my hands in an oaken bucket that had been filled with rainwater the night before. But Batist had cleaned a nutria in it for crab bait, and when I poured the water out it was red with blood.

At the office I called Adrien Glazier in New Orleans.

"Anything on the Scarlotti shooter?" I said.

"You figured out he's a French Canadian. You're ahead of us. What's the matter?" she said.

"Matter? He's going to kill somebody."

"If it will make you feel better, I already contacted Billy Holtzner and offered him Witness Protection. He goes, 'Where, on an ice floe at the South Pole?' and hangs up."

"Send some agents over here, Adrien."

"Holtzner's from Hollywood. He knows the rules. You get what you want when you come across. I told him the G's casting couch is nongender-specific. Try to have a few laughs with this stuff. You worry too much."

IT BEGAN TO RAIN just after sunset. The light faded in the swamp and the air was freckled with birds, then the rain beat on the dock and the tin roof of the bait shop and filled the rental boats that were chained up by the boat ramp. Batist closed out the cash register and put on his canvas coat and hat.

"Megan's daddy, the one got nailed to the barn? You know how many black men been killed and nobody ever been brought to cou't for it?" he said.

"Doesn't make it right," I said.

"Makes it the way it is," he replied.

After he had gone I turned off the outside lights so no late customers would come by, then began mopping the floor. The rain on the roof was deafening and I didn't hear the door open behind me, but I felt the cold blow across my back.

"Put your mop up. I got other work for you," the voice said.

I straightened up and looked into the seamed, rain-streaked face of Harpo Scruggs.

THIRTY-TWO

HIS FACE WAS BLOODLESS, SHRIVELED like a prune, glistening under the drenched brim of his hat. His raincoat dripped water in a circle on the floor. A blue-black .22 Ruger revolver, with ivory grips, on full cock, hung from his right hand.

"I got a magnum cylinder in it. The round will go through both sides of your skull," he said.

"What do you want, Scruggs?"

"Fix me some coffee and milk in one of them big glasses yonder." He pointed with one finger. "Put about four spoons of honey in it."

"Have you lost your mind?"

He propped the heel of his hand against the counter for support. The movement caused him to pucker his mouth and exhale his breath. It touched my face, like the raw odor from a broken drain line.

"You're listing," I said.

"Fix the coffee like I told you."

A moment later he picked up the glass with his left hand and drank from it steadily until it was almost empty. He set the glass on the counter and wiped his mouth with the back of his wrist. His whiskers made a scraping sound against his skin.

"We're going to Opelousas. You're gonna drive. You try to hurt me, I'll kill you. Then I'll come back and kill your wife and child. A man like me don't give it no thought," he said.

"Why me, Scruggs?"

" 'Cause you got an obsession over the man we stretched out on that barn wall. You gonna do right, no matter who you got to mess up. It ain't a compliment."

WE TOOK HIS PICKUP truck to the four-lane and headed north toward Lafayette and Opelousas. He didn't use the passenger seat belt but instead sat canted sideways with his right leg pushed out in front of him. His raincoat was unbuttoned and I could see the folds of a dark towel that were tied with rope across his side.

"You leaking pretty bad?" I said.

"Hope that I ain't. I'll pop one into your brisket 'fore I go under."

"I'm not your problem. We both know that."

With his left hand he took a candy bar from the dashboard and tore the paper with his dentures and began to eat the candy, swallowing as though he hadn't eaten in days. He held the revolver with his other hand, the barrel and cylinder resting across his thigh, pointed at my kidney.

The rain swept in sheets against the windshield. We passed through north Lafayette, the small, wood, galleried houses on each side of us whipped by the rain. Outside the city the country was dark green and sodden and there were thick stands of hardwoods on both sides of the four-lane and by the exit to Grand Coteau I saw emergency flares burning on the road and the flashers of emergency vehicles. A state trooper stood by an overturned semi, waving the traffic on with his flashlight.

"Was you ever a street cop?" Scruggs said.

"NOPD," I said.

"I was a gun bull at Angola, city cop, and road-gang hack, too. I done it all. I got no quarrel with you, Robicheaux."

"You want me to bring down Archer Terrebonne, don't you?"

"When I was a gun bull at Angola? That was in the days of the Red Hat House. The lights would go down all over the system and ole Sparky would make fire jump off their tailbone. There was this white boy from Mississippi put a piece of glass in my food once. A year later he cut up two other convicts for stealing a deck of cards from his cell. Guess who got to walk him into the Red Hat House?

"Lightning was crawling all over the sky that night and the current didn't work right. That boy was jolting in the straps for two minutes. The smell made them reporters hold handkerchiefs to their mouths. They was falling over themselves to get outside. I laughed till I couldn't hardly stand up."

"What's the point?"

"I'm gonna have my pound of flesh from Archer Terrebonne. You gonna be the man cut it out for me."

He straightened his tall frame inside his raincoat, his face draining with the effort. He saw me watching him and raised the barrel of the Ruger slightly, so that it was aimed upward at my armpit. He put his hand on the towel tied across his side and looked at it, then wiped his hand on his pants.

"Terrebonne paid my partner to shoot my liver out. I didn't think my partner would turn on me. I'll be damned if you can trust anybody these days," he said.

"The man who helped you kill the two brothers out in the Atchafalaya Basin?"

"That's him. Or was. I wouldn't eat no pigs that was butchered around here for a while . . . Take that exit yonder."

We drove for three miles through farmland, then followed a dirt road through pine trees, past a pond that was green with algae and covered with dead hyacinths, to a two-story yellow frame house whose yard was filled with the litter of dead pecan trees. The windows had been nailed over with plywood, the gallery stacked with hay bales that had rotted.

"You recognize it?" he asked.

"It was a brothel," I said.

"The governor of Lou'sana used to get laid there. Walk ahead of me."

We crossed through the back yard, past a collapsed privy and a cistern, with a brick foundation, that had caved outward into disjointed slats. The barn still had its roof, and through the rain I could hear hogs snuffing inside it. A tree of lightning burst across the sky and Scruggs jerked his face toward the light as though loud doors had been thrown back on their hinges behind him.

He saw me watching him and pointed the revolver at my face.

"I told you to walk ahead of me!" he said.

We went through the rear door of the house into a

gutted kitchen that was illuminated by the soft glow of a light at the bottom of a basement stairs.

"Where is Jessie Rideau?" I said.

Lightning crashed into a piney woods at the back of the property.

"Keep asking questions and I'll see you spend some time with her," he said, and pointed at the basement stairs with the barrel of the gun.

I walked down the wood steps into the basement, where a rechargeable Coleman lantern burned on the cement floor. The air was damp and cool, like the air inside a cave, and smelled of water and stone and the nests of small animals. Behind an old wooden icebox, the kind with an insert at the top for a block of tonged ice, I saw a woman's shoe and the sole of a bare foot. I walked around the side of the icebox and knelt down by the woman's side and felt her throat.

"You sonofabitch," I said to Scruggs.

"Her heart give out. She was old. It wasn't my fault," Scruggs said. Then he sat down in a wood chair, as though all his strength had drained through the bottoms of his feet. He stared at me dully from under the brim of his hat and wet his lips and swallowed before he spoke again.

"Yonder's what you want," he said.

In the corner, amidst a pile of bricks and broken mortar and plaster that had been prized from the wall with a crowbar, was a steel box that had probably been used to contain dynamite caps at one time. The lid was bradded and painted silver and heavy in my hand when I lifted it back on its hinges. Inside the box were a pair of handcuffs, two lengths of chain, a bath towel flattened inside a plastic bag, and a big hammer whose handle was almost black, as though stove soot and grease had been rubbed into the grain.

"Terrebonne's prints are gonna be on that hammer. The print will hold in blood just like in ink. Forensic man done told me that," Scruggs said.

"You've had your hands all over it. So have the women," I replied.

"The towel's got Flynn's blood all over it. So do them chains. You just got to get the right lab man to lift Terrebonne's prints."

His voice was deep in his throat, full of phlegm, his tongue thick against his dentures. He kept straightening his shoulders, as though resisting an unseen weight that was pushing them forward.

I removed the towel from the plastic bag and unfolded it. It was stiff and crusted, the fibers as pointed and hard as young thorns. I looked at the image in the center of the cloth, the black lines and smears that could have been a brow, a chin, a set of jawbones, eye sockets, even hair that had been soaked with blood.

"Do you have any idea of what you've been part of? Don't any of you understand what you've done?" I said to him.

"Flynn stirred everybody up. I know what I done. I was doing a job. That's the way it was back then."

"What do you see on the towel, Scruggs?"

"Dried blood. I done told you that. You carry all this to a lab. You gonna do that or not?"

He breathed through his mouth, his eyes seeming to focus on an insect an inch from the bridge of his nose. A terrible odor rose from his clothes.

"I'm going for the paramedics now," I said.

"A .45 ball went all the way through my intestines.

I ain't gonna live wired to machines. Tell Terrebonne I expect I'll see him. Tell him Hell don't have no lemonade springs."

He fitted the Ruger's barrel under the top of his dentures and pulled the trigger. The round exited from the crown of his head and patterned the plaster on the brick wall with a single red streak. His head hung back on his wide shoulders, his eyes staring sightlessly at the ceiling. A puff of smoke, like a dirty feather, drifted out of his mouth.

THIRTY-THREE

TWO DAYS LATER THE SKY was blue outside my office, a balmy wind clattering the palm trees on the lawn. Clete stood at the window, his porkpie hat on his head, his hands on his hips, surveying the street and the perfection of the afternoon. He turned and propped his huge arms on my desk and stared down into my face.

"Blow it off. Prints or no prints, rich guys don't do time," he said.

"I want to have that hammer sent to an FBI lab," I said.

"Forget it. If the St. Landry Parish guys couldn't lift them, nobody else is going to either. You even told Scruggs he was firing in the well."

"Look, Clete, you mean well, but—"

"The prints aren't what's bothering you. It's that damn towel."

"I saw the face on it. Those cops in Opelousas acted like I was drunk. Even the skipper down the hall."

"So fuck 'em," Clete said.

"I've got to get back to work. Where's your car?"

"Dave, you saw that face on the towel because you believe. You expect guys with jock rash of the brain to understand what you're talking about?"

"Where's your car, Clete?"

"I'm selling it," he said. He was sitting on the corner of my desk now, his upper arms scaling with dried sun blisters. I could smell salt water and sun lotion on his skin. "Leave Terrebonne alone. The guy's got juice all the way to Washington. You'll never touch him."

"He's going down."

"Not because of anything we do." He tapped his knuckles on the desk. "There's my ride."

Through the window I saw his convertible pull up to the curb. A woman in a scarf and dark glasses was behind the wheel.

"Who's driving?" I asked.

"Lila Terrebonne. I'll call you later."

AT NOON I MET Bootsie in City Park for lunch. We spread a checkered cloth on a table under a tin shed by the bayou and set out the silverware and salt and pepper shakers and a thermos of iced tea and a platter of cold cuts and stuffed eggs. The camellias were starting to bloom, and across the bayou we could see the bamboo and flowers and the live oaks in the yard of The Shadows.

I could almost forget about the events of the last few days.

Until I saw Megan Flynn park her car on the drive that wound through the park and stand by it, looking in our direction.

Bootsie saw her, too.

"I don't know why she's here," I said.

"Invite her over and find out," Bootsie said.

"That's what I have office hours for."

"You want me to do it?"

I set down the stack of plastic cups I was unwrapping and walked across the grass to the spreading oak Megan stood under.

"I didn't know you were with anyone. I wanted to thank you for all you've done and say goodbye," she said.

"Where are you going?"

"Paris. Rivages, my French publisher, wants me to do a collection on the Spaniards who fled into the Midi after the Spanish Civil War. By the way, I thought you'd like to know Cisco walked out on the film. It's probably going to bankrupt him."

"Cisco's stand-up."

"Billy Holtzner doesn't have the talent to finish it by himself. His backers are going to be very upset."

"That composite I gave you of the Canadian hit man, you and Cisco have no idea who he is?"

"No, we'd tell you."

We looked at each other in the silence. Leaves gusted from around the trunks of the trees onto the drive. Her gaze shifted briefly to Bootsie, who sat at the picnic table with her back to us.

"I'm flying out tomorrow afternoon with some friends. I don't guess I'll see you for some time," she said, and extended her hand. It felt small and cool inside mine.

I watched her get in her car, drawing her long khaki-clad legs and sandaled feet in after her, her dull red hair thick on the back of her neck.

Is this the way it all ends? I thought. Megan goes back to Europe, Clete eats aspirins for his hangovers and labors through all the sweaty legal mechanisms of the court system to get his driver's license back, the parish buries Harpo Scruggs in a potter's field, and Archer Terrebonne fixes another drink and plays tennis at his club with his daughter.

I walked back to the tin shed and sat down next to Bootsie.

"She came to say goodbye," I said.

"That's why she didn't come over to the table," she replied.

THAT EVENING, WHICH WAS Friday, the sky was purple, the clouds in the west stippled with the sun's last orange light. I raked stream trash out of the coulee and carried it in a washtub to the compost pile, then fed Tripod, our three-legged coon, and put fresh water in his bowl. My neighbor's cane was thick and green and waving in the field, and flights of ducks trailed in long V formations across the sun.

The phone rang inside, and Bootsie carried the portable out into the yard.

"We've got the Canadian identified. His name is Jacques Poitier, a real piece of shit," Adrien Glazier said. "Interpol says he's a suspect in at least a dozen assassinations. He's worked the Middle East, Europe, both sides in Latin America. He's gotten away with killing Israelis."

"We're not up to dealing with guys like this. Send us some help," I said.

"I'll see what I can do Monday," she said.

"Contract killers don't keep regular hours."

"Why do you think I'm making this call?" she said.

To feel better, I thought. But I didn't say it.

THAT EVENING I COULDN'T rest. But I didn't know what it was that bothered me.

Clete Purcel? His battered chartreuse convertible? Lila Terrebonne?

I called Clete's cottage.

"Where's your Caddy?" I asked.

"Lila's got it. I'm signing the title over to her Monday. Why?"

"Geraldine Holtzner's been driving it all over the area."

"Streak, the Terrebonnes might hurt themselves, but they don't get hurt by others. What does it take to make you understand that?"

"The Canadian shooter is a guy named Jacques Poitier. Ever hear of him?"

"No. And if he gives me any grief, I'm going to stick a .38 down his pants and blow his Jolly Roger off. Now, let me get some sleep."

"Megan told you she's going to France?"

The line was so quiet I thought it had gone dead. Then he said, "She must have called while I was out. When's she going?"

Way to go, Robicheaux, I thought.

THE SET THAT HAD been constructed on the levee at Henderson Swamp was lighted with the haloed brilliance of a phosphorus flare when Lila Terrebonne drove Clete's convertible along the dirt road at the top of the levee, above the long, wind-ruffled bays and islands of willow trees that were turning yellow with the season. The evening was cool, and she wore a sweater over her shoulders, a dark scarf with roses stitched on it tied around her head. She found her father with Billy Holtzner, and the three of them ate dinner on a cardboard table by the water's edge and drank a bottle of nonalcoholic champagne that had been chilled in a silver bucket.

When she left, she asked a grip to help her fasten down the top on her car. He was the only one to notice the blue Ford that pulled out of a fish camp down the levee and followed her toward the highway. He did not think it significant and did not mention the fact to anyone until later.

THE MAN IN THE blue Ford followed her through St. Martinville and down the Loreauville road to Cisco Flynn's house. When she turned into Cisco's driveway, a lawn party was in progress and the man in the Ford parked on the swale and opened his hood and appeared to onlookers to be at work on his engine.

On the patio, behind the house, Lila Terrebonne called Cisco Flynn a lowborn, treacherous sycophant, picked up his own mint julep from the table, and flung it in his face.

But on the front lawn a jazz combo played atop an elevated platform, and the guests wandered among the citrus and oak trees and the drink tables and the music that seemed to charm the pink softness of the evening into their lives. Megan wore her funny straw hat with an evening dress that clung to her figure like ice water, and was talking to a group of friends, people from New York and overseas, when she noticed the man working on his car.

She stood between two myrtle bushes, on the edge of the swale, and waited until he seemed to feel her eyes on his back. He straightened up and smiled, but the smile came and went erratically, as though the man thought it into place.

He wore a form-fitting long-sleeve gold shirt and blue jeans that were so tight they looked painted on his skin. A short-brim fedora with a red feather in the band rested on the fender. His hair was the color of his shirt, waved, and cut long and parted on the side so it combed down over one ear.

"It's a battery cable. I'll have it started in a minute," he said in a French accent.

She stared at him without speaking, a champagne glass resting in the fingers of both hands, her chest rising and falling.

"I am a big fan of American movies. I saw a lady turn in here. Isn't she the daughter of a famous Hollywood director?" he said.

"I'm not sure who you mean," Megan said.

"She was driving a Cadillac, a convertible," he said, and waited. Then he smiled, wiping his hands on a handkerchief. "Ah, I'm right, aren't I? Her father is William Holtzner. I love all his films. He is wonderful," the man said.

She stepped backward, once, twice, three times, the myrtle bushes brushing against her bare arms, then stood silently among her friends. She looked back at the man with gold hair only after he had restarted his car and driven down the road. Five minutes later Lila Terrebonne backed the Cadillac down the drive, hooking one wheel over the slab into a freshly watered flower bed, then shifted into low out on the road and floored the accelerator toward New Iberia. Her radio was blaring with rock 'n' roll from the 1960s, her face energized with vindication inside the black scarf, stitched with roses, that was tied tightly around her head.

THE MAN NAMED JACQUES Poitier caught up with her on the two-lane road that paralleled Bayou Teche, only one mile from her home. Witnesses said she tried to outrun him, swerving back and forth across the highway, blowing her horn, waving desperately at a group of blacks on the side of the road. Others said he passed her and they heard a gunshot. But we found no evidence of the latter, only a thread-worn tire that had exploded on the rim before the Cadillac skidded sideways, showering sparks off the pavement, into an oncoming dump truck loaded with condemned asbestos.

THIRTY-FOUR

IF THERE WAS ANY DRAMA at the crime scene later, it was not in our search for evidence or even in the removal of Lila's body from under the crushed roof of the Cadillac. Archer Terrebonne arrived at the scene twenty minutes after the crash, and was joined a few minutes later by Billy Holtzner. Terrebonne immediately took charge, as though his very presence and the slip-on half-top boots and red flannel shirt and quilted hunting vest and visor cap he wore gave him a level of authority that none of the firemen or paramedics or sheriff's deputies possessed.

They all did his bidding or sought sanction or at a minimum gave an explanation to him for whatever they did. It was extraordinary to behold. His attorney and family physician were there; also a U.S. congressman and a well-known movie actor. Terrebonne wore his grief like a patrician who had become a man of the people. A three-hundred-pound St. Mary Parish deputy, his mouth full of Red Man, stood next to me, his eyes fixed admiringly on Terrebonne.

"That ole boy is one brave sonofabuck, ain't he?" he said.

The paramedics covered Lila's body with a sheet and wheeled it on the gurney to the back of an ambulance, the strobe lights of TV cameras flowing with it, passing across Terrebonne's and Holtzner's stoic faces.

Helen Soileau and I walked through the crowd until we were a few feet from Terrebonne. Red flares burned along the shoulder of the road, and mist clung to the bayou and the oak trunks along the bank. The air was cold, but my face felt hot and moist with humidity. His eyes never registered our presence, as though we were moths outside a glass jar, looking in upon a pure white flame.

"Your daughter's death is on you, Terrebonne. You didn't intend for it to happen, but you helped bring the people here who killed her," I said.

A woman gasped; the scattered conversation around us died.

"You hope this will destroy me, don't you?" he replied.

"Harpo Scruggs said to tell you he'd be expecting you soon. I think he knew what he was talking about," I said.

"Don't you talk to him like that," Holtzner said, rising on the balls of his feet, his face dilating with the opportunity that had presented itself. "I'll tell you something else, too. Me and my new co-director are finishing our picture. And it's going to be dedicated to Lila Terrebonne. You can take your dirty mouth out of here."

Helen stepped toward him, her finger lifted toward his face.

"He's a gentleman. I'm not. Smart off again and see what happens," she said.

We walked to our cruiser, past the crushed, upside-down shell of Clete's Cadillac, the eyes of reporters and cops and passersby riveted on the sides of our faces.

I heard a voice behind me, one I didn't recognize, yell out, "You're the bottom of the barrel, Robicheaux."

Then others applauded him.

EARLY THE NEXT MORNING Helen and I began re-creating Lila Terrebonne's odyssey from the movie set on the levee, where she had dinner with her father and Billy Holtzner, to the moment she must have realized her peril and tried to outrun the contract assassin named Jacques Poitier. We interviewed the stage grip who saw the blue Ford pull out of the fish camp and follow her back down the levee; an attendant at a filling station in St. Martinville, where she stopped for gasoline; and everyone we could find from the Flynns' lawn party.

The New York and overseas friends of Megan and Cisco were cooperative and humble to a fault, in large part because they never sensed the implications of what they told us. But after talking with three guests from the lawn party, I had no doubt as to what transpired during the encounter between Megan and the French Canadian named Poitier.

Helen and I finished the last interview at a bed-and-breakfast across from The Shadows at three o'clock that afternoon. It was warm and the trees were speckled with sunlight, and a few raindrops were clicking on the bamboo in front of The Shadows and drying as soon as they struck the sidewalks.

"Megan's plane leaves at three-thirty from Acadiana Regional. See if you can get a hold of Judge Mouton at his club," I said.

"A warrant? We might be on shaky ground. There has to be intent, right?"

"Megan never did anything in her life without intending to."

OUR SMALL LOCAL AIRPORT had been built on the site of the old U.S. Navy air base outside of town. As I drove down the state road toward the hangars and maze of runways, under a partially blue sky that was starting to seal with rain clouds, my heart was beating in a way that it shouldn't, my hands sweating black prints on the steering wheel.

Then I saw her, with three other people, standing by a hangar, her luggage next to her, while a Learjet taxied around the far side of a parking area filled with helicopters. She wore her straw hat and a pink dress with straps and lace around the hem, and when the wind began gusting she held her hat to her head with one hand in a way that made me think of a 1920s flapper.

She saw me walking toward her, like someone she recognized from a dream, then her eyes fixed on mine and the smile went out of her face and she glanced briefly toward the horizon, as though the wind and the churning treetops held a message for her.

I looked at my watch. It was 3:25. The door to the Lear opened and a man in a white jacket and dark blue pants lowered the steps to the tarmac. Her friends picked up their luggage and drifted toward the door, glancing discreetly in her direction, unsure of the situation.

"Jacques Poitier stopped his car on the swale in front of your party. Your guests heard you talking to him," I said.

"He said his car was broken. He was working on it," she replied.

"He asked you if the woman driving Clete's Cadillac was Holtzner's daughter."

She was silent, her hair ruffling thickly on her neck. She looked at the open door of the plane and the attendant who waited for her.

"You let him think it was Geraldine Holtzner," I said.

"I didn't tell him anything, Dave."

"You knew who he was. I gave you the composite drawing."

"They're waiting for me."

"Why'd you do it, Meg?"

"I'm sorry for Lila Terrebonne. I'm not sorry for her father."

"She didn't deserve what happened to her."

"Neither did my father. I'm going now, unless you're arresting me. I don't think you can either. If I did anything wrong, it was a sin of omission. That's not a crime."

"You've already talked to a lawyer," I said, almost in amazement.

She leaned down and picked up her suitcase and shoulder bag. When she did, her hat blew off her head and bounced end over end across the tarmac. I ran after it, like a high school boy would, then walked back to her, brushing it off, and placed it in her hands.

"I won't let this rest. You've contributed to the death of an innocent person. Just like the black guy who died in your lens years ago. Somebody else has paid your tab. Don't come back to New Iberia, Meg," I said.

Her eyes held on mine and I saw a great sadness sweep through her face, like that of a child watching a balloon break loose from its string and float away suddenly on the wind.

EPILOGUE

THAT AFTERNOON THE WIND DROPPED and there was a red tint like dye in the clouds, and the water was high and brown in the bayou, the cypress and willows thick with robins. It should have been a good afternoon for business at the bait shop and dock, but it wasn't. The parking area was empty; there was no whine of boat engines out on the water, and the sound of my footsteps on the planks in the dock echoed off the bayou as though I were walking under a glass dome.

A drunk who had given Batist trouble earlier that day had broken the guardrail on the dock and fallen to the ramp below. I got some lumber and hand tools and an electric saw from the tin shed behind the house to repair the gap in the rail, and Alafair clipped Tripod's chain on his collar and walked him down to the dock with me. I heard the front screen door bang behind us, and I turned and saw Bootsie on the gallery. She waved, then went down into the flower bed with a trowel and a plastic bucket and began working on her knees.

"Where is everybody?" Alafair said out on the dock.

"I think a lot of people went to the USL game today," I replied.

"There's no sound. It makes my ears pop."

"How about opening up a couple of cans of Dr Pepper?" I said.

She went inside the bait shop, but did not come back out right away. I heard the cash register drawer open and knew the subterfuge that was at work, one that she used to mask her charity, as though somehow it were a vice. She would pay for the fried pie she took from the counter, then cradle Tripod in one arm and hand-feed it to him whether he wanted it or not, while his thick, ringed tail flipped in the air like a spring.

I tried to concentrate on repairing the rail on the dock and not see the thoughts that were as bright and jagged as shards of glass in the center of my mind. I kept touching my brow and temple with my arm, as though I were wiping off sweat, but that wasn't my trouble. I could feel a band of pressure tightening across the side of my head, just as I had felt it on night trails in Vietnam or when Bedcheck Charlie was cutting through our wire.

What was it that bothered me? The presence of men like Archer Terrebonne in our midst? But why should I worry about his kind? They had always been with us, scheming, buying our leaders, deceiving the masses. No, it was Megan, and Megan, and Megan, and her betrayal of everything I thought she represented: Joe Hill, the Wobblies, the strikers murdered at Ludlow, Colorado, Woody Guthrie, Dorothy Day, all those faceless working people whom historians and academics and liberals alike treat with indifference.

I ran the electric saw through a two-by-four and ground the blade across a nail. The board seemed to explode, the saw leaping from my hand, splinters embedding in my skin like needles. I stepped backward from the saw, which continued to spin by my foot, then ripped the cord loose from the socket in the bait-shop wall.

"You all right, Dave?" Alafair said through the screen.

"Yeah, I'm fine," I said, holding the back of my right hand.

Through the trees next to the bayou I saw a mud-splattered stake truck loaded with boxes of chrysanthemums coming down the road. The truck pulled at an angle across the boat ramp, and Mout' Broussard got out on the passenger's side and a tiny Hmong woman in a conical straw hat with a face like a withered apple got down from the other. Mout' put a long stick across his shoulders, and the woman loaded wire-bailed baskets of flowers on each end of it, then picked up a basket herself and followed him down the dock.

"You sell these for us, we gonna give you half, you," Mout' said.

"I don't seem to have much business today, Mout'," I said.

"Season's almost over. I'm fixing to give them away," he said.

"Put them under the eave. We'll give it a try," I said.

He and the woman lay the flowers in yellow and brown and purple clumps against the bait-shop wall.

Mout' wore a suit coat with his overalls and was sweating inside his clothes. He wiped his face with a red handkerchief.

"You doing all right?" he said to me.

"Sure," I said.

"That's real good. Way it should be," he said. He replaced the long stick across his shoulders and extended his arms on it and walked with the Hmong woman toward the truck, their bodies lit by the glow of the sun through the trees.

Why look for the fires that burn in western skies? I thought. The excoriated symbol of difference was always within our ken. You didn't have to see far to find it—an elderly black man who took pride in the fact he shined Huey Long's and Harry James's shoes or a misplaced and wizened Hmong woman who had fought the Communists in Laos for the French and the CIA and now grew flowers for Cajuns in Louisiana. The story was ongoing, the players changing only in name. I believe Jack Flynn understood that and probably forgave his children when they didn't.

I sat on a bench by the water faucet and tried to pick the wood splinters out of the backs of my hands. The wind came up and the robins filled the air with a sound that was almost deafening, their wings fluttering above my head, their breasts the color of dried blood.

"Are we still going to the show tonight?" Alafair said.

"You better believe it, you," I said, and winked.

She flipped Tripod up on her shoulder like a sack of meal, and the three of us went up the slope to find Bootsie.

...ed and forthcoming Oxford Handbooks

OXFORD MEDICAL PUBLIC

Oxford Handboo

Clinical Exa
and Practic

Publis

Oxford
Progran
Oxford
Medici
Oxforc
Oxfore
Science
Oxfore
Oxfor
Labora
Oxfor
Denti
Oxfor
Diagn
Oxfo
Exam
Oxfo
Haer
Oxfc
Imm
Oxfe
Med
Oxf
Med
Oxf
Ox
Pha
Ox
Reb
Ox
Spe
Ox
Su
O.
M
O
O
Pa
C
C
N
C
a
C
a

Oxford Handbook of
Clinical Examination and Practical Skills

2nd edition

Edited by

Dr James Thomas
Consultant Musculoskeletal Radiologist
Nottingham University Hospitals NHS
Trust, Nottingham, UK

and

Dr Tanya Monaghan
Academic Clinical Lecturer in Gastroenterology
NIHR Nottingham Digestive Diseases Centre Biomedical
Research Unit,
Nottingham University Hospitals NHS Trust,
Nottingham, UK

OXFORD
UNIVERSITY PRESS

OXFORD
UNIVERSITY PRESS

Great Clarendon Street, Oxford, OX2 6DP,
United Kingdom

Oxford University Press is a department of the University of Oxford.
It furthers the University's objective of excellence in research, scholarship,
and education by publishing worldwide. Oxford is a registered trade mark of
Oxford University Press in the UK and in certain other countries

© Oxford University Press 2014

The moral rights of the authors have been asserted

First Edition published in 2007
Second Edition published in 2014, Reprinted 2015, Reprinted 2016

Impression: 3

Published in the United States of America by Oxford University Press
198 Madison Avenue, New York, NY 10016, United States of America

British Library Cataloguing in Publication Data

Data available

Library of Congress Control Number: 2014931113

ISBN 978-0-19-959397-2

Printed in China by
C&C Offset Printing Co. Ltd

Oxford University Press makes no representation, express or implied, that the drug
dosages in this book are correct. Readers must therefore always check the product
information and clinical procedures with the most up-to-date published product
information and data sheets provided by the manufacturers and the most recent
codes of conduct and safety regulations. The authors and the publishers do not
accept responsibility or legal liability for any errors in the text or for the misuse or
misapplication of material in this work. Except where otherwise stated, drug dosages
and recommendations are for the non-pregnant adult who is not
breast-feeding.

Links to third party websites are provided by Oxford in good faith and
for information only. Oxford disclaims any responsibility for the materials
contained in any third party website referenced in this work.

Preface

Since the publication of the first edition of this book, we have been heartened by the many positive comments and emails from readers and have been very grateful for the suggestions for improvements and modifications. We have tried to incorporate as many of these as possible.

We have tried hard to update the text to reflect modern practice and to make changes which, only with the 20–20 vision of hindsight, could we see were needed.

We have tried to keep an eye on OSCE examinations and the reader will find new 'skills stations' throughout the book to add to the existing examination frameworks.

Several chapters, including respiratory, paediatrics, skin, and locomotor have been rewritten from scratch.

We have incorporated new chapters on the eyes, the obstetric assessment.

The 'important presentations' section of each systems chapter has been greatly expanded and referenced to our sister publications the *Oxford Handbooks Clinical Tutor Study Cards*.

The practical procedures chapter has been significantly expanded and updated.

The photographs throughout the book have been updated to reflect modern healthcare dress codes.

There is a brand new chapter on 'other investigations' so that the reader can understand what is involved in common tests and how to prepare patients for them.

Finally, the chapter order has been changed to highlight the importance of the 'core' system examinations of the cardiovascular, respiratory, abdominal, and nervous systems.

As always, we welcome any comments and suggestions for improvement from our reader—this book, after all, is for you.

James D Thomas
Tanya M Monaghan
2013

Acknowledgements

We would like to record our thanks to the very many people who have given their advice and support since the publication of the first edition.

For contributing specialist portions of the book, we thank Dr Caroline Bodey (Paediatrics), Dr Stuart Cohen (Skin, hair, and nails), Dr John Blakey (Respiratory), Dr A Abhishek (Locomotor) and Mr Venki Sundaram and Mr Farid Afshar (Eyes).

Once again, the elderly pages have been penned by the peerless Dr Richard Fuller who remains a steadfast supporter and is much appreciated.

This edition builds on the work of contributors to the first edition whose efforts deserve to be recorded again. Thanks then to Heid Ridsdale, Franco Guarasci, Jeremy Robson, Lyn Dean, Jonathan Bodansky, Mandy Garforth, and Mike Gaell.

For this edition, Michelle Jie, Muhammad Umer, and Dr Sandeep Tiwari kindly posed for new and updated photographs. Their bravery made the process easy and enjoyable. Our continued gratitude goes to our original models, Adam Swallow, Geoffrey McConnell, and our anonymous female model. We thank the staff at the Nottingham University Hospitals Medical Photography Department, in particular Nina Chambers for taking the photographs.

Additional diagrams for this edition, including the skin pictures, have been drawn by Dr Ravi Kothari and we thank him for his speedy and high-quality work.

As well as contributing some material for the procedures chapter, Dr Yutaro Higashi has remained a grounding force during this process. His wisdom and sagely advice throughout have been much appreciated.

Finally, we would like to thank the staff at Oxford University Press for originally trusting us with this project, especially Catherine Barnes and Elizabeth Reeves for their faith, support, and guidance.

Contents

How to use this book

The systems chapters

In each chapter, there are suggestions as to what questions to ask and how to proceed depending on the presenting complaint. These are not exhaustive and are intended as guidance. The history parts of each chapter should be used in conjunction with Chapter 2 to build a full and thorough history.

Practical procedures

This chapter describes those practical procedures that the junior doctor or senior nurse may be expected to perform. Some should only be performed once you have been trained specifically in the correct technique by a more senior colleague.

Reality versus theory

In describing the practical procedures, we have tried to be 'realistic'. The methods described are the most commonly used across the profession and are aimed at helping the reader perform the procedure correctly and safely within a clinical environment.

There may be slight differences, therefore, between the way that a small number of the procedures are described here and the way that they are taught in a clinical skills laboratory. In addition, local trusts may use different equipment for some procedures. The good practitioner should be flexible and make changes to their routine accordingly.

Data interpretation

A minority of the reference ranges described for some of the biochemical tests in the data interpretation chapter may differ very slightly from those used by your local laboratory—this is dependent on the equipment and techniques used for measurement. Any differences are likely to be very small indeed. If in doubt, check with your local trust.

Contributors

Dr A Abhishek
Consultant Rheumatologist,
Cambridge University Hospitals NHS Trust,
Cambridge, UK

Mr Farid Afshar
Specialty Registrar in Ophthalmology,
Severn Deanery, UK

Dr John Blakey
Senior Clinical Lecturer and Honorary Consultant in Respiratory Medicine,
Liverpool School of Tropical Medicine,
University of Liverpool,
Liverpool, UK

Dr Caroline Bodey
Specialist Registrar in Paediatric Neurodisability,
Leeds, UK

Dr Stuart N Cohen
Consultant Dermatologist,
Nottingham University Hospitals NHS Trust,
Nottingham, UK

Dr Richard Fuller
Associate Professor and Honorary Consultant Physician,
Leeds Institute of Medical Education,
University of Leeds,
Leeds, UK

Mr Venki Sundaram
Specialty Registrar in Ophthalmology,
London Deanery,
London, UK

Symbols and abbreviations

↑	increased
↓	decreased
↔	normal
▶	this fact or idea is important
~	approximately
⮎	cross-reference
❶	warning
℘	website
ABG	arterial blood gas
ACL	anterior cruciate ligament
ACSM	American College of Sports Medicine
ACTH	adrenocorticotrophic hormone
ADH	antidiuretic hormone
ADP	adenosine diphosphate
AED	automated external defibrillator
AITFL	anterior inferior tibiofibular ligament
AMD	age-related macular degeneration
AMTS	Abbreviated Mental Test Score
ANCOVA	analysis of covariance
ANOVA	analysis of variance
ANTT	aseptic non-touch technique
AP	antero-posterior
APC	argon plasma coagulation
APH	ante-partum haemorrhage
APKD	adult polycystic kidney disease
APL	antiphospholipid
AS	ankylosing spondylitis
ASD	atrial septal defect
ASIS	anterior superior iliac spine
ATFL	anterior talofibular ligament
ATLS	advanced trauma life support
ATP	adenosine triphosphate
AV	atrioventricular
AVN	avascular necrosis
a-vO$_2$ diff	arterio venous difference in oxygen concentration
BLa	blood lactate
BMD	bone mineral density

BMI	body mass index
BMR	basal metabolic rate
BPV	benign postural vertigo
BSL	British Sign Language
CABG	coronary artery bypass graft
CAH	congenital adrenal hyperplasia
CDC	Centers for Disease Control
CFL	calcaneofibular ligament
CHD	congenital heart disease
CHF	congestive heart failure
CHO	carbohydrate
CISS	Comité International des Sports des Sourds
CJD	Creutzfeldt–Jakob disease
CKD	chronic kidney disease
CMCJ	carpometacarpal joint
CNS	central nervous system
CON	concentric
COPD	chronic obstructive pulmonary disease
CP	cerebral palsy
CP	creatine phosphate
CPAP	continuous positive airways pressure
CP-IRSA	Cerebral Palsy International Sport and Recreation Association
CPK	creatine phosphokinase
CPN	community psychiatric nurse
CPPD	calcium pyrophosphate dihydrate deposition disease
CPR	cardio-pulmonary resuscitation
CRP	C-reactive protein
CRVO	central retinal vein occlusion
CSF	cerebrospinal fluid
CT	computed tomography
CTD	connective tissue disease
CVD	cardiovascular disease
DCO	doping control officer
DCS	diffuse cerebral swelling
DEXA	dual energy x-ray absorptiometry
DIPJ	distal interphalangeal joint
DKA	diabetic ketoacidosis
DLCO	carbon monoxide diffusion capacity
DM	diabetes mellitus
DVT	deep vein thrombosis

ECC	eccentric
ECG	electrocardiogram
ECRB	extensor carpi radialis brevis
ECRL	extensor carpi radialis longus
ECU	extensor carpi ulnaris
EDD	estimated date of delivery
EEA	energy expenditure for activity
EIA	exercise-induced asthma
EIB	exercise-induced bronchospasm
EMG	electromyography
EMR	endoscopic mucosal resection
ENMG	electoneuromyography
EPB	extensor pollicis brevis
EPO	erythropoietin
ESR	erythrocyte sedimentation rate
ESRD	end stage renal disease
ET	endotracheal
ETT	exercise tolerance test
EVH	eucapnic voluntary hyperpnoea
EWS	early warning score
FABER	flexion abduction external rotation
FBC	full blood count
FCU	flexor carpi ulnaris
FDS	flexor digitorum superficialis
$FeCO_2$	expired air carbon dioxide concentration
FeO_2	expired air oxygen concentration
FEV_1	forced expiratory volume in first second
FHR	fetal heart rate
FHx	family history
FiO_2	fraction of inspired oxygen
FNA	fine needle aspiration
FPL	flexor policis longus
FSH	follicle stimulating hormone
FVC	forced vital capacity
GA	general anaesthetic
GAD	generalized anxiety disorder
GALS	gait, arms, legs, spine
GCA	giant cell arteritis
GCS	Glasgow Coma Scale
GFR	glomerular filtration rate
GH	growth hormone

GnRH	gonadotrophin releasing hormone
GOJ	gastro-oesophageal junction
GORD	gastro-oesophageal reflux disease
GTN	glyceryl trinitrate
Hb	haemoglobin
HCC	hepatocellular carcinoma
hCG	human chorionic gonadotropin
Hct	haematocrit
HDL	high density lipoprotein
HE	hepatic encephalopathy
HHT	hereditary haemorrhagic telangiectasia
HIS	International Headache Society
HMB	beta-hydroxy-beta-methylbutyrate
HR	heart rate
HRT	hormone replacement therapy
HT	highly trained
IA	intra-arterial
IBD	inflammatory bowel disease
ICP	intracranial pressure
IGF-1	insulin-like growth factor 1
IHCD	Institute of Health and Care Development
IHD	ischaemic heart disease
IIH	idiopathic intracranial hypertension
IJV	internal jugular vein
IMB	intermenstrual bleeding
INO	internuclear ophthalmoplegia
INR	international normalized ratio
IUCD	intra-uterine contraceptive device
IOC	International Olympic Committee
IOP	intraocular pressure
IPJ	interphalangeal joint
ITB	ilio-tibial band
ITBFS	ilio-tibial band friction syndrome
IVP	intravenous pyelogram
IZ	injury zone
JVP	jugular venous pressure
LBC	liquid-based cytology
LDH	lactate dehydrogenase
LDL	low density lipoprotein
LH	luteinizing hormone
LMA	laryngeal mask airway

LMN	lower motor neuron
LMP	last menstrual period
LOC	loss of consciousness
LRT	lower respiratory tract
LSE	left sternal edge
LV	left ventricle
LVH	left ventricular hypertrophy
MANOVA	multivariate analysis of the variance
MCD	minimal change disease
MCL	medial collateral ligament
MCPJ	metacarpophalangeal joint
MCS	microscopy, culture, and sensitivity
MDI	metered dose inhaler
MDT	multi-disciplinary team
MELD	model for end-stage liver disease
MEN	multiple endocrine neoplasia
MG	myasthenia gravis
MI	myocardial infarction
MMSE	Mini-Mental State Examination
MPHR	maximum predicted heart rate
MRI	magnetic resonance imaging
MRSA	methicillin-resistant *Staphylococcus aureus*
MSU	mid-stream urine sample
MTPJ	metatarsophalangeal joint
MUST	Malnutrition Universal Screening Tool
NASH	non-alcoholic steatohepatitis
NGB	National Governing Body
NIV	non-invasive ventilation
NPL	no perception of light
NSAIDs	non-steroidal anti-inflammatory drugs
NSF	nephrogenic systemic fibrosis
OA	osteoarthritis
OCD	osteochondritis dissecans
OCP	oral contraceptive pill
OGD	oesophagogastroduodenoscopy
OHCM9	*Oxford Handbook of Clinical Medicine* 9th ed.
OHCS9	*Oxford Handbook of Clinical Specialties* 9th ed.
ORIF	open reduction and internal fixation
OSA	obstructive sleep apnoea
OTC	over-the-counter
PC	presenting complaint

PCL	posterior cruciate ligament
PCOS	polycystic ovary syndrome
PCR	phospho-creatine (energy system)
PCS	post-concussion syndrome
PDA	patent ductus arteriosus
PEFR	peak expiratory flow rate
PFJ	patello-femoral joint
Pi	inorganic phosphate
PIN	posterior interosseous nerve
PIPJ	proximal interphalangeal joint
PMH	past medical history
PNF	proprioneurofacilitation
POMS	profile of mood states
PPH	post-partum haemorrhage
PRICE	protection, rest, ice, compression, elevation
PSC	primary sclerosing cholangitis
PSIS	posterior superior iliac crest
PSYM	parasympathetic
PTFL	posterior talofibular ligament
PTH	parathyroid hormone
PTHrP	parathyroid hormone related protein
PV	*per vaginam*
Q	cardiac output
QID	four times a day (quater in die)
QSART	quantitative sudomotor axon reflex tests
RA	rheumatoid arthritis
RAPD	relative afferent pupillary defect
RBBB	right bundle branch block
RCC	red cell count
ROM	range of movement
RPE	retinal pigment epithelium
RR	respiratory rate
RSO	resting sweat output
RTA	road traffic accident
RV	residual volume
SA	sinoatrial
SAH	subarachnoid haemorrhage
SAID	specific adaptations to imposed demand
SARA	sexually acquired reactive arthritis
SBAR	situation, background, assessment, recommendation
SBP	spontaneous bacterial peritonitis

SCAT	Standardised Concussion Assessment Tool
SCBU	special care baby unit
SEM	sports and exercise medicine
SFJ	sapheno-femoral junction
SIJ	sacro-iliac joint
SLAP	superior labrum anterior to posterior
SLE	systemic lupus erythematosus
SLR	straight leg raise
SOB	shortness of breath
SPECT	single photon emission computed tomography
STD	sexually transmitted disease
SV	stroke volume
SVCO	superior vena cava obstruction
SYM	sympathetic
TAVI	transcatheter aortic valve implantation
TBI	traumatic brain injury
TFCC	triangular fibrocartilage complex
TGA	transposition of the great arteries
TLac	lactate threshold (aerobic/anaerobic threshold)
TLC	total lung capacity
TNF-α	tumour necrosis factor alpha
TOE	trans-oesophageal echo
TUE	therapeutic use exemption
UCL	ulnar collateral ligament
ULTT	upper limb tension test
UMN	upper motor neuron
URT	upper respiratory tract
URTI	upper respiratory tract infection
US	ultrasound
UT	untrained
UV	ultraviolet
VA	alveolar ventilation
VE	minute ventilation
VEGF	vascular derived growth factor
VI	visually impaired
VIP	vasoactive intestinal polypeptide
VMO	vastus medialis obliquus
VO$_2$	oxygen uptake
VT	ventricular tachycardia
WADA	World Anti-Doping Agency
WCC	white cell count

Communication skills

Introduction

Communication skills are notoriously hard to teach and describe. There are too many possible situations that one might encounter to be able to draw rules or guidelines. In addition, your actions will depend greatly on the personalities present, not least of all your own.

Using this chapter

Throughout this chapter, there is some general advice about communicating in different situations and to different people. We have not provided rules to stick to, but rather tried to give the reader an appreciation of the great many ways the same situation may be tackled.

Ultimately, skill at communication comes from practice and a large amount of common sense.

A huge amount has been written about communication skills in medicine. Most is a mix of accepted protocols and personal opinion—this chapter is no different.

Patient-centred communication

In recent years, there has been a significant change in the way healthcare workers interact with patients. The biomedical model has fallen out of favour. Instead, there is an appreciation that the patient has a unique experience of the illness involving the social, psychological, and behavioural effects of the disease.

The biomedical model

- Doctor is in charge of the consultation.
- Focus is on disease management.

The patient-centred model (see also Box 1.1)

- Power and decision-making is shared.
- Address and treat the whole patient.

Box 1.1 Key points in the patient-centred model

- Explore the disease and the patient's experience of it:
  - Understand the patient's ideas and feelings about the illness
  - Appreciate the impact on the patient's quality of life and psychosocial well-being
  - Understand the patient's expectations of the consultation.
- Understand the whole person:
  - Family
  - Social environment
  - Beliefs.
- Find common ground on management
- Establish the doctor–patient relationship
- Be realistic:
  - Priorities for treatment.
- Resources.

Becoming a good communicator

Learning

As in all aspects of medicine, learning is a lifelong process. One part of this, particularly relevant to communication skills and at the beginning of your career, is watching others.

The student should take every opportunity to observe doctor–patient and other interactions. Look carefully at how patients are treated by staff that you come across and consider every move that is made ... is that something that you could try yourself? Would you like to be treated in that way?

You should ask to be present during difficult conversations.

Instead of glazing over during consultations in clinic or on the ward round, you should watch the interaction and consider if the behaviours you see are worth emulating or avoiding. Consider how you might adjust your future behaviour.

'Cherry-pick' the things you like and use them as your own—building up your own repertoire of communication techniques.

Spontaneity versus learnt behaviours

If you watch a good communicator (in any field) you will see them making friendly conversation, spontaneous jokes, and using words and phrases that put people at ease. It seems natural, relaxed, and spontaneous.

Watching that same person interact with someone else can shatter the illusion as you see them using the very same 'spontaneous' jokes and other gambits from their repertoire.

This is one of the keys to good communication—an ability to judge the situation and pull the appropriate phrase, word, or action from your internal catalogue. If done well, it leads to a smooth interaction with no hesitations or misunderstandings. The additional advantage is that your mental processes are free to consider the next move, mull over what has been said, or consider the findings, whilst externally you are partially on 'auto-pilot'.

During physical examination, this is particularly relevant. You should be able to coax the wanted actions from the patient and put them at ease whilst considering the findings and your next step.

It must be stressed that this is *not* the same as lacking concentration—quite the opposite, in fact.

Essential considerations

Attitudes

Patients are entrusting their health and personal information to you—they want someone who is confident, friendly, competent, and above all, is trustworthy. See Box 1.2 for notes on confidentiality.

Personal appearance

First impressions count—and studies have consistently shown that your appearance (clothes, hair, make-up) has a great impact on the patients' opinion of you and their willingness to interact with you. Part of that intangible 'professionalism' comes from your image.

The white coat is no longer part of the medical culture in the UK. National guidance has widely been interpreted as 'bare below the elbow' with no long sleeves or jewellery. This does not mean that you should look scruffy, however. Many hospitals are now adopting uniforms for all their staff which helps solve some potential appearance issues. Fashions in clothing change rapidly but some basic rules still apply:

- Ensure you have a good standard of personal hygiene.
  - Any perfume or deodorant should not be overpowering
  - Many people believe men should be clean-shaven. This is obviously impossible for some religious groups and not a view shared by the authors. Facial hair should, however, be clean and tidy.
- Neutralize any extreme tastes in fashion that you may have.
- Men should usually wear a shirt. If a tie is worn, it should be tucked into the shirt when examining patients.
- Women may wear skirts or trousers but the length of the skirts should not raise any eyebrows.
- The belly should be covered—even during the summer.
- The shoulders, likewise, should usually be covered.
- Shoes should be polished and clean.
- Clean surgical scrubs may be worn if appropriate.
- Hair should be relatively conservatively styled and no hair should be over the face. It is advised to wear long hair tied up.
- Your name badge should be clearly visible—worn at the belt or on a lanyard around the neck is acceptable depending on hospital policy.
  - Note that lanyards should have a safety mechanism which will allow them to break open if pulled hard. Most hospitals supply these—be cautious about using your own lanyard from a shop or conference
  - Wearing a name badge at the belt means people have to look at your crotch – not necessarily ideal!
- Stethoscopes are best carried—worn at the neck is acceptable but a little pretentious, according to some views.
  - Try not to tuck items in your belt—use pockets or belt-holders for mobile phones, keys, and wallets.

▶ Psychiatry, paediatrics, and a handful of other specialties require a different dress code as they deal with patients requiring differing techniques to bond.

Timing

If in a hospital setting, make sure that your discussion is not during an allocated quiet time—or immediately before one is to start! You should also avoid mealtimes or when the patient's long-lost relative has just come to visit.

▶ If taking the patient from the bedside, ask the supervising doctor (if not you) and the nursing staff—and let all concerned know where you have gone in case the patient is needed.

Setting

Students, doctors, and others tend to see patients on busy wards which provide distractions that can break the interaction. Often this is necessary during the course of a busy day. However, if you are intending to discuss a matter of delicacy requiring concentration on both your parts, consider the following conditions:

- The room should be quiet, private, and free from disturbances.
- There should be enough seating for everyone.
- Chairs should be comfortable enough for an extended conversation.
- Arrange the seats close to yours with no intervening tables or other furniture.

Box 1.2 Confidentiality

As a doctor, healthcare worker, or student, you are party to personal and confidential information. There are certain rules that you should abide by and times when confidentiality must or should be broken. The essence for day-to-day practice is:

> Never tell anyone about a patient unless it is directly
> related to their care.

This includes relatives. Withholding information from family can be very difficult at times, particularly if a relative asks you directly about something confidential.

You can reinforce the importance of confidentiality to relatives and visitors. If asked by a relative to speak to them about a patient, you should approach the patient and ask their permission, preferably within view of the relative.

This rule also applies to friends outside of medicine. As doctors and others, we come across many amazing, bizarre, amusing, or uplifting stories on a day-to-day basis but, like any other kind of information, these should not be shared with anyone, however juicy the story is.

If you do intend to use an anecdote for some after-dinner entertainment, at the very least you should ensure that there is nothing in your story that could possibly lead to the identification of the person or persons involved.

Avoid medical jargon

The problem is that medics are so immersed in jargon that it becomes part of their daily speech. The patient may not understand the words or may have a different idea as to the meaning.

Technical words such as 'myocardial infarction' are in obvious need of avoidance or explanation. Consider terms such as 'exacerbate', 'chronic', 'numb', and 'sputum'—these may seem obvious in meaning to you but not to the patient. Be very careful to tease out the exact meaning of any pseudo-medical terms that the patient uses.

You may also think that some terms such as 'angina' and 'migraine' are well known—but these are very often misinterpreted.

Fear-words

There are certain words which immediately generate fear, such as 'cancer' and 'leukaemia'. You should only use these if you are sure that the patient wants to know the full story.

Beware, however, of avoiding these words and causing confusion by not giving the whole story.

You should also be aware of certain words that people will instinctively assume mean something more serious. For example, to most people a 'shadow' on the lung means cancer. Don't then use the word when you are talking about consolidation due to pneumonia!

The importance of silence

In conversations that you may have with friends or colleagues, your aim is to avoid silence using filler noises such as 'um' and 'ah' whilst pausing.

In medical situations, silences should be embraced and used to extract more information from the patient. Use silence to listen.

Practice is needed as the inexperienced may find this uncomfortable. It is often useful, however, to remain silent once the patient has answered your question. You will usually find that they start speaking again—and often impart useful and enlightening facts.

Remember the name

Forgetting someone's name is what we all fear but is easy to disguise by simple avoidance. However, the use of a name will make you seem to be taking a greater interest. It is particularly important that you remember the patient's name when talking to family. Getting the name wrong is embarrassing and seriously undermines their confidence in you.

Aside from actually remembering the name, it is a good idea to have it written down and within sight—either on a piece of paper in your hand or on the desk, or at the head of the patient's bed. To be seen visibly glancing at the name is forgivable.

Standing

Although this might be considered old-fashioned by some younger people, standing is a universal mark of respect. You should always stand when a patient enters a room and take your seat at the same time as them. You should also stand as they leave but, if you have established a good rapport during the consultation, this isn't absolutely necessary.

Greeting

Beware of 'good afternoon' and 'good morning'. These can be inappropriate if you are about to break some bad news or if there is another reason for distress. Consider instead a simple 'hello'.

Shaking hands

A difficult issue which, again, needs to be judged at the time.

Physical contact always seems friendly and warms a person to you—but a hand-shake may be seen as overly formal by some. It may be inappropriate if the patient is unable to reciprocate through paralysis or pain. Perhaps consider using some other form of touch—such as a slight guiding hand on their arm as they enter the room or a brief touch to the forearm.

Remember also that members of some religious groups may be forbidden from touching a member of the opposite sex.

Introductions

This is a potential minefield! You may wish to alter your greeting depending on circumstances—choose terms that suit you.

Title—them

Older patients may prefer to be called Mr or Mrs; younger patients would find it odd. Difficulty arises with females when you don't know their marital status. Some younger or married patients may find the term 'Ms' offensive.

Using the patient's first name may be considered too informal by some—whilst a change to using the family name mid-way through the encounter will seem very abrasive and unfriendly.

There are no rules here and common sense is required to judge the situation at the time. When unsure, the best option is always to ask.

Title—you

The title 'doctor' has always been a status symbol and a badge of authority—within the healthcare professions, at least. Young doctors may be reluctant to part with the title so soon after acquiring it but, in these days when consultations are becoming two-way conversations between equals, should you really introduce yourself as 'Dr'?

Many patients will simply call you 'doctor' and the matter doesn't arise. The authors prefer using first names in most circumstances but some elderly patients prefer—and expect—a certain level of formality so the situation has to be judged at the time.

Introducing yourself by the first name only seems too informal for most medical situations. Some young-looking students and doctors, however, may feel the need to introduce themselves using their title to avoid any misunderstanding of their role—particularly since the demise of the white coat. Perhaps worth considering is a longer introduction using both your names and an explanation along the lines of 'Hello, my name is Jane Smith, I am one of the doctors.'

General principles

Demeanour

Give the patient your full attention. Appear encouraging with a warm, friendly manner. Use appropriate facial expressions—don't look bored!

Define your role

Along with the standard introductions, you should always make it clear who you are and what your role is. You might also wish to say who your seniors are, if appropriate.

Be sure that anyone else in the room has also been introduced by name.

Style of questioning

Open questions versus closed questions

Open questions are those where any answer is possible. These allow the patient to give you the true answer in their own words. Be careful not to lead them with closed questions.

Compare 'How much does it hurt?' to 'Does it hurt a lot?' The former allows the patient to tell you how the pain feels on a wide spectrum of severity, the latter leaves the patient only two options—and will not give a true reflection of the severity.

Multiple choice questions

Often, patients have difficulty with an open question if they are not quite sure what you mean. A question about the character of pain, for example, is rather hard to form and patients will often not know quite what you mean by 'What sort of pain is it?' or 'What does it feel like, exactly?'

In these circumstances, you may wish to give them a few examples—but leave the list open-ended for them to add their own words. You must be very careful *not* to give the answer that you are expecting from them. For example, in a patient who you suspect has angina ('crushing' pain), you could ask, 'What sort of a pain is it…burning, stabbing, aching, for example…?'

Clarifying questions

Use clarifying questions to get the full details, particularly if there are terms used which may have a different meaning to the patient than to you.

Difficult questions

Apologise for potentially offensive, embarrassing, or upsetting questions ('I'm sorry to have you ask you this, but…').

Reflective comments

Use reflective comments to encourage the patient to go on and reassure them that you are following the story.

Staying on topic

You should be forceful but friendly when keeping the patient on the topic you want or moving the patient on to a new topic. Don't be afraid to interrupt them—some patients will talk for hours if you let them!

Eye-contact

▶ Make eye-contact and look at the patient when they are speaking.

Make a note of eye-contact next time you are in conversation with a friend or colleague.

In normal conversations, the speaker usually looks away whilst the listener looks directly at the speaker. The roles then change when the other person starts talking...and so on.

In the medical situation, whilst the patient is speaking, you may be tempted to make notes, read the referral letter, look at a test result, or similar—you should resist and stick to the 'normal' rules of eye-contact.

Adjusting your manner

You would clearly not talk to another doctor as you would someone with no medical knowledge. This is a difficult area, you should try to adjust your manner and speech according to the patient's educational level.

This can be extremely difficult—you should not make assumptions on intellect or understanding based solely on educational history.

A safe approach is to start in a relatively neutral way and then adjust your manner and speech based on what you see and hear in the first minute or two of the interaction—but be alert to whether this is effective and make changes accordingly.

Interruptions

Apologize to the patient if you are interrupted.

Don't take offence or get annoyed

As well as being directly aggressive or offensive, people may be thoughtless in their speech or manner and cause offence when they don't mean to. As a professional, you should rise above this and remember that apparent aggression may be the patient's coping mechanism, born from a feeling of helplessness or frustration—it is not a personal insult or affront.

Cross-cultural communication

Cultural background and tradition may have a large influence on disease management. Beliefs about the origin of disease and prejudices or stigma surrounding the diagnosis can make dealing with the problem challenging.

Be aware of all possible implications of a person's cultural background, both in their understanding of disease, expectations of healthcare, and in other practices that may affect their health.

Above all, be aware of prejudice—yours and theirs.

Body language: an introduction

Body language is rarely given the place it deserves in the teaching of communication skills. There are over 600 muscles in the human body; 90 in the face of which 30 act purely to express emotion. Changes in your position or expression—some obvious, others subtle—can heavily influence the message that you are communicating.

We've all met someone and thought 'I didn't like him' or alternatively 'she seemed trustworthy'. Often these impressions of people are not built on what is said but the manner in which people handle themselves. You subconsciously pick up cues from the other person's body. Being good at using body language means having awareness of how the other person may be viewing you and getting your subconscious actions and expressions under conscious control.

If done well, you can influence the other person's opinion of you, make them more receptive to your message, or add particular emphasis to certain words and phrases.

Touching

Touching is one of the most powerful forms of non-verbal communication and needs to be managed with care.

- *Greeting:* touch is part of greeting rituals in most cultures. It demonstrates that you are not holding a weapon and establishes intimacy.
- *Shaking hands:* there are many variations. The length of the shake and the strength of the grip impart a huge amount of information. For added intimacy and warmth, a double-handed grip can be used. For extra intimacy, one may touch the other's forearm or elbow.*
- *Dominance:* touch is a powerful display of dominance. Touching someone on the back or shoulder demonstrates that you are in charge—this can be countered by mirroring the action back.
- *Sympathy:* the lightest of touches can be very comforting and is appropriate in the medical situation where other touch may be misread as dominance or intimacy (you shouldn't hug a patient that you've only just met!). Display sympathy by a brief touch to the arm or hand.

Open body language

This refers to a cluster of movements concerned with seeming open. The most significant part of this is the act of opening—signalling a change in the way you are feeling. Openness demonstrates that you have nothing to hide and are receptive to the other person. Openness encourages openness.

This can be used to calm an angry situation or when asking about personal information.

The key is to not have your arms or legs crossed in any way.

---

* Watch the first few minutes of the 1998 film 'Primary Colors' which demonstrates the different uses of touch during handshakes.

- *Arms open:* either at your side or held wide. Even better, hold your hands open and face your palms to the other person.
- *Legs open:* this does not mean legs wide but rather not crossed. You may hold them parallel. The feet often point to something of subconscious interest to you—point them at the patient!

Emphasis

You can amplify your spoken words with your body—usually without noticing it. Actions include nodding your head, pointing, or other hand gestures. A gesture may even involve your entire body.

Watch newsreaders—often only their heads are in view so they emphasize with nods and turns of their heads much more than one would during normal conversation.

- *Synchrony:* this is key. Time points of the finger, taps of the hand on the desk, or other actions with the words you wish to emphasize.
- *Precision:* signal that the words currently being spoken are worth paying attention to with delicate, precise movements. You could make an 'O' with your thumb and index finger or hold your hands such that each finger is touching its opposite counterpart—like a splayed prayer position.

Eye level

This is a very powerful tool. In general, the person with their eye level higher is in control of the situation.

You can use this to your advantage. When asking someone personal questions or when you want them to open up, position yourself such that your eyes are below theirs—meaning they have to look down at you slightly. This makes them feel more in control and comfortable.

Likewise, anger often comes from a feeling of lack of control—put the angry person in charge by lowering your eye level—even if that means squatting next to them or sitting when they are standing.

Conversely, you may raise your eye level to take charge of a difficult situation: looking down on someone is intimidating. Stand over a seated person to demonstrate that you are in charge.

Watch and learn

There is much that could be said about body language. You should watch others and yourselves and consider what messages are being portrayed by non-verbal communication.

Stay aware of your own movements and consider purposefully changing what would normally be subconscious actions to add to, or alter, the meaning of your speech.

Interpreters

Official communicators are bound by a code of ethics, impartiality, and confidentiality—friends and relatives are not.

It is often impossible to be sure that a relative is passing on all that is said in the correct way.

Sometimes, the patient's children are used to interpret—this is clearly not advisable for a number of reasons. This not only places too much responsibility on the child but they may not be able to explain difficult concepts. In addition, conversations about sex, death, or other difficult topics may be unsuitable for the child to be party to.

Using an official interpreter

Before you start
- Brief the interpreter on the situation, clarify your role and the work of the department, if necessary.
- Allow the interpreter to introduce themselves to the patient and explain their role.
- Arrange seating so that the patient can see the interpreter and you equally.
- Allow enough time (at least twice as long as normal).

During the exchange
- Speak to the patient, not the interpreter. This may be hard at first, but you should speak to and look at the patient at all times.
- Be patient, some concepts are hard to explain.
- Avoid complex terms and grammar.
- Avoid jargon.
- Avoid slang and colloquialisms which may be hard to interpret correctly.
- Check understanding frequently.

Finishing off
- Check understanding.
- Allow time for questions.
- ▶ If the conversation has been distressing, offer the interpreter support and let their manager know.

Written information
- If interpreting written information, read it out loud. The interpreter may not necessarily be able to translate written language as easily.
- Many departments and charities provide some written information in a variety of languages—some also provide tapes. You should be aware of what your department has to offer.

Communicating with deaf patients

People who are hard of hearing may cope with the problem by using a hearing-aid, lip-reading, or using sign language. Whichever technique is used (if any), some simple rules should always apply:

- Speak clearly but not too slowly.
- Don't repeat a sentence if it is misunderstood—say the same thing in a different way.
- Write things down if necessary.
- Use plain English and avoid waffling.
- Be patient and take the time to communicate properly.
- Check understanding frequently.
- Consider finding an amplifier—many elderly medicine wards will have one available.

Lip-readers

Patients who are able to lip-read do so by looking at the normal movements of your lips and face during speech. Exaggerating movements or speaking loudly will distort these and make it harder for them to understand. In addition to the points already mentioned, when talking to lip-readers:

- Maintain eye-contact.
- Don't shout.
- Speak clearly but not too slowly.
- Do not exaggerate your oral or facial movements.

British Sign Language (BSL)

- It should be appreciated that BSL is not a signed version of English—it is a distinct language with its own grammar and syntax.
- For BSL users, English is a 2nd or 3rd language so using a pen and paper may not be effective or safe for discussing complex topics or gaining consent.
- Seek an official BSL interpreter, if possible, and follow the rules on working with interpreters.

Telephone communication

The essential rule of confidentiality is that you must not impart personal information to anyone without the express permission of the patient concerned—except in a few specific circumstances.

- You must not give out any confidential information over the telephone as you cannot be sure of the identity of the caller. All communication should be done face-to-face. This may cause difficulty if a relative calls to ask about the patient, but you should remain strict.
- If telephone communication is essential but you are in doubt as to the caller's identity, you may wish to take their number and call them back.

SBAR

SBAR was created as an easy to remember mechanism to frame conversations and install some uniformity into telephone communication, particularly those requiring a clinician's immediate attention and action. There are 4 sections to help you order the information with the right level of detail and reduce repetition.

S: Situation
- Identify yourself (name and designation) and where you are calling from.
- Identify the patient by name and the reason you are calling.
- Describe your concern in one sentence.

Include vital signs where appropriate.

B: Background
- State the admission diagnosis and date.
- Explain the background to the current problem.
- Describe any relevant treatment so far.

You should have collected information from the patient's charts, notes, and drug card and have this at your fingertips. Include current medication, allergies, pertinent laboratory results, and other diagnostic tests.

A: Assessment
- State your assessment of the patient including vital signs, early warning score (EWS), if relevant, and your overall clinical impression and concerns.

You should have considered what might be the underlying reason for the patient's current condition.

R: Recommendation
- 'I think the problem is . . .'.
- Explain what you need and the time-frame in which you need it.
- Make suggestions and clarify expectations.
- 'Is there anything else I should do?'
- ▶ Record the name and contact details of the person you have been speaking to.
- ▶ Record the details of the conversation in the patient's notes.

Other specific situations

Talking about sex

This is a cause of considerable embarrassment for the patient and for the inexperienced professional. Sexual questions are usually inappropriate to be overheard by friends or relatives—so ask them to leave. Your aim is to put the patient at ease and make their responses more forthcoming.

- The key is to ask direct, clear questions and show no embarrassment yourself.
- You should maintain eye-contact.
- You should also show no surprise whatsoever—even if the sexual practices described differ from your own or those that you would consider acceptable.
- Try to become au fait with sexual slang and sexual practices which you might not be familiar with previously.
  - A failure to understand slang may lead to an immediate barrier in the consultation.
- In general, you should not use slang terms first. You may wish to consider mirroring the patient's speech as you continue the conversation.

Angry patients

Use body language to take charge of the situation without appearing aggressive. Throughout the exchange, you should remain polite, avoiding confrontation, and resist becoming angry yourself.

- Look to your own safety first.
- Calm the situation then establish the facts of the case. Anger is often secondary to some other emotion such as loss, fear, or guilt.
- Acknowledge their emotions.
  - 'I can see this has made you angry'
  - 'It's understandable that you should feel like this.'
- Steer the conversation away from the area of unhappiness towards the positive and plans to move the situation forward.
- Don't incriminate colleagues—the patients may remember your throw-away comments which could come back to haunt you. Avoid remarks like 'he shouldn't have done that'.
- Emphasize any grounds for optimism, or plans for resolving the situation and putting things right.

Breaking bad news

Breaking bad news is feared by students and, indeed, no-one likes doing it. However, knowing that you have broken difficult news in a sensitive way and that you have helped the patient through a terrible experience can be one of the most uplifting aspects of working in healthcare.

Before you start

- Confirm all the information for yourself and ensure that you have all the information to hand, if necessary.
- Speak to the nursing staff to get background information on what the patient knows, their fears, and details of the relationship with any family or friends who may be present.

Choose the right place

- Pick a quiet, private room where you won't be disturbed.
- Ensure there is no intervening desk or other piece of furniture.
- Arrange the chairs so that everyone can be seen equally.
- Hand your bleep/mobile phone to a colleague.

Ensure the right people are present

- Invite a member of the nursing staff to join you—particularly if they have already established a relationship with the patient.
  - Remember, it is usually the nursing staff that will be dealing with the patient and relatives when you have left so they need to know exactly what was said.
- Would the patient like anyone present?

Establish previous knowledge

It is essential to understand what the patient already knows. The situation is very different in the case of a patient who knows that you have been looking for cancer to one who thinks their cough is due to a cold.

How much do they want to know?

This is key! Before you consider breaking bad news, you have to discover if the patient actually wants to hear it.

- Ask an open question such as:
  - 'What do you know so far?'
  - 'What have the other doctors/nurses told you?'
- You can also ask directly if they want to hear bad news. Say:
  - 'Are you the sort of person who likes to know all the available facts and details or would you rather a short version?'

Honesty, above all else

- Above all, you should be honest at all times. Never guess or lie.
- The patient may break your pre-prepared flow of information requiring you to think on your feet. Sometimes you simply can't stick to the rules above. If asked a direct question, you must be honest and straightforward.

Warning shots

You should break the news step-wise, delivering multiple 'warning shots'. This gives the patient a chance to stop you if they've heard enough, or to ask for more information. Keep your sentences short, clear, and simple.

You could start by saying that the test results show things are more 'serious' than first thought and wait to see their reaction. If they ask what you mean, you can tell them more, and so on.

▶ Inexperienced practitioners sometimes feel that they 'ought' to tell the patient the full story but they must understand that many people would much rather not hear the words said aloud—this is their coping strategy and must be respected.

Allow time for information to sink in

You should allow time for each piece of information to sink in, ensure that the patient understands all that has been said, and repeat any important information.

Remember also that patients will not be able to remember the exact details of what you have said—you may need to reschedule at a later time to talk about treatment options or prognosis.

Don't rush to the positive

When told of bad news, the patient needs a few moments to let the information sink in. Wait in silence for the patient to speak next.

The patient may break down in tears—in which case they should be offered tissues and the support of relatives, if nearby.

If emotionally distressed, the patient will not be receptive to what you say next—you may want to give them some time alone with a relative or nurse before you continue to talk about prognosis or treatment options.

Above all, you should not give false hope. The moment after the bad news has been broken is uncomfortable and you must fight the instinctive move to the positive with 'there are things we can do', 'on the plus side...', 'the good news is...', or similar.

Questions about time

'How long have I got?' is one of the most common questions to be asked—and the hardest to answer.

- As always, don't guess and don't lie.
- It's often impossible to estimate and is perfectly acceptable to say so. Giving a figure will almost always lead to you being wrong.
- Explain that it is impossible to judge and ask if there is any date in particular that they don't want to miss—perhaps they want to experience Christmas or a relative's birthday.

Ending the conversation

Summarize the information given, check their understanding, repeat any information as necessary, allow time for questions, and make arrangements for a follow-up appointment or a further opportunity to ask questions again.

Obviously, you shouldn't make promises that you can't keep. Don't offer to come back that afternoon if you're going to be in clinic!

Law, ethics, and consent

No discussion of communication skills would be complete without mention of confidentiality, capacity, and consent. It is also worth knowing the four bioethical principles about which much has been written elsewhere.

Four bioethical principles

- *Autonomy:* a respect for the individual and their ability to make decisions regarding their own health.
- *Beneficence:* acting to the benefit of patients.
- *Non-maleficence:* acting to prevent harm to the patient.
- *Justice:* 'fairness' to the patient and the wider community when considering the consequences of an action.

Confidentiality

Confidentiality is closely linked to the ethical principles described above. Maintaining a secret record of personal information shows respect for the individual's autonomy and their right to control their own information. There is also an element of beneficence where releasing the protected information may cause harm.

Breaking confidentiality

The rules surrounding the maintenance of confidentiality have been mentioned. There are a number of circumstances where confidentiality can, or must, be broken. The exact advice varies slightly between different bodies. See the links under 'further reading'. In general, confidentiality may be broken in the following situations:

- With the consent of the individual concerned.
- If disclosure is in the patient's interest but consent cannot be gained.
- If required by law.
- When there is a statutory duty such as reporting of births, deaths, and abortions and in cases of certain communicable diseases.
- If it is overwhelmingly in the public interest.
- If it is necessary for national security or where prevention or detection of a crime may be prejudiced or delayed.
- In certain situations related to medical research.

Consent and capacity

There are three main components to valid consent. To be competent (or have capacity) to give consent, the patient:

- Must understand the information that has been given.
- Must believe that information.
- Must be able to retain and weigh-up the information.

In addition, for consent to be valid, the patient must be free from any kind of duress.

▶ It should be noted that an assessment of capacity is valid for the specific decision in hand. It is not an all-or-nothing phenomenon—you cannot either have 'capacity' or not. The assessment regarding competence must be made for each new decision faced.

Young people and capacity
- All persons aged 18 and over are considered to be a competent adult unless there is evidence to the contrary.
- People aged between 16 and 18 are treated as adults (Family Law Reform Act 1969). However, the refusal of a treatment can be overridden by someone with parental responsibility or the courts.
- Children of 16 and younger are considered competent to give consent if they meet the three conditions mentioned previously. Their decisions can be, however, overridden by the courts or people with parental responsibility.

Gillick competence
In 1985, the well-known Gillick case was considered by the House of Lords and from this two principles (often known as the Fraser Guidelines) were established:
- A parent's right to consent to treatment on behalf of the child finishes when the child has sufficient understanding to give consent themselves (when they become 'Gillick competent').
- The decision as to whether the child is Gillick competent rests with the treating doctor.

Powers of attorney
People lacking mental capacity may need someone to manage their legal, financial, and health affairs. This is done through power of attorney as laid out in the Mental Capacity Act 2005.

Enduring powers of attorney (EPA)
Before 2007, people could grant EPA so a trusted person could manage their finances. Those with EPA do not have the right to make other decisions on a person's behalf.

Lasting powers of attorney (LPA)
Property and affairs LPA
Those with property and affairs LPA can make decisions regarding paying bills, collecting income and benefits, and selling property, subject to any restrictions or conditions the patient may have included.

Personal welfare LPA
This allows the 'attorney' to make decisions relating to living situation and other personal care. They can also make medical decisions *if this power has been expressly given in the LPA.*

Further reading
There are many other complex topics in this area and the law varies between countries and even between regions within the UK. We suggest the following as a good start:
- The British Medical Association: ℘ http://www.bma.org.uk
- The Medical Defence Union: ℘ http://www.the-mdu.com
- The Medical Protection Society: ℘ http://www.medicalprotection.org
- The UK Ministry of Justice: ℘ http://www.justice.gov.uk/
- The UK Department of Health: ℘ http://www.dh.gov.uk

The history

Using this book

This book is divided into chapters by organ system. In each chapter, there are suggestions as to how to proceed depending on the nature of the presenting complaint and notes on what you should especially ask about under each of the standard headings. These are not exhaustive and are intended as guidance to supplement a thorough history.

History taking

The history is a patient's account of their illness together with other relevant information that you have gleaned from them. Like all things in medicine, there is a tried and tested standard sequence which you should stick to and is used by all practitioners.

It is good practice to make quick notes whilst talking to the patient that you can use to write a thorough history afterwards—don't document every word they say as this breaks your interaction!

By the end of the history taking, you should have a good idea as to a diagnosis or have several differential diagnoses in mind. The examination is your chance to confirm or refute these by gaining more information.

History taking is not a passive process. You need to keep your wits about you and gently guide the patient into giving you relevant information using all the communication skills described in ➜ Chapter 1.

You should break the history down into headings and record it in the notes in this order—many people prefer to use the standard abbreviations (shown in Box 2.1) instead of writing out the heading in full.

Box 2.1 The standard history framework
- Presenting complaint (PC)
- History of presenting complaint (HPC)
- Past medical history (PMH)
- Drug history (DHx)
- Allergies/reactions
- Alcohol
- Smoking
- Family history (FHx)
- Social history (SHx)
- Systematic enquiry.

The outline in Box 2.1 is the authors' favoured method—slight variations exist. Remember to record the history thoroughly (see Box 2.2). See also notes on collateral histories in Box 2.3.

▶ Many people will put 'smoking' and 'alcohol' as part of the 'social history'. We feel that as these can have such an important impact on health they deserve their own spot and are more than simply 'what the patient does in their spare time'.

It is good practice in medicine to watch what other practitioners do and adapt the parts that you feel are done well to your own style, making them part of your own routine.

Box 2.2 Recording the history
- Documentation is a vital part of all medical interactions
- The history should be recorded in the patient's notes
- Remember, if it isn't written down, it didn't happen!

Box 2.3 Collateral histories

There are many situations when the patient may be unable to give a history (e.g. they are unconscious, delirious, demented, dysphasic, etc.). In these situations, you should make an effort to speak to all those who can help you fill in the gaps—not only regarding what happened to bring the patient to your attention now, but also regarding their usual medication, functional state, living arrangements, and so on.

When taking a history from a source other than the patient, be sure to document clearly that this is the case and why the patient is unable to speak for themselves.

Useful sources of information include:
- Relatives/cohabitants
- Close friends/room-mates
- The GP or other members of the primary care team
- The pharmacist
- The warden (if in sheltered accommodation)
- The staff at the nursing or residential home
- Anyone who witnessed the event.

Presenting complaint (PC)

- This is the patient's chief symptom(s) in their own words and should be no more than a single sentence.
  - ▶ Remember, this is the problem in the patient's words. 'Haemoptysis' is rarely a presenting complaint but 'coughing up blood' may well be.
- If the patient has several symptoms, present them as a list which you can expand on later in the history.
- Ask the patient an open question such as 'What's the problem?' or 'What made you come to the doctor?' Each practitioner will have their own style. You should choose a phrase that suits you and your manner (one of the authors favours 'tell me the story' after a brief introduction).
  - ❶ The question 'what brought you here?' usually brings the response 'an ambulance' or 'the taxi'—each patient under the impression that they are the first to crack this show-stopper of a joke. This is, therefore, best avoided.

History of the presenting complaint (HPC)

Here, you ask about and document the details of the presenting complaint. By the end of this, you should have a clear idea about the nature of the problem along with exactly how and when it started, how the problem has progressed over time, and what impact it has had on the patient in terms of their general physical health, psychology, social, and working lives.

This is best tackled in two phases:

First, ask an open question and allow the patient to talk through what has happened for about 2 minutes. Don't interrupt! Encourage the patient with non-verbal responses and make discreet notes. This also allows you to make an initial assessment of the patient in terms of education level, personality, and anxiety. Using this information, you can adjust your responses and interaction. It should also become clear to you exactly what symptom the patient is most concerned about.

In the second phase, you should revisit the whole story asking more detailed questions. It may be useful to say 'I'd just like to go through the story again, clarifying some details'. This is your chance to verify time-lines and the relationship of one symptom to another. You should also be careful to clarify pseudo-medical terms (exactly what does the patient mean by 'vertigo', 'flu', or 'rheumatism'?). Remember, this should feel like a conversation, not an interrogation!

▶ The standard features that should be determined for any symptom are shown in Box 2.4; the additional features regarding 'pain' are in Box 2.5.

See Box 2.6 for notes on the history of long-standing symptoms.

At the end of the history of presenting complaint, you should have established a *problem list*. You should run through this with the patient, summarizing what you have been told and ask them if you have the information *correct* and if there is *anything further* that they would like to share with you.

Box 2.4 For each symptom, determine:

- The exact nature of the symptom
- The onset:
  - The date it began
  - How it began (e.g. suddenly, gradually—over how long?)
  - If long-standing, why is the patient seeking help now?
- Periodicity and frequency:
  - Is the symptom constant or intermittent?
  - How long does it last each time?
  - What is the exact manner in which it comes and goes?
- Change over time:
  - Is it improving or deteriorating?
- Exacerbating factors:
  - What makes the symptom worse?
- Relieving factors:
  - What makes the symptom better?
- Associated symptoms.

Box 2.5 SOCRATES

The questions to ask about the characteristics of pain can be remembered with the mnemonic 'SOCRATES':

- S: Site (where is the pain worse? Ask the patient to point to the site with *one finger*)
- O: Onset (how did it come on? Over how long?)
- C: Character (i.e. 'dull', 'aching', 'stabbing', 'burning', etc.)
- R: Radiation (does the pain move or spread to elsewhere?)
- A: Associated symptoms (e.g. nausea, dyspepsia, shortness of breath)
- T: Timing (duration, course, pattern)
- E: Exacerbating and relieving factors
- S: Severity (scored out of 10, with '10' as the worst pain imaginable).

Box 2.6 Long-standing problems

If the symptom is long-standing, ask why the patient is seeking help now. Has anything changed? It is often useful to ask when the patient was last well. This helps focus their minds on the start of the problem which may seem distant and less important to them.

Past medical history (PMH)

Some aspects of the patient's past illnesses or diagnoses may have already been covered. Here, you should obtain detailed information about past illness and surgical procedures.

Ask if they're 'under the doctor for anything else' or have ever been to hospital before. Ensure you get dates and location for each event. There are some conditions which you should specifically ask patients about and these are shown in Box 2.7; see also the notes in Box 2.8.

For each condition, ask:
- When was it diagnosed?
- How was it diagnosed?
- How has it been treated?

For operations, ask about any previous anaesthetic problems.
   ❶ Ask also about immunizations and company/insurance medicals.

Box 2.7 PMH – ask specifically about:
- Diabetes
- Rheumatic fever
- Jaundice
- Hypercholesterolaemia
- Hypertension
- Angina
- Myocardial infarction
- Stroke or TIA
- Asthma
- TB
- Epilepsy
- Anaesthetic problems
- Blood transfusions.

Box 2.8 Don't take anything for granted!
- For each condition that the patient reports having, ask exactly how it was diagnosed (where? by whom?) and how it has been treated since
- For example, if the patient reports 'asthma', ask who made the diagnosis, when the diagnosis was made, if they have ever had lung function tests, if they have ever seen a chest physician at a hospital, if they are taking any inhalers
- Occasionally, the patient will give a long-standing symptom a medical name which can be very confusing. In this example, the patient's 'asthma' could be how they refer to their wheeze which is, in fact, due to congestive cardiac failure.

Drug history (DHx)

Here, you should list all the medications the patient is taking, including the dose, duration, and frequency of each prescription along with any significant side effects. If the patient is unsure, you should confirm with the GP or pharmacy. You should make a special note of any drugs that have been started or stopped recently.

You should also ask about compliance/adherence—does the patient know what dose they take? Do they ever miss doses? If they are not taking the medication—what's the reason? Do they have any compliance/adherence aids such as a pre-packaged weekly supply?

The patient may not consider some medications to be 'drugs' so specific questioning is required. Don't forget to ask about:

- Eye drops.
- Inhalers.
- Sleeping pills.
- Oral contraception.
- Over-the-counter drugs (bought at a pharmacy), vitamin supplements.
- Herbal remedies.
- 'Illicit' or 'recreational' drug use (record exactly what type of drug, route of administration, site, frequency of use, shared needles).

Allergies and reactions

This should be documented separately from the 'drug history' due to its importance.

Ask if the patient has any allergies or 'is allergic to anything' if they are unfamiliar with the term. Be sure to probe carefully as people will often tell you about their hay fever and forget about the rash they had when they took penicillin. Ask specifically if they have had any 'reactions' to drugs or medication.

▶ If an allergy is reported, you should obtain the exact nature of the event and decide if the patient is describing a true allergy, an intolerance, or simply an unpleasant side effect.

▶ All true allergies should be clearly recorded in the patient's case notes and drug chart.

Alcohol

Attempt to quantify, as accurately as you can, the amount and type of alcohol consumed daily/per week—and also establish if the consumption is spread evenly over the week or concentrated into a shorter period.

In the UK, alcohol is quantified in 'units' (1 unit = 10ml of alcohol).

In many European countries, and the US, alcohol is quantified as 'standard drinks'. In the US, a 'standard drink' contains 0.54 ounces of alcohol which is about 1.5 UK 'units'.

Units can be calculated as in Box 2.9 and Box 2.10.

If there is a suspicion of excess alcohol consumption, you may wish to use the quick 'CAGE and 'FAST' questionnaires shown in Boxes 2.11 and 2.12.

Recommended weekly alcohol consumption

- The Royal College of Physicians advises no more than 21 units per week for men and 14 units per week for women.
- The UK Department for Health advises alcohol consumption should not regularly exceed 3–4 units daily for men and 2–3 units daily for women.
- Both men and women should have at least 2 alcohol-free days per week.

Box 2.9 Calculating units

- You can work out how many units there are in any drink by multiplying the total volume of a drink (in ml) by its % alcohol by volume (ABV) or 'strength'. Divide the result by 1000
  - (Strength x volume)/1000
- Example:
  - 1 pint (568ml) of strong lager (ABV 5.2%)
  - = (5.2 x 568)/1000
  - = 2.95 units.

Box 2.10 Unit content of common drinks

- 1 unit = ½ pint of normal beer, single spirit shot
- 1.5 units = small glass of wine (125ml), bottle of alcopop
- 2 units = large bottle/can/pint normal beer, ½ pint of strong beer, medium glass of wine (175ml)
- 3 units = large bottle/can strong beer, large glass of wine (250ml)
- 9 units = bottle of wine
- 30 units = bottle of spirits.

Box 2.11 CAGE questionnaire

A positive response to any of the four questions may indicate someone at risk of alcohol abuse. A positive answer to two or more questions makes the presence of alcohol dependency likely.

- C: Have you ever felt that you should <u>C</u>ut down your drinking?
- A: Have you ever become <u>A</u>ngry when someone suggested that you should cut down?
- G: Do you ever feel <u>G</u>uilty about your drinking?
- E: Do you ever need an '<u>E</u>ye-opener' in the morning to steady your nerves or get rid of a hangover?

Box 2.12 FAST questionnaire (Fast Alcohol Screening Test)

- This questionnaire is used to identify hazardous drinking
- '1 drink' is defined as '1 unit' or ½ pint of beer, 1 glass of wine or 1 single spirit:

1. Men: How often do you have 8 or more drinks on one occasion?
1. Women: How often do you have 6 or more drinks on one occasion?

Never   Less than monthly   Monthly   Weekly   Daily

2. How often during the last year have you been unable to remember what happened the night before because you had been drinking?

Never   Less than monthly   Monthly   Weekly   Daily

3. How often during the last year have you failed to do what was normally expected of you because of drink?

Never   Less than monthly   Monthly   Weekly   Daily

4. In the last year, has a relative, or friend, or doctor, or other health worker been concerned about your drinking or suggested you cut down?

No   Yes, once   Yes, more than once

Scoring
- Question 1: never = not misusing alcohol; weekly/ daily = hazardous or harmful drinking. If other responses, go on to question 2
- Questions 1, 2, and 3: score each answer as 0, 1, 2, 3, 4 with never as 0 and daily as 4
- Question 4: no = 0; yes, once = 2; yes, more than once = 4
- Maximum score = 16.

The patient is misusing alcohol if the total score is more than 3.

Smoking

- Attempt to quantify the habit in 'pack-years'. 1 pack-year is 20 cigarettes per day for one year (e.g. 40/day for 1 year = 2 pack-years; 10/day for 2 years = 1 pack-year).
  - An alternative calculation which gets you the same result: (no. of cigarettes smoked per day x number of years)/20.
- Ask about previous smoking as many will call themselves non-smokers if they gave up yesterday or even on their way to the hospital or clinic. See Box 2.13 for notes on quantification.
- Remember to ask about passive smoking.
  - ❶ Be aware of cultural issues—smoking is forbidden for Sikhs, for example, and they may take offence at the suggestion.

Health problems related to tobacco

Cardiovascular
- Coronary heart disease.
- Peripheral vascular disease.
- Abdominal aortic aneurysm.

Respiratory
- COPD.
- Bronchitis.
- Pneumonia.

Neurological
- Cerebrovascular disease.

Sexual
- Erectile and ejaculatory dysfunction.

Neoplasias
- Oral cavity.
- Laryngeal.
- Pharyngeal.
- Bronchial/lung.
- Oesophageal.
- Gastric.
- Pancreatic.
- Renal.
- Cystic.
- Cervical.
- Acute myeloid leukaemia.

Other
- Infertility.
- Pre-term delivery.
- Still-birth.
- Low birth weight.
- Sudden infant death syndrome.

Some conditions where smoking can worsen symptoms

- Asthma.
- Chest infections including tuberculosis.
- Chronic rhinitis.
- Diabetic retinopathy.
- Optic neuritis.
- Hyperthyroidism.
- Multiple sclerosis.
- Crohn's disease.

Some conditions which smoking increases the risk of

- Dementia.
- Optic neuropathy.
- Cataracts.
- Macular degeneration.
- Pulmonary fibrosis.
- Psoriasis.
- Gum disease.
- Tooth loss.
- Osteoporosis.
- Raynaud's phenomenon.

Box 2.13 Haggling and the art of quantification

Smoking and alcohol histories are notoriously unreliable—alcohol especially so. The patient may be trying to please you or feel embarrassed about openly admitting their true consumption.

Gaining an accurate account of consumption can sometimes feel like haggling. There are two steps in this process.

Firstly, appear non-judgemental and resist acting surprised *in any way*, even in the face of liquor or tobacco consumption that you may consider excessive and unwise.

Secondly, if the patient remains reticent ('I smoke a few'), suggest a number—but start very high ('shall we say 60 a day?') and the patient will usually give you a number nearer the true amount ('oh no, more like 20'). If you were to start low, the same patient may only admit to half that.

Family history (FHx)

The FHx details:
- The make up of the current family, including the age and gender of parents, siblings, children, and extended family as relevant.
- The health of the family.

You should ask about any diagnosed conditions in other living family members. You should also document the age of death and cause of death for all deceased first-degree relatives and other family members if you feel it is appropriate.

It is worth noting that whilst many conditions run in families, some are due to a single gene disorder. If this is the case (such as Huntington's disease and cystic fibrosis) you should go back several generations for details of consanguinity and racial origins.

It may help to draw a family tree as shown in Box 2.14. These are particularly useful in paediatric assessments.

Social history (SHx)

This is your chance to document the details of the patient's personal life which are relevant to the working diagnosis, the patient's general well-being, and recovery/convalescence. It will help to understand the impact of the illness on the patient's functional status.

This is a vital part of the history but sadly, perhaps because it comes at the end, it is often given only brief attention. The disease, and indeed the patient, do not exist in a vacuum but are part of a community which they interact with and contribute to. Without these details, it is impossible to take an holistic approach to the patient's well-being.

Establish:
- Marital status, sexual orientation.
- Occupation (or previous occupations if retired).
  - You should establish the exact nature of the job if it is unclear—does it involve sitting at a desk, carrying heavy loads, travelling?
- Other people who live at the same address.
- The type of accommodation (e.g. house, flat—and on what floor).
- Does the patient own their accommodation or rent it?
- Are there any stairs? How many?
- Does the patient have any aids or adaptations in their house (e.g. rails near the bath, stairlift)?
- Does the patient use any walking aids (e.g. stick, frame, scooter)?
- Does the patient receive any help day-to-day?
  - Who from (e.g. family, friends, social services)?
  - Who does the laundry, cleaning, cooking, and shopping?
- Does the patient have relatives living nearby?
- What hobbies does the patient have?
- Does the patient own any pets?
- Has the patient been abroad recently or spent any time abroad in the past (countries visited, travel vaccination, malaria prophylaxis)?
- Does the patient drive?

Box 2.14 Family trees

Conventionally, males are represented by a square (□) and females by a circle (O). The patient that you are talking to is called the *propositus* and is indicated by a small arrow (↗).

Horizontal lines represent marriages or relationships resulting in a child. Vertical lines descend from these, connecting to a horizontal line from which the children 'hang'. You can add ages and causes of death.

Family members who have died are represented by a diagonal line through their circle or square (Ø, ⧄) and those with the condition of interest are represented by shaded shapes (●, ■).

See Figs 2.1 and 2.2 for examples of family trees.

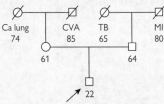

Fig. 2.1 Our patient is an only child and has no children, his parents are alive but all his grandparents have died of different causes.

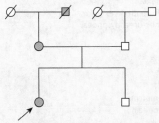

Fig. 2.2 Our patient suffers from colon cancer and has no children. She has a brother who is well. Her parents are both alive and her mother also has colon cancer. Of her grandparents, only her paternal grandfather is alive. Her maternal grandfather died of colon cancer.

Systematic enquiry (SE)

After talking about the presenting complaint, you should perform a brief screen of the other bodily systems.

This often proves to be more important than you expect, finding symptoms that the patient had forgotten about or identifying secondary, unrelated, problems that can be addressed.

The questions asked will depend on the discussion that has gone before. If you have discussed chest pain in the history of presenting complaint, there is no need to ask about it again.

General symptoms
- Change in appetite (loss or gain).
- Fever.
- Lethargy.
- Malaise.

Respiratory symptoms
- Cough.
- Sputum.
- Haemoptysis.
- Shortness of breath.
- Wheeze.
- Chest pain.

Cardiovascular symptoms
- Shortness of breath on exertion.
- Paroxysmal nocturnal dyspnoea.
- Chest pain.
- Palpitations.
- Ankle swelling.
- Orthopnoea.
- Claudication.

Gastrointestinal symptoms
- Weight loss or gain.
- Abdominal pain.
- Indigestion.
- Dysphagia.
- Odynophagia.
- Nausea.
- Vomiting.
- Change in bowel habit, diarrhoea, constipation.
- PR blood loss.

Genitourinary symptoms
- Urinary frequency.
- Polyuria.
- Dysuria.
- Haematuria.
- Nocturia.

Neurological symptoms
- Headaches.
- Dizziness.
- Tingling.
- Weakness.
- Tremor.
- Fits, faints, 'funny turns'.
- Black-outs.
- Sphincter disturbance.

Endocrine symptoms
- Heat or cold intolerance.
- Neck swelling (thyroid).
- Menstrual disturbance.
- Erectile dysfunction.
- Increased thirst.
- Sweating, flushing.
- Hirsutism.
- Muscle weakness.

Locomotor symptoms
- Aches, pains.
- Stiffness.
- Swelling.

Skin symptoms
- Lumps/bumps.
- Ulcers.
- Rashes.
- Other lesions (e.g. skin colour or texture change).
- Itch.

Sexual history

A detailed sexual history does not form part of the standard routine. However, if the patient complains of genitourinary symptoms, a full and thorough sexual history should be obtained.

This can be awkward for both the patient and the history taker. It should be undertaken in a sensitive, confident, and confidential manner. Before the discussion takes place, the patient should be reassured about the levels of privacy and confidentiality and that they are free to openly discuss their sexual life and habits.

Make no assumptions, remain professional, and try to use the patient's own words and language. Beware of cultural and religious differences surrounding both sex and talking about it.

You should approach a sexual history in a structured way.

Sexual activity

This should include an assessment of the risk of acquiring a sexually transmitted disease (STD).

You need to determine the number and gender of the patient's sexual partners, what their risk of having an STD is and what precautions (if any) were taken. Try asking the following questions:

- Do you have sex with men, women, or both?
- In the past 2 months, how many people have you had sex with?
- When did you last have sexual intercourse?
- Was it with a man or a woman?
- Were they a casual or regular partner?
- Where were they from?
- Do they use injected drugs?
- Do they have any history of STDs?
- How many other partners do you think they've had recently?
- In what country did you have sex?
- What kind of sex did you take part in (e.g. vaginal, anal, oral)?
- For each type of sex…did you use a condom?
- Does your partner have any symptoms?
- Have you had any other partners in the last 6 weeks?
  - If so, repeat the questions for each partner.

Previous history

You also need to establish the history of STDs for the patient.
- Have you had any other STDs?
- Have you ever had a sexual check-up?
- Have you ever been tested for HIV, hepatitis, or syphilis?
- Have you ever been vaccinated against hepatitis A or B?

Psychological factors

Concerns over loss of libido and sexual functioning may point to a complex psychological cause for the symptoms. Explore this delicately and ask about:

- A history of sexual abuse.
- Problems with the relationship.
- Sexual partners outside the relationship.
- Any other cause for anxiety.
- A history of depression or anxiety.

The elderly patient

Obtaining a history from older people might be regarded as no greater a task than from any patient—however cognitive decline, deafness, acute illness, and the middle of a night shift can make this difficult. Getting to grips with taking a good history from older people is a skill you will find useful in all other situations. Whilst the history is key for making diagnoses, it is an opportunity for so much more—your first interaction with an (older) patient sets important first impressions. A skilful history not only reaps diagnostic rewards, but marks you as a competent doctor who can gain trust, reassure, and communicate well with patients in any challenging situation (see Boxes 2.15 and 2.16 for more).

Box 2.15 Learning to listen

It can be tempting to ask lots of questions to obtain every fact in the history, particularly if you are rushed and faced with a clerking pro forma. Doing this will not only frustrate and offend your patient (because you clearly don't listen), but will also risk you missing important facts.

Instead, learn to stay quiet—and listen in detail to the history of the presenting complaint which may only be 3–4 minutes, but gives your patient a chance to be heard; seemingly irrelevant detail is often useful when patients have the chance to put it in context. It often saves you time, as other key information may emerge straight away and you can better focus the history.

Key points

- *Problem lists:* patients with chronic illness or multiple diagnoses may have more than one strand to their acute presentation. Consider breaking the history of the presenting complaint down into a problem list e.g. (1) worsening heart failure; (2) continence problems; (3) diarrhoea; (4) falls. This can often reveal key interactions between diagnoses you might not have thought about.
- *Drug history:* remember polypharmacy and that patients may not remember all the treatments they take. Be aware that more drugs mean more side effects and less concordance—so ask which are taken and why—(older) people are often quite honest about why they omit tablets. Eye drops, sleeping pills, and laxatives are often regarded as non-medicines by patients, so be thorough and ask separately—and avoid precipitating delirium due to acute withdrawal of benzodiazepines.
- *Past history:* as well as the traditional list of illnesses, remember to ask about recent admissions, whether to hospital or community/ intermediate care facilities. Do they see other disciplines in outpatients?
- *Functional history:* a comprehensive functional history is a cornerstone of your history taking in older people—we make no apologies for reminding you about this throughout this book. Diseases may not be cured or modified, but their key component—the effects on patients

and their lives—might be easily transformed through manipulation of activities of daily living. Remember to ask about formal and informal support for the patient at home—have things resulted in a crisis for the patient because a caring neighbour or friend is unwell? Be polite—and ask tactfully about benefits, including Attendance Allowance—many patients do not realize they might be eligible, so couch your questions with an explanation that advice might be available too.

- *Social history:* is exactly that, and should complement the functional history. Occupation (other than 'retired') can be of value when faced with a new diagnosis of pulmonary fibrosis or bladder cancer and may give your patient a chance to sketch out more about their lives. Enquire about family—don't assume that a relative may be able to undertake more help, as they may live far away; the patient may still have a spouse but be separated. Chat with patients about their daily lives—understanding interests and pursuits can help distract an unwell patient, give hope for the future, and act as a spur for recovery and meaningful rehabilitation. Learn to consider not just the patient and their acute illness, but a wider context that involves home, family, and potential issues such as carer strain.

Box 2.16 A note on narratives

Akin to 'learning to listen' is the recognition that many patients might not deliver their histories in a style that fits the traditional pattern described in this chapter. Pushing (older) patients through histories is not to be recommended. Elders will often discuss events and preferences with a constituted story, and it is important to recognize the value of this. Narrative analysis at its most simple—i.e. your ability to listen and interpret—is a vital skill for all clinicians. Listening to stories allows you to understand patients' preferences, hopes, and fears.

Remember also that older patients often have different views about what they want from their doctors. Their 'agendas' may differ hugely from what you think treatment plans should be, but they may not make their views known through fear of offending you. If you are unsure, always ask—learning to involve your patients in key decisions about their care will make you a better clinician.

General and endocrine examination

The eye in endocrine disease
Please turn to ➲ Chapter 9 for details of:
- Examination of the fundus.
- Eye signs in thyroid disease.
- The fundus in endocrine disease including diabetic retinopathy.

Approaching the physical examination

General conduct

Medical professionals are in a position of trust. It is generally assumed that you will act with professionalism, integrity, honesty, and with a respect for the dignity and privacy of your patients. In no part of the patient encounter is this more evident than at the physical examination.

People who you may have only just met will take off their clothes and allow you to look at and touch their bodies—something that would be completely unacceptable to many people in any other situation. They will, of course, be more comfortable with this if you have established an appropriate rapport during history taking. However, the communication does not stop at the end of the history. The manner in which you conduct yourself during the examination can make the difference between an effective examination and a formal complaint.

This is not to say that you should shy away from examining for fear of acting inappropriately and causing offence. In particular, you should not avoid examining members of the opposite sex, especially their intimate body parts, as there should be no sexual undertones in the relationship.

Projected confidence will be picked up by the patient, making them more at ease. Constant verbal and non-verbal communication should ensure that no misunderstandings occur. You should ensure that you have a chaperone present—another student, doctor, nurse, or other healthcare professional—whenever you perform any intimate examination. The chaperone should ideally be the same gender as the patient.

The format of the examination

The 'right' approach

One important rule is that you should always stand at the patient's right hand side. It is thought this gives them a feeling of control over the situation (most people are right handed), although there is no hard evidence to this effect. All the standard examination techniques are formulated with this orientation in mind.

The systems examinations

The physical examination can be broken into body systems—and this is the format of this book.

You often need to examine several systems at a time and it is then that you must combine your learnt techniques.

The examination framework

Each system examination is divided into 4 categories:
- Inspection (looking).
- Palpation (feeling).
- Percussion (tapping).
- Auscultation (listening).

In addition, there may be special tests and other added categories—but you will meet these as you go through the book.

First impressions

Diagnosis at first sight

From the first moment you set eyes on the patient, you should be forming impressions of their general state of health. It takes experience and practice to pick up all the possible clues but much can be gained by combining common sense with medical knowledge. Ask yourself:

- Is the patient comfortable or distressed?
- Is the patient well or ill?
- Is there a recognizable syndrome or facies?
- Is the patient well-nourished and hydrated?

Many of these features will be noted subconsciously—but you must make yourself consciously aware of them.

Bedside clues

In a hospital setting, there may be additional clues as to the patient's state of health in the objects around them. In other circumstances, look at objects that they are carrying or are visible in their pockets.

Examples include oxygen tubing, inhalers, GTN spray, insulin injections, glucose meter, or cigarettes.

Vital signs

It may also be appropriate to assess vital signs at an early stage. These usually include:

- Temperature.
- Blood pressure.
- Pulse.
- Oxygen saturation.
- Respiratory rate.
- Blood glucose.

Conscious level

If necessary, a rapid and initial assessment of a patient's conscious level can be made using the AVPU scale or the GCS.

Set-up

Before commencing a formal examination, introduce yourself, explain what you would like to do and obtain verbal consent.

- Ensure that the patient has adequate privacy to undress.
- Make sure that you will not be disturbed.
- Check that the examination couch or bed is draped/covered by a clean sheet or disposable towelling.
- If the patient is accompanied, ask them if they would like their companion(s) to stay in the room.
- Check that any equipment you will require is available (torch, cotton wool, tendon hammer, stethoscope, etc.).
- When ready, the patient should ideally be positioned supine with the head and shoulders raised to ~45°.

Colour

The colour of the patient, or parts of the patient, can give clues to their general state of health and to particular diagnoses. Look especially for evidence of pallor, central and peripheral cyanosis, jaundice, and abnormal skin pigmentation.

Pallor (paleness)

Facial pallor is often a sign of severe anaemia and is especially noticeable on inspecting the palpebral conjunctiva, nail beds, and palmar skin creases.

Ask the patient to look upward and gently draw down their lower eyelid with your thumb—the conjunctiva should be red/pink.

It is, however, an unreliable sign in shocked patients and those with vascular disease since peripheral vasoconstriction or poor blood flow causes skin and conjunctival pallor, even in the absence of blood loss.

Cyanosis

Cyanosis refers to a bluish discoloration of the skin and mucous membranes and is due to the presence of at least 2.5g/dl of deoxygenated haemoglobin in the blood.

Central cyanosis: the tongue appears blue due to an abnormal amount of deoxygenated blood in the arteries. This may develop in any lung disease in which there is a ventilation/perfusion mismatch such as chronic obstructive pulmonary disease ± cor pulmonale and massive pulmonary embolus. It will also occur in right to left cardiac shunts. Finally, polycythaemia and haemoglobinopathies (such as methaemoglobinaemia and sulphaemoglobinaemia) may give the appearance of cyanosis due to abnormal oxygen carriage.

Peripheral cyanosis: a bluish discoloration at the extremities (fingers, toes) only. It is usually due to a ↓ in blood supply or a slowing of the peripheral circulation. The latter commonly arises through exposure to cold, reduced cardiac output, or peripheral vascular disease.

Jaundice

Jaundice (icterus) refers to a yellow pigmentation of those tissues in the body which contain elastin (skin, sclerae, and mucosa) and occurs due to an ↑ in plasma bilirubin (visible at >35micromol/L).

Jaundice is best appreciated in fair-skinned individuals in natural daylight. Expose the sclera by gently holding down the lower lid and asking the patient to look upwards.

▶ Jaundice should not be confused with carotenaemia, which also causes a yellow discoloration of the skin, but the sclerae remain white.

Other abnormalities of coloration

You will meet other distinctive colour patterns through this book, a list here would be lengthy and probably unnecessary. These include the classic slate-grey appearance of haemochromatosis, the silver-grey coloration in argyria (silver poisoning), the ↑ skin-fold pigmentation seen in Addison's disease, and the non-pigmented patches of vitiligo.

Temperature

- Record the patient's temperature using either a mercury or electronic thermometer.
- The recording will depend on the site of measurement.
  - Normal oral temperature is usually considered to be 37°C
  - Rectal temperature is 0.5°C higher
  - Axillary temperature is 0.5°C lower.
- There is also a diurnal variation in body temperature.
  - Peak temperatures occur between 6pm and 10pm
  - Lowest temperatures occur between 2am and 4am.

High temperature

- The febrile pattern of most diseases also follows the diurnal variation described. Sequential recording of temperature may show a variety of patterns which can be helpful in diagnosis.
  - Persistent pyrexia may be a sign of malignant hyperthermia, a drug fever (e.g. halothane, suxamethonium), typhus, or typhoid fever
  - An intermittent pyrexia can be suggestive of lymphomas and pyogenic infections such as miliary TB
  - A relapsing high temperature or Pel–Ebstein fever occasionally occurs in patients with Hodgkin's disease and is characterized by 4–5 days of persistent fever which then returns to baseline before rising again.
- Also note any rigors (uncontrollable shaking) which may accompany high fever and are often considered characteristic of biliary sepsis or pyelonephritis, although can occur in the context of any sepsis.

Low temperature

- Hypothermia is a core (rectal) temperature of <35°C and occurs usually from cold exposure (e.g. near-drowning) or secondary to an impaired level of consciousness (e.g. following excess alcohol or drug overdose) or in the elderly (e.g. myxoedema).
- Patients may be pale with cold, waxy skin and stiff muscles, consciousness is often reduced.
- Patients typically lose consciousness at temperatures <27°C.

Hydration

You may already have obtained clues regarding hydration status from the history. For example, a patient may have been admitted with poor fluid intake and may feel thirsty. Sepsis, bleeding, or bowel obstruction and vomiting can also cause a person to become dehydrated.

Examination

- Begin with looking around the patient for any obvious clues including fluid restriction signs, catheter bag, or nutritional supplements.
- Inspect the face for sunken orbits (moderate–severe dehydration).
- *Mucous membranes:* inspect the tongue and mucous membranes for moisture.
  - Dehydration will cause these surfaces to appear dry.
- *Skin turgor:* assess by gently pinching a fold of skin on the forearm, holding for a few moments, and letting go.
  - If normally hydrated, the skin will promptly return to its original position, whereas in dehydration (reduced skin turgor), the skin takes longer to return to its original state
  - ❶ This sign is unreliable in elderly patients whose skin may have lost its normal elasticity.
- *Capillary refill:* test by raising the patient's thumb to the level of the heart, pressing hard on the pulp for 5 seconds, and then releasing. Measure the time taken for the normal pink colour to return.
  - Normal capillary refill time should be <2 seconds; a prolongation is indicative of a poor blood supply to the peripheries.
- *Pulse rate:* a compensatory tachycardia may occur in dehydration or in fluid overload.
- *Blood pressure:* check lying and standing blood pressure readings and look for a low blood pressure on standing (orthostatic hypotension) which may suggest dehydration.
- *JVP:* Assess the height of the JVP which is one of the most sensitive ways of judging intravascular volume (see ➲ Chapter 5).
  - The JVP is low in dehydration, but raised in fluid overload (e.g. pulmonary oedema).
- *Oedema:* another useful sign of fluid overload (think right heart failure, constrictive pericarditis, hypoalbuminaemia). Remember to test for both ankle and sacral oedema.

Oedema

Oedema refers to fluid accumulation in the tissues, particularly the subcutaneous layer, and implies an imbalance of the Starling forces (↑ intravascular pressure or reduced intravascular oncotic pressure) causing fluid to seep into the interstitial space.

Oedema will occur in hypoproteinaemic states (especially nephrotic syndrome, malnutrition, and malabsorption) and severe cardiac and renal failure.

Other causes of leg swelling are outlined in Box 3.1.

Examination

In ambulant patients, palpate the medial distal shaft of the tibia (the 'bare area') for oedema by gently compressing for up to 10 seconds with the thumb. If the oedema is 'pitting', the skin will show an indentation where pressure was applied which refills slowly.

▶ If oedema is present, note how far it extends proximally. What is the highest point at which you can detect oedema? Peripheral oedema may also involve the anterior abdominal wall and external genitalia.

When lying down, fluid moves to the new dependent area causing a 'sacral pad'. This can be checked for by asking the patient to sit forwards, exposing the lower back and sacral region, and again applying gentle pressure with your fingertips.

Box 3.1 Some causes of leg swelling

Local causes

- Cellulitis (usually unilateral)
- Ruptured Baker's cyst (usually unilateral)
- Occlusion of a large vein—i.e. thrombophlebitis, deep vein thrombosis (DVT), extrinsic venous compression
- Chronic venous insufficiency—pigmentation induration, inflammation, lipodermatosclerosis
- Lipomatosis
- Gastrocnemius rupture—swelling and bruising around the ankle joint and foot.

Systemic causes

- Congestive cardiac failure
- Hypoproteinaemia (nephrotic syndrome, liver cirrhosis, protein-losing enteropathy, kwashiorkor)
- Hypothyroidism
- Hyperthyroidism
- Drugs (e.g. corticosteroids, NSAIDs, vasodilators).

Lymphoedema

- This is non-pitting oedema associated with thickened and indurated skin
- It can be idiopathic or secondary to proximal lymphatic obstruction such as post surgery, metastatic cancer, or chronic infection.

Nutritional status

The nutritional status of the patient may be an important marker of disease and is often overlooked in physical examination.

There are simple clinical measures with can easily be undertaken to assess a patient's overall nutritional status.

General physical appearance

- Note the patient's overall body habitus; are they fat or thin?
- Do they appear to have recently lost or gained weight?
  - Weight loss can lead to muscle wasting seen as skeletal prominence, especially cheek bones, head of humerus, major joints, rib cage, and the bony landmarks of the pelvis.

Body weight and height

All patients should be weighed using accurate scales and have their height recorded (ideally using a stadiometer).

Body mass index

The body mass index (BMI) is a useful estimate of body fatness.

$$BMI = \frac{weight(kg)}{[height(m)]^2}$$

The World Health Organization has classified BMI as follows:

- 19–25 = normal.
- 25–30 = overweight.
- 30–40 = obese.
- >40 = extreme or 'morbid' obesity.

Regional fat distribution

A central distribution of fat (waist:hip circumference ratio of >1.0 in men and >0.9 in women) is associated with higher morbidity and mortality.

Skin fold thickness

Skin fold thickness is another useful method of assessing muscle and fat status and is usually measured at the triceps halfway between the olecranon and acromial processes. This is measured using specialist calipers.

The examiner should pinch a fold of skin and subcutaneous tissue between thumb and first finger and then apply the calipers to the skin fold. Three measurements are normally taken and the average calculated (normal values are 20mm in men and 30mm in women).

Mid-arm circumference

An additional method for estimating body fatness at the bedside is to measure mid-arm muscle circumference.

As with skin fold thickness, use the midpoint between the tip of the olecranon and acromial processes as your standard measurement point.

With the arm in a flexed right-angle position, take 3 tape measurements at this point before calculating the average. Standard age/sex charts are available.

Some conditions associated with malnutrition

- Any very ill patient.
- Malignancy.
- Metabolic disease (e.g. renal failure).
- Gastrointestinal disease (especially small bowel).
- Sepsis.
- Trauma.
- Post-surgery.
- Psychosocial problems (e.g. depression, anorexia nervosa, social isolation).

Some conditions associated with obesity

- Simple obesity ('biopsychosocial').
- Genetic e.g. Prader–Willi, Lawrence–Moon–Biedl syndrome.
- Endocrine (e.g. Cushing's syndrome, hypothyroidism).
- Drug-induced (e.g. corticosteroids).
- Hypothalamic damage due to tumour or trauma.

Lymph nodes

An examination of the lymph nodes forms part of the routine for most body systems. As there is no need to percuss or auscultate, examination involves inspection followed by palpation.

It should be remembered that there are a great many lymph nodes that are not accessible to the examining hand—for example, along the aorta, in the intestinal mesentery, and so on. There are several groups of lymph nodes that are accessible for the purposes of physical examination.

In the head and neck, these are located along the anterior and posterior aspects of the neck and on the underside of the jaw. In the upper limb and trunk, lymph nodes are located in the epitrochlear and axillary regions and in the lower limbs nodes can be examined in the inguinal and popliteal regions.

▶ Remember that the liver and spleen are often enlarged in the presence of generalized lymphadenopathy and these should be examined as in ➔ Chapter 7.

Inspection

Large nodes are often clearly visible on inspection, particularly if the enlargement is asymmetrical. If nodes are infected, the overlying skin may be red and inflamed.

Palpation

Lymph nodes should be palpated using the most sensitive part of your hands—the fingertips.

- *Head and neck (see Fig. 3.1):* the nodes should be palpated with the patient in an upright position and the examiner standing behind— similar to the examination of the thyroid gland.
- *Axillae (see Fig. 3.2):* To examine the nodes at the right axilla:
  - The patient should be sitting comfortably and you should stand at their right-hand side
  - Support their right arm abducted to 90° with your right hand
  - Examine the axilla with your left hand
  - To examine the nodes at the left axilla, perform the opposite manoeuvre.
- *Inguinal (see Fig. 3.3):* with the patient lying supine, palpate their inguinal region along the inguinal ligament—the same position as feeling for a hernia (➔ Chapter 7) or the femoral pulse (➔ Chapter 5).
  - There are 2 chains of superficial inguinal lymph nodes—a horizontal chain which runs just below the inguinal ligament and a vertical chain which runs along the saphenous vein.
- *Epitrochlear nodes:* place the palm of the right hand under the patient's slightly flexed right elbow and feel with your fingers in the groove above and posterior to the medial epicondyle of the humerus.
- *Popliteal:* best examined by passively flexing the knee and exploring the fossa with the fingers of both hands—much like feeling for the popliteal pulse.

Findings

Similar to the considerations to make when examining a lump (➋ Chapter 4), during palpation of lymph nodes, standard features should be assessed:

Site

- Important diseases such as both acute and chronic infections and metastatic carcinoma will cause localized lymphadenopathy depending on the site of primary pathology.
- It is often helpful to draw a diagram detailing exactly where the enlarged node is. See Box 3.2 for causes of generalized lymphadenopathy.

Number

- How many nodes are enlarged?
- Make a diagram and detail the palpable nodes clearly and carefully.

Size

- Normal nodes are not palpable.
- Palpable nodes, therefore, are enlarged.
  - You should measure their length and width.

Consistency

- Malignant lymph nodes feel unusually firm or hard and irregular.
- Enlarged nodes secondary to infection may feel 'rubbery'.

Tenderness

- Painful, tender nodes usually imply infection.

Fixation

- Nodes that are fixed to surrounding tissue are highly suspicious of malignancy.
- Matted glands may occur in tuberculous lymphadenopathy.

Overlying skin

- Inflamed nodes may cause redness and swelling in the overlying skin.
- Spread of a metastatic carcinoma into the surrounding tissue may cause oedema and surface texture changes.

Box 3.2 Some causes of generalized lymphadenopathy

- Haematological malignancies (e.g. lymphoma, acute, and chronic lymphatic leukaemia)
- Infections:
  - Viral (e.g. HIV, infectious mononucleosis, CMV)
  - Bacterial (e.g. tuberculosis, syphilis, brucellosis)
- Infiltrative diseases (e.g. sarcoidosis, amyloidosis)
- Autoimmune diseases (e.g. systemic lupus erythematosus, rheumatoid arthritis)
- Drugs (e.g. phenytoin causes a 'pseudolymphoma').

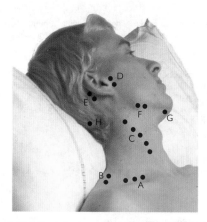

A = Supraclavicular
B = Posterior triangle
C = Jugular chain
D = Preauricular
E = Postauricular
F = Submandibular
G = Submental
H = Occipital

Fig. 3.1 Cervical and supraclavicular lymph nodes.

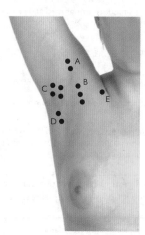

A = Lateral
B = Pectoral
C = Central
D = Subscapular
E = Infraclavicular

Fig. 3.2 Axillary lymph nodes.

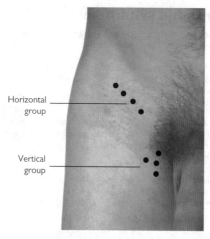

Horizontal group

Vertical group

Fig. 3.3 Inguinal lymph nodes.

Hands and upper limbs

Examination of the hands is an important part of all examination routines and may provide a huge number of diagnostic clues. It is also something that the student may be asked to perform on a regular basis.

You will meet various 'hand signs' throughout this book. Detailed hand examination is described in ➜ Chapters 8 and 10, the nervous system and the locomotor system, so is not repeated here. See also ➜ Chapter 4 for details of skin and nail signs in the hands.

Be sure to include assessment of:
- Both the dorsal surface and the palm.
- Skin colour.
- Discrete lesions.
- Muscles.
- Joints.
- Bony deformities.
- Nails.
- Remember to palpate and test movement and sensation.

After examining the hands, palpate both the radial and ulnar pulses.

Elbows

- Always examine the elbows to elicit any clues as to the cause of joint pathology.
- For example, there may be rheumatoid nodules, psoriatic plaques, xanthomata, or scars.

Recognizable syndromes

Some physical (especially facial) characteristics are so typical of certain congenital, endocrine, and other disorders that they immediately suggest the diagnosis.

Certain physical features of conditions can be appreciated on first inspection—enabling a 'spot diagnosis'. Most of these conditions have many other features which are not detailed here.

Down's syndrome (trisomy 21)

- *Facies:* oblique orbital fissures, epicanthic folds, hypertelorism (widely spaced eyes), conjunctivitis, lenticular opacities, small low-set ears, flat nasal bridge, mouth hanging open, protruding tongue (large, heavily fissured).
- *Hands:* single palmar crease (not pathognomonic), short broad hands, curved little finger, hyperflexible joints with generalized hypotonia.
- *Other:* mental deficiency, wide gap between 1st and 2nd toes, short stature, dementia of Alzheimer type, hypothyroidism.

Turner's syndrome (45 XO)

- *Facies:* micrognathia (small chin), epicanthic folds, low-set ears, fish-like mouth, hypertelorism, ptosis, strabismus.
- *Neck:* short, webbed neck, redundant skin folds at back of neck, low hairline.
- *Chest:* shield-like chest, widely spaced nipples.
- *Limbs:* short fourth metacarpal or metatarsal, hyperplastic nails, lymphoedema, increased carrying angle of the elbow.

Marfan's syndrome

Autosomal dominant condition caused by defects in fibrillin gene (ch15q).

- *Facies:* long, narrow face, high-arched palate, lens dislocation, heterochromia of iris, blue sclera, myopia.
- *Limbs:* tall stature, armspan > height, hyperextensibility of joints, recurrent dislocations.
- *Hands:* elongated fingers and toes (arachnodactyly).
- *Chest:* funnel or pigeon chest, kyphoscoliosis, aortic incompetence.
- *Other:* cystic disease of the lungs (spontaneous pneumothorax, bullae, apical fibrosis, aspergilloma and bronchiectasis), inguinal or femoral herniae.

Tuberous sclerosis

Also known as Bourneville's disease of the skin. Autosomal dominant condition localized to chromosomes 16 and 9.

- *Skin:* adenoma sebaceum (angiofibromata—papular, salmon-coloured eruption on centre of the face, especially at the nasolabial folds); shagreen patches (flesh-coloured, lumpy plaques found mostly on the lower back); ungal fibromata (firm, pink, periungual papules growing out from nail beds of fingers and toes); hypopigmented 'ash-leaf' macules (trunk and buttocks); café-au-lait macules and patches.

Neurofibromatosis type 1

Also known as von Recklinghausen's disease—autosomal dominant.
- *Skin:* neurofibromata (single, lobulated or pedunculated, soft, firm, mobile, lumps or nodules along the course of nerves), café-au-lait spots (especially in the axillae), axillary freckling.
- *Other:* kyphoscoliosis, nerve root involvement or compression, muscle wasting, sensory loss (Charcot's joints), plexiform neuroma, lung cysts.

Peutz–Jeghers syndrome

- *Skin:* sparse or profuse small brownish-black pigmented macules on lips, around mouth and on buccal mucosa, hands, and fingers.

Oculocutaneous albinism

- Marked hypomelanosis (pale skin), white hair or faintly yellow blonde.
- Nystagmus, photophobia, hypopigmented fundus, translucent (pink) iris.

Myotonic dystrophy*

- *Facies:* myopathic facies (drooping mouth and long, lean, sad, sleepy expression), frontal balding in men, ptosis, wasting of facial muscles (especially temporalis and masseter), cataracts.
- *Other:* wasting of sternomastoids, shoulder girdle, and quadriceps, areflexia, myotonia (percussion in tongue and thenar eminence, delay before releasing grip), cardiomyopathy, slurred speech, testicular atrophy, diabetes, intellect and personality deterioration in later stages.

Parkinson's disease*

- *Facies:* expressionless, unblinking face, drooling, titubation, blepharoclonus (tremor of eyelids when eyes gently closed).
- *Gait:* shuffling, festinant gait with reduced arm swing.
- *Tremor:* pill-rolling tremor, lead-pipe rigidity, cog-wheel rigidity, glabellar tap positive, small, tremulous, untidy hand writing (micrographia).

Osler–Weber–Rendu syndrome

Also known as hereditary haemorrhagic telangiectasia (HHT).
- *Facies:* telangiectasia (on face, around mouth, on lips, on tongue, buccal mucosa, nasal mucosa), telangiectasia may also be found on fingers. Associated with epistaxis, GI haemorrhage, iron-deficiency anaemia, haemoptysis.

Systemic sclerosis/CREST syndrome

- *Face/hands:* telangiectasia and pigmentation, pinched nose, perioral tethering, tight, shiny and adherent skin, vasculitis, atrophy of finger pulps, calcinosis (fingers), Raynaud's phenomenon.

---

* More detail in ➔ Chapter 8.

Vitamin and trace element deficiencies

Fat-soluble vitamins

Vitamin A (retinol)
- Found in dairy produce, eggs, fish oils, and liver.
- Deficiency causes night blindness, xerophthalmia, keratomalacia (corneal thickening), and follicular hyperkeratosis.

Vitamin D (cholecalciferol)
- Found in fish liver oils, dairy produce, and undergoes metabolism at the kidneys and the skin using UV light.
- Deficiency causes rickets (in children) and osteomalacia (in adults). Proximal muscle weakness may be evident.

Vitamin E (alpha-tocopherol)
- Widely distributed, green vegetables, and vegetable oils.
- Deficiency causes haemolytic anaemia (premature infants) and gross ataxia.

Vitamin K (K_1 = phylloquinine, K_2 = menaquinone)
- Widely distributed but particularly in green vegetables. Synthesized by intestinal bacteria.
- Deficiency causes coagulation defects seen as easy bruising and haemorrhage.

Water-soluble vitamins

Vitamin B_1 (thiamine)
- Found in cereals, peas, beans, yeast, and wholemeal flour. An essential factor in carbohydrate metabolism and transketolation reactions.
- Deficiency causes dry beri-beri (sensory and motor peripheral neuropathy), wet beri-beri (high output cardiac failure and oedema), and Wernicke–Korsakoff syndrome.

Vitamin B_2 (riboflavin)
- Found in wholemeal flour, meat, fish, and dairy produce. A coenzyme in reversible electron carriage in oxidation–reduction reactions.
- Deficiency gives angular stomatitis (fissuring and inflammation at the corners of the mouth), inflamed oral mucous membranes, seborrhoeic dermatitis, and peripheral neuropathy.

Vitamin B_3 (niacin)
- Found in fish, liver, nuts, and wholemeal flour.
- Deficiency causes pellagra: dermatitis, diarrhoea, and dementia.

Vitamin B_6 (pyridoxine)
- Widespread distribution, also synthesized from tryptophan.
- Deficiency causes peripheral neuropathy, convulsions, and sideroblastic anaemia. Deficiency may be provoked by a number of commonly used drugs (e.g. isoniazid, hydralazine, penicillamine) and is also seen in alcoholism and pregnancy.

Vitamin B₉ (folic acid)

- Deficiency can be caused by poor diet, malabsorption states, coeliac disease, Crohn's disease, gastrectomy, drugs (e.g. methotrexate, phenytoin), excessive utilization (e.g. leukaemia, malignancy, inflammatory disease).
- Consequences of deficiency include megaloblastic anaemia and glossitis.

Vitamin B₁₂ (cyanocobalamin)

- Causes of a deficiency are numerous and include partial or total gastrectomy, Crohn's disease, ileal resection, jejunal diverticulae, blind loop syndrome, and tapeworm.
- Deficiency causes megaloblastic anaemia, peripheral neuropathy, subacute combined degeneration of the spinal cord, depression, psychosis, and optic atrophy.

Vitamin C (ascorbic acid)

- Deficiency causes scurvy (perifollicular haemorrhage, bleeding swollen gums, spontaneous bruising, corkscrew hair, failure of wound healing), anaemia, and osteoporosis.

Trace elements

Copper

- Deficiency results in hypochromic and microcytic anaemia, neutropenia, impaired bone mineralization, Menkes' kinky hair syndrome (growth failure, mental deficiency, bone lesions, brittle hair, anaemia), sensory ataxia, muscle weakness, visual loss (optic neuropathy), peripheral neuropathy.
  - Usually caused by copper malabsorption.

Zinc

- Deficiency causes achondromatosis enterpathica (infants develop growth retardation, hair loss, severe diarrhoea, candida and bacterial infections), impaired wound healing, skin ulcers, alopecia, night blindness, confusion, apathy, and depression.

Magnesium

- Severe deficiency can cause cardiac arrhythmias, paraesthesia, and tetany.

Iodine

- Severe deficiency can cause cretinism (children), hypothyroidism, and goitre.

The elderly patient

For Nigel Hawthorne's on-screen King George III, examination by his doctor during an attack of porphyria was 'the very last resort' and viewed as an 'intolerable intrusion'. However, for older people, in whom the 'typical' presentations of illness may be subtle or unusual, a thorough physical examination is a cornerstone of assessment.

The value of a thorough physical examination can be underestimated by doctors, but be highly regarded as a therapeutic benefit by patients. This general overview complements the system-based chapters that follow, but the key message is repeated throughout—to reinforce the value of a comprehensive, holistic, and unrushed examination.

General points

Use your eyes
- A key question in your mind should be 'is the patient unwell?'
- Learn not to overlook key indices such as hypothermia and delirium which point to an acutely unwell patient.

Seek additional diagnoses
- Multiple illnesses are a typical feature of old age—seemingly incidental findings (to the presenting condition) are common, so look out for such things as:
  - Skin lesions (malignant?)
  - New/isolated patches of 'psoriasis' (Bowen's disease?)
  - Asymptomatic peripheral arterial disease.

Talk to your patient
- During the examination as well as during the history.
- As indicated, it is often of huge therapeutic benefit, of reassurance, engendering trust, and potentially gaining additional history—especially if an incidental lesion is discovered.

Key points

Observations
- Nurses spend time recording them—so do your colleagues the courtesy of recording them in the notes, *and act on them.*
- Many patients may run low blood pressures, often as a consequence of medications—a small drop from this point is easily overlooked, but may be the only sign of a myocardial infarction.
- Recognize the limits of temperature/fever—seriously unwell older people may actually be hypothermic.
- Recognize the limits of early warning scores for older people, especially with chronic diseases as you may be falsely reassured.

Hydration
- May be difficult to assess—reduction in skin turgor through changes in elasticity with age, dry mucous membranes (e.g. through mouth breathing), or sunken eyes (muscle wasting, weight loss) are useful in younger patients, but less reliable in elders.
  - ▶ A useful alternative is axillary palpation—are they sweating?

Skin and nail health
- Asteatosis and varicose eczema are common, but easily overlooked.
- Look out for typical lesions in atypical places—squamous cell carcinomas are notorious in this respect.
- Learn to look at footwear/toenails—is there onychogryphosis?

Nutrition
- Signs of weight loss are often obvious—ill-fitting clothes and dentures are good examples.

Joints
- Remember to look and examine—is the patient's mobility worse, or the reason for falling acute (pseudo) gout?

MMSE/AMTS
- Should be mandatory for the majority of patients.

Gait (where possible)
- Akin to mental state examination, should be undertaken whenever possible. See ➲ Chapter 10 for the 'get up and go' test.

Geriatric giants

So described by Bernard Isaacs, one of the key figures of contemporary geriatric medicine. Isaacs described five 'giants':
▶ These are not 'diagnoses', so avoid reaching them—but extremely common presentations of illness in older people, for which an underlying cause (or causes!) should be sought.
- Immobility.
- Instability.
- Incontinence.
- Intellectual impairment.
- Iatrogenic illness.

Information gathering

Faced with an acutely unwell, delirious patient, no old notes or GP letter and 'little to go on', it can be tempting to fall back on Isaacs' giants as a diagnosis. Make that extra effort to enquire of others for information which will reveal vital clues:
- Family and carers (e.g. care home staff): a real opportunity to update family, reassure or open up a conversation about other issues.
- IT: virtually all hospitals allow access to e-systems that record clinic letters, discharge notes, and results.
- GP surgeries: both for the Summary Care Record/current prescription and a discussion with one of the GPs, who is likely to know the patient better than you.
- Community services: you will often find that the rest of the multi-disciplinary team are ahead of you in liaising and gathering important information from homecare, district nurses, and intermediate care.

Symptoms in endocrinology

As hormones have an impact on every body system, it is therefore necessary to cover all areas of general health in history taking.

This section outlines some of the more important presenting symptoms in endocrine disease which should not be missed (if a high index of clinical suspicion is held regarding endocrine dysfunction), but it is by no means exhaustive.

Appetite and weight changes

Many people do not weigh themselves but may have noticed the consequences of weight change such as clothes becoming looser or tighter.

Lethargy

Lethargy or fatigue is a difficult symptom to pin down. Ask the patient how the tiredness impacts on their daily life. What are they able to do before needing to rest—and has this changed? Fatigue may be a feature of undiagnosed endocrine disease such as:

- Diabetes mellitus.
- Cushing's syndrome.
- Hypoadrenalism.
- Hypothyroidism.
- Hypercalcaemia.

▶ Consider depression and chronic disease of any other kind (anaemia, chronic liver and renal problems, chronic infection, and malignancy).

Bowel habit

Constipation is a common feature of hypercalcaemia and hypothyroidism. Hyperthyroidism and Addison's disease may give diarrhoea.

Urinary frequency and polyuria

Endocrine causes might include:

- Diabetes mellitus.
- Diabetes insipidus.
- Hyperglycaemia caused by Cushing's syndrome.
- Polyuria may also be seen in the presence of hypercalcaemia.

Thirst and polydipsia

Consider diabetes mellitus, diabetes insipidus, and hypercalcaemia.

Sweating

↑ perspiration may be seen during episodes of hypoglycaemia as well as in hyperthyroidism and acromegaly, and is associated with the other adrenergic symptoms of a phaeochromocytoma.

Pigmentation

Localized loss of pigmentation may be due to vitiligo—an autoimmune disorder associated with other endocrine immune diseases such as hypo- or hyperthyroidism, Addison's disease, and Hashimoto's thyroiditis.

- ↑ *pigmentation*: Addison's disease, Cushing's syndrome.
- ↓ *pigmentation*: generalized loss of pigmentation in hypopituitarism.

Hair distribution

See also 'Skin, hair, and nails', ➜ Chapter 4.

Hair loss

Decreased adrenal androgen production and loss of axillary and pubic hair in both sexes can be caused by:

- Hypogonadism.
- Adrenal insufficiency.

Hair gain

Hirsutism or excessive hair growth in a female may be due to endocrine dysfunction. Consider:

- Polycystic ovarian syndrome.
- Cushing's syndrome.
- Congenital adrenal hyperplasia.
- Acromegaly.
- Virilizing tumours.

Skin and soft tissue changes

Endocrine disorders cause many soft tissue changes including:

- *Hypothyroidism:* dry, coarse, pale skin with xanthelasma formation and, classically, loss of the outer 1/3 of the eyebrows.
- *Hyperthyroidism:* thyroid acropachy is seen only in hyperthyroidism due to Graves' disease. Features include finger clubbing and new bone formation at the fingers. Also pretibial myxoedema—reddened oedematous lesions on the shins (often the lateral aspects).
- *Hypoparathyroidism:* generally dry, scaly skin.
- *Diabetes mellitus:* xanthelasma, ulceration, repeated skin infections, necrobiosis lipoidica diabeticorum—shiny, yellowed lesions on the shins.
- *Acromegaly:* soft tissue overgrowth with skin tags at the axillae and anus, 'doughy' hands and fingers, acanthosis nigricans—velvety black skin changes at the axilla. (Acanthosis nigricans can also be seen in Cushing's syndrome, polycystic ovarian syndrome, and insulin resistance.)

Headache and visual disturbance

Visual field defects, cranial nerve palsies, and headache may be caused by space-occupying lesions within the skull. Pituitary tumours classically cause a bitemporal hemianopia by impinging on the optic chiasm.

Blurred vision is rather non-specific, but consider osmotic changes in the lens due to hyperglycaemia.

Alteration in growth

Hypopituitarism, hypothyroidism, growth hormone deficiency, and steroid excess may present with short stature. Tall stature may be caused by growth hormone excess or gonadotrophin deficiency.

Growth hormone excess in adults (acromegaly) causes soft tissue overgrowth. Patients may notice an increase in shoe size, glove size, or facial appearance (do they have any old photographs for comparison?).

Changes in sexual function

Women

Altered menstrual pattern in a female may be an early symptom suggestive of pituitary dysfunction. See ➲ Chapter 13 for more detail.

Men

In men, hypogonadism may result in loss of libido and an inability to attain or sustain an erection (see ➲ Chapter 12).

▶ Remember to look for non-endocrine causes of sexual dysfunction such as alcoholism, spinal cord disease, or psychological illness.

Flushing

Flushing may be a symptom of carcinoid or the menopause.

Ask about the nature of the flushing, any aggravating or relieving factors, and, importantly, any other symptoms at the time such as palpitations, diarrhoea, dizziness. Remember to take a full menstrual history.

The rest of the history

A full history should be taken (see Box 3.3 for the history in patients with diabetes). In a patient with endocrine symptoms, you should pay special attention to the following:

Drug history

As ever, a detailed medication history should be sought. Remember to ask especially about:

- Over-the-counter (OTC) medicines.
- Hormonal treatments—including the oral contraceptive pill, local, and systemic steroids.
- Amiodarone.
- Lithium.
- Herbal or other remedies.

Past medical history

- Any previous thyroid or parathyroid surgery.
- Any previous ^{131}I (radio-iodine) treatment or antithyroid drugs.
- Gestational diabetes.
- Hypertension.
- Any previous pituitary or adrenal surgery.

Family history

Ask especially about:

- Type II diabetes (Box 3.3).
- Related autoimmune disorders (pernicious anaemia, coeliac disease, vitiligo, Addison's disease, thyroid disease, type I diabetes).
  - Many patients will only have heard of these if they have a family member who suffers from them.
- Congential adrenal hyperplasia (CAH).
- Tumours of the MEN syndromes (Box 3.4).

Box 3.3 The diabetic history

As with other diseases, you should establish when the diagnosis was made (and how) and the course and treatment of the disease. There are additional questions relating to disease monitoring and diabetic complications that you should ask patients with diabetes:

- When was it first diagnosed?
- How was it first diagnosed?
- How was it first managed?
- How is it managed now?
- If on insulin—when was that first started?
- Are they compliant with a diabetic diet?
- Are they compliant with their diabetic medication?
- How often do they check their blood sugar?
- What readings do they normally get (if possible, ask to see their monitoring booklet)?
- What is their latest Hb_A1_c (many will know this)?
- Have they ever been admitted to hospital with diabetic ketoacidosis (DKA)?
- Do they go to a podiatrist or chiropodist?
- Have they experienced any problems with their feet? Do they use any moisturizers or cream on their feet?
- Do they attend a retinal screening program?
- Have they needed to be referred to an ophthalmologist?

If the patient is newly diagnosed with diabetes, ask about a history of weight loss (may differentiate type I and type II diabetes).

Box 3.4 The MEN syndromes

'Multiple endocrine neoplasias' which display autosomal dominant inheritance.

MEN 1

The 3 Ps:

- Parathyroid hyperplasia (100%)
- Pancreatic endocrine tumours (40–70%)
- Pituitary adenomas (30–50%).

MEN 2

- Medullary cell thyroid carcinoma (100%)
- Phaeochromocytoma (50%) and…
  - MEN 2a: parathyroid hyperplasia (80%)
  - MEN 2b: mucosal and bowel neuromas, marfanoid habitus.

General endocrine examination

It is not possible to perform an examination of the endocrine system in the same way that you may examine other organ systems. Usually, an endocrine examination is focused—looking for signs to confirm or refute differential diagnoses that you have developed.

See Box 3.5 for signs of tetany.

You may, however, perform a quick 'screening' general examination of a patient's endocrine status.

Hands/arms

Look at size, subcutaneous tissue, length of the metacarpals, nails, palmar erythema, sweating, and tremor. Note also skin thickness (thin skin in Cushing's, thick skin in acromegaly) and look for signs of easy bruising.

Pulse and blood pressure—lying and standing. Test for proximal muscle weakness (➔ Chapter 8).

Axillae

Note any skin tags, loss of hair, abnormal pigmentation, or acanthosis nigricans.

Face and mouth

Look for hirsutism, acne, plethora, or skin greasiness. Look at the soft tissues of the face for prominent glabellas (above the eyes) and enlargement of the chin (macrognathism). In the mouth, look at the spacing of the teeth and if any have fallen out. Note any buccal pigmentation and tongue enlargement (macroglossia). Normally, the upper teeth close in front of the lower set—reversal of this is termed 'prognathism'.

Eyes and fundi

See ➔ Chapter 9.

Neck

Note any swellings or lymphadenopathy. Examine the thyroid. Palpate the supraclavicular regions and note excessive soft tissue.

Chest

Inspect for any hair excess or loss, breast size in females and gynaecomastia in males. Note the nipple colour, pigmentation, or galactorrhoea.

Abdomen

Inspect for central adiposity/obesity, purple striae, hirsutism. Palpate for organomegaly. Look at the external genitalia to exclude any testicular atrophy in males or virilization (e.g. clitoromegaly) in women.

Legs

Test for proximal muscle weakness and make note of any diabetes-related changes.

Height and weight

Calculate the patient's BMI.

Box 3.5 Signs of tetany

Trousseau's sign

Inflate a blood pressure cuff just above the systolic pressure for 3 minutes. When hypocalcaemia has caused muscular irritability, the hand will develop flexor spasm.

Chvostek's sign

Gently tap over the facial nerve (in front of the tragus of the ear). The sign is positive if there is contraction of the lip and facial muscles on the same side of the face.

Examining the thyroid

The patient should be sitting upright on a chair or the edge of a bed.

Inspection

Look at the thyroid region. If the gland is quite enlarged (goitre), you may notice it protruding as a swelling just below the thyroid cartilage. The normal thyroid gland is usually neither visible nor palpable.

Thyroid gland

The gland lies ~2–3cm below the thyroid cartilage and has 2 equal lobes connected by a narrow isthmus.

If a localized or generalized swelling is visible, ask the patient to take a mouthful of water then swallow—watch the neck swelling carefully. Also ask the patient to protrude their tongue and watch the neck swelling.

- The thyroid is attached to the thyroid cartilage of the larynx and will move up with swallowing.
- Other neck masses such as an enlarged lymph node will hardly move.
- Thyroglossal cysts will not move with swallowing but will move upwards with protrusion of the tongue.

The rest of the neck

- Carefully inspect the neck for any obvious scars (thyroidectomy scars are often hidden below a necklace and are easily missed).
- Look for the JVP and make note of dilated veins which may indicate retrosternal extension of a goitre.
- Redness or erythema may indicate suppurative thyroiditis.

Palpation

Thyroid gland

Always begin palpation from behind. Stand behind the patient and place a hand either side of their neck. The patient's neck should be slightly flexed to relax the sternomastoids. 🛈 Explain what you are doing.

- Ask if there is any tenderness.
- Place the middle 3 fingers of either hand along the midline of the neck, just below the chin.
- Gently 'walk' your fingers down until you reach the thyroid gland.
  - The central isthmus is almost never palpable
- If the gland is enlarged, determine if it is symmetrical.
- Are there any discrete nodules?
- Assess the size, shape, and mobility of any swelling.
- Repeat the examination whilst the patient swallows.
  - Ask them to hold a small amount of water in their mouth—then ask them to swallow once your hands are in position.
- Consider the consistency of any palpable thyroid tissue:
  - Soft: normal
  - Firm: simple goitre
  - Rubbery hard: Hashimoto's thyroiditis
  - Stony hard: cancer, cystic calcification, fibrosis, Riedel's thyroiditis.
- Feel for a palpable thrill which may be present in metabolically active thyrotoxicosis.

The rest of the neck

Palpate cervical lymph nodes, carotid arteries (to check for patency—can be compressed by a large thyroid) and the trachea for deviation.

Percussion

- Percuss downwards from the sternal notch.
- In retrosternal enlargement the percussion note over the manubrosternum is dull as opposed to the normal resonance.

Auscultation

Apply the diaphragm of the stethoscope over each lobe of the thyroid gland and auscultate for a bruit.

- A soft bruit is indicative of increased blood flow which is characteristic of the hyperthyroid goitre seen in Graves' disease.
  - You may need to occlude venous return within the IJV to rule out a venous hum
  - Listen over the aortic area to ensure that the thyroid bruit is not, in fact, an outflow obstruction murmur conducted to the root of the neck.

Skills station 3.1

Instruction

Clinically assess this patient's thyroid status.

Model technique

- Clean your hands.
- Introduce yourself.
- Explain the purpose of examination, obtain informed consent.
- Ask for any painful areas you should avoid.
- Observe the patient's composure (relaxed/agitated/fidgety?).
- Measure the heart rate and note if the patient is in atrial fibrillation.
- Inspect the hands—erythema, warmth, thyroid acropathy (phalangeal bone overgrowth similar to pulmonary osteopathy).
- Feel the palms—sweaty/dry?
- Look for peripheral tremor—ask the patient to stretch out their arms with fingers out straight and palms down. Resting a piece of paper on the back of the hand can make a tremor more obvious.
- Inspect the face.
  - Exophthalmos, proptosis (➔ Chapter 9)
  - Hypothyroid features.
- Examine the eyes (➔ Chapter 9).
- Examine the thyroid and neck.
- Test tendon reflexes at the biceps and ankle (➔ Chapter 8).
- Test for proximal myopathy by asking the patient to stand from a sitting position.
- Look for pretibial myxoedema.
- Thank the patient and help them re-dress as necessary.

Examining the patient with diabetes

As diabetes has an impact on every body system, you can make the examination of a diabetic patient complex or simple depending on the circumstance.

In general, you should be alert to: cardiovascular disease, renal disease, retinal disease, peripheral neuropathy—especially sensory, health of insulin injection sites, the diabetic foot, secondary causes of diabetes (e.g. acromegaly, Cushing's syndrome, haemochromatosis), and associated hyperlipidaemia.

Framework for a thorough diabetic examination

General inspection
- Hydration.
- Weight.
- Facies associated with a known endocrine disease.
- Pigmentation (hyperpigmentation or patchy loss).

Legs
- Muscle wasting.
- Hair loss.
- Skin atrophy.
- Skin pigmentation.
- Leg ulceration (especially around pressure points and toes).
- Skin infections.

Injection sites
- Inspect and palpate for fat atrophy, fat hypertrophy, or local infection.

Associated skin lesions
- Necrobiosis lipoidica diabeticorum—look on the shins, arms, and back.
  - Sharply demarcated oval plaques with a shiny surface, yellow waxy atrophic centres, brownish-red margins, surrounding telangiectasia.
- Also look for granuloma annulare.

Hyperlipidaemia
- Eruptive xanthoma.
- Tendon xanthoma.
- Xanthelasma.

Neurological examination
- Visual acuity (**🕮** Chapter 9).
- Fundoscopy (**🕮** Chapter 9).
- Peripheral sensory neuropathy—evidence of injury, ulceration, and Charcot's joint formation.
- Test muscle strength (**➔** Chapter 8).
- Examine feet.

Cardiovascular examination
- Ideally a full cardiovascular examination including lying and standing blood pressure measurements.

The diabetic foot

The combination of peripheral vascular disease and peripheral neuropathy can lead to repeated minor trauma to the feet leading to ulceration and infection which are very slow to heal.

Using a 10g monofilament

A small, thin plastic filament, designed such that it bends under approximately 10g of pressure.

- Apply the filament to the patient's skin at the spots shown in Fig. 3.4a.
- Press firmly so that the filament bends (Fig. 3.4b).
- Hold the filament against the skin for ~1.5 seconds and ask the patient if they can feel it. The filament should not slide, stroke, or scratch.
- ❶ Do not press on ulcers, callouses, scars, or necrotic tissue.
  - The patient's feet are 'at risk' if they cannot feel the monofilament at any of the sites.

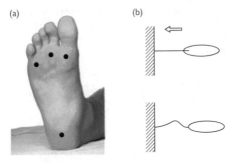

(a)   (b)

Fig. 3.4 (a) Sites to test with a 10g monofilament in the diabetic patient. (b) Apply the monofilament to the skin with enough force to make it bend.

Skills station 3.2

Instruction

Clinically assess the foot of this patient with diabetes.

Model technique

- Clean your hands.
- Introduce yourself.
- Explain the purpose of examination, obtain informed consent.
- Inspect, noting colour, ulceration, dryness, callous formation, evidence of infection.
- Evidence of injury—shoes rubbing?
- Are there any Charcot's joints?
  - Grossly abnormal and dysfunctional joints due to repeated minor trauma and poor healing due to a loss of pain sensation.
- 10g monofilament test.
- Test light-touch sensation, pain sensation, vibration sense, and proprioception.
- Palpate the peripheral pulses (dorsalis pedis and posterior tibial).
- Note the temperature of the skin on the dorsum and sole.
- Record capillary filling time.
- Thank the patient and help them re-dress as necessary.

Important presentations

Hypothyroidism

Causes

- Dietary iodine deficiency.
- Autoimmune thyroiditis (Hashimoto's thyroiditis).
- Lymphocytic thyroiditis (10% of post-partum women).
- Drugs (amiodarone, interferon alpha, thalidomide, dopamine, lithium).
- Radioactive iodine treatment.
- Surgical thyroid injury.
- External irradiation (e.g. for head and neck or breast cancer).
- Pituitary adenoma.

Symptoms

- Tiredness.
- Weight gain.
- Anorexia.
- Cold intolerance.
- Poor memory.
- Depression.
- Reduced libido.
- Goitre.
- Puffy eyes.
- Brittle hair.
- Dry skin.
- Arthralgia.
- Myalgia.
- Muscle weakness.
- Constipation.
- Menorrhagia.

Signs

- *General:* croaking voice, mental and physical sluggishness, pseudodementia, 'myxoedema madness'.
- *Inspection:* coarse cool dry skin (look for yellowish tint of carotenaemia 'peaches and cream' complexion), palmar crease pallor, peripheral cyanosis, puffy lower eyelids, loss of outer 1/3 of eyebrows, thinning of scalp hair, tongue swelling, xanthelasma.
- *Cardiovascular and chest:* mild hypertension, pericarditis, pleural effusion, low cardiac output, cardiac failure, bradycardia, small volume pulse.
- *Neurological:* carpal tunnel syndrome, peripheral neuropathy, cerebellar syndrome, proximal muscle weakness, myotonia, muscular hypertrophy, delayed ankle jerks, bilateral neural deafness (seen in congenital hypothyroidism).

Hyperthyroidism

Causes

- Graves' disease.
- Chronic thyroiditis (Hashimoto thyroiditis).
- Subacute thyroiditis (de Quervain thyroiditis).
- Postpartum thyroiditis.
- Drugs (iodine-induced, amiodarone).
- Bacterial thyroiditis.
- Postviral thyroiditis.
- Idiopathic.
- Toxic multinodular goitre.
- Malignancy (toxic adenoma, TSH-producing pituitary tumours).

Symptoms

- Weight loss.
- Increased appetite.
- Irritability.
- Restlessness.
- Muscle weakness.
- Tremor.
- Breathlessness.
- Palpitations.
- Sweating.
- Heat intolerance.
- Itching.
- Thirst.
- Vomiting.
- Diarrhoea.
- Eye complaints (Graves' ophthalmopathy).
- Oligomenorrhoea.
- Loss of libido.
- Gynaecomastia.

Signs:

- *General:* irritability, weight loss.
- *Inspection:* onycholysis, palmar erythema, tremor, sweaty palms, thyroid acropachy, hyperkinesis, gynaecomastia, pretibial myxoedema, Graves' ophthalmopathy.
- *Cardiovascular and chest:* resting tachycardia, high cardiac output, systolic flow murmurs.
- *Neurological:* proximal myopathy, muscle wasting, hyper-reflexia in legs.

Glucocorticoid excess (Cushing's syndrome)

- *Causes include:* high ACTH production from a pituitary adenoma and ectopic ACTH (e.g. small cell lung cancer). Primary hypercortisolaemia caused by adrenal hyperplasia, adrenal tumour (adenoma or carcinoma), exogenous steroids; ectopic CRF production (very rare), depression, alcohol-induced.
- *Symptoms:* weight gain (central/upper body), change in appearance, menstrual disturbance, thin skin with easy bruising, acne, excessive hair growth, muscle weakness, decreased libido, depression, insomnia.
- *Signs:* supraclavicular fat pads, 'moon face', thoracocervical fat pads ('buffalo hump'), centripetal obesity, hirsutism, thinning of skin, easy bruising, purple striae, poor wound healing, skin infections, proximal muscle weakness (shoulders and hips), ankle oedema, hypertension, fractures due to osteoporosis, hyperpigmentation (if raised ACTH), glycosuria.

Hypoadrenalism (Addison's disease)

- *Causes include:* autoimmune adrenalitis (>80% in UK), tuberculosis, metastatic malignancy, amyloidosis, haemorrhage, infarction, bilateral adrenalectomy, HIV.
- *Symptoms:* anorexia, weight loss, tiredness, nausea, vomiting, diarrhoea, constipation, abdominal pain, confusion, erectile dysfunction, amenorrhoea, dizziness, syncope, myalgia, arthralgia.
- *Signs:* skin pigmentation (especially on sun-exposed areas, mucosal surfaces, axillae, palmar creases, and in recent scars), cachexia, loss of body hair, postural hypotension, low-grade fever, dehydration.

Growth hormone excess (acromegaly)

- *Causes:* pituitary tumour (>95%), hyperplasia due to GHRH excess (very rare), tumours in hypothalamus, adrenal, or pancreas.
- *Symptoms:* headache, diplopia, change in appearance, enlarged extremities, deepening of voice, sweating, tiredness, weight gain, erectile dysfunction, dysmenorrhoea, galactorrhoea, snoring, arthralgia, weakness, numbness, paraesthesia, polyuria, polydipsia.
- *Signs:* prominent supraorbital ridges, large nose and lips, protrusion of lower jaw (prognathism), interdental separation, macroglossia, 'spade-like' hands, 'doughy' soft tissues, thick oily skin, carpal tunnel syndrome, hirsutism, bitemporal hemianopia (if pituitary tumour impinging on optic chiasm), cranial nerve palsies (particularly III, IV, and VI), hypertension.

Prolactinoma

A pituitary tumour (the most common hormone-secreting tumour).

- *Symptoms:* depend on age, sex, and degree of prolactinaemia. In females: oligomenorrhagia, vaginal dryness, dyspareunia, galactorrhoea. In males: loss of libido, erectile dysfunction, infertility, galactorrhoea. If before puberty, may have female body habitus and small testicles.
- *Signs:* visual field defects (bitemporal hemianopia?), cranial nerve palsies (III, IV, and VI), galactorrhoea. In males: small testicles and female pattern of hair growth.

Hypercalcaemia

- *Causes:* common—hyperparathyroidism, malignancy (PTHrP production or metastases in bone). Less common—vitamin D intoxication, granulomatous disease, familial hypocalciuric hypercalcaemia. Rare—drugs (e.g. bendrofluazide), hyperthyroidism, Addison's disease.
- *Symptoms:* depend largely on the underlying cause. Mild hypercalcaemia is asymptomatic. Higher levels may cause nausea, vomiting, drowsiness, confusion, abdominal pain, constipation, depression, muscle weakness, myalgia, polyuria, headache, and coma.
- *Signs:* often there are signs of the underlying cause. There are no specific signs of hypercalcaemia.

Hypocalcaemia

- *Causes:* hypoalbuminaemia, hypomagnesaemia, hyperphosphataemia, surgery to the thyroid or parathyroid glands, PTH deficiency or resistance, and vitamin D deficiency.
- *Symptoms:* depression, paraesthesia around the mouth, muscle spasms.
- *Signs:* carpopedal spasm (flexion at the wrist and the fingers) when blood supply to the hand is reduced by inflating a sphygmomanometer cuff on the arm (Trousseau's sign). Nervous excitability—tapping a nerve causes the supplied muscles to twitch (Chvostek's sign—tapping facial nerve at the parotid gland about 2cm anterior to the tragus of the ear causes the facial muscles to contract).

Polycystic ovarian syndrome (PCOS)

Abnormal metabolism of androgens and oestrogen with abnormal control of androgen production.

- *Symptoms:* oligomenorrhoea with anovulation and erratic periods, infertility. Some patients present complaining of hirsutism.
- *Signs:* obesity (50%), male-pattern hair growth, male-pattern baldness, increased muscle mass, deep voice, clitoromegaly, acanthosis nigricans.

Skin, hair, and nails

Introduction

The skin is a highly specialized organ with various physiological roles including protection from trauma, infection, and ultraviolet (UV) radiation; regulation of body temperature and fluid balance; detection of sensory stimuli; and synthesis of vitamin D.

The skin also plays a key function in social interaction so what might seem to be a trivial disease in terms of physical health, such as acne, can have devastating psychosocial consequences.

Anatomy and physiology

The skin comprises two layers: the epidermis and dermis. The fat layer below the skin is known as the subcutis.

Epidermis

This is a keratinizing, stratified squamous epithelium. The keratinocyte is the principal cell type. The basal layer of the epidermis is made up of cuboidal basal cells, which continually divide, generating new cells which migrate upwards towards the skin surface, from which they are eventually shed. This process takes 30–50 days, varying with body site. The epidermis forms a protective layer of keratin on the surface.

Other cell types in the epidermis include melanocytes, Langerhans cells, and Merkel cells.

- *Melanocytes:* reside in the basal layer and secrete melanin pigment into surrounding keratinocytes via long projections. Melanin helps to protect the skin from UV radiation. The number of melanin granules determines skin colour.
- *Langerhans cells:* important in the immune response, acting as antigen-presenting cells.
- *Merkel cells:* thought to be involved in touch sensation.

Dermis

This is a layer of connective tissue consisting of collagen and elastic fibres, which give rise to much of the tensile strength and elasticity of the skin. It is here where the skin appendages (hair follicles, sebaceous glands, eccrine and apocrine glands), nerves, and blood and lymphatic vessels lie.

- *The follicle:* a specialized tubular structure which opens on to the skin surface and produces hair. Follicles are present over virtually the entire body; some sites, such as the scalp, contain very dense numbers of large follicles. The arrector pili muscle connects the follicle to the dermis; its contraction pulls the hair more perpendicular to the skin.
- *Sebaceous glands:* attached to hair follicles. These secrete lipid-rich sebum, which waterproofs and lubricates the skin and hair.
- *Eccrine glands:* responsible for the production of sweat.
- *Apocrine glands:* structurally similar to eccrine glands. Their role in humans is not clear, but they are important in scent production in some mammals.

Subcutis

The subcutis acts as a lipid store and helps with insulation. It also contributes to body contour and shape.

Hair

Hair is comprised of keratin, a different form from that on the skin surface. Scalp hair is an example of *terminal* hair, which is coarse and pigmented, in contrast to fine vellus hair, found at sites such as the female face.

Hair growth

Hair growth is cyclical, with an active anagen phase, followed by the involutional catagen phase and then a resting telogen phase, at the end of which the hair is shed. At any given time, most hairs are in anagen phase, which typically lasts for upwards of 3 years. Although hair abnormalities may not seem particularly consequential to health, hair is of great importance in social interaction and sensitivity is required when dealing with patients with either too little or too much of it.

Nails

The nail plate is a sheet of keratin. Its main functions are protection of the fingertip and to improve dexterity. It is produced by the nail matrix, which lies mainly beneath the proximal nail fold, but is just visible in some nails as the pale lunula (or 'half-moon'). Nails grow continuously at an average rate of around 3mm per month though fingernails grow faster than toenails. Nail changes can provide clues to diagnosis of both dermatological and systemic disease.

The dermatological history

It is estimated that there are over 2000 different dermatological conditions. These can present with all manner of skin, hair, and nail changes and it is therefore difficult to be prescriptive when describing how to take a good dermatological history. It is hoped that the following will at least serve as a guide to elucidating the important elements, which include the **time course of the complaint**, its **evolution**, the **main symptoms**, **exacerbating or relieving factors**, and **associated features** or disease.

If an eruption is present, it is not necessary to elicit a detailed description of it from the patient (and rashes are notoriously difficult to describe anyway). However, if an eruption comes and goes, the history in some cases may still be diagnostic and should at the least provide important clues.

History of the presenting complaint

- When did the problem start?
- Where did it start?
  - Where is affected now?
- How have things changed since?
  - Is it a continuous or intermittent problem?
- Is it evolving (if so, how?) or stable?
- Is there any discharge or bleeding?
- Is there pain, itch, or altered sensation?
- Is there dryness or itching?
- Are there any obvious factors which trigger or exacerbate the problem? Possibilities include:
  - Sunlight
  - Extremes of temperature (itching is often worsened by heat)
  - Contact with certain substances (e.g. latex, rubber, metals, hair dye)
  - Work (e.g. occupational allergy or wet work leading to irritant contact dermatitis).
- Does anything relieve the symptoms?
  - e.g. sunlight, topical treatments, systemic drugs.
- What treatments have been tried?
  - What was effective or ineffective?
- Are there any systemic symptoms such as fever, malaise, joint pain, weight loss, or sore throat?

Past medical history

- Previous skin problems?
- Ask also about diabetes, connective tissue disease, inflammatory bowel disease, atopy (eczema, especially as a baby, asthma, hayfever)?

Allergies

- Remember to ask about the *nature* of any allergic reaction claimed.

Drug history
- Which drugs is the patient taking and for how long? See Box 4.1.
- If a drug reaction is possible, ask about recent courses of drugs not taken regularly (e.g. antibiotics, over-the-counter analgesics).
  - ❶ Bear in mind that there may be a delay of a few days to months before a drug eruption occurs
  - Immunosuppression can increase the risk of skin cancer.

Family history
- Ask especially about atopic diseases, psoriasis, skin cancer.

Social history
- Occupation (consider wet work, sun exposure, exposure to chemicals or plants).
- Hobbies.
- Pets (including pets of close friends and relatives).
- Living conditions—how many share the house/living space?
- Recent travel? Were appropriate vaccinations taken before leaving?
- Insect bites?
- Risk factors for sexually transmitted diseases? Take a full sexual history if relevant. ❶ Be delicate.

Psychosocial impact
- Ask about how the condition is affecting the patient.
- Physical symptoms such as pain or worsening in sunlight might curtail usual activities.
- Self-consciousness and embarrassment in a physically asymptomatic condition can still lead to enormous social handicap.

Box 4.1 Common culprits for drug eruption

Rashes can be caused by virtually any drug and mostly occur 1–2 weeks after the drug is started. The following are frequently responsible and should be viewed with suspicion in a patient with a rash compatible with drug eruption:
- Anticonvulsants
- Sulphonamides (e.g. trimethoprim, co-trimoxazole)
- Penicillins
- Allopurinol
- Non-steroidal anti-inflammatory drugs (NSAIDs).

Hair and nail symptoms

Hair loss

Alopecia is a clinical sign meaning hair loss: it is not a diagnosis. See Box 4.2 for more. In the history consider:

- Sudden or gradual?
  - Bear in mind that it is normal to lose up to 150 hairs per day from the scalp.
- Areas affected (scalp and/or body hair?).
- Diffuse or localized?
- Other scalp symptoms e.g. scaling, itch, soreness, crusting.
- Rashes elsewhere (e.g. lichen planus, cutaneous lupus).
- Other medical problems (e.g. systemic lupus, severe trauma, psychological stress or febrile illness in last few months).
- Family history of hair loss.

Excessive hair growth

Facial hair growth is common in post-pubertal women but many find this distressing. If the patient reports abnormal hair growth, treat as any other symptom but remember to ask about:

- FHx of a similar problem.
- DHx.
- For women, ask about the menstrual cycle (when was the last period? Are they regular or erratic?) and symptoms of virilization (e.g. voice change, clitoromegaly, new-onset acne).

Nail symptoms

The history for nail changes should be treated as other dermatological conditions.

However, seek evidence of skin or systemic conditions which can involve the nails (e.g. psoriasis, eczema, fungal infections). See also Box 4.3.

Box 4.2 Important disorders of hair loss
- *Male-pattern baldness:* commonly occurs from the 3rd decade. Hair is lost first from the frontotemporal region, then the crown
- *Female-pattern hair loss:* tends to occur post-menopause, but sometimes in much younger women; leads to thinning over the crown with preservation of the frontal hairline
- *Alopecia areata:* associated with organ-specific autoimmune disorders and tends to begin in the 2nd or 3rd decade. Sharply demarcated, non-inflammatory bald patches on the scalp. There may be pathognomonic 'exclamation mark' hairs which are a few millimetres long and thinner at the base. Eyebrows, beard, and body hair can also be affected. Nails may be slow-growing and pitted. Extreme examples include:
  - Alopecia totalis: loss of all scalp hair
  - Alopecia universalis: loss of all hair including on the body.
- *Telogen effluvium:* severe illness, high fever, or childbirth may synchronize all the hair follicles causing all hairs to enter the telogen phase at the same time, 3–6 months later. This leads to dramatic shedding and near-total hair loss, which then resolves
- *Scarring alopecia:* inflammatory lesions causing hair loss include lichen planus, burns, and infection. Scarring alopecia causes destruction of the follicles and is therefore permanent.

Box 4.3 Important nail disorders/signs
See also Chapter 3.
- *Splinter haemorrhages:* tiny, longitudinal streak haemorrhages under the nails caused by micro-emboli or trauma. Distal lesions can be a normal finding especially in manual workers
- *Pitting:* tiny indentations in the surface of the nail. A feature of psoriasis, lichen planus, and alopecia areata
- *Onycholysis:* separation of the nail plate from the nail bed; seen in psoriasis. Also caused by trauma, thyrotoxicosis, and certain drugs
- *Leukonychia:* white nails, seen in hypoalbuminaemia
- *Beau's lines:* transverse depressions in the nail. These represent arrested nail growth during a period of acute severe illness
- *Paronychia:* infection or inflammation of the nail folds, causing pain, redness, and swelling
- *Koilonychia:* spooning (concave indentation) of the nail, associated with severe iron deficiency
- *Clubbing:* see ➜ Chapter 3
- *Onychomycosis:* fungal nail infection causing the nail to become thickened, opaque, crumbly, and yellow. This may be indistinguishable from psoriatic nail changes
- *Longitudinal melanonychia:* a pigmented streak in the nail which may represent subungual melanoma, especially if Hutchinson's sign (pigmentation extending on to the proximal nail fold) is positive.

Examining the skin

Be wary of only focusing on the area identified by the patient—the whole organ needs to be examined.

After explaining and asking permission, ask the patient to undress to their underwear, to lie back comfortably on a couch or bed, and cover them with a sheet. Ensure that the room is warm and private and that you have adequate lighting—preferably in the form of an adjustable light source. You should have a chaperone—preferably one of the opposite sex to yourself.

General inspection of the skin

Begin by scanning the whole surface of the skin for any abnormal lesions. This can be done in any order but it will help you to build a pattern that you can consistently remember which does not miss any areas!

Remember to inspect those areas that are usually hidden:
- Inner thighs.
- Undersurfaces of female breasts.
- External genitalia.
- Axillae.
- Natal cleft (between the buttocks).

⓵ Remember also to inspect the mucosal surfaces of the mouth, nails, hair, and scalp.

Skin colour

Skin colour varies widely between individuals but should always be even in distribution with normal variation for sun-exposed surfaces.

Inspecting a focal lesion

▶ See also 'examining a lump' if the lesion is raised.

Inspect each lesion carefully and note:
- Grouped or solitary? If grouped, is there a pattern?
- Site.
- Distribution/location (symmetrical/asymmetrical? Peripheral? In only light-exposed areas? Dermatomal?).
- Colour.
- Shape.
- Size (diameter).
- Surface.
- Border.
- Nature of the surrounding skin.

For each of the previous points, describe as accurately as you can using dermatological terms. However, if a lesion is pear-shaped, it is perfectly acceptable to call it just that!

When noting the distribution, bear in mind what clothing (or lack of) is usually at that site and what other objects/substances that part of the body would come into contact with. (Consider especially belt buckles, watches, gloves, and jewellery.)

If the lesion is pigmented, some special considerations apply (see Box 4.4).

Palpation

Each lesion should be felt (remember to ask for—and be granted—permission first). It is rare to catch an infection from touching a rash or lesion and it's even rarer to see a dermatologist wearing gloves. Each situation should be judged at the time—gloves should be worn if there is bleeding or exudate present or if you are examining the genitalia.

For each lesion, note:

- Tenderness (watch the patient's face).
- Consistency.
- Temperature:
  • Use the back of your hand (inflamed lesions are usually hot).
- Depth/height.
- Mobility:
  • What skin layer is the lesion in and is it attached to any underlying or nearby structures?
  • Can it be moved in all directions or only in one or two?
  • Does it move with movement of underlying muscle or tendons?

Beyond the lesion

The skin condition must be seen in the context of the whole patient and other organ systems should be examined as necessary. Remember to palpate regional lymph nodes if appropriate (➔ Chapter 3).

Box 4.4 Describing pigmented lesions

When faced with a pigmented lesion, the key is to decide whether there is a possibility of melanoma, a potentially fatal cancer. See ➔ OHCM9. If so, the patient should be referred to a dermatologist or plastic surgeon for consideration of excision biopsy. Melanoma can arise in an existing naevus or *de novo*.

A useful system which can serve as a guide to whether a melanocytic lesion is clinically 'suspicious', as well as providing a framework for a description, is the ABCDE method. If one or more features are 'positive', melanoma is more likely. However, a history of change over time is also important. If in doubt, refer to a skin specialist.

ABCDE

- A: asymmetry
- B: irregular border
- C: irregular colour
- D: diameter >6mm
- E: (new) elevation.

Bear in mind that many pigmented lesions are not melanocytic. For example, seborrhoeic keratosis usually demonstrates a warty, fissured surface, and is well defined to the point of looking 'stuck on'. If you reach the end of ABCDE and feel that you haven't mentioned all the salient points, think of E also as 'Everything Else'.

Pictorial glossary of terms

A careful description often clinches the diagnosis in dermatology. All lesions should be documented in accepted dermatological terms (Figs 4.1–4.3).

Flat, non-palpable changes in skin colour

Macule
Small flat, non-palpable change in skin colour ≤ 0.5–1cm diameter 'Freckles' are pigmented macules

Patch
Large, flat, non-palpable change in skin colour

Elevation due to fluid in a cavity

Vesicle
Small blister (0.5–1cm) that contains clear fluid

Bulla
Large blister that contains clear fluid

Pustule
Visible collection of pus

Abscess
Localized collection of pus in cavity >1cm diameter

Elevation due to solid masses

Papule/papular
Small, solid, raised lesion ≥ 0.5–1cm in diameter, usually dome-shaped

Plaque
Larger superficial flat-topped raised area

Nodule
A dome-shaped solid lump, >0.5–1cm in diameter, that may project or be deep in the skin

Wheal (weal)
Pale area of dermal oedema, usually <2cm diameter, often surrounded by an erythematous flare

Loss of skin

Erosion
Partial epidermal loss Heals without scarring

Ulcer
Complete loss of epidermis and some dermis, may scar when heals

Fissure
A linear crack

Atrophy
Thinning of the epidermis and/or dermis

Fig. 4.1 Primary lesions. Images by Dr Ravi Kothari.

(a)
Surface changes

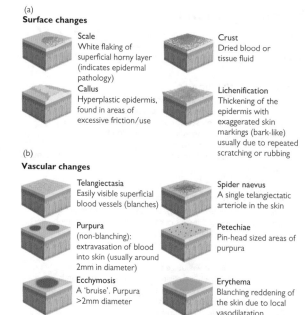

Scale
White flaking of superficial horny layer (indicates epidermal pathology)

Crust
Dried blood or tissue fluid

Callus
Hyperplastic epidermis, found in areas of excessive friction/use

Lichenification
Thickening of the epidermis with exaggerated skin markings (bark-like) usually due to repeated scratching or rubbing

(b)
Vascular changes

Telangiectasia
Easily visible superficial blood vessels (blanches)

Spider naevus
A single telangiectatic arteriole in the skin

Purpura
(non-blanching): extravasation of blood into skin (usually around 2mm in diameter)

Petechiae
Pin-head sized areas of purpura

Ecchymosis
A 'bruise'. Purpura >2mm diameter

Erythema
Blanching reddening of the skin due to local vasodilatation

Fig. 4.2 (a) Secondary lesions. (b) Vascular lesions. Images by Dr Ravi Kothari.

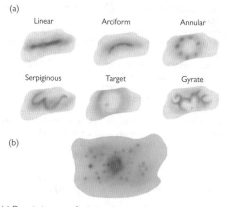

(a)

| Linear | Arciform | Annular |
| Serpiginous | Target | Gyrate |

(b)

Fig. 4.3 (a) Descriptive terms for lesion shapes and patterns of grouped lesions. (b) Confluence of grouped lesions. Note how the smaller lesions coalesce to form a larger lesion. Images by Dr Ravi Kothari.

Examining a lump

Any raised lesion or lump should be inspected and palpated as described previously. Note: position, distribution, colour, shape, size, surface, edge, nature of the surrounding skin, tenderness, consistency, temperature, and mobility.

Which layer is the lump in?

- Does it move with the skin? (Epidermal or dermal.)
- Does the skin move over the lump? (Subcutis.)
- Does it move with muscular contraction? (Muscle/tendon.)
- Does it move only in one direction? (Tendon or nerve.)
  - If the lesion belongs to a nerve, the patient may feel pins-and-needles in the distribution of the nerve when the lump is pressed.
- Is it immobile? (Bone.)

Additional characteristics to consider

- *Consistency:* e.g. stony, rubbery, spongy, soft. (Remember the consistency does not always correlate with the composition—a fluid-filled lump will feel hard if it is tense.)
- *Fluctuation:* press one side of the lump—the other sides may protrude.
- If the lump is solid, it will bulge at the opposite side only.
- *Fluid thrill:* this can only be elicited if the fluid-filled lesion is very large. Examine by tapping on one side and feeling the impulse on the other much as you would for ascites (see ➔ Chapter 7).
- *Translucency:* darken the room and press a lit pen-torch to one side of the lump—it will 'glow' illuminating the whole lump in the presence of water, serum, fat, or lymph. Solid lumps will not transilluminate.
- *Resonance:* only possible to test on large lumps. Percuss as you would any other part of the body (see ➔ Chapter 6) and listen (and feel) if the lump is hollow (gas-filled) or solid.
- *Pulsatility:* can you feel a pulse in the lump? Consider carefully if the pulse is transmitted from an underlying structure or if the lump itself is pulsating.
  - Use two fingers and place one on either side of the lump
  - If the lump is pulsating, it will be 'expansile' and your fingers will move up and outwards, away from each other
  - If the pulse is transmitted from a structure below, your fingers will move upwards but not outwards (see ➔ Chapter 7).
- *Compressibility:* attempt to compress the lump until it disappears. If this is possible, release the pressure and watch for the lump reforming. Compressible lumps may be fluid-filled or vascular malformations. Note, this is not 'reducibility'.
- *Reducibility:* a feature of herniae. Attempt to reduce the lump by manoeuvring its contents into another space (e.g. back into the abdominal cavity). Ask the patient to cough and watch for the lump reforming.

Auscultation

You should always listen with a stethoscope over any large lump, you could gain important clues regarding its origin and contents. Listen especially for:

- Vascular bruits.
- Bowel sounds.

Widespread skin eruptions

The 'DCM' method

'DCM' stands for distribution, configuration, and morphology, which are best presented in this order.

Distribution

- Where does the rash affect?
- Is there a pattern to it (e.g. predominantly extensor or flexor surfaces, photo-exposed distribution)?
- Is it broadly symmetrical?

Configuration

- If there are multiple lesions which comprise the rash, is there a pattern in the way these are aligned?
  - Are the lesions arranged in a line (linear), a ring (annular), or another recognizable shape?
  - Are there clusters of lesions, with spared skin in between?
- Bear in mind that most rashes will not display a specific configuration, but if you see one, it can be an important clue to the diagnosis.

Morphology

- Describe the actual features of the rash. For example, is it macular or are there papules or plaques?
- What colour is it?
- Are there discrete components and do they coalesce, or is there just a confluent area affected?

Finish by commenting on other features if relevant, such as abnormalities in the nails, hair, or mucous membranes.

Examining an ulcer

The approach to examining an ulcer is similar to any other skin lesion. Consider the site and size, as well as whether there are single or multiple lesions. If the shape of the ulcer, or position, is unusual or difficult to describe, make a drawing! See Box 4.5 for notes on leg ulcers.

Border

Assess the morphology of the border. See also Fig. 4.4. Some examples include:

- *Sloping:* these ulcers are usually shallow and a sloping edge implies that it is healing (e.g. venous ulcers).
- *Punched out:* this is full-thickness skin loss and typical of neuropathic ulceration and vasculitic lesions.
- *Undermined:* these extend below the visible edge creating a 'lip'. This is typical of pyoderma gangrenosum and infected ulceration such as TB.
- *Rolled:* here, the edge is mounded but neither everted or undermined and implies proliferation of the tissues at the edge of the ulcer. Basal cell carcinoma typically has a 'rolled' edge which is often described as 'pearly' in colour with thin overlying vessels.
- *Everted:* here the tissues at the edge of the ulcer are proliferating too fast, creating an everted lip. This is typical of neoplastic ulceration.

Most venous ulcers have a sloping border; arterial ulcers classically look 'punched out'; pyoderma gangrenosum (PG) and some pressure sores manifest an undermined border, meaning that the process extends beneath the edges of the actual ulcer. The border in PG also has a characteristic violaceous hue. If there is a rolled or heaped up edge, consider the possibility of a neoplastic ulcer: most types of skin cancer and some benign neoplasms can present with ulceration.

Depth

- Ulcers are loosely divided into superficial or deep; visible bone or tendon at the base certainly implies a deep ulcer, but use your judgement.

Base

- Healing ulcers have granulation tissue at the base; this appears moist, beefy red, and usually forms a cobble-stoned surface.
- Some ulcers will have surface slough, yellow or brown material which is sometimes mistaken for pus.

Surrounding skin

- Look for signs of chronic venous disease (e.g. peripheral oedema, varicose veins, haemosiderin deposition, lipodermatosclerosis, atrophie blanche) and arterial insufficiency (loss of hair, shiny, erythematous skin, cool peripheries).
  - Check peripheral pulses and capillary refill time if arterial disease is suspected.
- Assess the quality of surrounding skin: there may be incipient ulceration elsewhere or other damage to the skin such as blistering.

- Check that there is no cellulitis, but bear in mind that eczema (gravitational or contact) is very common around chronic leg ulcers.
  - If there is scaling and itch, this is a far more likely diagnosis than infection, and treatment should reflect this.
- If arterial or venous disease are possibilities, the ankle brachial pressure indices should be checked to confirm or refute an arterial component and to establish whether compression can be used safely.

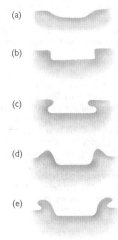

Fig. 4.4 Representation of some ulcer borders. (a) Sloping, (b) punched out, (c) undermined, (d) rolled, (e) everted.

Box 4.5 A word on leg ulcers

Leg ulcers are often a result of mixed venous and arterial disease; however, one pathology may predominate.

Venous ulceration

Venous hypertension causes fibrin to be laid down at the pericapillary cuff (lipodermatosclerosis), interfering with the delivery of nutrients to the surrounding tissues. There may be brown discoloration (haemosiderin deposition), eczema, telangiectasia and, eventually, ulcer formation with a base of granulation tissue and a serous exudate. Venous ulcers occur at the medial or lateral malleoli especially. These ulcers will often heal with time and care.

Arterial ulceration

Along with other symptoms and signs of leg ischaemia, there may be loss of hair and toenail dystrophy. Chronic arterial insufficiency may lead to deep, sharply defined, and painful ulcers which will not heal without intervention to restore blood supply. Arterial ulcers especially appear on the foot or mid-shin.

The elderly patient

Whilst the skin may be regarded as the largest organ of the body, it is sadly the one most often overlooked in any assessment of a patient. Many of the functional changes in ageing skin make it increasingly susceptible to injury, with delayed resolution of wounds and consequent ↑ in infection risk. Systemic illnesses often manifest in skin and nail changes, and astute assessment can resolve challenging diagnoses—e.g. erythema ab igne as a manifestation of hot water bottle use for abdominal pain and underlying pancreatic cancer or late onset ichthyosis associated with lymphoma. For acutely unwell older people, being alert to the existence and development of pressure ulcers can significantly reduce pain, immobility, and delays in their recovery.

History

- *Symptoms:* should be taken seriously. Whilst it is tempting to dismiss pruritus if there is no visible skin lesion, doing so risks missing a range of important diagnoses including iron-deficiency anaemia and liver disease. Attributing symptoms to age-related changes in the skin should be a diagnosis of exclusion by generalists (and avoid the term 'senile' pruritus—older people find it offensive). Always remember that many systemic diseases may first manifest through skin changes.
- *Pre-existing conditions:* carefully documenting the presence (and treatment plan) for pressure ulcers is the obligation of both medical and nursing staff. Do not shirk this responsibility—it is important to plan pressure care as critically as any other intervention. You should be particularly thorough in the presence of diabetes mellitus.
- *MRSA:* Has the patient received decolonization treatment as appropriate? Could the new rash reflect an allergy to administered topical treatment?
- *DHx:* important to ask about new changes in drugs and carefully document what an allergy or intolerance consists of—ring the patient's GP if needed. Consult the drug chart—watch for local reactions due to subcutaneous opiate infusions or skin necrosis due to low molecular weight heparins.
- *Functional history:* are overgrown toenails really a sign of self-neglect or more likely poor vision, arthritis, poor hand grip, or neuropathy? Consider asking about diet—particularly in care home residents.

Examination

- *General:* an assessment of pressure areas is paramount—ask and look for sore heels too (and prescribe heel pads if needed). Is the skin frail, intact, marked, or broken? Xerosis is extremely common, especially in states of dehydration. Prescribing emollients will earn the thanks of your patients (who may be uncomfortable and itching) and colleagues.
- *Oedema:* avoid hurting your patient—palpate gently. Is it gravitational? Are there signs of venous insufficiency or hypoalbuminaemia? Avoid rushing instantly to the diagnosis of heart failure.

- *Gravitational eczema:* often linked with oedematous change. Look out for pigmentation change and ensure emollients are prescribed. For patients who may receive compression bandaging/hosiery—check peripheral pulses/ankle brachial pressure index (ABPI) carefully. Carefully describe any ulceration present.
- *ECG stickers:* if you perform an ECG—remove the stickers immediately afterwards. Frail skin is easily torn and ulcerated when attempts at removal are made the next day merely due to the thoughtlessness of the person recording the ECG.
- *Subcutaneous fluids:* are a key intervention in some unwell older people. Get into the habit of inspecting infusion sites, and be watchful for pooling and microabscesses.

Skin malignancies

- *Common presentations:* we all spend significant amounts of time examining and talking to our patients. Don't overlook the typical ulceration of a basal cell carcinoma around the eye/nasal region, or forget to refer to colleagues in dermatology. If you suspect a skin cancer, explore previous occupation or lifestyle.
- *Atypical presentations:* of common problems in atypical sites are legion—so be thoughtful, and carefully examine areas where patients might not look or be able to see (e.g. scalp, back, calves). Examine nails particularly carefully for signs of systemic disease or subungual melanoma. Be careful about rushing to a diagnosis of psoriasis in a new, isolated plaque. This is more likely to be Bowen's disease, so seek expert review.

Presenting patterns

Skills station 4.1

Instruction

Describe your clinical findings and give the most likely diagnosis (Fig. 4.5).

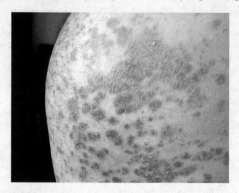

Fig. 4.5 Skin skill 1.

Model answer

This is a generalized, broadly symmetrical eruption mainly affecting the trunk with fewer lesions on the limbs and sparing of the face.

There is no specific configuration.

Morphologically, there are erythematous plaques with overlying silvery scale. These are small (5–10mm diameter), but are coalescing into larger plaques at some sites.

The diagnosis is guttate psoriasis.

Skills station 4.2

Instruction

Describe your clinical findings and give the most likely diagnosis (Fig. 4.6).

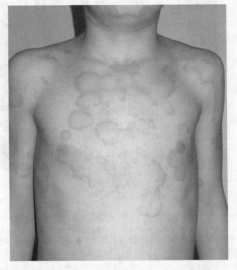

Fig. 4.6 Skin skill 2.

Model answer

This is a widespread, symmetrical eruption, which affects the trunk, arms, and face.

The lesions are markedly annular and polycyclic [having varying curves].

They comprise erythematous wheals of various sizes.

The diagnosis is urticaria.

Skills station 4.3

Instruction

Describe your clinical findings and give the most likely diagnosis (Fig. 4.7).

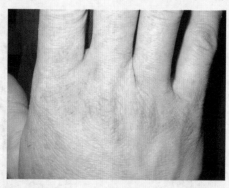

Fig. 4.7 Skin skill 3.

Model answer

This symmetrical eruption is confined to the dorsal aspect of the hands. The changes are diffuse and ill-defined so there is no specific configuration. There is xerosis, with some mild erythema, fine scaling, and some tiny fissures.

These changes are eczematous and the most likely diagnosis is irritant contact dermatitis.

Skills station 4.4

Instruction

Describe your clinical findings and give the most likely diagnosis (Fig. 4.8).

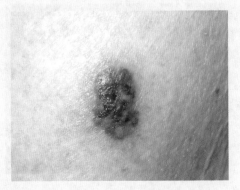

Fig. 4.8 Skin skill 4.

Model answer

This is a solitary, pigmented lesion on the upper back. It is asymmetrical with an irregular but clearly demarcated border; it has various colours including grey, dark brown, blue-black, and black; the size is 18x11mm and the lesion is elevated.

Other features comprise a moist, eroded surface and some surrounding erythema.

The lesion looks highly suspicious for malignant melanoma.

Skills station 4.5

Instruction

Describe your clinical findings and give the most likely diagnosis (Fig. 4.9).

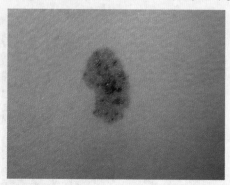

Fig. 4.9 Skin skill 5.

Model answer

This is a solitary, pigmented lesion.

It is broadly symmetrical, with a somewhat irregular but clearly defined border. There is a mid-brown, macular base studded with darker brown papules, the largest of which is central. It measures 15x8mm in diameter.

This is probably a benign, congenital naevus spilus (speckled naevus).

Skills station 4.6

Instruction

Describe your clinical findings and give the most likely diagnosis (Fig. 4.10).

Model answer

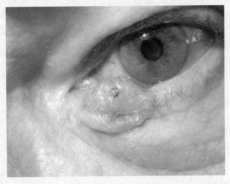

Fig 4.10 Skin skill 6.

This is a solitary 15mm lesion which straddles the left medial lower eyelid margin. It is a nodule with a rolled, pearly edge and some overlying telangiectasia. There is a small crusted area centrally.

The diagnosis is basal cell carcinoma.

Skills station 4.7

Instruction

Describe your clinical findings and give the most likely diagnosis (Fig. 4.11).

Model answer

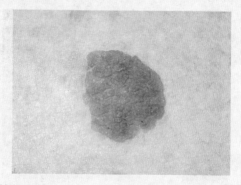

Fig. 4.11 Skin skill 7.

This is a pigmented lesion. It is symmetrical with a slightly irregular border, which is sharply defined to the extent that the lesion has a 'stuck on' appearance.

The colour is uniform mid-brown throughout the main part of the lesion, though there is also a skin-coloured component abutting this on the left.

The diameter is 12mm and the lesion is morphologically a plaque (i.e. elevated). The surface is fissured and warty.

This is a seborrhoeic keratosis.

The cardiovascular system

Introduction

The cardiovascular system is fundamentally rather straightforward and a good deal of information about its functioning can be gleaned from physical examination. The basic anatomy of the cardiovascular system should be familiar to readers. This is a summary of some points which have particular implications for the clinical assessment.

The heart

The heart rotates anticlockwise during embryonic development, finally settling such that the left ventricle lies almost entirely posteriorly and the right anteriorly—the whole seeming to hang in the chest, held by the aorta ('aorta' comes from the Greek 'aorte' meaning 'to suspend').

The myocardium is arranged in a complex spiral such that a contraction causes the heart to elongate and rotate slightly, hitting the anterior chest wall as it does—this can be felt as the apex beat.

All this movement is lubricated by a double-lined cavity filled with a very small amount of fluid that the heart sits in—the pericardial sac.

Heart sounds

As the ventricles contract, the tricuspid and mitral valves close, heard as the 1st heart sound. As the ventricles relax, intraventricular pressure drops and blood expelled into the great vessels begins to fall back, the aortic and pulmonary valves slam closed—this is heard as the 2nd heart sound. The sounds are often described as sounding like '*lub dub*'.

As each heart sound is, in fact, two valves closing, any mistiming will cause a double or 'split' heart sound as one valve closes shortly after the other. A split 2nd heart sound is normal in young adults and children. During inspiration, the intrathoracic pressure drops, drawing blood into the chest, ↑ delivery to the right side of the heart, and ↓ delivery to the left as it pools in the pulmonary veins. Consequently, the stroke volume will be greater on the right than the left and the right ventricular contraction will take slightly longer. Thus, the pulmonary valve will close very slightly later than the aortic valve, producing the split 2nd sound ('lub da-dub'). This is 'physiological splitting'.

Jugular venous pulse

There is no valve between the right heart and the large vessels supplying it. Thus, filling and contraction of the right atrium will cause a pressure wave to travel back through the feeding veins. This can actually be seen in the neck at the internal jugular vein.

Arteries

As the ventricle expels blood into the arteries, it sends a pulse wave to the periphery which can be felt. This is not the actual flow of blood from the ventricle at that contraction but a pressure wave. The shape and feel of the wave can be altered by the force of expulsion, any obstacles (such as the aortic valve), and the state of the peripheral vasculature.

The arteries have their own intrinsic elasticity, allowing a baseline, or diastolic, pressure to be maintained between each pulse wave.

Veins

Blood flows at a much lower pressure in the veins.

Above the level of the heart, gravity does most of the work in returning the blood. Below, blood return is facilitated by contraction of muscles surrounding the deep veins, helped by numerous one-way valves to prevent backflow. Blood moves initially from the surface to the deep veins before moving upwards, again mediated by one-way valves (if these valves become damaged, blood flows outward to the surface veins causing them to swell and look unsightly—varicose veins).

Blood return is also aided by a negative pressure created by blood being pumped out of the right ventricle—and therefore drawn in through the right atrium at each beat.

Chest pain

This is the most common—and most important—cardiovascular symptom. Patients who mention it may be surprised to find themselves whisked away for an ECG before they can say any more. It is usually possible to determine the probable cause of the pain from the history.

As for any other type of pain, the history must include the standard 'SOCRATES' questions (see ➲ Chapter 2):

- Nature (crushing, burning, aching, stabbing, etc.).
- Exact location.
- Any radiation.
- Severity (scored out of 10).
- Mode and rate of onset. What was the patient doing at the time?
- Change in the pain over time (and current score out of 10).
- Duration (if now resolved).
- Exacerbating factors (particularly, is it affected by respiration or movement?).
- Relieving factors (including the use of GTN).
- Associated symptoms (nausea, vomiting, sweating, belching, etc.).

Patients with a history of cardiac pain can also usually tell you whether the pain experienced is the same as, or different to, their 'usual' angina.

Angina

Full name 'angina pectoris', this is the pain caused by myocardial ischaemia. See Box 5.1 for the classic features.

'Angina' comes from the Latin for 'choking' and this is often what the patient describes. As the brain cannot interpret pain from the heart per se, it is felt over the central part of the anterior chest and can radiate up to the jaw, shoulder, or down the arms or even to the umbilicus. This pattern is due to the common embryological origins of the heart and these parts of the body. Some patients may experience angina pain *only* in the arm or jaw, for example.

The 'pain' of angina is usually an unfamiliar sensation; consequently, patients may be more comfortable with the term 'discomfort'.

In patients with known angina, a *change* in the nature of the symptoms is important.

Box 5.1 Classic features of angina

- Retrosternal
- 'Crushing', 'heaviness', or 'like a tight band'
- Worse with physical or emotional exertion, cold weather, and after eating
- Relieved by rest and nitrate spray (within a couple of minutes)
- Not affected by respiration or movement
- Sometimes associated with breathlessness.

▶ In addition, patients classically clench their right fist and hold it to their chest when describing the pain.

Myocardial infarction (MI)

Patients will know this as a 'heart attack'. The pain is similar to that of angina but much more severe, persistent (despite GTN spray), and associated with nausea, sweating, and vomiting. Patients may also describe a feeling of impending doom or death—'angor animi'.

Pericarditis

The commonest causes are viral or bacterial infection, MI, or uraemia.
- Constant retrosternal 'soreness'.
- Worse on inspiration (pleuritic).
- Relieved slightly by sitting forwards.
- Not related to movement or exertion.

Oesophageal spasm

Often mistaken for MI or angina.
- A severe, retrosternal burning pain.
- Onset often after eating or drinking.
- May be associated with dysphagia.
- May have a history of dyspepsia.
- May be relieved by GTN as this is a smooth muscle relaxant (hence the confusion with angina) but GTN will take up to 20 minutes to relieve this pain whereas angina is relieved within a few minutes.

Gastro-oesophageal reflux disease ('heartburn')

- Retrosternal, burning pain.
- Relieved by antacids, onset after eating.

Dissecting aortic aneurysm

Must be differentiated from an MI as thrombolysis here may prove fatal.
- Severe 'tearing' pain.
- Felt posteriorly—classically between the shoulder blades.
- Persistent, most severe at onset.
- Patient is usually hypertensive and 'marfanoid'.

Pleuritic (respiratory) pain

This is covered in more detail in ⭢ Chapter 6. May be caused by a wide range of respiratory conditions, particularly pulmonary embolus and pneumothorax.
- Sharp pain, worse on inspiration and coughing.
- Not central—may be localized to one side of the chest.
- No radiation.
- No relief with GTN.
- Associated with breathlessness, cyanosis, etc.

Musculoskeletal pain

May be caused by injury, fracture, chondritis, etc. Will be localized to a particular spot on the chest and worsened by movement and respiration. May be tender to palpation.

Tietze's syndrome is costochondritis (inflammation of the costal cartilages) at ribs 2, 3, and 4. Will be associated with tender swelling over the costo-sternal joints.

Breathlessness and oedema

Breathlessness and oedema are presented together here as, usually, they are linked pathophysiologically in the cardiovascular patient.

Excess tissue fluid caused by a failing heart will settle where gravity pulls it. In someone who is on their feet, it will settle in their ankles causing swelling. If the patient is bed bound, the swelling will occur about their sacrum and if the patient is lying down, fluid will collect on their lungs (pulmonary oedema) causing breathlessness.

Dyspnoea (breathlessness)

Dyspnoea is an abnormal awareness of one's breathing and is described in detail in ➲ Chapter 6. There are certain aspects of breathlessness that you should ask of the cardiovascular patient in particular.

As with everything, you must quantify the symptom if you are able so as to gauge its severity; this gives a baseline so that the effects of treatment or disease progression can be monitored. The New York Heart Association (NYHA) has devised a classification of breathlessness which is shown in Box 5.2. In practice, this is only used in clinical trials and it makes more sense to measure the functional result of breathlessness. Ask especially:

- How far can the patient walk on the flat before they have to stop ('march tolerance')?
- What about stairs and hills—can they make it up a flight?
- Are they sure that they stop due to breathlessness or is it some other reason (arthritic knees for example)?
- Has the patient had to curtail their normal activities in any way?

Orthopnoea

This is breathlessness when lying flat. Patients will not usually volunteer this as a symptom so ask them:

- How many pillows does the patient sleep with and has this changed?
  - Some patients may describe having to sleep sitting upright in a chair.
- If the patient sleeps with a number of pillows, ask why. Are they breathless when they lie down or is it for some other reason?

Paroxysmal nocturnal dyspnoea

This is episodes of breathlessness occurring at night—usually thought to be due to pulmonary oedema. Patients won't usually volunteer this information and will often react with surprised pleasure when you ask them about it.

Sufferers will experience waking in the night spluttering and coughing—they find they have to sit up or stand and many go to the window for 'fresh air' in an attempt to regain their normal breathing.

Ask:

- Do they wake up in the night coughing and trying to catch their breath?
- If so, glean as much detail as you can—including how often and how badly the symptom is disturbing the patient's sleep cycle.

Cough

Pulmonary oedema may cause a cough productive of frothy white sputum. This may be flecked with blood ('pink') due to ruptured bronchial vessels but this is not usually a worrying sign in itself.

Ankle oedema

As already mentioned, in ambulant patients fluid will collect at the ankles and cause swelling. It is often surprising just how severe the swelling can get before people seek medical attention. Ask:

* How long has this been going on for?
* Is it worse at any particular time of day? (Typically cardiac oedema is worse toward the evening and resolved somewhat overnight as the oedema redistributes itself.)
* Exactly how extensive is the swelling? Is it confined to the feet and ankles or does it extend to the shin, knee, thigh, or even the buttocks, genitalia, and anterior abdominal wall?
* Is there any evidence of abdominal swelling and ascites?

Box 5.2 NYHA classification of breathlessness

* *I* = nil at rest, some on vigorous exercise
* *II* = nil at rest, breathless on moderate exertion
* *III* = mild breathlessness at rest, worse on mild exertion
* *IV* = significant breathlessness at rest and worse on even slight exertion (the patient is often bed-bound).

Fatigue

A difficult symptom to determine as you'll find that most people will claim to be more tired than normal if asked. However, this pathological fatigue is caused by reduced cardiac output and decreased blood supply to muscles and needs to be taken seriously. Again, quantify and determine:

* Is the patient able to do less than they were previously?
* Is any decrease in activity due to fatigue or some other symptom (e.g. breathlessness)?
* What activities has the patient had to give up due to fatigue?
* What are they able to do before they become too tired?

Palpitations

To have palpitations is to have an awareness of one's own heart beating. This is one of the many situations in which the patient may have a very different idea of the word's meaning than you. You should spend some time teasing out exactly what they mean. Patients may be unfamiliar with the term and, instead, describe the heart 'jumping' or 'missing a beat'.

Attempt to determine:
- When did the sensation start and stop?
- How long did it last?
- Did it come on suddenly or gradually?
- Did the patient blackout? If so, for how long?
- Was the heartbeat felt as fast, slow, or some other pattern?
- Was it regular or irregular?
  - It is useful at this stage to ask the patient to tap out what they felt on their knee or a nearby table.
- What was the patient doing when the palpitations started?
- Is there any relationship to eating or drinking (particularly tea, coffee, wine, chocolate)?
- Could it have been precipitated or terminated by any medication?
- Has this ever happened before? If so, what were the circumstances?
- Any associated symptoms? (Chest pain, shortness of breath, syncope, nausea, dizziness.)
- Did the patient have to stop their activities or lie down?
- Was the patient able to stop the palpitations somehow? (Often, people discover they can terminate their palpitations with a vagal manoeuvre such as a Valsalva manoeuvre, a cough, or swallow.)

Syncope

This is a faint or a swoon. You must determine whether there truly was a loss of consciousness and not simply the feeling that the patient was about to faint (pre-syncope). In particular, can the patient remember hitting the floor? If there really was a loss of consciousness, attempt to gain a collateral history from witnesses.

Determine also:
- Was the onset gradual or sudden?
- How long was the loss of consciousness?
- What was the patient doing at the time? (Standing, urinating, coughing.)
- Were there any preceding or associated symptoms such as chest pain, palpitations, nausea, sweating (see previously)?
- Was there any relationship to the use of medication? (Antihypertensives and use of GTN spray are common culprits.)
- When the patient came round, were there any other symptoms remaining?
- Was there any tongue-biting or urinary or faecal incontinence?
- Was there any motor activity during the unconscious episode?
- How long did it take for the patient to feel 'back to normal'?

Claudication

This comes from the Latin 'claudicatio' meaning 'to limp'. These days, how-ever, it is used to describe muscle pain that occurs during exercise as a sign of peripheral ischaemia.

In true claudication, the patient describes the pain thus:

- Feels like a tight 'cramp' in the muscle.
- Usually occurs in the calf, thigh, buttock, and foot.
- Appears only on exercise.
- Disappears at rest.
- May also be associated with numbness or pins-and-needles on the skin of the foot (blood is diverted from the skin to the ischaemic muscle).

As always, you should attempt to quantify wherever possible. In this case, determine the 'claudication distance'—that is, how far the patient is able to walk before the pain starts. This will be useful in judging the severity of the disability and in monitoring the condition.

Rest pain

A similar pain to claudication, but this comes on *at rest* and is usually contin-uous—a sign of severe ischaemia. The patient may describe:

- Continuous, severe pain in the calf, thigh, buttock, or foot.
- 'Aching' in nature.
- Lasts through the day and night.
- Exacerbations of the pain may wake the patient from sleep.
- The patient may find slight relief by hanging the affected leg off the side of the bed.

The rest of the history

Cardiac risk factors

These are important aspects of the history that have an impact on the risk of cardiovascular disease. When documenting a history of a cardiovascular case, it is worth pulling these out of the usual order and documenting as a list with ticks/crosses and details where appropriate at the end of the presenting complaint. They should not then be repeated again later in the clerking.

- *Age:* increased risk with age.
- *Gender:* risk in males > females.
- *Obesity:* how heavy is the patient? (Calculate their BMI.)
- *Smoking:* quantify in pack-years. Don't be caught out by the 'ex-smoker' that gave up yesterday!
- *Hypertension:* find out when was it diagnosed? How was it treated? Is it being monitored?
- *Hypercholesterolaemia:* increasingly, patients will know about this, some will even know their last reading. When was it diagnosed? How is it treated and monitored?
- *Diabetes:* what type? When was it diagnosed? How is it treated and monitored? What are the usual glucose readings?
- *FHx:* particularly 1st degree relatives who have had cardiovascular events/diagnoses before the age of 60.

Past medical history

Ask especially about:

- Angina—if they have a GTN spray, ask how often they need to use it and whether this has changed significantly recently.
- MI—when? How was it treated?
- Ischaemic heart disease—how was the diagnosis made? Any angiograms? What other investigations has the patient had?
- Cardiac surgery—bypass? How many arteries?
- AF or other rhythm disturbance—what treatment? On warfarin?
- Rheumatic fever.
- Endocarditis.
- Thyroid disease.

Drug history

Take particular note of cardiac medication and attempt to assess compliance and the patient's understanding of what the medication does.

Social history

As in any other case, take note of the patient's employment—both how the disease has affected their ability to work and bear in mind how any cardiac diagnosis may affect the patient's employability.

Also record the home arrangements—are there any carers present, aids or adaptations, stairs, and so on.

Outline cardiovascular examination

The full examination framework is shown in Box 5.3. The order is not to be strictly adhered to but the authors feel that this is the easiest routine, working from the hands and face to more intimate areas of the body.

Positioning

The patient should be seated, leaning back to 45°, supported by pillows with their chest, arms, and ankles (if appropriate) exposed. Their head should be well supported allowing relaxation of the muscles in the neck. Ensure the room is warm and there is enough privacy. In an 'exam' condition, the patient should be undressed to their underwear.

If you intend to measure that patient's blood pressure seated and standing (remember to make the patient stand for 3 minutes before measuring), it may be wise to do this at the beginning of the examination.

Box 5.3 Framework for the cardiovascular examination

An example framework for a thorough examination of the cardiovascular system—the information in this chapter is presented in a slightly different order for the purpose of clarity.

This is the authors' recommendation. Other methods exist and none are right or wrong so long as nothing is missed.

- General inspection
- Hands
- Radial pulse
- Brachial pulse
- Blood pressure
- Face
- Eyes
- Tongue
- Carotid pulse
- Jugular venous pressure and pulse waveform
- Inspection of the precordium
- Palpation of the precordium
- Auscultation of the precordium
- Auscultation of the neck
- Dynamic manoeuvres (if appropriate)
- Lung bases
- Abdomen
- Peripheral pulses (lower limbs)
- Oedema.

General inspection and hands

General inspection

As always, take a step back and take an objective look at the patient.

- Do they look ill? If so, in which way?
- Are they short of breath at rest?
- Is there any cyanosis?
- What is their nutritional state?
  - Are they overweight?
  - Are they cachectic (underweight with muscle wasting)?
- Do they have features of any genetic syndrome such as Turner's, Down's, or Marfan's?

Hands

Take the patient's right hand in yours as if to greet them, look at it carefully and briefly compare with the other side. Look especially for:

- Temperature (may be cold in congestive cardiac failure).
- Sweat.
- The state of the nails.
  - Blue discoloration if peripheral blood flow is poor
  - Splinter haemorrhages (small streak-like bleeds in the nail bed) seen especially in bacterial endocarditis but may also be a sign of rheumatoid arthritis, vasculitis, trauma, or sepsis from any source.
- Finger clubbing.
  - Cardiac causes include infective endocarditis, and cyanotic congenital heart disease.
- Xanthomata.
  - Raised yellow lesions caused by a build-up of lipids beneath the skin
  - Often seen on tendons at the wrist.
- Osler nodes.
  - Rare manifestation of infective endocarditis (a late sign and the disease is usually treated before this develops)
  - Red, tender nodules on the finger pulps or thenar eminence.
- Janeway lesions.
  - Non-tender macular-papular erythematous lesions seen on the palm or finger pulps
  - A rare feature of bacterial endocarditis.

Peripheral pulses

For each peripheral pulse, you should attempt to detect the rate and rhythm of the pulsation. For the brachial and carotid pulsations in particular, you should also determine the volume and character (waveform) of the pulse.

Technique

Examination technique is illustrated in Fig. 5.1.

It is good practice *not* to use your thumb to feel pulses as you may mistake your own pulse (which can be felt weakly in the thumb) for the weak pulse of the patient—especially in the peripheral arteries.

Radial artery

Feeling for the waveform is not useful here as it is too far from the heart.

• Use your 1st and 2nd fingers to feel just lateral to the tendon of the flexor carpi radialis, medial to the radial styloid process at the wrist.

Brachial artery

• Feel at the medial side of the antecubital fossa, just medial to the tendinous insertion of the biceps.

Carotid artery

This is the best place to assess the pulse volume and waveform.

• Find the larynx, move a couple of centimetres laterally and press backwards medial to the sternomastoid muscle.
  • ❶ Be sure not to compress both carotids at once for fear of stemming blood flow to the brain—particularly in the frail and elderly.

Femoral artery

This is another useful place for assessing the waveform unless there is disease or abnormality in the abdominal aorta.

• The patient is usually undressed by this point in the examination and should be lying on a bed or couch with their legs outstretched.
• Ask them to lower their clothes a little more, exposing the groins.
• The femoral pulsation can be felt midway between the pubic tubercle and the anterior superior iliac spine.

Popliteal artery

This lies deep in the popliteal fossa and is surrounded by strong tendons. It can be difficult to feel and usually requires more pressure than you expect. There are several techniques but we recommend:

• With the patient lying flat and knees slightly flexed, press into the centre of the popliteal fossa with tips of the fingers of the left hand and use the fingers of the right hand to add extra pressure to these.

Posterior tibial artery

• Palpate at the ankle just posterior and inferior to the medial malleolus.

Dorsalis pedis

• This runs lateral to the exterior hallucis longus tendon on the superior surface of the foot between the bases of the 1st and 2nd metatarsals.

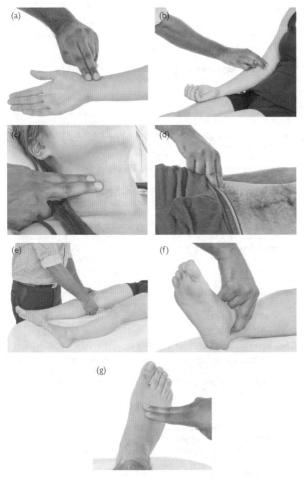

Fig. 5.1 Palpation of the peripheral pulses. (a) The radial pulse. (b) The brachial pulse. (c) The carotid pulse. (d) The femoral pulse. (e) The popliteal pulse. (f) The posterior tibial pulse. (g) The dorsalis pedis pulse.

Pulse rate

This should be expressed in 'beats per minute'. A rate <60bpm is called 'bradycardia' whilst 'tachycardia' is a pulse >100bpm. A normal healthy adult pulse rate should be ~60–100bpm.

The most accurate method is to count the pulse for a full minute. In practice, you count for a portion of this and calculate the rate by multiplication. Commonly, people count for 15 seconds and multiply by 4.

Rhythm

You should feel the pulse as long as it takes to be sure of the rhythm. In general, the pulse can be either regular or irregular but variations exist.

- *Regular:* a self-explanatory definition. It must be remembered that the pulse rate may decrease with inspiration and increase with expiration in the normal state.
- *Irregularly irregular:* this is a completely random pattern of pulsation and is synonymous with atrial fibrillation in which the atria twitch and contract in an irregular fashion sending electrical impulses to the ventricles (and therefore causing contraction and arterial pulsation) at random intervals.
- *Regularly irregular:* not quite the contradiction that it seems—you can have a non-regular pulse that occurs in some other regular pattern. For example, pulsus bigeminus will cause regular ectopic beats resulting in alternating brief gaps and long gaps between pulses. In Wenckebach's phenomenon, you may feel increasing time between each pulse until one is 'missed' and then the cycle repeats.
- *Regular with ectopics:* a very difficult thing to feel and be sure of without an ECG. A 'normal' regular heart rate may be intermittently interrupted by a beat that is out of step, making the pulse feel almost 'irregularly irregular'.

Character/waveform and volume

This is best assessed at the carotid artery. You are feeling for the speed at which the artery expands and collapses and force with which it does so. It takes some practice to master and it may be useful to imagine a graph such as those shown in Fig. 5.2. Some examples are:

- *Aortic stenosis:* a 'slow rising' pulse, maybe with a palpable shudder. Sometimes called 'anacrotic' or a 'plateau' phase.
- *Aortic regurgitation:* a 'collapsing' pulse which feels as though it suddenly hits your fingers and falls away just as quickly. You could try feeling at the brachial artery and raising the arm above the patient's heart. Sometimes referred to as a 'waterhammer' pulse.
- *Pulsus bisferiens:* a waveform with 2 peaks, found where aortic stenosis and regurgitation coexist.
- *Hypertrophic cardiomyopathy:* this pulse may feel normal at first but peter out quickly. Often described as 'jerky'.
- *Pulsus alternans:* an alternating strong and weak pulsation, synonymous with a severely impaired left ventricle in a failing heart.
- *Pulsus paradoxus:* pulse is weaker during inspiration (causes include cardiac tamponade, status asthmaticus, and constrictive pericarditis).

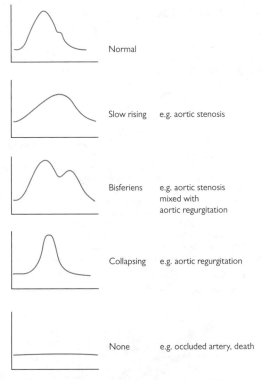

Fig. 5.2 Graphical representation of arterial pulse waveforms and their causes.

Other tests of arterial pulsation

These are not routinely performed unless the history and rest of the examination has made the examiner suspicious of the specific pathologies that they represent.

Radio-radial delay

You should feel both radial pulses simultaneously. In the normal state, the pulses will occur together. Any delay in the pulsation reaching the radial artery on one side may point to pathology such as an aneurysm at the aortic arch or subclavian artery stenosis.

Radio-femoral delay

You should palpate the radial and femoral pulses on the same side simultaneously. They should occur together. Any delay in the pulsation reaching the femoral artery may point to aortic pathology such as coarctation.

The face and neck

Face

Examine the patient's face at rest. It's a good idea to develop your own pattern for this. The authors recommend starting with an overview, moving to the eyes, the mouth, then the neck. The order is not important as long as all aspects are examined. Be sure to ask them to:

- Look up whilst you gently pull down one lower eyelid, exposing the conjunctiva.
- 'Open wide' and look inside their mouth.
- Protrude their tongue.

In the cardiovascular examination, you should be looking especially for:

- *Jaundice:* seen as a yellow discoloration of the sclera.
- *Anaemia:* seen as an unusually pale conjunctiva (practice needed here).
- *Xanthelasma:* yellow, raised lesions found particularly around the eyes, indicative of a high serum cholesterol.
- *Corneal arcus:* a yellow ring seen overlying the iris. Significant in patients <40 years but not in older persons.
- *Mitral facies:* rosy cheeks suggestive of mitral stenosis.
- *Cyanosis:* seen as a bluish discoloration of the lips and tongue.
- *High arched palate:* suggestive of diseases such as Marfan's syndrome.
- *Dental hygiene:* a common source of organisms causing endocarditis.

Carotid pulse

At this point in the routine, the carotid pulse should be examined.

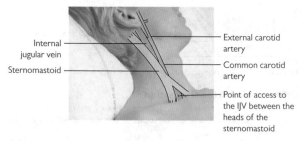

Internal jugular vein

Sternomastoid

External carotid artery

Common carotid artery

Point of access to the IJV between the heads of the sternomastoid

Fig. 5.3 The surface anatomy of the vasculature in the neck. Note that the IJV is partly hidden by the sternocleidomastoid at the base of the neck.

Jugular venous pressure

Theory

The jugular veins connect to the SVC and the right atrium without any intervening valves. Therefore, changes in pressure in the right atrium will transmit a pressure wave up these veins which can be seen in the neck. By measuring the height of the impulse, the pressure in the right side of the circulation can be expressed in centimetres.

It is often said that the JVP must only be measured in the internal jugular vein (IJV). This is not strictly the case. The external jugular vein (EJV) is easily seen as it makes a winding course down the neck (see Fig. 5.3). Its tortuous course means that impulses are not transmitted as readily or as reliably. It is for this reason that the IJV is used.

- The centre of the right atrium lies ~5cm below the sternal angle which is used as the reference point.
- The normal JVP is ~8cm of blood (therefore 3cm above the sternal angle). With the patient tilted back to 45°, the upper border of the pulse is just hidden at the base of the neck. This, therefore, is used as the standard position for JVP measurement.
- ▶ Remember, it is the vertical distance from the sternal angle to the upper border of the pulsation that must be measured.
- ▶ You must add 5cm to the figure to give the true JVP.

Examination

- With the patient lying back at 45°, expose the neck.
- Ask the patient to turn their head away from you (their left) and ensure that the neck muscles are relaxed.
- Look for the JVP and measure the *vertical* distance from the top of the pulsation to the sternal angle (see Fig. 5.4).
  - The result is often expressed along the lines of '3cm raised'
  - It must be remembered that that is a total JVP of 8cm after adding the extra 5cm that are not measured.
- Try to look upwards, along the line of the sternomastoid. Don't get too close and use oblique lighting to make the pulsation more obvious.

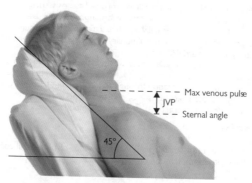

Fig. 5.4 Measuring the JVP. Measure the *vertical* distance.

Differentiating the jugular and carotid pulsations

The rules for differentiating the jugular and carotid pulsations are guides only and not always true. For example, in severe tricuspid regurgitation, the jugular pulse is palpable and is not easily abolished by compression. If proving difficult, test the hepatojugular reflex. See Table 5.1.

Table 5.1 Jugular and carotid pulsation

Jugular pulsation	Carotid pulsation
2 peaks (in sinus rhythm)	1 peak
Impalpable	Palpable
Obliterated by pressure	Hard to obliterate
Moves with respiration	Little movement with respiration

Hepatojugular reflux
- Watch the neck pulsation.
- Exert pressure over the liver with the flat of your right hand.
  - The JVP should rise by 2cm, the carotid pulse will not.

Character of the jugular venous pulsation

This is rather difficult without experience (Box 5.4). The jugular pulsation has 2 main peaks (see Fig. 5.5). You should establish the timing of the peaks in the cardiac cycle by palpating the carotid pulse at the same time. The key features are:
- *a wave*: caused by atrial contraction. Seen just before the carotid pulse.
- *c point*: slight AV-ring bulge during ventricular contraction.
- *x descent*: atrial relaxation.
- *v wave*: tricuspid closure and atrial filling.
- *y descent*: ventricular filling as tricuspid valve opens.

Findings
- *Raised JVP*: right ventricular failure, tricuspid stenosis, tricuspid regurgitation, superior vena cava obstruction, PE, fluid overload.
- *Large a waves*: caused usually by a hypertrophied right atrium (pulmonary hypertension, pulmonary stenosis, tricuspid stenosis).
- *Absent a wave*: atrial fibrillation.
- *'Cannon' a waves*: large, irregular waves caused by contraction of the atrium against a closed tricuspid valve. Seen in complete heart block.
- *Large v waves*: regurgitation through an incompetent tricuspid valve.
- *Sharp y descent*: characteristic of constrictive pericarditis.
- *Sharp x descent*: characteristic of cardiac tamponade.

Kussmaul's sign

The JVP will reduce during inspiration in the normal state. The JVP will rise during inspiration (Kussmaul's sign) in the presence of pericardial constriction, right ventricular infarction or, rarely, cardiac tamponade.

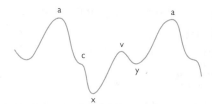

Fig. 5.5 Representation of the normal jugular venous pulsation.

Box 5.4 A word about honesty in learning

Students often find the JVP hard to see whilst they are learning the various examination techniques, which reminds the authors of an important point.

There is, in medicine, an almost overwhelming pressure to say 'yes' when asked 'can you see that?' by the teacher. You may be motivated by a fear of appearing stupid, taking too much of the tutor's time, or delaying the ward round further. This, however, is useful to no-one. The student fails to learn the correct technique or the correct identification of the sign and the teacher fails to discover that their demonstration is inadequate. Misconceptions are born and are passed from person to person.

The authors, therefore, urge students of medicine of all ages and at all stages to say 'no, please show me again' and we will all be better for it.

The precordium: inspection and palpation

The 'precordium' refers to that part of the chest overlying the heart.

Inspection

The patient should be lying at 45° with the chest exposed. Look for:
- Scars.
  - Sternal split is used to access the median structures and to perform coronary artery bypass surgery
  - A left lateral thoracotomy may be evidence of previous closed mitral valvotomy, resection of coarctation, or ligation of a patent ductus arteriosus.
- Any abnormal chest shape or movements.
- Pacemaker or implantable defibrillator.
  - Usually implanted over the left pectoral region.
- Any visible pulsations.

Palpation

Explain what you are doing and gain consent before touching.

General palpation

Place the flat of your right hand on the chest wall—to the left, then to the right of the sternum. Can you feel any pulsations?
- 'Heave': a sustained, thrusting pulsation usually felt at the left sternal edge.
  - Indicates right ventricular enlargement.
- 'Thrill': this is a palpable murmur felt as a shudder beneath your hand.
  - Caused by severe valvular disease
  - If systolic: aortic stenosis, ventricular septal defect, or mitral regurgitation
  - If diastolic: mitral stenosis.

Palpating the apex beat

This is the lowermost lateral point at which a definite pulsation can be felt. Usually at the 5th intercostal space in the mid-clavicular line (Fig. 5.6).
- Abnormal position of the apex beat: usually more lateral.
  - Caused by an enlarged heart or disease of the chest wall.
- No apex beat felt: usually caused by heavy padding with fat or internal padding with an over-inflated emphysematous lung.
  - Try asking the patient to lean forwards or laterally.
- ❶ Beware of dextrocardia. If no beat is felt, check on the right.

Character of the apex beat
This can only be learnt by experience, after having felt many 'normal' impulses. Some common abnormalities are:

- *Stronger, more forceful:* hyperdynamic circulation.
  - Causes include sepsis, anaemia.
- *Sustained:* impulse 'longer' than expected.
  - Causes include left ventricular hypertrophy, aortic stenosis, hypertrophic cardiomyopathy, and hyperkinesia.
- *Double impulse:* palpable atrial systole.
  - Characteristic of hyptertrophic cardiomyopathy.
- 'Tapping': this is the description given to a palpable 1st heart sound in severe mitral stenosis.
- *Diffuse:* a poorly localized beat.
  - Caused by left ventricular aneurysm.
- Impalpable.
  - Possible causes include emphysema, obesity, pericardial effusion, death.

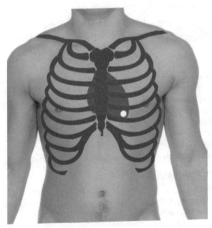

Fig. 5.6 Surface anatomy of the heart and most common location of the apex beat.

The precordium: auscultation

Technique

Different methods exist for this examination. A sensible approach would be to listen with the diaphragm at each area and then repeat using the bell. You can then 'go back' and concentrate on any abnormalities. You can then examine other areas looking for the features of certain murmurs and extra sounds.

- The 'bell' of the stethoscope is used to detect lower-pitched sounds, the diaphragm higher-pitched.
- You should auscultate at each of the four standard areas (Box 5.5, Fig. 5.7).

Box 5.5 The four areas

- *Mitral:* 5th intercostal space in the mid-axillary line (the apex)
- *Tricuspid:* 5th intercostal space at the left sternal edge
- *Pulmonary:* 2nd intercostal space at the left sternal edge
- *Aortic:* 2nd intercostal space at the right sternal edge.

❶ Note that these areas do not relate exactly to the anatomical position of the valves but are the areas at which the sound of each valve can be best heard.

Practice is needed here and many hearts should be listened to in order to be familiar with the normal sounds. The physiology behind the heart sounds and physiological splitting have been described and may be worth revisiting at this point.

If you are unsure which is the 1st and 2nd heart sound—or where a murmur is occurring—you can palpate one carotid pulse whilst listening to the heart—enabling you to 'feel' systole. The carotid pulsation occurs with S_1. (❶ Remember to only palpate one carotid pulse at a time.)

The heart sounds

1st heart sound (S_1)

Mitral valve closure is the main component of S_1 and the volume depends on the force with which it closes.

- *Loud:* forceful closing (mitral stenosis, tricuspid stenosis, tachycardia).
- *Soft:* prolonged ventricular filling or delayed systole (left bundle branch block, aortic stenosis, aortic regurgitation).
- *Variable:* variable ventricular filling (atrial fibrillation, complete heart block).

2nd heart sound (S_2)

- *Soft:* reduced mobility of aortic valve (aortic stenosis) or if leaflets fail to close properly (aortic regurgitation).
- *Loud:* aortic component loud in hypertension or congenital aortic stenosis (here the valve is narrowed but mobile). Pulmonary component loud in pulmonary hypertension.

Splitting of the 2nd heart sound
- *Exaggerated normal splitting:* caused by a delay in right ventricular emptying (right bundle branch block, pulmonary stenosis, ventricular septal defect, or mitral regurgitation).
- *Fixed splitting:* no difference in the extent of splitting between inspiration and expiration. Usually due to atrial septal defect.
- *Reversed splitting:* i.e. the pulmonary component of S_2 comes before the aortic component. Caused by a delay in left ventricular emptying (left bundle branch block, aortic stenosis, aortic coarctation).

3rd heart sound

This is a low frequency (can just be heard with the bell) sound just after S_2. Described as a 'triple' or 'gallop' rhythm. 'Da-da-dum' or 'ken-tuck-y'. Occurs at the end of rapid ventricular filling, early in diastole and is caused by tautening of the papillary muscles or ventricular distension.
- *Physiological:* soft sound heard only at the apex, normal in children and fit adults up to the age of 30.
- *Pathological:* indicates some impairment of left ventricular function or rapid ventricular filling (dilated cardiomyopathy, aortic regurgitation, mitral regurgitation, or constrictive pericarditis).
  - May be associated with a high-pitched pericardial knock.

4th heart sound

A late diastolic sound (just before S_1) caused by reduced compliance—or increased stiffness—of the ventricular myocardium. 'Da-lub dub' or 'Ten-ne-ssee'. Coincides with abnormally forceful atrial contraction and raised end diastolic pressure in the left ventricle.
- Never physiological.
  - Causes include hypertrophic cardiomyopathy and hypertension.

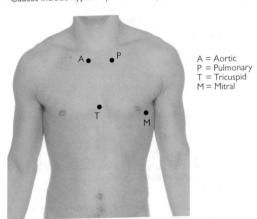

A = Aortic
P = Pulmonary
T = Tricuspid
M = Mitral

Fig. 5.7 The four standard areas for auscultation of the precordium and the valves that are best heard at each area.

Murmurs

These are 'musical' humming sounds produced by the turbulent flow of blood. For each murmur heard, you should determine:

- The timing.
- The site and radiation (where is it heard the loudest?).
- The loudness and pitch (see Box 5.6).
- The relationship to posture and respiration.

The timing of the murmur is particularly essential in establishing the sound's origin. You must decide whether the noise occurs in systole or diastole (you should feel the patient's pulse at the carotid artery to be sure) and then when, within that period, it occurs.

Systolic murmurs

Pansystolic

- This is a murmur that lasts for the whole of systole.
- Tends to be due to backflow of blood from a ventricle to an atrium (tricuspid regurgitation, mitral regurgitation).
- A ventricular septal defect will also cause a pansystolic murmur.

Ejection systolic

- These start quietly at the beginning of systole, quickly rise to a crescendo and decrescendo creating a 'whoosh' sound.
- Caused by turbulent flow of blood out of a ventricle (pulmonary stenosis, aortic stenosis, hypertrophic cardiomyopathy).
- Also found if flow is particularly fast (fever, fit young adults).

Late systolic

- Audible gap between S_1 and the start of the murmur which then continues until S_2.
- Typically tricuspid or mitral regurgitation through a prolapsing valve.

Diastolic murmurs

Early

- Usually due to backflow through incompetent aortic or pulmonary valves. Starts loudly at S_2 and decrescendos during diastole.
  - You can mimic this by whispering the letter 'R' out loud. Try it!

Mid-diastolic

- These begin later in diastole and may be brief or continue up to S_1.
- Usually due to flow through a narrowed mitral or tricuspid valve.
- Lower pitched than early diastolic murmurs.

Austin Flint murmur

- This is audible vibration of the mitral valve during diastole as it is hit by flow of blood due to severe aortic regurgitation.

Graham Steell murmur

- Pulmonary regurgitation secondary to pulmonary artery dilatation caused by increased pulmonary artery pressure in mitral stenosis.

Continuous murmurs

These are murmurs heard throughout both systole and diastole. Common causes include a patent ductus arteriosus or an arteriovenous fistula.

Radiation

The murmur can sometimes be heard in areas where heart sounds are not normally auscultated—the murmur will tend to radiate in the direction of the blood flow that is causing the sound.

For example, the murmur of aortic stenosis will radiate up to the carotids, a mitral regurgitation murmur may be heard in the left axilla.

Box 5.6 Grading the volume of a murmur

The experienced examiner should be able to give the murmur a 'grade' according to its loudness.

- 1 = very quiet (students will only hear it if they have already been told that it is there!)
- 2 = quiet but can be heard with a stethoscope wielded by an examiner with some experience
- 3 = moderate, easily heard
- 4 = loud, obvious murmur
- 5 = very loud and heard over the whole of the precordium. May be accompanied by a palpable thrill
- 6 = heard without the aid of a stethoscope.

Position

Some murmurs will become louder if you position the patient so as to let gravity aid the flow of blood creating the sound.

- *Aortic regurgitation* is heard louder if you ask the patient to sit up, leaning forwards, and listen at the left sternal edge.
- *Mitral stenosis* is louder if you ask the patient to lie on their left-hand side (listen with the bell at the apex).

Dynamic manoeuvres

Respiration

- Right-sided murmurs (e.g. pulmonary stenosis) tend to be louder during inspiration and quieter during expiration (increased venous return). Ask the patient to breathe deeply whilst you listen.
- Left-sided murmurs are louder during expiration.

Valsalva manoeuvre

- This is forceful expiration against a closed glottis.
- Replicate by asking the patient to blow into the end of a syringe, attempting to expel the plunger.
  - This will reduce cardiac output and cause most murmurs to soften
  - Murmurs of hypertrophic obstructive cardiomyopathy, mitral regurgitation, and mitral prolapse will get louder on release of Valsalva.

Extra sounds

These are added sounds that are often associated with a specific murmur—see Table 5.2.

Opening snap

The mitral valve normally opens immediately after S_2. In mitral stenosis, sudden opening of the stiffened valve can cause an audible high-pitched snap. This may be followed by the murmur of mitral stenosis. If there is no opening snap, the valve may be rigid.

- Best heard over the left sternal edge with the diaphragm of the stethoscope.

Ejection click

Similar to the opening snap of mitral stenosis, this is a high-pitched click heard early in systole caused by the opening of a stiffened semilunar valve (aortic stenosis). Associated with bicuspid aortic valves.

- Heard at the aortic or pulmonary areas and down the left sternal edge.

Mid-systolic click

Usually caused by mitral valve prolapse, this is the sound of the valve leaflet flicking backward (prolapsing) mid-way through ventricular systole. Will be followed by the murmur of mitral regurgitation.

- Best heard at the mitral area.

Tumour plop

A very rare finding due to atrial myxoma. If there is a pedunculated tumour in the atrium, it may move and block the atrial outflow during atrial systole causing an audible sound.

Pericardial rub

This is a scratching sound, comparable with creaking leather, heard with each heartbeat caused by inflamed pericardial membranes rubbing against each other in pericarditis. Louder as the patient is sitting up, leaning forward, and heard best in expiration.

Metallic valves

Patients who have had metallic valve replacement surgery will have an obviously audible mechanical 'click' corresponding to the closing of that valve. These can often be heard without the aid of a stethoscope and are reminiscent of the ticking crocodile in *Peter Pan*.

- Some valves have both opening and closing clicks.
- If a patient's valve click is unusually soft, this may indicate dysfunction e.g. thrombus or pannus.
- All patients with prosthetic valves will have a flow murmur when the valve is open.

Table 5.2 A selection of cardiac abnormalities and the expected clinical findings

Abnormality	Primary site of murmur	Radiation	Timing	Added sounds*	Graphical representation of the sounds
Aortic stenosis	'Aortic area' and apex	To carotid arteries	Ejection systolic	Ejection click (esp. bicuspid valve)	
Aortic regurgitation	Left sternal edge	Towards apex	Early diastolic	(Austin Flint murmur ⊙ p. 131)	
Mitral stenosis	Apex	Nil	Mid-diastolic	Opening snap	
Mitral regurgitation	Apex	Toward left axilla or base of left lung	Pansystolic	Mid-systolic click (if prolapsing)	
Tricuspid regurgitation	Lower left sternal edge	Lower right sternal edge, liver	Pansystolic		
Pulmonary stenosis	Upper left sternal edge	Left clavicular region	Ejection systolic		
Ventricular septal defect	Left sternal edge	Whole of the precordium	Pansystolic		

*Note that added sounds such as clicks and snaps may only be present in certain patients and should not be 'expected' when examining someone with a certain abnormality.

Examining beyond the chest

The lung bases
See ➔ Chapter 6. Look especially for crackles or sign of effusion.

The abdomen
See also ➔ Chapter 7. Look especially for:
- Hepatomegaly.
  - Is the liver pulsatile (severe tricuspid regurgitation)?
- Splenomegaly.
- Ascites.
- Abdominal aortic aneurysm.
- Renal bruits (renal artery stenosis).
- Enlarged kidneys.

Peripheral oedema
An abnormal increase in tissue fluid resulting in swelling—its causes are multiple but often due to heart failure. Oedema is under gravitational control so will gather at the ankles if the patient is standing or walking, at the sacrum if sitting, and in the lungs if lying (orthopnoea).
- Make a note of any peripheral swelling, examining both the ankles and the sacrum.
- Note if the oedema is 'pitting' (are you able to make an impression in it with your finger?—Best tested over the anterior of the tibia).
- Note how high the oedema extends (ankles, leg, thighs, etc.).
- If the oedema extends beyond the thighs, it is important to examine the external genitalia—particularly in men—where the swelling may cause outflow obstruction.

Varicose veins
Inspection

Varicosities appear as visible, dilated, tortuous, subcutaneous veins caused by the backflow of blood from the deep veins (usually a branch of the long saphenous vein).
- The patient should be examined in a standing position with the legs fully exposed.
- Venulectasias ('venous stars'): intradermal thread veins.
- Atrophie blanche: white skin scarring without ulceration.
- Evidence of venous hypertension:
  - Lipodermatosclerosis (sclerosis of the skin and subcutaneous fat results in tapering of the legs above the ankle)
  - Venous eczema
  - Skin discoloration: brown pigmentation of haemosiderin deposition
  - Venous ulcers.

Palpation
- There may be pitting oedema at ankle.
- Examine for tenderness or heat over the veins (thrombophlebitis).
- Phalen's test: palpable tender defects in deep fascia along course of vein at medial border of tibia.
- Check for a cough impulse.
- Ask the patient to cough. If there is a palpable pulsation in the varicosity, there may be valvular incompetence at the long saphenous vein in the groin.

Auscultation
- Listen over non-collapsible or large groups of varicosities to exclude an arteriovenous fistula.

Ultrasound
- The most reliable method of diagnosing and locating primary reflux, replacing the older clinical tests shown in Box 5.7.
- The probe is placed over the saphenofemoral junction (SFJ) 3–4cm below and lateral to pubic tubercle and saphenopopliteal junction whilst applying pressure to the calf and listening for reflux of 1–2 seconds.

Box 5.7 Older tests for varicose veins

▶ Doppler ultrasound has replaced these older, less reliable tests. These should not be performed and are presented here for historical interest.

Tap test
- With one hand resting on the medial calf along the course of a varicose vein, tap or flick the saphenofemoral junction (SFJ).
  - Transmission of the wave suggests intervening incompetent valves.

Trendelenburg test
- With the patient supine, empty the superficial venous system
- Press over the SFJ and ask the patient to stand whilst holding your finger in place.
  - If the veins do not fill, the site of incompetence is the SFJ
  - If the veins fill, there are incompetent perforators lower down.

Tourniquet test
- Uses the same principle as the Trendelenburg test, but a tourniquet is applied just below the SFJ and then caudally in a step-wise fashion until the vein-filling is prevented (this is the site of incompetence).

Perthe's test
- With a tourniquet over the SFJ, ask the patient to walk on tiptoes. The varicosities improve if the deep venous system is functional.

Important presentations

Valvular disease

Mitral stenosis

- *Symptoms:* dyspnoea, reduced exercise tolerance, cough productive of frothy (pink?) sputum, palpitations (often associated with atrial fibrillation and resultant emboli), dysphagia (oesophagus compressed by enlarged left atrium).
- *Signs:* palmar erythema, malar flush, 'tapping' apex beat, left parasternal heave, giant v waves in JVP, loud S_1, high-pitched early-diastolic (Graham Steell) murmur ± opening snap.

Mitral regurgitation

- *Symptoms:* acute dyspnoea and pulmonary congestion.
- *Signs:* thrusting apex beat displaced to the left (volume overload), possible systolic thrill at the apex, soft S_1, loud S_2 (pulmonary component), pansystolic murmur heard at the apex radiating to left axilla (best heard in the left lateral position) ± mid-systolic click.
- *Signs of decompensation:* small volume pulse, raised JVP, displaced thrusting apex with a systolic thrill, left parasternal heave, 3rd heart sound (Ken-tuc-ky), mid-diastolic flow murmur, bibasal crackles, peripheral oedema.

Mitral prolapse

- Displacement of an abnormally thickened mitral valve leaflet into the left atrium during systole, mimicking and leading to mitral regurgitation.
- Occurs in approximately 5% of the population.
- More common in females.
- *Signs:* mid-systolic click, late systolic murmur heard best at the apex.
  - Squatting delays the click and standing increases the murmur.

Aortic stenosis

- *Symptoms:* angina, syncope, dyspnoea, sudden death.
- *Signs:* small volume slow rising pulse ('pulsus tardus et parvus'), narrow pulse pressure, sustained and powerful apex beat (displaced if ventricular dysfunction and dilatation present), ejection systolic (crescendo-decrescendo) murmur heard at the left sternal edge and (loudest leaning forward at end-expiration) radiating to carotids, soft S_2.
- *Signs of decompensation:* raised JVP, left parasternal heave, gallop rhythym, bibasal crackles, peripheral oedema.

Aortic regurgitation

- *Symptoms:* similar to aortic stenosis.
- *Signs:* large volume 'collapsing' pulse which is exaggerated at the radial artery if you hold the patient's arm up ('waterhammer pulse'), wide pulse pressure, sustained and displaced apex beat, soft S_2, early diastolic murmur at the left sternal edge (often described as 'blowing' or decrescendo), you may also hear a 'pistol shot' sound over the femoral artery with severe aortic regurgitation. See Box 5.8.

Box 5.8 Eponymous signs in aortic regurgitation

- *Quincke's sign*: capillary nail bed pulsations
- *Corrigan's sign*: visible carotid pulsations
- *De Musset's sign*: head nodding with each heartbeat
- *Muller's sign*: pulsation of the uvula
- *Duroziez's sign*: diastolic femoral bruit when compressed distally
- *Traube's sign*: 'pistol shot' femorals
- *Austin Flint murmur*: mid-diastolic murmur heard at the apex, thought to be caused by a regurgitant jet interfering with the opening of the anterior mitral valve leaflet, mimicking the murmur of mitral stenosis
- *Rosenbach's sign*: pulsatile liver
- *Gerhardt's sign*: enlarged spleen.

Showing off

- Abraham Lincoln probably had Marfan's syndrome with his tall stature and long arms. In addition, a study of old photographs reveals that he had de Musset's sign. At the time when cameras had longer shutter times, President Lincoln's head-nodding caused his face to appear blurred in photographs when compared with those sitting around him
- *Prof. Heinrich Quincke*: German physician 1842–1922, also introduced the therapeutic lumbar puncture
- *Sir Dominic John Corrigan*: 1802–1880, was five-times President of the College of Physicians in Dublin
- *Alfred de Musset*: notable because de Musset's sign is named after the patient, not the doctor. De Musset was a French poet and novelist who died of syphilitic aortic regurgitation in 1857.

Tricuspid stenosis

Usually occurs along with mitral or aortic valvular disease (e.g. in rheumatic fever) and is often the less serious of the patient's problems.
- *Signs*: auscultation similar to that of mitral stenosis, hepatomegaly, pulsatile liver, and venous congestion.

Tricuspid regurgitation

- *Signs*: dilated neck veins, prominent v wave in JVP, pansystolic murmur louder on inspiration with a loud pulmonary component of S_2, left parasternal heave, pulsatile liver, peripheral and sacral oedema, ascites.

Pulmonary stenosis

- *Signs*: normal pulse with an ejection systolic murmur radiating to lung fields often with a palpable thrill over the pulmonary area. Other signs of right heart strain or failure.

Pulmonary regurgitation

- *Signs*: loud S_2 which may be palpable, early diastolic murmur heard at the pulmonary area and high at the left sternal edge.

Ventricular septal defect (VSD)

Large

- *Symptoms:* infant with breathlessness, poor feeding, and failure to thrive.
- *Signs:* As the pulmonary vascular resistance falls, a large defect may present with cardiac failure in the first few months of life.
  - Associated features include: low volume pulse, mid-diastolic murmur due to high flow through the mitral valve.

Small

- *Symptoms:* usually asymptomatic and called 'Maladie de Roger'.
- *Signs:* normal pulse, normal JVP, harsh pansystolic murmur at the lower left sternal edge, no evidence of decompensation.

Atrial septal defect (ASD)

The commonest congenital lesion and often an asymptomatic finding discovered on investigating a murmur.

Variants

- *Ostium primum:* 15% of cases may be associated with mitral and tricuspid regurgitation or a VSD. Usually identified early in childhood, associated with congenital syndromes (Down's, Noonan's, Klinefelter's), ECG shows RBBB with left axis deviation.
- *Ostium secundum:* 70% of cases. Usually central fossa ovalis defects, occasionally associated with mitral valve prolapse, ECG shows RBBB with right axis deviation.
- *Sinus venosus:* 15% of cases, defect in upper septum involving inflow from SVC or IVC, associated with defects of pulmonary drainage.

Symptoms

- *Symptoms of primum defect:* symptoms of heart failure in childhood with failure to thrive, chest infections, and poor development. In adults, there may be syncope (heart block) and symptoms of endocarditis.
- *Symptoms of secundum defect:* asymptomatic if small. Fatigue, dyspnoea, palpitations (atrial arrhythmias), recurrent pulmonary infections, right heart failure. Also migraine and paradoxical emboli.

Signs

- Irregularly irregular pulse (AF), apex beat undisplaced and palpable, fixed splitting of S_2, ejection systolic murmur at upper left sternal edge.
- *If haemodynamically significant:* irregularly irregular pulse (AF), apex beat displaced laterally, left parasternal heave (RV overload), systolic thrill over the pulmonary area, wide fixed splitting of S_2, ejection systolic murmur in the pulmonary area with ejection click (pulmonary artery dilatation), mid-diastolic rumble over tricuspid area (increased flow through the tricuspid valve from the large left-to-right shunt), pulmonary regurgitation.

Holt–Oram syndrome

- Triphalangeal thumb/other upper limb anomalies associated with ASD.
- Autosomal dominant (incomplete penetrance).

Patent ductus arteriosus (PDA)

A persistent embryonic connection between the pulmonary artery and the aorta. Blood flows from the aorta into the pulmonary artery giving:

- *Symptoms:* often asymptomatic. Severe cases—dyspnoea on exertion.
- *Signs:* bounding pulse, wide pulse pressure, displaced heaving apex beat, 'machinery' (continuous) murmur heard all over the precordium, S_2 not heard, systolic or diastolic thrill in the 2nd intercostal space on the left.

Coarctation of the aorta

A congenital narrowing of the aorta at, or beyond, the arch.

- *Symptoms:* usually asymptomatic. May include headache, epistaxis, dizziness, and palpitations. Claudication and leg fatigue are also features. The coarctation may also cause the heart to strain and give symptoms of congestive cardiac failure.
- *Signs:* large volume radial pulse, radio-radial or radio-femoral delay, blood pressure discrepancy between upper and lower limbs, superficial collateral vessels on the chest wall, 'heaving' undisplaced apex beat, thrill over the collaterals and in the suprasternal notch, systolic or continuous murmur heard in the left infraclavicular area anteriorly and the left infrascapular area posteriorly, weak femoral pulses. May also have underdeveloped lower limbs.
- *After surgical correction:* left thoracotomy scar, normal right radial pulse, weak left radial pulse, normal heart sounds, no radio-femoral delay.

Pericarditis

Causes include collagen diseases, TB, post-infarction, and idiopathic.

- *Symptoms of acute pericarditis:* constant retrosternal 'soreness', worse on inspiration (pleuritic), relieved slightly by sitting forwards, not related to movement or exertion.
- *If chronic, constrictive, may cause:* Kussmaul's sign, impalpable apex beat, S_3, hepatomegaly, splenomegaly, ascites ('pseudo-cirrhosis').

Pericardial effusion

- Pulsus paradoxus, raised JVP, impalpable apex beat, soft heart sounds, hepatomegaly, ascites, peripheral oedema.

Infective endocarditis

Bacteraemia can follow a wide range of events including dental work, brushing teeth, IV drug use, iatrogenic.

- *Symptoms:* malaise, lethargy, fevers, anorexia, weight loss, myalgia, arthralgia, heart failure, embolic stroke.
- *Signs:* pyrexia, petechial rash, splinter haemorrhages, Osler nodes (small, red/purple, raised, tender lesions often on finger pulps), Janeway lesions (irregular, flat, red, non-tender macules on palmar aspect of hands/feet), Roth spots ('cotton wool' spots on the retina), digital infarcts, digital clubbing, murmur, hepatosplenomegaly.

Hypertrophic cardiomyopathy

Inherited forms are usually autosomal dominant.

- *Symptoms:* can present with sudden cardiac death. Otherwise asymptomatic usually. If outflow obstruction: dyspnoea, reduced exercise tolerance, palpitations, syncope, chest pain.
- *Signs:* 'jerky' peripheral pulse with a steep upstroke, 'a' wave seen at JVP, forceful apex beat, ejection systolic murmur at the left sternal edge radiating to the axilla (does not radiate to the neck) and increases in intensity on Valsalva, 4th heart sound (in some cases).
- *Poor prognostic factors:* young age at diagnosis, family history of sudden death, syncopal symptoms, ventricular arrhythmias documented on ambulatory monitoring.

Congestive heart failure

In simple terms, this refers to the inability of the heart to maintain an adequate cardiac output for perfusion of vital organs with variable severity. It is usually described in terms of 'left' and 'right' heart failure but there is usually an element of both ('biventricular').

Left ventricular failure (LVF)

- *Symptoms:* may include shortness of breath on exertion, orthopnoea, paroxysmal nocturnal dyspnoea, cough with pink frothy sputum, fatigue, weight loss, muscle wasting, and anorexia.
- *Signs:* may appear tired, pale, sweaty, clammy, tachycardia, thready pulse, low blood pressure, narrow pulse pressure, displaced apex beat (murmur of an underlying valvular abnormality?), 3rd and 4th heart sounds, tachypnoea, crepitations at the lung bases.

Right ventricular failure (RVF)

- *Symptoms:* as LVF with peripheral oedema and facial swelling.
- *Signs:* many of those under LVF. Also raised JVP, hepatomegaly, ascites, peripheral (sacral?) oedema, pulsatile liver (if tricuspid regurgitation).

Subclavian steal syndrome

Subclavian steal 'phenomenon' is flow reversal in the left vertebral artery due to left subclavian artery occlusive disease proximal to the origin of the vertebral artery. If associated with transient neurological symptoms due to cerebral ischaemia, it is termed 'subclavian steal syndrome'.

- *Symptoms:* exercising the left arm produces muscle cramping, dizziness, vertigo, dysarthria, syncope, diplopia, nystagmus.
- *Signs:* evidence of left upper limb ischaemia (pallor, cyanosis, ulcers), left radial and brachial pulses weak, reduced systolic blood pressure in the left arm, supraclavicular bruit on the left.

Deep vein thrombosis (DVT)

Often confused with cellulitis and ruptured popliteal (Baker's) cyst.

- *Symptoms:* calf pain, swelling, and loss of use.
- *Signs:* warm, tense, swollen limb, erythema, dilated superficial veins, cyanosis. There may be palpable thrombus in the deep veins. Often pain on palpating the calf.

See also:

More information regarding the presentation and clinical signs of cardiovascular diseases to aid preparation for OSCE-type examinations and ward rounds can be found in the *Oxford Handbooks Clinical Tutor Study Cards*.

'Medicine' Study Card set:
- Mitral stenosis and regurgitation
- Aortic stenosis and regurgitation
- Mixed valve disease
- Prosthetic valves
- Ventricular septal defect
- Atrial septal defect
- Hypertrophic cardiomyopathy
- Coarctation of the aorta
- Persistent ductus arteriosus
- Fallot's tetralogy
- Dextrocardia
- Infective endocarditis.

'Surgery' Study Card set:
- Thoracic outlet syndrome
- Subclavian steal
- Carotid artery disease
- Superior vena cava obstruction
- Axillary vein thrombosis
- Deep vein thrombosis
- Ischaemic ulcer
- Abdominal aortic aneurysm
- Thrombophlebitis obliterans
- Raynaud's phenomenon
- Surgical arteriovenous (AV) fistulae
- Lymphoedema.

'Practical Procedures' Study Card set:
- Venepuncture
- Sampling from a central venous catheter
- Femoral venous catheter insertion
- Central venous access
- Arterial line insertion
- Recording a 12-lead ECG
- Carotid sinus massage
- Vagal manoeuvres
- Defibrillation
- DC cardioversion
- Temporary external pacing
- Pericardiocentesis
- Exercise tolerance testing.

The elderly patient

Geriatricians are equally interested in cardiovascular disease—with an age-ing population, the prevalence of cardiac, peripheral vascular, and stroke disease continues to rise. Whilst age is one of many risk factors for vascular disease, older people are one of the biggest groups to benefit from primary and secondary risk factor reduction—so be comprehensive in all assessments. A careful history is of far more use than an inaccurate one and list of physical findings.

History

- *Angina:* presents in a multitude of ways. Avoid labelling the symptoms as pain (which can irritate many patients) but listen to their complaints— 'discomfort', 'twinges', and 'aches' are equally common presentations. Many elders have few symptoms, and may present with sweating or breathlessness. Be astute and ask if these relate to exertion.
- *Orthopnoea:* ask why patients sleep on extra pillows—often due to other symptoms such as arthritis. Do they sleep upright in a chair?
- *Breathlessness:* relates to a low-output state and not necessarily to pulmonary oedema. Fatigue is a common presenting symptom and should not be overlooked. Exertional breathlessness may reflect an arrhythmia.
- *DHx:* Always a difficult balance of compliance, managing symptoms, achieving target doses, and avoiding side effects. Avoid rushing to 'optimize' doses and upsetting a careful regimen. Ask about beta-blocker eye drops—they can be absorbed systemically and exert significant effects.
- *Lifestyle:* don't forget to ask about smoking and seek opportunities to explore smoking cessation—it's never too late! Ask about alcohol; this may have a bearing on decisions around anticoagulation. Advice about healthy eating is often welcome, and more palatable than more tablets.
- *Functional history:* As ever, a key part of all histories. Targeted interventions—help with bathing to avoid over-exertion (and symptoms) can have significant impact.

Examination

- *General:* look out for clues—the breathless patient returning from the bathroom (check oxygen saturations!), the GTN spray close at hand, etc.
- *Auscultate and think:* especially about valve lesions. It is more valuable to assess how much a valvular problem is contributing to a patient's symptoms, and arrange investigations. Aortic valve replacement, CABG, or TAVI is often hugely successful in older people.
- *Oedema:* be careful when palpating—contrary to popular teaching, pitting and non-pitting oedema are painful! Could it be gravitational?
- *Peripheral pulses:* often overlooked, but a vital part of the examination. Document carefully, and look for skin changes and ulceration that might be causing significant problems, but not necessarily raised in the history.

Additional points
- *Alternative diagnoses:* Respiratory illnesses often overlap, and may mimic—e.g. pulmonary fibrosis and left ventricular failure. If things 'don't add up', or there is little response to treatment, revisit your diagnosis.

The respiratory system

Introduction

Anatomy

The respiratory tract extends from the nostrils to the alveoli but also includes the pulmonary parenchyma and vasculature and the musculoske-tetal structures required for ventilation. It is often divided for convenience into the upper respiratory tract (URT) which is the nose and pharynx, and the lower respiratory tract (LRT) which consists of the larynx and all distal structures.

Trachea, bronchi, and bronchioles

The trachea lies in the midline deep to the sternal notch and divides into the left and right main bronchi at the 'carina', at about the level of the sternal angle. There are about 25 further divisions before reaching the alveoli.

Lungs

The right lung has 3 lobes (upper, middle, and lower) whilst the left lung has 2 (upper and lower) to make room for the heart, but the lingular division of the upper lobe is effectively a 'left middle lobe '. Note that the oblique fissures run downwards from the back. Here's what this means when auscultating (see Fig. 6.1).

The diaphragm slants such that the inferior border of the lungs is at the 6th rib anteriorly but extends down to the 12th posteriorly.

Physiology

This is a complex system, the outline here is an aide-mémoire only.

Ventilation

- Central processing.
  - Pacemaker respiratory centre
  - Influence from higher voluntary centres, emotional centres, and circulating endocrine factors.
- Sensors.
  - Brainstem and aortic arch chemoreceptors
  - Lung stretch and cough receptors.
- Effectors.
  - Diaphragm
  - Intercostal muscles
  - Accessory muscles (e.g. sternocleidomastoids).

Contraction of effector muscles increases thoracic volume and air is drawn in, expiration is largely passive with air being expelled as the lungs recoil under their innate elasticity. During physiological stress, ventilation increases first by increasing tidal volume then by increasing rate: to fit more breaths into a minute, expiration must therefore become active.

Gas transfer

Getting enough air in is the first step, but we must also extract oxygen and get rid of carbon dioxide. Anything that impedes gas transfer has clinical implications:

- Inadequate global ventilation (e.g. muscular dystrophy).
- Inadequate local perfusion of ventilated area (e.g. PE).
- Inadequate local ventilation of perfused area (e.g. pneumonia).
- Thickened barrier to diffusion (e.g. pulmonary fibrosis).

Note that the degree of ventilation–perfusion mismatch will be altered by a patient's position and cardiac output.

Defence

Cough receptors in the pharynx and lower airways initiate a deep inspiration followed by expiration against a closed glottis and a sudden glottal opening. This causes a rapid, forceful expulsion of air.

Larger inhaled particles will impact on airway walls going round the many corners of the respiratory tract. Particles smaller than this might have time to sediment out from the air deep in the lungs (like inhaled medications), before they can be exhaled.

Most of the respiratory tract is lined with mucus secreted from goblet cells that catches these inhaled particles. This is continuously swept upwards like an escalator by cilia, towards the larynx where the mucus is swallowed (yes, we all do it).

In the smaller airways and alveoli, macrophages and a variety of secreted defensive proteins act against microbes at a microscopic level.

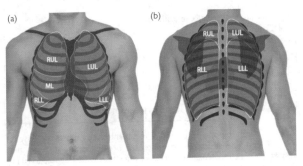

Fig. 6.1 Surface anatomy of the lungs. UL: upper lobe, ML: middle lobe, LL: lower lobe.

Dyspnoea

Defining dyspnoea

Shortness of breath (SOB), or dyspnoea, is the sensation that one has to use an abnormal amount of effort in breathing. Patients may describe 'breathlessness', an inability to 'get their breath', or being 'shortwinded'.

This is NOT the same as 'hypoxia'. A person can be breathless but have normal oxygen levels. Marathon runners crossing the finish-line are breathless but not blue.

'Tightness' is often described and may relate to airway narrowing as in asthma or may be chest pain, as in cardiac disease. Tease out exactly what the patient means.

🛈 Pleuritic and musculoskeletal chest pain is worse at the height of deep inspiration and patients may say 'I am not able to get my breath'. Thus, seemingly complaining of breathlessness, their actual problem is pain on inspiration. Ask if they feel unable to breathe deeply and for what reason (is it pain or some other sensation?). If all else fails, ask the patient to take a deep breath and watch what happens.

Onset and duration

How quickly did the SOB come on? (see Box 6.1)

Box 6.1 Some causes of dyspnoea by onset
- Abrupt
  - Pulmonary embolus
  - Pneumothorax
  - Acute exacerbation of asthma.
- Days/weeks
  - Asthma exacerbation
  - Pneumonia
  - Congestive cardiac failure.
- Months
  - Pulmonary fibrosis.
- Years
  - Chronic obstructive pulmonary disease.

Slower onsets are poorly reported. The patient often reports the onset of a *worsening* of breathlessness or when the breathlessness stopped them doing their benchmark daily activity. Ask when they were last able to run up the stairs and the real duration of breathlessness becomes apparent.

The nature of progression of breathlessness is also crucial: asthma may be long-standing and fluctuate greatly whereas fibrosis inexorably gets worse (often in a step-wise fashion).

Severity

Several classifications exist (see Box 6.2) but the key is to quantify in terms of progressive functional impairment whilst trying to keep it in context for the patient, e.g. 'Can you still mow the lawn without resting?', 'Do you have to walk slower than your friends?', 'Are you breathless getting washed and dressed in the morning?'

⊕ Be sure that activities are restricted by SOB as opposed to arthritic hips, knees, chest pain, or some other ailment.

Exacerbating and relieving factors

What makes the breathlessness worse? Can it be reliably triggered by a particular activity or situation? Remember orthopnoea (➔ p. 104) is not specific for heart failure: breathing whilst lying relies heavily on the diaphragm and also increases perfusion of the upper lobes (usually most badly damaged in COPD) so many people with dyspnoea are more breathless doing this.

What makes the dyspnoea better? Do inhalers or a break from work help?

Hyperventilation

Dysfunctional breathing, and particularly hyperventilation, is common generally and more so in people with genuine respiratory pathology. Hyperventilation ↓ blood CO_2 and so increases pH. This leads to symptoms of dyspnoea of rapid onset then:

- Early.
  - Paraesthesia in the lips and fingers
  - Light headedness
  - Chest pain or 'tightness'.
- Prolonged episode.
  - Bronchospasm
  - Post episode hypoxia (SpO_2 can be <85%).

Box 6.2 MRC Dyspnoea Score

- 1 = Not troubled by breathlessness except on strenuous exercise
- 2 = Short of breath when hurrying or walking up a slight hill
- 3 = Walks slower than contemporaries on level ground due to breathlessness, or has to stop for breath when walking at own pace
- 4 = Stops for breath after walking 100m or less on level ground
- 5 = Too breathless to leave the house, or breathless when dressing or undressing.

Cough and expectoration

Cough

A common, often overlooked and potentially miserable symptom in respiratory disease, usually caused by upper respiratory tract infection (URTI) and/or smoking. Duration of cough is important, as well as character, exacerbating factors, and whether any sputum is produced. See Tables 6.1a and 6.1b for some causes of cough.

Note that cough may be the only reported symptom of asthma.

Localizing the cough

This is not particularly useful, however patients are often keen to try to point out where they feel the cough originates.

Beyond the larynx, sensory innervation is such that localization is not possible. Patients often, therefore, point to their throat as the source of the cough.

Chronic cough

'Chronic cough' is that lasting >8 weeks and is often multi-factorial: common contributors are initial viral infection, asthma, post-nasal drip, gastro-oesophageal reflux disease, and medications (though it can be the first manifestation of interstitial lung disease or even lung cancer).

🛈 Smokers will have a chronic cough, particularly in the mornings, so a history of a change is important.

Sputum

Excess respiratory secretions that are coughed up. Patients will usually understand the term 'phlegm' better. Features to glean are:

- How often?
- How much?
- How difficult is it to cough up?
- Colour.
- Consistency and smell.

Attempt to quantify sputum production in terms of well-known objects such as tea-spoons, egg-cups, etc. 'Mucoid' sputum is white or clear in colour but can be grey in cigarette smokers. Yellow or green 'purulent' sputum is largely caused by inflammatory cells so usually indicates infection; although eosinophils in the sputum of asthmatics also discolour sputum, producing rubbery yellow plugs. See Table 6.2.

Haemoptysis

The coughing up of blood can vary from streaks to massive, life-threatening bleeds ('massive' haemoptysis = >500ml in 24 hours). Establish amount, colour, frequency, and nature of any associated sputum.

Haemoptysis is easily confused with blood originating in the nose, mouth, and GI tract (haematemesis). Ask about, and check for, bleeds in these areas also.

Causes of haemoptysis include infection, bronchiectasis, carcinoma, pulmonary embolus, and pulmonary vasculitis. 'Infective' causes will often produce blood-stained sputum as opposed to pure haemoptysis.

Table 6.1a Some clues to the origin of a cough (acute)

Cause	Character
Laryngitis	Cough with a hoarse voice
Tracheitis	Dry and very painful
Epiglottitis	'Barking'
LRTI	Purulent sputum, perhaps with pleuritic chest pain

Table 6.1b Some clues to the origin of a cough (chronic)

Cause	Character
Asthma	Chronic, paroxysmal, worse after exercise and at night
Oesophageal reflux	Dry and nauseating. Often first thing in the morning, after eating, or with prolonged talking
Pulmonary oedema	Clear sputum, worse on lying flat
Postnasal drip	Tickly, often with nasal blockage

Table 6.2 Some classical characteristics of sputum

Age	Heart rate
White/grey	Smoking
Green/yellow	Bronchitis, bronchiectasis
Green and offensive	Bronchiectasis, abscesses
Sticky, rusty	*Streptococcus pneumoniae* infection
Frothy, pink	Congestive cardiac failure
3 layers (mucoid, watery, rusty)	Severe bronchiectasis
Very sticky, often yellow	Asthma
Sticky, yellow but with large plugs	Allergic bronchopulmonary aspergillosis

Other respiratory symptoms

Wheeze

This is a whistling 'musical' sound emanating from narrow smaller airways. Occurs in inspiration and expiration, but usually louder and more prominent in the latter. Airway calibre is dynamic, and the external pressure in expiration means this is when airways are narrowest and when you'll hear wheeze. Cause may be any process that ↓ airway calibre:

- Airway muscle contraction: asthma.
- Reduced airway support tissue: COPD.
- Airway oedema: heart failure.
- Airway inflammation/mucus: bronchiectasis.

Stridor

A harsh 'crowing', predominantly inspiratory, sound with a largely constant pitch. Signals large airway narrowing, usually at the larynx or trachea, (e.g. vocal cord palsy, post intubation stenosis). Can precede complete airway obstruction (e.g. epiglottitis) so is treated as a medical emergency if the cause is unknown.

Chest pain

Chest pain is explored fully in ➜ Chapter 5.

Pleuritic pain

Pain arising from respiratory disease may be 'pleuritic' in nature: usually arising from the parietal pleura (the lungs have no pain fibres). It is felt as a severe, sharp pain at the height of inspiration or on coughing localized to a small area of chest wall. Note that patients will avoid deep breathing and may complain of 'breathlessness'.

Lung parenchymal pain

Pain from lung parenchymal lesions may be dull and constant. This is a sinister sign of malignancy spreading into the chest wall. Remember, though, that the stress placed through the chest wall by increased respiratory effort in other airways disease may cause ill-defined chest wall pain.

Diaphragmatic pain

Diaphragmatic pain may be felt at the ipsilateral shoulder tip whilst pain from the costal parts of the diaphragm may be referred to the abdomen.

Musculoskeletal pain

In general, muscular and costal lesions will be tender to touch over the corresponding chest wall and exacerbated by twisting movements—although this is not always the case. Costochondritis is a common cause of pleuritic pain of which Tietze's syndrome is a specific cause associated with pain and swelling of the superior costal cartilages.

Nerve root pain

May be due to spinal lesions or herpes zoster.

Somnolence

Sleepy people are often seen by respiratory physicians as the commonest pathological cause (obstructive sleep apnoea) usually requires commencement of nocturnal non-invasive ventilation.

Differentiate sleepiness from fatigue: think of how you feel after exercise and how you feel after being awake a long time (e.g. after a long-haul flight). Quantify how sleepy the patient is (see Epworth Score in Box 6.3).

Obstructive sleep apnoea (OSA)

This is caused by upper airway obstruction in susceptible individuals (overweight/retrognathic/relative macroglossia) as the palatal muscles become flaccid during REM sleep. Partial obstruction causes snoring then brief hypoxia as the obstruction becomes complete. Hypoxia is sensed and the patient wakes enough to return tone to their muscles and open their airway. This cycle is repeated many times per hour (sleepiness), the patient is restless and noisy (sleepy, irritated partner), and blood pressure doesn't fall at night (can give resistant hypertension).

Severe OSA leads to carbon dioxide retention, worsening somnolence, and early morning headaches.

Narcolepsy

Narcolepsy is less common than OSA but disabling and the diagnosis is often missed for years. Initially, patients experience weakening at the knees when experiencing sudden emotion (e.g. the punchline of a joke). This 'cataplexy' progresses to become more marked and widespread, sleep episodes suddenly occur at any time (e.g. mid-conversation), and dreams intrude into wakefulness. Strong genetic linkage.

Box 6.3 Epworth Sleepiness Scale

Ask the patient to choose a numbered grade for each situation and then add the numbers to give an overall score:

Grading
0 = would never doze or sleep
1 = slight chance of dozing or sleeping
2 = moderate chance of dozing or sleeping
3 = high chance of dozing or sleeping.

Situations
- Sitting and reading
- Watching TV
- Sitting inactive in a public place
- Being a passenger in a motor vehicle for an hour or more
- Lying down in the afternoon
- Sitting and talking to someone
- Sitting quietly after lunch (no alcohol)
- Stopped for a few minutes in traffic whilst driving.

Results
0–10 = Normal; 10–12 = borderline; 12–24 = abnormally sleepy

The rest of the history

Other key symptoms

Fever
Particularly at night may be a sign of infection such as TB, but remember fever is caused by inflammation so may arise from malignancy, PE, or a connective tissue disorder.

Weight loss
A common symptom of cancer, COPD, and chronic infection. Attempt to quantify any loss (how much in how long).

Peripheral oedema
Oedema manifesting as ankle swelling at the end of the day may be a sign of fluid retention due to chronic hypoxaemia ± hypoxia or right heart failure secondary to chronic lung disease (cor pulmonale). Older smokers with COPD often have coexisting cardiac disease.

Past medical history
- Vaccination for respiratory illnesses, particularly BCG.
- Previous respiratory infections especially TB before 1950 when surgery may have been performed resulting in lifelong deformity.
- X-ray abnormalities previously mentioned to the patient.
- Childhood (a 'chesty child' may have had undiagnosed asthma).
- Previous respiratory high dependency or ITU admissions and NIV.
- Multisystem disorders that affect the chest e.g. rheumatoid.

Drug history
Many medications can cause respiratory pathology – if unsure consult resources such as Pneumotox (🖰 http://www.pneumotox.com).
- What inhalers are used and how often? Check inhaler technique.
- Previous successful use of bronchodilators and steroids.
- Immunosuppressives including oral steroids predispose to (often atypical) infection.
- ACE inhibitors cause a dry cough.
- If O_2 therapy—cylinders or concentrator? How many hours a day?
- Illicit drug use (cannabis causes emphysema, many others are associated with respiratory disease).

Family history
- Asthma, eczema, and allergies.
- Inherited conditions (e.g. alpha-1-antitrypsin deficiency).
- Family contacts with TB.

Smoking
Attempt to quantify the habit in 'pack-years'. 1 pack-year is 20 cigarettes per day for one year. 20 cigarettes is roughly the same risk exposure as 0.5oz (12.5g) of tobacco.

Ask about previous smoking as many will call themselves ex-smokers if they gave up on their way to see you!

Remember to ask about passive smoking.

Alcohol

Alcoholics are at greater risk of chest infections and bingeing may result in aspiration pneumonia.

Social history

Pets

Animals are a common source of allergens. Remember birds and caged animals. Ask about exposure beyond the home in the form of close friends and relations, and hobbies such as pigeon fancying or horse riding.

Travel

Ask about travel (recent or previous) to areas where respiratory infections are endemic. Think particularly about TB. Remember *Legionella* can be caught from water systems and air-conditioning in developed countries. Pathogens common in other developed countries may be different to those in the UK (e.g. histoplasmosis in the USA) or show extensive antibiotic resistance.

Occupation

This is hugely important. Individual occupational diseases might be uncommon but collectively they represent a vast number of cases. Be alert to exposure to asbestos, coal, animals, metals and ores, cement dust, and organic compounds.

Trace the occupational history back as there may be a lag of >20 years between exposure and resultant disease. Remember that exposure may not be obvious and the patient may have been unaware of it at the time. Plumbers, builders, and electrical engineers may well have been exposed to asbestos in the past, as might their families, e.g. by washing clothes.

See Health and Safety Executive (HSE) website ♒ http://www.hse.gov.uk for more information.

General appearance

Respiratory patients may be short of breath and it may be easiest to examine them sitting at the edge of the bed as opposed to the classic position of sitting back at 45°. Choose a position comfortable to you both. They should be undressed to the waist. As ever, make sure you have introduced yourself and have clean hands.

As ever, a surprising amount of information can be obtained by observing the patient before laying on a finger.

Bedside clues

Look for evidence of the disease and its severity around the patient:
- Inhalers? Which ones? Spacer device?
- Nebulizer? NIV machine?
- Is the patient receiving O_2 therapy? If so, how much and by what method (i.e. face mask, nasal cannula, etc.)?
- Sputum pot? – look inside!
- Any mobility aids nearby?
- Look for cigarettes, lighter, or matches at the bedside or in a pocket.

Respiration

Watch the patient from the foot of the bed. Or watch them approach your clinic room.
- Do they appear out of breath at rest? or after undressing/walking in?
- Count the respiratory rate. At rest, this should be <15/minute.
  - Pretend to be checking the pulse if you think your observation is changing the patient's breathing pattern.
- Are the breaths of normal volume? (Patients with neuromuscular or fibrotic disease have more shallow and rapid breathing.)
- Expiration should be shorter than inspiration (about 2:1), but this will be reversed in obstructive lung diseases as the patient tries to prevent airway collapse from external pressure.
- Are they breathing through pursed lips? (increasing the end-expiratory pressure—an indication of chronic obstructive lung disease.)
  - Patients with airway obstruction have a high residual volume (↑ airway radial traction/incomplete expiration due to airway collapse).
- Are they using the accessory respiratory muscles (e.g. sternomastoids) or bracing their arms to splint their chest? (The classic position is sitting forwards, hands on knees.)
- Does the abdomen move out in inspiration? Or is a weakened diaphragm being drawn up and hence the abdomen inward (abdominal paradox)?

Abnormal breathing patterns
- Kussmaul's respiration: deep, sighing breaths. Systemic acidosis.
- Cheyne–Stokes breathing: a waxing and waning of breath amplitude and rate. Due to failure of the normal respiratory regulation in response to blood CO_2 levels. Commonly seen after cerebral insult (poor prognostic sign) or in heart failure (patient often relatively well).
- Other characteristic neurogenic ventilation patterns are described but are far less common.

Listen before 'auscultating'

- Is the speech limited by their breathlessness? If so, can they complete a full sentence?
- Listen for hoarseness as well as the gurgling of excess secretions.
- A nasal voice may indicate neuromuscular weakness.
- Listen for coughing (see previous pages) as well as stridor and wheeze.

Skills station 6.1

Instruction

Examine this patient's respiratory system.

Model technique

- Clean your hands.
- Introduce yourself.
- Explain the purpose of the examination, obtain informed consent.
- Ask for any painful areas that you should avoid.
- Note the patient's general appearance and demeanour.
- Note any bedside clues.
- Ask the patient to undress to the waist and sit comfortably at 45°.
- Measure the patient's respiratory rate and breathing pattern.
  - Some practitioners like to do this whilst pretending to feel the patient's radial pulse. In this way, the patient does not become self-conscious and breathes as they normally would.
- Examine the hands.
  - Note staining, cyanosis, clubbing, radial pulse
  - Assess for tremor.
- Examine the JVP.
- Look in the nose, mouth, and eyes.
- Feel for cervical, supraclavicular, and axillary lymph nodes.
- Inspect the chest.
- Assess mediastinal position and chest expansion, front and back.
- Percuss front and back, comparing sides.
- Auscultate front and back, comparing sides.
- You may wish to consider other bedside tests such as PEFR or simple spirometry.
- Thank the patient and help them re-dress if necessary.

Hands, face, and neck

Temperature
- Cold fingers indicate peripheral vasoconstriction or heart failure.
- Warm hands with dilated veins are seen in CO_2 retention.

Staining
Fingers stained with tar appear yellow/brown where the cigarette is held (nicotine is colourless and does *not* stain). This indicates smoking but is not an accurate indicator of the number of cigarettes smoked.

Cyanosis
This is a bluish tinge to the skin, mucous membranes, and nails, evident when >2.5g/dl of reduced haemoglobin is present (O_2 sat. about 85%). Easier to see in good, natural light.

Central cyanosis is seen in the tongue and oral membranes (severe lung disease, e.g. pneumonia, PE, COPD). Peripheral cyanosis is seen *only* in the fingers and toes and is caused by peripheral vascular disease and vasoconstriction.

Digital clubbing
↑ curvature of the nails. Early clubbing is seen as a softening of the nail bed (nail can be rocked from side to side) but this is very difficult to detect. Progressive clubbing leads to a loss of the nail angle at the base and eventually to a gross longitudinal curvature and deformity.

The most important respiratory causes are carcinoma and lung fibrosis but it is also seen in chronic sepsis (bronchiectasis, abscess, empyema, cystic fibrosis).

Pulse
Rate, rhythm, character. A tachycardic 'bounding' pulse = CO_2 retention.

Tremor
- *Fine tremor:* caused by use of β-agonist drugs (e.g. salbutamol).
- *Flapping tremor (asterixis):* flapping when holding the hands dorsiflexed with the fingers abducted (Fig. 6.2). Identical to the flap of hepatic failure. Late sign of CO_2 retention, so uncommon.

Blood pressure
Pulsus paradoxus. Causes: pericardial effusion, severe asthma (but there should be some other clues to severe asthma!).

JVP
See ➲ p. 117. Raised in pulmonary vasoconstriction or pulmonary hypertension and right heart failure. Markedly raised, without a pulsation, in superior vena cava obstruction with distended upper chest wall veins, facial and conjunctival oedema (chemosis).

Nose
Examine inside (nasal speculum) and out, looking for polyps (asthma), deviated septum, and lupus pernio (red/purple nasal swelling of sarcoid granuloma).

Mouth
Look especially for candidiasis (common in those on inhaled steroids or immunosuppressants).

Eyes

- *Conjunctiva:* evidence of anaemia?
- *Horner's syndrome:* caused by compression of the sympathetic chain in the chest cavity (tumour, sarcoidosis, fibrosis).
- *Iritis:* TB, sarcoidosis.
- *Conjunctivitis:* TB, sarcoidosis.

Lymph nodes

See ➲ Chapter 3 for full description of technique. Feel especially the anterior and posterior triangles, the supraclavicular areas. Don't forget the axillae receive lymph drainage from the chest wall and breasts (Fig. 6.3).

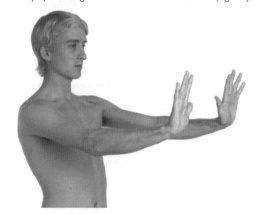

Fig. 6.2 Looking for a flapping tremor. Wrists are dorsiflexed and fingers abducted.

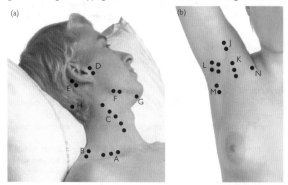

Fig. 6.3 Cervical, supraclavicular, and axillary lymph nodes. A: supraclavicular, B: posterior triangle, C: jugular chain, D: preauricular, E: postauricular, F: submandicular, G: submental, H: occipital, J: lateral, K: pectoral, L: central, M: subscapular, N: infraclavicular.

Inspection of the chest

Look at the shape and movement of the chest up-close.

Surface markings

Scars

May indicate previous surgery. Look especially in the mid-axillary lines for evidence of past chest drains. Remember a pnemonectomy can be undertaken with a relatively small lateral scar.

Radiotherapy

Radiotherapy will often cause lasting local skin thickening and erythema. Sites are usually marked with tattoo dots.

Veins

Look for unusually prominent surface vasculature suggesting obstructed venous return.

Shape

- *Deformity:* any asymmetry of shape? Remember to check the spine for scoliosis or kyphosis.
- *Surgery:* TB patients from the 1940s and 1950s may have had operations resulting in lasting and gross deformity (thoracoplasty).
- *Barrel chest:* a rounded thorax with ↑ AP diameter. Hyperinflation, a marker of chronic obstructive lung disease.
- *Pectus carinatum:* also called 'pigeon chest'. Sternum and costal cartilages are prominent and protrude from the chest. Can be caused by ↑ respiratory effort when the bones are still malleable in childhood—asthma, rickets.
- *Pectus excavatum:* also called 'funnel chest'. Sternum and costal cartilages appear depressed into the chest. A developmental defect, not usually of any clinical significance.
- *Surgical emphysema:* air in the soft tissues will appear as a diffuse swelling in the neck or around a chest drain site and will be 'crackly' to the touch.

Breathing pattern

Again, note the rate and depth of breathing as you did at the end of the bed (you only need formally time it once).

Movement

Observe chest wall movement during breathing at rest. Also, ask the patient to take a couple of deep breaths in and out and watch closely.

- Look for asymmetry. ↓ movement usually indicates lung disease on that side.
- ↓ movement globally is seen in COPD or neuromuscular conditions.
- Harrison's sulcus is a depression of the lower ribs just above the costal margins and is occasionally seen in the context of severe childhood asthma.

Palpation

Mediastinal position

Trachea

The trachea will shift as the mediastinum is pulled or pushed laterally (e.g. by fibrosis or mass). It should lie in the midline deep to the sternal notch.

You'll need to push down as well as back otherwise you are just checking the position in the neck: so warn the patient it will be uncomfortable. Use two fingers and palpate the sulci either side of the trachea at the same time. They should feel of identical size (Fig. 6.4).

The trachea often feels central even if there is pathology, but if you do feel a deviation it may be instructive and other signs should be sought.

Apex beat

Normally at the 5th intercostal space in the mid-clavicular line. However, the apex beat is difficult to localize in the presence of hyperexpanded lungs and it may be shifted to the left if the heart is enlarged.

Chest expansion

🚫 It is important to explain what you are doing here before grabbing hold of the patient's chest! See also Box 6.4.

Antero-posterior diameter

- Put both hands lightly on the anterior wall of the patient's chest above the nipples, fingers toward the clavicles.
- Ask the patient to breathe all the way out, then take a deep breath in: your hands should move equally.

Lateral diameter (from the front)

- Place both hands on the chest wall just below the level of their nipples, anchoring your fingers laterally at the sides (Fig. 6.5).
- Extend your thumbs so that they touch in the midline when the patient is in full expiration (or as near as you can if you have small hands or a large subject).
- Ask the patient to take a deep breath in. As they do this, watch your thumbs, they should move apart equally. Any ↓ in movement on one side should be visible.
  - It is easy to move your thumbs yourself in the expected direction. Beware of this and allow them to follow the movement of the chest.

Most sources recommend testing lateral expansion at the front and back: this is almost testing the same thing twice but is a good way of ensuring you had the right answer initially.

To test expansion posteriorly it is easiest to ask the patient to lean forward and place your hands on the chest wall with the thumbs pointing *down*. The procedure can then be repeated.

Tactile vocal fremitus

This is the vibration felt on the chest as the patient speaks. It gives the same information as vocal resonance testing so is now rarely tested.

Box 6.4 A word on the female chest

Breasts come in different shapes and sizes. The placement of your hands for this part of the examination should vary accordingly.

In particular, if faced with an older or particularly large-busted woman, it may be easier to place your hands above the breasts, at about the level of the 5th rib, rather than trying to reach below them.

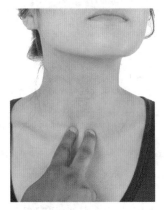

Fig. 6.4 Palpating the trachea. Methods vary and students are taught to use either one, two, or even three fingers. We suggest using two fingers to palpate the sulci either side of the trachea at the sternal notch. These should feel symmetrical.

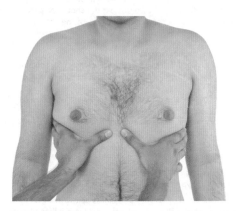

Fig. 6.5 Placement of the hands for testing chest expansion. Anchor with the fingers and leave the thumbs free-floating.

Percussion

Technique

This takes some practice to master so serves as a sound indicator of how much time a student has spent on the wards (it does also give extremely useful information in clinical practice!).

The aim is to tap the chest and listen to and feel for the resultant vibration (see Figs 6.6 and 6.7). For a *right-handed* examiner:

- Place the left hand on the chest wall, fingers separated and middle finger lying between the ribs.
- Press the middle finger firmly against the chest (students often don't press hard enough).
- Using the middle finger of the right hand, strike the middle phalanx of the middle finger of the left hand (Fig. 6.6). You'll have to hit yourself harder if the left hand is not firmly applied.
- The striking finger should be moved away again quickly as keeping it pressed on the left hand may muffle the noise.
- The right middle finger should be kept in the flexed position, the striking movement coming from the wrist (much like playing the piano).

🛈 Students quickly learn to keep the middle fingernail of their right hand well-trimmed!

- Practise on yourself, friends, and on objects around the house. You'll soon learn the different feel and sound produced by percussing over hollow and dense objects like the lung and the liver.
- In clinical practice, one should percuss each area of the lung, each time comparing right then left.
- Don't forget the apices which can be assessed by percussing directly onto the patient's clavicle (no left hand needed).
- If an area of dullness is heard (or felt) this should be percussed in more detail so as to map out the borders of the abnormality.

Findings

- Normal lung sounds 'resonant'.
- 'Dullness' is heard/felt over areas of ↑ density (consolidation, collapse, alveolar fluid, pleural thickening, peripheral abscess, neoplasm).
- 'Stony dullness' is the unique extreme dullness heard over a pleural effusion.
- 'Hyper-resonance' indicates areas of ↓ density (emphysematous bullae or pneumothorax).
  - COPD can create a globally hyper-resonant chest.

Normal dull areas

- There should be an area of dullness over the heart which may be diminished in hyperexpansion states (e.g. COPD or asthma).

The liver is manifested by an area of dullness below the level of the 6th rib anteriorly on the right. This will be lower with hyperinflated lungs.

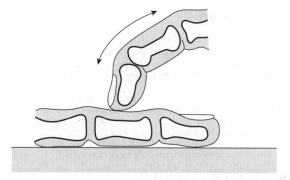

Fig. 6.6 Strike the middle phalanx of the middle finger of the left hand with the middle finger of the right hand. Withdraw the striking finger quickly so as not to muffle the sound and feel.

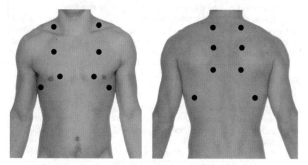

Fig. 6.7 Areas of the chest to percuss. Test right versus left for each area, front and back. You may examine the apices by percussing directly on the patient's clavicles—this does hurt a little, though.

Auscultation

Technique

The diaphragm of the stethoscope should be used except where better surface contact is needed in very thin or hairy patients.

- Ask the patient to 'take deep breaths in and out through the mouth'. See also Box 6.5.
- Listen to the whole of both inspiration and expiration.
- Listen over the same areas percussed, comparing left to right.
- If an abnormality is found, examine more carefully and define borders (see Table 6.3 for specific lobes).
- Listen for the breath sounds and any added sounds—and note at which point in the respiratory cycle they occur.

> ### Box 6.5 Patient performance
> Many patients have difficulty performing correctly here. They may take one deep breath and hold it, may breathe through the nose, or may take only one breath. Simple prompts ('keep going, in and out') will help. A brief demonstration will usually solve things if all else fails.
> ▶ Remember also that taking maximal forced breaths in and out will create additional noises in many healthy individuals, and will lead to symptoms from hyperventilation by the end of the examination. You may need to calm down your enthusiastic patients.

Findings

Breath sounds

- *Normal*: 'vesicular'. Produced by airflow in the large airways and larynx and altered by passage through the small airways before reaching the stethoscope. Often described as 'rustling'. Heard especially well in inspiration and early expiration.
- *Reduced sound*: if local = effusion, tumour, pneumothorax, pneumonia or lung collapse. If global = COPD or asthma.
  - ▶ The 'silent chest' is a sign of a life threatening asthma attack
- *Bronchial breathing*: caused by ↑ density of matter in the peripheral lung allowing sound from the larynx to the stethoscope unchanged. Has a 'hollow, blowing' quality, heard equally in inspiration and expiration, often with a brief pause between. (Think of a certain black-helmeted villain in a popular space movie franchise.)
  - A similar sound can be heard by listening over the trachea in the neck. Heard over consolidation, lung abscess at the chest wall, and dense fibrosis. Can be heard over squashed lung above a pleural effusion.

Added sounds

- *Wheeze (rhonchi)*: musical whistling sounds caused by narrowed airways. Heard in expiration:
  - Different calibre airways = different pitch note. Asthma and COPD can cause a chorus of notes termed 'polyphonic wheeze'
  - Monophonic 'wheeze' indicates a single airway is narrowed, usually by a foreign body or carcinoma.

- *Crackles (crepitations, rales):* caused by air entering collapsed airways and alveoli producing an opening snap or by mucus moving. Heard in inspiration:
  - 'Coarse' crackles made by larger airways opening and sound like the snap and pop of a certain breakfast cereal. Causes: fluid or infection
  - 'Fine' crackles occur later in inspiration. They sound like the tear of 'Velcro®' and can also be reproduced by rolling the hair at your temples between the thumb and forefinger. Usually fluid or fibrosis
  - The 'deciduous' crackles of bronchiectasis are of predominantly coarse type but fall away in volume and depth of note on inspiration
  - ❶ Crackles are often a normal finding at the lung bases, If so, they will clear after asking the patient to cough.
- *Rub:* creaking sound likened to the bending of new leather or the crunch of a footstep in fresh snow—once you've heard it you'll remember. Heard best at the height of inspiration, and may be very well localized. Caused by inflamed pleural surfaces rubbing against each other.
  - Causes: pneumonia, pulmonary embolism with infarction
  - ❶ Movement of the stethoscope on the chest wall sounds similar.

Vocal resonance

- Auscultatory equivalent of vocal fremitus.
- Sound transmitted though solid material (consolidated or collapsed lung) travels much better than through healthy air-filled lung, so phonation is more clearly heard.
- Ask the patient to say 'ninety-nine' or 'one, one, one' and listen over the same areas as before.
- Lower pitched sounds transmit particularly well so create a vocal 'booming' quality (this is why the original German 'neun und neunzig' works better than 'ninety nine').
- Marked ↑ resonance, such that a whisper can be clearly heard is termed 'whispering pectoriloquy'.

Table 6.3 Auscultating specific lung lobes

Lobe	Where to listen
Upper	Anteriorly, nipple level and above
Right middle/left lingula	Anterolaterally
Lower	Posteriorly

Important presentations

Pneumonia

Inspection
- Look for sputum pot at bedside.
- Tachypnoeic, tachycardic, or hypotensive?
- Warm peripheries.
- Bounding pulse.
- Sweaty and clammy.

Palpation
- Reduced expansion on the affected side.
- Increased tactile vocal fremitus if consolidation.

Percussion
- Dull.

Auscultation
- Coarse crackles, localized.
- Bronchial breathing (possible).
- Whispering pectoriloquy.
- Reduced air entry.
- Increased vocal resonance.

Lobar collapse

Palpation
- Mediastinal shift towards the abnormality.
- Potentially ↓ chest wall movement locally.

Percussion
- Dullness to percussion restricted to affected lobe.

Auscultation
- ↓ breath sounds usually.

Pleural effusion

Inspection
- Reduced chest expansion unilaterally (if large).

Palpation
- Trachea may be pushed away from the effusion.
- Apex beat:
  - A large right effusion will displace the cardiac apex to the left
  - A large left effusion may make the apex beat difficult to palpate.

Percussion
- 'Stony dull'.

Auscultation
- Markedly reduced breath sounds.
- Reduced vocal resonance.
- Collapsed or consolidated lung above the effusion may produce an overlying region of bronchial breathing.

Pneumothorax

Inspection

- No mediastinal shift (only occurs with a tension pneumothorax).
- Chest wall asymmetry may be evident with a large pneumothorax (greater volume on affected side).

Percussion

- Hyper-resonant.

Auscultation

- ↓ breath sounds on affected side.
- ↓ vocal resonance on affected side.

Interstitial fibrosis

Inspection

- Patients may be cyanosed.
- There may also be signs of connective tissue disease or skin changes of radiotherapy.
- Clubbing is common.

Palpation

- Trachea may move towards the fibrosis in upper lobe disease.
- ↔ or ↓ chest wall movement.

Percussion

- ↔ percussion note.

Auscultation

- ↔ breath sounds.
- ↔ vocal resonance usually, may be increased if dense fibrosis.
- Fine 'Velcro®' crackles.

COPD

Inspection

- Inhalers at the bedside.
- Sputum pot?
- Thin skin with bruising (use of steroids).
- Use of accessory muscles/brace position.
- Tachypnoea.
- No mediastinal shift.
- Chest hyper-expanded with little additional excursion.
- Prolonged expiration and pursed lip breathing.

Percussion

- May be globally hyper-resonant to percussion.

Auscultation

- ↓ breath sounds globally, may be additional polyphonic wheeze.
- ↓ vocal resonance usually in the upper lobes (where bullae are commonest).
- Heart sounds often quiet.

Bronchiectasis

Inspection

- Often copious sputum (usually purulent, may contain blood).
- Digital clubbing may be present.
- Low BMI.

Palpation

- No mediastinal shift.
- Chest wall expansion equal.

Percussion

- Percussion resonant.

Auscultation

- Mixed, predominant coarse crackles.
- Often additional polyphonic wheeze.
- Vocal resonance normal.

Neuromuscular insufficiency

Intrinsic muscle weakness or damaged innervations.

Inspection

- Non-respiratory signs of neuromuscular illness (e.g. altered phonation, limited mobility).
- Rapid shallow breathing, sometimes with abdominal paradox.

Palpation

- Chest wall expansion equal but limited excursion.

Percussion

- Percussion note resonant.

Auscultation

- Breath sounds normal.
- Basal crackles common from atelectasis (impaired cough).

See also:

More information regarding the presentation and clinical signs of respiratory diseases, to aid preparation for OSCE-type examinations and ward rounds, can be found in the *Oxford Handbooks Clinical Tutor Study Cards*.

'Medicine' Study Card set:

- Chronic obstructive pulmonary disease
- Interstitial lung disease
- Lobectomy
- Pleural effusion
- Pneumothorax
- Previous tuberculosis
- Pneumonia
- Obstructive sleep apnoea
- Cystic fibrosis
- Kartagener's syndrome
- Bronchiectasis
- Superior vena cava obstruction
- Chronic cor pulmonale.

The elderly patient

Up to 60% of older people may suffer respiratory symptoms, but less readily see their doctors about them. Lung function declines with age and exertional breathlessness rises, often with concurrent (non-respiratory) illnesses. Careful, thoughtful assessment is therefore vital.

History

- *Clarify diagnosis:* not all disease in elders is COPD and many older people are lifelong non-smokers. Asthma and pulmonary fibrosis are often underdiagnosed.
- *Fatigue:* often associated with chronic respiratory illnesses and may be more disabling to individuals than respiratory symptoms themselves.
- *DHx:* should be comprehensive and 'dovetail' other medical problems. Anticholinergic drugs (e.g. atrovent) may precipitate glaucoma or worsen bladder and bowel symptoms, so be thorough. Ask about vaccinations—many miss their annual 'flu vaccine through hospitalization. Consider vaccination in hospital.
- *Nutrition and mood:* under-nutrition is common with chronic diseases and those in long-term care, impacting on illnesses with higher resting metabolic rates (e.g. COPD). Low mood is similarly common and should be sought.
- *SHx:* functional history is paramount and may reveal key interventions. A thorough occupational history is vital; many people do not know they have worked/lived with someone exposed to e.g. asbestos.

Examination

- *General:* poorly fitting clothes/dentures may point to weight loss (under-nutrition, chronic disease, malignancy).
- *Hands:* arthritis/other deformities may make inhaler use difficult and point to related diagnoses (e.g. rheumatoid lung disease). Clubbing may not be present in later onset pulmonary fibrosis.
- *Chest:* beware 'basal crepitations' which are common in older age. Pick out discriminating signs—tachypnoea, position of crackles, added sounds, etc.
- *Inhaler technique:* key examination; may reveal why prior treatments were unsuccessful.

Diagnoses not to be missed

- *Asthma:* up to 8% of over-60s, but under-recognized and under-treated. Spirometry is a key investigation.
- *Tuberculosis:* increased in the elderly—through reactivation, chronic illness, under-nutrition. Presents non-specifically—cough, lethargy, weight loss.
- *Smoking status:* The patient may be on long-term oxygen, but may still smoke! Consider nicotine withdrawal as a cause of agitation in hospitalized older patients. They may not be able to go out to smoke, and nicotine patches (on discussion with senior nursing and medical staff) may be very helpful.

Chapter 7

The abdomen

Introduction

The abdomen includes the perineum, external and internal genitalia, and the inguinal regions. The male and female genitalia are discussed later in this book.

Boundaries

The abdomen is defined as the region lying between the thorax above and the pelvic cavity below. The anterior abdominal wall is bounded by the 7th to 12th costal cartilages and the xiphoid process of the sternum superiorly and the inguinal ligaments and pelvic bones inferiorly.

The abdominal cavity is separated from the thoracic cavity by the diaphragm. There is no such delineation, however, between the abdomen and the pelvis and, as a consequence, definitions vary.

Abdominal contents

The abdomen contains structures which form part of just about every body system.

The *digestive* organs of the oesophagus, stomach, small intestine, large intestine, and the associated organs (liver, gallbladder and biliary system, exocrine pancreas) all lie within the abdomen. The *endocrine* portion of the pancreas, the adrenal glands and gonads represent the endocrine system. From the *cardiovascular* system: the abdominal aorta with its important branches to the liver, spleen, intestine, kidneys, and lower limbs. The *immunological* system is represented by the spleen, the multiple lymph nodes surrounding the aorta and intestines, and the MALT tissue within the intestine itself. The whole of the *urinary system* is present (kidneys, ureters, bladder, and urethra).

It is worth remembering that, much like the thorax, the abdomen is lined by a rather thin layer of membranous tissue: the peritoneum. This is a double lining—the 'parietal' peritoneum covers the internal surface of the abdominal walls whilst the 'visceral' peritoneum covers the organs. Between the two layers (the 'peritoneal cavity') is a small amount of fluid which acts a lubricant allowing the abdominal contents to move against each other as the body changes position or, for example, as the gut contorts with peristalsis.

A select few organs lie behind the peritoneum on the posterior abdominal wall. They are the pancreas, a portion of the duodenum, the ascending and descending colon, and the kidneys.

Abdominal regions

The anterior abdominal wall is artificially divided into nine portions for descriptive purposes. Four imaginary lines can be drawn (see Fig. 7.1):
- One horizontal line between the anterior superior iliac spines.
- One horizontal line between the lower border of the ribs.
- Two vertical lines at the mid-clavicular point.

To make life easier, the abdomen can also be simply divided into four quadrants by imagining one horizontal and one vertical line crossing at the umbilicus (see Fig. 7.2).

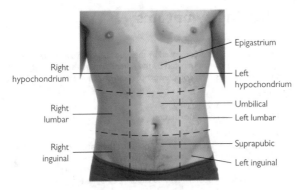

Epigastrium

Right
hypochondrium

Left
hypochondrium

Right
lumbar

Umbilical

Left lumbar

Right
inguinal

Suprapubic

Left inguinal

Fig. 7.1 The nine segments of the anterior abdominal wall. Students should familiarize themselves with these, along with the organs lying in each area.

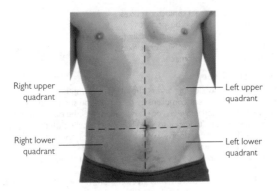

Right upper
quadrant

Left upper
quadrant

Right lower
quadrant

Left lower
quadrant

Fig. 7.2 The four quadrants of the abdomen.

Swallowing symptoms

Physiology of swallowing

The swallowing process is controlled by the medulla initially and by an autonomous peristaltic reflex coordinated by the enteric nervous system in the mid- and distal-oesophagus. This complex process can be divided into three phases:

Oral phase

- Food enters the oral cavity.
- Mastication and bolus formation.

Oro-pharyngeal phase

- Tongue elevates and propels the bolus to the pharynx.
- The soft palate elevates to seal the nasopharynx.
- The larynx and hyoid bone move anteriorly and cranially.
- Epiglottis moves posteriorly and caudally to close the respiratory tract.
- Respiration pauses.
- Pharynx shortens.

Oesophageal phase

- Upper oesophageal sphincter relaxes.
- Bolus passes into the oesophagus.
- Oesophagus contracts sequentially (peristalsis).
- Lower oesophageal sphincter relaxes.
- Bolus enters the stomach.

Dysphagia history

This is difficulty swallowing and is the principal symptom of oesophageal disease. When a patient complains of dysphagia you should establish:

- *Level of obstruction:* where does the patient feel the obstruction?
  - Patients can often point to a level on the chest although the sensation usually correlates poorly with the actual level of obstruction.
- *Onset:* How quickly did the symptoms emerge?
  - Obstruction caused by cancer may progress rapidly over a few months
  - Benign peptic stricture may give very long history of GORD with slowly progressive dysphagia.
- *Time course:* is the symptom intermittent or constant?
  - Present for only the first few swallows: lower oesophageal ring, spasm?
  - Progressive: cancer, stricture, achalasia.
- *Solids/liquids:* solids, liquids or both affected?
  - Both solids and liquids being affected equally suggests a motor cause (achalasia, spasm)
  - Solids affected more than liquids suggests some physical obstruction is more likely (e.g. cancer).
- *Associated symptoms:* heartburn (leads to oesophageal strictures), weight loss, wasting, fatigue (perhaps suggestive of cancer). Coughing and choking suggest 'pharyngeal dysphagia' due to motor dysfunction (e.g. motor neuron disease causing bulbar- or pseudobulbar palsy).

Types of dysphagia

See Box 7.1 for a list of causes.

Oropharyngeal

Also called 'high' dysphagia. Patients have difficulty initiating a swallow and often feel as though the cervical/neck area is the level of apparent obstruction.

Symptoms relate to both the dysphagia itself and likely underlying causes. These may include:

- Difficulty initiating swallow.
- Nasal regurgitation.
- Coughing.
- Nasal speech.
- Diminished cough reflex.
- Choking.
  - Due to laryngeal penetration and aspiration. Note that aspiration may occur without coughing in the neurologically impaired.
- Dysarthria and diplopia.
  - Due to underlying neurological diagnosis. Ask about other neurological symptoms and perform a full neurological examination (see ➲ Chapter 8).
- Halitosis.
  - Caused by large residue-containing Zenker's diverticulum. Also seen in advanced (end-stage) achalasia or long-term obstruction.

Oesophageal

Also called 'low' dysphagia. Patients find the site of apparent obstruction difficult to localize and may often point to their neck when the obstruction is actually within the distal oesophagus (e.g. in achalasia).

Box 7.1 Causes of dysphagia

Oropharyngeal

- Mechanical and obstructive: infections (e.g. retropharyngeal abscess), enlarged thyroid, lymphadenopathy, Zenker's diverticulum, reduced muscle compliance (e.g. myositis, fibrosis), malignancy, large cervical osteophytosis
- Neuromuscular: stroke, Parkinson's disease, bulbar palsy, motor neuron disease, multiple sclerosis, myasthenia gravis, muscular dystrophy
- Other: poor dentition, oral ulcers, xerostomia.

Oesophageal

- Mucosal disease: peptic stricture, oesophageal rings and webs (e.g. Plummer–Vinson syndrome), oesophageal tumours, chemical injury, radiation injury, infectious oesophagitis, eosinophilic oesophagitis
- Mediastinal disease: tumours, infection (e.g. TB, histoplasmosis), cardiovascular (e.g. vascular compression)
- Smooth muscle/innervation disease: achalasia (e.g. idiopathic, Chagas disease), scleroderma, post-surgical (e.g. post-fundoplication, antireflux devices, gastric banding).

Odynophagia

This is pain on swallowing and usually reflects a severe inflammatory process involving the oesophageal mucosa or, rarely, the oesophageal musculature.

The character may range from a dull retrosternal ache to a sharp, stabbing pain with radiation through to the back. Severity can be such that patients feel unable to swallow their own saliva. Causes are shown in Box 7.2.

Box 7.2 Causes of odynophagia

- Chemical irritation
  - Acid
  - Alkali.
- Drug-induced oesophagitis
  - Antibiotics (e.g. doxycycline)
  - Potassium chloride
  - Quinidine
  - Iron sulphate
  - Zidovudine
  - NSAIDs.
- Radiation oesophagitis
- Infectious oesophagitis
- Healthy patients: *Candida albicans*, herpes simplex
- Immunocompromised patients: fungal (*Candida*, histoplasmosis), viral (herpes simplex, cytomegalovirus, HIV, EBV), *Mycobacteria* (*tuberculosis*, *avium-complex*), protozoan (*Cryptosporidium*, *Pneumocystis jiroveci*), idiopathic ulceration
- Severe ulcerative oesophagitis secondary to gastro-oesophageal reflux disease (GORD)
- Oesophageal carcinoma.

Globus sensation

This is the sensation of a 'lump' or tightness in the throat and is usually not related to swallowing. Patients may describe this as a 'tightness', 'choking', or 'strangling feeling' as if something is caught in the throat.

- Present between meals.
- Swallowing solids or large liquid boluses may give temporary relief.
- Exacerbated by emotional stress.
- ❶ Dysphagia and odynophagia are not present.

The cause of globus sensation is often unclear and may be a combination of physiological and psychological factors. Anxiety, panic disorder, depression, and somatization are often present. Physiological tests of oesophageal motility are often normal.

A combination of biological factors, hypochondriacal traits, and learned fear following an episode of choking can increase the symptom.

Heartburn and acid reflux

Also known as gastro-oesophageal reflux disease (GORD). It is caused by the regurgitation of stomach contents into the oesophagus due to an incompetent anti-reflux mechanism at the gastro-oesophageal junction. See also Box 7.3.

Typical features
- Site: mid-line, retrosternal.
- Radiation: to the throat and occasionally the infra-scapular regions.
- Nature: 'burning'.
- Aggravating factors: worse after meals and when performing postures which raise the intra-abdominal pressure (bending, stooping, lying supine). Also worse during pregnancy.
- Associated symptoms: Often accompanied by acid or bitter taste (acid regurgitation) or sudden filling of the mouth with saliva* ('waterbrash').

Acid reflux may be worsened by certain foods (alcohol, caffeine, chocolate, fatty meals) and some drugs (calcium channel blockers, anticholinergics) which act to reduce the GOJ sphincter pressure.

🛈 Hiatus hernia is another important cause of reflux symptoms—be sure to enquire about this in the history.

Box 7.3 Causes of heartburn

Decreased lower oesophageal sphincter pressure
- Foods
  - Fats, sugars, chocolate, onions, coffee, alcohol.
- Cigarette smoking
- Medication
  - Calcium channel blockers, nitrates, diazepam, theophylline, progesterone, anti-cholinergics.

Direct mucosal irritation
- Foods
  - Citrus fruits, tomato-based foods, spicy foods, coffee.
- Medication
  - Aspirin, NSAIDs, tetracycline, quinidine, potassium chloride, iron.

Increased intra-abdominal pressure
- Bending over
- Lifting
- Straining at stool
- Exercise.

Other
- Lying supine
- Lying on the right
- Red wine
- High emotion.

---

* The salivary glands can produce 10ml of saliva/minute. The 'oesophageo-salivary response'.

Nausea and vomiting

Definitions

Nausea

- A feeling of sickness—the inclination to vomit.
- Usually occurs in waves.
- May be associated with retching or heaving.
- Can last from seconds to days depending on the cause.

Vomiting (emesis)

- The forceful expulsion of the gastric contents by reflex contractions of the thoracic and abdominal muscles.
- Usually follows nausea and autonomic symptoms such as salivation.

Onset

Over what time period have the symptoms developed?

- *Acute:* cholecystitis, gastroenteritis, recreational drug use, pancreatitis.
- *Chronic:* metabolic disorders, gastroparesis, gastro-oesophageal reflux, pregnancy, medications.

Timing

You should be clear on exactly when the vomiting tends to occur—particularly its relation to meals.

- *Before breakfast:* alcohol, raised intracranial pressure, pregnancy, uraemia.
- *During or immediately after eating:* psychiatric causes (also peptic ulcer disease, pyloric stenosis).
- *1–4 hours after a meal:* gastric outlet obstruction, gastroparesis.
- *Continuous:* conversion disorder, depression.
- *Irregular:* major depression.

Nature of the vomitus

Although unpleasant, you should enquire about the exact nature of any vomited material and attempt to see a sample, if possible.

- *Undigested food:* achalasia, oesophageal disorders (e.g. diverticulum, strictures).
- *Partially digested food:* gastric outlet obstruction, gastroparesis.
- *Bile:* proximal small bowel obstruction.
- *Faeculent/malodorous:* fistula, obstruction.
- *Large volume:* >1.5L in 24hrs, more likely physical than psychiatric.

Associated symptoms and their causes

- *Malignancy:* weight loss.
- *Viral:* diarrhoea, myalgia, malaise, headache.
- *Central neurologic:* headache, neck stiffness, vertigo, focal neurological signs/symptoms.
- *Gastroparesis:* early satiety, post-prandial bloating, abdominal discomfort.
- *Cyclical vomiting syndrome:* repetitive migraine headaches, symptoms of irritable bowel syndrome.

Vomiting blood (haematemesis)

Presence of blood indicates bleeding in the upper gastrointestinal tract (oesophagus, stomach, duodenum). See Box 7.4. Ask about:

- The amount of blood and exact nature of it:
  - *Large volume* of fresh, red blood suggests active bleeding (co-incident liver disease and/or heavy alcohol intake may suggest bleeding oesophageal varices, abdominal pain and heartburn may suggest a gastric or oesophageal source such as peptic ulceration or GORD)
  - *Small streaks* at the end of prolonged retching may indicate minor oesophageal trauma at the GOJ (Mallory–Weiss tear)
  - *Coffee-grounds:* looking like small brown granules, this is the term used for blood that has been 'altered' by exposure to stomach acid, implying that the bleeding has ceased or is relatively modest.
- Previous bleeding episodes, treatment, and outcome (e.g. previous surgery?).
- Cigarette smoking.
- Use of drugs such as aspirin, clopidogrel, NSAIDs, and warfarin.
- ❶ Remember to ask about weight loss, dysphagia, abdominal pain, and melaena (consider the possibility of neoplastic disease).

Box 7.4 Causes of upper GI bleeding

- Peptic ulceration
- Oesophagitis
- Gastritis/erosions
- Erosive duodenitis
- Varices
- Portal hypertensive gastropathy
- Malignancy
- Mallory–Weiss tear
- Vascular anomalies (e.g. angiodysplasia, AV malformation)
- Connective tissue disorders (e.g. Ehlers–Danlos syndrome)
- Vasculitis
- Bleeding diathesis.

Vomiting bile

Assess the presence or absence of bile. Remember that bile comes largely in two colours—the green pigment (biliverdin) often seen to colour the vomitus in the absence of undigested food. The yellow pigment (bilirubin) appears as orange, often occurring in small lumps.*

Undigested food without bile suggests a lack of connection between the stomach and the small intestine (e.g. pyloric obstruction).

---

* This is the answer to the age-old question 'why are there always carrots in vomit?' The orange globules are, in fact, dyed with bilirubin. We suggest saving that fact for your next dinner party.

Abdominal pain

As with any pain, work through the 'SOCRATES' questions (see ➲ Chapter 2) to establish the site, onset, character, radiation, associated symptoms, timing, exacerbating/relieving factors, and severity.

Site

Pain from most abdominal organs cannot be felt directly—the sensation is 'referred' to areas of the abdominal wall according to the organ's embryological origin (see Box 7.5 and Fig. 7.3). See Box 7.6 for some characteristic pains.

- Ask the patient to point to the area affected.
  - Patients often find this challenging and may indicate a wide area. In this case, ask them to 'use one finger' and point to the area of maximum intensity.

Box 7.5 Sites of abdominal pain and embryologic origins

- *Epigastric:* foregut (stomach, duodenum, liver, pancreas, gallbladder)
- *Periumbilical:* midgut (small and large intestines including appendix)
- *Suprapubic:* hindgut (rectum and urogenital organs).

▶ A very localized pain may originate from the parietal peritoneum. e.g. appendicitis—may begin as an umbilical pain (referred from the appendix) then 'move' to the right iliac fossa as the inflammation spreads to the peritoneum overlying the appendix.

Radiation

Ask the patient if the pain is felt elsewhere or if they have any other pains (they may not associate the radiated pain with the abdominal pain).

Some examples include:

- *Right scapula:* gallbladder.
- *Shoulder-tip:* diaphragmatic irritation.
- *Mid-back:* pancreas.

Character

Ask the patient what sort of pain it is. Give some examples if they have trouble but be careful not to lead the patient. A couple of examples include:

- *Colicky:* this is pain that comes and goes in waves and indicates obstruction of a hollow, muscular-walled organ (intestine, gallbladder, bile duct, ureter).
- *Burning:* may indicate an acid cause and is related to the stomach, duodenum, or lower end of the oesophagus.

Exacerbating/relieving factors

Ask the patient what appears to make the pain better or worse—or what they do to get rid of the pain if they suffer from it often.

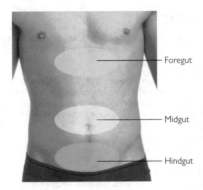

Fig. 7.3 Typical sites of pain according to embryologic origin.

Box 7.6 Some characteristic pains

- *Renal colic:* colicky pain at the renal angles and loins, which are tender to touch, radiating to the groins/testicles/labia. Typically, the patient writhes, unable to find a position that relieves the pain
- *Bladder pain:* a diffuse severe pain in the suprapubic region
- *Prostatic pain:* a dull ache which may be felt in the lower abdomen, rectum, perineum, or anterior thighs
- *Urethral pain:* variable in presentation ranging from a 'tickling' discomfort to a severe sharp pain felt at the end of the urethra (tip of the penis in males) and exacerbated by micturition. Can be so severe that patients attempt to 'hold on' to urine
- *Small bowel obstruction:* colicky central pain associated with vomiting, abdominal distension, and/or constipation
- *Colonic pain:* as under 'small bowel' but sometimes temporarily relieved by defaecation or passing flatus
- *Bowel ischaemia:* dull, severe, constant, right upper quadrant/central abdominal pain exacerbated by eating
- *Biliary pain:* severe, constant, right upper quadrant/epigastric pain that can last hours and is often worse after eating fatty foods
- *Pancreatic pain:* epigastric, radiating to the back and partly relieved by sitting up and leaning forward
- *Peptic ulcer pain:* dull, burning pain in the epigastrium. Typically episodic at night, waking the patient from sleep. Exacerbated by eating and sometimes relieved by consuming milk or antacids.

Bowel habit

Patients should be asked how often they open their bowels and if this has changed recently. Ask also about the other symptoms on these pages.

Constipation

A disorder that can mean different things to different people. Normal bowel habit ranges from three times/day to once every three days.

'Constipation' is the passage of stool <3 times/week, or stools that are hard or difficult to pass. Some causes are shown in Box 7.7.

A thorough history should include:
- Duration of constipation
- Frequency of bowel action
- Stool size and consistency
- Straining, particularly at the end of evacuation
- Associated symptoms (nausea, vomiting, weight loss)
- Pain on defaecation
- Rectal bleeding
- Intercurrent diarrhoea?
- Fluid and fibre intake
- Depression, lack of exercise
- DHx (prescription and over-the-counter)
  • Codeine, antidepressants, aluminium, and calcium antacids.
- Metabolic or endocrine diseases
  • Thyroid disorders, hypercalcaemia, diabetes, phaechromocytoma.
- Neurological problems
  • Autonomic neuropathy, spinal cord injury, multiple sclerosis, Hirschsprung's disease.

Diarrhoea

Defined as an increase in stool volume (>200ml daily) and frequency (3/day). Also a change in consistency to semi-formed or liquid stool. Some causes are shown in Boxes 7.8 and 7.9.

You should establish the time course since acute diarrhoea is suggestive of infection. Ask especially about:
- Colour, consistency, offensive smell, ease of flushing
- Duration
- Does the diarrhoea disturb the patient's sleep?
- Is there any blood, mucus, or pus?
- Associated pain or colic?
- Is there urgency?
- Nausea, vomiting, weight loss?
- Any difference if the patient fasts?
  • No change in 'secretory' diarrhoea—e.g. E. coli, Staph. aureus
  • Disappears on fasting: 'osmotic' diarrhoea.
- Foreign travel
- Recent antibiotics.

Box 7.7 Some causes of constipation

- Low-fibre diet
- Physical immobility (e.g. stroke, Parkinson's disease)
- Functional bowel disease (constipation-predominant irritable bowel syndrome)
- Drugs (e.g. opiates, iron, antidepressants, aluminium, antacids)
- Metabolic and endocrine diseases (e.g. hypothyroidism, hypercalcaemia, hypokalaemia, diabetes mellitus, porphyria, phaeochromocytoma)
- Neurological disorders (e.g. autonomic neuropathy, spinal cord injury, multiple sclerosis)
- Colonic stricture
- Anorectal disease (e.g. anal fissure—causes pain to the extent that the patient may avoid defaecating altogether)
- Habitual neglect
- Depression
- Dementia.

Box 7.8 Some causes of diarrhoea

- *Malabsorption:* may cause steatorrhoea, a fatty, pale stool which is extremely odorous and difficult to flush
- *Increased intestinal motility:* hyperthyroidism, irritable bowel syndrome
- *Exudative:* inflammation of the bowel causes small volume, frequent stools, often with blood or mucus (e.g. colonic carcinoma, Crohn's disease, ulcerative colitis)
- *Osmotic:* large volume of stool which disappears with fasting. Causes include lactose intolerance, gastric surgery
- *Secretory:* high volume of stool which persists with fasting. No pus, blood, or excessive fat. Causes include: gastrointestinal infections, carcinoid syndrome, villous adenoma of the colon, Zollinger–Ellison syndrome, VIP (vasoactive intestinal polypeptide)-secreting tumour
- *Other:* drugs (especially antibiotics), laxative abuse, constipation and faecal impaction (overflow), small bowel or right colonic resection.

Box 7.9 Fat malabsorption (steatorrhoea)

A common feature of pancreatic insufficiency. Also caused by coeliac disease, inflammatory bowel disease, blind bowel loops, and short bowel syndrome.

You should be aware of these features and explore them all fully if one is mentioned by the patient:

- Pale stool
- Offensive smelling
- Poorly formed
- Difficult to flush (floats).

Rectal bleeding and melaena

There are many causes of PR blood loss but, as always, a detailed history will help. See Box 7.10 for some causes. In taking the history, determine:

- The amount
  - Small amounts can appear dramatic, colouring toilet water red.
- The nature of the blood (red, brown, black)
- Is it mixed with the stool or 'on' the stool?
- Is it spattered over the pan, with the stool or only seen on the paper?
- Any associated features (mucus may indicate inflammatory bowel disease or colonic cancer).

Melaena

This is jet-black, tar-like and pungent-smelling stool representing blood from the upper GI tract (or right side of the large bowel) that has been 'altered' by passage through the gut.

The presence of melaena is often queried in hospital in-patients but those who have smelt true melaena rarely forget the experience!

Ask about iron supplementation or bismuth-containing compounds—cause blackened stools but without the melaena smell or consistency.

Box 7.10 Some causes of lower GI bleeding

- Haemorrhoids
- Anal fissure
- Diverticular disease
- Colorectal carcinoma
- Colorectal polyp
- Angiodysplasia
- Inflammatory bowel disease
- Ischaemic colitis
- Meckel's diverticulum
- Small bowel disease (e.g. tumour, diverticula, intussusception, Crohn's)
- Solitary rectal ulcer
- Haemobilia (bleeding into the biliary tree).

Mucus

Clear, viscoid secretion of the mucous membranes. Mucus contains epithelial cells, leukocytes, and various salts suspended in water.

The presence of mucus in, or on, stools may indicate:

- Inflammatory bowel disease
- Solitary rectal ulcer
- Small or large bowel fistula
- Colonic villous adenoma
- Irritable bowel syndrome.

Flatus

Small amounts of gas frequently escape from the bowel via the mouth (eructation) and anus and the notable excess of this is a common feature of both functional and organic disorders of the gastrointestinal tract.

Often associated with abdominal bloating and caused by the colonic bacterial fermentation of poorly absorbed carbohydrates.

Excessive flatus is a particular feature of:

- Hiatus hernia.
- Peptic ulceration.
- Chronic gallbladder disease.
- Air-swallowing (aerophagy).
- High-fibre diet.
- Lactase deficiency.
- Intestinal malabsorption.

Tenesmus

This is the feeling of the need to open the bowels with little or no stool actually passed. The sensation may be constant or intermittent and is usually accompanied by pain, cramping, and involuntary straining.

Causes include:

- Inflammatory bowel disease.
- Anorectal abscess.
- Infective colitis.
- Colorectal tumours/polyps.
- Radiation proctitis.
- Irritable bowel syndrome.
- Thrombosed haemorrhoids.

Generalized abdominal swelling

The five classic causes of abdominal swelling ('the 5 Fs'):

- Fat.
- Fluid (see also Box 7.11).
- Flatus.
- Faeces.
- Fetus.

To these, you should also add 'tumour' and another 'F': Functional (irritable bowel syndrome).

Box 7.11 Ascites in decompensated liver disease

- In decompensated cirrhosis, a combination of portal (sinusoidal) hypertension and Na and H_2O retention favours the transudation of fluid into the peritoneal cavity (ascites)
- The resultant swelling may be unsightly—it can also cause shortness of breath by putting pressure on the diaphragm from below, particularly when supine and may be associated with pleural effusions.

Jaundice and pruritus

Jaundice

Jaundice ('icterus') is a yellow pigmentation of skin, sclera, and mucosae caused by excess bilirubin in the tissue. See Box 7.12 for some causes and Box 7.13 for other causes of skin yellowing.

Jaundice results from interference in the normal metabolism of bilirubin (including uptake, transport, conjugation, and excretion). Ask about:

- The colour of the urine (dark in cholestatic jaundice due to renal excretion of conjugated bilirubin).
- The colour and consistency of the stools (pale in cholestatic jaundice).
- Abdominal pain (e.g. caused by gallstones).

Ask especially about:

- Previous blood transfusions.
- Past history of jaundice, hepatitis, pancreatitis, or biliary surgery.
- Drugs (e.g. antibiotics, NSAIDs, oral contraceptives, phenothiazines, herbal remedies, anabolic steroids). See also Box 7.14.
- Intravenous drug use.
- Tattoos and body piercing.
- Foreign travel and immunizations.
- Sexual history.
- FHx of liver disease.
- Alcohol consumption.
- Any personal contacts who also have jaundice.
- Occupational exposure to hepatotoxins.

Box 7.12 Causes of jaundice

Pre-hepatic (unconjugated hyperbilirubinaemia)
- Overproduction: haemolysis; ineffective erythropoiesis
- Impaired hepatic uptake: drugs (contrast agents, rifampicin), congestive cardiac failure
- Impaired conjugation: Gilbert's syndrome, Crigler–Najjar syndrome.

Hepatic (conjugated hyperbilirubinaemia)
- Infection: viral hepatitis, CMV, liver abscess, septicaemia
- Alcohol and toxins: carbon tetrachloride, fungi (*Amanita phalloides*)
- Drug-induced hepatitis: paracetamol, anti-tuberculosis drugs (isoniazid, rifampicin, pyrazinamide), statins, sodium valproate, halothane
- Metabolic: haemochromatosis, α_1-antitrypsin deficiency, Wilson's disease, Rotor syndrome
- Vascular: Budd–Chiari, right-sided heart failure.

Post-hepatic (conjugated hyperbilirubinaemia)
- Luminal: gallstones
- Mural: cholangiocarcinoma, sclerosing cholangitis, primary biliary cirrhosis, choledochal cyst
- Extra-mural: pancreatic cancer, lymph nodes at porta hepatis
- Drugs: antibiotics (flucloxacillin, fusidic acid, co-amoxiclav, nitrofurantoin), steroids, sulphonylureas, chlorpromazine, prochlorperazine.

Pruritus

This is itching of the skin and may be either localized or generalized. The mechanism is not fully understood but is likely due to increased bile acid levels secondary to cholestasis.

It has many causes—it is particularly associated with cholestatic liver disease (e.g. primary biliary cirrhosis, sclerosing cholangitis).

Box 7.13 Some other causes of yellowing of the skin

- Carotenodermia: excess ingestion of carotene (orange vegetables such as carrots, squash)
  - The pigment is concentrated on the palm, soles, forehead, and nasolabial folds but spares the sclerae.
- Lycopenodermia: excessive ingestion of lycopene-containing red foodstuffs (e.g. tomato)
- Quinacrine
- Excessive exposure to phenols.

Box 7.14 Drug history in liver disease

Think about drugs that can precipitate hepatic diseases and remember to ask about over-the-counter drugs. For example:

- *Hepatitis:* halothane, phenytoin, chlorothiazides, pyrazinamide, isoniazid, methyl dopa, HMG CoA reductase inhibitors ('statins'), sodium valproate, amiodarone, antibiotics, NSAIDs
- *Cholestasis:* chlorpromazine, sulphonamides, sulphonylureas, rifampicin, nitrofurantoin, anabolic steroids, oral contraceptive pill
- *Fatty liver:* tetracycline, sodium valproate, amiodarone
- *Acute liver necrosis:* paracetamol.

🚫 Ask also about previous blood transfusions.

Appetite and weight

Loss of appetite and changes in weight are rather non-specific symptoms but should raise suspicion of a serious disease if either is severe, prolonged, or unexpected. Be aware of triggers for concern (Box 7.15) and consider using the 'MUST' score (Box 7.16) for those at risk of malnutrition.

Important notes on appetite and weight

- ▶ Remember that weight loss has many causes outside of the abdomen and a thorough systems enquiry should be conducted.
- Weight loss may not be noticed by patients if they don't regularly weigh themselves—ask about clothes becoming loose.
- ❶ Remember that the patient may have been intentionally losing weight—throwing you off the scent. Ask if the loss is 'expected'.
- Ascites weighs 1kg/L and some patients with liver failure may have 10–20L of ascites, masking any 'dry weight' loss.
- The combination of weight loss with increased appetite may suggest malabsorption or a hypermetabolic state (e.g. thyrotoxicosis).
- In every case, you should calculate the patient's BMI (see ➔ Chapter 3).

Box 7.15 Triggers for concern

Closer nutritional assessment and follow-up should be considered if:
- Poor intake for longer than 1–2 weeks
- Weight loss of >10%.

Questions to ask

- Ask the patient about their eating habit and average daily diet.
- When the symptom was first noticed.
- Quantify the problem. In the case of weight loss, determine exactly how and over what time period.
- The cause of the anorexia—does eating make the patient feel sick?
- Does eating cause pain (e.g. gastric ulcer, mesenteric angina, pancreatitis)?
- Any accompanying symptoms including:
  - Abdominal pain
  - Nausea
  - Vomiting
  - Fever
  - Menstrual irregularities
  - Low mood.

Ask also about:
- The colour and consistency of stools (e.g. steatorrhoea?).
- Urinary symptoms.
- Recent change in temperature tolerance.

Box 7.16 The 'MUST' score

The 'Malnutrition Universal Screening Tool' has been designed to help identify adults who are underweight and at risk of malnutrition, as well as those who are obese. This score was developed by the Malnutrition Advisory Group (MAG), a committee of the British Association for Parenteral and Enteral Nutrition (BAPEN).

Further information is available at http://www.bapen.org.uk

The five 'MUST' steps

1 Calculate body mass index (BMI) from weight and height.

Kg/m²	Score
BMI >20	= 0 (>30 = obese)
18.5 – 20	= 1
<18.5	= 2

2 Determine unplanned weight loss (%) in past 3–6 months.

%	Score
<5	= 0
5–10	= 1
>10	= 2

3 Consider the effect of acute disease.

If patient is acutely ill and there has been or is likely to have been no nutritional intake for >5 days, score 2

4 Add scores from 1, 2 & 3 together to give overall risk of malnutrition.

Total score = 0	- low risk
= 1	- medium risk
= 2 or more	- high risk

5 Initiate appropriate nutritional management.

Using local management guidelines, prepare appropriate care plan.

Reproduced from Webster-Gandy J, Madden A, Holdsworth M, *Oxford Handbook of Nutrition and Dietetics* 2e, (2012) with permission from Oxford University Press. ('MUST' Screening tool produced by the Malnutrition Advisory Group. With permission from the British Association for Parenteral and Enteral Nutrition.)

Lower urinary tract symptoms

See also Box 7.17 for other points in the urinary history.

Urinary frequency

This is the passing of urine more often than is normal for the patient.
- How many times in a day? How much urine is passed each time?
  - Is patient producing more urine than normal or simply feeling the urge to urinate more than normal?

Urgency

This is the sudden need to urinate, a feeling that the patient may not be able to make it to the toilet in time. Ask about the volume expelled.

Nocturia

Urination during the night. Does the patient wake from sleep to urinate? How many times a night? How much urine is expelled each time?

Urinary incontinence

The loss of voluntary control of bladder emptying. Patients may be hesitant to talk about this so try to avoid the phrase 'wetting yourself'. You could ask about it immediately after asking about urgency, 'Do you ever feel the desperate need to empty your bladder? Have you ever not made it in time?' or by asking about a 'loss of control'.

There are five main types of urinary incontinence:
- *True:* total lack of control of urinary excretion. Suggestive of a fistula between the urinary tract and the exterior or a neurological condition.
- *Giggle:* incontinence during bouts of laughter. Common in young girls.
- *Stress:* leakage associated with a sudden increase in intra-abdominal pressure of any cause (e.g. coughing, laughing, sneezing).
- *Urge:* intense urge to urinate such that the patient is unable to get to the toilet in time. Causes include over-activity of the detrusor muscle, urinary infection, bladder stones, and bladder cancer.
- *Dribbling or overflow:* continual loss of urine from a chronically distended bladder. Typically in elderly males with prostate disease.

Terminal dribbling

A male complaint and usually indicative of prostate disease. This is a dripping of urine from the urethra at the end of micturition, requiring an abnormally protracted shake of the penis and may cause embarrassing staining of clothing.

Hesitancy

Difficulty in starting to micturate. The patient describes standing and waiting for the urine to start flowing. Usually due to bladder outflow obstruction caused by prostatic disease or strictures.

Dysuria

'Pain on micturition' usually described by the patient as 'burning' or 'stinging' and felt at the urethral meatus.
- Ask whether it is throughout or only at the end ('terminal dysuria').

Haematuria

The passage of blood in the urine. Always an abnormal finding.

- Remember that 'microscopic haematuria' will be undetectable to the patient, only showing on dip-testing.

Incomplete emptying

This is the sensation that there is more urine left to expel at the end of micturition. Suggests detrusor dysfunction or prostatic disease.

Intermittency

The disruption of urine flow in a stop–start manner. Causes include prostatic hypertrophy, bladder stones, and ureterocoeles.

Oliguria

Oliguria is scanty or low-volume urination and is defined as the excretion of <400ml urine in 24 hours. Causes can be physiological (dehydration) or pathological (intrinsic renal disease, shock, or obstruction).

Anuria

Anuria is the absence of urine formation and you should attempt to rule out urinary tract obstruction as a matter of urgency. Other causes include severe intrinsic renal dysfunction and shock.

Polyuria

This is excessive excretion of large volumes of urine and must be carefully differentiated from urinary frequency (the frequent passage of small amounts of urine).

Causes vary widely but include the ingestion of large volumes of water (including hysterical polydipsia), diabetes mellitus (the osmotic effect of glucose in the tubules encourages more urine to be made), failure of the action of ADH at the renal tubule (as in diabetes insipidus), and defective renal concentrating ability (e.g. chronic renal failure).

Remember also to ask the patient about the use of diuretic medication.

Box 7.17 Other points in the urinary history

- Loin pain (urinary calculi, urinary retention, pyelonephritis, renal tumours)
- Back pain (e.g. bony metastases from prostate cancer)
- Systemic symptoms of acute kidney injury or chronic renal failure (anorexia, vomiting, fatigue, pruritus, peripheral oedema)
- Past medical history: neurologic diseases causing bladder dysfunction, previous abdominal or pelvic surgery causing bladder denervation
- Drug history (nephrotoxins)
- Family history of renal failure or polycystic kidney disease
- Occupational history (industrial carcinogens causing bladder cancer)
- Foreign travel (exposure to schistosomiasis).

The rest of the history

As well as points from the history described elsewhere in this chapter under the individual symptoms, you should make note of the following in a full and thorough history:

Past medical history

Ask especially about:
- Previous surgical procedures including peri- and postoperative complications and anaesthetic complications.
- Chronic bowel diseases (e.g. IBD including recent flare-ups and treatment to date).
- Possible associated conditions (e.g. diabetes with haemochromatosis).

Drug history

See notes on the drug history described previously under each presenting symptom.

Smoking

Smokers are at increased risk of peptic ulceration, oesophageal cancer, and colorectal cancer. Smoking may also have a detrimental outcome on the natural history of Crohn's disease. There is some evidence that smoking may protect against ulcerative colitis.

Alcohol

As always, a detailed history is required—see ➔ Chapter 2.

Family history

Ask especially about a history of inflammatory bowel disease, coeliac disease, peptic ulcer disease, hereditary liver diseases (e.g. Wilson's, haemochromatosis), bowel cancer, jaundice, anaemia, splenectomy, and cholecystectomy.

Social history
- Risks of exposure to hepatotoxins and hepatitis through occupation.
- Tattoos.
- Illicit drug use (especially sharing needles).
- Social contacts with a similar disease (particularly relevant to jaundice).
- Recent foreign travel.

Dietary history
- Amount of fruit, vegetables, and fibre in the diet.
- Evidence of lactose intolerance.
- Change in symptoms related to eating certain food groups.
- Sensitivities to wheat, fat, caffeine, gluten.

Outline examination

As always, ensure adequate privacy. Ideally the patient should be lying flat with the head propped on a single pillow, arms lying at the sides.

The abdomen should be exposed at least from the bottom of the sternum to the symphysis pubis—preferably the whole upper torso should be uncovered. Do not expose the genitalia unless needed later.

The examination should follow an orderly routine. The authors' suggestion is shown in Box 7.18. It is standard practice to start with the hands and work proximally—this establishes a 'physical rapport' before you examine more delicate or embarrassing areas.

> **Box 7.18 Framework for the abdominal examination**
> - General inspection
> - The hands
> - The arms
> - The axillae
> - The face
> - The chest
> - Inspection of the abdomen
> - Palpation of the abdomen
>   - Light
>   - Deep
>   - Specific organs
>   - Examination of the hernial orifices
>   - External genitalia.
> - Percussion (± examination of ascites)
> - Auscultation
> - Digital examination of the anus, rectum ± prostate.

General inspection

Look at the patient from the end of the bed to assess their general health and look for any obvious abnormalities described in ➲ Chapter 3 before moving closer. Look especially for:
- High or low body mass.
- The state of hydration.
- Fever.
- Distress.
- Pain.
- Muscle wasting.
- Peripheral oedema.
- Jaundice.
- Anaemia.

Inspection: hands

Take the patient's right hand in yours and examine carefully for the signs described here.

Nails

See also **⊃** Chapter 4.

- *Leukonychia:* whitening of the nail bed due to hypoalbuminaemia (e.g. malnutrition, malabsorption, hepatic disease, nephritic syndrome).
- *Koilonychia:* 'spooning' of the nails making a concave shape instead of the normal convexity. Causes include congenital and chronic iron deficiency.
- *Muehrcke's lines:* these are transverse white lines. Seen in hypo-albuminaemic states including severe liver cirrhosis.
- *Digital clubbing:* Abdominal causes are cirrhosis, inflammatory bowel disease, and coeliac disease.
- *Blue lunulae:* a bluish discoloration of the normal lunulae seen in Wilson's disease.

Palms

- *Palmar erythema:* 'liver palms'. A blotchy reddening of the palms of the hands, especially affecting the thenar and hypothenar eminences.
  - Can also affect the soles of the feet
  - Associated with chronic liver disease, pregnancy, thyrotoxicosis, rheumatoid arthritis, polycythaemia, and (rarely) chronic leukaemia. It can also be a normal finding.
- *Dupuytren's contracture:* this is thickening and fibrous contraction of the palmar fascia. In early stages, palpable irregular thickening of the fascia is seen, especially that overlying the 4th and 5th metacarpals.
  - Can progress to a fixed flexion deformity of the fingers starting at the 5th and working across to the 3rd or 2nd
  - Often bilateral, it may also affect the feet
  - Seen especially in alcoholic liver disease but may also be seen in manual workers (or may be familial).
- *Anaemia:* pallor in the palmar creases suggests significant anaemia.

Inspection: upper limbs

The upper limb

Examine the arms for any signs of:

- *Bruising:* may be a sign of:
  - Hepatocellular damage and the resulting coagulation disorder
  - Thrombocytopenia due to hypersplenism
  - Marrow suppression with alcohol.
- *Petechiae:* pin-prick bleeds which do not blanch with pressure. Possibly a sign of thrombocytopenia.
- *Muscle wasting:* seen as a decrease in muscle mass, possibly with overlying skin hanging loosely. A late manifestation of malnutrition and often seen in patients with chronic alcoholic liver disease.
- *Scratch marks (excoriations):* suggests itch (pruritus) is present and may be the only visible feature of early cholestasis.
- *Iatrogenic features:* be careful not to miss arteriovenous (AV) fistulae or haemodialysis catheters.

Hepatic flap (asterixis)

- Characteristic of encephalopathy due to liver failure. This is identical to the flap seen in hypercapnic states (see Box 7.19).
- Ask the patient to stretch out their hands in front of them with the hands dorsiflexed at the wrists and fingers outstretched and separated.
  - The patient should hold that position for at least 15 seconds
  - If 'flap' is present, the patient's hands will move in jerky, irregular flexion/extension at the wrist and MCP joints
  - The flap is nearly always bilateral. May be subtle and intermittent.

Hepatic encephalopathy in a patient with previously compensated liver disease may have been precipitated by infection, diuretic medication, electrolyte imbalance, diarrhoea or constipation, vomiting, centrally acting drugs, upper GI bleeding, abdominal paracentesis, or surgery.

The axillae

Examine carefully for lymphadenopathy and acanthosis nigricans (a thickened blackening of the skin, velvety in appearance. May be associated with intra-abdominal malignancy).

Box 7.19 Other causes of asterixis

- Uraemia
- Azotaemia
- CO_2 toxicity
- Electrolyte abnormalities (hypoglycaemia, hypokalaemia, hypomagnesaemia)
- Drug intoxication (barbiturates, phenytoin, alcoholism).

Inspection: face

Eyes

Ask the patient to look ahead whilst you look at their eyes and orbits. Ask the patient to look up whilst you gently retract the lower lid with a finger, looking at the sclera and conjunctiva. Look especially for:

- *Jaundice:* a yellow discoloration of the sclera. Usually the first place that jaundice can be seen. Particularly useful in a patient with dark skin tones in whom jaundice would not be otherwise obvious.
- *Anaemia:* pallor of the conjunctivae.
- *Kayser–Fleischer rings:* best seen with a slit lamp in an ophthalmology clinic. A greenish-yellow pigmented ring just inside the cornea–scleral margin due to copper deposition. Seen in Wilson's disease.
- *Xanthelasma:* raised yellow lesions caused by a build-up of lipids beneath the skin—especially at the nasal side of the orbit.

Mouth

Ask the patient to show you their teeth then 'open wide' and look carefully at the state of the teeth, the tongue and the inner surface of the cheeks. You should also subtly attempt to smell the patient's breath.

- *Angular stomatitis:* a reddening and inflammation at the corners of the mouth. A sign of thiamine, vitamin B12, and iron deficiencies.
- *Circumoral pigmentation:* hyperpigmented areas surrounding the mouth. Seen in Peutz–Jeghers syndrome.
- *Dentition:* note false teeth or if there is evidence of tooth decay.
- *Telangiectasia:* dilatation of the small vessels on the gums and buccal mucosa. Seen in Osler–Weber–Rendu syndrome.
- *Gums:* look especially for ulcers (causes include coeliac disease, inflammatory bowel disease, Behçet's disease, and Reiter's syndrome) and hypertrophy (caused by pregnancy, phenytoin use, leukaemia, scurvy [vitamin C deficiency], or inflammation [gingivitis]).
- *Breath:* smell especially for:
  - Fetor hepaticus: a sweet-smelling breath
  - Ketosis: sickly sweet 'pear-drop' smelling breath
  - Uraemia: a fishy smell.
- *Tongue:* look especially for:
  - *Glossitis:* smooth, erythematous swelling of the tongue. Causes include deficiencies of iron, vitamin B12, and folate deficiencies
  - *Macroglossia:* enlarged tongue. Causes include amyloidosis, hypothroidism, acromegaly, Down's syndrome, and neoplasia
  - *Leukoplakia:* a white thickening of the tongue and mucous membranes. A premalignant condition caused by smoking, poor dental hygiene, alcohol, sepsis, and syphilis
  - *Geographical tongue:* painless red rings and lines on the surface of the tongue looking rather like a map. Can be caused by vitamin B2 (riboflavin) deficiency or may be a normal variant
  - *Candidiasis:* 'thrush'. A fungal infection of the oral membranes seen as creamy white curd-like patches which can be scraped off revealing erythematous mucosa below. Causes include immunosuppression, antibiotic use, poor oral hygiene, iron deficiency, and diabetes.

Inspection: neck and chest

The neck

Examine the cervical and supraclavicular lymph nodes as in ➋ Chapter 3.

Look especially for a supraclavicular node on the left-hand side which, when enlarged, is called Virchow's node (Troisier's sign—suggestive of gastric malignancy).

The chest

Look at the anterior chest and notice especially:

- *Spider naevi*: telangiectatic capillary lesions.
  - A central red area with engorged capillaries spreading out from it in a 'spidery' manner
  - Caused by engorgement of capillaries from a central 'feeder' vessel
  - If the lesion is truly a spider naevus, it will be completely eliminated by pressure at the centre using a pen-point or similar and will fill outwards when the pressure is released
  - Can range in size from those that are only just visible up to 5 or 6mm in diameter
  - Found in the distribution of the superior vena cava (Fig. 7.4)
  - A normal adult is 'allowed' up to 5 spider naevi
  - Causes include chronic liver disease and oestrogen excess.
- *Gynaecomastia*: the excessive development of male mammary glands due to ductal proliferation such that they resemble post-pubertal female breasts.
  - This is often embarrassing for the patient so be sensitive
  - Caused by alcoholic liver disease, congenital adrenal hyperplasia, and several commonly used drugs including spironolactone, digoxin, and cimetidine
  - Can also be seen during puberty in the normal male.

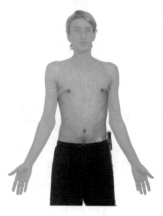

Fig. 7.4 Distribution of drainage to the superior vena cave and the area to look for spider naevi. The normal adult may have up to five such lesions.

Inspection: abdomen

Abdominal distension

Does the abdomen look swollen? Consider the 5 Fs and note the state of the umbilicus. (Everted? Deep?)

Focal swellings

Treat an abdominal swelling as you would do any other lump and bear in mind the underlying anatomy and possible organ involvement.

Divarication of the recti

Particularly in the elderly and in patients who have had abdominal surgery, the twin rectus abdominis muscles may separate laterally on contraction, causing a bulge through the resultant mid-line gap.

- Ask the patient to lift their head off the bed or to sit up slightly and watch for the appearance of a longitudinal midline bulge.

Prominent vasculature

If veins are seen coursing over the abdomen, note their exact location.
- Attempt to map the direction of blood flow within them:
  - Place 2 fingers at one end of the vein and apply occlusive pressure
  - Move 1 finger along the vein, emptying it in a 'milking' action
  - Release the pressure from one finger and watch for flow of blood
  - Repeat, emptying blood in the other direction
  - Due to the venous valves, you should be able to determine the direction of blood flow in that vein.
- Inferior flow of blood suggests superior vena cava obstruction.
- Superior flow of blood suggests inferior vena cava obstruction.
- Flow radiating out from the umbilicus ('caput medusae') indicates portal vein hypertension (porto-systemic shunting occurs through the umbilical veins which become engorged).

Peristaltic waves

Usually only seen in thin, fit, young individuals. A very obvious bowel peristalsis is seen as rippling movements beneath the skin and may indicate intestinal obstruction.

Striae

'Stretch marks' are pink or white streaky lines caused by changes in the tension of the abdominal wall. These may be normal in rapidly growing pubescent teens. Also seen in obesity, pregnancy ('striae gravidarum'), ascites, and following rapid weight loss or abdominal paracentesis.

Skin discoloration

There are 2 classical patterns of bruising/discoloration indicating the presence of retroperitoneal blood (seen especially in pancreatitis):
- *Cullen's sign:* discoloration at the umbilicus and surrounding skin.
- *Grey Turner's sign:* discoloration at the flanks.

Stomas

Inspection

Use the following system to describe or identify a stoma.

- Site?
- Bag covering?
- Appearance:
  - Healthy mucous lining? What colour?
  - Spouted or flush to skin?
  - One orifice (end) or two (loop)?
- Content (e.g. urine, formed stool, semi-formed or liquid stool).
- Any other abdominal scars?
- Any drains or healed stoma sites?
- Look for evidence of complications:
  - Early: necrosis (black/brown discoloration), infection
  - Late: parastomal hernia, prolapse, stenosis, retraction, obstruction, skin erosions, bleeding.

Common types of stoma

- *Ileostomy:* may be 'loop' or 'end'.
  - End: total/partial colectomy (e.g. inflammatory bowel disease, familial adenomatous polyposis, total colonic Hirschsprung's disease)
  - Loop: to protect distal anastomosis (e.g. partial colectomy, formation or ileorectal pouch).
- *Colostomy:* may be 'loop' or 'end'.
  - End: Hartmann's procedure, abdominoperitoneal resection
  - Loop: rectal trauma, colovaginal or perianal fistula.
- *Urostomy/ileal conduit:* one or both ureters are diverted to a short length of ileum which is disconnected and brought to the skin (usually follows radical lower urinary tract surgery).
  - Spouted, prominent mucosal folds, dark pink/red, right-sided
  - ⓘ Indistinguishable from ileostomy unless the output is seen.
- *Gastrostomy/duodenostomy/jejunostomy:* surgically or endoscopically created connection between the stomach/duodenum/jejunum and the anterior abdominal wall. For feeding and/or drainage (stomach).
  - Narrow calibre, flush to skin with little visible mucosa, usually at left upper quadrant. Fitted with indwelling tubes or access devices.

Other stomas

- *Caecostomy or typhlostomy:* loop stoma in the caecum.
- *Appendicostomy or caecostomy tube:* used in paediatrics to allow administration of proximal enemas.
- *Cholecystostomy:* communication between the gallbladder and anterior abdominal wall (drainage of gallbladder contents).
- *Nephrostomy:* tube that exits through flank region and drains urine from the renal pelvis.

Abdominal scars 1: open surgery

See Fig. 7.5 for common surgical scars.

Upper- and lower-midline laparotomy

A standard elective and emergency incision.

- *Upper:* gastric, splenic surgery.
- *Lower:* gynaecological surgery (e.g. hysterectomy, oophorectomy), urological surgery (e.g. cystectomy, prostatectomy) or colorectal surgery (e.g. sigmoidectomy, anterior resection).
- *Full laparotomy:* performed in emergencies and for surgery that may involve both regions (e.g. right or left hemicolectomy).

Roof-top or Mercedes-Benz incision

- Classically used for partial hepatectomies, liver transplants, or pancreatic surgery, e.g. Whipple's procedure or necrosectomy.

Kocher incision

- Classical incision for an open cholecystectomy.

Paramedian incision

- Now rarely used; previously used for colorectal surgery.
- Can take longer to perform and risks greater blood loss than midline laparotomy.
- Point at which the internal oblique aponeurosis splits round the rectus abdominis.

Inguinal incision

- Inguinal hernia repair and orchidectomies.
- May be left- or right-sided.

Gridiron and Lanz incisions

- Used for appendectomy.
- The Lanz is more transverse, extends more medially and is closer to the anterior superior iliac spine.

Femoral incision

- Used to access the femoral triangle, especially the femoral artery.
  - If bilateral, often due to femoral–femoral bypass or endovascular aneurysm repair
  - If unilateral, look for further scars around the knee (for femoral–popliteal or femoral–distal bypass).

Pfannenstiel incision

- Classically used for C-section or abdominal hysterectomy.

Hockey-stick incision

- Classically used for renal transplants.
- The scar may not include the (vertical) laparotomy component depending on the surgeon.

Nephrectomy incision

- Used for partial or complete nephrectomy.

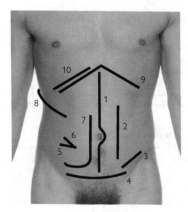

Fig. 7.5 Common surgical scars. 1. Midline laparotomy. 2. Paramedian incision. 3. Left inguinal incision. 4. Pfannenstiel incision. 5. Lanz incision. 6. Gridiron incision. 7. Hockey-stick incision. 8. Nephrectomy incision. 9. Roof-top or, with additional superior incision, 'Mercedes-Benz' incision. 10. Kocher incision.

Abdominal scars 2: laparoscopic

Laparoscopic or 'key-hole' surgery uses several small incisions for the insertion of the instruments. There will be a site for the camera insertion and at least 2 other 'ports' for the graspers.

The port site scars are often arranged in a loose semicircle around the internal operation site. See also Box 7.20.

If you work out where the camera and graspers are pointing, you can guess the possible operations based on your anatomy knowledge. See Fig. 7.6.

Laparoscopic cholecystectomy
- This is now the most common method of removing the gallbladder. Complications can include bile leaks, retained stones in the common bile duct (CBD), damage to the CBD, and bleeding.

Laparoscopic right hemicolectomy
- Left-sided port site placed at lateral margin of rectus abdominis.
- The RUQ port site is expanded to allow removal of the colon. The anastomosis may be performed through any port.

Laparoscopic left hemicolectomy, sigmoidectomy, or anterior resection
- Right-sided port site placed at lateral margin of rectus abdominis.
- The LIF port site is expanded to allow removal of the colon and insertion of end-to-end circular stapler to join the rectum and cut end of bowel together again.

Laparoscopic inguinal hernia repair
- Both the left and right inguinal canals are usually accessed through the same midline port sites.

Laparoscopic appendicectomy
- The figure demonstrates one possible placement.
- Another common port placement is moving the LIF port to the RIF at the level of the umbilicus to allow traction of the appendix.

Laparoscopic nephrectomy
- One of the port sites is expanded to allow removal of the organ.

Box 7.20 More on laparoscopic technique
- In general an open technique or Hassan technique is used
  - A small infra-umbilical incision is made and the linea alba incised with direct visualization of the peritoneum. A finger is then inserted prior to the trocar to sweep away any adhesions
  - A pneumoperitoneum is maintained between 12–15mmHg.
- *Risks:* damage to other organs, diathermy burns to areas away from the operation site (perforations or bile leaks), converting to open surgery.

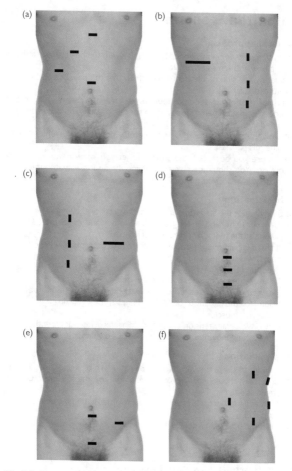

Fig. 7.6 Common laparoscopic surgical scars. (a) cholecystectomy, (b) right hemicolectomy, (c) left hemicolectomy, sigmoidectomy, or anterior resection, (d) inguinal hernia repair, (e) appendicectomy, (f) nephrectomy.

Palpation: general

General approach

The patient should be positioned lying supine with the head supported by a single pillow and arms at their sides.

Squat by the side of the bed or couch so that the patient's abdomen is at your eye level.

Each of the four quadrants should be examined in turn with light, and then deep palpation before focusing on specific organs. The order they are examined in doesn't matter—find a routine that suits you.

▶ Ask the patient if there is any area of tenderness and remember to examine this part last.

▶ Before you begin, ask the patient to let you know if you cause any discomfort. You should be able to examine the abdomen without looking at it closely. Instead, you should watch the patient's face for signs of pain.

Light palpation

For this, you use the finger tips and palmar aspects of the fingers.

- Lay your right hand on the patient's abdomen and gently press in by flexing at the metacarpo-phalangeal joints.
- If there is pain on light palpation, attempt to determine whether the pain is worse when you press down or when you release the pressure ('rebound tenderness').
- If the abdominal muscles seem tense, determine whether it is localized or generalized. Ensure the patient is relaxed—it may be helpful for the patient to bend their knees slightly, relaxing the abdominal muscles.
  - An involuntary tension in the abdominal muscles—apparently protecting the underlying organs—is called 'guarding'.

Deep palpation

Once all four quadrants are lightly palpated, re-examine using more pressure. This should enable you to feel for any masses or structural abnormalities.

- If a mass is felt, treat it as you would any other lump (see Boxes 7.21 and 7.22).
- It is often possible to detect the putty-like consistency of stool in the sigmoid colon.

Box 7.21 Which layer is the mass in?

- *Epidermal or dermal:* moves with the skin
- *Subcutis:* skin moves over the mass
- *Muscle/tendon:* moves with muscular contraction
- Ask the patient to raise their head and shoulders off the bed
  - Intra-abdominal: more difficult to palpate when abdominal muscles are tensed.
- *Bone:* immobile.

Box 7.22 Characteristics of abdominal masses

- *Consistency:* the consistency does not always correlate with the composition. A fluid-filled lump will feel hard if it is tense
- *Fluctuation:* press one side of the lump, the opposite side may protrude
- *Fluid thrill:* this can only be elicited if the fluid-filled lesion is very large
  - Examine by tapping on one side and feeling the impulse on the other much as you would for ascites.
- *Translucency:* darken the room and press a lit pen-torch to one side of the lump. It will 'glow' in the presence of water, serum, fat, or lymph
  - Solid lumps will not transilluminate.
- *Resonance:* only possible to test on large lumps. Percuss and listen (and feel) if the lump is hollow (gas-filled) or solid
- *Pulsatility:* consider carefully if the pulse is transmitted from an underlying structure or if the lump itself is pulsating
- *Compressibility:* attempt to compress the lump until it disappears. If this is possible, release the pressure and watch for the lump reforming
  - Compressible lumps may be fluid-filled or vascular malformations
  - Note, this is not the same as 'reducibility'.
- *Reducibility:* A feature of herniae. Attempt to reduce the lump by maneouvring its contents back into the abdominal cavity. Ask the patient to cough and watch for the lump reforming.

Palpation: aorta

The abdominal aorta may be palpated in the midline above the umbilicus, particularly in thin people. If felt:

- Place each hand either side of the outermost palpable margins.
- Measure the distance between your fingers. Normal = 2–3cm.
- Is it pulsatile/expansile in itself (in which case your fingers will move outwards) or is the pulsation transmitted through other tissue (in which case your fingers will move upwards)? See Fig. 7.7.

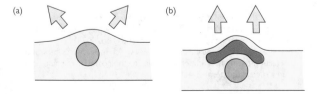

Fig. 7.7 Palpating a pulsatile mass. If expansile (a), your fingers move outwards. If the pulsatility is being transmitted (b), your fingers will move upwards.

Palpation: liver and gallbladder

Liver

The normal liver extends from the 5th intercostal space on the right of the midline to the costal margin, hiding under the ribs so is often not normally palpable—don't worry if you can't feel it.

- Using the flat of the right hand, start palpation from the right iliac fossa.
- You should angle your hand such that the index finger is aligned with the costal margin (Fig. 7.8).
- Exert gentle pressure and ask the patient to take a deep breath.
- With each inward breath, your fingers should drift slightly superiorly as the liver moves inferiorly with the diaphragm.
  - Relax the pressure on your hand slightly at the height of inspiration.
- If the liver is just above the position of your hand, the lateral surface of your index finger will strike the liver edge and glide over it with a palpable 'step'.
- If the liver is not felt, move your hand 1–2cm superiorly and feel again.
- Repeat the process, moving towards the ribs until the liver is felt.

If a liver edge is felt, you should note:

- How far below the costal margin it extends in finger-breadths or (preferably) centimetres and record the number carefully.
- The nature of the liver edge (is the surface smooth or irregular?).
- The presence of tenderness.
- Whether the liver is pulsatile.

Findings

- It is often possible to palpate the liver just below the costal margin at the height of inspiration in normal, healthy, thin people.
- An enlarged liver has many causes (see ➔ p. 205).
- A normal liver may be palpable in patients with COPD or asthma in whom the chest is hyper-expanded or in patients with a subdiaphragmatic collection.
- The liver may also be palpable in the presence of 'Riedel's lobe'—a normal variant in which a projection of the liver arises from the inferior surface of the right lobe.
  - More common in females
  - Commonly mistaken for a right kidney or enlarged gallbladder.

Gallbladder

Lies at the right costal margin at the tip of the 9th rib, at the lateral border of the rectus abdominis (Fig. 7.9). Normally only palpable when enlarged due to biliary obstruction or acute cholecystitis (Box 7.23).

- Felt as a bulbous, focal, rounded mass which moves with inspiration.
- Position the right hand perpendicular to the costal margin and palpate in a medial to lateral direction.

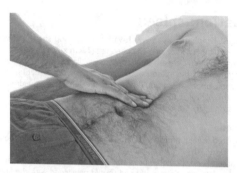

Fig. 7.8 Palpation of the liver—align the lateral surface of the index finger with the costal margin and palpate from the right iliac fossa to the ribs in a step-wise fashion.

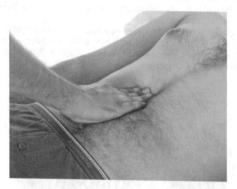

Fig. 7.9 Palpation of the gallbladder—the examining hand should be perpendicular to the costal margin at the tip of the 9th rib (where the lateral border of the rectus muscle meets the costal cartilages).

Box 7.23 Gallbladder signs

Murphy's sign

A sign of cholecystitis—pain on palpation over the gallbladder during deep inspiration. Only positive if there is NO pain on the left at the same position.

Courvoisier's law

In the presence of jaundice, a palpable gallbladder is probably NOT caused by gallstones.

Palpation: spleen

The largest lymphatic organ which varies in size and shape between individuals—roughly the size of a clenched fist (12cm x 7cm).

Normally hidden beneath the left costal cartilages and impalpable.

Enlargement of the spleen occurs in a downward direction, extending into the left upper quadrant (and even the left lower quadrant) across towards the right iliac fossa. Causes of splenomegaly, hepatosplenomegaly and hepatomegaly are outlined in Boxes 7.24, 7.25, and 7.26.

Technique

- Palpated using a similar technique to that used to examine the liver (see Fig. 7.10).
- Your left hand should be used to support the left of the ribcage posterolaterally. Your right hand should be aligned with the fingertips parallel to the left costal margin.
- Start palpation just below the umbilicus in the midline and work towards the left costal margin asking the patient to take a deep breath in and feeling for the movement of the spleen under your fingers— much like palpating the liver.
- The inferior edge of the spleen may have a palpable 'notch' centrally which will help you differentiate it from any other abdominal mass.
- If a spleen is felt, measure the distance to the costal border in finger-breadths or (preferably) centimetres.

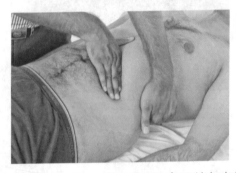

Fig. 7.10 Palpation of the spleen—align the fingertips of your right hand with the left costal border and start palpating just below the umbilicus working towards the left upper quadrant.

Box 7.24 Causes of splenomegaly

- *Infection:* EBV, CMV, HIV, viral hepatitis, any cause of septicaemia, subacute bacterial endocarditis, typhoid, brucellosis, tuberculosis, leptospirosis, histoplasmosis, malaria, leishmaniasis, trypanosomiasis
- *Haematological:* myeloid and lymphatic leukaemia, lymphoma, spherocytosis, thalassaemia, sickle cell (splenic infarcts may cause a small spleen in late disease), autoimmune haemolytic anaemia, idiopathic thrombocytopenic purpura
- *Infiltration:* glycogen storage diseases, Gaucher's disease
- *Congestive:* hepatic cirrhosis, congestive heart failure, portal vein thrombosis, splenic vein thrombosis, Budd–Chiari syndrome
- *Other:* amyloidosis, cysts, hamartomas, connective tissue disorders (e.g. RA, SLE, sarcoidosis).

Box 7.25 Causes of hepatosplenomegaly

- *Hepatic:* Chronic liver disease with portal hypertension (if cirrhotic, liver may be impalpable)
- *Infection:* EBV, CMV, viral hepatitis, infective endocarditis
- *Infiltration:* amyloidosis, Gaucher's disease
- *Haematological:* lymphoma, leukaemia, pernicious anaemia, myeloproliferative disease
- *Endocrine:* acromegaly, thyrotoxicosis
- *Granulomatous conditions:* tuberculosis, sarcoidosis, Wegener's granulomatosis
- *Other causes:* malaria, kala-azar, schistosomiasis.

Box 7.26 Causes of hepatomegaly

- Cirrhosis
- Congestive cardiac failure
- Neoplastic: secondary and primary (e.g. hepatoma)
- Infective: acute viral hepatitis, liver abscess, hydatid cyst
- Polycystic disease
- Tricuspid regurgitation (pulsatile hepatomegaly)
- Budd–Chiari syndrome
- Haemochromatosis
- Infiltrative: amyloidosis, sarcoidosis.

Palpation: kidneys and bladder

The kidneys are retroperitoneal, lying on the posterior abdominal wall either side of the vertebral column between T12 and L3 vertebrae. They move slightly inferiorly with inspiration. The right kidney lies a little lower than the left (displaced by the liver).

Palpation is 'bimanual' (both hands). You may be able to feel the lower pole of the right kidney in normal, thin people. Take care not to mistake splenomegaly for an enlarged kidney (see Table 7.1).

Technique

- Place your left hand behind the patient at the right loin.
- Place your right hand below the right costal margin at the lateral border of the rectus abdominis.
- Keeping the fingers of your right hand together, flex them at the metacarpo-phalangeal joints pushing deep into the abdomen (Fig. 7.11).
- Ask the patient to take a deep breath—you may be able to feel the rounded lower pole of the kidney between your hands, slipping away when the patient exhales.
- This technique of using one hand to move the kidney toward the other is called renal ballottement.
- Repeat the procedure for the left kidney—leaning over and placing your left hand behind the patient's left loin (Fig. 7.12).

Findings

- Unilateral palpable kidney: hydronephrosis, polycystic kidney disease, renal cell carcinoma, acute renal vein thrombosis, renal abscess, acute pyelonephritis (see 'important presentations').
- Bilateral palpable kidneys: bilateral hydronephrosis, bilateral renal cell carcinoma, polycystic kidney disease, nephrotic syndrome, amyloidosis, lymphoma, acromegaly.

Table 7.1 Differentiating splenomegaly from an enlarged left kidney

Enlarged spleen	Enlarged kidney
Impossible to feel above	Can feel above the organ
Has a central 'notch' on the leading edge	No notch – but you may feel the central hilar notch medially
Moves early on inspiration	Moves late on inspiration
Moves inferomedially on inspiration	Moves inferiorly on inspiration
Not ballottable	Ballottable
Dullness to percussion	Resonant percussion note due to overlying bowel gas
May enlarge toward the umbilicus	Enlarges inferiorly lateral to the midline

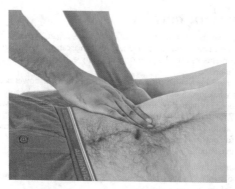

Fig. 7.11 Palpation of the right kidney.

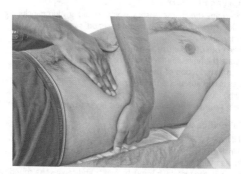

Fig. 7.12 Palpation of the left kidney.

Bladder

The urinary bladder is not palpable when empty. As it fills, it expands superiorly and may reach as high as the umbilicus if very full.

It may be difficult to differentiate it from an enlarged uterus or ovarian cyst. The full bladder will be:

- A palpable, rounded mass arising from behind the pubic symphysis.
- Dull to percussion.
- You will be unable to feel below it.
- Pressure on the full bladder will make the patient feel the need to urinate.

Palpation: herniae

A hernia is an abnormal protrusion of a structure, organ, or part of an organ out of the cavity in which it belongs. A hernia can usually be 'reduced', i.e. its contents returned to the original cavity either spontaneously or by manipulation.

Abdominal herniae are usually caused by portions of bowel protruding through weakened areas of the abdominal wall. In the abdomen, herniae usually occur at natural openings or weak spots such as surgical scars. See Box 7.27 for some rarer hernia types.

Most abdominal herniae have an expansile cough impulse—asking the patient to cough will increase the intra-abdominal pressure causing a visible or palpable impulse.

Strangulation: herniae that cannot be reduced (irreducible) may become fixed and swollen as their blood supply is occluded causing ischaemia and necrosis of the herniated organ.

An approach to herniae

- Determine the characteristics as you would any lump including position, temperature, tenderness, shape, size, tension, and composition.
- Make note of the characteristics of the overlying skin.
- Palpate the hernia and feel for a cough impulse.
- Attempt reduction of the hernia.
- Percuss and auscultate the hernia (listening for bowel sounds or bruits).
- Always remember to examine the same site on the opposite side.

Hernial orifice anatomy

Inguinal canal

The inguinal canal extends from the pubic tubercle to the anterior superior iliac spine. In the male, it carries the spermatic cord (vas deferens, blood vessels, and nerves). In the female, it is much smaller and carries the round ligament of the uterus.

The internal ring is an opening in the transversalis fascia lying at the mid-inguinal point, halfway between the anterior superior iliac spine and the pubic symphysis (about 1.5cm above the femoral pulse).

The external ring is an opening of the external oblique aponeurosis and is immediately above and medial to the pubic tubercle.

- Direct inguinal hernia: this is herniation at the site of the external ring.
- Indirect inguinal hernia: this is the most common site (85% of all herniae). More likely to strangulate than direct inguinal herniae.

Femoral canal

The femoral canal is the small component of the femoral sheath medial to the femoral vessels and contains loose connective tissue, lymphatic vessels, and lymph nodes. It is bordered anteriorly by the inguinal ligament, the pectineal ligament posteriorly, the femoral vein laterally, and the lacunar ligament medially.

Femoral herniae are protrusions of bowel or omentum through this space. They are more common in middle-aged and elderly women and can easily strangulate due to the small, rigid opening they pass through.

Examining an inguinal hernia

Inspection

- Look for visible swelling at both groins.
- Ask the patient to cough and watch for swellings.
  - Minor bulging of the inguinal canal is normal (Malgaigne's bulges).
- Look for scars in relation to previous open repair (groin) and laparoscopic repair (around umbilicus).

Palpation

- Ask the patient if there is any pain.
- Examine the scrotum and its content.
- Examine any lump carefully.
- Ask patient to cough and feel for an expansile cough impulse.
- Ask if the lump is normally reducible.
  - Lie patient down on couch to allow gravity to help reduction. Try to reduce hernia or ask patient to reduce it for you.

Relate the swelling to the bony landmarks

- Place a finger on the pubic tubercle and ask patient to cough.
  - Inguinal herniae will be superior and medial to your finger
  - Femoral herniae will be inferior and lateral to your finger
- Place 2 fingers at the midpoint between anterior superior iliac spine and pubic tubercle (the internal ring). Ask patient to cough.
  - This will prevent an indirect inguinal hernia appearing, whereas a direct inguinal hernia will appear.

Auscultation

- Listen over any swelling for bowel sounds.

Examining a femoral hernia

Inspection

- Lump in the groin.
  - Below and lateral to the pubic tubercle
  - Medial to the femoral artery (palpate for the pulsation).
- Flattening/obliteration of the inguinal skin crease.
- Overlying skin appears normal in colour/texture.

Palpation

- Firm smooth, spherical lump.
  - Tender if strangulated.
- Non-reducible.
- Often no cough impulse.

Percussion and auscultation

- A resonant percussion note and active bowel sounds imply strangulated bowel.
  - Femoral herniae commonly contain greater omentum.

Incisional hernia

- Be sure to examine the patient standing and lying supine. Incisional herniae account for 10–15% of all herniae.
- Peak incidence is at 5 years following surgery.

Inspection

- A lump arising from the site of a previous incision.

Palpation

- A positive cough impulse is present.
- Note the size, site, shape, and constituents.
- Assess whether the hernia is reducible, if so palpate the edges to quantify the defect's size.
  - If irreducible, the lump may be an incarcerated or strangulated hernia.

Auscultation

- Active bowel sounds point to bowel in the hernial sac.

Completion

- A full abdominal examination should be conducted, looking for signs of deep infection and for a cause of raised intra-abdominal pressure.

Paraumbilical hernia

- A hernia in the linea alba, just superior or inferior to the umbilicus
- Male:female ratio = 1:5.
- Risk factors include obesity, multiparity, and advancing age.

Inspection

- Bulge beside the umbilicus.
- The umbilicus is often distorted into a crescent shape.

Palpation

- The lump is separate from the umbilicus and should be reducible.
  - ▶ Examine the patient standing and make careful note of the size, site, shape, and constituents of the lump.
- A positive cough impulse may be present.
  - Absence of a cough impulse does not exclude a hernia.
- ▶ Now examine the patient lying supine.
- Assess if the hernia is reducible; if so, palpate the edges to quantify the defect's size.

Percussion

- Resonance to percussion implies bowel is present in the hernia sac.

Auscultation

- Active bowel sounds point to bowel in the hernia sac.

Completion

- A full abdominal examination should be conducted, looking for causes of raised intra-abdominal pressure.

Spigelian hernia

- Also known as semi-lunar line herniae.
- Occurs through bands of the internal oblique muscle as it enters the semilunar line (sometimes called Spigel's line). Protrudes along the lateral border of the rectus sheath.
- Most occur below the umbilicus, adjacent to the line of Douglas.

Inspection

- A swelling at the lateral border of the rectus abdominis muscle.
  - Difficult to assess with the patient supine. Ask them to stand
  - May need patient to direct you to lump especially in the obese.

Palpation

- Positive cough impulse.
- Overlying skin is normal.
- May or may not be reducible.

Percussion and auscultation

- A resonant percussion note and active bowel sounds suggest herniated bowel.
  - If the hernia contains greater omentum only, there will be no positive findings on auscultation.

Further examination

- The whole abdomen should be examined, looking for potential causes of raised intra-abdominal pressure and abdominal masses.
- If the hernia contains strangulated bowel, there may be abdominal distension.

Box 7.27 Some other types of hernia

- *Maydl's hernia:* two adjacent loops of bowel in the sac; the portion in the abdomen is at risk if strangulation occurs
- *Sliding (en-glissade) hernia:* the sac is partially formed by retroperitoneal tissue
- *Richter's hernia:* a knuckle of bowel wall is strangulated
- *Littre's hernia:* a protrusion of a diverticulum into a hernia sac (50% inguinal, 20% femoral). Classically contains Meckel's diverticulum
- *Amyand's hernia:* the appendix enters the hernial sac and can become occluded leading to appendicitis
- *De Garengeot's hernia:* a rare subtype in which the appendix is incarcerated within a femoral hernia.

Percussion

In the examination of the abdomen, percussion is useful for:

- Determining the size and nature of enlarged organs or masses.
- Detecting shifting dullness.
- Eliciting rebound tenderness.

Organs or masses will appear as dullness whereas a bowel full of gas will seem abnormally resonant. Good technique comes with experience. Practise percussing out your own liver.

Examining for ascites

If fluid is present in the peritoneal cavity (ascites), gravity will cause it to collect in the flanks when the patient is lying flat—this will give dullness to percussion laterally with central resonance as the bowel floats.

Ascites will give a distended abdomen, often with an everted umbilicus. If you suspect the presence of ascites:

- Percuss centrally to laterally with the fingers spread and positioned longitudinally.
- Listen (and feel) for a definite change to a dull note.

There are then 2 specific tests to perform:

*Shifting dullness**

- Percuss centrally to laterally until dullness is detected. This marks the air-fluid level in the abdomen.
- Keep your finger pressed there as you:
  - Ask the patient to roll onto the opposite side (i.e. if dullness is detected on the right, roll the patient to their left-hand side)
  - Ask the patient to hold the new position for half a minute
  - Repeat percussion moving laterally to central over your mark.
- If the dullness truly was an air-fluid level, the fluid will now be moved by gravity away from the marked spot and the previously dull area will be resonant.

Fluid thrill

In this test, you are attempting to detect a wave transmitted across the peritoneal fluid. This is only really possible with massive ascites.

- You need an assistant for this test (you can ask the patient to help).
- Ask your assistant to place the ulnar edge of one of their hands in the midline of the abdomen.
- Place your left hand on one side of the abdomen, about level with the midclavicular line.
- With your right hand, flick the opposite side of the patient's abdomen (Fig. 7.13).
- If a 'fluid thrill' can be detected, you will feel the ripple from the flick transmitted as a tap to your left hand.
  - The assistant's hand is important—it prevents transmission of the impulse across the surface of the abdominal wall.

---

* This is also the punch-line to the medical student joke: 'What's the definition of a ward round?'

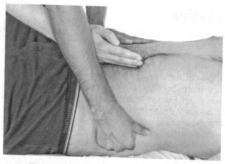

Fig. 7.13 Testing for a fluid thrill. Ask an assistant to place their hand centrally on the abdomen, this prevents transmission of the impulse through the abdominal wall.

Liver

- Percuss to map the upper and lower borders of the liver—note the length, in centimetres, at the midclavicular line.

Spleen

- Percussion from the left costal margin towards the midaxillary line and the lower left ribs may reveal dullness suggestive of splenic enlargement that could not normally be palpated.

Kidneys

- Useful in differentiating an enlarged kidney from an enlarged spleen or liver.
- The kidneys lie deep in the abdomen and are surrounded by perinephric fat which makes them resonant to percussion.
- Splenomegaly or hepatomegaly will appear dull.

Bladder

- Dullness to percussion in the suprapubic region may be helpful in determining whether an ill-defined mass is an enlarged bladder (dull) or distended bowel (resonant).

Auscultation

An important part of the abdominal examination which should not be skipped.

Bowel sounds

These are low-pitched gurgling sounds produced by normal gut peristalsis. They are intermittent but will vary in timing depending on when the last meal was eaten. Practise listening to as many abdomens as possible to understand the normal range of sounds.

Listen with the diaphragm of the stethoscope just below the umbilicus.

- *Normal:* low-pitched gurgling, intermittent.
- *High-pitched:* often called 'tinkling'. These sounds are suggestive of partial or total bowel obstruction.
- *Borborygmus:* this is a loud low-pitched gurgling that can even be heard without a stethoscope. (The sounds are called 'borborygmi'.) Typical of diarrhoeal states or abnormal peristalsis.
- *Absent sounds:* if no sounds are heard for 2 minutes, there may be a complete lack of peristalsis—i.e. a paralytic ileus or peritonitis.

Bruits

These are sounds produced by the turbulent flow of blood through a vessel—similar in sound to heart murmurs. Listen with diaphragm of the stethoscope.

Bruits may occur in normal adults but raise the suspicion of pathological stenosis (narrowing) when heard throughout both systole and diastole. There are several areas you should listen at on the abdomen:

- Just above the umbilicus over the aorta (abdominal aortic aneurysm).
- Either side of the midline just above the umbilicus (renal artery stenosis).
- At the epigastrium (mesenteric stenosis).
- Over the liver (AV malformations, acute alcoholic hepatitis, hepatocellular carcinoma).

Friction rubs

These are creaking sounds like that of a pleural rub heard when inflamed peritoneal surfaces move against each other with respiration.

Listen over the liver and the spleen in the right and left upper quadrants respectively.

Causes include hepatocellular carcinoma, liver abscesses, recent percutaneous liver biopsy, liver or splenic infarction and STD-associated perihepatitis (Fitz–Hugh–Curtis syndrome).

Venous hums

Rarely, it is possible to hear the hum of venous blood flow in the upper abdomen over a caput medusa secondary to porto-systemic shunting of blood.

'Per rectum' examination

This is an important part of the examination and should not be avoided simply because it is considered unpleasant. It is particularly important in patients with symptoms of PR bleeding, tenesmus, change in bowel habit, and pruritus ani.

▶ Remember: 'If you don't put your finger in it, you may put your foot in it!'

Before you begin

Explain to the patient what is involved and obtain verbal consent. Choose your words carefully, adjusting your wording to suit the patient! Favourite phrases include 'tail-end', 'back-passage', and 'bottom'. Say that you need to examine their back passage 'with a finger'. Warn that it 'probably won't hurt' but may feel 'cold' and 'a little unusual'.

You should ask for another member of staff to chaperone.

As you proceed, explain each stage to the patient.

Equipment

- Chaperone.
- Non-sterile gloves.
- Tissues.
- Lubricating jelly (e.g. Aquagel®).

Technique

- With informed verbal consent obtained, ensure adequate privacy.
- Uncover the patient from waist to knees.
- Ask the patient to lie in the left lateral position with their legs bent such that their knees are drawn up to their chest and their buttocks facing towards you—preferably projecting slightly over the edge of the bed/couch.
- Ensure that there is a good light source—preferably a mobile lamp.
- Put on a pair of gloves.
- Separate the buttocks carefully by lifting the right buttock with your left hand.
- Inspect the perianal area and anus.
  - Look for rashes, excoriations, skin tags, anal warts, fistulous openings, fissures, external haemorrhoids, abscesses, faecal soiling, blood, and mucus.
- Ask the patient to strain or 'bear down' and watch for the projection of pink mucosa of a rectal prolapse.
- Lubricate the tip of your right index finger with the jelly.
- Begin by placing the pulp of your right index finger against the anus in the midline and press in firmly but slowly.
  - Most anal sphincters will reflexly tighten when touched but will quickly relax with continued pressure.
- When the sphincter relaxes, gently advance the finger into the anal canal.
- Assess anal sphincter tone by asking the patient to clench your finger.

- Rotate the finger backwards and forwards covering the full 360°, feeling for any thickening or irregularities.
- Push the finger further—up to the hilt if possible—to the rectum.
- Examine all 360° by moving the finger in sweeping motions. Note:
  - The presence of thickening or irregularities of the rectal wall
  - The presence of palpable faeces—and its consistency
  - Any points of tenderness.
- Next, in the male, identify the prostate gland which can be felt through the anterior rectal wall.
  - The normal prostate is smooth-surfaced, firm with a slightly rubbery texture measuring 2–3cm diameter. It has two lobes with a palpable central sulcus.
- Gently withdraw your finger and inspect the glove for faeces, blood, or mucus and note the colour of the stool, if present.
- Tell the patient that the examination is over and wipe any faeces or jelly from the natal cleft with the tissues. Some patients may prefer to do this themselves.
- Thank the patient and ask them to redress. You may need to help.

Findings

If any mass or abnormality is identified on the exterior or interior of the areas examined, its exact location should be noted. It is conventional to record as the position on a clock face with 12 o'clock indicating the anterior side of the rectum at the perineum.

- *Benign prostatic hyperplasia:* the prostate is enlarged but the central sulcus is preserved, often exaggerated.
- *Prostate cancer:* the gland loses its rubbery consistency and may become hard. The lateral lobes may be irregular and nodular. There is often distortion or loss of the central sulcus. If the tumour is large and has spread locally, there may be thickening of the rectal mucosa either side of the gland creating 'winging' of the prostate.
- *Prostatitis:* the gland will be enlarged, boggy, and very tender.

Procedure tips

- If the patient experiences severe pain, with gentle pressure on the anal opening, consider: anal fissure, ischiorectal abscess, anal ulcer, thrombosed haemorrhoid, or prostatitis.
- In this situation, you may have to apply local anaesthetic gel to the anal margin before proceeding. If in doubt, ask a senior.

Important presentations

Hepatomegaly

Once hepatomegaly is found, examine for splenomegaly and evidence of other features which may help determine the cause. See also Boxes 7.28, 7.29, and 7.30.

Examination findings

- Pallor/anaemia.
  - Haemolysis, chronic liver disease, malignancy, marrow failure, infective endocarditis.
- Jaundice.
  - Haemolysis, chronic liver disease, hepatitis.
- Lymphadenopathy.
  - Lymphoma, metastatic disease, leukaemia, myeloproliferative disorders, connective tissue disorders, tuberculosis, viral hepatitis, infectious mononucleosis.
- Cachexia.
  - Malignancy, TB.
- Petechial rash.
  - Thrombocytopenia in cirrhosis, leukaemia.
- Herpes zoster, oral candidiasis.
  - Immunocompromised state in leukaemia, lymphoma, TB.
- Stigmata of chronic liver disease.
  - Spider naevi, palmar erythema, leukonychia, digital clubbing, gynaecomastia.
- Peripheral oedema.
  - Cirrhosis, right heart failure, hypoalbuminaemia.
- Raised JVP.
  - Right heart failure.

Further examination: abdomen

- Look for visible masses, prominent veins, caput medusa.
- Palpate in each quadrant for tenderness and masses.
- Palpate specifically for the kidneys, gallbladder, and presence of ascites.
- Auscultate for murmurs over the liver.

Causes

- Infective: EBV, CMV, hepatitis, liver abscess, malaria, leptospirosis, amoebiasis, hydatid cyst, actinomycosis.
- Neoplastic: hepatocellular carcinoma (HCC), metastasis, myeloma, leukaemia, lymphoma, haemangioma.
- Metabolic: haemochromatosis, amyloidosis, glycogen storage diseases (e.g. Hunter syndrome, Gaucher's disease, Niemann–Pick disease), fat.
- Congenital: Riedel's lobe, polycystic disease.
- Other: alcohol, right heart failure, Budd–Chiari syndrome, sarcoidosis.

Box 7.28 Causes of hepatomegaly by degree of enlargement

Mild

- Infection: hepatitis, HIV, EBV, hydatid disease
- Other: biliary obstruction, and the causes below.

Moderate

- Haematological: lymphoma, myeloproliferative disorders
- Infiltration: amyloidosis
- Haemochromatosis, and the causes of massive hepatomegaly below.

Massive

- Malignancy: HCC, metastasis
- Haematological: myeloproliferative disorders
- Vascular: right-sided heart failure, tricuspid regurgitation
- Alcoholic liver disease and fatty infiltration.

Box 7.29 Causes of hepatomegaly by other examination findings

Irregular surface

- Malignancy (e.g. HCC, metastasis), cirrhosis
- Hydatid cysts, amyloid, sarcoid granulomas.

Pulsatility

- Vascular: tricuspid regurgitation, vascular malformation e.g. AVM
- Malignancy: HCC.

Tenderness

- Infection: hepatitis, malaria, EBV, hepatic abscess
- Malignancy: HCC, metastasis (stretching of liver capsule)
- Vascular: right-sided heart failure, Budd–Chiari syndrome
- Biliary obstruction, ascending cholangitis.

Box 7.30 A word on chronic liver disease

- *Cirrhosis* is a histological diagnosis that may also be suggested by non-invasive tests such as serum markers and ultrasonographic elastography
- The main prognostic tests of *function* are bilirubin, prothrombin time, creatinine, and sodium levels (as reflected in MELD and UKELD severity scores).

Chronic liver disease

Examination findings: general inspection

Look for:

- Pallor (anaemia).
- Tattoos, needle track marks (may suggest viral hepatitis).
- Digital clubbing.
- Terry's nails (proximal 2/3 of nail plate white with distal 1/3 red).
- Muehrcke's lines.
- Palmar erythema.
- Spider naevi (number and size correlate with severity).
- Gynaecomastia.
- Generalized muscle wasting.
- Loss of body hair.
- Testicular atrophy.
- Evidence of alcohol misuse.
  - Dupuytren's contracture
  - Parotid enlargement
  - Cerebellar signs (past-pointing, ataxic gait).
- Signs of decompensated liver disease.
  - Jaundice, purpura, asterixis.

Examination findings: abdominal inspection

- Distension (ascites; a paraumbilical hernia may be visible).
- Caput medusa.
- Look also for scars, drain sites.

Palpation, percussion, and auscultation

- Palpate for hepatomegaly, splenomegaly.
- Percuss for liver span, spleen, shifting dullness, fluid thrill.
- Auscultate for either hepatic arterial bruit or venous hum (in portal hypertension; Cruveilhier-Baumgarten murmur).

Aetiology

- Toxins: alcohol and other drugs (e.g. amiodarone, methotrexate).
- Viral: hepatitis B and C, CMV, EBV.
- Metabolic: non-alcoholic steatohepatitis (NASH), haemochromatosis, Wilson's disease, α_1-antitrypsin deficiency.
- Autoimmune: autoimmune hepatitis, primary biliary cirrhosis, primary sclerosing cholangitis.

Clinical spectrum of alcoholic liver disease

- Alcohol withdrawal syndrome including delirium tremens.
- Wernicke's encephalopathy.
  - Confusion, ataxia, and ophthalmoplegia
- Alcoholic fatty liver.
  - Fatty liver on ultrasound, abnormal liver enzymes on biochemistry with good synthetic function
- Alcoholic hepatitis.
  - Jaundice, raised liver enzymes, coagulopathy, encephalopathy
- Cirrhosis with portal hypertension.

Hepatic encephalopathy

- Neuropsychiatric disorder in patients with liver dysfunction (personality changes, intellectual impairment, reduced consciousness).
- Diversion of portal blood into the systemic circulation via collaterals leads to a lack of hepatic detoxification.
- Exposure of the brain to excessive concentrations of ammonia can cause neurotoxicity.
- Severity can be graded by the West Haven classification (Box 7.31).
- ❶ Ammonia levels don't always correlate with severity.
  - Other toxins implicated include mercaptans, short-chain fatty acids, and phenol.

Epidemiology and prognosis

- In decompensated cirrhosis, the risk of developing HE is 20% per year.
- At any time, 30–45% of people with cirrhosis exhibit evidence of HE.
- Development of HE is associated with a poor prognosis and strongly predicts short-term mortality in acute liver failure.

Common precipitants

- Increased nitrogen load: constipation, gastro-intestinal bleeding, blood transfusion, azotaemia, infection, hypokalaemia.
- Decreased toxin clearance: dehydration (fluid restriction, diuretics, abdominal paracentesis, diarrhoea, vomiting), hypotension (bleeding, systemic vasodilatation), anaemia, portosystemic shunts.
- Altered neurotransmission: benzodiazepines, psycho-active drugs.
- Hepatocellular damage: continued alcohol use, hepatocellular carcinoma.

Box 7.31 West Haven classification

- *Grade 0:* encephalopathy without clinically overt cognitive dysfunction, can be demonstrated by neuropsychological studies
  - Minor memory problems, no changes in behaviour. No asterixis.
- *Grade 1:* trivial lack of awareness, altered mood/behaviour, sleep disturbance, shortened attention span, impaired performance of addition or subtraction
  - Tremor, constructional apraxia, incoordination.
- *Grade 2:* lethargy or apathy, disorientation, inappropriate behaviour, slurred speech
  - Asterixis, ataxia.
- *Grade 3:* somnolence to semi-stupor but responsive to verbal stimuli, significant confusion, gross disorientation
  - Asterixis usually absent, hyperreflexia.
- *Grade 4:* coma with or without response to painful stimuli
  - Decerebrate posture.

Jaundice

Some causes of jaundice are shown in Box 7.32.

Examination: inspection

- Inspect the sclera and conjunctiva.
  - Using the left thumb, pull on the patient's lower eyelid and ask them to look towards the ceiling
  - Inspect the soft palate with a pen torch in cases of doubt (bilirubin is avidly taken up by tissues that are rich in elastin)
- Check for signs of chronic liver disease.
- Look for body piercings and tattoos (hepatitis risk).

Examination: palpation

- Palpate the abdomen for tenderness, masses, and organomegaly (including the gallbladder).

Examination: percussion

- Percuss for the liver, spleen, and presence of ascites.

Examination: completion

- Perform a digital rectal examination to look for pale stools (post-hepatic) or melaena (GI bleed complication).
- Examine the external genitalia for hair growth and testicular size (atrophic in chronic liver disease).
- Examine the hernial orifices.
- Carry out a urinary dipstick test for bilirubin (post-hepatic).

Box 7.32 Causes of jaundice

Pre-hepatic (unconjugated hyperbilirubinaemia)

- Overproduction: haemolysis; ineffective erythropoiesis
- Impaired hepatic uptake: drugs (contrast agents, rifampicin), congestive cardiac failure
- Impaired conjugation: Gilbert's syndrome, Crigler–Najjar syndrome.

Hepatic (conjugated hyperbilirubinaemia)

- Infection: viral hepatitis, leptospirosis, liver abscess, septicaemia
- Alcohol and toxins: carbon tetrachloride, fungi (*Amanita phalloides*)
- Drug-induced hepatitis: paracetamol, anti-tuberculosis drugs (isoniazid, rifampicin, pyrazinamide), statins, sodium valproate, halothane
- Metabolic: haemochromatosis, α_1-antitrypsin deficiency, Wilson's disease, Rotor syndrome
- Vascular: Budd–Chiari, right-sided heart failure.

Post-hepatic (conjugated hyperbilirubinaemia)

- Luminal: gallstones
- Mural: cholangiocarcinoma, sclerosing cholangitis, primary biliary cirrhosis, choledochal cyst
- Extra-mural: pancreatic cancer, lymph nodes at porta hepatis
- Drugs: antibiotics (flucloxacillin, fusidic acid, co-amoxiclav, nitrofurantoin).

Gallstones

Some causes of gallstones are shown in Box 7.33.

Background and epidemiology

- Stones form due to the supersaturation of bile constituents, usually cholesterol.
- Affects 10% of the population (and 2% of children).
- Incidence increases with age (40% of women >80 years).
- Male:female ratio roughly 1:2.
- Typical patient: '5 Fs' (female, forty, fair, fat, fertile).

Examination: inspection

There may be no signs of gallstones. Look for risk factors and complications.

- Jaundice?
- Scars of open or laparoscopic cholecystectomy (see separate topics).
- If the patient has recently had surgery, a T-tube and drain may be visible.
  - A flexible tube arising from the right upper quadrant.

Examination: palpation

- Examine for a palpable gallbladder.

Murphy's test

- Using 2 fingers, palpate just below the costal margin in the right upper quadrant and maintain the position whilst the patient takes a deep breath. Note any tenderness.
- Repeat the procedure in the left upper quadrant.
- If the patient experiences tenderness only when the right side is palpated, the test is positive.
  - Indicates acute cholecystitis, ascending cholangitis, empyema.

Box 7.33 Conditions predisposing to gallstones

- *Haemolysis:* sickle cell, hereditary spherocytosis, thalassaemia, pernicious anaemia, prosthetic heart valves
- *Metabolic:* diabetes, obesity, pancreatic disease, cystic fibrosis, hypercholesterolaemia, hyperparathyroidism, hypothyroidism, pregnancy
- *Cholestasis:* hepatitis, Caroli's disease, parasitic infection, prolonged fasting (e.g. TPN), methadone use
- *Malabsorption:* (×10 risk of stone formation) inflammatory bowel disease (especially Crohn's), small bowel resection, bypass surgery
- *Other:* muscular dystrophy.

Ascites

Definition and aetiology

- Ascites is more than 25ml of fluid within the peritoneal cavity.
- Common causes: cirrhosis with portal hypertension, peritoneal carcinomatosis.
- Less common causes: hepatocellular carcinoma, Budd–Chiari syndrome, congestive cardiac failure, pancreatitis, and tuberculosis.

Ascites complicating advanced cirrhosis

- Ascites often marks the first sign of hepatic decompensation.
  - Occurs in >50% over 10 years of follow-up, worsens the course of disease, and reduces survival substantially
  - If ascites becomes refractory to diuretics, 50% die within 1 year.
- Spontaneous bacterial peritonitis (SBP) is a frequent and serious complication of cirrhotic ascites and is defined as an ascitic neutrophil count >250 cells/mm^3.

Examination: inspection

- If there is gross ascites, the abdomen may be distended.
  - Look for bulging of the flanks in a supine patient (fluid accumulates in the paracolic gutters).
- Look for signs of chronic liver disease:
  - Hands: clubbing, leukonychia, bruising, palmar erythema, Dupuytren's contracture, hepatic flap, scratch marks
  - Face: anaemia, jaundice, xanthelasma, parotid enlargement, glossitis
  - Neck: Troisier's sign/Virchow's node (intra-abdominal malignancy)
  - Trunk: spider naevi, gynaecomastia
  - Abdomen: distended superficial veins, caput medusa.

Examination: palpation

- Palpate in each quadrant for tenderness and masses.
  - Palpation for organomegaly may be difficult in gross ascites.

Examination: percussion

- Percuss borders of the liver, spleen, bladder, and any masses.
- Shifting dullness.
- Fluid thrill test.

Examination: completion

- Examine the hernial orifices, lymph nodes and cardiovascular system (peripheral oedema and pleural effusion).

Primary biliary cirrhosis

- Autoimmune liver disease characterized by progressive destruction of intrahepatic bile ducts with cholestasis, portal inflammation and fibrosis.
- May lead to cirrhosis, its complications, and eventually to liver transplantation or death.
- Predominantly affects females in their 5th to 7th decades.

History

- Majority are asymptomatic.
- Fatigue (multifactorial: autonomic dysfunction, sleep disturbance, and excessive daytime somnolence, depression).
- Pruritus (typically precedes onset of jaundice by months to years. Develops independently of degree of cholestasis and stage of disease).
- Vague right upper quadrant pain.
- Night blindness, bony pain, easy bruising, fat-soluble vitamin malabsorption (A, D, E, and K).

Examination: inspection

Look for:

- Scratch marks.
- Pigmentation.
- Digital clubbing.
- Arthropathy (involving small joints).
- Xanthelasma.
- Xanthoma.
- Evidence of decompensated liver disease:
  - Jaundice
  - Abdominal distension
  - Dilated abdominal veins
  - Hepatomegaly
  - Splenomegaly
  - Ascites
  - Encephalopathy
  - Flapping tremor (asterixis).

Associated autoimmune conditions

- Look for evidence of: rheumatoid arthritis, thyroid dysfunction, Sjögren's syndrome, scleroderma, systemic lupus erythematosus, coeliac disease.

Haemochromatosis

- Autosomal recessive condition causing an abnormal accumulation of iron in the parenchymal organs, leading to organ toxicity.
- Gene for most genetic haemochromatosis (GH), called 'HFE', lies on short arm of chromosome 6. The two major mutations are C282Y and H63D. Defective hepcidin (iron-regulatory hormone) gene expression or function may underlie most forms of non-HFE associated GH.
- Carrier state ~1:10; frequency of homozygosity ~1:200/400 but penetrance is low (higher with co-factors such as excess alcohol).
- Male preponderance; menstruation has protective effect in females.

Symptoms

- Often vague and non-specific.
  - Weakness, fatigue, lethargy, apathy, weight loss.
- Organ specific: arthralgia, abdominal pain (hepatomegaly), amenorrhoea, loss of libido, impotence (pituitary dysfunction, hepatic cirrhosis), shortness of breath (CCF).
- Impaired memory, mood swings, and irritability.

Examination findings

A patient with haemochromatosis may show any of the following clinical features:

- Hepatomegaly.
- Cutaneous stigmata of liver disease (palmar erythema, jaundice, spider naevi).
- Signs of portal hypertension (splenomegaly, ascites).
- Arthritis and joint swelling.
  - Especially 2nd, 3rd metacarpophalangeal joints, wrists, hips, and knees.
- Shortness of breath, oedema, raised JVP (dilated cardiomyopathy).
- Arrhythmias (conduction abnormalities).
- Altered pigmentation.
  - Bronzing or 'slate-grey' due to iron and melanin deposition.
- Scars in cubital fossae (previous venesection).
- Hair loss.
- Hypogonadism (testicular atrophy, loss of axillary and pubic hair).
- Increased blood and urine glucose levels (diabetes mellitus secondary to iron toxicity of pancreatic beta cells).
- Signs of hypothyroidism (see separate topic).

Wilson's disease

Definition and epidemiology
- Wilson's disease or hepatolenticular degeneration is a rare autosomal recessive inherited disorder of copper metabolism characterized by excessive deposition of copper in the liver, brain, and other tissues.
- Affects about 1 in 30,000 people, often manifesting as liver disease in children and adolescents and as a neuropsychiatric illness in young adults.

Pathogenesis
- The transport of copper by the P-type ATPase is defective due to one of several mutations (>300 identified) occurring within the ATP7B gene.
- This gene has been mapped to chromosome 13q14.3.
- Intestinal copper absorption and transport into the liver are intact, whilst incorporation into caeruloplasmin and excretion into bile are impaired.

Clinical features
Wilson's can cause a variety of clinical findings. A patient may present with any of the clinical features described here.
- Neurological.
  - Dysarthria
  - Dystonia
  - Tremor
  - Incoordination
  - Parkinsonian symptoms (rigidity, bradykinesia)
  - Poor hand-writing
  - Abnormal eye movements
  - Polyneuropathy.
- Hepatic.
  - Acute hepatitis, chronic active hepatitis
  - Cirrhosis
  - Fulminant hepatic failure.
- Psychiatric.
  - Irritability or anger, emotional lability
  - Hyperkinetic behaviour
  - Mania, depression
  - Psychosis
  - Impaired concentration
  - Personality changes.
- Ophthalmic: Kayser–Fleischer rings.
  - Deposition of copper in Descemet's membrane at the limbus of the cornea; greenish gold-brown, may be readily visible with the naked eye or can be identified on slit-lamp examination
  - Seen in nearly all with neurological signs of Wilson's disease
  - Sunflower cataracts (visible only with slit lamp).
- Other (<10% patients).
  - Endocrine, renal, cardiac, skeletal manifestations.

Peutz–Jeghers syndrome

Background and epidemiology

- Peutz–Jeghers syndrome is due to germline mutations of the STK11 gene and is characterized by intestinal hamartomatous polyps and mucocutaneous melanocytic macules.
- Autosomal dominant, with variable penetrance. Incidence is estimated at between 1 in 50,000 to 1 in 200,000 live births.
- The disease carries an increased risk of gastrointestinal and other cancers, including pancreas, breast, cervix, ovary, uterus, lung, and testis.
- Patients have a 93% cumulative risk of cancer by the age of 64; roughly half die from cancer by the age of 57. Rapid increase in risk >50 years.
- Differential diagnosis is shown in Box 7.34.

Examination: inspection

- Pigmented macules of 1–5mm in diameter.
- Most commonly around the mouth, crossing the vermilion border of the lip.
- Dark brown to black (reminiscent of freckles).
- They may be present also on the hands and feet, and around the umbilicus, genitalia, and anus.
  - Similar lesions often occur on the buccal mucosa.
- A prolapsed rectal polyp may be seen.

Examination: other systems

- Abdomen: inspect for scars (e.g. resulting from surgery for intussusceptions or malignancy).
- A rectal mass due to a polyp may be palpable.
- Testicular masses also occur: examine the testicles and check the chest for gynaecomastia (as a result of a Sertoli cell tumour).
- In females, the breasts should be assessed for masses.

Box 7.34 Differential diagnosis of Peutz–Jeghers syndrome

- *Laugier–Hunziker syndrome:* peri-oral and intra-oral pigmentation, but lacks systemic manifestations
- *Cronkhite–Canada syndrome:* intestinal polyposis and freckle-like lesions; presents in older individuals and the skin lesions are more extensive
- *Addison's disease:* hypotension, hyper-pigmentation of skin and gums, hyponatraemia, and hyperkalaemia
- *McCune–Albright syndrome:* precocious puberty, café-au-lait lesion, fibrous dysplasia of bones including the femur, tibia, pelvis, and skull
- *Familial adenomatous polyposis and Gardner syndrome:* numerous adenomatous colonic polyps. Gardner variant includes multiple extra-colonic polyps such as osteomas and desmoid tumours.

Appendicitis

Epidemiology

- The diagnosis is clinical, therefore investigations are only needed to exclude other pathology.
- Lifetime risk 7%.
- Overall mortality 0.2–0.8% but higher in >70yrs due to diagnostic delay.
- After the first 36 hours, perforation risk is 16–36%, with 5% risk for every subsequent 12 hours.

Examination: inspection

- Fever.
- Pain on movement.
- Flexion of the right hip and a reluctance to extend it.
- Flushed appearance.
- Dry tongue.
- Fetor oris.
- Ask the patient to point to the site of pain with one finger.
  - Classically this is McBurney's point (2/3 of the way along a line between the umbilicus and the right anterior superior iliac spine).

Examination: palpation

- Tenderness and (guarding) at the right iliac fossa.
  - Maximal tenderness may be over McBurney's point.
- Percussion tenderness in the RIF.
- Rovsing's test.
  - Press the left iliac fossa and ask the patient if and where they feel pain
  - If pain is felt at the right iliac fossa, the test is positive.
- ▶ Rebound tenderness. Testing for this should be avoided as this is painful and does not add to the diagnosis.

Other tests

- PR or PV examinations: tenderness on the right may indicate appendicitis, but examination may be normal (see also Box 7.35).
- Psoas sign: extension of the hip stretches the psoas and is painful if irritated by a nearby inflamed appendix (especially retrocaecal).
- Obturator sign: suprapubic pain on flexion and internal rotation of the right hip. Due to obturator internus irritation by inflamed appendix.

Box 7.35 Findings by appendix position

- *Retrocaecal (75%):* right loin/right iliac fossa pain and tenderness. Guarding may be absent. Psoas sign may be present
- *Pelvic (20%):* suprapubic pain, urinary frequency, diarrhoea. Bladder irritation may give haematuria and urinary leukocystosis. Abdominal tenderness may be minimal; rectal and vaginal tenderness predominate
- *Pre-ileal and post-ileal (5%):* may have few signs and symptoms. Ileitis may lead to vomiting.

Ulcerative colitis (UC)

Definition and epidemiology

- UC is an idiopathic inflammatory bowel disease characterized by colonic mucosal inflammation and a chronic relapsing course.
- UC extends uninterrupted from the anal verge to involve part or all of the colon. Apart from backwash ileitis, the small bowel is not involved.
- Bimodal distribution with peaks at 15–30 years and in the 6th decade.
- Three times more common in non-smokers (some relapse on quitting).

Associated conditions

- Primary sclerosing cholangitis, cholangiocarcinoma, amyloidosis, uric acid renal stones.

History

- Depends on extent and activity of the disease.
  - Bloody diarrhoea, mucous discharge, faecal urgency, tenesmus, colicky abdominal pain, fever, malaise, anorexia, weight loss.

Inspection: general

Physical examination is often unremarkable, unless the patient is presenting acutely.

- Aphthous ulcers.
- Glossitis.
- Pallor (anaemia is common).
- Peripheral oedema.
- Digital clubbing.
- Ocular inflammation (uveitis, episcleritis, scleritis).
- Cushingoid features (if steroid use).
- Enteropathic arthropathy (large joint arthritis, seronegative spondyloarthropathy: sacroiliitis, ankylosing spondylitis).
- Erythema nodosum (15%).
- Pyoderma gangrenosum (1–2%).

Inspection: abdomen

- May be surgical scars (e.g. from hemicolectomy).
- Stomas or healed stoma sites.
- Abdominal drains or healed drain sites.

Palpation

- May find distended, tense abdomen.

Percussion

- Hyper-resonance (if abdomen distended).

Auscultation

- Tinkling bowel sounds (in obstruction).

Crohn's disease

Definition and epidemiology

- Idiopathic inflammatory bowel disease characterized by transmural, granulomatous inflammation anywhere from mouth to anus (most common at ileocaecum). It has a chronic, relapsing/remitting course.
- Age of onset is bimodal with peaks at 15–30 and 60–80 years.
- Smoking increases risk x3–4.

Intestinal complications

- Malnutrition, fistulae, colorectal adenocarcinoma (Crohn's colitis), short bowel syndrome (following surgical resection).

Extra-intestinal complications

- Hepatic: fatty change, chronic active hepatitis, cirrhosis, amyloidosis.
- Biliary tract: gallstones, sclerosing cholangitis, cholangiocarcinoma.
- Renal: uric acid stones, oxalate stones.
- Musculoskeletal: enteropathic arthropathy, osteoporosis.
- Ocular: uveitis, episcleritis, scleritis.
- Dermatological: erythema nodosum, pyoderma gangrenosum.
- Haematological: anaemia (Fe, B_{12}, and folate deficiency), thrombosis.

History

- Abdominal pain, diarrhoea, weight loss, fever, malaise, anorexia.

Inspection: general

- Aphthous ulcers.
- Glossitis.
- Pallor (anaemia is common).
- Peripheral oedema.
- Digital clubbing.
- Ocular inflammation (uveitis, episcleritis, scleritis).
- Cushingoid features (if steroid use).
- Enteropathic arthropathy (large joint arthritis, seronegative spondyloarthropathy: sacroiliitis, ankylosing spondylitis).
- Erythema nodosum (15%), pyoderma gangrenosum (1–2%).

Inspection: abdomen and perineum

- Multiple surgical scars.
- Stomas or healed stoma sites.
- Enterocutaneous fistulae.
- Perianal skin tags, fissures, ulceration, sinuses.
- Abdominal drains or healed drain sites.

Palpation

- May find distended, tense abdomen, mass (especially in right iliac fossa), hepatomegaly.

Percussion

- Hyper-resonance (if abdomen distended).

Auscultation

- Increased bowel sounds (in acute exacerbations).

Perianal disease

Haemorrhoids

- Hypertrophied endoanal cushions (causing symptoms).
- Clinical features: acute prolapse and inflammation with associated perianal lump, soreness, and irritation. May bleed. Chronic: bleeding and pruritus ani.
- Sites: primary (3, 7, 11 o'clock in the supine position; the locations of the main anal blood vessel pedicles).
- Classification (Lord's):
  - 1st degree: bleeding, no prolapse
  - 2nd degree: prolapse, spontaneous reduction
  - 3rd degree: prolapse, digital reduction.

Fissure in ano

- A superficial linear tear in the anoderm distal to the dentate line commonly caused by passage of hard stool. Almost always in the midline: 90% posterior, 10% anterior.
- Clinical features: identified on inspection, often too painful to perform PR. Causes acute severe, localized 'knife-like' pain during defaecation with associated deep throbbing pain for minutes or hours after (pelvic floor spasm). Blood is often seen on the paper when wiping.

Perianal abscess

- Definition: abscess within the soft tissues surrounding the anal canal.
- Clinical features: gradual onset, constant localized perianal pain. Associated swelling with tenderness and possible discharge.

Fistula in ano

- Definition: abnormal communication between the anorectal lining and the perineal or vaginal epithelium. Nearly always caused by a previous anorectal abscess. Other less common causes include trauma, Crohn's disease, carcinoma, radiation therapy, and tuberculosis.
- Clinical features: perianal or perineal pain, swelling and erythema of perianal skin, fever, tachycardia, discharge.
- Goodsall's rule: if the external opening is posterior to a line drawn transversely through the anus (in the supine position), the opening will be in the midline and thus have a curved tract. If the opening is anterior to this line it will have a radial tract.

Rectal prolapse

- Definition: protrusion of either the rectal mucosa or the entire wall of the rectum (complete prolapse). Mainly occurs in the elderly and young children.
- Clinical features: obvious, large perineal lump, dark red/blue with surface mucosa and, occasionally, some surface ulceration. Pain, constipation, faecal incontinence, mucous discharge, or rectal bleeding may occur.

Nephrotic syndrome

Nephrotic syndrome is a clinical syndrome, not a diagnosis.

Nephrotic syndrome is a tetrad of:
- Proteinuria >3g/24 hours.
- Oedema.
- Hypoalbuminaemia.
- Hyperlipidaemia.

Common causes of nephrotic syndrome in adults
- Minimal change disease (MCD).
- Membranous nephropathy.
- Focal segmental glomerulosclerosis.
- Diabetic glomerulosclerosis.

Other causes of nephrotic syndrome
- Renal amyloidosis, lupus nephritis, mesangiocapillary glomerulonephritis, collapsing glomerulopathy (HIV-associated nephropathy), light chain deposition disease.

Other causes of bilateral swollen legs
- Right ventricular failure.
- Lymphoedema.
- Hypoalbuminaemia.
- Hepatic failure.

Complications
- Increased risk of thromboembolism (loss of anticoagulant factors in the urine).
  - Those with albumin <20g/L are often anticoagulated with warfarin.
- Renal vein thrombosis.
  - Suspect if the patient develops loin pain, haematuria, and an acute deterioration in their renal function.
- Pulmonary emboli.
- Infection (loss of immunoglobulin and complement).
- Hypercholesterolaemia.

Examination findings
- Extensive oedema.
- Periorbital swelling.
  - Typically worse in the morning.
- Bilateral pitting oedema of the lower limbs.
  - Usually symmetrical
  - May extend up to the abdomen.
- Also look for evidence of:
  - Pulmonary oedema
  - Pleural effusion
  - Ascites.

Chronic kidney disease (CKD)

Common causes in the UK

- Diabetes mellitus.
- Glomerulonephritis e.g. IgA nephropathy.
- Reflux nephropathy.
- Obstructive uropathy.
- Renovascular disease.
- Hypertension.
- Polycystic kidney disease.

Other causes

- Myeloma, renal amyloidosis, systemic lupus erythematosus (SLE), vasculitis, tubulointerstitial nephritis, scleroderma, other inherited renal diseases e.g. Alport's disease, oxalosis, cystinosis.

History

Many patients with CKD are asymptomatic. Symptoms usually develop at an advanced stage and include:

- Fatigue, weakness (secondary to anaemia).
- Breathlessness (due to fluid overload, acidosis).
- Anorexia, vomiting, metallic taste in mouth (due to uraemia).
- Pruritus.
- Restless legs.
- Bone pain.
- Leg swelling.

Examination findings

A patient with CKD may have no specific clinical findings or they may have a number of clinical features:

- Pallor (due to chronic anaemia).
- A lemon tinge to the skin (due to uraemia).
- Scratch marks from pruritus.
- Hyertension.
- A pericardial rub (uncommon, due to uraemia).
- Pleural effusions.
- Palpable kidneys (causes include polycystic kidney disease, hydronephrosis).
- Bilateral lower limb oedema (fluid overload or heavy proteinuria).
- Distended bladder?

Evidence that the patient is being prepared for dialysis

- An arteriovenous fistula either at the wrist or in the antecubital fossa (usually in the non-dominant arm) for haemodialysis.
- A peritoneal dialysis catheter situated in the abdomen.

Transplanted kidney

- A renal transplant is the most favourable and desired form of renal replacement therapy for patients with end-stage renal disease (ESRD).
- Simultaneous pancreas–kidney transplants are performed in patients with type 1 diabetes and stage 5 CKD (see Box 7.36).
- Following a renal transplant, patients are required to take life-long immunosuppression to prevent graft rejection.
- Transplanted kidneys may be from a deceased or a living donor.
- A transplanted kidney will lie in either the left or right iliac fossae.

Examination: inspection

- Look around the bedside for clues that the patient has diabetes.
- There may be lipoatrophy or lipohypertrophy at insulin injection sites.
- Look for other complications of severe diabetes including signs of visual impairment due to diabetic retinopathy and peripheral vascular disease.

Examination: abdomen

- A firm mass palpable deep to a diagonal scar.
  - It is possible that a patient may have had more than one transplant and could have a transplanted kidney in each iliac fossa
  - An extended Lanz incision in either iliac fossa is called a Rutherford–Morrison incision
  - The renal artery is usually anastomosed to the internal or external iliac artery and the renal vein to the external iliac vein. The ureter is attached separately to the patient's bladder.
- Looks for scars of previous nephrectomy (midline, chevron, or loin).

Evidence of end-stage renal disease

- An arteriovenous fistula either at the wrist or in the antecubital fossa (Cimino–Brescia fistula).
- Small scars near the umbilicus consistent with previous peritoneal dialysis catheter placement.
- Small scars beneath the clavicle on either side of the chest which might suggest previous tunnelled dialysis catheter placement.
- A scar at the base of the neck consistent with parathyroidectomy (for advanced renal bone disease).

Box 7.36 Simultaneous pancreas–kidney transplant (SPK)

- A curved (bucket-handle) scar across the lower abdomen extending between the iliac fossae with a mass palpable in each
- The pancreas is usually transplanted into the right iliac fossa and the kidney into the left.

Adult polycystic kidney disease

- Adult polycystic kidney disease (APKD) is the commonest inherited form of renal disease with a prevalence of around 1 in 1000.
- APKD is inherited in an autosomal dominant manner.
- 25–40% of patients will have no family history.
- Polycystic kidneys are usually not difficult to miss on examination.

History

- Flank or loin pain from enlarged or infected cysts.
- Nocturia and polyuria (loss of urinary concentrating ability).
- Hypertension.
- Low grade proteinuria, persistent microscopic haematuria +/− frank haematuria.
- Uraemic symptoms if the patient presents late.

Examination findings

- Bilaterally enlarged kidneys with irregular surfaces (see Box 7.37).
  - Ballotable flank masses which move caudally with inspiration and the examining hand can 'get above'.
- There may also be an enlarged liver with an irregular, lobulated edge.
- Look for evidence of end-stage renal disease.

Evidence of advanced or end-stage renal disease (ESRD)

- A scar in the iliac fossa and a mass consistent with a renal transplant.
- An arteriovenous fistula either at the wrist or in the antecubital fossa (usually in the non-dominant arm) for haemodialysis.
- A peritoneal dialysis catheter situated in the abdomen or a scar consistent with previous catheter placement.
- A scar at the base of the neck consistent with parathyroidectomy (for advanced renal bone disease).
- Small scars beneath the clavicle on either side of the chest which might suggest previous tunnelled dialysis catheter placement.

APKD associations

- Cysts of other organs notably the liver, spleen, and pancreas.
- Cardiac abnormalities: mitral valve prolapse, aortic regurgitation.
- Intracranial aneurysms which on rupture present as subarachnoid haemorrhage. Patients are screened for these only if there is a strong positive family history of intracranial bleeding.
- Colonic diverticula, abdominal and inguinal herniae.

Box 7.37 Other causes of bilateral renal enlargement

- Bilateral hydronephrosis
- Amyloidosis (hepatosplenomegaly?)
- Tuberous sclerosis (adenoma sebaceum or shagreen patches?)
- Von Hippel–Lindau disease.

See also:

More information regarding the presentation and clinical signs of abdominal diseases to aid preparation for OSCE-type examinations and ward rounds can be found in the *Oxford Handbooks Clinical Tutor Study Cards*.

'Medicine' Study Card set:
- Chronic liver disease
- Hepatic encephalopathy
- Autoimmune hepatitis
- Primary biliary cirrhosis
- Haemochromatosis
- Wilson's disease
- Chronic kidney disease
- Lymphadenopathy
- Nephrotic syndrome.

'Surgery' Study Card set:
- Abdominal mass
- Inguinal hernia
- Femoral hernia
- Incisional hernia
- Paraumbilical hernia
- Spigelian hernia
- Abdominal stomas
- Appendicitis
- Jaundice
- Ascites
- Peutz–Jeghers syndrome
- Gallstones
- Perianal disease.

Both the 'Medicine' and 'Surgery' Study Card sets:
- Hepatomegaly
- Splenomegaly
- Ulcerative colitis
- Crohn's disease
- Adult polycystic kidney disease
- Transplanted kidney
- Single palpable kidney.

The elderly patient

Gastrointestinal disease presents as a huge spectrum in elders, encompassing nutrition, oral care, and continence in addition to the range of presentations described in this chapter. Whilst many older people suffer gastrointestinal symptoms, often due to underlying illnesses or the effect of medication, they may be embarrassed about discussing them. Thoughtful and holistic assessment is paramount, and simple interventions can pay dividends.

History

- *Oral care:* is often overlooked, but a key part of any assessment. Dentures may be ill-fitting or lost, and dietary intake can suffer as a consequence, and hospital inpatients are particularly prone to losing their dentures.
- *Clarify symptoms and diagnoses:* does the patient really have an irritable bowel? Many patients may describe themselves as having such diagnoses, but take the time to clarify what this means. Recent changes of bowel habit must always be treated seriously.
- *Constipation:* this can often lead to serious decline in patients. This is often easily remediable.
- *Weight and nutrition:* ask yourself why has the patient lost weight? The range of diagnoses is broad, but contemplate mood, dietary habits, and functional abilities in your assessments.
- *Drug history:* always consider the side effects of medication—analgesics and constipation, recent antibiotics, and diarrhoea – has the patient recently been in hospital (could the diarrhoea represent *C. difficile* infection?). Ask about over-the-counter drugs including NSAIDs (topical drugs too!) and aperients.
- *Continence:* another key part of the assessment; try to discuss sensitively and determine if there factors additional to any GI disturbance, including mobility, cognition, and visual problems. This dovetails with the ever-important functional history.

Examination

- *General:* look out for signs of weight loss—wasting, poorly fitting clothes, etc. For inpatients, a completed weight chart and careful consideration may alleviate some of the problems of poor nutrition and acute illness.
- *Look in the mouth:* as a range of diagnoses is often apparent. Denture care should be assessed (poor cleaning associated with recurrent stomatitis), and other problems such as oral candidiasis are obvious.
- *Observe:* for other signs of systemic disease that might point to the cause of the gastrointestinal symptoms (e.g. multiple telangiectasia, valvular heart disease in GI bleeding).
- *Examine:* thoroughly for lymphadenopathy. Remember to examine hernial orifices: the cause of abdominal pain may be instantly obvious—and correctable.
- *Rectal examination:* vital—changes in bowel habit, continence, iron-deficiency anaemia, bladder symptomatology all indicate this.

Diagnoses not to be missed

- *Functional bowel disorders:* tend to be less common in older people, so always consider underlying organic problems. Endoscopic examinations are often well tolerated and have a good diagnostic yield.
- *Biliary sepsis:* is the 3rd most common source of infection in older people (after chest and urine sepsis), and may lack many of the salient presenting features described previously in this chapter. Be alert to this possibility when considering differential diagnoses and choosing antibiotics.

The nervous system

Presenting symptoms

The history is key in many neurological cases. If the patient cannot give a complete story (e.g. when describing a loss of consciousness or seizure), collateral histories should be gained from any witnesses to the event(s)—relatives, friends, the GP, or even passers-by.

An approach to neurological symptoms

Symptoms can vary wildly in neurology and the intricacies of a few are discussed below. For all symptoms, you should try to understand:

- The exact nature of the symptom.
- The onset (Sudden? Slow—hours? Days? Weeks? Months?).
- Change over time (Progressive? Intermittent? Episodes of recovery?).
- Precipitating factors.
- Exacerbating and relieving factors.
- Previous episodes of the same symptom.
- Previous investigations and treatment.
- Associated symptoms.
- Any other neurological symptoms.

Dizziness

Narrow the exact meaning down without appearing aggressive or disbelieving. This term is used by different people to describe rather different things including:

- A sense of rotation = 'vertigo'.
- 'Swimminess' or 'lightheadedness'—a rather nonspecific symptom which can be related to pathology in many different systems.
- 'Pre-syncope'—the rather unique feeling one gets just prior to fainting.
- Incoordination—many will say they are dizzy when, in fact, they can't walk straight due to either ataxia or weakness.

Headache

This should be treated as you would any other type of pain. Establish character, severity, site, duration, time course, frequency, radiation, aggravating and relieving factors, and associated symptoms.

- Ask about facial and visual symptoms. (Some different types of headaches are described in Box 8.1.)

Numbness and weakness

These two words are often confused by patients—describing a leg as 'numb' when it is *weak* with normal sensation.

Also, patients may report 'numbness' when, in fact, they are experiencing pins-and-needles or pain.

Tremor

Here, you should establish if the tremor occurs only at rest, only when attempting an action or both. Is it worse at any particular time of the day? The severity can be established in terms of its functional consequence (can't hold a cup/put food to mouth?).

Again, establish exactly what is being described. A tremor is a shaking, regular, or jerky involuntary movement.

Syncope

This is discussed in ➜ Chapter 5.

Falls and loss of consciousness (LOC)

An eyewitness account is vital. Establish also whether the patient actually lost consciousness or not. People often describe 'blacking out' when in fact they simply fell to the ground (drop attacks have no LOC). An important question here is 'can you remember hitting the ground?'

Ask about preceding symptoms and warning signs—they may point towards a different organ system (sweating or weakness could be a marker of hypoglycaemia; palpitations may indicate a cardiac dysrhythmia).

Seizures

Very difficult even for experienced history-takers! Establish early on if there was any impairment of consciousness and seek collateral histories. Lay persons usually consider 'seizure' = 'fit' = tonic–clonic seizure. Doctors' understanding of 'seizure' may be rather different. A surprising number of people also suffer 'pseudoseizures' which are non-organic and have a psychological cause.

A few points to consider:

- Syncopal attacks can often cause a few tonic–clonic jerks which may be mistaken for epilepsy.
- True tonic–clonic seizures may cause tongue-biting, urinary and faecal incontinence, or all of the above.
- People presenting with pseudoseizure can have true epilepsy *as well* and vice versa.

Visual symptoms

Commonly visual loss, double vision, or photophobia (pain when looking at bright lights). Here, establish exactly what is being experienced—'double vision' (diplopia) is often complained of when, in fact, the vision is blurred or sight is generally poor (amblyopia) or clouded.

See ➜ Chapter 9 for more on visual symptoms.

The rest of the history

▶ Remember to ask if the patient is right- or left-handed (consider disability from loss of function and may also be useful when thinking about cerebral lesions).

Direct questioning

- Headaches (see Box 8.1).
- Fits, faints and 'funny turns', and 'blackouts'.
- Visual symptoms.
- Pins-and-needles, tingling.
- Numbness.
- Weakness.
- Incontinence, constipation, or urinary retention.

Past medical history

▶ A birth history is important here, particularly in patients with epilepsy. Brain injury at birth has neurological consequences.

A thorough history is required, as always, but enquire especially about:

- Hypertension—if so, what treatment?
- Diabetes mellitus—what type? What treatment?
- Thyroid disease.
- Mental illness (e.g. depression).
- Meningitis or encephalitis.
- Head or spinal injuries.
- Epilepsy, convulsions, or seizures.
- Cancers.
- HIV/AIDS.

Drug history

Ask especially about:

- Anticonvulsant therapy (current or previous), oral contraceptive pill, steroids, anticoagulants, anti-platelet agents.

Family history

A thorough history, as always, is important. Ask about neurological diagnoses and evidence of missed diagnoses (seizures, blackouts, etc.).

Tobacco, alcohol

As important here as in any other system.

Social history

- Occupation—neurological disease can impact significantly on occupation so ask about this at an early stage—some suggest right at the beginning of the history. Also ask about exposure to heavy metals or other neurotoxins.
- Driving?—Many neurological conditions have implications here.
- Ask about the home environment thoroughly (will be very useful when considering handicaps and consequences of the diagnosis).
- Ask about support systems—family, friends, home-helps, day centre visits, etc.

Box 8.1 Some characteristic headaches

Tension headache
- Bilateral—frontal, temporal
- Sensation of tightness radiating to neck and shoulders
- Can last for days
- No associated symptoms.

Subarachnoid haemorrhage
- Sudden, dramatic onset 'like being hit with a brick'
- Occipital initially—may become generalized
- Associated with neck stiffness and sometimes photophobia.

Sinusitis
- Frontal, felt behind the eyes or over the cheeks
- Ethmoid sinusitis is felt deep behind the nose
- Overlying skin may be tender
- Worse on bending forwards
- Lasts 1–2 weeks. Associated with coryza.

Temporal (giant cell) arteritis
- Diffuse, spreading from the temple—unilateral
- Tender overlying temporal artery (painful brushing hair)
- ?jaw claudication whilst eating
- ?blurred vision—can lead to loss of vision if severe and untreated.

Meningitis
- Generalized
- Associated with neck stiffness and signs of meningism
- Nausea, vomiting, photophobia.
  - Purpuric rash is caused by septicaemia, not meningitis *per se*.

Cluster headache
- Rapid onset, usually felt over one eye
- Associated with a blood-shot, watering eye, and facial flushing
- May also have rhinorrhoea (runny nose)
- Last for a few weeks at a time.

Raised intracranial pressure
- Generalized headache, worse when lying down, straining, coughing, on exertion, or in the morning
- Headache may wake the patient in the early hours
- May be associated with drowsiness, vomiting, and focal neurology.

Migraine
- Unilateral—rarely crosses the midline
- Throbbing/pounding headache
- Associated with photophobia, nausea, vomiting, and neck stiffness
- May have preceding aura.

The outline examination

It is easy to get bogged down in some of the complexities of the neuro-logical examination but it is not something to be afraid of. Students should embrace it—practise often, as a competent neurological examination is a sure sign of someone who has spent plenty of time on the wards. (See Box 8.2.)

> **Box 8.2 Examination framework**
>
> The neurological examination can be complex and lengthy. The following is a brief outline of an approach to a 'full' neurological examination.
> - Inspection, mood, conscious level
> - Speech and higher mental functions
> - Cranial nerves II–XII
> - Motor system
> - Sensation
> - Coordination
> - Gait
> - Any extra tests
> - Other relevant examinations.
>   - Skull, spine, neck stiffness, ear drums, blood pressure, anterior chest, carotid arteries, breasts, abdomen, lymph nodes.

General inspection and mental state

The neurological exam should start with any clues that can be gleaned from simply looking at, and engaging with, the patient.
- Are they accompanied by carers—and how do they interact with those people?
- Do they use any walking aids or other forms of support?
- Any abnormal movements?
- Observe the gait as they approach the clinic room, if able.
- Any speech disturbance?
- What is their mood like?
  - A detailed mood assessment is not necessary here
  - Ask the patient how they feel
  - What is the state or their clothing, hair, skin, and nails?
  - Is there any restlessness, inappropriately high spirits, or pressure of speech?
  - Are they obviously depressed with disinterest?
  - Are they denying any disability?

Cognitive function

Neurological diseases may affect function such that patients' appearance or communication skills are at odds with their educational level—formal assessment allows for any future change to be noted and monitored.

The Abbreviated Mental Test Score (10 points)

This serves as a brief screening tool (see Box 8.3). A more detailed, 30 point, score is shown in ➲ Box 16.12.

▶ Approach this gently—you may offend a patient by testing them without warning or explanation. Always explain the purpose of the questions—and ask their permission to proceed.

Box 8.3 Abbreviated Mental Test Score	
1. Date of birth	• 'What is your date of birth?'
2. Age	• 'How old are you?'
3. Time	• 'What time is it?'
	• Correct to the nearest hour.
4. Year	• 'What year is it now?'
	• Note that hospital patients often lose track of the day or month not the year.
5. Place	• 'Where are we?' or 'What is this place?'
	• The name of the hospital/clinic/surgery.
6. Head of state	• 'Who's the Prime Minister at the moment?'
	• A name is required. Such descriptions as 'That man in all the trouble' won't do—even if it is potentially correct!
7. War II	• 'What year did the Second World War start?'
8. 5-minute recall	• Tell the patient an address (often '42 West Street' is used) and ask them to repeat it back to you to ensure they've heard it correctly. Ask them to remember it. Five minutes later, ask them to recall the address.
	• They must remember the address *in full* to score the point.
9. 20–1	• 'Count backward from 20 down to 1.'
	• Patients sometimes need a prompt here 'Like this: 20, 19, 18, and so on'.
10. Recognition	• 'What job do I do?' and 'What job does this man/woman do?'
	• *Both* must be correct to score a point.

Hints and tips

- If thinking of an address for the patient to remember—be careful not to give out your own!
- Beware of repeating the test too often. Patients may well remember '42 West Street' from the last time it was asked!

Speech and language

Speech and language difficulties, especially expressive dysphasia, may be extremely distressing for the patient and their family. This topic must be approached with caution, reassurance, and a calm seriousness in the face of possibly bizarre and amusing answers to questions.

Examination

- Speech and language problems may be evident from the start of the history and require no formal testing. You should briefly test language function by asking the patient to read or obey a simple written command (e.g. close your eyes) and write a short sentence.
- If apparently problematic, speech can be tested formally by asking the patient to respond to progressively harder questions: yes/no questions, simple statements or instructions, more complicated sentences, and finally by asking them to repeat complex phrases or tongue-twisters.
- Before jumping to conclusions, ensure that the patient is not deaf (or that their hearing-aid is working) and that they can usually understand the language you are speaking.

Dysarthria

A defect of articulation with language function intact (writing will be unaffected). There may be a cerebellar lesion, an LMN lesion of the cranial nerves, an extrapyramidal lesion, or a problem with muscles in the mouth and jaws or their nerve supply.

- Listen for slurring and the rhythm of speech.
- Test function of different structures by asking the patient to repeat:
  - 'Yellow lorry' or words with 'D', 'L', and 'T' (*tongue* function)
  - 'Peter Piper picked a pickle' or words with 'P' and 'B' (*lip* function).
- *Cerebellar lesions:* slow, slurred, low volume with equal emphasis on all syllables ('scanning').
- *Facial weakness:* speech is slurred.
- *Extrapyramidal lesions:* monotonous, low volume and lacking in normal rhythm.

Dysphonia

Defective volume—huskiness. Usually from laryngeal disease, laryngeal nerve palsy or, rarely, muscular disease such as myasthenia gravis.

May also be 'functional' (psychological).

Dysphasia

This is a defect of language, not just speech, so reading and writing may also be affected (some patients attempt to overcome speaking difficulties with a notepad and pen only to be bitterly disappointed).

There are four main types of dysphasia:

Expressive dysphasia

Also called 'anterior', 'motor', or 'Broca's' dysphasia. (See Box 8.4.)
- Lesion in Broca's area (frontal lobe), involved in language production.
- Understanding remains intact.
- Unable to answer questions appropriately.
- Speech is non-fluent, broken with abnormal word ordering.
- Unable to repeat sentences.

> **Box 8.4 Communicating in expressive dysphasia**
>
> This can be very distressing for patients.
> Relatives and others often try to get the patient to write things down,
> unaware that the problem is *language*, and are disappointed to find the
> attempts at writing are just as garbled as the speech.
> Some helpful tips include:
> - Do not pretend to understand, tell the patient what you can and
>   cannot guess at and ask if you've got it right
> - Encourage other means of communication including body language
>   and hand signals. The patient is often still able to draw diagrams.

Receptive dysphasia

Also called 'posterior', 'sensory', or 'Wernicke's' dysphasia.
- Lesion in Wernicke's area creates problems understanding spoken or
  written language (dyslexia) and problems with word-finding.
- Unable to understand commands or questions.
- Speech is fluent with lots of meaningless grammatical elements.
- May contain meaningless words.
- Unable to repeat sentences.
- Patients are often unaware of their speech difficulty and will talk
  nonsense contentedly—although may become frustrated with other
  people's lack of understanding.
  - 'Jargon dysphasia' describes a severe form of receptive dysphasia
    containing only meaningless words ('neologisms') and sounds
  - Paraphasia is the substitution of one word with another.

Conductive dysphasia

Lesion in the arcuate fasciculus and/or other connections between the two
primary language areas.
- Patient can comprehend and respond appropriately.
- Unable to repeat a sentence.

Nominal dysphasia

- All language function is intact *except* for naming of objects.
- Caused by lesion at the angular gyrus.
- Patient may function with 'circumlocution' (e.g. says 'that thing that
  I write with' if unable to say 'pen').

Global dysphasia

- Both Broca's and Wernicke's areas affected. The patient is unable to
  speak or understand speech at all.

Cranial nerve examination

The following part of the chapter describes the individual examination of each cranial nerve in turn. In practice (and in exam circumstances), these are usually examined together in a fluid manner.

The student should know the ins and outs of each cranial nerve examination and develop their own method of going from one to the next that suits them and the patients.

Cranial nerves II, III, IV, and VI

The examination of the II (optic), III (oculomotor), IV (trochlear), and VI (abducens) nerves is covered in detail in ➔ Chapter 9.

Turn to the eye chapter for:
- Visual acuity.
- Visual fields.
- The pupils.
- Eye movements.
  - III, IV, and VI palsies
  - Other eye movement disorders.
- Ophthalmoscopy and the use of the ophthalmoscope.
  - Anterior segment examination
  - Posterior segment examination (including fundoscopy).

Cranial nerve I: olfactory

Applied anatomy

Sensory: smell
Motor: none

Fibres arise in the mucous membrane of the nose. Axons pass across the cribiform plate to the olfactory bulb. The olfactory tract runs backwards below the frontal lobe and projects, mainly, in the uncus of the ipsilateral temporal lobe.

Note: olfactory epithelium also contains free nerve endings of the 1st division of cranial nerve V.

Examination

Not routinely tested unless the patient complains of a loss of sense of smell (anosmia) and exhibits other signs suggestive of a frontal or temporal lobe cause (e.g. tumour).

- *Casual:* take a nearby odorous object (e.g. coffee or chocolate) and ask the patient if it smells normal.
- *Formal:* a series of identical bottles containing recognizable smells are used. The patient is asked to identify them. Commonly used agents: coffee, vanilla, camphor, vinegar.
- Test each nostril separately and determine if any loss of smell is uni- or bilateral.

Findings

- *Bilateral anosmia:* usually nasal, not neurological.
  - Causes include upper respiratory tract infection, trauma, smoking, old age, and Parkinson's disease. Less commonly, tumours of the ethmoid bones or congenital ciliary dysmotility syndromes.
- *Unilateral anosmia:* mucus-blocked nostril, head trauma, subfrontal meningioma.

▶ Hints and tips

Peppermint, ammonia, and menthol stimulate the free trigeminal endings so are not a good test of cranial nerve I.

Cranial nerve V: trigeminal

Applied anatomy

Sensory: facial sensation in three branches—ophthalmic (V1), maxillary (V2), mandibular (V3). Distribution shown in Fig. 8.1

Motor: muscles of mastication

Nerve originates in the pons, travels to trigeminal ganglion at the petrous temporal bone and splits. V_1 passes through the cavernous sinus with III and exits via the superior orbital fissure; V_2 leaves via the infraorbital foramen (also supplies the palate and nasopharynx); V_3 exits via the foramen ovale with the motor portion.

Examination

Inspection

Inspect the patient's face—wasting of the temporalis will show as hollowing above the zygomatic arch.

Testing motor function

- Ask the patient to clench their teeth and feel both sides for the bulge of the masseter and temporalis.
- Ask the patient to open their mouth wide—the jaw will deviate towards the side of a V lesion.
- Again ask them to open their mouth but provide resistance by holding their jaw closed with one of your hands.

Testing sensory function

- Assess light touch for each branch and ask the patient to say 'yes' if they can feel it.
  - Choose three spots to test on each side to make the examination easy to remember—forehead, cheek, and mid-way along jaw.
- For each branch, compare left to right. Ignore minor differences (it's rather difficult to press with exactly the same force each time!).
- Test pin-prick sensation at the same spots using a sterile pin.
- Temperature sensation is not routinely tested—consider only if abnormalities in light touch or pin-prick are found. Use specimen tubes or other small containers full of warm or cold water.

Findings

- Wasting of muscles: long-term V palsy, MND, myotonic dystrophy.
- Loss of all sensory modalities: V ganglion lesion (?herpes zoster).
- Loss of light touch only—with loss of sensation on ipsilateral side of the body: contralateral parietal lobe (sensory cortex) lesion.
- Loss of light touch in V only: lesion at sensory root pons.
- Loss of pin-prick only—along with contralateral side of body: ipsilateral brainstem lesion.
- Loss of sensation in a 'muzzle' distribution (nose, lips, anterior cheeks): damage to the lower part of the spinal sensory nucleus (syringomyelia, demyelination).

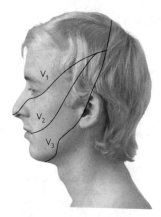

Fig. 8.1 Distribution of the sensory branches of the trigeminal nerve. V_1 = ophthalmic, V_2 = maxillary, V_3 = mandibular. Note that V_1 extends to the vertex and includes the cornea and V_3 does not include the angle of the jaw.

Reflexes

Jaw jerk

- 🛈 Explain to the patient what is about to happen as this could appear rather threatening.
- Ask the patient to let their mouth hang loosely open.
- Place your finger horizontally across their chin and tap your finger with a patella hammer.
- Feel and watch jaw movement.
  - There should be a slight closure of the jaw but this varies widely in normal people. A brisk and definite closure may indicate a UMN lesion above the level of the pons (e.g. pseudobulbar palsy).

Corneal reflex

Afferent = V_1, efferent = VII.

- Ask the patient to look up and away from you.
- Gently touch the cornea with a wisp of cotton wool. Bring this in from the side so it cannot be seen approaching.
- Watch both eyes. A blink is a normal response.
  - No response = ipsilateral V_1 palsy
  - Lack of blink on one side only = VII palsy.
- ▶ Watch out for contact lenses!—will give reduced sensation. Ask the patient to remove them first.

▶ Hints and tips

- Note the sensory distribution! The angle of the jaw is **not** supplied by V_3 but by the great auricular nerve (C2, C3).
- When testing the corneal reflex, touch the **cornea** (overlies the iris), not the conjunctiva (overlies the sclera).

Cranial nerve VII: facial

Applied anatomy

Sensory: external auditory meatus, tympanic membrane, small portion of skin behind ear. Special sensation: taste anterior 2/3 of tongue
Motor: muscles of facial expression, stapedius
Autonomic: parasympathetic supply to lacrimal glands

The nucleus lies in the pons, the nerve leaves at the cerebellopontine angle with VIII. The nerve gives off a branch to the stapedius at the geniculate ganglion whilst the majority of the nerve leaves the skull via the stylomastoid foramen and travels through the parotid gland.

Examination

Muscles of facial expression

Here, you test both left and right at the same time. Some patients have difficulty understanding the instructions—the authors recommend a quick demonstration following each command allowing the patient to mirror you (e.g. 'puff out your cheeks like this...'). This exam can be rather embarrassing—the examiner pulling equally strange faces lightens the mood and aids the patient's co-operation and enthusiasm. (See Fig. 8.2.)

- Look at the patient's face at rest. Look for asymmetry in the nasolabial folds, angles of the mouth, and forehead wrinkles.
- Ask the patient to raise their eyebrows ('look up!') and watch the forehead wrinkle.
- Attempt to push their eyebrows down and note any weakness.
- Ask the patient to 'close your eyes tightly'. Watch, then test against resistance with your finger and thumb. 'Don't let me pull them apart.'
- Ask the patient to blow out their cheeks. Watch for air escaping on one side.
- Ask the patient to bare their teeth. 'Show me your teeth!' Look for asymmetry.
- Ask the patient to purse their lips. 'Whistle for me!' Look for asymmetry. The patient will always smile after whistling (see below).

The 'whistle-smile' sign

A failure to smile when asked to whistle (whistle-smile negative) is usually due to 'emotional paresis' of the facial muscles and is synonymous with Parkinsonism.

External auditory meatus

This should be examined briefly if only VII is examined—can be done as part of VIII if examining all the cranial nerves.

Taste

This is rarely tested outside specialist clinics.

- Each side is tested separately by using cotton buds dipped in the solution of choice applied to each side of the tongue in turn. Be sure to swill the mouth with distilled water between each taste sensation.
- Test: sweet, salty, bitter (quinine), and sour (vinegar).

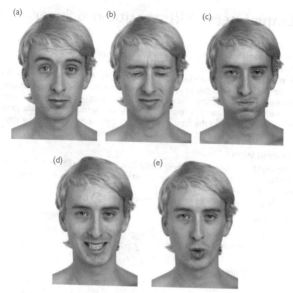

Fig. 8.2 Testing the muscles of facial expression as described on ➔ p. 254.
(a) Eyebrows; (b) eyelids; (c) puffing out the cheeks; (d) baring teeth; (e) whistle.

Findings

- *Upper motor nerve lesion:* will cause loss of facial movement on the contralateral side but with preservation of forehead wrinkling—both sides of the forehead receive bilateral nervous supply. (Unilateral = CVA, etc. Bilateral = pseudobulbar palsy, motor neuron disease).
- *Lower motor nerve lesion:* will cause loss of all movement on the ipsilateral side of the face (unilateral = demyelination, tumours, Bell's palsy, pontine lesions, cerebellopontine angle lesions; bilateral = sarcoid, GBS, myasthenia gravis).
- *Bell's palsy:* idiopathic unilateral LMN VII paresis.
- *Ramsay–Hunt syndrome:* unilateral paresis caused by herpes at the geniculate ganglion (look for herpes rash on the external ear).

▶ Hints and tips

- *Bell's phenomenon* is the upward movement of the eyeballs when the eye closes. This occurs in the normal state but can be clearly seen if the eyelids fail to close due to VII palsy.
- VII palsy does *not* cause eyelid ptosis.
- Longstanding VII palsy can cause fibrous contraction of the muscles on the affected side resulting in more pronounced nasolabial fold (the reverse of the expected findings).
- Bilateral VII palsy will cause a sagging, expressionless face and is often missed.

Cranial nerve VIII: vestibulocochlear

Applied anatomy

Sensory: hearing (cochlear), balance/equilibrium (vestibular)

Motor: none

The 8th nerve comprises two parts. The cochlear branch originates in the organ of Corti in the ear, passes through the internal auditory meatus to its nucleus in the pons. Fibres pass to the superior gyrus of the temporal lobes.

The vestibular branch arises in the utricle and semicircular canals, joins the auditory fibres in the facial canal, enters the brainstem at the cerebellopontine angle, and ends in the pons and cerebellum.

Examination

Enquire first about symptoms—hearing loss/changes or balance problems. Peripheral vestibular lesions cause ataxia during paroxysms of vertigo but not at other times.

- Begin by inspecting each ear as described in ➲ Chapter 11.

Hearing

Test each ear separately. Cover one by pressing on the tragus or create white noise by rubbing your fingers together at the external auditory meatus.

Simple test of hearing

- Whisper a number into one ear and ask the patient to repeat it.
- Repeat with the other ear.
- Be careful to whisper at the same volume in each ear (the end of expiration is best) and at the same distance (about 60cm).

Rinne's test

- Tap a 512Hz* tuning fork and hold adjacent to the ear (air conduction, Fig. 8.3a).
- Then apply the base of the tuning fork to the mastoid process (bone conduction)—see Fig. 8.3b.
- Ask the patient which position sounds louder.
  - Normal = air conduction > bone conduction = 'Rinne's positive'
  - In neural (or perceptive) deafness, Rinne's test will remain positive
  - In conductive deafness, the findings are reversed (bone > air).

Weber's test

- Tap a 512Hz tuning fork and hold the base against the vertex or forehead at the midline (see Fig. 8.3c).
- Ask the patient if it sounds louder on one side.
  - In neural deafness, the tone is heard better in the intact ear
  - In conductive deafness, the tone is heard better in the affected ear.

---

* This is the 'C' above 'middle C' for those who like to know such things.

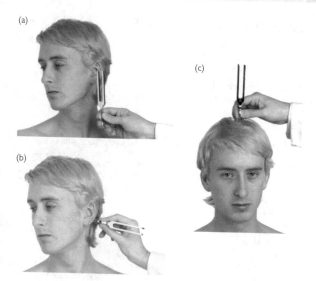

Fig. 8.3 (a) Testing air conduction. (b) Testing bone conduction. (c) Position of the tuning fork for Weber's test.

Vestibular function

Turning test

- Ask the patient to stand facing you, arms outstretched.
- Ask them to march on the spot, then close their eyes (continue marching).
- Watch!
  - The patient will gradually turn toward the side of the lesion—sometimes will turn right round 180°.

Hallpike's manoeuvre

A test for benign positional vertigo (BPV). Do **not** test those with known neck problems or possible posterior circulation impairment.

- Warn the patient about what is to happen.
- Sit the patient facing away from the edge of the bed such that when they lie back their head will not be supported (over the edge).
- Turn their head to one side and ask them to look in that direction.
- Lie them back quickly—supporting their head so that it lies about 30° below the horizontal.
- Watch for nystagmus (affected ear will be lowermost).
- Repeat with the head turned in the other direction.
  - No nystagmus = normal
  - Nystagmus, with a slight delay (~10 secs) and fatigable (can't be repeated successfully for ~10–15 minutes) = BPV
  - Nystagmus, no delay, and no fatiguing = central vestibular syndrome.

Cranial nerves IX and X

The 9th (glossopharyngeal) and 10th (vagus) nerves are considered together as they have similar functions and work together to control pharynx, larynx, and swallow.

Applied anatomy: IX

Sensory: pharynx, middle ear. Special sensation: taste on posterior 1/3 of tongue
Motor: stylopharyngeus
Autonomic: parotid gland
Originates in the medulla, passes through the jugular foramen.

Applied anatomy: X

Sensory: tympanic membrane, external auditory canal, and external ear. Also proprioception from thorax and abdomen
Motor: palate, pharynx, and larynx
Autonomic: carotid baroreceptors
Originates in medulla and pons, leaves the skull via jugular foramen.

Examination

Pharynx

- Ask the patient to open their mouth and inspect the uvula (use a tongue depressor if necessary). Is it central or deviated to one side? If so, which side?
- Ask the patient to say 'aah'. Watch the uvula. It should move upwards centrally. Does it deviate to one side?

Gag reflex

This is unpleasant for the patient and should only be tested if a IX or X nerve lesion is suspected (afferent signal = IX, efferent = X).

- With the patient's mouth open wide, gently touch the posterior pharyngeal wall on one side with a tongue depressor or other sterile stick.
- Watch the uvula (it should lift up).
- Repeat on the opposite side.
- Ask the patient if they felt the 2 touches—and was there any difference in sensation?

Larynx

- Ask the patient to cough—normal character? Gradual onset/sudden?
- Listen to the patient's speech—note volume, quality, and whether it appears to fatigue (quieter as time goes on).
- Test swallow:
  - At each stage, watch the swallow action—two phases or one smooth movement? Delay between fluid leaving mouth (oral phase) and pharynx/larynx reacting (pharyngeal phase)? Any coughing/choking? Any 'wet' voice?
  - ▶ Terminate the test at the first sign of the patient aspirating
  - Offer the patient a teaspoon of water to swallow. Repeat × 3
  - Offer the patient a sip of water. Repeat × 3
  - Offer the patient the glass for a mouthful of water. Repeat × 3.

Findings

Uvula

- Moves to one side = X lesion on the *opposite* side.
- No movement = muscle paresis.
- Moves with 'aah' but not gag and ↓ pharyngeal sensation = IX palsy.

Cough

- Gradual onset of a deliberate cough = vocal cord palsy.
- 'Wet', bubbly voice and cough (before the swallow test) = pharyngeal and vocal cord palsy (X palsy).
- Poor swallow and aspiration = combined IX and X or lone X lesion.

Cranial nerve XI: accessory

Applied anatomy

Sensory: none
Motor: sternocleidomastoids and upper part of trapezii
The accessory nerve is composed of 'cranial' and 'spinal' parts.

The cranial accessory nerve arises from the nucleus ambiguus in the medulla. The spinal accessory nerve arises from the lateral part of the spinal cord down to C5 as a series of rootlets. These join together and ascend adjacent to the spinal cord, passing through the foramen magnum to join with the cranial portion of the accessory nerve. It leaves the skull via the jugular foramen.

The cranial portion joins with the vagus nerve (X).

The spinal portion innervates the sternocleidomastoids and the upper fibres of the trapezii.

▶ Note that each cerebral hemisphere controls the ipsilateral sternocleidomastoid and the contralateral trapezius.

Examination

The cranial portion of the accessory nerve cannot be tested separately.
- Inspect the sternocleidomastoids. Look for wasting, fasciculation, hypertrophy, and any abnormal head position.
- Ask the patient to shrug their shoulders and observe.
- Ask the patient to shrug again, using your hands on their shoulders to provide resistance.
- Ask the patient to turn their head to each side, first without and then with resistance (use your hand on their cheek).

Findings

Isolated accessory nerve lesions are very rare. XI lesions usually present as part of a wider weakness or neurological syndrome.
- Bilateral weakness: with wasting caused by muscular problems or motor neuron disease.
- Unilateral weakness (trapezius and sternomastoid same side): suggests a peripheral neurological lesion.
- Unilateral weakness (trapezius and sternomastoid of opposite sides): usually with hemiplegia suggests a UMN lesion ipsilateral to the weak sternomastoid.

Hints and tips

- Remember that the action of the sternocleidomastoid is to turn the head to the *opposite* side (e.g. poor head turning to the *left* indicates a weak *right* sternocleidomastoid).
- When providing resistance to head turning, be sure to press against the patient's cheek. Lateral pressure to the jaw can cause pain and injury, particularly in the elderly and frail.

Cranial nerve XII: hypoglossal

Applied anatomy

Sensory: none

Motor: muscles of the tongue

Nucleus lies on the floor of IV ventricle. Fibres pass ventrally, leaving the brainstem lateral to the pyramidal tracts. Leaves the skull via the hypoglossal foramen.

Examination

- Ask the patient to open wide and inspect the tongue on the floor of the mouth. Look for size and evidence of fasciculation.
- Ask the patient to protrude the tongue. Look for deviation or abnormal movements.
- Ask the patient to move the tongue in and out repeatedly, then side to side.
- To test for subtle weakness, place your finger on the patient's cheek and ask them to push against it from the inside using their tongue.

Findings

- An LMN neuron lesion will cause fasciculation on the affected side and a deviation towards the affected side on protrusion. There will also be a weakness on pressing the tongue away from the affected side.
- A unilateral UMN lesion will rarely cause any clinically obvious signs.
- A bilateral UMN lesion will give a small, globally weak tongue with reduced movements.
- A bilateral LMN lesion (e.g. motor neuron disease) will also produce a small, weak tongue.
- A rapid 'in and out' movement on protrusion (trombone tremor) can be caused by cerebellar disease, extra-pyramidal syndromes, and essential tremor.

▶ Hints and tips

- Rippling movements may be seen if the tongue is held protruded for long periods. This is normal and should not be mistaken for fasciculation.

Motor: applied anatomy

The motor system is complex and a detailed description is beyond the scope of this book. What follows is a brief overview. (See Box 8.5 also.)

Cortex

The primary motor area is the precentral gyrus of the cerebrum and it is here, along with adjacent cerebral areas, that initiation of voluntary movement occurs. Muscle groups are represented by areas of the cortex from medial to lateral as shown in Fig. 8.4. The size of the area dedicated to muscle corresponds with the precision of movement (= the number of motor units) that are involved.

Pyramidal (direct) pathways

These are concerned with precise, voluntary movements of the face, vocal cords, hands, and feet.

The simplest pathways consist of two neurons. The first 'upper motor neuron' (UMN) originates in the cerebral cortex, passes down through the internal capsule, brainstem, and spinal cord where it synapses with a 'lower motor neuron' (LMN). This, in turn, leaves the cord to synapse with the skeletal muscle fibres.

- There are three pyramidal tracts:
- *Lateral corticospinal:* control of precise movement in the hands and feet and represents 90% of the UMN axons. These cross over (decussate) in the medulla oblongata before continuing to descend so that nerves from the right side of the brain control muscles on the left of the body and vice versa.
- *Anterior corticospinal:* control of the neck and trunk and holds 10% of the UMN axons. These do not cross in the medulla but descend in the anterior white columns of the spinal cord. They decussate at several spinal levels and exit at the cervical and upper thoracic segments.
- *Corticobulbar:* voluntary muscles of the eyes, face, tongue, neck, and speech. Terminate at nuclei in the pons and medulla, some crossed, others not. Control of cranial nerves III, IV, V, VI, VII, IX, X, XI, and XII.

Extrapyramidal (indirect) pathways

All the other descending pathways. These are complex circuits involving the cortex, limbic system, basal ganglia, cerebellum, and cranial nerve nuclei. There are five major tracts controlling precise movements of the hands and feet, movement of the head and eyes in response to visual stimuli, muscle tone, and truncal stability and balance.

Basal ganglia/nuclei: complex circuits concerned with the production of automatic movement, planning movement sequences. Also appear to inhibit intrinsically excitable circuits.

Cerebellum

Involved in learning and performing skilled, automatic movements (e.g. running, playing the piano), posture, and balance. Monitors intention, receives signals as to actual movements, compares the difference, and makes corrective adjustments.

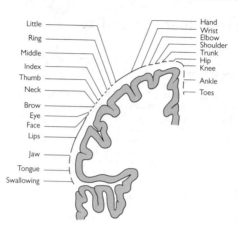

Fig. 8.4 Coronal section through the motor cortex showing the representation of different muscle groups. Note the larger areas given to those muscles performing precise movements—hands, face, lips.

Box 8.5 Functional weakness

Large parts of the neurological examination rely on the cooperation of the patient. Occasionally, patients give the appearance of neurological disability which does not exist—for any number of psychiatric or psychosocial reasons. The examination here is very difficult even for very experienced practitioners. Consider a 'functional' component to the problem if you see:

- Abnormal distribution of weakness
- Normal reflexes and tone despite weakness
- Movements are variable and power erratic
- Variation is seen on repeat testing.

❗ Careful! Don't jump to conclusions. Do not assume symptoms are functional if they are unusual. All patients should be given the benefit of the doubt. 'Functional' weakness is a diagnosis largely of exclusion.

Motor: inspection and tone

Inspection

As for any other system, the examination begins when you first set eyes on the patient and continues through the history taking.

- Any walking aids or abnormal gait?
- Shake hands—abnormalities of movement? Strength? Relaxation?
- Any abnormal movements when sitting?
- Any obvious weaknesses (e.g. hemiplegia)?
- Does the patient have good sitting balance?

Inspection can then be formalized at the examination stage of the encounter. The patient should be seated or lying comfortably with as much of their body exposed as possible. Look at all muscle groups for:

- Abnormal positioning—due to weakness or contractures.
- Wasting.
- Fasciculation (irregular contractions of small areas of muscle).

Make a point of inspecting the shoulder girdle, small muscles of the hand, quadriceps, anterior compartment of lower leg and ankle.

Look at the foot for contractures or abnormalities of shape.

Tone

The aim is to test resting tone in the limbs. This takes practice and the feel of normal, ↓, or ↑ tone can only be learned through experience. (See Fig. 8.5.)

❶ The assessment can be difficult as it relies on the patient being relaxed and telling the patient to relax usually has the opposite effect! They can be distracted by a counting task or told to relax the limb 'as if you're asleep'. However, distracting the patient with light conversation is a generally successful ploy. You should also repeat the following manoeuvres at different speeds and intervals to catch the patient at an unguarded moment.

Arms

- Take the patient's hand in yours (as if shaking it) and hold their elbow with your other hand (see Fig. 8.5a). From this position, you can:
  - Pronate and supinate the patient's forearm
  - Roll the patient's wrist through 360°
  - Flex and extend the patient's elbow.

Legs

- *Hip:* with the patient lying flat, legs straight, hold on to the patient's knee and roll it from side to side (see Fig. 8.5b).
- *Knee:* with the patient in the same position, put your hand behind the patient's knee and raise it quickly (Fig. 8.5c). Watch the heel—it should lift from the bed/couch slightly if tone is normal.
- *Ankle:* holding the foot and the lower leg, flex and dorsiflex the ankle (Fig. 8.5d).

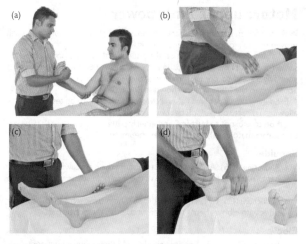

Fig. 8.5 Testing tone. (a) Testing the upper limb. (b) Testing tone at the hip.
(c) Testing tone at the knee. (d) Testing tone at the ankle.

Findings

- *Normal tone:* slight resistance in movement (feel through experience).
- ↓ *tone:* 'flaccid' due to LMN or cerebellar lesions or myopathies.
- ↑ *tone:*
  - *Spasticity (clasp-knife rigidity):* the limb appears stiff. With ↑ pressure, there is a sudden 'give' and the limb moves. Seen in UMN lesions
  - *Rigidity (lead-pipe):* the limb is equally stiff through all movements
  - *Rigidity (cogwheel):* an extrapyramidal sign, caused by a tremor superimposed on a rigid limb. The limb moves in a stop–go halting fashion
  - *Gegenhalten:* (paratonia) seen in bilateral frontal lobe damage and catatonic states. Tone ↑ with ↑ pressure from the examiner—the patient appears to be resisting movement
  - *Myotonia:* a slow relaxation after action—when asked to make a fist, the patient is unable to release it quickly and will be slow to let go of a hand-shake (e.g. myotonic dystrophy)
  - *Dystonia:* the limb or head has an abnormal posture that looks rather uncomfortable.

Motor: upper limb power

▶ As for the muscles of the face, the examiner should demonstrate each movement, mirroring the patient (see Fig. 8.6).

This also allows each action that the patient makes to be opposed by the same (or similar) muscle groups in the examiner—test their fingers against your fingers and so on. Each muscle group should be graded from 0 to 5 according to the MRC system shown in Box 8.6.

Examining the upper limbs also allows for both sides to be tested at once, allowing a direct comparison between left and right.

❶ Be careful not to hurt frail and elderly patients or those with osteoarthritis, rheumatoid arthritis, and other rheumatological disease.

Shoulder

- *Abduction:* (C5). Ask the patient to abduct their arms with elbows bent. 'Arms up like a chicken!' Ask them to hold still as you attempt to push their arms down.
- *Adduction:* (C6, C7). The patient should hold their arms tightly to their sides with elbows bent. You attempt to push their arms out.

Elbow

- *Flexion:* (C5, C6). The patient should hold their elbows bent and supinated in front of them. Hold the patient at the elbow and wrist and attempt to extend their arm. 'Don't let me straighten your arm!'
- *Extension:* (C7). Patient holds position above as you resist extension at the elbow by pushing on their distal forearm/wrist. 'Push me away!'

Wrist

- *Flexion:* (C6, C7). With arms supinated, the patient should flex the wrist and hold as you attempt to extend it by pulling from your own wrists.
- *Extension:* (C6, C7). The opposite manoeuvre to that above. The patient holds their hand out straight and resists your attempts to bend it.

Fingers

- *Flexion:* (C8). Ask the patient to squeeze your fingers or (better) ask the patient to grip your fingers palm-to-palm (see Fig. 8.6c) and resist your attempts to pull their hand open.
- *Extension:* (C7, C8). Ask the patient to hold their fingers out straight—you support their wrist with one hand and attempt to push their fingers down with the side of your hand over their first interphalangeal joints.
- *Abduction:* (T1). Ask the patient to splay their fingers out and resist your attempts to push them together.
- *Adduction:* (T1). Holding the patient's middle, ring, and little finger with one hand and their index finger with the other, ask the patient to pull their fingers together or place a piece of paper between their outstretched fingers and ask them to resist your attempts to pull it away.

Pronator drift

A useful test of subtle weakness. The patient is asked to hold their arms outstretched in front, palms upwards and eyes closed. If one side is weak, the arm will pronate and slowly drift downwards.

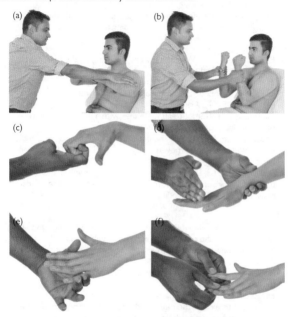

Fig. 8.6 Testing power in the upper limbs. (a) Shoulder movements. (b) Elbow movements. (c) Finger flexion. (d) Finger extension. (e) Finger abduction. (f) Finger adduction.

Box 8.6 Medical Research Council (MRC) power classification

- 5 = Normal power
- 4 = Movement against resistance but not 'full' normal power
- 3 = Movement against gravity, but not against resistance
- 2 = Movement with gravity eliminated (e.g. can move leg side to side on bed but not lift it)
- 1 = Muscle contractions but no movement seen
- 0 = No movement or muscular contraction

► The authors see an increasing number of power scores such as '4+' and '4–' in patients' notes. We find it hard to believe that someone can differentiate between 4+, 4 and 4–. There are either some very impressive clinicians about or people are attempting to be a little too precise in their scoring. Stick to whole numbers as described above.

Motor: lower limb power

The patient should be seated on a couch or bed with their legs outstretched in front of them. The limbs should be exposed as much as possible so that contractions of the muscles can be seen. (See Fig. 8.7.)

Again, power is tested for each muscle group on one side then the other, comparing left with right and scored according to the MRC scale.

Hip

- *Flexion:* (L1, L2, L3). With the lower limbs lying on the bed/couch, the patient is asked to raise each leg, keeping the knee straight. The examiner can oppose the movement by pushing down on the thigh just above the knee. 'Stop me from pushing down!'
- *Extension:* (L5, S1). Ask the patient to keep their leg pressed against the bed as you attempt to lift it—either with a hand beneath the calf or the ankle. 'Stop me lifting your leg up!'
- *Abduction:* (L4, L5, S1). Ask the patient to move their leg out to the side as you oppose the movement with a hand on the lateral thigh. 'Stop me pushing your legs together!'
- *Adduction:* (L2, L3, L4). With the legs central, put your hand on the medial thigh and attempt to pull the leg out to the side against resistance. 'Don't let me pull your legs apart!'

Knee

- *Flexion:* (L5, S1). Take hold of the patient's knee with one hand and their ankle with the other and flex the leg to about 60°. (The patient may think you want them to resist this so often a quick instruction 'bend at the knee' is required.) Ask the patient to bend their leg further ('stop me straightening your leg out') and oppose the movement at their ankle.
- *Extension:* (L3, L4). With the patient's leg in the position above, ask the patient to extend their leg ('push me away', 'straighten your leg out') as you oppose it. Alternatively, attempt to bend the patient's leg from a straightened starting position.

Ankle

- *Plantar flexion:* (S1, S2). With the patient's leg out straight and ankle relaxed, put your hand on the ball of the foot and ask the patient to push you away. 'Push down and stop me pushing back!'
- *Dorsiflexion:* (L4, L5). From the starting position above, hold the patient's foot just above the toes and ask them to pull their foot backwards. Patients often attempt to move their entire leg here so 'cock your foot back and stop me pushing your foot down' with an accompanying hand gesture helps.

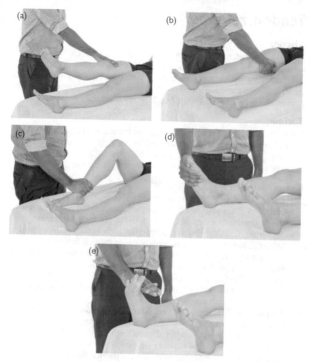

Fig. 8.7 Testing power in the lower limb against resistance. (a) Flexing the hip. (b) Extending the hip. (c) Flexing/extending the knee. (d) Plantar flexion at the ankle. (e) Dorsiflexion at the ankle.

Tendon reflexes

Theory

The sudden stretch of a muscle is detected by the muscle spindle which initiates a simple 2 neuron reflex arc, causing that muscle to contract.

Tendons are struck with a tendon hammer (causing a sudden stretch of the muscle) and the resultant contraction observed. In LMN lesions or myopathies, the reflex is ↓ or absent, but ↑ or 'brisk' in UMN lesions.

Technique

For each reflex, test the right, then left and compare. The hammer should be held at the far end of the handle and swung in a loose movement from the wrist (Fig. 8.8). The patient should be relaxed (see notes on patient relaxation under 'inspection and tone' earlier in this chapter).

Examination

- *Biceps:* (C5, C6). With the patient seated, lie their arms across their abdomen. Place your thumb across the biceps tendon and strike it with the tendon hammer as above. Watch the biceps for contraction.
- *Supinator:* (C5, C6). The muscle tested is actually the brachioradialis. With the patient's arms lying loosely across their abdomen, put your fingers on the radial tuberosity and tap with the hammer. The arm will flex at the elbow. If brisk, the fingers may also flex.
- *Triceps:* (C7). Taking hold of the patient's wrist, flex their arm to ~90°. Tap the triceps tendon about 5cm superior to the olecranon process of the ulna. Watch the triceps.
- *Fingers:* (C8). This is only present if tone is pathologically ↑. With your palm up and the patient's arm pronated, lie their fingers on yours. Strike the back of your fingers. The patient's fingers will flex.
- *Knee:* (L3, L4). With the patient's leg extended, use one hand behind their knee to lift their leg to ~60°. Tap the patella tendon and watch the quadriceps. If brisk, proceed to testing for clonus here:
  - *Knee clonus:* with the patient's leg extended, place your thumb and index finger over the superior edge of the patella. Create a sudden downward (toward the feet) movement, and hold. Watch the quadriceps. Any beat of clonus here is abnormal.
- *Ankle:* (S1, S2). With the hip flexed and externally rotated and the knee flexed to ~90°, hold the foot and tap the Achilles tendon. Watch the calf muscles for contraction/ankle flexion.
  - Alternatively, with the leg extended and relaxed, place your hand on the ball of the foot and strike your hand with the hammer.

Reinforcement

If the reflex is absent, it can sometimes be elicited by asking the patient to perform a 'reinforcing' action which acts to increase the activity of neurons in the spinal cord. This effect is short-lived, however, so you should aim to test the reflex in the first 10 seconds of the reinforcement.

- For upper limb reflexes, ask the patient to clench their teeth.
- For lower limb reflexes, ask the patient to lock their fingers together, pulling in opposite directions.

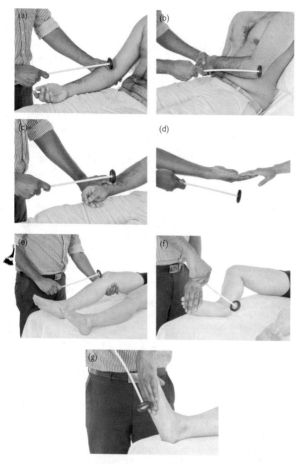

Fig. 8.8 Testing tendon reflexes. (a) Biceps. (b) Triceps. (c) Supinator. (d) Fingers. (e) Knee. (f) Ankle. (g) Alternative method for ankle.

Recording tendon reflexes

These are usually recorded as a list—or often by applying the numbers to the appropriate area of a stick-man sketch

- 0 = absent
- ± = present only with reinforcement
- 1+ = reduced/less than normal
- 2+ = normal
- 3+ = brisk/more than normal.

Other reflexes

In normal practice, the plantar response is the only one of the following routinely tested.

Plantar response

(L5, S1, S2.) This is sometimes, inappropriately, called the Babinski reflex.

- The patient should be lying comfortably, legs outstretched.
- Warn the patient that you are about to touch the sole of their foot.
- Stroke the patient's sole—with an orange stick or similar disposable item (don't use your fingernail!).
- You should stroke from the heel, up the lateral aspect of the sole to the base of the 5th toe. If there is no response, the stroke can be continued along the ball of the foot to the base of the big toe.
- Watch the big toe for its *initial* movement.
  - Normal response is plantar flexion of the big toe
  - Upper motor nerve lesions will cause the big toe to dorsiflex. This is 'the Babinski response'.
- Document your findings using arrows:
  - ↓ for plantar flexion, ↑ for dorsiflexion, – for an absent response.
- If the leg is withdrawn and the heel moves in a 'ticklish' reaction, this is called a 'withdrawal' response and the test should be repeated.

Ankle clonus

- A rhythmical contraction of a muscle when suddenly stretched—a sign of hyperreflexia due to UMN lesion. With the patient lying on the bed, knee straight and thigh slightly externally rotated, suddenly dorsiflex the foot. More than three beats of clonus—as long as the foot is held dorsiflexed—is abnormal.

Abdominal reflex

(The upper segments are supplied by T8–T9, the lower by T10–T11.) This test relies on observing the abdominal muscles and is, therefore, less easy in those with a covering of fat. It is also less obvious in children, the elderly, multiparous patients, or those who have had abdominal surgery.

- The patient should be lying on their back, abdomen exposed.
- Using an orange stick or similar, stroke each of the 4 segments of the abdomen, in a brief movement towards the umbilicus.
- As each segment is stroked, abdominal muscles will reflexly contract.
- Summarize the findings diagrammatically using a simple 2×2 grid and indicating the presence or absence of a response by marking '+' and '–' respectively. ('±' for an intermediate response).

Cremasteric reflex

(L1, L2.) Due to its nature, this reflex is very rarely tested and requires a full explanation and consent from the patient first.

- With the male patient standing and naked from the waist down, you should lightly stroke the upper aspect of their inner thigh.
- The ipsilateral cremaster muscle contracts and the testicle will briefly rise.

Primitive reflexes

These are reflexes seen in the newborn—but may still be present in a few normal adults. They return somewhat in the elderly but are seen mainly in frontal lobe disease and encephalopathy.

The primitive reflexes are not routinely tested unless the examiner is looking specifically for frontal lobe signs or Parkinson's disease.

Glabellar tap

- Using your index finger, repeatedly tap (gently) the patient's forehead between the eyebrows.
- If normal, the patient will blink only with the first three or four taps.

Palmo-mental reflex

- You should stroke the patient's palm, using sharp firm pressure from the radial side to the ulnar.
- Watch the patient's chin.
- If the reflex is present, there will be a contraction of the ipsilateral mentalis seen in the neck and chin.

Grasp reflex

- Gently stroke your fingers over the patient's palm in a radial–ulnar direction, telling the patient *not* to grip your hand.
- If present, the patient will involuntarily grasp your hand and seemingly refuse to let go.

Snout (or pout) reflex

- With the patient's eyes closed, gently tap their lips with your fingers or (very cautiously) with a patellar hammer.
- An involuntary puckering of the lips is a positive reflex.

Suckling reflex

- With the patient's eyes closed, gentle stimulation at the corner of their mouth will result in a suckling action at the mouth. The patient's head may also turn towards the stimulus.

Sensory: applied anatomy

The sensory system, like the rest of the nervous system, is vastly complex. The following is a simplified explanation which should provide enough background to make sense of the examination technique and findings.

Spinal roots and dermatomes

A spinal nerve arises at each spinal level, containing sensory and motor neurons serving a specific segment of the body. The area of skin supplied by the sensory neurons corresponding to each spinal level can be mapped out—each segment is called a dermatome. See Figs 8.10 and 8.11.

There is considerable overlap such that loss of sensation in just one dermatome is usually not testable (and textbooks show a marked variation in dermatome maps!). Medical students should strive to become familiar with the dermatomal distribution at an early stage.

Somatic sensory pathways

There are two main spinal pathways for sensory impulses. The clinical importance of these can be seen in spinal cord damage and is summarized later in this chapter.

Posterior columns

These convey light touch, proprioception, and vibration sense—as well as stereognosis (the ability to recognize an object by touch), weight discrimination, and kinaesthesia (the perception of movement).

Nerves from receptors extend up the ipsilateral side of the spinal cord to the medulla, their axons forming the 'posterior columns' (fasciculus gracilis and fasciculus cuneatus). The second order neurons decussate (cross over) at the medulla and travel in the medial lemniscus to the thalamus. From there, the impulse is conveyed to the sensory cortex.

Spinothalamic tract

This carries pain and temperature sensation. From a clinical point of view, the important difference here is that the first-order neurons synapse in the posterior grey horn on joining the spinal cord. The second order neurons then cross over and ascend the contralateral side of the cord in the spinothalamic tract to the thalamus.

The sensory cortex

This is located at the postcentral gyrus, just posterior to the motor cortex. Much like the motor strip, the areas receiving stimuli from various parts of the body can be mapped out (see Fig. 8.9). A lesion affecting one area will cause sensory loss in the corresponding body area on the contralateral side (see sensory pathways above).

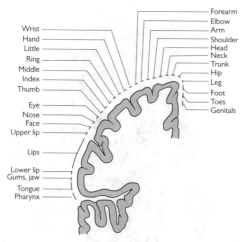

Fig. 8.9 The sensory cortex map showing areas corresponding to the different parts of the body. Note the large areas given over to the fingers and lips.

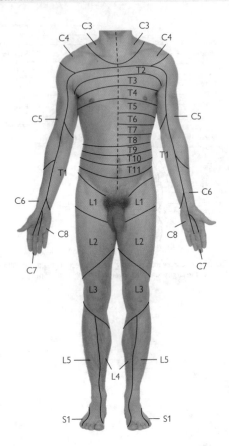

Fig. 8.10 The dermatomes (anterior view). Students would do well to be familiar with these diagrams, particularly the limbs—note important landmarks to aid recall. (C7 covers the middle finger, T4 lies at the level of the nipples, T10 over the umbilicus.)

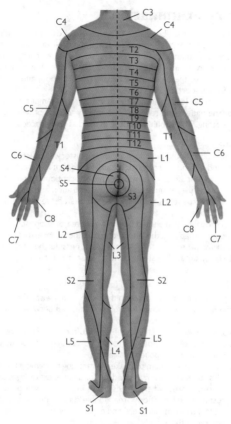

Fig. 8.11 The dermatomes (posterior view).

Sensory examination

This examination can be difficult—as it requires concentration and cooperation on the part of both the patient and the examiner. The results depend on the patient's response and are, therefore, partly subjective. Many patients prove unreliable witnesses due to a lack of understanding or attempts to please the examiner. Education, explanation, and reassurance are, therefore, important at all times.

Often, sensory loss (particularly vibration and temperature) is not noticed by the patient and revealing it during the course of an examination may be upsetting. This should be borne in mind as you proceed.

Technique

Your examination should be influenced by the history. In practice, only light touch is tested as a quick 'screening' exam if no deficit is expected.

If you are to test vibration sense and proprioception, it may be best to test these first as they require the least concentration and can be used by you to assess the patient's reliability as a witness before testing the other sensory modalities.

For each modality, you should begin at any area of supposed deficit and work outwards, mapping the affected area—then move to a systematic examination from head to toe. Always test one side then the other for each limb/body area. You should aim, at least, to test one spot in each dermatome.

Light touch

With the patient's eyes closed, touch their skin with a wisp of cotton wool and ask them to say 'yes' when it is felt. The interval between each touch should be irregular and unpredictable.

- In practice, a gentle touch with a finger is often used. However, this risks testing 'pressure' not 'light touch' sensation—it is also harder to ensure equal force is applied in all areas.
- ❶ Do not, as many seem to, make tiny stroking movements on the skin—this stimulates hair fibres and, again, is not a test of 'light touch'.
- ❶ Be aware of areas where ↓ sensation is expected (e.g. foot calluses).
- After testing each limb/body area, double check with the patient 'did that feel the same all over?' and explore any areas of abnormal sensation more thoroughly before moving on.

Sensory inattention

- This is a subtle but often clinically important sign of parietal lobe dysfunction. The patient feels a stimulus on the affected part—but not when there is competition from a stimulus on the opposite side.
- Ask the patient to close their eyes and to tell you if they feel a touch on their left or right—use any body part—commonly hands and feet as a quick 'screen'.
- Touch the right hand, then the left hand, then both.
- The touches should be repeated randomly to confirm the result.
  - e.g. in a right-sided parietal lesion, the patient will feel both left and right stimuli but when both sides are touched, they will not be able to feel the stimulus on the left.

Vibration sense

A 128Hz tuning fork (compare with CN-VIII) is used.

- Ask the patient to close their eyes, tap the tuning fork and place the base on a bony prominence—ask if the patient can feel the *vibration*.
- If 'yes', confirm by taking hold of the tuning fork with your other hand to stop the vibration after asking the patient to tell you when the vibration ceases.
- As always, compare left to right and work in a systematic fashion, testing bony prominences to include:
  - Finger tip, wrist, elbow, shoulder, anterior superior iliac spine, tibial tuberosity, metatarsophalangeal joint, and toes.

Proprioception

Testing proprioception in the way described below is rather crude and results must be interpreted with the rest of the history and examination.

Loss of position sense is usually distal. Start by testing the patient's big toe as below. This technique can be used at any joint.

- With the patient's eyes closed and leg relaxed, grasp the distal phalanx of the big toe from the sides.
- Whilst stabilizing the rest of the foot, you should move the toe up and down at the joint.
- Ask the patient if they can feel any movement—and in which direction.
- Flex and extend the joint, stopping at intervals to ask the patient whether the toe is 'up' or 'down'.
- If proprioception is absent, test other joints, working proximally
- ▶ The toe is gripped from the sides—if held incorrectly, pressure on the nail may suggest the toe is pressed down and so on.
- ▶ Normal proprioception should allow the patient to identify very subtle movements which are barely visible.

Pin-prick

Use a disposable pin or safety pin—not a hypodermic needle as these break the skin.

- Test as you would for light touch, gently pressing the pin on the skin.
- Test each dermatome in a systematic way, mapping out abnormalities.
- On each touch, ask the patient to say whether it feels *sharp* or *dull*.
- Occasionally test the patient's reliability as a witness with a negative control by using the opposite (blunt) end of the pin.

Temperature

- This is not routinely tested outside of specialist clinics. Loss of temperature sensation may be evident from the history (accidental burns?).
- When tested, test tubes or similar vessels containing hot and ice-cold water are used—and each dermatome tested as above.
- Remember to ensure the exterior of the tube is dry.

Coordination

Coordination should be tested in conjunction with gait. Cerebellar lesions cause incoordination on the ipsilateral side. For each of the following, compare performance on the left and right. (See Box 8.7 for cerebellar syndrome.)

Upper limbs

Finger–nose test

- Ask the patient to touch the end of their nose with their index finger.
- Hold your own finger out in front of them—at arm's reach from the patient—and ask them to then touch the tip of your finger with theirs.
- Ask them to move between their nose and your finger (Fig. 8.12).
- Look for intention tremor (worse as it approaches the target) and 'past-pointing' (missing the target entirely).
- The test can be made more difficult by moving the position of your finger each time the patient touches their nose.

Rapid alternating movements

- (This is hard to describe and should be demonstrated to the patient.) Ask the patient to repeatedly supinate and pronate their forearm keeping the other arm still such that they clap their hands palm-to-palm, then back-to-palm and so on (see Fig. 8.13).
- Alternatively, ask them to mimic screwing in a light-bulb.
  - Slow and clumsy = dysdiadochokinesis.
- ❶ This is the inability to perform rapidly alternating movements (dia-doke = Greek for succession).

Rebound

- From a resting (arms at their side) position, the patient should be asked to quickly abduct their arms and stop suddenly at the horizontal.
  - In cerebellar disease, there will be delay in stopping and the arm will oscillate about the intended final position.
- Alternatively, pull on the patient's flexed arms (as if testing elbow flexion power) and suddenly let go. If lacking coordination, the patient will hit him/herself in the face. This test does little for doctor–patient trust and rapport and is rarely performed for obvious reasons (!).

Lower limbs

Heel–shin test

- With the patient sitting, legs outstretched, ask them to slide the heel of one foot up and down the shin of the other leg at a moderate pace.
  - A lack of coordination will manifest as the heel moving side to side about the intended path
  - In sensory—as opposed to cerebellar—ataxia (lack of proprioception), patients will perform worse with their eyes closed.

Foot tapping

- The patient taps your hand with their foot as fast as possible.
- NB The non-dominant side performs poorly in normal individuals.

Fig. 8.12 Testing rapidly alternating movements. This can be rather hard to describe to a patient—a brief demonstration is usually required.

Box 8.7 Cerebellar syndrome

Examination findings
- Eye movements show a loss of smooth pursuit
  - This is the most subtle sign of cerebellar disease in the eyes.
- There is (may be) nystagmus
  - Note the direction of the gaze and the direction of the nystagmus.
- The patient is dysarthric
  - Note any dysarthria or the classical monotonous 'scanning' speech.
- Tone is reduced
  - Reduced in pure cerebellar disease but may be increased if cerebellar signs coexist with other disease (e.g. posterior circulation stroke, MS).
- Intention tremor
  - Perform finger–nose test.
- Dysdiadochokinesis
- Trunkal unsteadiness
  - Ask the patient to sit forward with their arms across their chest.
- Lower limb incoordination.
  - Ask the patient to place one heel on their knee on the other side, run it down their shin, pick it up and place it on their knee and repeat.

Gait
- Unsteady broad-based gait
  - If the patient is steady, assess tandem gait (walking with one foot placed in front of the other).

Extras
- Examine tendon reflexes
  - These may be reduced or pendular in cerebellar disease, or increased with coexisting disease (as above).

Some peripheral nerves

Peripheral nerve lesions may occur in isolation (e.g. trauma, compression, neoplasia) or as part of a wider pathology (e.g. mononeuritis multiplex). The following sections describe the signs following lesions of a selection of peripheral nerves. (See Boxes 8.8–8.10.)

Upper limb

Median nerve (C6–T1)

- *Motor:* muscles of the anterior forearm, except flexor carpi ulnaris, and 'LOAF' (lateral two lumbricals, opponens pollicis, abductor pollicis brevis, and flexor pollicis brevis).
- *Sensory:* thumb, anterior index and middle fingers as well as some of the radial side of the palm (see Fig. 8.13).

Ulnar nerve (C8–T1)

- *Motor:* all the small muscles of the hand except LOAF (see above) and flexor carpi ulnaris.
- *Sensory:* ulnar side of hand, little finger and half of ring finger (see Fig. 8.13).

Radial nerve (C5–C8)

- *Motor:* triceps, brachioradialis, and extensors of the hand.
- *Sensory:* a small area over the anatomical snuff box—hard to test.

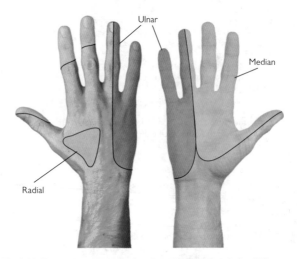

Fig. 8.13 Sensory distribution of the major peripheral nerves in the hand. There is considerable overlap and the small area supplied by the radial nerve may not be detectable clinically.

Box 8.8 Median nerve palsy

Inspection
- Inspect the forearm carefully, looking for signs of rheumatoid arthritis, osteoarthritis, and any scars
- Wasting of the thenar eminence?
- Sign of benediction?
  - The index and middle fingers are held out straight despite flexion of the other fingers, rather like a Catholic blessing
  - Due to paralysis of flexor digitorum profundus.
- The thumb is held in abduction in the plane of the palm.
  - Also known as a 'simian thumb' or sometimes 'monkey paw'.

Tone
- Normal

Power
- Weakness of the thenar eminence
  - Abduction, flexion, and opposition of the thumb.
- Weakness of flexion at the terminal IP joint of the index finger
- The 'pen-touching test':
  - Place the patient's hand flat, palm up
  - Hold your pen (or similar object) just above the thumb and ask the patient to lift the thumb vertically to touch the pen, without moving the rest of their hand
  - In median nerve palsy, they will not be able to do this (weakness of flexor pollicis brevis).
- Oschner's clasping test:
  - Ask the patient to clasp their hands together with fingers interlocking
  - The index finger will fail to flex in median nerve palsy (weakness of flexor digitorum profundus).

Sensation
- Loss of sensation over the thumb, anterior index and middle fingers, and the radial side of the palm (see Fig. 8.13)

Tinel's test
- Percussion over the median nerve at the carpal tunnel causes tingling in the distribution of the nerve
  - Tinel's *sign* is paraesthesia in a nerve distribution caused by percussion of that nerve and applies to any nerve.

Phalen's test
- Ask the patient to hold both wrists flexed for 60 seconds
  - This produces an exacerbation of the paraesthesia – relieved by relaxing the wrist (positive in 50% of patients).

Tourniquet test
- A sphygmomanometer pumped to just above systolic pressure on the ipsilateral arm for 1–2 minutes reproduces the symptoms.

Box 8.9 Ulnar nerve palsy

Inspection

- Wasting of the dorsal interossei and hypothenar eminence
  - If the neuropathy is long-standing
- 'Ulnar claw'
  - Extension at the phalangeal-metacarpal joints and flexion at the interphalangeal joints – usually little finger first, then ring finger.
- The patient may be complaining of pain, usually in the forearm or elbow.

Tone

- Normal

Power

- Weakness of all the small muscles of the hand, except 'LOAF' (lateral two lumbricals, opponens pollicis, abductor pollicis brevis, flexor pollicis brevis)
- Weak abduction of the index finger
- Ulnar muscles in the forearm may be weak:
  - Flexor digitorum profundus of the fourth and fifth digits which flexes the distal phalanges
  - Flexor carpi ulnaris which flexes the wrist in the medial direction.
- **Froment's sign:** ask the patient to pinch a piece of paper between thumb and index finger or make a fist; this will be weak and the thumb will flex as it is unable to abduct (Fig. 8.14)
- Test thumb abduction to rule out a C8/T1 nerve root lesion.

Reflexes

- Normal tendon reflexes

Sensation

- Loss of sensation over the medial aspect of the hand, little finger, and medial half of the ring finger.

(a)    (b)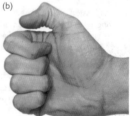

Fig. 8.14 Froment's sign (a) normal. (b) Froment's positive. Jules Froment has the credit for this following his 1915 paper in La Press Medicale. The sign was actually described first in 1904 by Breeman.

Box 8.10 Radial nerve palsy

Inspection

- Carefully inspect the upper limbs
- Radial nerve palsy is the classic cause of wrist drop.

Tone

- Normal

Power

- Weakness of triceps (elbow extension) in very proximal lesions
- Weakness of brachioradialis (elbow flexion with the forearm partially pronated)
- Test power in the extensor muscles of the wrist, fingers at the MCP joints, and thumb
  - Weakness in some or all of these
  - Sparing of finger abduction and thenar eminence muscles (thumb abduction at right angles to the palm—see median nerve palsy).
- Remember that to test finger abduction, fingers must be extended.
  - Place hand on a flat surface to test if there is finger drop.

Reflexes

- Absent or weak triceps reflex in very proximal lesions (and also C7 root lesions)

Sensation

- Sensory loss in a small area over the dorsal aspect of the hand at the anatomical snuff box
  - This is very hard to test and as there is considerable overlap in the sensory distribution to the hand, the small area supplied by the radial nerve may not be clinically detectable.

Lower limb

Lateral cutaneous nerve of the thigh (L2–L3)

- Motor: none.
- Sensory: the lateral aspect of the thigh (see Fig. 10.15a).
- Examining a lesion:
  - There may be some sensory loss as indicated but, in practice, this is very hard to test.

Common peroneal nerve (L4–S2)

- Motor: anterior and lateral compartments of the leg.
- Sensory: the dorsum of the foot and anterior aspect of the leg.
- Examining a lesion:
  - 'Foot-drop' with corresponding gait. Weakness of foot dorsiflexion and eversion. Preserved inversion. (Fig. 10.15b)
  - NB in an L5 lesion, there will be a similar deficit but also a weakness of inversion, hip abduction, and knee flexion.

Femoral nerve (L2–L4)

- Motor: quadriceps.
- Sensory: medial aspect of thigh and leg (see Fig. 10.15d).
- Examining a lesion:
  - Weakness of knee extension is only slightly affected—hip adduction is preserved
  - Stretch: with the patient lying prone, abduct the hip, flex the knee, and plantar-flex the foot. The stretch test is positive if pain is felt in the thigh/inguinal region.

Sciatic nerve (L4–S3)

- Motor: all the muscles below the knee and some hamstrings.
- Sensory: posterior thigh, ankle, and foot (see Fig. 10.15c).
- Examining a lesion:
  - Foot drop and weak knee flexion
  - Knee jerk reflex is preserved but ankle jerk and plantar response are absent
  - Stretch test: with the patient lying supine, hold the ankle and lift the leg, straight, to 90°. Once there, dorsiflex the foot. If positive, pain will be felt at the back of the thigh.

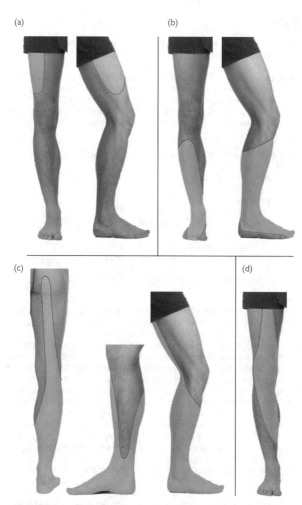

Fig. 8.15 Distribution of the sensory component of some lower limb nerves. (a) Lateral cutaneous nerve of the thigh. (b) Common peroneal nerve. (c) Sciatic nerve. (d) Femoral nerve.

Gait

This is easily missed from the neurological examination—it is often difficult to test in a crowded ward or cramped consulting room. However, you should try to incorporate it into your assessment.

Gait can be observed informally as the patient makes their way to the clinic room or returns to their chair on the ward. Watch the patient stand—and use the same opportunity for Romberg's test. (See Box 8.11.)

A patient may be simply lacking in confidence and this will be evident later. Do not test if you suspect a severe problem with balance.

Examination

- Ask the patient to walk a few metres, turn, and walk back to you.
- Note especially:
  - Use of walking aids
  - Symmetry
  - Size of paces
  - Lateral distance between the feet
  - How high the feet and knees are lifted
  - Bony deformities
  - Disturbance of normal gait by abnormal movements.
- You may want to consider asking the patient to:
  - Walk on tip-toes (inability = S1 or gastrocnemius lesion)
  - Walk on their heels (inability = L4/L5 lesion—foot drop).

Findings

- *Hemiplegia:* one side will be obviously weaker than the other with the patient tilting pelvis to lift the weak leg which may swing out to the side. Gait may be unsafe without the use of walking aid.
- *'Scissoring':* if both legs are spastic (cerebral palsy, MS), toes drag on floor, trunk sways from side to side, and legs cross over on each step.
- *Parkinsonism:* flexed posture with small, shuffling steps. No or little arm-swing. Difficulty starting, stopping, and turning. Gait seems hurried ('festinant') as legs attempt to prevent body falling forwards.
- *Cerebellar ataxia:* broad-based (legs wide) gait with lumbering body movements and variable distance between steps. Difficulty turning.
- *Sensory ataxia:* (loss of proprioception.) Patient requires more sensory input to be sure of leg position so lifts legs high. ('high-stepping') and stamps feet down with a wide-based gait—may also watch legs as they walk. Romberg's positive.
- *Waddling:* (weakness of proximal lower limb muscles.) Patient fails to tilt pelvis as normal so ↑ rotation to compensate—also at the shoulders. May also see ↑ lumbar lordosis.
- *Foot drop:* (L4/L5 lesion, sciatic, or common peroneal nerves.) Failure to dorsiflex the foot leads to a 'high-stepping' gait with ↑ flexion at the hip and knee. If bilateral, may indicate peripheral neuropathy.

- *Apraxic:* (usually frontal lobe pathology such as normal pressure hydrocephalus or cerebrovascular disease.) Problems with gait even if all other movements may be normal. Patient may appear frozen to the spot and unable to initiate waking. Movements are disjointed once walking.
- *Marche à petits pas:* (diffuse cortical dysfunction.) Upright posture, small steps with a normal arm-swing.
- *Painful gait:* the cause will normally be obvious from the history. The patient limps with an asymmetrical gait due to painful movement.
- *Functional:* (also known as hysterical.) Gait problems will be variable and inconsistent, often with bizarre and elaborate consequences. May fall without causing injury. Often worse when watched.

Box 8.11 Romberg's sign

A further test of proprioception. Usually tested at the time of gait examination, as the patient will be standing at this point. When proprioception is lost in the lower limbs, patients can often stand and move normally as long as they can see the limb in question.

🚫 Perform this with care—only if you are able to prevent the patient falling and injuring themselves

- Ask the patient to stand. You stand facing them
- Ask the patient to close their eyes.

If there is loss of proprioception, the patient will lose their balance and start to fall—if so, ask them to open their eyes immediately, if they haven't already done so, and help them regain their balance without injury.

The unconscious patient

History

- Eye-witness account? State of clothing—loss of continence?
- Look for alert necklace/bracelet. Look in wallet, purse, etc.

Examination

- *ABC:* (covered in detail in other Oxford Handbooks).
  - Airway patent? Should the patient be in the recovery position?
  - Measure respiratory rate, note pattern of breathing. Is O_2 needed?
  - Cyanosis? Feel pulse. Listen to chest. Measure heart rate, BP.
- *Skin:* look for injury, petechial haemorrhage, evidence of IV drug use.
- *Movements/posture:*
  - Watch! Is the patient still or moving? All four limbs moving equally?
  - Any abnormal movements—fitting, myoclonic jerks?
  - Test tone and compare both sides
  - Squeeze the nail bed to test the response to pain (all four limbs)
  - Test tendon reflexes and plantar response
  - *Decorticate posture:* (lesion above the brainstem.) Flexion and internal rotation of the arms, extension of the lower limbs
  - *Decerebrate posture:* (lesion in the midbrain.) Extension at the elbow and wrist, pronation of the forearm, lower limbs extended.
- *Consciousness:* attempt to wake the patient by sound. Ask their name. If responsive, are they able to articulate appropriately?—Note the best response. ⓘ Be aware of possible dys- or aphasia which may cause an inappropriate response in an otherwise alert individual.
  - Score level of consciousness according to the GCS or AVPU (Boxes 8.12 and 8.13).
- *Neck:* do not examine if there may have been trauma. Test for meningeal irritation—these signs ↓ as coma deepens.
- *Head:* inspect for signs of trauma and facial weakness. Test pain sense.
- *Battle's sign:* bruising behind the ear = a base of skull fracture.
- *Ears/nose:* look for CSF leakage or bleeding. Test any clear fluid for glucose (positive result = CSF). Inspect eardrums.
- *Tongue/mouth:* Look for cuts on the tongue (seizures), corrosive material around the mouth. Smell breath for alcohol or ketosis. Test the gag reflex—absent in brainstem disease or deep coma.
- *Eyes:*
  - Pupils: measure size in mm. Are they equal? Test direct and consensual light responses. Pupils ↑ with atropine, tricyclic antidepressants, and amphetamine; ↓ with morphine and metabolic coma
  - Test corneal reflex
  - Fundi: look especially for papilloedema and retinopathy.
  - Doll's head manoeuvre: take the patient's head in your hands and turn it from side to side. The eyes should move to stay fixed on an object—indicates an intact brainstem.
- *Rest of the body:* a brief but thorough exam. Look especially for trauma, fractures, signs of liver disease, and added heart sounds.
- *Other bedside tests:* test urine, capillary glucose, and temperature.

Box 8.12 Glasgow Coma Scale (GCS)

This is an objective score of consciousness. Repeated testing is useful for judging whether coma is deepening or lifting. There are three categories as below. Note that the lowest score in each is '1' meaning that the lowest possible GCS = 3 (even if the patient is dead!)

Eye opening (max 4 points)

Spontaneously open	4
Open to (any) verbal stimulus	3
Open in response to painful stimulus	2
No eye opening at all	1

Best verbal response (max 5 points)

Conversing and orientated (normal)	5
Conversing but disorientated and confused	4
Inappropriate words (random words, no conversation)	3
Incomprehensible sounds (moaning, etc.)	2
No speech at all	1

Best motor response (max 6 points)

Obeying commands (e.g. raise your hand)	6
Localizing to pain (moves hand towards site of stimulus)	5
Withdraws to pain (pulls hand away from stimulus)	4
Abnormal flexion to pain (decorticate posturing)	3
Abnormal extension to pain (decerebrate posturing)	2
No response at all	1

Box 8.13 AVPU

A much more simplified score used in rapid assessment of consciousness and often by non-specialist nurses in monitoring conscious level.

A = Alert
V = responds to Voice
P = responds to Pain
U = Unresponsive

Important presenting patterns

Neck stiffness

Caused by a number of conditions provoking painful extensor muscle spasm including: bacterial and viral meningitis, subarachnoid haemorrhage, Parkinsonism, raised intracranial pressure, cervical spondylosis, cervical lymphadenopathy, and pharyngitis. (See Box 8.14 also.)

▶ None of the following tests should be conducted if there is suspicion of cervical injury or instability.

Examination

- Lie the patient flat.
- Taking their head in your hands, gently rotate it to the sides in a 'no' movement, feeling for stiffness.
- Lift the head off the bed and watch the hips and knees—the chin should easily touch the chest.

Brudzinski's sign

- When the head is flexed by the examiner, the patient briefly flexes at the hips and knees—a test for meningeal irritation.

Kernig's sign

- A further test of meningeal irritation.
- With the patient lying flat, flex their hip and knee, holding the weight of the leg yourself.
- With the hip flexed to 90°, extend the knee joint so as to point the leg at the ceiling.
- If 'positive', there will be resistance to leg straightening (caused by hamstring spasm as a result of inflammation around the lumbar spinal roots) and pain felt at the back of the neck.

Lhermitte's phenomenon

- A test for an intrinsic lesion in the cervical cord (not meningeal irritation).
- When the neck is flexed as above, the patient feels an electric shock-like sensation down the centre of their back.

Upper motor and lower motor nerve lesions

Upper motor neuron (UMN) lesions

Defined as damage *above* the level of the anterior horn cell—anywhere from the spinal cord to the primary motor cortex.

- No muscle wasting (although will have disuse atrophy in long-term weakness).
- ↑ tone. 'Spasticity' (clasp-knife) due to stretch reflex hypersensitivity.
- Typical pattern of weakness is termed 'pyramidal':
  - Upper limbs: weak abductors and extensors
  - Lower limbs: weak adductors and flexors.
- ↑ tendon reflexes and clonus. Up-going plantar response.

Lower motor neuron (LMN) lesions

- Muscle wasting, fasciculation.
- ↓ tone.
- Flaccid weakness.
- ↓ tendon reflexes. Plantar response may be down-going or absent.

Box 8.14 Hemiplegia: examination findings

Inspection
- Are there any scars from a brain biopsy or craniotomy?

Tone
- Tone increased unilaterally

Power
- If examining the upper limbs, ask the patient to hold out their arms with their palms facing the ceiling. Ask them to close their eyes
  - Note any failure to fully raise and supinate the arm and any pronator drift with the eyes closed.
- Power is reduced in a pyramidal distribution:
  - Flexors stronger than extensors in upper limb
  - Extensors stronger than flexors in lower limb.

Reflexes
- Brisk tendon reflexes on the affected side
- Remember to examine for clonus which may be present on the affected side.

Sensation
- There may be sensory loss, usually on the side of the weakness
  - If crossed and dissociated pin-prick/vibration and joint position sense, this localizes the lesion to the brainstem.

Gait
- If the patient can walk, gait will be spastic on the affected side with a foot drop, difficulty flexing the knee resulting in swinging the leg round
- A pyramidal posture of the upper limb may be exaggerated.

Motor neuron disease (MND)

See ➲ *OHCM9*. MND is a disease of the anterior horn cells of the motor pathway. It is progressive and eventually leads to respiratory failure and death. Most MND is sporadic but there are genetic forms of the disease. The most common is the autosomal dominantly inherited SOD mutation.

MND may present as 4 different phenotypes, described in Box 8.15.

Inspection
- Look around the patient for communication aids, walking aids, and wheelchairs.
- Look carefully at the limbs for muscle wasting and fasciculation.
- Is there a gastrostomy tube *in situ*?

Cranial nerves
- Patient may be dysarthric.
- Facial weakness.
- Weakness of neck flexion and extension.
- The tongue shows fasciculation.
  - Ask the patient to move the tongue quickly; a spastic tongue will not fasciculate but will be weak and move slowly.
- There is lip, tongue, and palatal weakness.
  - Ask the patient to say 'M, M, M', 'L, L, L', and 'K, K, K'.
- Jaw jerk is brisk.

Peripheral nerves
- On examination of peripheral tone, power and tendon reflexes, there is a mixture of upper and lower motor neuron signs.
  - Commonly muscle wasting and fasciculation with brisk reflexes and possibly extensor (up-going) plantar responses.
- Sensory examination is normal.

Box 8.15 MND presentations

MND may *present* as four different phenotypes in the early stages:

Amyotrophic lateral sclerosis
- Clinical presentation described above
- Most common type with the classical mix of upper and lower motor neuron features.

Bulbar presentation
- Bulbar symptoms with preservation of limb function in the early stages; poor prognosis due to early respiratory involvement

Progressive muscular atrophy
- Purely lower motor neuron signs

Primary lateral sclerosis
- Purely upper motor neuron signs.

Myotonic dystrophy

- The myotonic dystrophies are multisystem disorders in which myopathy and myotonia are prominent features (see Box 8.16).
- Myotonia is continued involuntary muscle contraction after voluntary effort has ceased.

Inspection
- Bilateral partial ptosis.
- Slack, open mouth due to jaw weakness.
- Frontal balding.
- Expressionless face.
- Cataracts (look with an ophthalmoscope).

Tone
- Normal.

Power
- Distal muscle weakness (especially hands and foot drop).
- *Myotonia:* ask the patient to squeeze their hand tightly shut and then quickly release it; note the slow relaxation of the muscles.
- *Percussion myotonia:* tap the thenar eminence with a tendon hammer; the abductor pollicis brevis will contract and very slowly relax.

Reflexes
- Reduced or absent.

Sensation
- Normal.

Associated features
- Cardiac conduction abnormalities and cardiomyopathy.
- Testicular atrophy.
- Endocrine disturbance (most commonly type II diabetes mellitus).
- Cognitive difficulties: intellectual and personality deterioration.
- Hypersomnolence.

Box 8.16 Myotonic dystrophies

Myotonic dystrophy type 1
- Autosomal dominant inheritance with genetic 'anticipation' (subsequent generations develop more severe symptoms earlier in life)
- It is an unstable trinucleotide CGT repeat on chromosome 19 in the myotonin protein kinase gene.

Myotonic dystrophy type 2
- Autosomal dominant inherited condition with a slightly different presentation to 'classic' MD
- Patients do not have facial weakness
- Limb weakness is proximal rather than distal
- Clinically milder than type 1, although patients also have cataracts and may have cardiac conduction abnormalities.

Parkinson's disease

Parkinsonism is a pattern of symptoms comprising an akinetic–rigid syndrome. Parkinsonism has a number of causes including drug-induced and other intracranial pathologies.

Parkinson's disease (PD) is a neurodegenerative disease with loss of dopaminergic cells in the substantia nigra with Lewy body formation. PD is essentially a clinical diagnosis (currently). (See Box 8.17 for abnormal movements.)

Inspection
- 'Mask-like' facies with little or no expression.
- Reduced blink rate.
- Is there a head tremor?
  - yes–yes or no–no; associated with essential/dystonic tremor **not** Parkinson's disease.
- Speech is low-volume and monotonous.
- Examine for tremor with arms at rest and in posture.
  - PD tremor is asymmetrical
  - Usually said to be 'pill-rolling' and worse at rest, but can present with an asymmetrical postural tremor.

Tone
- Examine tone feeling for asymmetrical cogwheel rigidity.

Power/function
- Examine repetitive hand movements such as walking the thumb along the fingers.
  - Encourage the patient to make big, quick movements to be sure of eliciting bradykinesia if present.
- Use synkinesis (active movement of the opposite limb) to exaggerate tremor, cogwheeling or bradykinesia.

Gait
- Difficulty initiating gait.
- Loss of arm swing on one side.
- Shuffling gait.
- Difficulty turning.
- Unsteadiness/loss of postural reflexes.

Extras
- Examine pursuit and doll's eye movements.
  - Could this be a Parkinson's plus syndrome like progressive supranuclear palsy?

Box 8.17 Abnormal movements

- *Akathisia:* motor restlessness with a feeling of muscle quivering and an inability to remain in a sitting position
- *Athetosis:* slow, writhing, involuntary movements often with flexion, extension, pronation, and supination of the fingers and wrists
- *Blepharospasm:* intermittent spasm of muscles around the eyes
- *Chorea:* non-rhythmical, dance-like, spasmodic movements of the limbs or face. Appear pseudo-purposeful (the patient often hides the condition by turning a spasm into a voluntary movement—e.g. the arm suddenly lifts up and the patient pretends they were adjusting their hair)
- *Dyskinesia:* repetitive, automatic movements that stop only during sleep
- *Tardive dyskinesia:* dyskinetic movements often of the face (lip-smacking, twisting of the mouth). Often a side effect of neuroleptic therapy
- *Dystonia:* markedly ↑ tone often with spasms causing uncomfortable-looking postures
- *Hemiballismus:* violent involuntary flinging movements of the limbs on one side—rather like severe chorea
- *Myoclonus:* brief, shock-like movement of a muscle or muscle-group
- *Pseudoathetosis:* writhing limb movements (often finger/arm) much like athetosis but caused by a loss of proprioception. The arm returns to the normal position when the patient notices it straying
- *Myokymia:* continuous quivering and rippling movements of muscles at rest like a 'bag of worms'. Facial myokymia: especially near the eyes
- *Tic:* repetitive, active, habitual, purposeful contractions causing stereotyped actions. Can be suppressed for brief periods with effort
- *Titubation:* rhythmical contraction of the head. May be either 'yes–yes' or 'no–no' movements
- *Tremor:* repetitive, alternating movements, usually involuntary.

Spinal cord lesions

As neurons in some spinal cord tracts relate to the contralateral side of the body, others the ipsilateral side, certain types of spinal cord damage will give predictable patterns of motor and sensory loss.

Complete section of the cord

- Loss of all modalities below the level of the lesion.

Hemisection of the cord

Also known as 'Brown-Sequard syndrome'.*

- Motor: below the level of the lesion, UMN pattern of weakness on ipsilateral side with brisk tendon reflexes.
- Sensory: below the level of the lesion:
  - Contralateral loss of pain and temperature sensation
  - Ipsilateral loss of light touch, vibration sense, and proprioception
  - (Light touch may remain intact as some fibres travel in the spinothalamic tract.)

Posterior column loss

- Loss of vibration sense and proprioception on both sides below the level of the lesion.

Subacute combined degeneration of the cord

'Posterolateral column syndrome' often due to vitamin B_{12} deficiency.

- Loss of vibration sense and proprioception on both sides below the level of the lesion.
- UMN weakness in lower limbs, *absent* ankle reflexes.
- (Also peripheral sensory neuropathy, optic atrophy and dementia.)

Anterior spinal artery occlusion

- Loss of pin-prick and temperature sensation below the lesion.
- Intact light touch, vibration sense, and proprioception.

Syringomyelia

Longitudinal cavity (syrinx) in the central part of the spinal cord.

- Wasting of the small muscles of the hands, ulnar border of upper limb.
- Loss of pain and temperature sensation over the neck, shoulders, and arms in a 'cape' distribution (look for scars and cuts).
- Intact vibration sense, proprioception, and light touch.
- Atrophy and areflexia in the upper limbs.
- UMN weakness in the lower limbs.
- Look also for scoliosis due to weakness of paravertebral muscles.

---

* Charles Edward Brown-Sequard discovered this while studying victims of failed murder attempts amongst traditional cane cutters in Mauritius.

Cauda equina syndrome

- The cauda equina is the name given to the descending nerve roots which extend from the termination of the spinal cord at the conus (which occurs at about L1) caudally to the final nerve root exits.
- Cauda equina syndrome is characterized by:
  - Pain in the lower back (although this is variable)
  - Bladder and bowel disturbance (as well as sexual dysfunction)
  - Saddle anaesthesia
  - Variable paralysis and sensory disturbance of the lower limbs.
- ▶ Acute herniation of a lumbar disc compressing the cauda equina and causing sphincter disturbance and paralysis is a surgical emergency and needs to be decompressed immediately to prevent long-term consequences.

Inspection

- Carefully inspect the lower limbs; with long-standing problems there may be muscle wasting.
  - Upper limbs will be normal.
- Note the presence of a catheter suggesting bladder dysfunction.

Tone

- Normal or reduced.

Power

- Normal in the upper limbs.
- Reduced in the lower limbs.
  - May be complete paralysis or weakness in a nerve root distribution
  - May be unilateral or bilateral.

Reflexes

- Tendon reflexes may be reduced or absent.
- Flexor (down-going) plantar responses.

Sensation

- Saddle anaesthesia (around the perineum and buttocks).
  - Compression of the sciatic nerve roots
  - May be unilateral or bilateral.

Disturbance of higher functions

A selection of testable consequences of cortical lesions:

Parietal lobe

- Sensory and visual inattention.
- Visual field defects.
- Agnosias (lack of sensory perceptual abilities).
  - *Hemi-neglect*—patient ignores one side of their body
  - *Asomatognosia*—patient fails to recognize own body part
  - *Anosognosia*—patient is unaware of neurological deficits
  - *Finger agnosia*—patient is unable to show you different fingers when requested (e.g. 'show me your index finger')
  - *Astereognosis*—inability to recognize an object by touch alone
  - *Agraphaesthesia*—inability to recognize letters or numbers when traced on the back of the hand
  - *Prosopagnosia*—inability to recognize faces (test with family members or famous faces from a nearby magazine).
- Apraxias (inability to perform movements or use objects correctly).
  - *Ideational apraxia*—performs tasks but makes mistakes (i.e. puts tea into kettle and pours milk into cup)
  - *Ideomotor apraxia*—unable to perform task but understands what is required
  - *Dressing apraxia*—inability to dress correctly (test with a dressing gown). One of a number of apraxias named after the action tested.
- *Gerstmann's syndrome:* Right–left dissociation, finger agnosia, dysgraphia (writing defect), dyscalculia (test with serial 7s).

Temporal lobe

- Memory loss—confabulation (invented stories and details).

Frontal lobe

- Primitive reflexes.
- Concrete thinking (unable to explain proverbs—e.g. ask to explain what 'a bird in the hand is worth two in the bush' means).
- Loss of smell sensation.
- Gait apraxia.

Myasthenia gravis (MG)

MG is an autoimmune disease of the neuromuscular junction.

- Antibodies bind to the acetylcholine receptor, blocking acetylcholine.
- 50–60% of patients present with ocular symptoms, but only 10% of patients have isolated ocular MG.
- Disease onset is bimodal; young (15–30 years) or old (60–75 years).
- 90% develop generalized MG which can be fatal if the respiratory muscles are affected.

Inspection

- Look carefully at the eyes. Is there unilateral or bilateral ptosis? If so, check the pupils. In MG they are equal and reactive.
- Are the eyes conjugate as you inspect?
- Is there an eye patch indicating diplopia?
- Inspection of the limbs will usually be normal.

Cranial nerves

- Diplopia, worsening at the extremes of gaze.
  - Ask the patient if they have double vision and the direction of the double vision (i.e. horizontal, vertical, skewed).
- Is there any ophthalmoplegia and in which direction of gaze?
- Fatigable ptosis.
  - Hold your finger above the patient's eye-line and ask them to look up at it for 30 seconds
  - Watch their eyes
  - If fatigable ptosis and/or upgaze is present, their eyes will slowly fall back and the eyelids will begin to close.
- Facial weakness.
- Test by asking the patient to screw their eyes shut, purse their lips and open their jaw, all against resistance.
- Neck flexion and extension weakness.
- Dysarthria.
- Dysphagia.
  - Ask the patient about swallowing difficulties—do not test unless under controlled conditions.

Power

- Fatigable weakness of the proximal arm muscles.
  - Test power in shoulder abduction
  - Ask the patient to raise and lower their arms 20 times
  - Recheck power (will have weakened).

Differential diagnoses

- Unilateral ptosis and complex ophthalmoplegia: partial third nerve palsy.
- Bilateral ptosis: myotonic dystrophy.
- Bilateral facial weakness: Guillan–Barré syndrome, muscular dystrophy.
- Proximal muscle weakness: myopathy, muscular dystrophy.
- Dysarthria: stroke, motor neuron disease.

Multiple sclerosis (MS)

- MS is a cell-mediated auto-immune condition characterized by repeated episodes of inflammation of the nervous tissue in the brain and spinal cord, causing loss of the insulating myelin sheath.
- UK prevalence is 100–140 per 100,000 with approximately 2500–3000 new diagnoses per year (or 50–60 a week).
- MS is more common in women with female-to-male ratio 2–3:1.
- MS is usually diagnosed in persons aged 15–45 years; however, it can occur in any age.
- 4% of people with a 1st degree relative with multiple sclerosis will develop the condition.
- 20% of MS patients have an affected relative.

Examination

- The presentation is highly variable depending on the site of the inflammation with lower and upper motor neuron signs, sensory system deficits, and cranial nerve palsies. A full and thorough systems examination is essential.

Recognized patterns

- *Relapsing/remitting:* symptoms come and go, 80% of patients at onset.
- *Secondary progressive:* gradually more or worsening symptoms with fewer remissions. 50% of those with relapsing/remitting MS develop secondary progressive MS during the first 10 years of the illness.
- *Primary progressive:* from the beginning symptoms gradually develop and worsen over time (10–15% of people at onset).

Clinical symptoms and signs

- *Motor:* weakness of variable severity including mono-, para-, hemi-, and quadri-paresis. Spasticity resulting in spastic gait. Facial myokymia (unusual fine undulating wave-like facial twitching).
- *Sensory:* dysaesthesic pain, paraesthesia, numbness, Lhermitte's sign, severe decrease or loss of vibratory sense and proprioception, positive Romberg's test.
- *Cranial nerves:* CN V most frequently involved followed by VII, III, and VIII. Isolated cranial nerve palsies are not frequent. Combined cranial nerve palsies are rare in MS. Symptoms might include trigeminal neuralgia. Signs such as taste and smell dysfunction frequently found if specifically looked for.
- *Cerebellar signs:* incoordination including dysdiadochokinesis, failure of heel–shin test, ataxic gait, scanning speech, loss of balance.
- *Ocular:* reduced visual acuity, colour blindness, complete loss of vision (1 in 35 cases), retrobulbar pain, blurred vision, diplopia, nystagmus, internuclear ophthalmoplegia, central scotomata and other visual field defects, oscillopsia, relative afferent pupillary defect (Marcus Gunn pupil), optic disc pallor and atrophy, Uhthoff's phenomenon (worsening of vision in optic neuritis during a fever, in hot weather, or after exercise).
- *Other:* neuropathic and musculoskeletal pain; bladder, bowel, and sexual dysfunction; fatigue; cognitive and emotional problems; heat sensitivity due to loss of thermoregulation manifesting as excess sweating, etc.

See also:

More information regarding the presentation and clinical signs of neurological diseases to aid preparation for OSCE-type examinations and ward rounds can be found in the *Oxford Handbooks Clinical Tutor Study Cards*.

'Medicine' Study Card set:

- Proximal myopathy
- Motor neuron disease
- Myasthenia gravis
- Cervical myelopathy
- Median, ulnar, and radial nerve palsies
- Wasting of the small muscles of the hand
- Syringomyelia
- Polymyositis
- Parkinson's disease
- Friedreich's ataxia
- Charcot–Marie–Tooth disease
- Subacute combined degeneration of the cord
- Brown-Sequard syndrome
- Tabes dorsalis
- Cerebellopontine angle syndrome
- Wallenberg's syndrome
- Cranial nerve palsies
- Bulbar palsy
- Pseudobulbar palsy.

The elderly patient

Diagnosing and managing neurological illness can be complex, but the combination of cognitive failure and the effects of an ageing neurological system can present significant challenges for clinicians.

Presentations of neurological disease are varied, and the range of diagnoses diverse. Epilepsy, Parkinsonism, and dementias are all common problems in older age—so resist the temptation to restrict your diagnoses to stroke or TIA.

History

- *Witness histories:* are vital. Many patients may attend with vague symptoms that may be underplayed. Partial complex seizures may be very difficult to diagnose—so pursue witness histories from families, neighbours, home care staff, etc. Enquire not just about the present incident, but also prior function and any decline.
- *Drug history:* falls are a common presentation and often multifactorial. Always remember to ask about any drugs that may lower blood pressure, even if the primary cause of the fall is due to neurological disease.
- *Intercurrent illness:* may precipitate further seizures or make pre-existing neurological signs seem worse. Don't rush to diagnose a worsening of the original problem—careful assessment pays dividends.
- *Cognition and mood disorders:* often complicate presentations. Look for clues in the history and ask witnesses.
- *Functional history:* a key part of the neurological history. The disease itself may be incurable—functional problems often are not.

Examination

- *Observe:* Non-verbal clues may point to mood or cognitive disorders. Handshakes and facial expressions are an important part of the examination.
- *Think:* about patterns of illness, and attempt to identify if there are single or multiple lesions. There may often be more than one diagnosis—e.g. cerebrovascular disease and peripheral neuropathy due to diabetes.
- *Assess cognition:* use a scale you are comfortable with such as the Abbreviated Mental Test Score (➔ AMTS p. 247; ➔ MMSE p. 513)—but remember no half marks! Note that the original format of the MMSE is now copyrighted, so may be less readily available.
- *Gait:* even simple observation of a patient's walking can reap rewards. Always include it in your examination where practicable and note why if unable.
- *Therapy colleagues:* sharing observations is a useful practice. Therapists are a huge fount of knowledge and experience so seek to learn from them and how they assess patients.

Additional points

- *Communicating diagnoses:* many diagnoses—e.g. dementia and motor neuron disease—can be devastating, so be thoughtful in your approach. Clarify what the patient knows, and what has already been said—learn first from your seniors how to explain the diagnosis, and more importantly talk about its impact. It is also vital to reassure—many patients with benign essential tremors are terrified that they may have Parkinson's disease.
- *Managing uncertainty:* many diagnoses are not clear, especially in the early stages of diseases. Try to resist labelling your patients when a diagnosis is unclear; be open about uncertainty—patients often cope with it better than their doctors.

The eyes

Important symptoms

The ophthalmic history has extra sections: past ophthalmic history and family ophthalmic history (see Boxes 9.1 and 9.2). Specific symptoms related to the eyes include:

Redness

Ask specifically about:
- Associated factors (discharge, watering).
  - Mucopurulent discharge suggests bacterial infection.
- Pain (sharp, dull).
  - Aching: anterior segment inflammation, acute glaucoma.
- Foreign body sensation.
  - Epithelial defect, foreign body.
- Photophobia.
- Blurred vision.
- Contact lens wear.
- History of trauma.

Diplopia

See Box 9.3.
- Is it actually double or blurred?
  - Patients complain of 'double vision' without true diplopia.
- Duration/age of onset.
- Monocular or binocular?
- Variable or constant?
- Horizontal, vertical, or mixed?
  - Horizontal: III, VI nerve palsies
  - Vertical: IV nerve palsy
  - Variable: myasthenia gravis
  - Progressive: thyroid eye disease.

Visual loss

- Unilateral or bilateral?
  - Uniocular: suggestive of ocular or optic nerve pathology
  - Binocular: lesions at or posterior to the optic chiasm.
- Extent.
  - Severe visual loss can occur with optic neuropathies
  - Unilateral, segmental visual loss: retinal disorders such as retinal detachment and branch retinal vein occlusion.
- Speed of onset.
  - Sudden suggests ischaemic causes
  - Gradual is more typical of compressive causes
  - Progression over a few hours to days can occur in optic neuritis.

Colour vision abnormalities

- Often a feature of optic nerve disease.
- Congenital red–green colour discrimination deficiency is seen in 5–8%.
- Blue–yellow is rarely due to congenital colour deficiency so a causation should be sought.

Flashing lights

- 'Photopsia' is the perception of light in the absence of a light stimulus.
- Monocular or binocular?
  - Monocular is typically due to vitreoretinal pathology
  - Binocular is usually a cortical phenomenon.

Causes:

- Mechanical retinal stimulation (posterior vitreous detachment, tears) or external compression.
- Subretinal pathology (choroidal neovascularization, uveitis, choroidal tumours).
- Cortical ischaemia (migraine or TIA).
- Visual hallucinations.

Other symptoms

Ask also about:

- Glare.
- Haloes or starbursts.
- Floaters.
- Night-driving problems.
- Increased myopia.

Box 9.1 Some causes of pain

- Gritty, sharp pain: corneal epithelial defect (abrasion, keratitis)
- Ache, photophobia: iritis
- Pain on eye movement: optic neuritis
- Scalp tenderness, jaw claudication: temporal arteritis
- Nausea, vomiting: acute angle closure glaucoma, raised intracranial pressure (papilloedema).

Box 9.2 Some causes of floaters

- Weiss ring following posterior vitreous detachment
- Vitreous condensation
- Vitreous haemorrhage
- Liberated pigment cells associated with retinal tears
- Inflammatory cells
- Tumour cells
- Asteroid hyalosis.

The rest of the history

Systems enquiry

Use this to explore symptoms that may point to a systemic disease with ocular manifestations

- Multiple sclerosis: weakness, paraesthesia bladder dysfunction.
- Thyroid eye disease: heat intolerance, weight loss, irritability, anxiety.
- Myasthenia gravis: dysphagia, weakness worse at the end of the day.
- Embolic disease: atherosclerotic disease, arrhythmias.
- Acoustic neuroma: hearing loss, tinnitus, balance problems.
- Rheumatologic and collagen vascular diseases: arthralgia, rashes.

Past medical history

- Diabetes.
- Hypertension.
- Atopy (allergic conjunctivitis).
- Rheumatologic disease (dry eye, corneal melt, scleritis).
- Neurological diseases (VII palsy, exposure keratopathy).
- Metabolic disease (hypercalcaemia).

Past ocular history

- Past ophthalmic surgery.
    - Intraocular (endothelial dysfunction)
    - Refractive (post-laser-assisted stromal *in situ* keratomileusis [LASIK], dry eye, flap dehiscence).
- Does the patient wear glasses?
- Does the patient wear contact lenses?
    - Type
    - Overnight wear?
    - Cleaning regimen (including use of tap water)?
    - Swimming with lenses in?
- Trauma (physical, chemical, radiation).
- Infection.
    - Herpes simplex keratitis
    - Herpes zoster ophthalmicus.

Drug history

- Topical steroid (cataract, glaucoma, herpetic geographic ulcer).
- Toxicity to preservatives/drop allergy.
- Ethambutol, isoniazid, amiodarone, and ciclosporin can cause optic neuropathy.
- Recreational drug use is important, particularly in atypical pupil abnormalities.

Family history

- Family history of multiple sclerosis is common in patients with optic neuritis.
- Contact with infection, conjunctivitis.
- Inherited corneal dystrophies.
- Glaucoma.

Family ophthalmic history

- Ask about any eye diseases which run in the family (e.g. glaucoma, inherited retinal dystrophies).

Social history

Ask especially about:
- Occupation and hobbies: this is very important and needed to understand patient's visual requirements (sports, driving, reading).
- Country of previous residence (sun exposure, poor sanitation).
- Lead and carbon monoxide can cause optic nerve dysfunction.
- Possibility of sexually transmitted diseases (e.g. syphilis, HIV/AIDS).

Box 9.3 Some causes of diplopia

Horizontal: VI nerve palsy
- Impairment of abduction due to lateral rectus palsy
- Horizontal diplopia worse on looking towards the side of the lesion.

Vertical: IV nerve palsy
- Diplopia worse on looking down due to superior oblique palsy
- Ipsilateral hypertropia, worse on looking away from the side of the lesion and on ipsilateral head tilt
- Reduced depression in adduction.

Mixed: III nerve palsy
- May be partial or complete
- Pupil involving or sparing, ± ptosis
- Palsy of all extraocular muscles except lateral rectus and superior oblique.

Mechanical
- Ductions and versions equally reduced
- Causes: thyroid eye disease, trauma (orbital wall/floor fracture), idiopathic orbital inflammatory disease, tumour.

Myasthenia gravis
- 'The great masquerader'
- Intermittent diplopia, variable severity
  - Often worse end of the day/after exercise
  - ± ptosis.
- Ice-pack test: recheck ptosis after placing ice pack on closed eyelid for 2 minutes. Positive if significant improvement of ptosis (>2mm).

Decompensating phoria
- Intermittent but with constant pattern

Monocular
- High refractive disparity between eyes (anisometropia, astigmatism)
- Corneal opacities or ectasias
- Lens subluxation
- Iris defects: trauma, laser peripheral iridotomies.

Visual acuity

It is important to remember the path light takes that enables vision. Any interruption to this pathway can lead to loss of vision (see Box 9.4).

Visual axis – applied anatomy

With an understanding of the anatomy, defects in the visual field enable the localization of a lesion within the visual pathway.

- Light passes through the cornea, anterior chamber, pupil, lens, and vitreous chamber before hitting the retina.
- The optic nerve begins at the retina (and is the only part of the central nervous system that can be directly visualized). The nerve passes through the optic foramen and joins its fellow nerve from the other eye at the 'optic chiasm' just above the pituitary fossa. Here, the fibres from the nasal half of the retina cross over (decussate). They continue in the optic tract to the lateral geniculate body. From there, they splay out such that those from the upper retina pass through the parietal lobe and the others through the temporal lobe.
- 🚹 Students easily get confused here and would do well to get to grips with this at an early stage! Because of the refraction at the lens, images are represented on the retina upside-down and back-to-front. Therefore, the nasal half of the retina receives input from the temporal part of the visual field in each eye, whilst the temporal half of the retina receives input from the nasal half of the eye.
- Fibres from the nasal halves of the retinas cross, so, for example, the left side of the brain receives input from the right side of vision (the left temporal retina and the right nasal retina) and vice versa.

Testing visual acuity

Snellen chart (Fig. 9.1)

In good light conditions, stand the patient 6m from a Snellen chart.

- Test each eye in turn unaided or with the glasses they normally use for distance vision.
  - Repeat the test with a pinhole. Any improvement in vision implies an uncorrected refractive error (rather than ocular pathology).
- Record the lowest line that can be read (allow two errors per line).
  - The number associated with the letters indicates the distance from which a person with normal sight would be expected to read.
- Record the visual acuity as the distance from the chart followed by the number at the lowest letters read.
  - For example, if the patient has read the '36' line from a distance of 6 metres, the visual acuity is '6/36'.

Poor vision

If the patient is unable to see the Snellen chart at all, see if they can:

- Count fingers (CF).
- See hand movements (HM).
- See light (PL).
  - If the patient is unable to see light then record as 'NPL' (no perception of light).

Box 9.4 Some causes of visual loss

Cornea
- Dry eyes, corneal abrasion, corneal ulcer, herpetic keratitis, corneal oedema (acute angle closure glaucoma), keratoconus

Anterior chamber
- Iritis, hyphaema, hypopyon

Lens
- Cataract

Vitreous chamber
- Vitreous haemorrhage, vitritis

Retina
- Branch/central artery or vein occlusion, retinal detachment, macular degeneration, macular oedema, hypertensive retinopathy

Optic nerve
- Optic neuritis, ischaemic optic neuropathy, papilloedema

Optic chiasm
- Pituitary tumour, meningioma

Optic tract
- CVA, tumour

Occipital cortex
- CVA, tumour.

Skills station 9.1

Instruction

Examine this patient's optic nerve function.

Model technique
- Clean your hands
- Introduce yourself
- Explain the purpose of examination, obtain informed consent
- Sit facing the patient
- Measure visual acuity for distance and near
- Measure colour vision (e.g. Ishihara colour plates)
- Check for an RAPD (relative afferent pupillary defect)
- Examine the optic disc looking for any disc swelling, haemorrhage, atrophy, collateral vessels, and cupping
- Perform perimetry (confrontation, manual, automated) to detect any characteristic field defects
- Thank the patient.

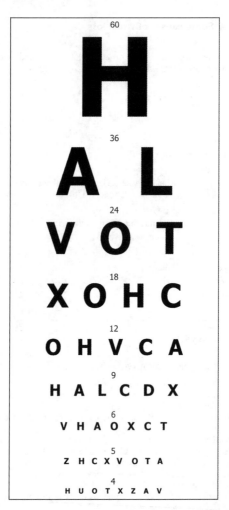

Fig. 9.1 Schematic example of a Snellen chart (reproduced with permission from *Oxford Handbook of Ophthalmology*).

LogMAR chart
This is an alternative method of checking distance vision. It has advantages over Snellen charts overcoming the 'crowding' phenomenon by having five letters on each line with equal spacing (see Fig. 9.2).

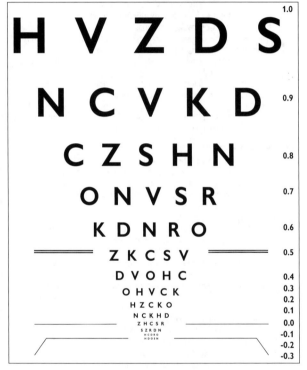

Fig. 9.2 Schematic example of LogMAR chart (reproduced with permission from *Oxford Handbook of Ophthalmology*).

Visual fields

Testing the visual field

Gross defects and visual neglect (inattention)

- Sit opposite the patient, 1m apart, eyes level.
- Test first for gross defects and visual neglect with both eyes open.
  - Ask the patient to look directly at you ('look at my nose')
  - Ask 'is any part of my face missing?'
  - Raise your arms up and out to the sides so that one hand is in the upper right quadrant of your vision and one in the upper left
  - Move one index finger, whilst looking straight at you, to point to the hand which is moving
  - Test with the right, left, and then both hands
  - Test the lower quadrants in the same way
  - If visual neglect is present, the patient will be able to see each hand moving individually but report seeing only one hand when both are moving (compare with sensory inattention).

Testing each eye

- In the same position as above, ask the patient to cover their right eye while you close your left and ask them to look into your right eye.
  - (If you were now to trace the outer borders of your vision in the air halfway between yourself and the patient, it should be almost identical to the area seen by the patient.)
- Test each quadrant individually:
  - Stretch your arm out and up so that your hand is just outside your field of vision, an equal distance between you and the patient
  - Slowly bring your hand into the centre (perhaps wiggling one finger) and ask the patient to say 'yes' as soon as they can see it
  - ❶ Make sure they keep looking at your right eye
  - You should both be able to see your hand at the same time.
- Test upper right and left, lower right and left individually, bringing your hand in from each corner of vision at a time.
  - Ensure that the patient remains looking directly at you (many will attempt to turn and look at the hand if not prompted correctly).
- Map out any areas of visual loss in detail, finding borders. Test if any visual loss extends across the midline horizontally or vertically.
- Test each eye in turn (you both may require a short break between eyes as this requires considerable concentration).
- Repeat the above procedure with a red-headed pin or similar small red object to map out areas of visual loss in more detail.
  - Ask the patient to say 'yes' when they see the pin as red
  - Start by mapping out the blind spot which should be 15° lateral from the centre at the midline (this tests both your technique and the patient's reliability as a witness before proceeding).
- Decide if any defect is of a quadrant, half the visual field or another shape and in which eye, or both.
- Record by drawing the defect in two circles representing the patient's visual fields as shown in Fig. 9.3.

Common visual field defects

Compare the defects below with the corresponding number on Fig. 9.3.

- *Tunnel vision:* a constricted visual field (glaucoma or retinal damage).
  - 'Tubular' vision is often functional.
- *Enlarged blind spot:* caused by papilloedema.
- *Unilateral visual loss:* (1) blindness in one eye caused by devastating damage to the eye, its blood supply, or optic nerve.
- *Scotoma:* a 'hole' in the visual field (macular degeneration, vascular lesion or toxins).
  - If bilateral, may indicate a very small defect in the corresponding area of the occipital cortex (e.g. multiple sclerosis).
- *Bitemporal hemianopia:* (2) the nasal half of both retinas and, therefore, the temporal half of each visual field is lost (damage to the centre of the optic chiasm such as pituitary tumour, craniopharyngioma, suprasellar meningioma).
- *Binasal hemianopia:* the nasal half of each visual field is lost (rare).
- *Homonymous hemianopia:* (3) commonly seen in stroke patients. The right or left side of vision in both eyes is lost (e.g. the nasal field in the right eye and the temporal field in the left eye). If the central part of vision (the macula) is spared, the lesion is likely in the optic radiation; without macula sparing, the lesion is in the optic tract.
- *Homonymous quadrantanopia:* corresponding quarters of the vision are lost in each eye.
  - Upper quadrantanopias (4) suggest a lesion in the temporal lobe
  - Lower quadrantanopias (5) suggest a lesion in the parietal lobe.

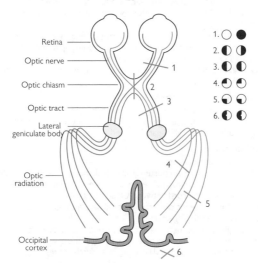

Fig. 9.3 Representation of the visual pathway from the retina to the occipital cortex showing visual field loss according to site of lesion.

The pupils

Pupillary abnormalities include irregular pupil size and impaired reflexes to light and accommodation. (See Boxes 9.5 and 9.6.)

Applied anatomy

Pupil size is controlled by the autonomic nervous system.

- Pupil constriction (miosis) via parasympathetic nerves through innervation of the sphincter pupillae.
- Pupil dilation (mydriasis), via the dilator pupillae muscle is under sympathetic control.

Light reflex (parasympathetic system)

- Nasal retinal fibres cross at the chiasm and connect to the contralateral pretectal nucleus, which innervates both Edinger–Westphal nuclei (see Fig. 9.4).
- Temporal retinal fibres connect to the ipsilateral pretectal nucleus, which again innervates both Edinger–Westphal nuclei.
  - This quadruple innervation ensures that both pupils constrict when light is shone in either eye.
- The parasympathetic preganglionic motor fibres connect the Edinger–Westphal nucleus to the ciliary ganglion.
- The postganglionic fibres connect the ciliary ganglion to the sphincter pupillae via the short ciliary nerves.

Relative afferent pupillary defect (RAPD)

- Light shining into an eye will lead to constriction of the ipsilateral pupil, the 'direct' reflex, but also constriction of the contralateral eye, the 'consensual' reflex.
- If there is a defect in the afferent pathway (e.g. optic nerve damage), shining a light into the affected eye will cause both pupils to initially dilate.
- An RAPD can still be detected if one eye is pharmacologically dilated. One should observe the undilated pupil to assess whether an initial dilatation occurs.

Near reflex (parasympathetic system)

Looking at a near target activates the 'near reflex' which comprises accommodation, convergence, and miosis. The final pathways are as for the light reflex, e.g. third nerve, ciliary ganglion, and short ciliary nerves.

Sympathetic system

This involves three neurons:

- *Central:* descends from posterior hypothalamus through the ipsilateral brainstem to the ciliospinal centre of Budge in the intermediolateral horn of the spinal cord between C8 and T2 (see Fig. 9.5).
- *Preganglionic:* ascends close to the apical pleura to terminate in the superior cervical ganglion in the neck.
- *Postganglionic:* ascends along internal carotid artery, joining the ophthalmic division of the trigeminal nerve in the cavernous sinus. It terminates in the dilator pupillae muscle via the long ciliary nerve.

Testing for RAPD

- With the patient sitting opposite, shine a pen-torch into one eye for 2–3 seconds.
- Quickly swing the light into the other eye.
- Watch for an initial pupillary dilatation (RAPD).

Testing the accommodation reflex

- With the patient sitting opposite you, hold up an accommodative target (e.g. page of a book) approximately 30cm in front of the patient.
- Watch for pupil constriction.
- If in doubt, ask the patient to look at something distant over your shoulder and then at the page again.

Skills station 9.2

Instruction

Examine this patient's pupils.

Model technique

- Clean your hands
- Introduce yourself
- Explain the purpose of examination, obtain informed consent
- Sit facing the patient
- Ask the patient to fixate on a distant target
- Look for any anisocoria (difference in pupil size), heterochromia (difference in iris colour), ptosis, or ocular deviation
- Dark response
  - Measure pupil sizes with ruler and then dim room lights and repeat measurements.
  - If anisocoria is present, the larger pupil in bright conditions is likely to be the abnormal one and vice versa
- Check direct pupil light response in each eye
  - Shine a torch and observe the pupil reaction in that eye
- Check consensual pupil response
  - Shine a torch into one eye and observe the pupil reaction in the other eye.
- Check for a relative afferent pupillary defect (RAPD)
- Check accommodation reflex
- Thank the patient and help them re-dress as necessary.

In a full examination:

- If possible, examine patient on slit lamp looking for vermiform iris movements (in Adie's pupil)
- Perform eye-movements examination looking for associated nerve palsies
- Perform full neurological examination, particularly checking for decreased deep tendon reflexes (in Holmes–Adie–Moore syndrome).

Pupil abnormalities

Relative afferent pupillary defect (RAPD)

This results from lesions in the anterior visual pathway.

⚠ Corneal opacities or cataract do not cause a RAPD.

Causes include:
- Optic neuropathy (e.g. optic neuritis, compressive lesions).
- Gross retinal pathology (e.g. central retinal vein occlusion (CRVO), retinal detachment).
- Optic chiasm and tract lesions (infarcts, demyelination).

Horner's syndrome

Oculosympathetic palsy (interruption of the cervicothoracic sympathetic chain at a 1st, 2nd, or 3rd order neuron level). Multiple causes, depending on site of lesion.
- Unilateral mild ptosis.
- Ipsilateral anhydrosis (decreased sweating).
- Ipsilateral iris heterochromia (different or lighter coloured iris if the lesion is congenital or long-standing).
- Mild miosis.
- Normal or slight delay of pupillary dilatation.
- No relative afferent pupillary defect.

Argyll Robertson pupil

Caused by neurosyphilis.
- Constricted and irregular pupils (asymmetric).
- No reaction to light.
- Brisk constriction to accommodation.

Holmes–Adie–Moore syndrome (or Adie's pupil)

Denervation of the sphincter pupillae and ciliary muscles, probably following viral illness. Usually seen in middle-aged females.
- Dilated pupil (mydriasis).
  - Anisocoria (difference in pupil size) greater in the light.
- Poor response to light and accommodation.
- Deep tendon reflexes may be reduced or absent.

Pupil involving 3rd nerve palsy

Causes include subdural haematoma with uncal herniation, posterior communicating artery aneurysm, tumour, vasculitis.
- Fixed dilated pupil, ptosis, eye held 'down and out' with restricted eye movements.

Box 9.5 Light-near dissociation

Absent or sluggish response to light but normal accommodation reflex
- Afferent conduction defect (e.g. optic neuropathy)
- Holmes–Adie–Moore pupil
- Argyll Robertson pupil
- Aberrant third nerve regeneration
- Myotonic dystrophy
- Parinaud dorsal midbrain syndrome.

Box 9.6 Some other causes of abnormal pupils

Pupil is constricted
- Pharmacological (alcohol, opiates, antipsychotics)
- Chronic Adie's pupil
- Iritis.

Pupil is dilated
- Pharmacological (atropine, LSD, psilocybin mushrooms, cocaine, amphetamines, SSRI antidepressants)
- Iris trauma.

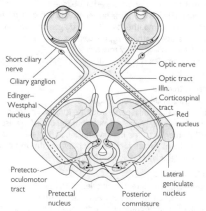

Fig. 9.4 Light reflex pathway. Reproduced with permission from *Training in Ophthalmology* by Sundaram et al.

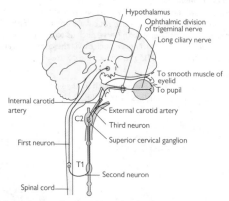

Fig. 9.5 Sympathetic pupil pathway. Reproduced with permission from *Training in Ophthalmology* by Sundaram et al.

Eye movements

Eye movements are controlled by three cranial nerves: oculomotor (III), trochlear (IV), and abducens (VI). There are also supranuclear centres that control conjugate eye movements or 'versions', where both eyes move in synchrony (see Fig. 9.6 and Box 9.7).

Applied anatomy

Third (III) nerve: oculomotor

- *Motor:* levator palpebrae superioris, superior rectus, medial rectus, inferior rectus, inferior oblique. (All the extrinsic muscles of the eye except the lateral rectus and superior oblique.)
    - The III nerve has two motor nuclei: the main motor nucleus and the accessory parasympathetic nucleus (Edinger–Westphal nucleus).
- *Autonomic:* parasympathetic supply to the constrictor (sphincter) pupillae of the iris and ciliary muscles.
- The nuclear complex is in the midbrain at the level of the superior colliculus.

Fourth (IV) nerve: trochlear

- *Motor:* contralateral superior oblique.
    - It is the thinnest cranial nerve with the longest intracranial course and the only cranial nerve to exit from the dorsal brainstem.
- Nucleus lies inferior to the III nerve nuclei, at the level of the inferior colliculus in the midbrain. It receives input from the vestibular system and medial longitudinal fasciculus (MLF).

Sixth (VI) nerve: abducens

- *Motor:* ipsilateral lateral rectus muscle.
- The nucleus lies beneath the 4th ventricle. It connects with the nuclei of the III and IV cranial nerves through the medial longitudinal fasciculus.

Horizontal eye movements

- Horizontal eye movements are controlled by the horizontal gaze centre in the pontine paramedian reticular formation (PPRF). This connects to the ipsilateral sixth nerve nucleus to abduct the eye and also the contralateral third nerve nucleus via the contralateral median longitudinal fasciculus (MLF) to adduct the contralateral eye.

Vertical eye movements

- Vertical eye movements are controlled by the vertical gaze centre in the rostral interstitial nucleus of the MLF.

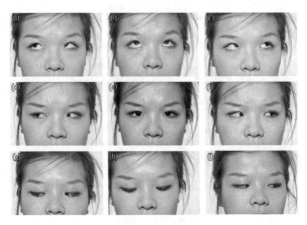

Fig. 9.6 The nine positions of gaze, including looking straight ahead (neutral position).

Box 9.7 Normal and abnormal eye movements

- *Ductions:* normal monocular movements including adduction, abduction, elevation, depression, intorsion, and extorsion
- *Versions:* normal binocular, conjugate eye movements where both eyes move in the same direction
- *Vergences:* normal binocular eye movements in which the eyes move synchronously in opposite directions (e.g. convergence)
- *Phorias:* eye deviations which are not obvious during normal binocular vision (when the retinal images are 'fused'). They can 'decompensate' when the patient is tired and become obvious or can be seen when binocular vision is prevented (e.g. covering one eye)
- *Tropias:* obvious deviations. For example:
  - Esotropia = inward deviation
  - Exotropia = divergent squint.

Examining eye movements

Observe

- Position yourself opposite the patient and assess their head posture.
- Look for ptosis (drooping of the eyelid).
- Shine a pen-torch into each eye from a central position in front of the nose and look for asymmetry of the corneal reflections.
  - Both should be approximately central. If the reflection is nasal to the pupil the eye is exotropic. If it is temporal it is esotropic.

Cover test

This is used to assess for phorias (see Box 9.3). These are eye deviations which are compensated for during normal binocular vision.

- Ask the patient to look at a distant target.
- Cover each eye in turn with your hand and watch for movement of the other eye. If the non-covered eye moves to take fixation, there is a phoria and the direction of movement gives a clue as to the type:
  - Inward movement = exotropia (eye had been outward)
  - Outward = esotropia (eye had been inward)
  - Down = hypertropia (eye had been up)
  - Up = hypotropia (eye had been down).

Uncover test

- Remove the cover and watch for movement in the eye that is revealed.
  - See cover test above for interpretation of the movements.

Alternate cover test

- Repeatedly cover each eye for a few seconds moving quickly between each eye so one is always covered.
  - Watch for any eye deviation and recovery.

Voluntary eye movements

- Ask the patient if they have any diplopia in primary position (looking straight at you).
- Sitting opposite the patient, ask them to follow a target (e.g. your finger tip or pen-torch) without moving their head.
  - Sometimes, your hand on their chin helps to hold the head still.
- Examine the nine positions of gaze as in Fig. 9.6.
  - Avoid the extremes of gaze
  - Ask if they have double vision in each position
  - Watch for failure of eye movements or abnormal movements (e.g. nystagmus)
  - Perform a cover test in each position.

Saccades

- Hold two targets either side of the patient (your thumb of one hand and a finger of your other hand works well).
- Ask the patient to look rapidly between the two targets.
  - Often a quick demonstration helps
  - Movements should be accurate, smooth, and rapid.
- Repeat for the vertical meridian (holding targets above and below the midline).

Convergence
- Hold a target approximately 1m in front of the patient and ask them to fix on it.
- Slowly bring the target towards the patient and watch their eyes.
  - The eyes should converge slowly, symmetrically, and smoothly.

Skills station 9.3

Instruction

Examine this patient's eye movements.

Model technique
- Clean your hands
- Introduce yourself
- Explain the purpose of examination, obtain informed consent
- Sit facing the patient
- Ask the patient if they have any visual problems
- Perform a brief examination of visual acuity and visual fields
  - Asking a blind patient to follow your finger will not work!
- Ask the patient to look straight at you
- Make note of the patient's head position and any evidence of ptosis
- Ask the patient to look at your nose
  - Look for any obvious asymmetry in eye position (strabismus)
- With the patient's eyes in neutral position, perform the cover–uncover test
- Examine voluntary eye movements
- Perform the cover–uncover test in each of the nine positions of gaze if necessary
- Test saccadic eye movements
- Test convergence
- Thank the patient.

III, IV, and VI palsies

Oculomotor (III) palsy

Clinical features

- Ptosis.
- Affected eye is exotropic and hypotropic ('down and out').
- Ophthalmoplegia in all directions other than laterally and inferiorly (Fig. 9.7).
- Mydriasis (pupillary dilation—variable).
  - The fibres which control pupil constriction lie near the surface of the nerve and are supplied by surface blood vessels, thus are vulnerable to compressive lesions. Pupil dilatation distinguishes 'medical' third nerve palsy from 'surgical' (compressive) nerve palsy.

Causes

- 20–45% microvascular causes (with diabetes and hypertension).
- 15–20% intracranial aneurysms (often posterior communicating artery).
- Trauma.
- Tumours.
- Demyelination.
- Vasculitis.
- Congenital.

Trochear (IV) palsy

Clinical features

- Vertical diplopia (worse on downgaze).
- Slight external rotation of affected eye (head may be tilted to opposite side to compensate).
- Hypertropia (eye sits higher than contralateral side).
  - Worse on contralateral gaze and ipsilateral head tilt.
- Limitation of depression in adduction.

Causes

- 30–40% due to head trauma.
- 20% microvascular disease (often improves within 3–4 months).
- Congenital (common, although not usually symptomatic until adult life).
- Others: haemorrhage, infarction, demyelination, tumours, infection.

Abducens (VI) palsy

Clinical features

- Inability to abduct the affected eye.
- Diplopia (worse when looking in direction of paretic muscle and worse for distance than near).

Causes

- Microvascular lesions (most common).
- Other causes: demyelination, infarction, raised intracranial pressure, tumours, meningeal infection, aneurysm (basilar artery), inflammatory processes.

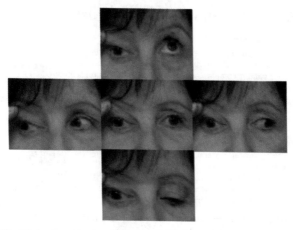

Fig. 9.7 A patient with right oculomotor (III) palsy, shown in five directions of gaze.

Combined nerve palsies

The cavernous sinus

All three nerves involved in oculomotor control, with sympathetic fibres to the iris and the ophthalmic and maxillary divisions of the trigeminal nerve pass through here. Common lesions include: carotico-cavernous fistula; expanding pituitary tumour; cavernous sinus thrombosis—associated with proptosis and injection of conjunctival vessels (chemosis); aneurysm.

The orbit

A complex range of ophthalmoplegias can result from any compressive lesion located within the orbit. Proptosis may be present with variable optic nerve involvement. Many lesions may directly impinge upon the extraocular muscles as well as the innervating nerves.

Superior orbital fissure

The superior orbital fissure transmits all the nerves supplying the extra-ocular muscles along with the ophthalmic division of the trigeminal nerve. Inflammation or a lesion at the superior orbital fissure leads to Tolosa–Hunt syndrome—a complex unilateral ophthalmoplegia associated with anaesthesia over the forehead and ocular pain.

Other eye movement disorders

Internuclear ophthalmoplegia (INO)

An interruption of the medial longitudinal fasciculus (MLF) that interconnects the nuclei of cranial nerves III and VI on opposite sides.

The patient complains of horizontal diplopia due to impaired adduction on the affected side.

Unilateral lesions
- Impaired adduction in the ipsilateral eye.
- Nystagmus is often seen in the abducting eye (Box 9.8).

Bilateral lesions
- May appear bilaterally exotropic (eyes look laterally).
- Vertical nystagmus.
- Impaired visual pursuit.
- Convergence is intact in posterior lesions and absent in anterior and mesencephalic lesions.

Parapontine reticular formation (PPRF) lesions

The PPRF is responsible for conjugate movements in horizontal gaze.
- Horizontal gaze paresis towards the affected side.
- Preservation of vertical gaze.

Causes: vascular disease, demyelinating disease, tumour.

'One and a half syndrome'

INO with the addition of a lesion in the PPRF or the ipsilateral VI nucleus.
- Conjugate gaze palsy to the side ipsilateral to the lesion (this is the 'one') and an inability to adduct the eye on the affected side when looking contralaterally (this is the 'half').

Parinaud's (dorsal midbrain) syndrome

- Impaired upgaze in both eyes giving convergence, retraction of the globe into the orbit, and nystagmus.
- Light-near dissociation.
  - The near response is intact but the light response is slow.
- Lid retraction (Collier's sign).

Causes: demyelination, arteriovenous malformation, tumour, enlarged 3rd ventricle, vascular disease affecting the midbrain, meningitis.

Box 9.8 Nystagmus

Nystagmus is involuntary rhythmic oscillation of the eyes and may have a number of appearances

- Direction: vertical, horizontal, upbeat, downbeat, rotatory
- Speed of away movement: slow, fast
- Speed of corrective movement
- *Pendular nystagmus:* oscillation is the same speed in both directions
- *Jerk nystagmus:* different speeds in different directions. The 'direction' of the nystagmus is determined by the fast phase.

Sensory deprivation nystagmus

- A pendular type of nystagmus due to a lack of visual stimulus
- Seen in a number of conditions including: congenital cataract, ocular albinism, aniridia, congenital optic nerve abnormalities.

Motor nystagmus

- Usually present at birth or very early in life. Not present whilst asleep. Decreases with convergence.

Latent nystagmus

- Bilateral jerk nystagmus which is only present when one eye is covered
- The fast phase of the jerk is away from the occluded eye.

Dissociated nystagmus

- Different pattern of nystagmus seen in the two eyes
- Causes include: INO, posterior fossa pathology.

Downbeat nystagmus

- A jerk nystagmus. Fast phase is down, slow upbeat. Null point in upgaze
- Associated with diseases of the craniomedullary junction: MS, stroke, syringomyelia, Arnold–Chiari malformation, lithium toxicity.

Gaze-evoked nystagmus

- Seen in particular directions of gaze and not in the primary position
- If physiological, it should be fatiguable and symmetrical
- Pathological causes: drugs, lesions of the brainstem and posterior fossa.

Upbeat nystagmus

- Seen in the primary position of gaze
- Causes: Wernicke's encephalopathy, drugs, lower brainstem lesions.

Vestibular nystagmus

- Another type of jerk nystagmus secondary to vestibular disease Often a rotary component. The fast phase away is from the side of the lesion. Check for associated tinnitus, vertigo, or hearing loss.

Anterior segment examination

This is ideally performed with a slit lamp, but all the findings should be visible with an ophthalmoscope.

Set the dial to +10 to focus on the anterior segment.

Even without an ophthalmoscope you can gain a lot of information using a pen-torch and a blue filter (Box 9.9).

Examination routine

- Check for RAPD (see p. 319).
- General inspection.
  - General habitus
  - Facial asymmetry
  - Skin lesions (e.g. herpes).
- Lids.
  - Position: ptosis, entropion (inverted lid), ectropion (everted lid)
  - Examine the lashes, looking for blepharitis or other lesions
  - Look for lumps, erythema, swelling
  - Evert the upper and lower lids, looking at the conjunctiva and fornices. Look especially for foreign bodies, papillae, follicles, symblepharon (partial or complete adhesion of the palpebral conjunctiva of the eyelid to the bulbar conjunctiva of the globe).
- Conjunctiva.
  - Look for: hyperaemia, haemorrhage, chemosis (oedema), lumps, abrasions, foreign bodies, pterygia (benign growth of conjunctiva).
- Sclera.
  - Look for: colour, hyperaemia, swelling.
- Cornea.
  - Raise the lid to examine entire cornea
  - Instil a drop of 2% fluorescein and look for epithelial defects which will fluoresce green under a blue light.
- Anterior chamber.
  - Gauge the depth
  - Check for cells, fibrin, flare, blood (hyphaema), pus (hypopyon).
- Iris.
  - Note: colour, shape, movement, atrophy.
  - Use retroillumination to check for transillumination defects.
- Lens.
  - Look for: cataract, intraocular lens. Note position, movement.
- Anterior vitreous.
  - Focus behind the lens and ask the patient to look up, down, and then straight ahead to view the vitreous
  - Check for cells (small white deposits), 'tobacco dust' (pigment indicative of retinal tear), blood.

Box 9.9 Using a slit lamp

Only ophthalmologists will be expected to be proficient with a slit-lamp microscope. We include this for those that wish to impress:

- Check the slit lamp is plugged in and turn the switch on the left-hand side to get a light beam
  - If it is not working, check the bulb.
- Adjust the eye pieces to your interpupillary diameter (IPD) and dial in your own refraction for each eye piece
- Choose the light beam from the switch at the top (bright light, bright light with heat filter, normal light, green light, blue light)
  - Start with the normal light with a thin beam and then use the bright light with filter when required
  - Adjust the width, height, angle, and orientation of the light beam.
- Adjust the height of the patient's chair and your own to ensure they are at comfortable heights for you both
  - The height of the slit lamp can be adjusted with a lever under the table
- Ask the patient to place their chin in the rest and press their forehead against the bar. Ensure it is a comfortable height for them
- Adjust the height of the chin rest to align the patient's eyes with mark on the slit lamp
- Move the slit lamp slowly towards the patient and use the joystick for fine adjustments to get the eye in focus
  - You can twist the joystick to raise or lower the light beam
- Examine the anterior segment as on ⊃ p. 330.
  - You can increase the magnification by turning the switch beneath the eye pieces.

Direct illumination

- Using a coaxial light (angling the light) will allow greater evaluation of the cornea and anterior segment
- Check for cells.
  - Use a coaxial light and focus on the centre of the anterior chamber with the blackness of the pupil in the background
  - Cells will look like small dust particles visible in the light beam rising and falling in the aqueous flow.

Retroillumination

- Shorten the bright light beam and direct straight ahead through the pupil onto the retina. As the light is reflected you can assess lens opacities (dilated pupil) or iris transillumination defects.

Posterior segment examination

The posterior segment is the part of the eye deep to the lens and includes the vitreous, optic disc, and the retina (see Box 9.10).

Direct ophthalmoscopic examination of the fundus is a vital part of any neurological examination but often avoided by students as it is considered difficult.

The direct ophthalmoscope gives a greatly magnified view of the fundus but gaining a view of the peripheral retina beyond the equator requires examination with the slit lamp or the indirect ophthalmoscope.

For a complete ophthalmoscopic examination it is often worth dilating the pupil by instilling a few drops of mydriatic (1% tropicamide or 1% cyclopentolate) into the inferior conjunctival sac.

🛈 If you plan to dilate the pupil, ask the patient if they have any history of angle closure glaucoma or episodes of seeing haloes around lights at night-time. If you suspect this, or the anterior chamber of the eye appears shallow, it is best to err on the side of caution—dilating the pupil could occlude the drainage angle and precipitate an acute attack.

Using an ophthalmoscope

- Introduce yourself, explain the procedure to the patient, and gain informed consent.
- Ensure the room is dimly lit and, ideally, sit opposite the patient.
  - This can be performed with the patient lying down.
- Familiarize yourself with the ophthalmoscope. Choose a large-aperture light and adjust the brightness so as not to dazzle your patient.
- Ask the patient to focus on a distant object and keep their eyes still (relaxes accommodation as much as possible).
- Set the refraction to +10.
- Look through the ophthalmoscope ~30cm away from the patient and bring the light in nasally from the temporal field to land on the pupil..
  - The pupil will appear red and opacities in the visual axis will appear as black dots or lines
  - By cycling through the different lenses of the ophthalmoscope, you should be able to gain an impression of where these opacities lie. Possible locations are the cornea, aqueous, lens (and its anterior and posterior capsules), and vitreous.
- Approach the patient from 15 degrees keeping in mind the angle the optic nerve enters the eye.
  - Be careful not to block the view of their other eye which maintains fixation and allows them to keep their eyes still.
- With the +10 setting you can examine the anterior segment.
  - By gradually ↓ the power of the lens you can examine the cornea, iris, and lens in turn.
- Ask the patient to look up, down, and then straight ahead to view the vitreous.
- As you approach, dial the refraction to 0 or to your own refraction.
- Find a blood vessel and adjust the focus as necessary. Follow the blood vessel, as it increases in diameter to the optic disc. If you don't find it try following it in the other direction.

- Examine the optic disc, noting:
  - Cup:disc ratio
  - Colour
  - Shape
  - Margin
  - Rim
  - Abnormal vasculature.
- Examine all 4 quadrants.
- Examine the macula.
  - Ask the patient to look directly at the light.

Box 9.10 What to look for on ophthalmoscopy

Vitreous

- Cells (appear as small white particles)
- Pigment
- Blood
- Asteroid hyalosis (calcium deposits in the vitreous)
- Weiss ring (posterior vitreous detachment).

Macula

- Dot/blot haemorrhages
- Microaneurysms
- Exudates
- Cotton-wool spots
- Oedema.

Vessels

- Venous beading
- Venous loops
- Intraretinal microvascular abnormalities (IRMAs)
- New vessels (very thin, tortuous vessels)
- 'Silver wiring' (arteries appear to have a shiny, silver strip)
- Arteriovenous nipping (veins are 'pinched' as arteries pass over)
- Macroaneurysm.

Peripheral retina

- Degenerations
- Tears
- Retinal detachment
- Pigmentation
- Laser/cryotherapy scars
- Chorioretinal scars
- Tumours.

Eye trauma

Being faced with a patient who has sustained trauma can be disconcerting but by maintaining a systematic approach you will not miss any important signs. It is critical in cases of assault that you document your findings accurately with drawings/images as cases may involve legal proceedings (see Box 9.11).

The history

Take a complete history but specifically include.
- Date and time of injury.
- Mechanism of injury: blunt, sharp, high velocity.
- Visual symptoms: blurring, floaters, flashing lights, diplopia.
- Don't forget other facial/systemic injuries.

Examination routine

- Visual acuity (best corrected and pin-hole).
- Pupils: equal and reactive?
- RAPD?
- Lids: swelling, bruising, laceration?
- Anterior segment examination.
  - In cases of suspected globe rupture, keep manipulation to the absolute minimum.
- Conjunctiva: laceration, subconjunctival haemorrhage?
- Cornea: is it clear?
  - Apply a drop of 2% fluorescein and examine under a blue light. Epithelial defects will fluoresce green (Siedel test).
- Anterior chamber: cells, blood (hyphaema), disparity in depth compared to the other eye.
- Lens: opacity, check for any movement as the patient moves their eye.
- Vitreous: haemorrhage?
- Retina: commotio retinae (white/blanched areas of retina), haemorrhage, retinal tears/detachment, choroidal rupture.
- Optic disc: check function and appearance.

Box 9.11 Some clinical presentations of trauma

Chemical injury

Alkalis are more dangerous than acids, causing greater cellular disruption and can penetrate deep into the stroma and beyond

- Check the pH in both eyes
- Irrigate first, complete the assessment later
- Check for limbal ischaemia (blanching of limbal conjunctival vessels)
- Check corneal clarity: haze develops with severe chemical injury
- Other clinical features: chemosis, epithelial defect, anterior uveitis.

Foreign body

These may be penetrating and perforating (enter and exit)

- Establish the risk of penetrating injury from the history
- Examine for signs of perforation: reduced visual acuity, epithelial defect (Siedel positive), irregular pupil, iris defect, lens defect
- Evert the lids, dilate, and examine for vitreous haemorrhage or retinal foreign body.

Corneal foreign body

- Patients complain of a sensation of something in their eye. Also photophobia, watering, blurred vision
- Look for: conjunctival hyperaemia, visible corneal foreign body ± rust ring or infiltrate, ± anterior uveitis.

Corneal abrasion

- Conjunctival hyperaemia, corneal epithelial defect, relief of pain with topical anaesthetic, improved vision with a pin-hole.

Traumatic hyphaema

- History of blunt trauma
- Blood in anterior chamber, ± traumatic mydriasis (dilated pupil), irregular pupil (pupil sphincter damage).

Globe rupture: anterior

- History of severe injury
- Subconjunctival haemorrhage, herniation of uveal tissue, shallow anterior chamber, hyphaema, ± corneal oedema, endophthalmitis.

Globe rupture: posterior

- History of severe injury
- Subconjunctival haemorrhage, deep anterior chamber compared to non-injured eye, vitreous haemorrhage, retinal haemorrhage, retinal detachment, endophthalmitis.

Orbital fracture

- History of blunt trauma (e.g. tennis ball)
- Clinical features: blurred vision, ± diplopia, periorbital bruising haemorrhage, hyphaema, painful restricted eye movements, infraorbital hypoaesthesia (infraorbital nerve damage associated with orbital floor fractures), enophthalmos, surgical emphysema.

The red eye

Approach

- A careful history must be taken including previous ophthalmic history, systems review, and family history of eye disease.
- Examine the eyes systematically:
  - Visual acuity
  - Pupil responses
  - Lids
  - Conjunctiva/sclera
  - Cornea (add fluorescein and examine under a cobalt blue light for an epithelial defect)
  - Anterior chamber
  - Iris
  - Lens.
- Always record the patient's visual acuity for distance and near with their appropriate prescription.
  - ▶ Don't forget to check both eyes.
- Can the vision be improved with a pin-hole?

Red flags

- ▶ A red eye in a contact lens wearer should be assumed to be microbial keratitis until proven otherwise and should be seen by an ophthalmologist the same day.
- A significant reduction in visual acuity not corrected by a pin-hole or the patient's glasses should be regarded as sinister.

Causes of the red eye

Conjunctivitis
See Box 9.12.

Uveitis
- Inflammation of the uveal tract (iris, ciliary body, and choroid).
- Anterior uveitis usually presents with circumcorneal injection and photophobia, watering, blurring of the vision.
- Aggressive uveitis may lead to the iris sticking to the lens. This (posterior synechiae) may give the pupil a small irregular appearance.
- In severe cases, pus may form in the anterior chamber (hypopyon).

Microbial keratitis (corneal ulcer)
- *Symptoms:* discomfort, often history of prolonged contact lens wear, photophobia, blurred vision.
- *Signs:* infected conjunctiva, corneal ulcer, ± anterior chamber cells.

Herpes simplex keratitis
- *Symptoms:* pain and photophobia. Often the eye waters, there may be a history of cold sores.
- *Signs:* a branching dendritic ulcer is visible on the surface of the cornea with fluorescein under a cobalt blue light.

Episcleritis

- Inflammation of the layer superficial to the sclera, deep to conjunctiva.
- *Symptoms:* bruised, tender feeling, watering.
- *Signs:* the inflamed vessels in the episclera are superficial and can be moved by touch unlike the deeper scleral vessels. Sometimes nodular.

Scleritis

- May be seen in association with connective tissue diseases (Wegener's granulomatosis, rheumatoid disease, polyarteritis nodosa).
- *Symptoms:* severe eye pain that keeps the patient awake at night.
- *Signs:* the sclera may thin revealing the choroid below as a blue tinge.

Subconjunctival haemorrhage

- Redness is usually the only symptoms and sign.
- Check for hypertension or a bleeding disorder.

Acute angle closure

- ▶ An emergency.
- Systemic features include nausea, vomiting, and headache.
  - A typical history includes blurred vision and haloes around lights.
- Clinical features: significant reduction in vision; red, infected eye. Fixed, mid-dilated and oval-shaped pupil, hazy cornea due to oedema.
- Raised intraocular pressure makes the eye feel hard (compare sides).

Box 9.12 Conjunctivitis

Bacterial

- *Symptoms:* acute red eye, grittiness, burning, discharge, no visual loss
- *Signs:* infected conjunctiva, mucopurulent discharge, clear cornea.

Viral

- *Symptoms:* acute red eye, watering, often starts in one eye and then spreads to other eye
- *Signs:* red eye, watering, ± chemosis, ± eyelid oedema, ± pseudo-membrane, corneal subepithelial opacities, tender lymphadenopathy.

Chlamydial

- *Symptoms:* unilateral or bilateral mucopurulent discharge, red eye (may become chronic), ± urethritis (may be asymptomatic)
- *Signs:* red eye, mucopurulent discharge, ± peripheral corneal infiltrates, tender lymphadenopathy.

Allergic

- *Symptoms:* itching is the key symptom, bilateral redness, watering, associated 'hay fever' symptoms (sneezing, nasal discharge)
- *Signs:* lid oedema, 'pinkish' conjunctivae, papillae.

Ophthalmia neonatorum

- Conjunctivitis occurring in the first month of life, commonly acquired during birth. It is a notifiable disease in the UK
- *Clinical features:* mucopurulent discharge, ± chemosis, lid oedema, keratitis.
  - *Chlamydial:* onset 4–28 days after birth
  - *Gonococcal:* hyperacute onset (1–3 days after birth).

Eye signs in thyroid disease

Examination

Inspection
- Look at the patient's eyes from the front, side, and from above (see Box 9.13).
- Note whether the sclera is visible above or below the iris and whether the eyeball appears to sit forward (proptosis—best seen from above).
- Note the health of the conjunctiva and sclera looking especially for any ulceration or conjunctivitis.
- Ensure both eyes can close (failure is a medical emergency).

Visual fields
It is wise to perform a quick screening test of the visual fields.

Eye movements
Test eye movements in all directions.

Lid lag (von Graefe's sign)
- Hold your finger high and ask the patient to look at it and follow it with their eyes as it moves (keeping their head still).
- Quickly move your hand downwards—in this way the patient is made to look upwards and then quickly downwards.
- Watch the eyes and eyelids—do they move smoothly and together?
  - If lid lag is present, the upper eyelid seems to lag behind the movement of the eye, allowing white sclera to be seen above the iris as the eye moves downward.

Findings

Proptosis
- Protrusion of the globes as a result of an increase in retro-orbital fat, oedema, and cellular infiltration.
- It can be formally assessed using 'Hertel's exophthalmometer'.

Exophthalmos
This is a more severe form of proptosis. Sclera becomes visible below the lower edge of the iris (the inferior limbus). In very severe cases, the patient may not be able to close their eyelids and can develop:
- Corneal ulceration.
- Chemosis (oedema of the conjunctiva and sclera caused by obstruction of the normal venous and lymphatic drainage).
- Conjunctivitis.

Lid retraction
The upper eyelid is retracted such that you are able to see white sclera above the iris when the patient looks forwards.

Caused by ↑ tone and spasm of levator palpebrae superioris as a result of thyroid hormone excess (Dalrymple's sign).

Lid lag
Described above. Caused by sympathetic overstimulation of the muscles supplying the upper eyelid—seen in thyroid hormone excess.

Box 9.13 Eye signs of thyrotoxicosis and Graves' disease

A common misconception is that proptosis and exophthalmos are caused by thyrotoxicosis. This is not the case. Proptosis and exophthalmos may be seen in 50% of patients with thyrotoxicosis due to Graves' disease. However, the proptosis may persist once thyroid hormone levels have been normalized.

Eye signs of thyrotoxicosis

- Lid retraction
- Lid lag.

Eye signs of Graves' disease (Graves' ophthalmopathy)

- Periorbital oedema and chemosis
- Proptosis/exophthalmos
- Ophthalmoplegias (particularly of upward gaze)
- Lid retraction and lid lag *only* when thyrotoxicosis is present.

Visual blurring may indicate optic neuropathy; therefore, fundoscopy should be performed.

Important presentations

Painful loss of vision

- Trauma.
  - Corneal foreign body, corneal abrasion, traumatic hyphaema, penetrating injury, globe rupture.
- Corneal ulcer.
- Herpes simplex keratitis.
- Anterior uveitis.
- Endophthalmitis.
- Scleritis.
- Giant cell arteritis (GCA).

Acute painless loss of vision

Vitreous haemorrhage
- *Clinical features:* impaired or no fundal view, ± reduced red reflex.
- *Causes:* retinal detachment, diabetic retinopathy.

Wet age-related macular degeneration
- See elsewhere in this chapter.

Central or branch retinal vein occlusion
- *Clinical features:* widespread or hemispheric retinal haemorrhages, ± cotton-wool spots, exudates, disc swelling, macular oedema.
- *Common causes:* hypertension, diabetes, hyperlipidaemia.
- *Other causes:* vasculitis (e.g. Behçet's, sarcoidosis, systemic lupus erythematosus), clotting disorders (e.g. protein S or C deficiency, antiphospholipid syndrome), multiple myeloma, glaucoma.

Central or branch retinal arterial occlusion
- *Symptoms:* sudden loss of vision, may have symptoms of GCA, 10% of patients have preceding amaurosis fugax.
- *Signs:* pale retina, cherry red spot, retinal vessel emboli.
- Causes:
  - Atherosclerotic: hypertension, diabetes, smoking, hyperlipidaemia
  - Embolic: carotid/aortic artery disease, cardiac valve disease
  - Haematological: protein C deficiency, antiphospholipid syndrome, lymphoma, leukaemia
  - Inflammatory: GCA, SLE, polyarteritis nodosa, Wegener's granulomatosis
  - Other: oral contraceptive, trauma, migraine.

Anterior ischaemic optic neuropathy (AION)
- May be arteritic (temporal arteritis or GCA) or non-arteritic (hypertension, diabetes, anaemia, smoking, hyperlipidaemia).

Temporal arteritis or giant cell arteritis (GCA)
- *Symptoms:* headache, scalp tenderness, jaw claudication, neck pain, fever, malaise, joint pains.
- *Signs:* tender, non-pulsatile temporal artery, relative afferent pupillary defect, swollen optic disc.
  - +/− central retinal arterial occlusion, cranial nerve palsies.

Retinal detachment
- *Clinical features:* floaters, flashing lights, loss of vision/visual field defect.
- *Risk factors:*
  - Ocular: history of trauma, cataract surgery, myopia
  - Systemic: Stickler syndrome, Marfan's syndrome, Ehlers–Danlos syndrome.

Hypertensive retinopathy

Clinical features

▶ Findings depend on classification grade of retinopathy.
- Focal/generalized arteriolar constriction and straightening (Fig. 9.8).
- Arteriosclerosis leading to changes at arterio-venous (AV) crossing points: 'AV nipping' or 'nicking' (the arteriole crosses over the top of the vein) and silver-wiring of retinal arterioles.
- Microaneurysms.
- Cotton-wool spots indicating ischaemia.
- Retinal haemorrhages; usually flame shaped.
- Exudate; often in macular star pattern.
- Arterial macroaneurysms.
- Disc oedema.
- Tortuous vessels in malignant hypertension.

Classification
- *Grade 1:* mild generalized arteriolar constriction and narrowing.
- *Grade 2:* more severe narrowing with AV nipping.
- *Grade 3:* features of grade 1 and 2 plus retinal haemorrhages, exudates, microaneurysms, cotton-wool spots.
- *Grade 4:* all of the features described above with the presence of optic disc swelling ± macular oedema.

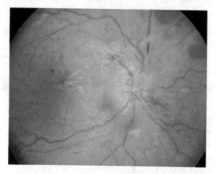

Fig. 9.8 Hypertensive retinopathy.

Diabetic retinopathy

Diabetes mellitus is the commonest cause of blindness in the working population. The best predictor of diabetic retinopathy is the duration of the disease (see Figs 9.9–9.11).

Pathogenesis

Microangiopathy primarily affecting pre-capillary arterioles, capillaries, and post-capillary venules. There is loss of pericytes, damage to the vascular endothelial cells, deformation of red blood cells with increased aggregation leading to microvascular occlusion and leakage.

Clinical features

Fundus findings are usually bilateral and broadly symmetrical. Abnormalities depend on the severity of disease and findings may include:

- Microaneurysms.
- Dot and blot haemorrhages.
- Lipid exudates.
- Venous beading.
- Intraretinal microvascular abnormalities (IRMAs).
- Cotton-wool spots (CWSs).
- New vessels at the disc or elsewhere (NVD/NVE).
- Tractional retinal detachment.
- Macular oedema and thickening (diabetic maculopathy).

Classification

The Early Treatment Diabetic Retinopathy Study provides a classification for the grading of diabetic retinopathy, dividing the disease into non-proliferative (NPDR) and proliferative (PDR) groups. The UK National Screening Committee classification is listed in brackets.

Non-proliferative

- *Mild*: at least one microaneursym (R1).
- *Moderate*: haemorrhages or microaneurysms present, lipid exudates, venous beading, IRMAs (R2).
- *Severe (the '4:2:1' rule)*: haemorrhages or microaneurysms in all four quadrants. Venous beading in two or more quadrants. IRMAs in at least one quadrant (R2).
- *Very Severe*: two or more of the 'severe' features above (R2).

Proliferative

- *Early PDR*: new vessels (NV) on the retina; either at the disc (NVD) or elsewhere (NVE) (R3).
- *High-Risk PDR*: new vessels on the disc (NVD) occupying 1/4 to 1/3 or more of the disc area. Any NV and vitreous or preretinal haemorrhage. (R3) Treatment is argon laser panretinal photocoagulation.

Diabetic maculopathy

- Retinal oedema within 500µm of the centre of the fovea.
- Hard exudates within 500µm of the fovea, adjacent retinal thickening.
- Retinal oedema ≥1 disc diameter in size within 1 disc diameter of the centre of the fovea.

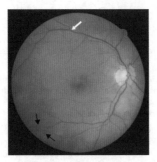

Fig. 9.9 Non-proliferative diabetic retinopathy. White arrow shows a microaneurysm, black arrows show haemorrhages.

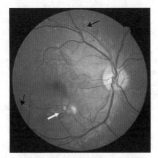

Fig. 9.10 Proliferative diabetic retinopathy. White arrow shows new vessels growing into a cotton-wool spot. Black arrows show dot haemorrhages.

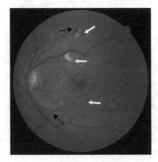

Fig. 9.11 Diabetic maculopathy. White arrows show hard exudates, black arrows show haemorrhages. New vessels can also be seen growing into the macula.

Glaucoma

Glaucoma is an optic neuropathy associated with raised intraocular pressures leading to irreversible optic nerve damage. It is usually asymptomatic and is often detected incidentally but can lead to blindness.

Applied physiology
- Aqueous humour is produced by the ciliary body and mainly drains through the trabecular meshwork but there is also drainage through uveoscleral routes.
  - Normal intraocular pressure = 8–21mmHg.

Primary angle closure
- Narrowing of the anterior chamber drainage angle prevents aqueous fluid outflow resulting in increased intraocular pressure (IOP).
- *Acute:* classically a red, painful eye; hazy cornea due to oedema; fixed, mid-dilated, oval pupil; reduced vision; headache, nausea, and vomiting.
- *Chronic/subacute:* may give a history of haloes around lights at night; often indistinguishable from open angle glaucoma unless anterior chamber viewed with gonioscopy.

Primary open angle
- Aqueous fluid outflow is reduced despite anterior chamber angle remaining open.
  - Most common form of glaucoma in patients >50 years.
- *Risk factors:* increased IOP, reduced central corneal thickness, Afro-Caribbean origin, increased age, affected 1st-degree relative.
- *Other risk factors:* hypertension, diabetes, myopia.

Secondary glaucoma
- Angle may be open or closed but the pathology results from a separate ocular condition or its treatment.

Normal tension/pressure glaucoma
- Open angle and glaucomatous field loss and disc changes despite an IOP falling within the 'normal' range.

Conditions leading to secondary glaucoma
- Uveitis:
  - Trabeculitis: chronic inflammation of the trabecular meshwork resulting in reduced aqueous outflow
  - Iris bombé: iris adhesions to the anterior capsule of the lens (posterior synechiae) through 360° following anterior uveitis can result in bowing forward of the iris, from trapped aqueous, closing the drainage angle.
- *Rubeosis:* ischaemic insults to the eye (retinal vein/artery occlusions, diabetes) can lead to new blood vessel growth/bleeding in the anterior chamber angle obstructing aqueous outflow.
- *Trauma:* damage to the drainage angle from blunt trauma can lead to scarring of the trabecular meshwork.

Age-related macular degeneration (AMD)

AMD is the leading cause of blindness registration in the western world. There are two main types. The common dry form is associated with gradual visual loss, while the much less common wet or neovascular AMD is associated with rapid and more severe visual loss.

Dry AMD

- Progressive atrophic changes of the macula characterized by the presence of drusen, extracellular material deposited between the retinal pigment epithelium (RPE) and the underlying Bruch's membrane.
- There is resulting loss of the RPE and photoreceptor layers of the retina.

Wet AMD

- Accounts for 10% of cases of AMD and is the most common cause of blindness in the Western world.
- New vessels grow from the choroidal vasculature and enter the retina forming a choroidal neovascular membrane (CNV), which can leak fluid or blood at the macula leading to scarring and visual loss.

Symptoms

- Central visual loss (gradual or sudden).
- Distortion (metamorphopsia: straight lines look wavy and distorted).
- Scotoma.

Signs

- Hard drusen (well-demarcated yellow lesions).
- Soft drusen (ill-defined paler lesions which may become confluent).
- Pigmentation.
- Subretinal or intraretinal haemorrhage.
- Exudate.

Risk factors

- Age.
- Family history.
- Female sex.
- Caucasian.
- Smoking.
- Hyptertension.
- Cardiovascular disease.
- Hypercholesterolaemia.

Cataract

The lens is a biconvex, transparent, avascular structure enclosed by a capsule. Lens fibres are continually laid down throughout life so the lens is the only eye structure that continues to grow. With time the lens loses its transparency leading to cataract formation, which is universal with increasing age (see Fig. 9.12).

Common symptoms
- Gradual deterioration of vision.
  - Difficulty reading.
- Glare from oncoming car headlights.

Risk factors
The majority of cataracts are senile, but cataracts may be associated with a number of systemic diseases including:
- Diabetes mellitus: usually cortical or posterior subcapsular cataracts. Patients are usually younger and the cataract can progress relatively quickly.
- Disorders of calcium homeostasis.
- Uveitis.
- Intraocular tumours.
- Angle closure glaucoma.
- Wilson's disease: so-called 'sunflower cataract' due to their shape. Green-brown in colour and secondary to copper deposition.

Subtypes of acquired cataract
- *Nuclear sclerosis:* central lens discoloration tends to affect distance vision to a greater extent than near vision.
- *Cortical cataract:* results from deterioration of younger lens fibres within the outer cortex of the lens. This may take on a variety of appearances including spokes and vacuoles.
- *Subcapsular cataract:* may form either anteriorly or posteriorly within the lens epithelial cells. Posterior tends to affect near vision more than distance vision.

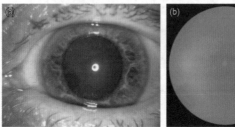

Fig. 9.12 (a) Cataract seen externally. (b) Attempted fundoscopy through mature white cataract.

See also:

More information regarding the presentation and clinical signs of eye diseases to aid preparation for OSCE-type examinations and ward rounds can be found in the *Oxford Handbooks Clinical Tutor Study Cards.*

'Medicine' Study Card set:

- The red eye
- Diabetic retinopathy
- Hypertensive retinopathy
- Optic disc swelling
- Glaucoma
- Optic atrophy
- Cataracts
- Central retinal vein occlusion
- Retinal detachment
- Angioid streaks
- Age-related macular degeneration
- Cytomegalovirus retinitis
- Myelinated nerve fibres
- Asteroid hyalinosis
- Visual field defects
- Nystagmus
- Ptosis
- Holmes–Adie–Moore syndrome
- Argyll Robertson pupils
- Internuclear ophthalmoplegia.

The locomotor system

Introduction

Joints

A joint is a connection or point of contact between bones, or between bone and cartilage. Joints are classified according to the type of material uniting the articulating surfaces, and the degree of movement they allow.

There are three types of joints (Boxes 10.1 and 10.2):
- *Fibrous joints (syndesmosis):* held together by fibrous (collagenous) connective tissue, are 'fixed' or 'immoveable'. They do not have a joint cavity. Examples include sutures between the bones of the skull.
- *Cartilagenous joints (synchondrosis):* held together by cartilage, are slightly moveable, and again have no joint cavity. Examples include the symphysis pubis, and intervertebral discs.
- Synovial joints (diarthrodial joint): covered by cartilage with a synovial membrane enclosing a joint cavity. These are freely moveable, and are the most common joint type, being typical of limb joints.

Synovial joints

Cartilage

Hyaline articular cartilage covers the intra-articular surface of the bones, ↓ friction at the joint, and facilitates shock absorption. Not all intra-articular bone is covered by hyaline cartilage; the part not covered by hyaline articular cartilage is the bare area of the joint and is the target site for erosions in inflammatory arthritis (e.g. rheumatoid arthritis).

Some synovial joints have an additional fibrocartilaginous disc (e.g. meniscus at the knee), or a fibrocartilaginous labrum (e.g. hip, shoulder).

Capsule and synovial membrane

A sleeve-like bag (fibrous capsule lined with synovial membrane) surrounds the synovial joint.

The inner synovial membrane secretes synovial fluid which has a number of functions including lubrication, and supply of nutrients to the cartilage (which is avascular and lacks pain fibres). The fluid contains phagocytic cells that remove microbes and debris within the joint cavity.

Ligaments are thickened portions of joint capsule. However, some ligaments may be distinct from the capsule.

Entheses

The bony attachment of capsules, ligaments, or tendons is called the enthesis. Entheseal inflammation (enthesitis) is the hallmark of sero-negative inflammatory arthritis (e.g. psoriatic arthritis, ankylosing spondylitis).

Tendon sheaths

Tendons e.g. those of flexor digitorum superficialis and profundus, biceps etc, are also covered by synovial sheaths called tenosynovium. This may get inflamed (tenosynovitis) due to mechanical (e.g. some cases of de Quervain's tenosynovitis), or autoimmune (e.g. lupus, rheumatoid arthritis) conditions. The Achilles tendon, one of the largest tendons in the body, does not have a tenosynovium, and is only covered by a thin layer of connective tissue: the *paratenon*.

Box 10.1 Types of synovial joint

There are different types of synovial joints and some of the more important types are:

- *Hinge:* movement occurs primarily in a single plane (e.g. elbow, knee, and interphalangeal joints)
- *Ball and socket:* allows movement around three axes: flexion/extension, abduction/adduction, rotation (e.g. shoulder and hip)
- *Pivot:* a ring of bone and ligament surrounds the surface of the other bone allowing rotation only (e.g. atlanto-axial joint between C1 and C2 vertebrae, and the connection between the radius and ulna)
- *Gliding:* flat bone surfaces allow side to side and backwards and forwards movements (e.g. between carpals, tarsals, sternum and clavicle and the scapula and clavicle)
- *Saddle:* similar to a hinge joint but with a degree of movement in a second plane (e.g. base of thumb).

Box 10.2 Movements at synovial joints

Angular movements

- *Flexion:* a decrease in the angle between the articulating bones (e.g. bending the elbow = elbow flexion)
- *Extension:* an increase in the angle between the articulating bones (e.g. straightening the elbow = elbow extension)
- *Abduction:* movement of a bone away from the midline (e.g. moving the arm out to the side = shoulder abduction)
- *Adduction:* movement of a bone towards the midline (e.g. bring the arm in to the side of the body = shoulder adduction).

Rotation

Movement of a bone about its longitudinal axis

- *Internal or medial rotation:* rotating a bone towards the midline (e.g. turning the lower limb with extended knee such that the toes point inwards = internal rotation at the hip)
- *External or lateral rotation:* rotating a bone away from the midline (e.g. turning the lower limb with extended knee such that the toes point outwards = external rotation at the hip).

Special movements

These occur at specific joints only

- *Pronation:* moving the forearm as if turning a dial anticlockwise
- *Supination:* moving the forearm as if turning a dial clockwise
- *Dorsiflexion:* moving the ankle to bring the dorsum of the foot towards the tibia (i.e. pointing the foot upwards)
- *Plantar flexion:* moving the ankle to bring the plantar surface in line with the tibia (i.e. pointing the foot downward)
- *Inversion:* tilting the soles of the feet inwards to face each other
- *Eversion:* tilting the soles of the feet outwards away from each other
- *Protraction:* moving the mandible forward
- *Retraction:* moving the mandible backward.

Important locomotor symptoms

As with any system, a carefully and accurately compiled history can be very informative and may point to a diagnosis even before examination or laboratory tests.

Pain

Pain is the most common symptom in problems of the locomotor system, and should be approached in the same manner as any other type of pain.

Pain may arise from articular structures, peri-articular structures, or may be referred from other sites. (See Boxes 10.3–10.5.)

Determine the character, onset, site, radiation, severity, periodicity, exacerbating and relieving factors (with particular reference to how it is influenced by rest and activity), and diurnal variation. Pain due to mechanical/degenerative arthropathies increases with joint use, whereas pain due to inflammatory arthropathy improves with joint use.

- Pain in a joint is called arthralgia.
- Pain in a muscle is called myalgia.

Character

- Bone pain is typically experienced as boring, penetrating, and is often worse at night. Causes include Paget's disease, tumour, chronic infection, avascular necrosis, and osteoid osteoma.
- Pain associated with a fracture is usually sharp and stabbing in nature, and is often exacerbated by movement.
- Shooting pain is suggestive of nerve entrapment (e.g. disc prolapse).

Onset

- Acute-onset pain is often a manifestation of infections such as septic arthritis, or of crystal arthropathy (e.g. gout).
- Osteoarthritis, ankylosing spondylitis, and rheumatoid arthritis usually cause a slower (insidious) onset of pain.

Site

Determine the exact site of maximal pain if possible, and of any associated lesser pains. Ask the patient to point to the site of maximal pain.

Remember that the site of pain is not necessarily the site of pathology; often the pain is referred. Referred pain is due to inability of the cerebral cortex to distinguish between sensory messages from embryologically related sites. For example, hip pain is frequently referred down the thigh, towards the knee; and pain from the cervical spine is referred to the shoulder region. Referred pain is usually poorly localized, and is worsened by movement of the affected joint (not of the joint to which it is referred).

Box 10.3 Some causes of hip pain
- *Anterior (groin):* hip arthropathy, avascular necrosis, ilio-psoas bursitis, disc prolapse pressing on L1–L2 nerve root, inguinal or femoral hernia
- *Medial:* adductor enthesopathy, inguinal or femoral hernia
- *Lateral:* trochanteric bursitis, abductor enthesopathy (greater trochanteric pain syndrome), meralgia paresthetica
- *Posterior:* inflammatory back pain due to sacro-iliitis (frequently reported as buttock pain), ischial bursitis, spinal stenosis, and disc prolapse pressing on L3–L5, and sacral nerve roots.

Box 10.4 Some causes of knee pain
- *Chondromalacia patellae:* softening of the patellar articular cartilage and is felt as anterior knee pain after prolonged sitting. Usually seen in young people
- *Osteochondritis dissecans:* usually associated with trauma resulting in an osteochondral fracture which forms a loose body in the joint with underlying necrosis
- *Osgood–Schlatter's disease:* arises as a result of a traction injury of the tibial epiphysis which is classically associated with a lump over the tibia
- *Other causes:* osteoarthritis, trauma, bursitis, tendonitis, rheumatoid arthritis, infection, malignancy.

Box 10.5 Some other causes of arthralgia
Shoulder
- Rotator cuff disorders (e.g. tendonitis, rupture, adhesive capsulitis/ frozen shoulder)
- Referred pain: e.g. cervical, mediastinal, cardiac
- Arthritis: glenohumeral, acromioclavicular.

Elbow
- Epicondylitis (lateral = tennis elbow; medial = golfer's elbow)
- Olecranon bursitis
- Referred pain from neck/shoulder (e.g. cervical spondylosis)
- Osteo- and rheumatoid arthritis.

Mechanical/degenerative back pain
- Arthritis
- Trauma
- Infection
- Ankylosing spondylitis
- Spondylolisthesis
- Disc prolapse, lumbar spinal/lateral recess stenosis
- Spinal tumours
- Metabolic bone disease.

Stiffness

This is a subjective inability or difficulty in moving a joint.

▶ If stiffness predominates without significant joint pain, consider spasticity or tetany. Look for hypertonia and other upper motor neuron signs.

Ask the patient:

- When is the stiffness worst?
  - 'Early morning stiffness', improving as the day goes by, is characteristically associated with inflammatory joint disease (e.g. rheumatoid arthritis, ankylosing spondylitis). This often takes hours before maximal improvement with activity
  - Early morning stiffness may be present in non-inflammatory joint diseases (e.g. osteoarthritis). In these cases, patients report a shorter duration of stiffness before improvement (often <20 minutes).
- Which joints are involved?
  - Stiffness predominates in hands and feet in rheumatoid arthritis; in shoulder and pelvic girdle in polymyalgia rheumatica; and in the buttocks and lower back in ankylosing spondylitis.
- How long does it take to 'get going' in the morning?
- How is the stiffness related to rest and activity?
  - Stiffness in inflammatory joint disease tends to worsen with rest, and improves with activity. However, in non-inflammatory joint disease, stiffness is exacerbated by activity and it is typically worse at the end of the day.

Swelling

Joint swelling can be due to a variety of factors including inflammation of the synovial lining, an ↑ in the volume of synovial fluid, hypertrophy of bone, or swelling of structures surrounding the joint.

This symptom is particularly significant in the presence of joint pain and stiffness. Establish:

- Which joints are affected (small or large)?
- Is the distribution symmetrical or not?
- What was the nature of onset of the swelling?
  - Rapid onset: haematoma, acute crystal synovitis, haemarthrosis (trauma, anticoagulants, or any underlying bleeding disorder)
  - Slow onset (over days to weeks) suggests inflammatory arthritis.
- Are the joints always swollen or does the swelling come and go?
- Is there any associated pain?
- Do the joints feel hot to touch?
- Is there erythema? (Common in infective, traumatic, and crystal arthropathies.)
- Have the joints in question sustained any injuries?
- Does the whole finger or toe swell up like a sausage? (Dactylitis.)

Crepitus

A crunching sound and feeling on moving the joint.

Distinguish crepitus from other articular/peri-articular noises like cracking, clonking, popping, and snapping which are usually not pathological.

Locking, triggering, and giving way

Locking
Locking is the sudden inability to complete a certain movement and suggests a mechanical block or obstruction usually caused by a loose body or torn cartilage within the joint. This frequently occurs at the knee.

Triggering
A similar phenomenon to locking. This may occur at the fingers, when there is an inability to actively extend the digit completely. This is usually due to thickening of the flexor tendon sheath but may occur in the context of trauma or other pathology to the extensor tendons. The triggering finger can be extended passively by the patient or the examiner.

Giving way
Patients with degenerative arthritis affecting the lower limb joints (typically the knee or ankle) often report a feeling of instability when weight-bearing. This is described as a sensation of 'giving way', a subjective sensation which may or may not be associated with falls.

Deformity
Acute deformity may arise with a fracture or dislocation. Chronic deformity is more typical of bone malalignment and may be partial/subluxed or complete/dislocated. (See Box 10.6.)

Establish:
- The time frame over which the deformity has developed.
- Any associated symptoms such as pain and swelling.
- Any resultant loss of function? (What is the patient unable to do now, which he or she could do before?).

Box 10.6 Some terminology of joint deformity

Valgus
The bone or part of limb distal to the joint is deviated laterally.
For example, a valgus deformity at the knees would give 'knock knees' that tend to meet in the middle despite the feet being apart.

Varus
Here, the bone or part of limb distal to the joint is deviated medially.
For example, a varus deformity at the knees would give 'bow legs' with a gap between the knees even if the feet are together.

Weakness
Always enquire about the presence of localized weakness (peripheral nerve lesion) or generalized weakness (systemic cause).

In some patients, subjective weakness may result from pain. This is often seen in patients with polymyalgia rheumatica who report 'weakness' around their hips and shoulders.

Sensory disturbance

Ask about the exact distribution of any numbness or paraesthesia as well as documenting any exacerbating and relieving factors.

Loss of function

This is the inability to perform an action (disability) and is distinguished from the term 'handicap' which is the social/functional result or impact that disability has on the individual's life.

Loss of function can be caused by a combination of muscle weakness, pain, mechanical factors, and damage to the nerve supply.

The questions you ask will depend partly on the patient's occupation. It is also essential to gain some insight into the patient's mobility (can they use stairs? How they cope with personal care such as feeding, washing, and dressing? Can they manage shopping and cooking?).

Affect and sleep

Patients with chronic musculoskeletal conditions may have, or develop, low mood. Therefore, targeted enquiries should be made about the patient's mood.

Similarly, these patients may have reduced and/or poor quality of sleep. Chronic sleep deprivation results in increased pain sensitivity, increasing the perception of pain. If pronounced, this may result in chronic widespread pain (e.g. fibromyalgia).

You may enquire about sleep in the following ways:

- How is your sleep?
- Do you have problems falling asleep?
- Do you frequently wake up at night? If so, why?
- Is your sleep refreshing?

Extra-articular features

Several locomotor disorders (e.g. rheumatoid arthritis, SLE) cause extra-articular or multisystem features, some of which are outlined below:

- Systemic symptoms: low-grade fever, weight loss, fatigue, lethargy.
- Skin rash: vasculitic, photosensitive, nail-fold infarcts, alopecia (see ➔ Chapter 4).
- Oral:
  - Dry mouth (Sjögren's syndrome)
  - Ulcers (non-scarring: SLE; scarring: Behçet's disease).
- Raynaud's phenomenon (primary, SLE, systemic sclerosis).
- Urethritis (Reiter's syndrome).
- Scarring oro-genital ulcers (Behçet's disease).
- Eye symptoms:
  - Dry eyes (Sjögren's syndrome)
  - Episcleritis, scleritis, scleromalacia perforans (rheumatoid arthritis)
  - Uveitis (sero-negative inflammatory arthirtis).
- Cardiorespiratory: breathlessness (pulmonary fibrosis?), pericarditis, and pleurisy (rheumatoid arthritis); aortic regurgitation (ankylosing spondylitis).
- Neurological:
  - Nerve entrapment (rheumatoid arthritis)
  - Migraine, depression, psychosis (SLE)
  - Stroke (anti-phospholipid antibody syndrome).

The rest of the history

Past medical history

Ask about all previous medical and surgical disorders and enquire specifically about any previous history of trauma or musculoskeletal disease. (See Box 10.7.)

Family history

It is important to note any FHx of illness, especially those locomotor conditions with a heritable element:

- Osteoarthritis.
- Rheumatoid arthritis.
- Osteoporosis.
- Psoriasis.
- SLE.
- Sero-negative spondarthropathy.

Note that the seronegative spondyloarthropathies (e.g. ankylosing spondylosis) are more prevalent in patients with the HLA B27 haplotype.

Drug history

Take a full DHx including all prescribed and over-the-counter (including herbal) medications. Attempt to assess the efficacy of each treatment, including all those past and present.

Ask about any side effects of any drugs taken for locomotor disease including:

- Gastric upset associated with non-steroidal anti-inflammatory drugs.
- Long-term side effects of steroid therapy such as skin thinning, osteoporosis, myopathy, infections, and avascular necrosis.

Ask also about medication with known adverse musculoskeletal effects including:

- Statins: myalgia, myositis, and myopathy.
- ACE inhibitors: myalgia.
- Anticonvulsants: osteomalacia.
- Quinolone: tendinopathy.
- Diuretics, aspirin, alcohol: gout.
- Procainamide, hydralazine, isoniazid: drug-induced lupus.

▶ It is also worth bearing in mind that illicit drugs may ↑ the risk of developing infectious diseases such as tuberculosis, HIV, and hepatitis, all of which can cause musculoskeletal symptoms.

Smoking and alcohol

As always, full smoking and alcohol histories should be taken.

Social history

This should form a natural extension of the functional enquiry and should include a record of the patient's occupation if not already noted, as well as ethnicity.

- *Certain occupations* predispose to specific locomotor problems.
  - Mechanically demanding occupations result in osteoarthritis in the mechanically loaded joints
  - Repetitive strain injury is seen in office workers
  - Vibrating power tools predispose to hand-vibration syndrome
  - Fatigue fractures may be seen in athletes.
- *Ethnicity* is relevant as there is an overrepresentation of lupus and TB in the Asian population, both of which are linked to a variety of locomotor complaints.
- *Age:* if the patient is an older person, make a note about the activities of daily living, how mobile the patient is, and if there are any home adaptations such as a chair lift or railings.
- Remember to ask about home care or other supports.
- Where appropriate, take a *sexual history*. This is important because reactive arthritis or Reiter's syndrome may be caused by sexually transmitted diseases such as chlamydia and gonorrhoea. Where applicable, take a history of risk factors for HIV and hepatitis.

Box 10.7 Screening history

If the locomotor system is not the main area of concern, you may wish to take a very short screening history in the form of three questions:
- Do you have any pain or stiffness in your muscle, joints, or back?
- Are you able to dress yourself completely without any difficulty?
- Are you able to walk up and down stairs without any difficulty?

If any of these questions reveal a problem, the issue should be explored in more detail.

Outline locomotor history

As with other systems, organizing the clinical data (and your thoughts) into a structured framework can be crucial in clinching the diagnosis (see Box 10.8).

Box 10.8 Structure of a musculoskeletal history

- Presenting complaint(s)
  - How many joints are affected?
  - Establish their locations and timeline
- What is the pattern of joint involvement?
  - Single episode
  - Episodic/intermittent
  - Progressive/additive
- Extra-articular features
- Past medical history
- Family history
- Allergies
- Drug history
- Smoking
- Alcohol
- Social history.

Formulations

At the end of a locomotor history, you should be able to identify:

- Key locomotor symptoms.
- Number of joints involved (see Box 10.9).
- Location of joint involvement (see Box 10.10).
- Onset and progression of joint involvement (see Box 10.11).

This allows you to formulate a clinical diagnosis in most instances.

Box 10.9 Diagnoses by number of joints involved

One joint (monoarthritis)

- Crystal arthropathy
- Haemarthrosis
- Infection
- Degenerative
- Post-traumatic
- A mono-articular presentation of an oligo- or polyarthritis.

2–4 joints (oligoarthritis)

- Inflammatory arthritis (rheumatoid, psoriatic, reactive, ankylosing spondylitis)
- Infection (endocarditis, acute rheumatic fever)
- Osteoarthritis.

>5 joints (polyarthritis)

- Inflammatory (rheumatoid, psoriatic, SLE)
- Osteoarthritis.

Box 10.10 Diagnoses by pattern of involvement

Rheumatoid arthritis
- MCPJs, PIPJs, wrist, and MTPJs
  - Typically does not affect DIPJs & 1st CMCJ.

Psoriatic arthritis
- Typically affects DIPJs more commonly than other hand joints
  - May sometimes mimic RA.

Ankylosing spondylitis
- Sacro-iliac joints, spine, shoulder, and hips

SLE
- MCPJs and wrists

Osteoarthritis
- Knees, 1st CMCJ, DIPJ, PIPJ, spinal apophyseal joints, hips, and ankle

Gout
- 1st MTPJ, IPJs, knees, and ankles

Calcium pyrophosphate dihydrate deposition disease (CPPD)
- Knees, wrist, MCPJs.

Box 10.11 Diagnoses by onset and progression

Single attack of acute arthritis
- Reactive arthritis, first presentation of crystal or inflammatory arthritis, septic arthritis

Multiple completely resolving episodes
- Crystal synovitis (gout, acute CPP crystal synovitis), palindromic rheumatoid arthritis

Persistent or progressive 'additive' joint involvement
- Rheumatoid arthritis (typically symmetric), seronegative inflammatory arthritis (typically asymmetric)
  - Progression may be over months or years.

Persistent or progressive sacro-iliac joint and spinal involvement
- Sero-negative spondarthropathy
  - Peripheral large joint oligo-arthritis may also occur.

One joint involved after the other over years
- Osteoarthritis
  - Progressive involvement of several IPJs over a period of few months may occur at disease onset in 'nodal' OA. This typically occurs in post-menopausal women.

Outline locomotor examination

A full examination of the entire locomotor system can be long and complicated.

In this chapter, we have broken the examination down into the following joints/regions: hand (including wrist), elbow, shoulder, spine, hip, knee, ankle, and foot. (See Box 10.12.)

Box 10.12 Examination framework

The examination of each joint should follow the standard format:
- Look
- Feel
- Move
  - Active
  - Passive.
- Special tests
- Function.

Limitation of active movement alone reflects underlying pathology of the tendons and muscle surrounding the joint, but limitation of both active and passive movement suggests an intrinsic joint problem.

▶ In a thorough locomotor examination, you should examine the joints 'above' and 'below' the symptomatic one. For example, for an elbow complaint, also examine the shoulder and wrist.

The GALS screen

The overall integrity of the locomotor system can be screened very quickly by using the 'GALS' method of assessment. (See Box 10.13.)

You may also use the GALS screen to make a quick, 'screening' examination of the whole locomotor system in order to identify which joints or regions require to be examined in more detail.

The GALS screen consists of four components:
- **G** = Gait.
- **A** = Arms.
- **L** = Legs.
- **S** = Spine.

Box 10.13 Modified GALS screen

The GALS screen was devised as a quick screen for abnormality in the absence of symptoms.* With apologies to the original authors, below is a slightly modified version:

Gait
- Watch the patient walk, turn, and then walk back
  - There should be symmetry and smoothness of movement and arm swing with no pelvic tilt and normal stride length. The patient should be able to start, stop, and turn quickly.

Arms (sitting on couch)
- *Inspection:* look for muscle wasting and joint deformity at the shoulders, elbows, wrists, and fingers. Squeeze across the 2nd–5th metacarpals—there should be no tenderness
- *Shoulder abduction:* 'raise your arms out sideways, above your head'. Normal range 170–180°
- *Shoulder external rotation:* 'touch your back between your shoulder blades'
- *Shoulder internal rotation:* 'touch the small of your back'. Should touch above T10
- *Elbow extension:* 'straighten your arms out'. Normal is 0°
- *Wrist and finger extension:* the prayer sign
- *Wrist flexion and finger extension:* the reverse prayer sign
- *Power grip:* 'make a tight fist'—should hide fingernails
- *Precision grip:* 'put your fingertips on your thumb'.

Legs (lying on couch)
- *Inspection:* look for swelling or deformity at the knee, ankle, and foot as well as quadriceps muscle wasting. Squeeze across the metatarsals—there should be no tenderness
- *Hip and knee flexion:* test passively and actively. Normal hip flexion is 120°, normal knee flexion is 135°
- *Hip internal rotation:* normal is 90° at 45° flexion
- *Knee:* bulge test and patellar tap
- *Ankle:* test dorsiflexion (normal 15°) and plantar flexion (normal 55°).

Spine (standing)
- *Inspection from behind:* look for scoliosis, muscle bulk at the paraspinals, shoulders, and gluteals, level iliac crests
- *Inspection from the side:* look for normal thoracic kyphosis and lumbar and cervical lordosis
- *Tenderness:* feel over the mid-supraspinatus—there should be no tenderness
- *Lumbar flexion:* 'touch your toes'. Normal is finger–floor distance <15cm. Lumbar expansion (Schober's test)
- *Cervical lateral flexion:* 'put your ear on your shoulder'.

*Doherty et al. (1992). *Annals Rheum Dis* 51: 1165–9.

Hand

Hand examination is an important part of all examination routines. This section focuses on hand examination with an emphasis on the locomotor system. The reader should refer to ➲ Chapters 4 and 8 on skin, hair, and nails and the nervous system for other components of hand examination (Fig. 10.3).

Inspection

Look around the room, or at the patient for any functional aids, or adaptations. Begin by exposing the forearms up to the elbows, and sit facing the patient. Inspect the dorsal surface first, asking the patient to place their hands flat, palms down on a pillow with fingers and thumbs resting on the pillow. Then, inspect the palms. Look for:

Skin and nails

- Skin colour.
  - Erythema (acute gout, acute CPP crystal arthritis, infection)
  - Digital ischaemia: pallor or bluish discoloration.
- Skin thickness.
  - Thin skin: corticosteroid use
  - Callosities: mechanically demanding occupation
  - Tight shiny skin, sclerodactyly: systemic sclerosis.
- Discrete skin lesions.
  - Vasculitis
  - Psoriasis
  - Gottron's papules (dermatomyositis)
  - Ulcers (systemic sclerosis—typically on fingertips).
- Other soft-tissue lesions.
  - Rheumatoid nodules (along extensor tendons)
  - Gouty tophi (near interphalangeal joints on fingers).
  - Ganglion (near wrist).
- Scars.
  - Wrist fusion: dorsal median longitudinal scar on wrist
  - MCPJ replacement: dorsal longitudinal scar on MCPJs
  - Tendon transfer: dorsal longitudinal scar.
- Nails:
  - Clubbing: hypertrophic pulmonary osteo-arthropathy
  - Splinter haemorrhage: infective endocarditis, vasculitis, physical trauma (digital trauma in mechanically demanding occupations may also result in occasional splinters in the distal nail bed)
  - Onycholysis (psoriasis, hyperthyroidism)
  - Pitting of the nail plate (psoriasis)
  - Nail-fold capillary telangiectasia and peri-ungual erythema: dermatomyositis, SLE, systemic sclerosis.

Muscle wasting:

Look at the interossei and forearm muscles.

Attitude, deformity, and swelling
- Inspect each of the following joint groups sequentially (see Box 10.14):
  - Distal interphalangeal (DIP)
  - Proximal interphalangeal (PIP)
  - Metacarpophalangeal (MCP)
  - Wrist.
- You may also ask the patient to make a fist and look at the MCP heads.
  - Normally, there is a depression ('valley') between neighbouring MCP heads which become 'filled in' with MCPJ synovitis.
- Ask the patient to hold their hand in front of their chest with elbow and shoulders flexed and wrist extended. In this position, look for:
  - Volar subluxation of the carpus in RA
  - Wrist drop in radial nerve palsy
  - Finger drop due to ruptured finger extensor tendons.

Palmar abnormalities
As well as the features noted on the dorsal aspect, look for:
- Scar of carpal tunnel decompression: volar mid-line longitudinal scar.
- Thenar or hypothenar wasting.
- Palmar erythema (RA, liver disease, corticosteroid use).
- Nodules near the distal palmar crease (Dupuytren's contracture gives thickened palmar fascia).
- Tendon nodules: usually occur at the level of MCPJ heads, associated with triggering.
- Gouty tophi (fingertips).
- Calcinosis cutis (fingertips; seen in limited cutaneous systemic sclerosis).
- Digital pits (fingertips; seen in diffuse cutaneous systemic sclerosis).

Box 10.14 Some finger and wrist deformities

- *Swan neck:* fixed flexion at the DIPJ and hyperextension at the PIPJs—associated with rheumatoid arthritis
- *Boutonnière:* hyperextension at the DIPJ and flexion at the PIPJs—associated with rheumatoid arthritis
- *Z-shaped thumb:* flexion at the MCPJ of the thumb, hyperextension at the interphalangeal joint—associated with RA
- *Ulnar deviation at MCPJs:* a feature of rheumatoid arthritis and other conditions, the fingers are deviated medially (toward the ulnar aspect of the forearm) at the MCPJs
- *Wrist subluxation:* volar subluxation of carpus (RA)
- *Wrist deviation:* radial deviation is frequently seen in RA
- *Heberden's nodes:* postero-lateral bony swelling (due to osteophytes) at the DIPJs—a feature of osteoarthritis
- *Bouchard's nodes:* similar to Heberden's nodes, but at the PIPJs—a feature of osteoarthritis
- *Dorsal bar:* merging of Heberden's or Bouchard's nodes at the IPJs
- *Telescopic fingers:* advanced destruction of IPJs. The finger may be elongated when it is pulled out passively. There is concentric wrinkling of the skin. Seen in advanced psoriatic arthritis.

Palpation

🛈 Ask the patient if there is any tenderness and palpate those areas last.

- Using the dorsum of your hands, feel for temperature change over the wrists, thumb-base, MCPJs, and IPJs.
  - As a rule, skin in the peripheries gets cooler distally.
- Palpate any abnormalities identified on inspection.
- Perform an MCPJ squeeze (as in GALS) to screen for MCPJ synovitis.
- Depress the ulnar styloid (piano key sign) to check for the integrity of the inferior radio-ulnar joint and its supporting ligaments.
- Assess for skin thickening.
  - Gently pick the skin on the dorsum of the hand between your thumb and index finger to make a skin fold
  - If you are not able to make a skin fold, try to move the skin over the underlying soft-tissue structures.
- Palpate finger flexor tendons on the palmar aspect for thickening.

Movement

Before assessing movement, ask the patient if they have any pain. Test active, and then passive movements.

Active movements

- *Wrist extension:* test with the 'prayer sign' manoeuvre. Ask the patient to place their hands, palm to palm, in front of them with fingers extended as in Fig. 10.1.
- *Wrist flexion:* test with the 'reverse prayer' position. Ask the patient to place their hands back to back in front of them with fingers extended as in Fig. 10.2.
- *Wrist abduction:* with elbows flexed at 90°, palm facing up, and forearm fixed, ask the patient to point their fingers outwards.
- *Wrist adduction:* with elbows flexed at 90°, palm facing up, and forearm fixed, ask the patient to point their fingers inwards.
- *Finger flexion:* ask the patient to make a fist.
  - Also observe for range of movement. Normally a patient should be able to dig their finger nails into their palms
  - Detailed assessment of IPJ flexion may be carried out if necessary. Fix the proximal phalanx to assess PIPJ flexion (flexor digitorum superficialis) and the distal phalanx to assess DIPJ flexion.
- *Finger extension:* ask the patient to straighten their fingers out. Also tested with the prayer and reverse prayer positions. Triggering of the finger may be revealed during extension.
- *Thumb movements:* assess flexion, extension, abduction, adduction, opposition (see ➜ Chapter 8).

Passive movements

- Move each joint and assess the range of movement and watch for any pain.
- Feel for crepitus, especially over the base of the thumb.

Function

Testing function is a vital part of any hand examination and should not be overlooked. Ask the patient to:

- Write their name.
- Pour a glass of water.
- Fasten and unfasten a button. Pick a coin up from a flat surface.

Fig. 10.1 The prayer position.

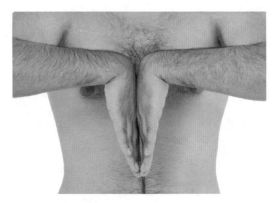

Fig. 10.2 The reverse prayer position.

Skills station 10.1

Instruction

Examine this patient's hands.

Model technique

- Clean your hands
- Introduce yourself
- Explain the purpose of examination, obtain informed consent
- Ask for any painful areas you should avoid
- Ask the patient to expose the distal upper limb including the forearm, wrist, and hand
- Sit opposite and ask the patient to position their hands on a pillow, palms facing down
- Inspect the dorsum of the hand, wrist, and forearm. Look at the elbow
- Feel for temperature over the joint areas (proximal to distal) using the dorsum of your hands
  - Compare opposite sides simultaneously
- Palate the wrist, MCPJs, and IPJs for swelling and tenderness
- Ask the patient to turn their hands over
- Inspect the palmar surfaces of the hand, wrist, and forearm
- Assess active, then passive movements
- Examine sensation (see ➔ Chapter 8)
  - Examine the median, ulnar, and radial nerves specifically
- Examine power (see ➔ Chapter 8)
- Test reflexes (see ➔ Chapter 8)
- Check the radial and ulnar artery pulsations
- Assess function
  - Ask the patient to write and do up some buttons
- Thank the patient.

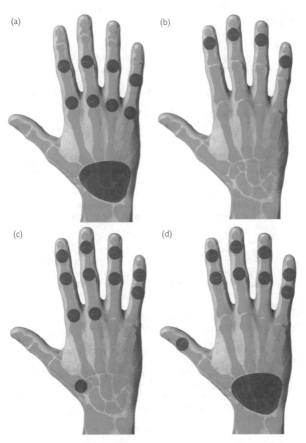

Fig. 10.3 Patterns of joint involvement. (a) Rheumatoid arthritis. (b) Psoriatic arthritis. (c) Osteoarthritis. (d) Gout.

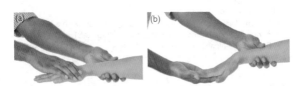

Fig 10.4 Assessing resisted active motion. (a) Wrist extension; (b) wrist flexion.

Elbow

Look
Look around the bed for any mobility aids or other clues. Ask the patient to stand, make sure both upper limbs are exposed, and look at the patient from top to toe.

Inspect the elbow from the front, side, and behind, with the patient's arm hanging by side, the forearm supine, and note:

- Skin change (e.g. psoriatic plaques).
- Skin or subcutaneous nodules (e.g. rheumatoid nodules, gouty tophi).
- Scars.
- Deformities:
  - Varus (cubitus varus): can be caused by a supracondylar fracture
  - Valgus (cubitus valgus): can be caused by non-union of a lateral condylar fracture or Turner's syndrome
  - Fixed flexion deformity (inability to straighten the elbow completely): can be caused by synovitis in inflammatory arthritis or by joint damage in inflammatory arthritis or osteoarthritis.
- Muscle wasting.
- Swelling.
  - Synovial swelling is seen on the lateral aspect of elbow, around the radial head, or around the posterior para-olecranon fossa (felt lateral and medial to the olecranon process)
  - Bursal swelling occurs at the olecranon bursa posteriorly.

Feel
▶ Always ask about pain before getting started.
Palpate the joint posteriorly and laterally and feel for:

- Temperature.
- Subcutaneous nodules (rheumatoid nodules, gouty tophi).
- Swelling.
  - Soft swelling may be due to olecranon bursitis (e.g. sepsis, gout)
  - Boggy swelling suggests synovial thickening (e.g. rheumatoid)
  - Hard swelling suggests a bony deformity
  - If fluid is present, attempt to displace it on either side of olecranon.
- Tenderness.
  - Carefully palpate the joint margin and epicondyles. Note the exact location of any pain.
- Crepitus.
  - Palpate posterolaterally during flexion/extension and pronation/supination.
- Ulnar nerve.
  - Feel medially for ulnar nerve subluxation (occurs with a 'snap' during flexion/extension; palpate medially for this)
  - Palpate the ulnar nerve for any thickening.

Move

🚫 Check that there is good shoulder function before attempting to assess elbow movements.

▶ Remember to test passive movements (you do the moving) and active movements (the patient does the moving) at each stage. Test active movements before passive movements.

- Ask the patient to place their arms on the back of their head.
- Next, assess elbow flexion and extension with the upper arm fixed.
  - Remember to compare with the opposite side.
- With the elbows tucked into the sides and flexed to a right angle, test the radio-ulnar joints for pronation (palms towards floor) and supination (palms towards the ceiling).
  - This position fixes the upper arm, and prevents any trick movement of the upper arm across the abdomen.

Resisted active motion

- With the elbow flexed at 90° and prone, hold the patient's forearm still. Ask the patient to extend their wrist against resistance (Fig. 10.4).
  - This reproduces pain in lateral epicondylitis (tennis elbow).
- In the same position, ask the patient to flex the wrist against resistance.
  - This reproduces pain in medial epicondylitis (golfer's elbow).
- With the elbow flexed at 90° ask the patient to supinate, or flex their elbow against resistance.
  - This causes pain in distal bicipital tendonitis.

Measure

- Measure elbow flexion and extension in degrees from the neutral position (i.e. consider a straight elbow joint to be 0°).
- The normal ranges of movements at the elbow are:
  - 0–150° for flexion/extension
  - 0–85° for pronation
  - 0–90° for supination.

Function

Observe the patient pour a glass of water and then put on a jacket.

Shoulder

Look

Look around for any aids or adaptations. Ask the patient to remove any covering clothing and expose the upper limbs, neck, and chest. Scan the patient from top to toe. Inspect from the front, side, and behind.

Look especially for:

- Scars.
- Bruising or other skin/subcutaneous tissue changes.
- Contours.
  - Look for winging of the scapula, prominence of the acromioclavicular joint and muscle wasting in the deltoid or short rotators which overlie the upper and lower segments of the scapula (rotator cuff pathology)
  - Generalized atrophy of shoulder muscle suggests painful shoulder arthropathy, or brachial neuritis.
- Joint swelling.
  - This may be a clue to acute bleeds, effusions, pseudogout, or sepsis
  - Sub-deltoid/subacromial bursa swelling appears on the lateral aspect of the shoulder.
- Attitude/deformity: Look at the position of both shoulders looking for evidence of dislocation.
  - Posterior dislocation: the arm is held in an internal rotation
  - Anterior dislocation: the arm is displaced antero-inferiorly
  - In advanced glenohumeral arthropathy, the attitude of shoulder is internal rotation, and adduction.
- ▶ Remember to inspect the axillary regions.

Feel

▶ Always ask about pain before getting started.

Make note of any temperature changes, tenderness, or crepitus. Standing in front of the patient:

- Palpate the soft tissues and bony points in the following order: sternoclavicular joint, clavicle, acromioclavicular joint, acromial process, head of humerus, coracoid process, glenohumeral joint, spine of scapula, greater tuberosity of humerus.
- Check the interscapular area for pain.
- Palpate the supraclavicular area for lymphadenopathy.

Move

▶ Remember to test active movements (the patient does the moving) before passive movements (you do the moving) at each stage.

Compound movements

These may be employed as screening tests to assess shoulder dysfunction. See Fig. 10.5.

- Ask the patient to put both hands behind the head (flexion, external rotation, and abduction).
- Ask the patient to reach up their back with the fingers to touch a spot between their shoulder blades (extension, internal rotation, and adduction).

Glenohumeral movements

❗ To test true glenohumeral movement, anchor the scapula by pressing firmly down on the top of the shoulder. After about 70° of abduction, the scapula rotates on the thorax—movement is scapulothoracic.

Quantify any movement in degrees (measure).

- *Flexion:* ask the patient to raise their arms forwards above their head.
- *Extension:* straighten the arms backwards as far as possible.
- *Abduction:* move the arm away from the side of the body until the fingertips are pointing to the ceiling.
- *Adduction:* ask the patient to move the arm inwards towards the opposite side, across the trunk.
- *External rotation:* with the elbows held close to the body and flexed to 90°, ask the patient to move the forearms apart in an arc-like motion in order to separate the hands as widely as possible.
- *Internal rotation:* ask the patient to bring the hands together again across the body (loss of external rotation suggests adhesive capsulitis).

Special tests

Testing for a rotator cuff lesion/tendonitis: 'the painful arc'

Ask the patient to abduct the shoulder against light resistance.

Pain in early abduction suggests a rotator cuff lesion and usually occurs between 40–120°. This is due to a damaged and inflamed supraspinatus tendon being compressed against the acromial arch. Similar symptoms may also occur in subacromial bursitis.

Testing for acromioclavicular arthritis

If there is pain during a high arc of movement (starting around 90°) and the patient is unable to raise their arm straight up above their head to 180°, even passively, this is suggestive of acromioclavicular arthritis.

Function

Ask the patient to scratch the centre of their back or to put on a jacket.

(a)   (b)

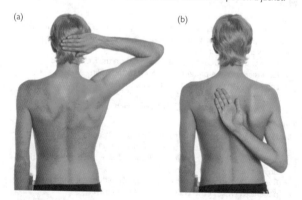

Fig 10.5 Compound movements. (a) Flexion, external rotation, and abduction. (b) Extension, internal rotation, and adduction.

Spine

Look

Scan around the room for any clues such as a wheelchair or walking aids. Watch how the patient walks into the room or moves around the bed area. Study their posture, paying particular attention to the neck.

Ask the patient to strip down to their underwear. Ask the patient to walk, turn around, and walk back. Inspect from front, the side, and behind in both the standing and sitting positions.

Look especially for:

- Scars.
- Pigmentation.
- Abnormal hair growth.
- Unusual skin creases.
- Muscle spasm.
- Height of iliac crest on each side.
- Asymmetry including abnormal spinal:
  - *Kyphosis:* convex curvature—normal in the T-spine
  - *Lordosis:* concave curvature—normal in the L- and C-spines
  - *Scoliosis:* side-to-side curvature away from the midline. This may be postural (corrects on anterior flexion) or structural (unchanged or worsened on flexion).

▶ A 'question mark' spine with exaggerated thoracic kyphosis and a loss of lumbar lordosis is classic of ankylosing spondylitis.

Feel

Palpate each spinous process noting any prominence or step and feel the paraspinal muscles for tenderness and spasm. Apply firm pressure using your thumb to elicit tenderness arising from facet joint arthritis.

You should also make a point of palpating the sacro-iliac joints.

Move

C-spine

Assess active movements of the cervical spine first. These include flexion, extension, lateral flexion, and rotation. It is often helpful to demonstrate these movements yourself.

- *Flexion:* ask the patient to put their chin on their chest (0–80°).
- *Extension:* ask the patient to look up to the ceiling (0–50°).
- *Lateral flexion:* ask the patient to lean their head sideways, placing an ear on their shoulder (0–45°).
- *Rotation:* ask the patient to look over each shoulder (0–80°).

T- and L-spine

- *Flexion:* ask the patient to touch their toes, keeping knees straight.
- *Extension:* ask the patient to lean backwards (10–20°).
- *Lateral flexion:* ask the patient to bend sideways, sliding each hand down their leg as far as possible.
- *Rotation:* anchor the pelvis (put a hand on either side) and ask the patient to twist at the waist to each side in turn.

Measure

Schober's test

This is useful measurement of lumbar flexion.

- Ask the patient to stand erect with normal posture and identify the level of the posterior superior iliac spines on the vertebral column.
- Make a small pen mark at the midline 5cm below and 10cm above this.
- Now instruct the patient to bend at the waist to full forward flexion.
- Measure the distance between the two marks using a tape measure.
- The distance should have increased to >20cm (an increase of >5cm).

Modified Schober's test

- As above but only the 10cm segment above the level of posterior superior iliac spines is measured. Increase >3.5cm on flexion is normal.

Chest expansion

- See ➲ Chapter 6. Expiration to peak inspiration should be ≥5cm.

Occiput to wall distance

- Ask the patient to stand upright with their heels and back touching the wall, looking straight forward with the chin at the usual carrying level.
- Ask them to try to touch the wall with the back of their head.
- Measure the distance between the occiput and the wall.
  - Any gap suggests thoracic kyphosis or fixed cervical flexion.

Other measurements

Students will not be expected to perform the following, but should be aware that they are used in patients with spondyloarthropathies.

- Tragus to wall distance.
- Cervical rotation (in degrees).
- Lateral flexion (measure of lumbar spine mobility).

Special tests

Sciatic nerve stretch test

This test is used to look for evidence of nerve root irritation (Fig. 10.6).

- With the patient lying supine, hold the ankle and lift the leg, straight, to 70–80°. Once at 70–80°, or at an angle at which pain is felt, dorsiflex the foot (Bragard test). If positive, pain will be felt at the back of the thigh, radiating to below the knee.
  - The pain may be relieved by knee flexion, returning the foot to a neutral position, or by reducing the degree of flexion at the hip.
- A positive stretch test suggests tension of the nerve roots supplying the sciatic nerve, commonly over a prolapsed disc (L4/5 or L5/S1).

Femoral nerve stretch test

With the patient lying prone, extend the hip, flex the knee, and plantar-flex the foot. The stretch test is positive if pain is felt in the thigh/inguinal region.

Sacro-iliac joint distraction test

- With the patient lying supine, apply firm outward pressure to both iliac crests at the anterior superior iliac spines.
  - Pain in the buttocks suggests sacro-iliac joint arthropathy.

Skills station 10.2

Instruction

Examine this patient's spine.

Model technique

- Clean your hands
- Introduce yourself
- Explain the purpose of examination, obtain informed consent
- Ask for any painful areas you should avoid
- Ask the patient to undress to underwear
- Ask the patient to walk. Watch the gait
- With the patient standing, inspect from back and side
- Palpate the spinous processes individually
- Test active movements
- Perform Schober's test
  - If positive, perform other tests to assess restriction in spinal movements
- Ask the patient to lie on the examination couch
- Perform the straight leg raise test
- Examine sensation and reflexes in the lower limbs
- Assess function
  - Ask the patient to pick something up from the floor
  - Ask about how they manage to turn in bed
- Thank the patient.

(a)

(b)

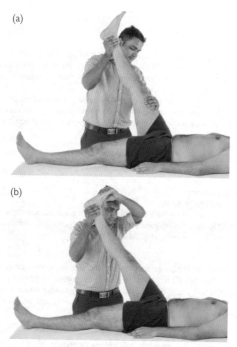

Fig. 10.6 Sciatic nerve stretch test. (a) With the patient supine, hold the ankle and lift the leg, straight, to 70–80° or until pain is felt. (b) Dorsiflex the foot (Bragard test). If positive, pain will be felt at the back of the thigh, radiating to below the knee.

Hip

Look

Expose the whole lower limb. Look around the room for any aids or devices such as orthopaedic shoes or walking aids. If they have not done so already, ask the patient to walk and note the gait. Note if there is evidence of a limp or obvious pain.

Pay attention to the position of the limbs (e.g. external rotation, pelvic tilting, standing with one knee bent, or foot held plantar-flexed/in equinus).

With the patient in the standing position, inspect from the front, side, and behind. Look for:

- Scars.
- Sinuses.
- Asymmetry of skin creases.
- Swelling.
- Muscle wasting.
- Deformities/attitude.
  - Patients with structural hip arthropathy (e.g. advanced osteoarthritis) tend to hold the hip joint in flexion, external rotation, and abduction. A similar posture is adopted in hip synovitis.

Feel

Feel for bony prominences such as the anterior superior iliac spines and greater trochanters. Check that they are in the expected position.

Palpate the soft tissue contours and feel for any tenderness in and around the joint (usually elicited lateral to the femoral pulse) and over the greater trochanter.

Move

Ask the patient if they have any pain before examining.

▶ Fix the pelvis by using your left hand to stabilize the contralateral anterior superior iliac spine since any limitation of hip movement can easily be hidden by movement of the pelvis.

Active movements

With the patient *supine*:

- *Flexion:* ask the patient to flex the hip until the knee meets the abdomen, normal is around ~100–135°.
- *Abduction:* with the patient's leg held straight, ask them to move it away from the midline, normal is 30–40°.
- *Adduction:* with the patient's leg held straight, ask them to move it across the midline, normal is ~30°.
- *Internal rotation:* ask the patient to keep the knees together and point the feet towards each other, normal is 30°.
- *External rotation:* ask the patient to keep the knees together and point the feet as far apart as possible, normal is 15–30°.

With the patient *prone*:

- *Extension:* ask the patient to raise each leg off the bed, normal is 15–30°. (This movement is not routinely measured in clinical practice.)

Passive movements

Most should be assessed by the examiner as for active movements whilst the patient is in a relaxed state. With the patient supine:

- *Passive flexion:* flex the hip and knee simultaneously. (This relaxes the hamstrings and avoids performing a 'straight leg raising test'.)
- *Passive external and internal rotation:* flex the knee and hip to 90°, hold the knee with one hand, and move the ankle away or towards the midline with the other.
  - In hip arthropathy, internal rotation of the hip is the first movement to be restricted.
- *Passive abduction and adduction:* examine with the limb in neutral.

Measure (limb length)

⚠ True shortening, in which there is loss of bone length, must not be confused with apparent shortening due to a deformity at the hip.

Technique

- With the patient supine, place the pelvis square and the lower limbs in comparable positions in relation to the pelvis.
- Measure the distance from the anterior superior iliac spine to the medial malleolus on each side (true length).
  - Apparent length is measured from a midline structure such as the xiphisternum (or the umbilicus) to the medial malleolus.
- A difference of 1cm is considered abnormal.

Special tests

Trendelenberg test

This is useful as an overall assessment of the function of the hip and will expose dislocations or subluxations, weakness of the abductors, shortening of the femoral neck, or any painful disorder of the hip.

- Ask the patient to stand up straight without any support.
- Ask them to raise their left leg by bending the knee.
- Watch the pelvis (should normally rise on the side of the lifted leg).
- Repeat the test with the patient standing on the left leg.
  - A *positive test* is when the pelvis falls on the side of the lifted leg indicating hip instability on the supporting side (i.e. the pelvis falls to the left = right hip weakness).

Thomas's test

A fixed flexion deformity of the hip (often seen in osteoarthritis) can be hidden when the patient lies supine by tilting the pelvis and arching the back. Thomas's test will expose any flexion deformity.

- With the patient supine, feel for a lumbar lordosis (palm upwards).
- With the other hand, flex the opposite hip and knee fully to ensure that the lumbar spine becomes flattened.
  - If a fixed flexion deformity is present, the affected leg flexes too (measure the angle relative to the bed).
- Remember to repeat the test on the other hip.

Function

Assess gait. See ➲ Chapter 8.

Knee

Look

Scan the room for any walking aids or other clues and inspect the patient standing. The lower limbs should be completely exposed except for underwear so that comparisons can be made.

Compare one side to the other and look for:

- Deformity (e.g. genu valgus, genu varus, fixed flexion, or hyperextension 'genu recurvatum').
- Scars or wounds to suggest infection past or present?
- Muscle wasting (quadriceps).
- Swelling (including posteriorly).
- Erythema.
- Look for loss of the medial and lateral dimples around the knees which suggest the presence of an effusion.

Feel

▶ Always ask about pain before getting started. Always compare sides. With the patient lying supine:

- Palpate for temperature using the back of the hand.
- Ask if the knee is tender on palpation.
- Feel around the joint line while asking the patient to bend the knee slightly.
- Palpate the collateral ligaments (either side of the joint).
- Feel the patellofemoral joint (by tilting the patella).

Examining for a small effusion—the 'bulge sign'

- With the knee extended and the quadriceps relaxed, gently milk any synovial fluid from suprapatellar pouch downwards into the retropatellar space (Fig. 10.7).
- Now, holding the patella still, empty the medial joint recess using a wiping motion of your palm.
  - This will milk any fluid into the lateral joint recess.
- Now apply a similar wiping motion to the lateral recess and…
- Watch the medial recess.
  - If there is fluid present, a distinct bulge should appear on the flattened, medial surface as it is milked out of the lateral side.

Examining for a large effusion—the 'patellar tap'

If the effusion is tense or large, the bulge sign is absent as you will be unable to empty either recess of fluid—use the patellar tap instead.

- Move any fluid from the medial and lateral compartments into the retropatellar space (Fig. 10.8).
  - Apply firm pressure over the suprapatellar pouch with the flat of the hand and use your thumb and index finger placed either side of the patella to push any fluid centrally.
- With the first one or two fingers of the other hand, push the patella down firmly.
  - If fluid is present, the patella will bounce off the lateral femoral condyle behind. You will feel it being pushed down and then 'tap' against the femur.

Move

▶ Remember to test active movements (the patient does the moving) before passive movements (you do the moving) at each stage. Quantify any movement in degrees (measure).

- *Flexion:* ask the patient to maximally flex the knee, normal ~135°.
- *Extension:* ask the patient to straighten the leg at the knee.
- *Hyperextension:* assess by watching the patient lift the leg off the bed and then, holding the feet stable in both hands above the bed/couch, ask the patient to relax. Ensure that you are not causing the patient any discomfort.
- *Passive movements:* Feel over the knee with one hand for any crepitus.

Measure

The visual impression of wasting of the quadriceps can be confirmed by measuring the circumference of the thighs at the same level using a fixed bony point of reference e.g. 25cm above the tibial tubercle.

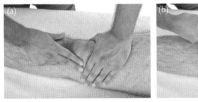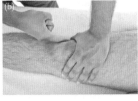

Fig. 10.7 Examining for the 'bulge sign'. (a) Wipe any fluid from the medial joint recess. (b) Wipe the fluid back out of the lateral joint recess and watch the medial side.

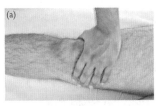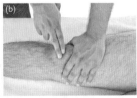

Fig. 10.8 Testing for 'patellar tap'. (a) Use the palmar surface, thumb, and index finger of one hand to move any fluid into the retropatellar space. (b) Attempt to 'tap' the patella on the femur using the other hand.

Special tests

Testing for medial and lateral collateral ligament instability

Normally, the joint should move no more than a few degrees laterally, excessive movement suggests a torn or stretched collateral ligament.

- With the patient's legs extended, take the foot in your right hand.
- Hold the patient's extended knee firmly with the other hand.
- Attempt to bend the knee medially (varus) whilst feeling the lateral knee joint line.
  - This tests the lateral collateral ligament.
- Attempt to bend the knee laterally (valgus), feeling the medial joint line.
  - This tests the medial collateral ligament.
- Repeat the above with the knee at 30° flexion.
  - In this position, only the lateral and medial collateral ligaments (and not the cruciates) contribute to varus–valgus stability at the knee.

Anterior and posterior drawer tests

These test the anterior and posterior cruciate ligaments. These ligaments prevent the distal part of the knee moving anteriorly and posteriorly.

- Ensure the patient is lying in a relaxed supine position.
- Ask the patient to flex the knee to 90°.
  - In an anterior cruciate ligament tear, the tibia sags posteriorly in this position ('sag sign').
- You may wish to position yourself perched on the patient's foot to stabilize the leg. Warn the patient about this first!.
- Wrap your fingers around the back of the knee using both hands, positioning the thumbs over the patella pointing towards the ceiling.
- Push up with your index fingers to ensure the hamstrings are relaxed.
- The upper end of the tibia is then pulled forwards and pushed backwards in a rocking motion.
  - Normally, there should be very little or no movement seen
  - Excessive anterior movement reflects anterior cruciate laxity
  - Excessive posterior movement denotes posterior cruciate laxity.

McMurray's test

A test for meniscal tears (Fig. 10.9a).

- With the patient lying supine, bend the hip and knee to 90°.
- Grip the heel with your right hand and press on the medial and lateral cartilage with your left hand.
- Internally rotate the tibia on the femur and slowly extend the knee.
- Repeat but externally rotate the distal leg whilst extending the knee.
- Repeated with varying degrees of knee flexion.
  - If a meniscus is torn, a tag of cartilage may become trapped and cause pain and an audible (and palpable) 'click'.

Apley's test

Another test for meniscal tears. If 'positive', the test will produce pain.

- Position the patient prone with the knee flexed to 90° (Fig. 10.9b).
- Stabilize the thigh with your left hand.
- With the right hand, grip the foot and rotate or twist it whilst pressing downwards in a 'grinding motion'.

Fig. 10.9 Testing for meniscal tears. (a) McMurray's test. (b) Apley's grinding test.

Skills station 10.3

Instruction

Examine this patient's knees.

Model technique
- Clean your hands
- Introduce yourself
- Explain the purpose of examination, obtain informed consent
- Ask for any painful areas you should avoid
- Ask the patient to expose their lower limbs including the ankles and feet, and stand up
- Look for knee alignment and swellings
- Ask the patient to walk. Watch the gait
- Ask the patient to lie on the couch. Inspect the knees again
- Palpate the knees for warmth
- Examine for effusions
- Feel for localized tenderness
- Test active and passive movements
- Test for integrity of the cruciate and collateral ligaments
- To assess function, ask the patient to stand from sitting and ask how they find climbing stairs.

Ankle and foot

Look

Expose the lower limbs and make note of any walking or other aids. Take a moment to also examine the footwear for any adaptations, abnormal wear, or stretching.

Examine the feet and ankles with the patient lying on a couch or bed. Look from front, sides, back, and inspect the plantar surface.

Also examine the feet and ankle when the patient is standing up. Look from front, sides, and back. If you think the patient can, ask them to stand on tip-toes and then on their heels while you watch the foot from behind and from the sides.

Finally, watch the patient walk.

Look for:

- Skin or soft-tissue lesions including calluses, swellings, ulcers and scars.
- Muscle wasting at the calf and lower leg.
- Swellings.
- Deformities.
- Examine the nails carefully for any abnormalities such as fungal infections or in-growing toenails. ▶ Don't forget to look between the toes.

You may also wish to inspect for evidence of other abnormalities such as clubbing of the feet (talipes equinovarus).

Swellings

- *Ankle synovitis:* diffuse anterior swelling ± lateral or medial extension.
- *Tenosynovitis:* tubular swelling oriented longitudinally along a tendon.
  - Anterior: tibialis anterior, extensor hallucis, or extensor digitorum
  - Posterior to medial malleolus: tibialis posterior, flexor digitorum, or flexor hallucis
  - Posterior to lateral malleolus: peroneal tendons.
- *Achilles tendinopathy/tear, retrocalcaneal and retroachilles bursitis:* posterior to calcaneum.

Deformities

Deformities involving the arch and hindfoot are better appreciated with the patient standing. Look for:

- *Hallux valgus:* 'bunion'. Medial deviation of the 1st metatarsal and lateral deviation and/or rotation of the great toe. Commonly bilateral.
- *Hammer toes:* flexion deformity at the PIPJ of the affected toe(s) (commonly the 2nd toe), hyperextension of the MTPJ and DIPJ. Caused by an overpull of the extensor digitorum longus tendon.
- *Claw toes:* Extension contracture with dorsal subluxation of the MTPJ, flexion deformities of the PIPJ and DIPJ.
  - Often idiopathic. Often elderly females with diabetes or RA.
- *Mallet toes:* A flexed DIPJ (commonly the 2nd toe). May exist in conjunction with a claw-toe deformity.
- *Pes planus (flat foot):* a lack of the normal plantar arches.
  - Physiologic pes planus (but not pathologic) may correct when standing on tip-toes.
- *Pes cavus (high-arched foot):* exaggeration of the plantar arches.

Feel

▶ Always ask about pain before getting started.

- Assess the skin temperature and compare over both the feet.
- Look for areas of tenderness, particularly over the ankle bony prominences (lateral and medial malleoli, MTPJs, interphalangeal joints, and heel) as well as the metatarsal heads.
- Squeeze across the MTPJs, and assess pain and movement.
- Remember to palpate any swelling, oedema, or lumps.

Move

The ankle and foot is a series of joints which function as a unit.

▶ Remember to test passive movements (you do the moving) and active movements (the patient does the moving) at each stage.

Active movements should be performed with the patient's legs hanging over the edge of the bed.

- *Ankle dorsiflexion:* ask the patient to point their toes to their head (normal ~20°).
- *Ankle plantar flexion:* ask the patient to push the toes down towards the floor 'like pushing on a pedal' (normal ~45°).
- *Inversion:* (subtalar joint between the talus and calcaneum). Ask the patient to turn their sole inward (you may have to demonstrate this (normal ~20°).
- *Eversion:* as inversion but turn the sole outwards, away from the midline (normal ~10°).
- *Toe flexion:* ask the patient to curl their toes.
- *Toe extension:* ask the patient to straighten the toes.
- *Toe abduction:* ask the patient to fan out their toes as far as possible.
- *Toe adduction:* ask the patient to hold a piece of paper between their toes.

Passive movements

Palpate for crepitus. Whilst checking inversion and eversion passively, grasp the ankle with one hand and with the other, grasp the heel, and turn the sole inwards towards the midline and then outwards.

Measure

Calf circumference can be measured bilaterally to check for any discrepancies which may highlight muscle wasting/hypertrophy (e.g. 10cm below the tibial tuberosities).

Special tests

Simmond's test

This test is used to assess for a ruptured Achilles tendon.

- Ask the patient to kneel on a chair with their feet hanging over the edge. Squeezes both calves.
  - Normally the feet should plantar-flex. If the Achilles tendon is ruptured, there will be no movement on the affected side.

Function

It is also helpful to observe the patient's gait with and without shoes. Be sure to ask the patient if they are able to do this first.

Important presentations

Rheumatoid arthritis (RA)

RA is a chronic inflammatory multisystem autoimmune disease mediated by pro-inflammatory cytokines such as tumour necrosis factor alpha (TNF-α) and may associate with antibodies such as rheumatoid factor and anti-CCP. However, it is worth remembering that between 30–40% of patients with rheumatoid arthritis are not positive for rheumatoid factor. A smaller proportion of patients (10–20%) does not develop anti-CCP antibodies.

Usually the onset of symptoms in RA is over a few days to a few weeks, and the progression is slow. Additional joints are involved over weeks and months. It can rarely have an acute onset (over a day or two). The course can be episodic with complete resolution between attacks (palindromic). The clinical features of RA can be divided into articular and extra-articular features summarized below.

Demographics
- Affects around 1–3% of the population.
- Occurs in all races.
- Peak age of onset in the 4th and 5th decades.
- Female:male ratio ~3:1.

Articular features
RA usually presents as a symmetrical polyarthritis affecting the wrists and small joints of the hands and feet. Occasionally, a patient presents with a mono- or oligo-arthritis of larger joints such as the knees, wrists, shoulders, or elbows. Common symptoms are joint pain, stiffness, and swelling which are typically worse in the morning and improve as the day progresses.

Signs of RA
Synovitis involving the wrists (dorsal swelling), metacarpo-phalangeal (filling in of gaps between the MCP heads) and proximal interphalangeal joints (lateral expansion of IPJs), with sparing of the distal interphalangeal and 1st carpometacarpal joints.

With modern and aggressive treatment of synovitis, joint destruction and resulting deformities are not common in patients developing RA in the last decade. However, these deformities may be present in the patients who have had the disease for some years or in some with aggressive uncontrolled RA.

Inspection:
- Symmetric swelling of proximal interphalangeal (PIP) joints.
- Symmetric swelling of metacarpo-phalangeal (MCP) joints.
  - Ask the patient to make a fist; subtle swelling of MCP joints is seen as filling in of the 'valleys' between metacarpal heads.
- Ulnar deviation at MCP joints.
- Thin skin with scars. (Long-term corticosteroid use.)
- Wasting of intrinsic muscles.

- *Tuck sign:* tubular swelling due to extensor tenosynovitis, seen on the dorsal aspect of wrist and on finger extension.
- Swan-neck deformity.
  - Hyperextension of PIPJ and flexion of DIPJ.
- Boutonnière deformity.
  - Flexion at PIPJ, extension at DIPJ.
- Volar subluxation at MCP and wrist joints.
- Rheumatoid nodules on extensor tendons, joints, sites of mechanical irritation (elbow, toe, and heel).

Palpation:
- Warmth and tenderness at DIP, PIP, MCP, and wrist joints (if active).
- 'Doughy' feeling of synovial proliferation at joints.
- *Piano key sign:* up and down movement of the ulnar styloid in response to pressure from examiners' fingers.

Extra-articular features of RA
Extra-articular features are the systemic manifestations of RA which are unique to, and caused by, the immune-pathological process of RA.

Common:
- Rheumatoid nodules: common at sites of pressure (elbows and wrists). Associated with more severe disease and rheumatoid factor positivity.
- Sjögren's syndrome (keratoconjunctivitis sicca).
- Raynaud's phenomenon.
- Interstitial lung disease (pulmonary fibrosis, pulmonary nodules).
- Pleurisy/pleural effusions.
- Episcleritis/scleritis.

Uncommon:
- Neurological features:
  - Mononeuritis multiplex
  - Peripheral neuropathy.
- Cardiac features:
  - Pericarditis/pericardial effusions.
- *Systemic features* (fever, malaise, weight loss, and lymphadenopathy).

Rare:
- Vasculitis:
  - Nail-fold infarcts
  - Cutaneous ulceration
  - Digital gangrene.
- Skin lesions:
  - Pyoderma gangrenosum.
- Lung features:
  - Caplan's syndrome (massive lung fibrosis in RA patients with pneumoconiosis)
  - Obliterative bronchiolitis
  - Felty's syndrome (RA, splenomegaly, and neutropenia).
- Amyloidosis (proteinuria, hepatosplenomegaly).

Complications of RA

Extra-articular features of RA should be distinguished from 'complications'. These are consequences of joint inflammation, systemic inflammation, or drug treatment and include:

- Anaemia (Box 10.15).
- Cataracts (chloroquine, steroids).
- Peripheral nerve entrapment (e.g. carpal tunnel syndrome).
- Cervical myelopathy (atlanto-axial subluxation).
- Palmar erythema, skin thinning, and muscle wasting (synovitis in nearby joints).

Recently, non-Hodgkin's lymphoma (systemic inflammation), ischaemic heart disease (systemic inflammation), osteoporosis, and a propensity to lower respiratory tract infections have been recognized as complications of RA.

Box 10.15 Causes of anaemia in RA

- Anaemia of chronic disease
- GI bleeding
  - Non-steroidal anti-inflammatory drugs (NSAIDs) or corticosteroid use.
- Bone marrow suppression
  - Disease-modifying anti-rheumatic drugs (e.g. methotrexate).
- Megaloblastic anaemia
  - Due to folic acid deficiency or pernicious anaemia.
- Macrocytic anaemia.
  - Methotrexate, azathioprine.

Osteoarthritis

Osteoarthritis is a chronic disorder of synovial joints characterized by focal cartilage loss and an accompanying reparative bone response.

It represents the single most important cause of locomotor disability with a prevalence which is ↑ with age, and has a female preponderance.

Secondary causes of OA include:

- Trauma (fracture, meniscal, or cruciate injury).
- Inflammatory arthritis (e.g. RA).
- Abnormalities in articular contour (hip and acetabular dysplasias) or alignment (varus or valgus knee malalignment).
- Generalized or localized hypermobility (Ehlers–Danlos syndrome, Marfan's syndrome, benign hypermobility syndrome).
- Previous septic arthritis.
- Avascular necrosis.

Symptoms

Common symptoms include swelling, deformity, stiffness, weakness, and pain which is normally worse after activity and relieved by rest.

Inspection
- Posterolateral swelling at the distal interphalangeal (DIP) (Heberden's nodes) and proximal interphalangeal (PIP) (Bouchard's nodes) with characteristic radial or ulnar deviation of the phalanx.
- Squaring of thumb base, wasting of thenar eminence observed on the volar aspect (1st carpometacarpal joint).

Inspection (knee)
Patient standing, examine from front. Look for:
- Varus and valgus deformity.
- Suprapatellar and infrapatellar effusion.
- Quadriceps wasting.
- Fixed flexion at knee with the patient lying supine.

Palpation (hands)
- Cool bony swelling at IPJs.
- Joint line tenderness at IPJ and 1st CMCJ.

Paget's disease (osteitis deformans)

A disorder of bone remodelling characterized by ↑ osteoclast and osteoblast activity, leading to accelerated bone resorption and disorganized bone formation.

Paget's disease is more common in males and affects around 1–2% of the Caucasian adults >55 years. It occurs more commonly in the UK than anywhere else in the world. The exact aetiology remains unknown, however a number of factors have been implicated, including a slow viral infection such as paromyxovirus. The axial skeleton is preferentially affected; common sites of involvement include the pelvis, femur, lumbar spine, skull, and tibia in a descending order of frequency.

Important clinical features and complications
Common
- Pain: bone pain, not joint pain. Pain is present day and night and is not made worse by joint movements.
- Deformity.
  - Enlargement of the skull
  - Exaggerated thoracic kyphosis
  - Anterior bowing of the tibia
  - Lateral bowing of the femur.
- Fractures.
- Hearing loss (ossicle involvement, or VIII nerve compression).

Less common
- Spinal stenosis.
- Nerve compression syndromes.

Rare
- Hypercalcaemia during immobilization.
- Cardiac failure.
- Sarcomatous change.
- Hydrocephalus.
- Cord compression.

Crystal arthropathies

Gout

A disorder of purine metabolism. Characterized by hyperuricaemia due to either overproduction or underexcretion of uric acid. Prolonged hyperuricaemia (Box 10.16) leads to the deposition of urate crystals in synovium, connective tissues, and the kidney. These crystals are then shed leading to acute gout.

Gout is associated with metabolic syndrome (central obesity, insulin resistance, hypertension, and ischaemic heart disease).

Most patients are middle aged or older with risk factors for gout such as renal failure, excess alcohol intake, and diuretic usage. Causes of premature gout include renal failure, solid organ transplant with immunosuppression with calcineurin inhibitors, haematological malignancy, and inherited errors of metabolism.

Clinical features of acute gout

- Sudden onset (hours) of severe pain and swelling classically in the great toe MTPJ, worse at night, and associated with redness.
- Occasionally multiple joints are involved e.g. knees, ankles ± systemic symptoms.
- Some patients (frequently elderly and those on diuretics) present with large-joint (knee, ankle, shoulder, or wrist) involvement or with polyarticular gout.

Clinical features of chronic (tophaceous) gout

- Tophi (deposits of urate crystal) occur in:
  - The digits (at IPJs, finger pulp). In the presence of osteoarthritis, gouty tophi preferentially occur at the IPJs affected by Heberden's or Bouchard's nodes.
  - Near the 1st metatarsophalangeal joint
  - In bursae (e.g. olecranon bursa)
  - Near the Achilles tendon
  - In tendon sheaths
  - On the helix (ear). In hands, gouty tophi preferentially occur at the IPJs affected by Heberden's or Bouchard's nodes.

Calcium pyrophosphate deposition (CPPD)

CPPD may occur in the cartilage (chondrocalcinosis), joint capsule, and tendons. Established risk factors include ↑ age (>60 years) and osteoarthritis. If CPPD is present in those <55 years or is florid and polyarticular, the patient should be screened for haemochromatosis, hypophosphataemia, hypomagnesaemia, and hyperthyroidism.

Knees, wrists, MCPJs, and hips are the most commonly involved joints. CPPD may present as:

- *Asymptomatic:* chondrocalcinosis.
- *Acute CPP crystal arthritis (formerly 'pseudogout'):* the commonest cause of acute mono-arthritis in the elderly.
- *CPPD and OA:* symptoms of OA with or without superimposed episodes of acute synovitis.
- *Chronic CPP crystal inflammatory arthritis:* uncommon.

Box 10.16 Causes of hyperuricaemia

More common in the summer months due to reduced fluid intake and increased fluid loss.

- Drugs: diuretics, ethanol, salicylates, pyrazinamide, ethambutol, nicotinic acid, and ciclosporin
- Chronic renal failure
- Myeloproliferative and lymphoproliferative disorders (↑ purine metabolism)
- Obesity
- Hypertension
- Hypothyroidism
- Hyperthyroidism
- Familial
- Excessive dietary purines.

Spondyloarthropathies

These include ankylosing spondylitis, psoriatic arthritis, reactive arthritis, and enteropathic arthritis. This is a group of related and overlapping forms of inflammatory arthritis which characteristically lack rheumatoid factor and are associated with HLA B27. They present at any age, though young males are primarily affected.

They also share a number of key clinical features:
- Enthesitis (an enthesis is the insertion of a tendon, ligament, or joint capsule onto a bone).
- Sacroiliitis.
- Dactylitis.
- Peripheral arthritis predominantly affecting the large joints.

Ankylosing spondylitis

Ankylosing spondylitis usually develops in early adulthood with a peak age of onset in the mid-20s, and is 3 times more common in males.

Common symptoms
- Back pain (which may be localized to the buttocks) and stiffness which are typically worse in early hours of the night (2am–5am) and on waking up in the morning.
  - Pain recurs after long periods of rest and is relieved by activity. Patients report a dramatic response to NSAIDs, which remains the first line of treatment.
- Chest pain may be present as a result of T-spine involvement as well as enthesitis at the costochondral joints.
- Pain, swelling, and stiffness may be present in peripheral joints affected by inflammatory arthritis e.g. shoulders, hips, knees, and ankles.

Musculoskeletal features/signs
- 'Question mark' posture (loss of lumbar lordosis, fixed kyphosis of the T-spine, compensatory hyperextension of the C-spine).
- Protuberant abdomen.
- Schober's test positive.
- Sacroiliac joint tenderness. (SIJ distraction test may be positive.)
- Achilles tendonitis.
- Plantar fasciitis.

Some extra-skeletal features
- Anterior uveitis.
- Aortic regurgitation.
- Apical lung fibrosis.
- AV block.
- Amyloidosis (secondary).
- Weight loss.

In some cases, a fracture may occur through the rigid spine and involve the intervertebral discs. A similar lesion may be produced by inflammatory granulation tissue. These are known as disco-vertebral or 'Andersson' lesions.

Psoriatic arthritis

Psoriatic arthropathy affects up to 10% of patients with psoriasis and may precede or follow the skin disease.▶ Importantly the arthropathy does not correlate with the severity of the skin lesions.

There are five main subtypes of psoriatic arthropathy:
- Asymmetrical distal interphalangeal joint arthropathy.
- Asymmetrical large joint mono- or oligo-arthropathy.
- Spondyloarthropathy and sacroiliitis (usually asymmetric).
- Rheumatoid-like hands (clinically identical to RA but seronegative).
- Arthritis mutilans (a destructive form with telescoping of the fingers).

Associated clinical features
- Psoriatic plaques (extensor surfaces, scalp, behind the ears, navel and natal clefts).
- Nail involvement (pitting, onycholysis, discoloration, and thickening).
- Dactylitis (sausage-shaped swelling of the digits due to tenosynovitis).
- Enthesitis.

Reactive arthritis
- An aseptic arthritis, strongly linked to a recognized episode of infection. Common causes are gut and genitourinary pathogens.
- It mainly affects young adult males and usually presents with an asymmetric oligoarthritis. Symptoms start a few days to a few weeks after the infection.
- Enthesitis and dactylitis are other common features.
- Extra-articular features include urethritis, conjunctivitis, and skin lesions.

Reiter's syndrome

A form of reactive arthritis associated with the classic triad of:
- Arthritis.
- Urethritis.
- Conjunctivitis.

It often follows dysenteric infections such as shigella, salmonella, campylo-bacter, and yersinia or infections of the genital tract. Other findings which may be encountered are mouth ulceration, circinate balanitis, keratoderma blennorrhagica (pustular-like lesions found on the palms or soles) and plantar fasciitis.

Enteropathic arthritis

Enteropathic arthritis is a peripheral or axial arthritis and is the commonest extra-intestinal manifestation of inflammatory bowel disease. Patients are usually young adults and there is no gender predisposition. The musculo-skeletal manifestations include:
- Sacroiliitis (symmetric usually).
- Peripheral arthritis.
- Dactylitis.
- Enthesopathy (Achilles, plantar fascia, costovertebral, costosternal).

Only a minority of patients (7%) are HLA B27 positive. Enteropathic spon-dyloarthropathy does not typically correlate with the severity of bowel disease. However, in some cases, the peripheral arthritis has been shown to improve if the affected bowel is resected.

Osteoporosis

Osteoporosis is a systemic skeletal disorder involving ↓ bone mass (osteopenia) and micro-architectural deterioration, resulting in an ↑ risk of fracture (Box 10.17). Classification (and treatment) is based on measurement of the bone mineral density (BMD), with comparison to that of a young healthy adult.

The underlying pathology is related to an imbalance between the osteoblasts producing bone and the osteoclasts removing bone which ultimately produces net bone loss. By the World Health Organization definition, patients with a BMD of <2.5 standard deviations below the mean of young adult BMD of the same gender have osteoporosis.

Primary osteoporosis

- 95% of osteoporosis in women, 70–80% osteoporosis in men.
- Seen in postmenopausal women and elderly men.
- No single underlying cause of osteoporosis. However, patients may have several risk factors including:
  - Older age (>50 years)
  - Female gender
  - Low dietary calcium and vitamin D intake
  - FHx of osteoporosis
  - Parental history of hip fracture
  - BMI <19 kg/m^2
  - Delayed menarche
  - Premature menopause
  - Sedentary lifestyle
  - Excess caffeine intake.

Secondary osteoporosis

- Has an identifiable underlying cause of osteoporosis (see Box 10.17).
- In addition, patients may have other identifiable risk factors as for primary osteoporosis.

Clinical features

- The process leading to osteoporosis is asymptomatic.
- The condition is diagnosed usually after the patient has a fragility fracture.
  - A fragility fracture is a fracture caused by falling from a standing height or less
  - Common sites of osteoporotic fracture include femoral neck, wrist, and vertebrae
  - Vertebral fracture may be asymptomatic sometimes, being diagnosed only when the patient has a spinal radiograph for kyphosis, loss of height, or for unrelated reasons.

Box 10.17 Secondary causes of osteoporosis
- Prolonged immobilization/weightlessness
- Malignancy
- GI diseases: malabsorption syndrome, IBD, liver disease, anorexia nervosa
- Rheumatologic diseases: RA, SLE, AS
- COPD
- Genetic diseases: cystic fibrosis, Ehlers–Danlos syndrome
- Endocrine diseases: diabetes type 1, hyperparathyroid, hyperthyroid, hyperprolactinaemia, Cushing's syndrome, hypogonadism
- Drugs: corticosteroids, phenytoin, long-term heparin
- Alcohol (>recommended daily allowance) and smoking.

See also:
More information regarding the presentation and clinical signs of locomotor diseases to aid preparation for OSCE-type examinations and ward rounds can be found in the *Oxford Handbooks Clinical Tutor Study Cards*.

'Medicine' Study Card set:
- Rheumatoid arthritis
- Osteoarthritis
- Psoriatic arthritis
- Ankylosing spondylitis
- Paget's disease
- Tophaceous gout
- Marfan's syndrome
- Systemic sclerosis
- Vasculitides
- Systemic lupus erythematosus
- Rickets.

'Surgery' Study Card set:
- Dupuytren's contracture
- Hammer toe
- Claw toes
- Mallet toe
- Mallet finger
- Trigger finger
- Olecranon bursitis
- Swellings around the knee
- Osteochondroma
- Pes cavus
- Charcot's joint
- Hallux valgus.

The elderly patient

Rheumatological diseases represent a huge spectrum of illness in older people, often complicating and concurrent with other diseases—e.g. the impact of severe arthritis on COPD; or heart failure, or the effect of hip or knee arthritis on recovery after acute stroke. Arthritis and osteoporosis are two major factors in the 'geriatric giants' of immobility and instability—pertinent reminders of the widespread effect of locomotor illness with advancing age.

History

- *Method of presentation:* can vary, ranging from the fall that leads to a femoral neck fracture or a referral 'off legs' or with declining mobility. Older people will often have an existing diagnosis of some form of arthritis—the difficulty is not in the diagnosis, but understanding the impact on everyday life. Locomotor illnesses are a key part of such presentations, and attention to these illnesses is vital. However, it is important to remember that presentations such as falls are multifactorial—try to work out how locomotor illness contributes to mobility or falls risk.
- *Intercurrent illness:* may often precipitate gout or particularly pseudogout. Equally important are those illnesses that disturb carefully balanced homeostasis, leading to a fall and fracture. Your task is not just to treat the consequence of the fall, but also to look at why it happened in the first place.
- *Septic joints:* can be notoriously difficult to diagnose at times. Unilateral large joint swelling/acute arthritis should ring alarm bells instantly, especially if the patient is unwell. Myriad causes contribute to back pain, but never forget deep-seated infection such as discitis or osteomyelitis which may be a consequence of something as innocuous as a urinary infection.
- *DHx:* as ever, a keystone of any assessment. Consider the side-effect profile of NSAIDs, or whether gout has been precipitated by the effects of diuretics or low-dose aspirin. If your patient has sustained a fragility fracture due to osteoporosis, are they on appropriate treatment? Never forget the number of older people whose arthritis is successfully treated with disease-modifying drugs—and understand the effects of such drugs (and the need to prescribe concurrent folic acid with methotrexate—don't forget!).
- *Activities, occupation, and interests:* overlaps with the functional history, a key message of these sections. Multi-disciplinary assessment is vital in terms of tailoring rehabilitation, aids, and future care where appropriate. Ask too about hobbies and interests—improving balance, minimizing pain, and maximizing function may allow patients to carry on with activities that are a key part of their lives (and might represent an opportunity for continued exercise or rehabilitation).

Examination

- *General:* the signs are often very clear, but despite this, easily overlooked. The need here is for a careful and thoughtful assessment of function as well as disease activity. Always be solicitous of your patient's comfort—and examine carefully, explaining what you wish to do to avoid misunderstanding and pain.
- *Pattern of disease:* look out for typical patterns of disease, and also single joint pathology. Look at ankles, feet, and back—it takes only a little more time to undertake a good examination, but is depressingly common to see patients with poor balance and falls with a clerking that details no locomotor assessment.
- *Disease activity:* be careful when palpating—but look to see if an acute exacerbation of joint disease may well have contributed to the current presentation.
- *Gait and balance:* often overlooked, but a vital part of the examination. Learn (e.g. from the ward physiotherapist) how to undertake the 'get up and go test' (Box 10.18), a well-validated test of gait and balance. This assessment should overlap with neurological assessment when appropriate. (See Box 10.19.)

Box 10.18 Get up and go

An easy test to do, and one which gives a wealth of information. Ask the patient to perform the following 3-part task:

- Rise to standing from a chair
- Walk 3 metres
- Turn and return to the chair.

This is not a pure observer role for the clinician—you must make an assessment of safety and be on hand to support the patient if needed.

Box 10.19 A word on labels and respect

It is a sad fact that we still see patients labelled with awful terms such as 'acopia' or 'social admission' after failing and/or falling at home. They are not to be used as they reflect:

- Your (and your seniors') limited thinking
- Missed diagnoses
  - Such as infections, overmedication, pain, fractures.
- A lack of respect.
  - Older people would almost certainly prefer not to be in hospital and it is extremely rare that the reason for admission is their 'fault'.

▶ Do your best for them with as thorough and detailed an assessment as you would do for any other patient presentation.

▶ Consider using your own 'family and friends test'. Would you be satisfied if these labels were attached to an older person you knew who had been admitted acutely to hospital?

The ear, nose, and throat

Introduction

Ear

The ear is involved in both balance and hearing and is divided into the external, middle, and inner ear.

The external ear

This is composed of the pinna (auricle), external auditory meatus, and the lateral wall of the tympanic membrane.

The auricle is divided into the antihelix, helix, lobe, tragus, and concha and is composed of fibrocartilage; the ear lobe is adipose only.

The tympanic membrane is a thin, grey, oval, semitransparent membrane at the medial end of the external acoustic meatus ~1cm in diameter. It detects air vibrations (sound waves). These tiny movements are then transmitted to the auditory ossicles.

The middle ear

This lies in the petrous part of the temporal bone and is connected to the nasopharynx via the Eustachian tube. It connects with the mastoid air cells. The tympanic cavity contains three tiny bones (ossicles: the malleus, incus, and stapes) which transmit vibrations to the cochlea and two small muscles (stapedius and tensor tympani). The chorda tympani branch of the facial nerve passes through here before it exits the skull.

The inner ear (vestibulocochlear organ)

This is involved in the reception of sound and the maintenance of balance. It consists of a series of interconnecting bony-walled fluid-filled chambers (vestibule, semicircular canals, and cochlea). Within the bony labyrinth is a further series of interconnecting membranous chambers (membranous labyrinth: saccule, utricle, cochlear duct, and semicircular ducts).

The vestibule and semicircular canals contain the peripheral balance organs. These have connections to the cerebellum and are important in the maintenance of posture and fixed gaze. The sensory impulses are conducted by the cochlear and vestibular divisions of cranial nerve VIII.

Nose and paranasal sinuses

The main functions of the nose and nasal cavities are olfaction, respiration, and air filtration.

The upper 1/3 of the external nose is bony; the rest is cartilaginous. The inferior surface holds the anterior nares (nostrils) which are separated from each other by the bony/cartilaginous nasal septum. The lateral wall of each cavity supports a series of three ridges called turbinates (superior, middle, and inferior).

The paranasal sinuses are air-filled extensions of the nasal cavity. They are named according to the bones in which they are located: frontal, ethmoid, sphenoid, and maxilla (see Fig. 11.1). Their purpose is thought to include protection of intracranial structures and the eyes from trauma, as an aid to vocal resonance, and reduction of skull weight.

Mouth and throat

The oral cavity comprises the lips, the anterior 2/3 of the tongue, hard palate, teeth, and alveoli of the mandible and maxilla.

The tongue is involved with mastication, taste, swallowing (deglutination), and articulation. Two sets of teeth develop within a lifetime. The first set is deciduous (milk teeth). The incisors are the first to erupt at ~6 months; the rest follow within 3 years. In the permanent set, the first molar or central incisor erupts first (~6 years), the second molar erupts ~11 years of age; the third molar emerges ~18 years (wisdom teeth).

The pharynx is divided into three parts: nasopharynx, oropharynx, and hypopharynx. The nasopharynx lies posterior to the nose and superior to the soft palate. The oropharynx lies posterior to the oral cavity, extending from the soft palate to the epiglottis, and contains the tonsils. The hypopharynx lies posterior to the larynx, extending from the epiglottis to the inferior border of the cricoid cartilage, where it is continuous with the oesophagus.

The larynx lies at the level of the bodies of C3–C6 vertebrae. It connects the inferior part of the pharynx with the trachea. It functions to prevent food and saliva entering the respiratory tract and as a phonating mechanism for voice production. It is supported by a framework of hyaline cartilage connected by ligaments. The thyroid cartilage is the largest of the laryngeal cartilages and can be seen as the 'Adam's apple'. The nervous supply of the larynx is from cranial nerve X (sensory and motor).

The epiglottis is attached to the thyroid cartilage and occludes the laryngeal inlet during swallowing.

Salivary glands

The main salivary glands are the parotid, submandibular, and sublingual. The sublingual glands are the smallest and their ducts open on to the floor of the mouth—as do the ducts of the submandibular glands. The parotid glands are the largest. The parotid ducts cross the masseter muscles and open into the oral cavity opposite the upper 2nd molar teeth.

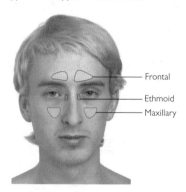

— Frontal

— Ethmoid

— Maxillary

Fig. 11.1 The surface anatomy of the facial sinuses.

Symptoms of ear disorders

Otalgia

You should take a standard 'pain' history as in ❷ Chapter 2.

Ask about associated discharge, hearing loss, previous ear operations, or ear syringing, use of cotton buds, trauma, swimming, and air travel.

▶ Remember that the ear has a sensory supply from cranial nerves V, IX, X, and the 2nd and 3rd cervical nerves so otalgia may be referred from several other areas (Box 11.1).

Box 11.1 Some causes of otalgia

Otological
- Acute otitis externa
- Acute otitis media
- Perichondritis
- Furunculosis
- Trauma
- Neoplasm
- Herpes zoster (Ramsay Hunt syndrome).

Non-otological (referred)
- Cervical spine disease
- Tonsillitis
- Dental disease
- Temporo-mandibular joint disease
- Neoplasms of the pharynx or larynx.

Otorrhoea

This is discharge from the external auditory meatus. Ask about other ear symptoms, when the discharge began, and any precipitating or exacerbating factors. Ask especially about the nature of the discharge:
- *Watery:* eczema, CSF.
- *Purulent:* acute otitis externa.
- *Mucoid:* chronic suppurative otitis media with perforation.
- *Mucopurulent/blood-stained:* trauma, acute otitis media, cancer.
- *Foul-smelling:* chronic suppurative otitis media ± cholesteatoma.

Dizziness

The term 'dizziness' can mean different things to different people and must be distinguished from light-headedness, pre-syncope, and pure unsteadiness. Two features of the dizziness suggest that it arises from the vestibular system:
- Vertigo (a hallucination of movement, most commonly rotational).
- Dizziness related to movement or position change.

Both these symptoms can occur together, separately in time, or alone in different people. Disequilibrium (unsteadiness or veering) may accompany vestibular dizziness.

Important points from the history

You should obtain a precise history, aiming to establish whether or not the dizziness is due to vestibular disease (Box 11.2). Ask about:

- The nature and severity of the dizziness.
- Whether it is persistent or in intermittent 'attacks'.
- The duration of attacks (seconds, hours, or days).
- The pattern of events since the onset.
- Relation to movement or position, especially lying down.
- Associated symptoms (e.g. nausea, vomiting, hearing change, tinnitus, headaches).
- DHx including alcohol.
- Other ear problems or previous ear surgery.

Peripheral vestibular lesions

Vertigo caused by vestibular problems is most commonly rotational, but may be swaying or tilting. Whether it is movement of the person or surroundings is irrelevant.

Any rapid head movement may provoke the dizziness, but dizziness provoked by lying down, rolling over, or sitting up is specific to benign paroxysmal positional vertigo.

Central vestibular lesions

These are not always easy to distinguish on the history but vertigo is not so marked and gait disturbances and other neurological symptoms and signs would suggest this.

Box 11.2 Some causes of dizziness

Otological
- Benign paroxysmal positional vertigo
- Ménière's disease
- Vestibular neuronitis
- Trauma (surgery or temporal bone fracture)
- Perilymph fistula
- Middle ear infection
- Otosclerosis
- Syphilis
- Ototoxic drugs
- Acoustic neuromas.

Non-otological
- These are often more disequilibrium than dizziness
- Ageing (poor eyesight and proprioception)
- Cerebrovascular disease
- Parkinson's disease
- Migraine
- Epilepsy
- Demyelinating disorders
- Hyperventilation
- Drugs (e.g. cardiovascular, neuroleptic drugs, and alcohol).

Hearing loss

Deafness or total hearing loss is unusual. Hearing loss is usually described as being mild, moderate, or profound.

Hearing loss may be conductive, sensorineural, mixed, or non-organic.

Conductive hearing loss may be due to pathology of the ear canal, eardrum, or middle ear. Sensorineural hearing loss is caused by disease in the cochlea or the neural pathway to the brain. (See Box 11.3.)

You should take a full history as in ➔ Chapter 2. In particular, note:

- *PC:* As well as the usual questions, establish:
  - The time and speed of onset
  - Is it partial or complete?
  - Are both ears affected or just one?
  - Is there associated pain, discharge, or vertigo?
- *PMH:* especially tuberculosis and septicaemia.
- *FHx:* hearing loss may be inherited (e.g. otosclerosis).
- *DHx:* certain drugs, particularly those which are toxic to the renal system, affect the ear (e.g. aminoglycosides, some diuretics, cytotoxic agents). Salicylates and quinine show reversible toxicity.
- *SHx:* occupation and leisure activities should not be overlooked. Prolonged exposure to loud noise (e.g. heavy industrial machinery) can lead to sensorineural hearing loss. Levels of 90dB or greater require ear protection.

Box 11.3 Some causes of hearing loss

Conductive

- Wax
- Otitis externa, if ear is full of debris
- Middle ear effusion
- Trauma to ossicles
- Otosclerosis
- Chronic middle ear infection (current or previous)
- Tumours of the middle ear.

Sensorineural

- Presbyacusis
- Vascular ischaemia
- Noise exposure
- Inflammatory/infectious diseases (e.g. measles, mumps, meningitis, syphilis)
- Ototoxicity
- Acoustic tumours (progressive unilateral hearing loss, but may be bilateral).

Non-organic hearing loss

🚺 Only diagnose after fully excluding an organic cause. In such cases, there may be a discrepancy between the history and clinical and audiometric findings.

Tinnitus

As well as the full standard history, ask the patient about the character of the tinnitus, associated hearing loss, how the tinnitus bothers them (i.e. is sleep or daily living affected) and any previous history of ear disease as well as the full standard history. (See Box 11.4.)

- *Rushing, hissing, or buzzing* tinnitus is the commonest and usually associated with hearing loss. It is caused by pathology in the inner ear, brainstem, or auditory cortex (although it can sometimes appear with conductive hearing loss).
- *Pulsatile* tinnitus is caused by noise transmitted from blood vessels close to the ear. These include the internal carotid artery and internal jugular vein (the latter can be diagnosed by abolition of the noise by pressure on the neck). Occasionally, pulsatile tinnitus can be heard by an observer by using a stethoscope over the ear or neck.
- *Cracking and popping* noises can be associated with dysfunction of the Eustachian tube or rhythmic myoclonus of the muscles in the middle ear or attached to the Eustachian tube.

▶ Remember to distinguish tinnitus from complex noises (e.g. voices, music) which may constitute auditory hallucinations.

Box 11.4 Some causes of tinnitus

- Presbyacusis
- Noise-induced hearing loss
- Ménière's disease
- Ototoxic drugs, trauma
- Any cause of conductive hearing loss
- Acoustic neuromas.

Pulsatile tinnitus

- Arterial aneurysms
- Arteriovenous malformations.

Injury to the ear

- Trauma may be self-inflicted, especially in children, when foreign bodies inserted in the ear can damage the meatal skin or the eardrum.
- Head injuries can cause temporal bone fractures, with bleeding from the ear and may be associated with dislocation of the ossicles, or may involve the labyrinth causing severe vertigo and complete deafness.
- Temporary or permanent facial nerve palsy may also occur.

Deformity of the ear

- This may be either congenital or acquired (usually traumatic).
- Complete or partial absence of the pinna (anotia or microtia), accessory auricles (anterior to the tragus), or a pre-auricular sinus. Protruding ears may cause social embarrassment and can be surgically corrected.
- Small auricles are seen in Down's syndrome—often with a rudimentary or absent lobule.

Symptoms of nasal disorders

Nasal obstruction

As well as the full standard history (➲ Chapter 2), establish:

- Is the nose blocked constantly or intermittently?
  - Constant: long-standing structural deformity such as deviated septum, nasal polyps, or enlarged turbinates
  - Intermittent: allergic rhinitis or common cold.
- Unilateral or bilateral obstruction?
- Associated nasal discharge.
- Relieving or exacerbating factors.
- Use of nose drops or any other 'per-nasal' substance (e.g. glue-sniffing or drug-snorting).
- ► Don't miss a previous history of nasal surgery.

Nasal discharge

Ask about the specific character of the discharge which is often very helpful in deciding aetiology. See Box 11.5.

ⓘ The terms 'catarrh' and 'postnasal drip' should be reserved only for complaints of nasal discharge pouring backwards into the nasopharynx.

Epistaxis

This is a nasal haemorrhage or 'nose-bleed'. The anterior septum, known as Little's area, is the point of convergence of the anterior ethmoidal artery, the septal branches of the sphenopalatine and superior labial arteries, and the greater palatine artery. A common site of bleeding.

Epistaxis is most commonly due to spontaneous rupture of a blood vessel in the nasal mucous membrane.

Your history should explore the possible causes (see Box 11.6).

Distinguish between anterior bleed (blood running out of the nose, usually one nostril) and posterior bleed (blood running into the throat or from both nostrils).

Sneezing

Sneezing is a very frequent accompaniment to viral upper respiratory tract infection and allergic rhinitis. It is commonly associated with rhinorrhoea and itching of the nose and eyes.

Ask about exacerbating factors and explore the time-line carefully, looking for precipitants.

Disorders of smell

Patients may complain of a ↓ sense of smell (hyposmia) or, more rarely, a total loss of smell (anosmia). Ask about the exact timing of the hyposmia and any other associated nasal symptoms.

- *Anosmia:* most commonly caused by nasal polyps but may be caused by head injury disrupting the olfactory fibres emerging through the cribriform plate. It may also complicate a viral upper respiratory tract infection (viral neuropathy).
- *Cacosmia:* the hallucination of an unpleasant smell and may be caused by infection interfering with the olfactory structures.

Nasal deformity

Nasal deformity may occur as a result of a trauma causing pain ± swelling ± epistaxis ± displacement of nasal bones and septum.

Disruption of the bones and nasal septum may produce a 'saddle' deformity. Other causes of a 'saddle' nose include Wegener's granulomatosis, congenital syphilis, and long-term snorting of cocaine.

Acne rosacea can cause an enlarged, red, and bulbous rhinophyma. Widening of the nose is an early feature of acromegaly.

Nasal and facial pain

Facial pain is not normally due to local nasal causes. More frequently, it is related to infection within the sinuses, trigeminal neuralgia, dental sepsis, migraine, or mid-facial tension pain.

Box 11.5 Some causes of nasal discharge

Watery or mucoid
- Allergic rhinitis
- Infective (viral) rhinitis
- Vasomotor rhinitis
- A unilateral copious watery discharge may be due to CSF rhinorrhoea.

Purulent
- Infective rhinosinusitis
- Foreign body (especially if unilateral).

Blood stained
- Tumours (with unilateral symptoms)
- Bleeding diathesis
- Trauma.

Box 11.6 Some causes of epistaxis

- Trauma from nose picking, nasal surgery, cocaine use, or infection
- Prolonged bleeding may be caused by hypertension, alcohol, anticoagulants, coagulation defects, Waldenström's macroglobulinaemia, Wegener's granulomatosis, and hereditary telangiectasia
- Neoplasia and angiomas of the postnasal space and nose may present with epistaxis.

Symptoms of throat disorders

Oral pain

- The commonest cause of pain in the oral cavity is dental caries and periodontal infection. Periodontal disease can cause pain on tooth-brushing and is associated with halitosis.
- Gum disease is a common cause of oral pain.
- In elderly patients, dentures may cause pain if improperly sized or if they produce an abnormal bite.
- Take a full pain history as in ➜ Chapter 2 and ask about other mouth/throat symptoms.

Throat pain

- A sore throat is an extremely common symptom. You should clarify the full nature of the pain as discussed in ➜ Chapter 2. It is important to establish exactly where the pain is felt.
  - Throat pain often radiates to the ear because the pharynx and external auditory meatus are innervated by the vagus (X) nerve.
- Most acute sore throats are viral in origin and are associated with rhinorrhoea and a productive cough. Consider infectious mononucleosis in teenagers.
- Acute tonsillitis is associated with systemic symptoms such as malaise, fever, and anorexia.
- You should consider malignancy in all chronically sore throats in adults.
  - Ask about symptoms associated with cancer such as dysphagia, dysphonia, weight loss, and a history of smoking or excessive alcohol.

Lumps in the mouth

Lips

- The lips are a common site for localized malignancy, e.g. BCC, SCC.

Tongue

- Lumps here are nearly always neoplastic

Oral cavity

- Blockage of a minor salivary gland might give rise to a cystic lesion called a ranula and is usually sited in the floor of the mouth.
  - Most malignant lesions on the floor of the mouth present late: pain, dysphagia, and odynophagia (pain on swallowing) are common symptoms. The buccal lining is also another very common site for cancer.

Globus pharyngeus

This is the sensation of a lump in the throat (globus pharyngeus or globus syndrome). It is important to ask about symptoms of gastro-oesophageal reflux or postnasal drip.

It is occasionally associated with a malignancy. You should ask about dysphagia, odynophagia, hoarseness, and weight loss.

Lumps in the neck

Neck lumps are usually secondary to infection but a minority are due to malignant disease. The most common cause of neck swelling is lymph node enlargement. A comprehensive history and examination of the head and neck is important.

▶ In the adult, it is worth remembering that metastatic neck disease may represent spread from structures below the clavicle including lung, breast, stomach, pancreas, kidney, prostate, and uterus. If malignancy is suspected, the history and examination should include a search for symptoms and signs in other systems.

As well as the full standard history, ask especially about:

- The duration of the swelling.
- Progression in size.
- Associated pain or other symptoms in the upper aerodigestive tract:
  - Odynophagia
  - Dysphagia
  - Dysphonia.
- Systemic symptoms (weight loss, night sweats, malaise).
- Smoking and alcohol habits.

Dysphonia

This is an alteration in the quality of the voice. There are several causes which your history should be aimed at identifying including:

- *Inflammatory:* acute laryngitis, chronic laryngitis (chronic vocal abuse, alcohol, smoke inhalation).
- *Neurological:*
  - Central: pseudobulbar palsy, cerebral palsy, multiple sclerosis, stroke, Guillain–Barré syndrome, head injury
  - Peripheral: lesions affecting X and recurrent laryngeal nerves (e.g. lung cancer, post-thyroidectomy, cardiothoracic, and oesophageal surgery), myasthenia gravis, motor neuron disease.
- *Neoplastic:* laryngeal cancer for example.
- *Systemic:* rheumatoid arthritis, angiogenic oedema, hypothyroidism.
- *Psychogenic:* these are dysphonias in the absence of laryngeal disease and mainly occur due to an underlying anxiety or depression (i.e. musculoskeletal tension disorders, conversion voice disorders). Like all other non-organic disorders, you must rule out organic pathology.

Halitosis

This is offensive-smelling breath. It is commonly caused by poor dental hygiene or diet. Tonsillar infection, gingivitis, pharyngeal pouch, and chronic sinusitis with purulent postnasal drip can also cause bad breath.

Stridor

This is a noise from the upper airway (see also ➲ Chapter 6) and is caused by narrowing of the trachea or larynx.

The main causes of stridor in adults are laryngeal cancer, laryngeal trauma, epiglottitis, and cancer of the trachea or main bronchus.

Examining the ear

Inspection and palpation

- Briefly inspect the external structures of the ear, paying particular attention to the pinna, noting its shape, size, and any deformity.
- Carefully inspect for any skin changes suggestive of cancer.
- Don't forget to look behind the ears for any scars or a hearing aid.
- Pull on the pinna and ask the patient if it is painful.
  - Infection of the external auditory meatus.
- Palpate the area in front of the tragus and ask if there is any pain.
  - Temporo-mandibular joint disease.
- Look for any discharge (Fig. 11.2).

Otoscopy

The otoscope (or auroscope) allows you to examine the external auditory canal, the eardrum, and a few middle ear structures.

The otoscope

The otoscope consists of a light source, a removable funnel-shaped speculum, and a viewing window which often slightly magnifies the image (Fig. 11.3).

On many otoscopes, the viewing window can be slid aside to allow insertion of instruments (e.g. scrapers and swabs) down the auditory canal.

Technique

The following is the method for examining the patient's right ear. Examination of the left ear should be a mirror-image of this.

- Introduce yourself and clean your hands.
- Explain the procedure to the patient and obtain verbal consent.
- Turn the light source on.
- Place a clean speculum on the end of the scope.
- Gently pull the pinna upwards and backwards with your left hand.
  - This straightens out the cartilaginous part of the canal allowing easier passage of the scope.
- Holding the otoscope in your right hand, place the tip of the speculum in the opening of the external canal. Do this under direct vision before looking through the viewing window.
- Slowly advance the otoscope whilst looking though it.
  - It is often helpful to stabilize the otoscope by extending the little finger of the right hand and placing it on the patient's head.
- Inspect the skin of the auditory canal for signs of infection, wax, and foreign bodies.
  - If wax is causing obstruction, it may be necessary to perform ear syringing before continuing.
- Examine the tympanic membrane (Fig. 11.4).
  - A healthy eardrum should appear greyish and translucent
  - Look for the light reflex. This is the reflection off the surface of the drum visible just below the malleus
  - Notice any white patches (tympanosclerosis) or perforation
  - A reddened, bulging drum is a sign of acute otitis media
  - A dull grey, yellow drum may indicate middle ear fluid.

Testing auditory and vestibular function

See cranial nerve VIII in ➲ Chapter 8.

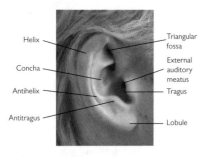

Helix — Triangular fossa

Concha — External auditory meatus

Antihelix — Tragus

Antitragus — Lobule

Fig. 11.2 The surface anatomy of the normal ear.

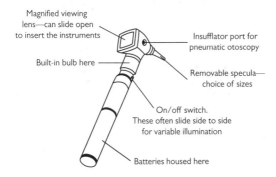

Magnified viewing lens—can slide open to insert the instruments

Insufflator port for pneumatic otoscopy

Built-in bulb here

Removable specula—choice of sizes

On/off switch. These often slide side to side for variable illumination

Batteries housed here

Fig. 11.3 A standard otoscope.

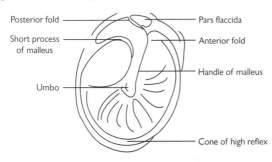

Posterior fold — Pars flaccida

Short process of malleus — Anterior fold

Handle of malleus

Umbo

Cone of high reflex

Fig. 11.4 The appearance of the normal eardrum on otoscopy.

Examining the nose

See Box 11.7 for rhinitis.

External inspection

- Inspect the external surface and appearance of the nose noting any disease or deformity.
- Stand behind the patient and look down, over their head to detect any deviation.

Palpation

- Gently palpate the nasal bones and ask the patient to alert you to any pain.
- If a visible deformity is present, palpate to determine if it is bony (hard and immobile) or cartilaginous (firm but compressible).
- Feel for facial swelling and tenderness.
  - Tenderness suggests underlying inflammation.

Nostril patency

Assess whether air moves through both nostrils effectively.

- Push on one nostril until it is occluded.
- Ask the patient to inhale through their nose.
- Then repeat on the opposite side.
  - Air should move equally well through each nostril.

Internal examination

The postnasal space (nasopharynx) can be examined using fine-bore endoscopy. This is done by trained professionals; the student or non-specialist should examine the anterior portion of the nose only.

- Ask the patient to tilt their head back.
- Push up slightly on the tip of the nose with the thumb.
  - You should now be able to see just inside the anterior vestibule.
- In adults, you can use a nasal speculum to widen the nares allowing easier inspection.
- Pinch the speculum closed, place the prongs just inside the nostril, and release your grip gently allowing the prongs to spread apart.
- Look at:
  - The colour of the mucosa
  - The presence and colour of any discharge
  - The septum (which should be in the midline)
  - Any obvious bleeding points, clots, crusting, or perforation
  - The middle and inferior turbinates along the lateral wall for evidence of polypoid growth, foreign bodies, and other soft tissue swelling.

Testing olfaction

This is described under cranial nerve I in ➲ Chapter 8.

Box 11.7 Rhinitis

Allergic rhinitis
- Inhaled allergens cause an antigen-antibody type I hypersensitivity reaction
- Common allergens:
  - Pollen (including from grass) and flowering trees: seasonal allergic rhinitis (hayfever)
  - Animal dander*, dust mites**, and feathers: perennial allergic rhinitis
  - Digested allergens such as wheat, eggs, milk, and nuts are also rarely involved.
- The main symptoms include:
  - Bouts of sneezing
  - Profuse rhinorrhoea due to activity of glandular elements
  - Postnasal drip
  - Nasal itching
  - Nasal obstruction due to nasal vasodilatation and oedema.

Non-allergic (vasomotor) rhinitis
- This has all the clinical features of allergic rhinitis but the nose is not responding to an antigen-antibody type I reaction
- The reactions tend to be to inhaled chemicals such as deodorants, perfumes, or smoke, although alcohol and sunlight can provoke symptoms
- Allergies can coexist and some people seem to have an instability of the parasympathetic system in the nose with excessive secretion of watery mucus and congestion (vasomotor rhinitis).

* Cat allergy is actually an allergy to one of the proteins in feline saliva—their fur is covered in it through licking.
** Actually an allergy to dust mite faeces.

Examining the nasal sinuses

The reader should revisit the anatomy of the sinuses and Fig. 11.1. The frontal and maxillary sinuses are the only two that can be examined, albeit indirectly.

Palpation
- Palpate and percuss the skin overlying the frontal and maxillary sinuses.
- Tap on the upper teeth (which sit in the floor of the maxillary sinus).
  - In both of the above, pain suggests inflammation (sinusitis).

Examining the mouth and throat

Ensure that the room is well lit. You should have an adjustable light-source. An otoscope or pen-torch should be adequate for non-specialists. (See Fig. 11.5.)

Inspection

- *Face:* look at the patient's face for obvious skin disease, scars, lumps, signs of trauma, deformity, or facial asymmetry (including parotid enlargement).
- *Lips, teeth, gums:* inspect the lips at rest first.
  - Ask the patient to open their mouth and take a look at the buccal mucosa, teeth, and gums (see Box 11.8)
  - Note signs of dental decay or gingivitis
  - Ask the patient to evert the lips and look for any inflammation, discoloration, ulceration, nodules, or telangiectasia.
- *Tongue and floor of the mouth:* inspect the tongue inside and outside the mouth. Look for any obvious growths or abnormalities.
  - Included in this should be an assessment of cranial nerve XII
  - Ask the patient to touch the roof of the mouth with their tongue
  - This allows you to look at the underside of the tongue and floor of the mouth.
- *Oropharynx:* to look at the posterior oropharynx, ask the patient to say 'Aaah' (elevates the soft palate).
  - Using tongue depressor may provide a better view
  - Uvula: should hang down from the roof of the mouth, in the midline. With an 'Aaah' the uvula rises up. Deviation to one side may be caused by cranial nerve IX palsy, tumour, or infection.
- *Soft palate:* look for any cleft, structural abnormality, or asymmetry of movement and note any telangiectasia.
- *Tonsils:* inspect the tonsils noting their size, colour, and any discharge.
  - The tonsils lie in an alcove between the posterior and anterior pillars (arches) on either side of the mouth.

Palpation

This is reserved for any abnormal or painful areas which you have detected on initial inspection.

- Put on a pair of gloves and palpate the area of interest with *both* hands (one hand outside on the patient's cheek or jaw and the other inside the mouth).

The rest of the neck

Palpate the cervical and supraclavicular lymph nodes (➲ Chapter 3), thyroid (➲ Chapter 3), and look for any additional masses.

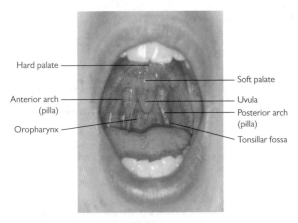

Hard palate —

Anterior arch (pilla) —

Oropharynx —

Soft palate

Uvula

Posterior arch (pilla)

Tonsillar fossa

Fig. 11.5 The normal appearance of the oral cavity.

Findings

- *Mucosal inflammation:* bacterial, fungal (candidiasis), and viral (e.g. herpes simplex) infections, or after radiotherapy treatment.
- *Oral candidiasis:* think radiotherapy, use of inhaled steroids, and immunodeficiency states (e.g. leukaemia, lymphoma, HIV).
- *Gingivitis:* inflammation of the gums may occur in minor trauma (teeth brushing), vitamin and mineral deficiency, or lichen planus.
- *Tonsillitis:* mucopus on the pharyngeal wall implies bacterial infection. Think of infectious mononucleosis in teenagers, particularly if the tonsils are covered with a white pseudomembranous exudate.
  - Acute tonsillitis is often associated with systemic features of malaise, fever, anorexia, cervical lymphadenopathy, and candidiasis.

Box 11.8 Gum changes in systemic conditions

- Chronic lead poisoning: punctate blue lesions
- Phenytoin treatment: firm and hypertrophic gums
- Scurvy: gums are soft and haemorrhagic
- Cyanotic congenital heart disease: gums are spongy and haemorrhagic.

Important presentations

Otitis externa

- Inflammation of the outer ear.
- Commonly caused by bacterial infection of the ear canal (e.g. *Streptococci*, *Staphylococci*, *Pseudomonas*) and fungi.
  - Heat, humidity, swimming, and any irritants causing pruritus can all predispose a patient to otitis externa.
- Often occurs in patients with eczema, seborrhoeic dermatitis, or psoriasis due to scratching.
- Symptoms can vary from irritation to severe pain ± discharge.
- Pressure on the tragus or movement of the auricle may cause pain.
- *'Malignant otitis externa'*: very aggressive form caused by a spreading osteomyelitis of the temporal bone (usually *Pseudomonas pyocaneus*).

Furunculosis

- An infection of hair follicles in the auditory canal.
- Presents with severe throbbing pain exacerbated by jaw movement with pyrexia and often precedes rupture of an abscess.

Otitis media and glue ear

- Inflammation of the middle ear, usually following an URTI.
- In the early stages, the eardrum becomes retracted as the Eustachian tube is blocked, resulting in an inflammatory middle ear exudate.
- If there is infection, pus builds up causing the middle ear pressure to rise and this is seen on otoscopy as bulging of the eardrum.
- The eardrum may eventually rupture if untreated.

Complications

- Include: inflammation in the mastoid air cells (mastoiditis), labyrinthitis, facial nerve palsy, extradural abscess, meningitis, lateral sinus thrombosis, cerebellar and temporal lobe abscess.

Chronic suppurative otitis media

- Associated with a central persistent perforation of the pars tensa. The resulting otorrhoea is usually mucoid and profuse in active infection.

Glue ear

- (Otitis media with effusion) is the commonest cause of acquired conductive hearing loss in children (peaks between 3–6 years).
- Higher incidence in patients with cleft palate and Down's syndrome.
- The aetiology is usually Eustachian tube dysfunction with thinning of the drum.

Cholesteatoma

- Destructive disease consisting of overgrowth of stratified squamous epithelial tissue in the middle ear and mastoid causing erosion of local structures and the introduction of infection.
- When infected, there may be a foul-smelling discharge.
- Bone destruction and marked hearing loss can occur.
- May be complicated by meningitis, cerebral abscesses, and VII palsy.

Ménière's disease

- Also known as endolymphatic hydrops.
- Distension of the membranous labyrinthine spaces.
  - The exact cause is not known.
- Symptoms: attacks of vertigo with prostration, nausea, vomiting, a fluctuating sensorineural hearing loss at the low frequencies, tinnitus, and aural fullness or pressure in the ear.
- Attacks tend to occur in clusters with quiescent periods between.
  - Each attack only lasts a few hours and the patient usually has normal balance between. Over years, the hearing gradually deteriorates in the affected ear.

Vestibular neuronitis

- Typically associated with sudden vertigo, vomiting, and prostration.
- The symptoms are exacerbated by head movement.
- Often follows a viral illness in the young or a vascular lesion in the elderly.
- No deafness or tinnitus.
- Vertigo lasts for several days, but complete recovery of balance can take months, or may never be achieved.

Otosclerosis

- A localized disease of bone which affects the capsule of the inner ear.
  - Vascular, spongy bone replaces normal bone around the oval window and may fix the footplate of the stapes
  - Both ears are affected in >50% of patients.
- Otoscopic examination is usually normal.
- There may be progressive conductive deafness manifesting after the second decade, possibly with tinnitus and, rarely, vertigo.
- Pregnancy and lactation aggravate the condition.
- There is often a strong FHx.

Benign positional vertigo

- Attacks of sudden-onset rotational vertigo provoked by lying flat or turning over in bed.
- Caused by crystalline debris in the posterior semicircular canal.
- Can follow an upper respiratory tract infection or head injury, but often there may be no preceding illness.
- Hallpike's manoeuvre is diagnostic (see ➔ Chapter 8).
- If diagnosed, the person should have an Epley manoeuvre which is often curative.
  - This repositions the debris in the posterior semicircular canal into the utricle.

Labyrinthitis

- Localized infection of the labyrinth apparatus.
  - Difficult to distinguish clinically from vestibular neuronitis, unless there is hearing loss due to cochlear involvement.

Acoustic neuromas

- Benign tumours of the vestibular element of cranial nerve VIII.
- Usually present in middle age and occur more frequently in females.
- Bilateral neuromas occur in 5% of patients.
- The early symptoms are unilateral or markedly asymmetric, progressive sensorineural hearing loss and tinnitus.
- Vertigo is rare but patients with large tumours may have ataxia.

Presbyacusis (senile deafness)

- Progressive loss of hair cells in the cochlea with age, resulting in a loss of acuity for high-frequency sounds.
- It usually becomes clinically noticeable from the age of 60–65 years.
  - The degree of loss and age of onset are variable.
- Hearing is most affected in the presence of background noise.

Glomus jugulare tumour

- A highly vascular tumour arising from 'glomus jugulare' tissue lying in the bulb of the internal jugular vein or the mucosa of the middle ear.
- Usually presents with a hearing loss or pulsatile tinnitus.
- Examination may show a deep red mass behind the eardrum.
- Occasionally associated with other tumours such as phaeochromocytomas, or carotid body tumours.

Nasal polyps

- Nasal polyps are pale, greyish, pedunculated, oedematous mucosal tissue which project into the nasal cavity.
  - Most frequently arise from the ethmoid region and prolapse into the nose via the middle meatus
  - Nearly always bilateral.
- In the majority of cases, they are associated with non-allergic rhinitis and late-onset asthma.
- Other causes to consider include:
  - Chronic paranasal infection
  - Neoplasia (usually unilateral ± bleeding)
  - Cystic fibrosis
  - Bronchiectasis.
- The main symptoms are watery anterior rhinorrhoea, purulent postnasal drip, progressive nasal obstruction, anosmia, change in voice quality, and taste disturbance.

Septal perforation

- May be idiopathic or be caused by trauma (especially post-op nasal surgery), infection (e.g. tuberculosis, syphilis), neoplasia (SCC, BCC, malignant granuloma), and inhaling cocaine and toxic gases.
- The main clinical complaints include crusting, recurrent epistaxis, and a whistling respiration.

Tonsillitis

- Acute tonsillitis is uncommon in adults in comparison to its frequency in children.
- The diagnosis is made from the appearance of the tonsils which are enlarged with surface exudates.
- The patient is usually systemically unwell with pyrexia, cervical lymphadenopathy, dysphagia, halitosis, and abdominal pain in children.
- Complications include peritonsillar abscess (quinsy) and retropharyngeal abscess.

Laryngitis

- Frequently associated with an URTI and is self-limiting.
- May be associated with secondary infection with *Staph.* and *Strep.*
- Patient typically complains of hoarseness, malaise, and fever.
  - There may also be odynophagia, dysphagia, and throat pain.

Epiglottitis

- 🛈 This is a medical emergency.
- Caused by group B *Haemophilus influenzae.*
- Characterized by gross swelling of the epiglottis and is primarily seen in 3–7-year-olds, although adults may also be affected.
- Clinical features include pyrexia, stridor, sore throat, and dysphagia.

Croup (laryngotracheobronchitis)

- The majority of cases are viral (parainfluenza or respiratory syncytial virus). It mainly occurs between the ages of 6 months and 3 years.

Branchial cyst

- This is an embryological remnant of the branchial complex during development of the neck.
- Located in the anterior triangle just in front of the sternomastoid.
- Presentation is typically at the age of 15–25 years.
- For more, see the *Oxford Handbooks Clinical Tutor: Surgery.*

See also:

More information regarding the presentation and clinical signs of ENT diseases to aid preparation for OSCE-type examinations and ward rounds can be found in the *Oxford Handbooks Clinical Tutor Study Cards.*

'Surgery' Study Card set:
- Thyroglossal cyst
- Branchial cyst
- Pharyngeal pouch
- Tumours of the parotid
- Diffuse parotid enlargement
- Submandibular calculi.

The male reproductive system

Notes
This chapter describes the history and examination related to male sexual function. Urinary and prostatic history and examination can be found in 'the abdomen' ⊃ Chapter 7.

Introduction

Anatomy

The male reproductive system consists of a pair of testes, a network of excretory ducts (epididymis, ductus deferens, and ejaculatory tracts), seminal vesicles, prostate, bulbo-urethral glands, and penis.

The penis

The penis consists of erectile tissue contained within two dorsally placed corpora cavernosa and the corpus spongiosum which lies on their ventral surface. The corpora are attached proximally to the inferior pubic rami. The corpus spongiosum expands distally to form the glans penis and surrounds the urethra.

The three corpora are contained within a fibrous tubular sheath of fascia and covered by freely mobile (and elastic) skin. A loose fold of skin, the prepuce or 'foreskin', extends distally to cover the glans penis.

The scrotum

This is a muscular out-pouching of the lower part of the anterior abdominal wall. It contains the testes, epididymis, and lower ends of the spermatic cords. The scrotum acts as a 'climate-control system' for the testes. Muscles in the wall of the scrotum, in conjunction with muscle fibres in the spermatic cord, allow it to contract and relax moving the testicles closer to or further away from the body.

The testes

These are paired, ovoid organs measuring 4 x 3 x 2cm, found within the scrotal sac. The testes are made up of masses of seminiferous tubules which are responsible for producing spermatozoa. Interstitial cells (Leydig cells) lying between these tubules produce the male sex hormones.

In the fetus, the testes develop close to the kidneys in the abdomen, then descend caudally through the inguinal canal to reach the scrotum at ~38 weeks' gestation.

Each testis is covered by an outer fibrous capsule (tunica albuginea). Laterally and medially lies the visceral layer of the tunica vaginalis (a closed serous sac—an embryonic derivative of the processus vaginalis which normally closes before birth). The posterior surface of the testis is devoid of tunica vaginalis and is pierced by numerous small veins that form the pampiniform plexus. Also the seminiferous tubules converge here to form the efferent tubules with eventually give rise to the epididymis.

Spermatic cord

This suspends the testis in the scrotum and contains structures running between the testis and the deep inguinal ring (the ductus deferens, arteries, veins, testicular nerves, and epididymis).

The cord is surrounded by the layers of the spermatic fascia (internal spermatic fascia) formed from the transversalis fascia, the cremasteric fascia formed from fascia covering the internal oblique, and the external spermatic fascia formed from the external oblique aponeurosis).

The cremasteric fascia is partly muscular. Contraction of this (the cremaster muscle) draws the testis superiorly. The raising and lowering of the testis acts to keep it at a near-constant temperature.

Epididymis

This is a convoluted duct 76cm in length lying on the posterior surface of the testis. It is a specialized part of the collecting apparatus where spermatozoa are matured before travelling up the vas deferens to join the ducts draining the seminal vesicles, known as the ejaculatory ducts.

The seminal vesicles are paired organs that lie on the posterior surface of the bladder and contribute the majority of the fluid that makes up semen along with fructose, ascorbic acid, amino acids, and prostaglandins.

Prostate gland

This is a firm, walnut-sized structure which lies inferior to the bladder, encircling the urethra. Many short ducts produce fluid which is emptied into the urethra and makes up a proportion of semen.

Bulbo-urethral glands

These are small, pea-sized glands located near the base of the penis.

In response to sexual stimulation, the bulbo-urethral glands secrete an alkaline mucus-like fluid which neutralizes the acidity of the urine in the urethra and provides a small amount of lubrication for the tip of the penis during intercourse.

Sex hormones

Three hormones are the regulators of the male reproductive system:

- FSH is produced in the anterior pituitary gland and stimulates spermatogenesis by its action on Sertoli cells.
- LH is produced in the anterior pituitary gland and stimulates the production of testosterone from Leydig cells.
- Testosterone is produced in the testis and adrenal gland and aids the development of male secondary sexual characteristics and spermatogenesis.

The male sexual response

There are four stages of the sexual response:

- *Excitement or arousal:* under control of the parasympathetic nervous system. During this, the penis becomes engorged with blood and stands out from the body. Other changes include an ↑ in heart rate, blood pressure, respiratory rate, and skeletal muscle tone.
- *Plateau:* continued sexual stimulation maintains the changes made in the arousal phase. This can last from a few seconds to many minutes.
- *Orgasm:* In males, this is the briefest stage and is mediated by the sympathetic nervous system. Rhythmic contractions of the perineal muscles, the accessory glands, and peristaltic contraction of the seminal ducts result in ejaculation. This is usually followed by a refractory period during which another erection cannot be achieved—this varies from minutes to hours and lengthens with advancing age.
- *Resolution:* blood pressure, heart rate, respiratory rate, and muscle tone return to the un-aroused state. Accompanied by a sense of relaxation.

Symptoms

Urethral discharge

If the patient complains of discharge from the end of their penis, or 'mucus', establish:

- The amount.
- The colour.
- The presence of blood.
- The relationship between the discharge and urination or ejaculation.
- Is there any pain?
- Are there any other symptoms—such as conjunctivitis, arthralgia?
- Has the patient recently had symptoms of gastroenteritis?

You should also determine when this symptom was first noticed and how that relates to any sexual contacts that the patient has had and the possibility of exposure to STIs.

Rashes, warts, ulcers

Treat a genital lesion as you would any other rash (see ➲ Chapter 4). Ask also about:

- Similar lesions elsewhere (e.g. mouth, anus).
- Foreign travel.

You should determine the risk of recent exposure to STDs as previously.

Testicular pain

This is often felt as a deep burning and accompanied by nausea. Treat as pain in any other location (see ➲ Chapter 2). Also ask about associated genital symptoms such as testicular swelling, dysuria, or haematuria.

Common causes include: testicular torsion, mumps, orchitis, and epididymitis. Remember the possibility of cancer.

Impotence

This term simply serves to confuse and is best avoided by doctors. Patients may use 'impotence' to mean a number of different sexual problems. Ask specifically if the patient means:

- Difficulty in either achieving or maintaining an erection (erectile dysfunction).
- Difficulty in ejaculating semen (ejaculatory dysfunction).
- Difficulty in reaching orgasm (orgasmic dysfunction).

▶ Remember that an erection is not necessary for men to reach orgasm or to ejaculate.

Erectile dysfunction

Erectile dysfunction is the inability to gain and maintain an erection for satisfactory completion of sexual activities.

If a patient complains of erectile dysfunction, this needs to be explored in more detail. Establish particularly if the lack of function is related to a particular partner, a particular situation, or is constant. Ask:

- Are you able to get an erection at all?
- Do you wake with an erection in the morning?
- Are you able to get an erection to masturbate?

If the cause is psychological, patients will often still wake with an erection (the so-called 'morning glory') but not be able to perform in a sexual situation. This can be tested with a sleep-study if necessary.

Psychological factors should be explored delicately.

Organic causes for erectile dysfunction include atherosclerosis, diabetes mellitus, multiple sclerosis, pelvic fractures, urethral injury, or other endocrine dysfunction.

DHx is important here. Drugs associated with erectile dysfunction include: barbiturates, benzodiazepines, phenothiazines, lithium, antihypertensives (e.g. β-blockers), alcohol, oestrogens, methadone, and heroin.

Loss of sexual desire (libido)

This can be the first sign of a pituitary tumour—but the cause is more often deeply rooted in the patient's psychology. Ask:

- How often do you shave your face?
- Has this changed recently?
- Do you have any muscle wasting or pain?

Explore any issues there may be surrounding the sexual partner and the patient's relationship with them.

Infertility

Around 10% of couples have difficulty in conception. Male infertility accounts for 1/3 of childless relationships. This is a huge topic and not within the scope of this book.

Relevant information to ascertain includes:

- The age of both partners.
- The length of time they have been trying to conceive.
- The presence of existing children belonging to both partners.
- Frequency and timing of intercourse.
- Any erectile, ejaculatory, or orgasmic dysfunction.
- DHx of both partners.
- Factors suggestive of endocrine malfunction as above under 'loss of sexual desire'.
- Smoking and alcohol consumption.
- Menstrual history from partner (Box 12.1).

Box 12.1 The rest of the history

A full history needs to be taken as described in ➔ Chapter 2. The following may have particular relevance here:

PMH

Ask especially about:

- Sexually transmitted diseases
- Orchitis
- Inguinal, scrotal, and testicular injury/surgery
- Urethral/penile injury.

Smoking and alcohol

Detailed histories should be taken as described elsewhere in this book.

Examining the male genitalia

Explain to the patient that you would like to examine the penis and testes and reassure them that the procedure will be quick and gentle.

You should have a chaperone present, particularly if you are female.

Ensure that the examination room is warm and that you will not be disturbed. With the patient on a bed or couch, raised to a comfortable height, ask them to pull their clothing down. You should be able to see the genitalia and lower part of the patient's abdomen at the very least.

The penis

Inspection

Make a careful inspection of the organ noting particularly:

- Size.
- Shape.
- Presence or absence of a foreskin.
- Colour of the skin.
- The position and calibre of the urethral meatus (see Box 12.2).
- Any discharge.
- Any abnormal curvature.
- Any scaling, scabbing, or other superficial abnormality such as erythema or ulceration—particularly at the distal end (glans).

Palpation

Palpate the whole length of the penis to the perineum and note the state of the dorsal vein which is usually easily seen stretching the length of the penis at the dorsal midline. Note also any abnormalities of the underlying tissues (e.g. firm areas) which may not be visible—this may represent the plaques of Peyronie's disease.

Retract the foreskin to expose the glans penis and urethral meatus. The foreskin should be supple, allowing smooth and painless retraction. Look especially for any secretion or discharge and collect a specimen if possible. The patient may be able to 'milk' the shaft of the penis to express the secretion.

There is often a trace of smegma underlying the foreskin. This is a normal finding.

🕦 Remember to replace the foreskin at the end of the examination.

▶ Note that in the presence of phimosis, the foreskin will be non-retractile and attempts may cause considerable pain.

Box 12.2 Hypospadias

Hypospadias is the abnormal, ventral, positioning of the urethral meatus. It is more common than many realize, seen in 1 in 250 males. In the vast majority, the hypospadias is slight. Patients may have a 'hooded foreskin' with the meatus at the very edge of the glans or a very slightly ventral meatus which is covered by a normal foreskin.

Slight hypospadias has no effect on sexual function but may be a cause of anxiety and embarrassment resulting in psychosexual problems once the patient is aware that his penis is 'different'.

The scrotum and its contents

See ➋ p. 428.

The perineum and rectum

Don't overlook the perineum, anal canal, and rectum. In particular, a digital rectal examination should be performed as described in ➋ Chapter 7 with particular attention to feeling the prostate and seminal vesicles.

The local lymphatics

- Lymph from the skin of the penis and scrotum drains to the inguinal lymph nodes (Fig. 12.1).
- Lymph from the covering of the testes and spermatic cord drains initially to the internal, then common, iliac nodes.
- Lymph from the body of the testes drains to the para-aortic lymph nodes—these are impalpable.
- Your examination is not complete without a careful palpation of the inguinal lymph nodes. This is best done with the patient lying comfortably on a bed or couch.
- If any swelling is found, it should be described in the same way as any lump (see ➋ Chapter 4).

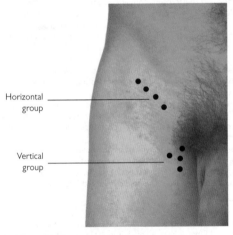

Fig. 12.1 Diagrammatic representation of the inguinal lymph nodes.

The scrotum and contents

Examining the scrotum and scrotal contents is best done with the patient standing up.

Inspection

Make a careful examination of the scrotal skin. It is usually wrinkled, slightly more pigmented than the rest of the patient's body, and should be freely mobile on the testes.

One testis usually hangs lower than the other. Remember to lift the scrotum, inspecting the inferior and posterior aspects.

Look especially for:
- Oedema.
- Sebaceous cysts.
- Ulcers.
- Scabies.
- Scars.

Palpation

The scrotal contents should be *gently* supported with your left hand and palpated with the fingers and thumb of your right hand. It may help to ask the patient to hold their penis to one side (see Fig. 12.2).

- Check that the scrotum contains two testes.
  - Absence of one or both testes may be due to previous excision, failure of the testis to descend, or a retractile testis
  - If there appears to be a single testis, carefully examine the inguinal canal for evidence of a discrete swelling that could be an undescended testis.
- Make careful note of any discrete lumps or swellings of the testis.
  - Any swelling in the body of the testis must be considered to be suggestive of a malignancy.
- Compare the left and right testes, noting the size and consistency.
  - The testes are normally equal in size, smooth, with a firm, rubbery consistency. If there is a significant discrepancy, ask the patient if he has ever noticed this.
- Feel for the epididymis which lies posterolaterally.
- The vas can be distinguished from the rest of the cord structures, lying along the posterior aspect of the bundle and feels firm and wire-like. It runs from the epididymis to the external inguinal ring.

Scrotal swellings

If a lump is palpated (see also Boxes 12.3 and 12.4):
- Decide if the lump is confined to the scrotum. Are you able to feel above it? Does it have a cough impulse? Is it fluctuant? (You will be unable to 'get above' swellings that descend from the inguinal canal.)
- Define the lump as any other mass as described in → Chapter 4.
- Transillumination is often important here. Darken the room and shine a small torch through the posterior part of the swelling (see Fig. 12.3).
  - A solid mass remains dark while a cystic mass or fluid will transilluminate.

(a)

(b)

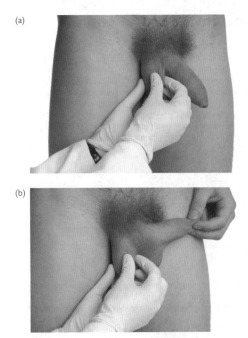

Fig. 12.2 (a) Examine the scrotum with the patient standing and use both hands. It is sometimes preferable to ask the patient to hold their penis aside (b).

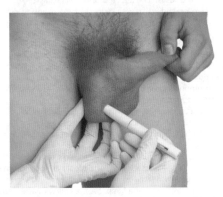

Fig. 12.3 Attempt to transilluminate any swelling by shining a small torch through it. NB Unlike the figure above, the room should be darkened.

Important presentations

Testicular torsion

This presents in a very similar way to orchitis and is often difficult to distinguish although the onset is much more sudden in torsion. Twisting of the testis on the spermatic cord ('torsion') will cause ischaemia and severe pain. Usually occurs in young adults and teenagers with a peak age of 14. Torsion is usually due to an internal rotation, towards the midline.

▶ This is a urological emergency. If the testicle is left in this condition without being untwisted (with appropriate analgesia), surgical removal of the testis may be necessary. Immediate surgical referral is advised if this is suspected.

Rough salvage rates are:
- <6 hours: 80–100%.
- 6–12 hours: 76%.
- 12–24 hours: 20%.
- >24 hours: 0%.

Inspection
- Patient usually exhibits signs of distress or pain.
- Hemi-scrotum may be swollen and erythematous compared to opposite side.

Palpation
- Testis will be exquisitely tender and often slightly swollen.
  - May be higher than normal and horizontal in orientation.
- Epididymis may be palpated anteriorly and spermatic cord may be thickened.
- Cremasteric reflex may be absent.

Orchitis

Inflammation of the testis. The affected organ will hang higher in the scrotum, may be swollen and warm with redness of the overlying skin. It will be very tender to palpation. The patient may be systemically unwell with fever.

Testicular tumour

This should be at the top of your list of differential diagnoses in the case of an intra-scrotal mass. 90% are germ cell tumours (of which 48% are seminomas and 42% non-seminomatous germ cell tumours e.g. teratomas). Teratomas commonly occur between the ages of 20–30 years while seminomas are more common between 30–40 years.

Look for constitutional symptoms and signs suggestive of neoplastic disease such as malaise, wasting, and anorexia as well as leg swelling (venous or lymphatic obstruction), lymphadenopathy, or an associated abdominal mass.

Symptoms include a gradually enlarging, painless testicular lump. A dull ache or heaviness is not unusual. 10% of patients are asymptomatic. 10% present with symptoms related to metastatic disease. 10% give a history of trauma prior to discovery of a lump. 5% present with acute scrotal pain secondary to intratumoural haemorrhage.

Inspection
- Swollen or asymmetrical hemi-scrotum compared to opposite side.
- Patient may appear cachexic.
- There may be gynaecomastia (due to trophoblastic elements secreting human chorionic gonadotropin e.g. Leydig and Sertoli cell tumours).

Palpation
- A hard, non-tender, irregular, non-transilluminable mass in the testis or even replacing testis.
  - Should be able to palpate above mass
  - Assess the epididymis, spermatic cord, and scrotal wall.
- ❶ The lump may be impalpable if there is an associated hydrocoele.

Box 12.3 Differential diagnosis of scrotal lumps
- *Indirect inguinal hernia:* has cough impulse, reduces with direct pressure or lying down and examiner cannot 'get above' the swelling
- *Epididymal cyst:* swelling confined to epididymis, should be able to palpate normal testis
- *Testicular tumour:* usually hard, craggy mass in body of testis (but can invade surrounding structures)
- *Varicocoele:* feels like a 'bag of worms', often disappears on lying down
- *Sebaceous cyst:* smooth and fixed to scrotal skin. Able to palpate scrotal contents separately
- *Epididymo-orchitis:* tender, painful swelling of testis and epididymis. May have erythema of scrotal skin
- *Testicular torsion:* sudden onset of severe pain with exquisitely tender testis, thickened spermatic cord, and horizontal testicular lie
- *Gumma of testis:* rare and secondary to syphilis. Feels round, hard, insensitive ('like a billiard ball')
- *Carcinoma of scrotal skin:* irregular and fixed to scrotal skin, may be associated with inguinal lymphadenopathy.

Box 12.4 Differential diagnosis of an epididymal lump
- *Epididymo-orchitis:* usually tender, painful swelling of testis and epididymis. May have erythema of scrotal skin
- *Tuberculous epididymo-orchitis:* usually painless and non-tender, epididymis is hard with an irregular surface. The spermatic cord is thickened and the vas deferens feels hard and irregular (like a string of beads)
- *Sperm granuloma:* seen in roughly 1 in 500 men who have undergone vasectomy. Congested sperm and fluid extravasates from the end of the vas deferens, is recognized by the immune system as 'foreign' and initiates an inflammatory reaction giving a palpable 'lump'. These are usually painless and can be felt as separate to the testis.

Hydrocoele

This is fluid entrapment in the tunica vaginalis causing usually painless swelling of the scrotum—the size of which can be considerable. Hydrocoele will surround the testis making it impalpable. It will transilluminate.

As well as congenital abnormalities in the inguinal canal, hydrocoele can be caused by trauma, infection, and neoplastic disease.

Inspection

- Swollen hemi-scrotum compared to opposite side.
- Usually no abnormality of scrotal skin.

Palpation

- Hemi-scrotal content will usually be painless and swollen with a tense, smooth surface.
- Unable to palpate testis separately from swelling.
- Superior margin can be palpated (i.e. you can 'get above it').
- Spermatic cord is palpable separately.
- Cough reflex is present.
- Swelling can be transilluminated.

Epididymal cysts

These are harmless, painless swellings arising behind, and separate from, the testis itself. If aspirated, the fluid may appear opalescent, like lime water, because a few sperm are present. The aetiology is unknown.

Occasionally they occur as a complication of vasectomy, in which case they are full of sperm and are termed 'spermatocoeles'.

Inspection

- The hemi-scrotum may be swollen compared to opposite side.

Palpation

- No abnormality of scrotal skin.
- Examination of the testis is normal.
- A firm, loculated, painless mass can be felt within the epididymis, the rest of the epididymis may not be palpable.
  - Superior margin can be palpated (i.e. you can 'get above it').
- The mass can be transilluminated.
  - Normally only demonstrable in large cysts
  - No transillumination if cyst contains sperm.

Varicocoele

A dilatation of the veins of the pampiniform plexus of the spermatic cord. Found in 15% of men in the general population and 40% of men with infertility. Either bilateral or unilateral, the left side is affected in 90%.

Incompetent valves in the internal gonadal veins lead to retrograde blood flow, vessel dilatation, and tortuosity of pampiniform plexus.

Inspection

Hemi-scrotum may be swollen compared to opposite side when standing.

Palpation

- Usually no abnormality of scrotal skin.

- If moderate or large in size, a mass of dilated and tortuous veins will be felt above testis around the spermatic cord (described as feeling like a 'bag of worms').
  - If no mass is palpated, ask patient to perform Valsalva manoeuvre (strain down). Small varicocoeles will then be palpable
  - Examine the patient lying supine; the mass will decompress and disappear.
- The testis and epididymis are palpable separately.
- The testis may be atrophied.

Varicocoeles and renal malignancy
- 5% of renal cell carcinomas present with acute left varicocoele due to obstruction of the testicular vein by tumour in the left renal vein.
- In the presence of a left-sided varicocoele, the abdomen should be examined for a renal mass and the patient should be asked about pain and haematuria.
- Abdominal/renal ultrasound should be considered.

Phimosis

This is a narrowing of the end of the foreskin which prevents its retraction over the glans penis.

This can cause difficulty with micturition and lead to recurrent balanitis. It may cause interference with erections and sexual intercourse.

Causes include congenital, infection, trauma, and inflammation (balanitis).

Paraphimosis

In this case, the foreskin can be retracted but then cannot be replaced over the glans. This results in oedema which limits its movement still further. If left in this condition, it can become necrotic or gangrenous.

Commonly occurs in men 15–30 years old. A frequent complication of urinary catheterization if the practitioner fails to replace the foreskin after the procedure is performed.

Balanitis and balanoposthitis

Balanitis is inflammation of the glans penis. Balanoposthitis is inflammation of the glans and the foreskin. Such inflammation presents as redness, swelling, and pain of the affected parts, often with difficulty of retracting the foreskin.

Causes include *Candida albicans* (especially in patients with diabetes), herpes infection, carcinoma, drug eruptions, and poor hygiene.

Priapism

This is a painful, persistent erection and a serious feature of sickle-crisis.

Other causes include: leukaemia, drugs (e.g. psychotropics), neurogenic (e.g. diseases of the spinal cord).

Penile ulcers

Conditions causing ulceration of the genitalia include herpes simplex (vesicles followed by ulceration), syphilis (non-tender ulceration), malignancy (e.g. squamous cell carcinoma—non-tender), Behçet's syndrome.

The elderly patient

Many of the messages in this page overlap with those in the female reproductive system pages and we would encourage you to regard them as a 'whole'.

It is important to recognize that bladder carcinoma and diseases of the prostate are some of the most common urogenital problems faced by older men, remember to screen for such problems in any assessment. For prostate diseases, it is also important to be alert that awareness by patients is equally high, so expect questions and a wish to be involved in treatment decisions. Equally so, many of these problems are faced by patients with cognitive impairment, in whom history may be limited and thorough assessment is vital. (See Box 12.5.)

Retain a holistic outlook on male urogenital problems, and you're less likely to miss delirium because of acute epididymo-orchitis—a not uncommon presentation!

❶ It is also important to remember that studies report that 60% of men and 30% of women over the age of 80 still engage in some form of regular sexual activity. Avoiding these issues can cause major problems to be overlooked, with 70% of men over the age of 70 experiencing impotence—so try not to make assumptions when seeing older people with sexual health problems.

History

- *Explore:* the history. Even for patients with prostate disease, how will the effects of treatment (e.g. transurethral resection of the prostate (TURP)) affect relationships or sexual activity? Keep your thought processes open when assessing continence problems—there may be an irritative/unstable bladder component alongside obstructive symptoms.
- *PMH:* vascular diseases, metabolic, and neurological illnesses may all be underpinning diagnoses when faced with impotence. Could the new presentation of balanitis indicate diabetes?
- *DHx:* aside from obvious culprits (e.g. diuretics) consider the effects of antidepressants, digoxin, and antihypertensives on both bladder and sexual function.
- *SHx and sexual history:* always take an appropriate functional history, particularly if there are continence problems. Consider alcohol and tobacco in relation to impotence, and undertake a detailed occupational history if the patient presents with haematuria (bladder cancer?). Have the confidence to take a sexual history if there are problems with erectile or ejaculatory dysfunction—as indicated earlier, many older people have active sex lives and you're more likely to be embarrassed about taking the history than they are recounting it.

Examination
- *General:* alongside the detailed examination considered earlier in this chapter, keep in mind the need for a general examination—focusing on mood and neurological assessment in particular.
- *Cognition:* a key part of this assessment, and particularly for continence and erectile dysfunction problems.
- *Urogenital:* think subtly: in older men, orchitis may present with declining mobility, delirium, or falls—so never forget to undertake a thorough examination in elders, even when there is apparently little to indicate it! For patients with urinary catheters, whether short- or long-term, examination is a mandatory part of assessment.

Box 12.5 A note on (recurrent) urinary tract infections

Most readers will have already seen many older patients with this common (and often over-diagnosed) problem.

Whilst many diagnoses are made on clinical suspicion, it is vital to undertake urinalysis and obtain urine for microscopy and culture to confirm the presence of urinary tract infections (UTIs). The reasoning is two-fold—avoiding rushing to a label of UTI as the cause of delirium or mobility decline will reduce the chance of missing the correct diagnosis. Similarly, a proven culture diagnosis of UTI aids prescribing, and helps identify recurrent infections. Recognizing the latter may reveal underlying diagnoses and reduce discomfort or even hospitalization for some patients.

So, when faced with recurrent infections, be assiduous and request urine cytology (to look for bladder cancers), ultrasound (for structural abnormalities), and discuss the value of cystoscopy and rotating/long-term antibiotics with urology colleagues.

The female reproductive system

The obstetric assessment

The obstetric history and examination is covered in
➔ Chapter 14.

Introduction

The pelvis

The bony pelvis is composed of the two pelvic bones with the sacrum and coccyx posteriorly. The pelvic brim divides the 'false pelvis' above (part of the abdominal cavity) and the 'true pelvis' below.

- *Pelvic inlet:* also known as the pelvic brim. Formed by the sacral promontory posteriorly, the iliopectineal lines laterally and the symphysis pubis anteriorly.
- *Pelvic outlet:* formed by the coccyx posteriorly, the ischial tuberosities laterally and the pubic arch anteriorly. The pelvic outlet has three wide notches. The sciatic notches are divided into the greater and lesser sciatic foramina by the sacrotuberous and sacrospinous ligaments which can be considered part of the perimeter of the outlet clinically.
- *The pelvic cavity:* lies between the inlet and the outlet. It has a deep posterior wall and a shallow anterior wall giving a curved shape.

The contents of the pelvic cavity

The pelvic cavity contains the rectum, sigmoid colon, coils of the ileum, ureters, bladder, female reproductive organs, fascia, and peritoneum.

Female internal genital organs

Vagina

The vagina is a thin-walled distensible, fibromuscular tube that extends upwards and backwards from the vestibule of the vulva to the cervix. It is ~8cm long and lies posterior to the bladder and anterior to the rectum.

The vagina serves as an eliminatory passage for menstrual flow, forms part of the birth canal, and receives the penis during sexual intercourse.

The fornix

This is the vaginal recess around the cervix and is divided into anterior, posterior, and lateral regions which, clinically, provide access points for examining the pelvic organs.

Uterus

The uterus is a thick-walled, hollow, pear-shaped muscular organ consisting of the cervix, body, and fundus. In the nulliparous female, it is ~8cm long, ~5cm wide, and ~2.5cm deep. The uterus is covered with peritoneum forming an anterior uterovesical fold, a fold between the uterus and rectum termed the pouch of Douglas, and the broad ligaments laterally.

The uterus receives, retains, and nourishes the fertilized ovum.

Uterine orientation

In most females, the uterus lies in an anteverted and anteflexed position.

- *Anteversion:* the long axis of the uterus is angled forward.
- *Retroversion:* the fundus and body are angled backwards and therefore lie in the pouch of Douglas. Occurs in about 15% of the female population. A full bladder may mimic retroversion clinically.
- *Anteflexion:* the long axis of the body of the uterus is angled forward on the long axis of the cervix.
- *Retroflexion:* the body of the uterus is angled backward on the cervix.

Fallopian tubes

The Fallopian or 'uterine' tubes are paired tubular structures, ~10cm long. The Fallopian tubes extend laterally from the cornua of the uterine body, in the upper border of the broad ligament and open into the peritoneal cavity near the ovaries. The Fallopian tube is divided into four parts:

- *Infundibulum:* distal, funnel-shaped portion with finger-like 'fimbriae'.
- *Ampulla:* widest and longest part of tube outside the uterus.
- *Isthmus:* thick-walled with a narrow lumen and therefore, least distensible part. Enters the horns of the uterine body.
- *Intramural:* that part which pierces the uterine wall.

The main functions of the uterine tube are to receive the ovum from the ovary, provide a site where fertilization can take place (usually in the ampulla), and transport the ovum from the ampulla to the uterus. The tube also provides nourishment for the fertilized ovum.

Ovaries

The ovaries are whitish-grey, almond-shaped organs measuring ~4cm x 2cm which are responsible for the production of the female germ cells, the ova, and the sex hormones, oestrogen and progesterone.

They are suspended on the posterior layer of the broad ligament by a peritoneal extension (mesovarium) and supported by the suspensory ligament of the ovary (a lateral extension of the broad ligament and mesovarium) and the round ligament which stretches from the lateral wall of the uterus to the medial aspect of the ovary.

Perineum

- The perineum lies inferior to the pelvic inlet and is separated from the pelvic cavity by the pelvic diaphragm.
- Seen from below with the thighs abducted, it is a diamond-shaped area bounded anteriorly by the pubic symphysis, posteriorly by the tip of the coccyx and laterally by the ischial tuberosities.
- The perineum is artificially divided into the anterior urogenital triangle containing the external genitalia in females and an anal triangle containing the anus and ischiorectal fossae.

Female external genital organs

These are sometimes collectively known as the 'vulva'. It consists of:

- *Labia majora:* a pair of fat-filled folds of skin extending on either side of the vaginal vestibule from the mons towards the anus.
- *Labia minora:* a pair of flat folds containing a core of spongy connective tissue with a rich vascular supply. Lie medial to the labia majora.
- *Vestibule of the vagina:* between the labia minora, contains the urethral meatus and vaginal orifice. Receives mucous secretions from the greater and lesser vestibular glands.
- *Clitoris:* short, erectile organ; the female homologue of the male penis. Like the penis, a crus arises from each ischiopubic ramus and joins in the midline forming the 'body' capped by the sensitive 'glans'.
- *Bulbs of vestibule:* two masses of elongated erectile tissue, ~3cm long, lying along the sides of the vaginal orifice.
- *Greater and lesser vestibular glands.*

The menstrual cycle

Menstruation is the shedding of the functional superficial 2/3 of the endometrium after sex hormone withdrawal. This process, which consists of three phases, is typically repeated ~300–400 times during a woman's life. Coordination of the menstrual cycle depends on a complex interplay between the hypothalamus, the pituitary gland, the ovaries, and the uterine endometrium.

Cyclical changes in the endometrium prepare it for implantation in the event of fertilization and menstruation in the absence of fertilization. It should be noted that several other tissues are sensitive to these hormones and undergo cyclical change (e.g. the breasts and the lower part of the urinary tract).

The endometrial cycle can divided into three phases.

Phases of the menstrual cycle

The first day of menses is considered to be day 1 of the menstrual cycle.

The proliferative or follicular phase

This begins at the end of the menstrual phase (usually day 4) and ends at ovulation (days 13–14). During this phase, the endometrium thickens and ovarian follicles mature.

The hypothalamus is the initiator of the follicular phase. Gonadotrophin-releasing hormone (GnRH) is released from the hypothalamus in a pulsatile fashion to the pituitary portal system surrounding the anterior pituitary gland. GnRH causes release of follicle stimulating hormone (FSH). FSH is secreted into the general circulation and interacts with the granulosa cells surrounding the dividing oocytes.

FSH enhances the development of 15–20 follicles each month and interacts with granulosa cells to enhance aromatization of androgens into oestrogen and oestradiol.

Only one follicle with the largest reservoir of oestrogen can withstand the declining FSH environment whilst the remaining follicles undergo atresia at the end of this phase.

Follicular oestrogen synthesis is essential for uterine priming, but is also part of the positive feedback that induces a dramatic preovulatory luteinizing hormone (LH) surge and subsequent ovulation.

The luteal or secretory phase

The luteal phase starts at ovulation and lasts through to day 28 of the menstrual cycle.

The major effects of the LH surge are the conversion of granulosa cells from predominantly androgen-converting cells to predominantly progesterone-synthesizing cells. High progesterone levels exert negative feedback on GnRH which, in turn, reduces FSH/LH secretion.

At the beginning of the luteal phase, progesterone induces the endometrial glands to secrete glycogens, mucus, and other substances. These glands become tortuous and have large lumina due to increased secretory activity. Spiral arterioles extend into the superficial layer of the endometrium.

In the absence of fertilization by day 23 of the menstrual cycle, the superficial endometrium begins to degenerate and consequently ovarian hormone levels decrease. As oestrogen and progesterone levels fall, the endometrium undergoes involution.

If the corpus luteum is not rescued by human chorionic gonadotropin (hCG) hormone from the developing placenta, menstruation occurs 14 days after ovulation. If conception occurs, placental hCG maintains luteal function until placental production of progesterone is well established.

The menstrual phase

This phase sees the gradual withdrawal of ovarian sex steroids which causes slight shrinking of the endometrium, and therefore the blood flow of spiral vessels is reduced. This, together with spiral arteriolar spasms, leads to distal endometrial ischaemia and stasis. Extravasation of blood and endometrial tissue breakdown lead to onset of menstruation.

The menstrual phase begins as the spiral arteries rupture, releasing blood into the uterus and the apoptosing endometrium is sloughed off.

During this period, the functionalis layer of the endometrium is completely shed. Arteriolar and venous blood, remnants of endometrial stroma and glands, leukocytes and red blood cells are all present in the menstrual flow.

Shedding usually lasts ~4 days.

The gynaecological history

It is important to remember that many females can be embarrassed by having to discuss their gynaecological problems, so it is vital to appear confident, friendly, and relaxed.

Although there are parts particular to this history, most of it is the same as the basic outline described in ➲ Chapter 2 and we suggest that readers review that chapter before going on. We detail here those parts that may differ from the basic format.

History of presenting complaint

More detailed questioning will depend on the nature of the presenting complaint. Ascertain:

- The exact nature of the symptom.
- The onset.
  - When and how it began (e.g. suddenly, gradually—over how long?)
  - If long-standing, why is the patient seeking help now?
- Periodicity and frequency.
  - Is the symptom constant or intermittent?
  - If intermittent, how long does it last each time?
  - What is the exact manner in which it comes and goes?
  - ▶ How does it relate to the menstrual cycle?
- Change over time.
- Exacerbating and relieving factors.
- Associated symptoms.
- The degree of functional disability caused.

Menstrual history

- Age of menarche (first menstrual period).
  - Normally about 12 years but can be as early as 9 or as late as 16.
- Date of last menstrual period (LMP).
- Duration and regularity of periods (cycle).
  - Normal menstruation lasts 4–7 days
  - Average length of menstrual cycle is 28 days (i.e. the time between first day of one period and the first day of the following period) but can vary between 21 and 42 days in normal women.
- Menstrual flow: whether light, normal, or heavy.
- Menstrual pain: whether occurs prior to or at the start of bleeding.
- Irregular bleeding.
  - e.g. intermenstrual blood loss, post-coital bleeding, etc.
- Associated symptoms.
  - Bowel or bladder dysfunction, pain.
- Hormonal contraception or HRT.
- Age at menopause (if this has occurred).

Past gynaecological history

- Previous cervical smears, including date of last smear, any abnormal smear results, and treatments received.
- Previous gynaecological problems and treatments including surgery and pelvic inflammatory disease.

Contraception

It is essential to ask sexually active women of reproductive age about contraception, including methods used, duration of use and acceptance, current method, as well as future plans.

Past obstetric history

- Gravidity and parity.

Document the specifics of each pregnancy:
- Current age of the child and age of mother when pregnant.
- Birth weight.
- Complications of pregnancy, labour, and puerperium.
- Miscarriages and terminations. Note gestation time and complications.

Past medical history

Pay particular attention to any history of chronic lung or heart disease and make note of all previous surgical procedures.

Drug history

Ask about all medication/drugs taken (prescribed, over-the-counter, and illicit drugs). Record dose and frequency, as well as any known drug allergies.
▶ Make particular note to ask about the oral contraceptive pill (OCP) and hormone replacement therapy (HRT) if not done so already.

Family history

Note especially any history of genital tract cancer, breast cancer, and diabetes.

Social history

Take a standard SHx including living conditions and marital status.
This is also an extra chance to explore the impact of the presenting problem on the patient's life—in terms of their social life, employment, home life, and sexual activity.

Abnormal bleeding

Menorrhagia

This is defined as >80ml of menstrual blood loss per period (normal = 20–60ml) and may be caused by a variety of local, systemic, or iatrogenic factors. Menorrhagia is hard to measure, but periods are considered 'heavy' if they lead to frequent changes of sanitary towels. See Box 13.1.

As well as the standard questions for any symptom, ask about:

- The number of sanitary pads/towels used per day and the 'strength' (absorbency) of those pads.
- Bleeding through to clothes or onto the bedding at night ('flooding').
- The need to use two pads at once.
- The need to wear double protection (i.e. pad and tampon together).
- Interference with normal activities.
- ▶ Remember to ask about symptoms of iron-deficiency anaemia such as lethargy, breathlessness, and dizziness.

Dysmenorrhoea

This is pain associated with menstruation—thought to be caused by ↑ levels of endometrial prostaglandins during the luteal and menstrual phases of the cycle resulting in uterine contractions. The pain is typically cramping, localized to the lower abdomen and pelvic regions, and radiating to the thighs and back. See Box 13.2.

Dysmenorrhoea may be primary or secondary:

- Primary: occurring from menarche.
- Secondary: occurring in females who previously had normal periods (often caused by pelvic pathology).

When taking a history of dysmenorrhoea, take a full pain history, a detailed menstrual history, and ask especially about the relationship of the pain to the menstrual cycle. Remember to ask about the functional consequences of the pain—how does it interfere with normal activities?

Intermenstrual bleeding (IMB)

Intermenstrual bleeding is uterine bleeding which occurs between the menstrual periods. See Box 13.3 for causes.

As for all these symptoms, a full standard battery of questions should be asked, a full menstrual history, past medical and gynaecological histories, and sexual history.

Ask also about the association of the bleeding with hormonal therapy, contraceptive use, and previous cervical smears.

Post-coital bleeding

This is vaginal bleeding precipitated by sexual intercourse. It can be caused by similar conditions to intermenstrual bleeding. Take a full and detailed history as always.

See Box 13.4 for causes.

Box 13.1 Some causes of menorrhagia

- Hypothyroidism
- Intra-uterine contraceptive device (IUCD)
- Fibroids
- Endometriosis
- Polyps—cervix, uterus
- Uterine cancer
- Infection (STDs)
- Previous sterilization
- Warfarin therapy
- Aspirin
- Non-steroidal anti-inflammatory drugs (NSAIDs)
- Clotting disorders (e.g. von-Willebrand's disease).

Box 13.2 Some causes of dysmenorrhoea

- Pelvic inflammatory disease
- Endometriosis
- Uterine adenomyosis
- Fibroids
- Endometrial polyps
- Premenstrual syndrome
- Cessation of oral contraceptive.

Box 13.3 Some causes of intermenstrual bleeding

Obstetric
- Pregnancy, ectopic pregnancy, gestational trophoblastic disease

Gynaecological
- Vaginal malignancy, vaginitis, cervical cancer, adenomyosis, fibroids, ovarian cancer

Iatrogenic
- Anticoagulants, corticosteroids, antipsychotics, tamoxifen, SSRIs, rifampicin, and anti-epileptic drugs (AEDs).

Box 13.4 Some causes of post-coital bleeding

Similar to intermenstrual bleeding, as well as:
- Vaginal infection:
  - Chlamydia
  - Gonorrhoea
  - Trichomaniasis
  - Yeast.
- Cervicitis.

Amenorrhoea

This is the absence of periods and may be 'primary' or 'secondary'. See Box 13.5 for causes.

- *Primary:* failure to menstruate by 16 years of age in the presence of normal secondary sexual development or failure to menstruate by 14 years in the absence of secondary sexual characteristics.
- *Secondary:* normal menarche, then cessation of menstruation with no periods for at least 6 months.

▶ Amenorrhoea is a normal feature in prepubertal girls, pregnancy, during lactation, postmenopausal females, and in some women using hormonal contraception.

History taking

A full and detailed history should be taken. Ask especially about:
- Childhood growth and development.
- If secondary amenorrhoea:
  - Age of menarche
  - Cycle days
  - Day and date of LMP
  - Presence or absence of breast soreness
  - Mood change immediately before menses.
- Chronic illnesses.
- Previous surgery (including cervical surgery which can cause stenosis and more obviously oophorectomy and hysterectomy).
- Prescribed medications known to cause amenorrhoea such as phenothiazines, domperidone, and metoclopramide (produce either hyperprolactinaemia or ovarian failure).
- Illicit or 'recreational' drugs.
- Sexual history.
- Social history including any emotional stress at school/work/home, exercise and diet—include here any weight gain or weight loss.
- Systems enquiry: include vasomotor symptoms, hot flushes, virilizing changes (e.g. increased body hair, greasy skin, etc.), galactorrhoea, headaches, visual field disturbance, palpitations, nervousness, hearing loss.

Postmenopausal bleeding

This is vaginal bleeding occurring >6 months after the menopause. It requires reassurance and prompt investigation as it could indicate the presence of malignancy. See Box 13.6 for some causes.

As well as all the points outlined under 'amenorrhoea', ask about:
- Local symptoms of oestrogen deficiency such as vaginal dryness, soreness, and superficial dyspareunia.
- Itching (pruritus vulvae—more likely in non-neoplastic disorders).
- Presence of lumps or swellings at the vulva.

Cervical or endometrial malignancy

Often present with profuse or continuous vaginal bleeding or with a blood-stained offensive discharge.

Box 13.5 Some causes of amenorrhoea
- *Hypothalamic:* idiopathic, weight loss, intense exercise
- *Hypogonadism from hypothalamic or pituitary damage:* tumours, craniopharyngiomas, cranial irradiation, head injuries
- *Pituitary:* hyperprolactinaemia, hypopituitarism
- *Delayed puberty:* constitutional delay
- *Systemic:* chronic illness, weight loss, endocrine disorders (e.g. Cushing's syndrome, thyroid disorders)
- *Uterine:* Müllerian agenesis
- *Ovarian:* PCOS, premature ovarian failure (e.g. Turner's syndrome, autoimmune disease, surgery, chemotherapy, pelvic irradiation, infection)
- *Psychological:* emotional stress at school/home/work.

Box 13.6 Some causes of postmenopausal bleeding
- Cervical carcinoma
- Uterine sarcoma
- Vaginal carcinoma
- Endometrial hyperplasia/carcinoma/polyps
- Cervical polyps
- Trauma
- Hormone replacement therapy
- Bleeding disorder
- Vaginal atrophy.

Pelvic pain and dyspareunia

As with any type of pain, pelvic pain may be acute or chronic. Chronic pelvic pain is often associated with dyspareunia.

Dyspareunia is painful sexual intercourse and may be experienced superficially at the area of the vulva and introitus on penetration or deep within the pelvis. Dyspareunia can lead to failure to reach orgasm, the avoidance of sexual activity, and relationship problems.

Box 13.7 Gynaecological versus gastrointestinal pain

Distinguishing between pain of gynaecological and gastrointestinal origin is often difficult. This is because the uterus, cervix, and adnexa share the same visceral innervation as the lower ileum, sigmoid colon, and rectum. You should be careful in your history to rule out a gastrointestinal problem and keep an open mind.

History taking

When taking a history of pelvic pain or dyspareunia, you should obtain a detailed history as for any type of pain (➔ Chapter 2). Carefully differentiate from gastrointestinal pain (Box 13.7). Some causes of dyspareunia are shown in Box 13.8.

You also need to establish the relationship of the pain to the menstrual cycle. Ask also about:

- Date of LMP.
- Cervical smears.
- Intermenstrual or post-coital bleeding.
- Previous gynaecological procedures (e.g. IUCD, hysteroscopy).
- Previous pelvic inflammatory disease or genitourinary infections.
- Previous gynaecological surgery (adhesion formation?).
- Vulval discharge.
- A detailed sexual history (➔ Chapter 2) should also include contraceptive use and the degree of impact the symptoms have on the patient's normal life, and psychological health.

Box 13.8 Some causes of dyspareunia

- Scars from episiotomy
- Vaginal atrophy
- Vulvitis, vulvar vestibulitis
- Pelvic inflammatory disease
- Ovarian cysts
- Endometriosis
- Varicose veins in pelvis
- Ectopic pregnancy
- Infections (STIs)
- Bladder or urinary tract disorder
- Cancer in the reproductive organs or pelvic region.

Vaginal discharge

Vaginal discharge is a common complaint during the child-bearing years. As well as the standard questions, ask about:
- Colour, volume, odour, and presence of blood.
- Irritation.
- ▶ Don't forget to ask about diabetes and obtain a full DHx including recent antibiotic use—both of which may precipitate candidal infection.
- Obtain a full sexual history (◐ Chapter 2). A full gynaecological history should include history of cervical smear testing, use of ring pessaries, and recent history of surgery (increased risk of vesicovaginal fistulae).
- ▶ Lower abdominal pain, backache, and dyspareunia suggest PID.
- ▶ Weight loss and anorexia may indicate underlying malignancy.

Physiological vaginal discharge

Physiological discharge is usually scanty, mucoid, and odourless. It occurs with the changing oestrogen levels during the menstrual cycle (discharge increases in quantity mid-cycle and is a physiological sign of ovulation) and pregnancy.

It may arise from vestibular gland secretions, vaginal transudate, cervical mucus, and residual menstrual fluid.

Pathological vaginal discharge

This usually represents infection (trichomonal or candidal vaginitis) and may be associated with pruritus or burning of the vulval area.
- *Candida albicans:* the discharge is typically thick and causes itching.
- *Bacterial vaginitis:* the discharge is grey and watery with a fishy smell. Seen especially after intercourse.
- *Trichomonas vaginalis:* the discharge is typically profuse, opaque, cream-coloured, and frothy. It also has a characteristic 'fishy' smell. This may also be accompanied by urinary symptoms, such as dysuria and frequency.

Vulval symptoms

The main symptom to be aware of is itching or irritation of the vulva (pruritus vulvae). It can be debilitating and socially embarrassing. Embarrassment often delays the woman seeking advice. See Box 13.10 for some other vulval conditions.

Causes include infection, vulval dystrophy, neoplasia, and other dermatological conditions. Ask especially about:

- The nature of onset, exacerbating and relieving factors.
- Abnormal vaginal discharge.
- History of cervical intraepithelial neoplasia—CIN (thought to share a common aetiology with vulval intraepithelial neoplasia—VIN).
- Sexual history.
- Dermatological conditions such as psoriasis and eczema.
- Symptoms suggestive of renal or liver problems.
- Diabetes.

Urinary incontinence

This is an objectively demonstrable involuntary loss of urine that can be both a social and hygienic problem.

The two most common causes of urinary incontinence in females are *genuine stress incontinence* (GSI) and *detrusor over-activity* (DO). Other less commonly encountered causes include mixed GSI and DO, sensory urgency, chronic voiding problems, and fistulae.

When taking a history of urinary incontinence, ascertain under what circumstances they experience the symptom. Remember to ask about the functional consequences on the patient's daily life.

Genuine stress incontinence

Patients notice small amounts of urinary leakage with a cough, sneeze, or exercise. One third may also admit to symptoms of DO.

Ask about:
- Number of children (increased risk with increased parity).
- Genital prolapse.
- Previous pelvic floor surgery.

Detrusor over-activity

Urge incontinence, urgency, frequency, and nocturia. Ask about:
- History of nocturnal enuresis.
- Previous neurological problems.
- Previous incontinence surgery.
- Incontinence during sexual intercourse.
- DHx (see note under 'the elderly patient').

Overflow incontinence

Voiding disorders can result in chronic retention leading to overflow incontinence and increased predisposition to infection. The patient may complain of hesitancy, straining, poor flow, and incomplete emptying in addition to urgency and frequency.

Fistulae

Suspect if incontinence is continuous during the day and night.

Genital prolapse

Genital prolapse is descent of the pelvic organs through the pelvic floor into the vaginal canal. In the female genital tract, the type of prolapse is named according to the pelvic organ involved. Some causes are outlined in 13.9. Some examples include:

- Uterine: uterus.
- Cystocoele: bladder.
- Vaginal vault prolapse: apex of vagina after hysterectomy.
- Enterocoele: small bowel.
- Rectocoele: rectum.

Mild degrees of genital prolapse are often asymptomatic. More extensive prolapse may cause vaginal pressure or pain, introital bulging, a feeling of 'something coming down', as well as impaired sexual function.

Uterine descent often gives symptoms of backache especially in older patients.

There might be associated symptoms of incomplete bowel emptying (rectocoele) or urinary symptoms such as frequency or incomplete emptying (cystocoele or cysto-urethrocoele).

Box 13.9 Some causes of genital prolapse

- *Oestrogen deficiency states:* such as advancing age and the menopause (atrophy and weakness of the pelvic support structures)
- *Childbirth:* prolonged labour, instrumental delivery, fetal macrosomia, ↑ parity
- *Genetic factors:* e.g. spina bifida
- *Chronic raised intra-abdominal pressure:* e.g. chronic cough, constipation.

Box 13.10 Some other common vulval conditions

- *Dermatitis:* atopic, seborrhoeic, irritant, allergic, steroid-induced (itch, burning, erythema, scale, fissures, lichenification)
- *Vulvovaginal candidiasis:* itch, burning, erythema, vaginal discharge
- *Lichen sclerosus:* itch, burning, dyspareunia, white plaques, atrophic wrinkled surface
- *Psoriasis:* remember to look for other areas of psoriasis; scalp, natal cleft, nails
- *Vulval intraepithelial neoplasia:* itch, burning, multifocal plaques
- *Erosive vulvovaginitis:* erosive lichen planus, pemphigoid, pemphigus vulgaris, fixed drug eruption (chronic painful erosion and ulcers with superficial bleeding)
- *Atrophic vaginitis:* secondary to oestrogen deficiency (thin, pale, dry vaginal epithelium. Superficial dyspareunia, minor vaginal bleeding, and pain).

Outline gynaecological examination

Explain to the patient that you would like to examine their genitalia and reproductive organs and reassure them that the procedure will be quick and gentle.

You should have a chaperone present, preferably female.

As always, ensure that the room is warm and well lit, preferably with a moveable light source and that you will not be disturbed.

The examination should follow an orderly routine. The authors' suggestion is shown in Box 13.11. It is standard practice to start with the cardiovascular and respiratory systems—this not only gives a measure of the general health of the patient but establishes a 'physical rapport' before you examine more delicate or embarrassing areas.

Box 13.11 Framework for the gynaecological examination

- General inspection
- Cardiorespiratory examination
- Abdominal examination
- Pelvic examination
  - External genitalia—inspection
  - External genitalia—palpation
  - Speculum examination.
- Bimanual examination ('PV' examination).

General inspection and other systems

Always begin with a general examination of the patient (as described in ➋ Chapter 3) including temperature, hydration, coloration, nutritional status, lymph nodes, and blood pressure. Note especially:

- Distribution of facial and body hair, as hirsutism may be a presenting symptom of various endocrine disorders.
- Height and weight.
- Examine the cardiovascular and respiratory systems in turn.

Abdominal examination

A full abdominal examination should be performed (see ➋ Chapter 7). Look especially in the periumbilical region for scars from previous laparoscopies and in the suprapubic region where transverse incisions from caesarean sections and most gynaecological operations are found.

Pelvic examination

The patient should be allowed to undress in privacy and, if necessary, to empty her bladder first.

Set-up and positioning

Before starting the examination, always explain to the patient what will be involved. Ensure the abdomen is covered. Ensure good lighting and remember to wear disposable gloves.

Ask the patient to lie on her back on an examination couch with both knees bent up and let her knees fall apart—either with her heels together in the middle or separated.

The lithotomy position, in which both thighs are abducted and feet suspended from lithotomy stirrups is usually adopted when performing vaginal surgery.

Examination of the external genitalia

- Uncover the mons to expose the external genitalia making note of the pattern of hair distribution.
- Apply a lubricating gel to the examining finger.
- Separate the labia from above with the forefinger and thumb of your left hand.
- Inspect the clitoris, urethral meatus, and vaginal opening.
- Look especially for any:
  - Discharge
  - Redness
  - Ulceration
  - Atrophy
  - Old scars.
- Ask the patient to cough or strain down and look at the vaginal walls for any prolapse.

Palpation

- Palpate the length of the labia majora between the index finger and thumb.
  - The tissue should feel pliant and fleshy.
- Palpate for Bartholin's gland with the index finger of the right hand just inside the introitus and the thumb on the outer aspect of the labium majora.
  - Bartholin's glands are only palpable if the duct becomes obstructed resulting in a painless cystic mass or an acute Bartholin's abscess. The latter is seen as a hot, red, tender swelling in the posterolateral labia majora.

Speculum examination

Speculum examination is carried out to see further inside the vagina, to visualize the cervix, or take a cervical smear or swabs.

There are different types of vaginal specula (see Fig. 13.1) but the commonest is the Cusco's or bivalve speculum. See Box 13.12.

Inserting the speculum

- Explain to the patient that you are about to insert the speculum into the vagina and provide reassurance that this should not be painful.
- Warm the speculum under running water and lubricate it with a water-based lubricant.
- Using the left hand, open the lips of the labia minora to obtain a good view of the introitus.
- Hold the speculum in the right hand with the main body of the speculum in the palm (see Fig. 13.2) and the closed blades projecting between index and middle fingers.
- Gently insert the speculum into the vagina held with your wrist turned such that the blades are in line with the opening between the labia.
- The speculum should be angled downwards and backwards due to the angle of the vagina.
- Maintain a posterior angulation and rotate the speculum through 90° to position handles anteriorly.
- When it cannot be advanced further, maintain a downward pressure and press on the thumb piece to hinge the blades open exposing the cervix and vaginal walls.
- Once the optimum position is achieved, tighten the thumbscrew.

Findings

Inspect the cervix which is usually pink, smooth, and regular.

- Look for the external os (central opening) which is round in the nulliparous female and slit-shaped after childbirth.
- Look for cervical erosions which appear as strawberry-red areas spreading circumferentially around the os and represent extension of the endocervical epithelium onto the surface of the cervix.
- Identify any ulceration or growths which may suggest cancer.
- Cervicitis may give a mucopurulent discharge associated with a red, inflamed cervix which bleeds on contact. Take swabs for culture.

Removing the speculum

This should be conducted with as much care as insertion. You should still be examining the vaginal walls as the speculum is withdrawn.

- Undo the thumbscrew and withdraw the speculum.
  - ❶ The blades should be held open until their ends are visible distal to the cervix to avoid causing pain.
- Rotate the open blades in an anticlockwise direction to ensure that the anterior and posterior walls of the vagina can be inspected.
- Near the introitus, allow the blades to close taking care not to pinch the labia or hairs.

(a) (b)

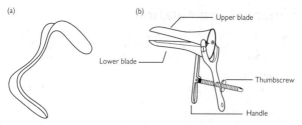

Fig. 13.1 (a) Sim's speculum—used mainly in the examination of women with vaginal prolapse. (b) Cusco's speculum.

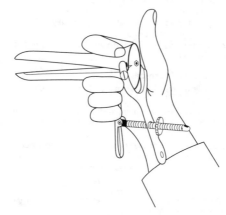

Fig. 13.2 Hold the speculum in the right hand such that the handles lie in the palm and the blades project between the index and middle fingers.

Box 13.12 A word about specula

Many departments and clinical areas now use plastic/disposable specula. These do not have a thumbscrew but a ratchet to open/close the blades. Take care to familiarize yourself with the operation of the speculum *before* starting the examination.

Bimanual examination

Digital examination helps identify the pelvic organs. Ideally the bladder should be emptied, if not already done so by this stage.

This examination is often known as *per vaginam* or simply 'PV'.

Getting started

- Explain again to the patient that you are about to perform an internal examination of the vagina, uterus, tubes, and ovaries and obtain verbal consent.
- The patient should be positioned as described previously.
- Expose the introitus by separating the labia with the thumb and forefinger of the gloved left hand.
- Gently introduce the lubricated index and middle fingers of the right hand into the vagina.
  - Insert your fingers with the palm facing laterally and then rotate 90° so that the palm faces upwards
  - The thumb should be abducted and the ring and little finger flexed into the palm (see Fig. 13.3).

Vagina, cervix, and fornices

- Feel the walls of the vagina which are slightly rugose, supple, and moist.
- Locate the cervix—usually pointing downwards in the upper vagina.
  - The normal cervix has a similar consistency to the cartilage in the tip of the nose
  - Assess the mobility of the cervix by moving it from side to side and note any tenderness ('excitation') which suggests infection.
- Gently palpate the fornices either side of the cervix.

Uterus

- Place your left hand on the lower anterior abdominal wall about 4cm above the symphysis pubis.
- Move the fingers of your right 'internal' hand to push the cervix upwards and simultaneously press the fingertips of your left 'external' hand towards the internal fingers.
  - You should be able to capture the uterus between your two hands.
- Note the features of the uterine body:
  - Size: a uniformly enlarged uterus may represent a pregnancy, fibroid, or endometrial tumour
  - Shape: multiple fibroids tend to give the uterus a lobulated feel
  - Position
  - Surface characteristics
  - Any tenderness
  - ▶ Remember that an anteverted uterus is easily palpable bimanually but a retroverted uterus may not be.
- Assess a retroverted uterus with the internal fingers positioned in the posterior fornix.

Ovaries and Fallopian tubes

- Position the internal fingers in each lateral fornix (finger pulps facing the anterior abdominal wall) and place your external fingers over each iliac fossa in turn.
- Press the external hand inwards and downwards and the internal fingers upwards and laterally.
- Feel the adnexal structures (ovaries and Fallopian tubes), assessing size, shape, mobility, and tenderness.
  - Ovaries are firm, ovoid, and often palpable. If there is unilateral or bilateral ovarian enlargement, consider benign cysts (smooth and compressible) and malignant ovarian tumours
  - Normal Fallopian tubes are impalpable
  - There may be marked tenderness of the lateral fornices and cervix in acute infection of the Fallopian tubes (salpingitis).

Masses

It is often not possible to differentiate between adnexal and uterine masses. However, there are some general rules:

- Uterine masses may be felt to move with the cervix when the uterus is shifted upwards while adnexal masses will not.
- If suspecting an adnexal mass, there should be a line of separation between the uterus and the mass, and the mass should be felt distinctly from the uterus.
- Whilst the consistency of the mass may help to distinguish its origin in certain cases, an ultrasound may be necessary.

Finishing the examination

- Withdraw your fingers from the vagina.
  - Inspect the glove for blood or discharge.
- Re-drape the genital area and allow the patient to re-dress in privacy—offer them assistance if needed.

(a) (b)

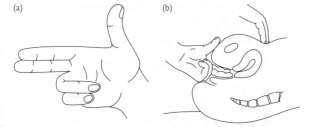

Fig. 13.3 (a) Correct position of the fingers of the right hand for *per vaginum* examination. (b) Bimanual examination of the uterus.

Taking a cervical smear

We describe the technique for obtaining a sample for 'liquid-based cytology' (LBC), now used by the majority of units in the UK.

Equipment

- Cusco's specula of different sizes.
- Disposable gloves.
- Request form.
- Sampling device: plastic broom (Cervex-Brush®).
- Liquid-based cytology vial: preservative for sample.
- Patient information leaflet.

Procedure

- Introduce yourself, confirm the patient's identity, ensure patient understands the purpose of the procedure and has been given patient information leaflet.
- Explain the procedure and obtain informed consent.
- Ensure a chaperone is available during the examination.
- Write the patient's identification details on LBC vial.
- Ask the patient to lie on her back on an examination couch with both knees bent up and let her knees fall apart: either with her heels together in the middle or separated.
- Warm the speculum under running water and lubricate it with a water-based lubricant.
- Using the left hand, open the lips of the labia minora to obtain a good view of the introitus.
- Hold the speculum with the main body of the speculum in the palm and the closed blades projecting between index and middle fingers.
- Gently insert the speculum into the vagina held with your wrist turned such that the blades are in line with the opening between the labia.
- The speculum should be angled downwards and backwards due to the angle of the vagina.
- Maintain a posterior angulation and rotate the speculum through 90° to position handles anteriorly.
- When it cannot be advanced further, maintain a downward pressure and press on the thumb piece to hinge the blades open exposing the cervix and vaginal walls.
- Ensure entire cervix is clearly visualized and note any obvious abnormalities or irregularity.
- Once in optimum position, tighten the thumbscrew.
- Insert the plastic broom so that the central bristles of the brush are in the endocervical canal, the outer bristles in contact with the ectocervix.
- Using pencil pressure, rotate the brush five times clockwise (Fig. 13.4).
  - The bristles are bevelled to scrape cells only on clockwise rotation.
- Rinse the brush thoroughly in the preservative (ThinPrep®) or break off brush into the preservative (SurePath®).
- Undo the thumbscrew and withdraw the speculum.
- ❗ The blades should be held open until their ends are visible distal to the cervix to avoid causing pain.

- Rotate the open blades in an anticlockwise direction to ensure that the anterior and posterior walls of the vagina can be inspected.
- Near the introitus, allow the blades to close taking care not to pinch the labia or hairs.
- Allow the patient to re-dress in privacy.

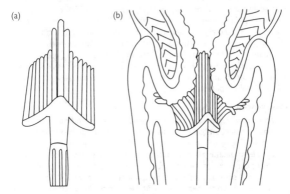

(a)   (b)

Fig. 13.4 (a) The end of a typical cervix-brush. (b) Representation of how to use a Cervex-Brush®. Note that the longer, central bristles are within the cervical canal whilst the outer bristles are in contact with the ectocervix.

Documentation

- Date, time, indication, informed consent obtained.
- Those present, including chaperone.
- Date of last menstrual period and use of hormonal treatments.
- Date of last smear and any abnormal results.
- Any abnormalities identified.
- Any immediate complications.
- Signature, printed name, and contact details.

Procedure tips

- Cervical smears should not be performed during pregnancy.
  - The increase in cervical mucus (and resultant decrease in the number of cells obtained) usually renders the sample inadequate and the results unreliable.
- Neither abnormal vaginal bleeding or discharge or a visible or palpable cervical lesion is an indication for a cervical smear per se as it is a test for cervical atypia which is asymptomatic. However, a speculum examination should be performed to inspect the cervix and infection screening offered.
  - A cervical smear can be offered to women who have not had a normal test within the usual screening period.
- Ensure the patient knows when and how she will receive the results of the test and who to contact in case of problems.

The elderly patient

It is easy to be seduced into thinking that the principal focus should be on very 'medical' diagnoses such as urinary tract infections, which contribute to significant morbidity (and mortality) in older people.

Continence issues are sadly overlooked in most clinical assessments. Large-scale surveys of prevalence have shown up to 20% of women over 40 reporting difficulties with continence; so whilst more common in older people, you should always be mindful of problems in younger adults too.

Although continence issues are one of the 'Geriatric Giants' of disease presentation, it is important to recall the physiology of the postmenopausal changes—such as vaginal atrophy (Box 13.13) and loss of secretions—which can complicate urinary tract infections, continence, and utero-vaginal prolapse in older patients.

Assessment

- *Tact and understanding:* although problems are common, patients may be reluctant to discuss them, or have them discussed in front of others. Engaging in a discussion about bladder and/or sexual function can seem daunting—but if done empathetically, remembering never to appear to judge, or be embarrassed—you may reveal problems that have seriously affected your patient's quality of life. Treating problems such as these, even with very simple interventions, can be of immeasurable value to the patient.
- *Holistic assessment of urinary problems:* learn to think when asking about bladder function, and work out a pattern of dysfunction—e.g. bladder instability or stress incontinence. Remember that bladder function may be disrupted by drugs, pain, lack of privacy. Continence issues may reflect poor mobility, visual and cognitive decline.
- *Genital symptoms:* never forget to consider vaginal or uterine pathology—view postmenopausal bleeding with suspicion. Discharges may represent active infection (if candida—consider diabetes) or atrophic vaginitis.
- *Past medical history:* pregnancies and previous surgery in particular may help point to a diagnosis of stress incontinence. Are urinary tract infections recurrent—has bladder pathology been excluded?
- *Drugs:* many are obvious—diuretics and anticholinergics; some are more subtle—sedatives may provoke nocturnal loss of continence. Does your patient drink tea or coffee?
- *Tailored functional history:* the cornerstone of any assessment you perform. This largely relates to bladder function—is the lavatory up or down? How are the stairs? Does your patient already have continence aids—bottles/commodes/pads—and do they manage with them?

Box 13.13 A word on atrophic vaginitis

Up to 40% of postmenopausal women will have symptoms and signs of atrophic vaginitis and the vast majority will be elderly and may be reluctant to discuss this with their doctors. A result of oestrogen deficiency, the subsequent increased vaginal pH, and thinned endometrium lead to both genital and urinary symptoms and signs. A decrease in vaginal lubrication presents with dryness, pruritus, and discharges, accompanied by an increase rate of prolapse. Urinary complications can result in frequency, stress incontinence, and infections.

Careful physical examination often makes the diagnosis clear with labial dryness, loss of skin turgidity, and smooth, shiny vaginal epithelium. A range of treatment options including topical oestrogens, simple lubricants, and continued sexual activity when appropriate are all key interventions to manage this common condition.

The obstetric assessment

History taking in obstetrics

Although there are parts particular to this history, most is the same as the basic outline described in ➜ Chapter 2 and we suggest that readers review that chapter before going on.

Demographic details

- Name, age, and date of birth.
- Gravidity and parity—see Boxes 14.2 and 14.3.

Estimated date of delivery (EDD)

The EDD can be calculated from the last menstrual period (LMP) by Naegele's rule*, which assumes a 28-day menstrual cycle (see Box 14.1).

Box 14.1 Calculating the EDD

- Subtract 3 months from the first day of the LMP
- Add on 7 days and 1 year.

If the normal menstrual cycle is <28 days, or >28 days, then an appropriate number of days should be subtracted from or added to the EDD. For example, if the normal cycle is 35 days, 7 days should be added to the EDD.

It is important to also consider at this point any detail that may influence the validity of the EDD as calculated from the LMP; such as:

- Was the last period normal?
- What is the usual cycle length?
- Are the patient's periods usually regular or irregular?
- Was the patient using the oral contraceptive pill in the three months prior to conception? If so, calculations based on her LMP are unreliable.

Current pregnancy

Ask about the patient's general health and that of her fetus. If there is a presenting complaint, the details should be documented in full. Also ask about:

- Fetal movements:
  - Not usually noticed until 20 weeks' gestation in the first pregnancy and 18 weeks' in the second or subsequent pregnancies.
- Any important laboratory tests or ultrasound scans.
  - Include dates and details of all the scans, especially the first scan (dating or nuchal translucency scan).

---

* Named after the German obstetrician, Franz Naegele following its publication in his *Lehrbuch der Geburtshuelfe* published for midwives in 1830. The formula was actually developed by Harmanni Boerhaave. Boerhaave H. (1744) Praelectiones Academicae in Propias Institutiones Rei Medicae. Von Haller A, ed. Göttingen: Vandehoeck. 5 (part 2): 437.

Box 14.2 Gravidity and parity

These terms can be confusing and, although it is worth knowing the definitions and how to use them, they should be supplemented with a detailed history and not relied on alone as you may miss subtleties which alter your outlook on the case.

Gravidity

- The number of pregnancies (including the present one) to *any* stage

Parity

- The number of live births (at any stage of gestation) and stillbirths after 24 weeks' gestation
  - Pregnancies terminating before 24 weeks' gestation can be written after this number with a plus sign.

Examples

- A woman who is currently 20 weeks pregnant and has had two normal deliveries* = Gravida 3, Para 2
- A woman who is not pregnant and has had a single live birth and one miscarriage at 17 weeks = Gravida 2, Para 1+1
- A woman who is currently 25 weeks pregnant, has had 3 normal deliveries, one miscarriage at 9 weeks, and a termination at 7 weeks = Gravida 6, Para 3+2.

Twins

There is some controversy as to how to express twin pregnancies. Most people suggest that they should count as 1 for gravidity and 2 for parity—but you should check your local practice on this.

Box 14.3 A word about deliveries

*The verb 'to deliver' is often misused by students of obstetrics as it is often misused by the population at large.

Babies are not delivered.

In fact, the mothers are 'delivered of' the child—as in being relieved of a burden.

Check your nearest dictionary!

Past obstetric history

Ask about all of the patient's previous pregnancies including miscarriages, terminations, and ectopic pregnancies.

For each pregnancy, note:
- Age of the mother when pregnant.
- Antenatal complications.
- Duration of pregnancy.
- Details of induction of labour.
- Duration of labour.
- Presentation and method of delivery.
- Birth weight and sex of infant.

Also enquire about any complications of the puerperal period. The puerperium is the period from the end of the 3rd stage of labour until involution of the uterus is complete (about 6 weeks).

Possible complications include:
- Postpartum haemorrhage.
- Infections of the genital and urinary tracts.
- Deep vein thrombosis.
- Perineal complications such as breakdown of the perineal wounds.
- Psychological complications (e.g. postnatal depression).

Past gynaecological history

- Record all previous gynaecological problems with full details of how the diagnosis was made, treatments received, and the success or otherwise of that treatment.
- Record the date of the last cervical smear and any previous abnormal results.
- Take a full contraceptive history.

Past medical history

Note especially those conditions which may have an impact on the pregnancy including:
- Diabetes.
- Endocrine disorders such as thyroid disorders or Addison's disease.
- Asthma.
- Epilepsy.
- Hypertension and heart disease.
- Renal disease.
- Infectious diseases such as TB, HIV, syphilis, and hepatitis.
  - Identification of such conditions will allow the obstetrician to consider early referral to a specialist for shared care.
- All previous operative procedures.
- Blood transfusions and receipt of other blood products.
- Psychiatric history—may extend beyond 'simple' postnatal depression.

Drug history

- Take a full drug history which should include all prescribed medication, over-the-counter medicines, and illicit drugs.
- Record any drug allergies and their nature.
- If currently pregnant, ensure the patient is taking 400 micrograms of folic acid daily until 12 weeks' gestation to reduce the incidence of spina bifida.

Family history

- Ask about any pregnancy-related conditions such as congenital abnormalities, problems following delivery, etc.
- Ask also about a FHx of diabetes.
- ▶ Ask especially if there are any known hereditary illnesses. Appropriate counselling and investigations such as chorionic villus sampling or amniocentesis may need to be offered.

Social history

As well as the full standard social history, ask about:

- Her partner—age, occupation, health.
- How stable the relationship is.
- If she is not in a relationship, who will give her support during and after the pregnancy?
- Ask if the pregnancy was planned or not.
- If she works, enquire about her job and if she has any plans to return to work.

Bleeding

During pregnancy

Treat as any symptom. In addition, you should build a clear picture of how much blood is being lost, when and how it is affecting the current pregnancy (Boxes 14.6 and 14.7).

After establishing an exact time-line and other details about the symptom, ask about:

- Exact nature of the bleeding (fresh/old).
- Amount of blood lost.
  - Number of sanitary pads used daily.
- Presence of clots (and, if present, size of those clots).
- Presence of pieces of tissue in the blood.
- Presence of mucoid discharge.
- Fetal movement.
- Associated symptoms such as abdominal pain (associated with placental abruption; placenta praevia is painless).
- Possible trigger factors—recent intercourse, injuries.
- Any history of cervical abnormalities—and the result of the last smear.

After pregnancy

This is called 'post-partum haemorrhage' or PPH (Boxes 14.4 and 14.5).

- *Primary PPH:* >500ml of blood loss within 24 hours following delivery.
- *Secondary PPH:* any excess bleeding between 24 hours and 6 weeks post delivery. (No amount of blood is specified in the definition.)

▶ Take a full history as for bleeding during pregnancy. Ask also about symptoms of infection—an important cause of secondary PPH.

Box 14.4 Risk factors for post-partum haemorrhage

Nulliparity, multiparity, polyhydramnios, prolonged labour, multiple gestation, previous PPH or APH, pre-eclampsia, coagulation abnormalities, genital tract lacerations, Asian or Hispanic ethnicity.

Box 14.5 Some causes of post-partum haemorrhage

Primary
Uterine atony (most frequent cause), genital tract trauma, coagulation disorders, retained placenta, uterine inversion, uterine rupture.

Secondary
Retained products of conception, endometritis, infection.

Box 14.6 Some causes of vaginal bleeding in early pregnancy

We suggest the reader turns to the *Oxford Handbook of Obstetrics and Gynaecology*[1] for more detail.

Ectopic pregnancy
- *Symptoms:* light bleeding, abdominal pain, fainting if pain and blood loss is severe
- *Signs:* closed cervix, uterus slightly larger and softer than normal, tender adnexal mass, cervical motion tenderness.

Threatened miscarriage
- *Symptoms:* light bleeding. Sometimes: cramping, lower abdominal pain
- *Signs:* closed cervix, uterus corresponds to dates. Sometimes, uterus is softer than normal.

Complete miscarriage
- *Symptoms:* light bleeding. Sometimes: light cramping, lower abdominal pain and a history of expulsion of products of conception
- *Signs:* uterus smaller than dates and softer than normal. Closed cervix.

Incomplete miscarriage
- *Symptoms:* heavy bleeding. Sometimes: cramping, lower abdominal pain, partial expulsion of products of conception
- *Signs:* uterus smaller than dates and cervix dilated.

Molar pregnancy
- *Symptoms:* heavy bleeding, partial expulsion of products of conception which resemble grapes. Sometimes: nausea and vomiting, cramping, lower abdominal pain, history of ovarian cysts
- *Signs:* dilated cervix, uterus larger than dates and softer than normal.

Box 14.7 Some causes of bleeding in 2nd/3rd trimesters (>24 weeks)

This is known as 'antepartum haemorrhage' (APH). See the *Oxford Handbook of Obstetrics and Gynaecology*[1] for more detail.

Placenta praevia

The placenta is positioned over the lower pole of the uterus, obscuring the cervix. Bleeding is usually after 28 weeks and often precipitated by intercourse. Findings may include a relaxed uterus, fetal presentation not in pelvis, and normal fetal condition.

Placental abruption

This is detachment of a normally located placenta from the uterus before the fetus is delivered. Bleeding can occur at any stage of the pregnancy. Possible findings include a tense, tender uterus, reduced or absent fetal movements, fetal distress, or absent fetal heart sounds.

[1] Collins et al. (2013). *Oxford Handbook of Obstetrics and Gynaecology*. OUP, Oxford.

Abdominal pain

A full pain history should be taken as in ➲ Chapter 2 including site, radiation, character, severity, mode and rate of onset, duration, frequency, exacerbating factors, relieving factors, and associated symptoms.

History taking

Take a full obstetric history and systems enquiry. Ask especially about a past history of pre-eclampsia, pre-term labour, peptic ulcer disease, gallstones, appendicectomy, and cholecystectomy.

Causes

❶ Remember that the pain may be unrelated to the pregnancy so keep an open mind. Causes of abdominal pain in pregnancy include:

Obstetric
- Preterm/term labour.
- Placental abruption.
- Ligament pain.
- Symphysis pubis dysfunction.
- Pre-eclampsia/HELLP syndrome.
- Acute fatty liver of pregnancy.

Gynaecological
- Ovarian cyst rupture, torsion, haemorrhage.
- Uterine fibroid degeneration.

Gastrointestinal
- Constipation.
- Appendicitis.
- Gallstones.
- Cholecystitis.
- Pancreatitis.
- Peptic ulceration.

Genitourinary
- Cystitis.
- Pyelonephritis.
- Renal stones.
- Renal colic.

Labour pain

This is usually intermittent, regular in frequency, and associated with tightening of the abdominal wall.

Hypertension

Hypertension is a common and important problem in pregnancy and you should be alert to the possible symptoms which can result from it such as headache, blurred vision, vomiting and epigastric pain after 24 weeks, convulsions or loss of consciousness.

Pregnancy-induced hypertension

- Two readings of diastolic blood pressure 90–110, 4 hours apart after 20 weeks' gestation.
- No proteinuria.

Mild proteinuric pregnancy-induced hypertension

- Two readings of diastolic blood pressure 90–110, 4 hours apart after 20 weeks' gestation.
- Proteinuria 2+.

Severe proteinuric pregnancy-induced hypertension

- Diastolic blood pressure 110 or greater after 20 weeks' gestation.
- Proteinuria 3+.
- Other symptoms may include:
  - Hyper-reflexia
  - Headache
  - Clouding of vision
  - Oligura
  - Abdominal pain
  - Pulmonary oedema.

Eclampsia

- Convulsions associated with raised blood pressure and/or proteinuria beyond 20 weeks' gestation.
- May be unconscious.

Minor symptoms of pregnancy

These so-called 'minor' symptoms of pregnancy are often experienced by a number of woman as normal changes occur. This is not to say that they should be ignored as they may point to pathology.

Nausea and vomiting

- The severity varies greatly and is more common in multiple pregnancies and molar pregnancies.
- Persistence of vomiting may suggest pathology such as:
  - Infections
  - Gastritis
  - Biliary tract disease
  - Hepatitis.

Heartburn/gastro-oesophageal reflux

- Heartburn is a frequent complaint during pregnancy due partially to compression of the stomach by the gravid uterus.

Constipation

- Often secondary to ↑ progesterone.
- Improves with gestation.

Shortness of breath

- Due to dilatation of the bronchial tree secondary to ↑ progesterone.
  - Peaks at 20–24 weeks
  - The growing uterus also has an impact.
- Other possible causes (such as pulmonary embolus) need to be considered.

Fatigue

- Very common in early pregnancy.
  - Peaking at the end of the first trimester.
- Fatigue in late pregnancy may be due to anaemia.

Insomnia

- Due to anxiety, hormonal changes, and physical discomfort.

Pruritus

- Generalized itching in the third trimester may resolve after delivery.
- Biliary problems should be excluded.

Haemorrhoids

- May resolve after delivery.

Varicose veins

- Especially at the feet and ankles.

Vaginal discharge

- Exclude infection and spontaneous rupture of the membranes.

Pelvic pain

- Stretching of pelvic structures can cause ligament pain which resolves in the second half of the pregnancy.
- Symphysis pubis dysfunction causes pain on abduction and rotation at the hips and on mobilization.

Backache

- Often first develops during the 5–7th months of pregnancy.

Peripheral paraesthesiae

- Fluid retention can lead to compression of peripheral nerves such as carpal tunnel syndrome.
- Other nerves can be affected, e.g. lateral cutaneous nerve of the thigh.

Outline obstetric examination

Explain to the patient that you would like to examine their womb and baby and reassure them that the procedure will be quick and gentle.

You should have a chaperone present, particularly if you are male.

As always, ensure that the room is warm and well lit, preferably with a moveable light source and that you will not be disturbed.

As for the gynaecological examination, you should follow an orderly routine. The authors' suggestion is shown on ➲ p. 475. It is standard practice to start with the cardiovascular and respiratory systems—this not only gives a measure of the general health of the patient but also establishes a 'physical rapport' before you examine more delicate or embarrassing areas (Box 14.8).

General inspection

Always begin with a general examination of the patient (as in ➲ Chapter 3) including:

- Temperature.
- Hydration.
- Coloration.
- Nutritional status.
- Lymph nodes.
- Blood pressure.

Note especially:

- Any brownish pigmentation over the forehead and cheeks known as chloasma.
- Distribution of facial and body hair, as hirsutism may be a presenting symptom of various endocrine disorders.
- Height, weight, and calculate BMI.
- ▶ Blood pressure should be measured in the left lateral position at 45° to avoid compression of the inferior vena cava by the gravid uterus.
- ⓘ Anaemia is a common complication of pregnancy so examine the mucosal surfaces and conjunctivae carefully.

Examining other systems

- Examine the cardiovascular and respiratory systems in turn (see ➲ Chapters 5 and 6).
  - Flow murmurs are common in pregnancy and, although usually of no clinical significance, must be recorded in detail.
- A routine breast examination is not normally indicated unless a female patient complains of breast symptoms, in which case you must carefully look for any pathology such as cysts or solid nodules.

Box 14.8 Framework for the obstetric examination

- General inspection
- Cardiorespiratory examination
- Abdominal inspection
- Abdominal palpation
  - Uterine size
  - Fetal lie
  - Fetal presentation
  - Engagement
  - Amniotic fluid estimation.
- Auscultation of the fetal heart
- Vaginal examination
- Perform bedside urinalysis (particularly protein) if able.

Abdominal inspection

Look for the abdominal distension caused by the gravid uterus rising from the pelvis. Look also for:

- Asymmetry.
- Fetal movements.
- Surgical scars.
  - Pubic hairline (transverse suprapubic Pfannenstiel incision)
  - Paraumbilical region (laparoscopic scars).
- Cutaneous signs of pregnancy including:
  - Linea nigra (black line) which stretches from the pubic symphysis upwards in the midline
  - Red stretch marks of current pregnancy (striae gravidarum)
  - White stretch marks (striae albicans) from a previous pregnancy
  - Other areas that can undergo pigmentation in pregnancy include the nipples, vulva, umbilicus, and recent abdominal scars.
- Umbilical changes:
  - Flattening as pregnancy advances
  - Eversion secondary to increased intra-abdominal pressure (e.g. caused by multiple pregnancies or polyhydraminios).

Palpation

Before palpating the abdomen, always enquire about any areas of tenderness and visit those areas last.

Palpation should start as for any standard abdominal examination (➲ Chapter 7) before proceeding to more specific manoeuvres in an obstetric examination.

Uterine size

▶ The symphysial–fundal height (cm) = weeks of gestation.

The distance from the symphysis pubis to the upper edge of the uterus provides an estimation of gestational age and is objectively measured and expressed in centimetres as the *symphysial–fundal* height (Box 14.9 and Fig. 14.1).

Between 16–36 weeks, there is a margin of error of ±2cm, ±3cm at 36–40 weeks, and ±4cm at 40 weeks onwards.

Technique

- 🕛 You need a tape measure for this—don't start without it!
- Use the ulnar border of the left hand to press firmly into the abdomen just below the sternum.
- Move the hand down the abdomen in small steps until you can feel the fundus of the uterus.
- Locate the upper border of the bony pubic symphysis by palpating downward in the midline starting from a few centimetres above the pubic hair margin.
- Measure the distance between the two points that you have found in centimetres using a flexible tape measure.

> **Box 14.9 Uterine size: milestones**
> - The uterus first becomes palpable at 12 weeks' gestation
> - 20 weeks' gestation = at the level of the umbilicus
> - 36 weeks' gestation = at the level of the xiphisternum.

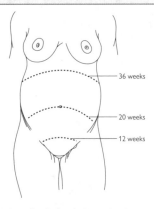

Fig. 14.1 A guide to the surface landmarks for uterine size.

Fetal lie

This describes the relationship between the long axis of the fetus and the long axis of the uterus and, in general, can be:

- *Longitudinal:* the long axis of the fetus matches the long axis of the uterus. Either the head or the breech will be palpable over the pelvic inlet.
- *Transverse:* the fetus lies at right angles to the uterus and the fetal poles are palpable in the flanks.
- *Oblique:* the long axis of the fetus lies at an angle of 45° to the long axis of the uterus, the presenting part will be palpable in one of the iliac fossae.

Examination technique

The best position is to stand at the mother's right side, facing her feet.

- Put your left hand along the left side of the uterus.
- Put your right hand on the right side of the uterus.
- Palpate towards the midline with one and then the other hand.
  - Use 'dipping' movements with flexion of the MCP joints to feel the fetus within the amniotic fluid.
- You should feel the fetal back as firm resistance or the irregular shape of the limbs.
- You should now palpate more widely using the 2-handed technique above to stabilize the uterus and attempt to locate the head and the breech.
  - The head can be felt as a smooth, round object that is ballotable— that is, it can be 'bounced' (gently) between your hands
  - The breech is softer, less discrete, and is not ballotable.

Fetal presentation

This is the part of the fetus that presents to the mother's pelvis. Possible presenting parts include:

- *Head:* cephalic presentation. One option in a longitudinal lie.
- *Breech:* podalic presentation. The other option in a longitudinal lie.
- *Shoulder:* seen in a transverse lie.

Examination technique

- Stand at the mother's right side, facing her feet.
- Place both hands on either side of the lower part of the uterus.
- Bring the hands together firmly but gently.
  - You should be able to feel either the head, breech, or other part as described above under 'fetal lie'.

Paulik's grip

It is also possible to use a one-handed technique (Paulik's grip) to feel for the presenting part—this is best left to obstetricians. In this, you use a cupped right hand to hold the lower pole of the uterus. This is possible in ~95% of pregnancies at about 40 weeks.

Engagement

When the widest part of the fetal skull is within the pelvic inlet, the fetal head is said to be 'engaged'.

In a cephalic presentation, palpation of the head is assessed and expressed as the number of fifths of the skull palpable above the pelvic brim. A fifth is roughly equal to a finger breath on an adult hand.

- The head is engaged when 3 or more fifths are within the pelvic inlet—that is when 2 or fewer fifths are palpable.
- When 3 or more fifths are palpable, the head is not engaged.

Number of fetuses

The number of fetuses present can be calculated by assessing the number of fetal poles (head or breech) present.

- If there is one fetus present, 2 poles should be palpable (unless the presenting part is deeply engaged).
- In a multiple pregnancy, you should be able to feel all the poles except one—as one is usually tucked away out of reach.

Amniotic fluid/liquor volume estimation

The ease with which fetal parts are palpable can give an indication as to the possibility of reduced or increased amniotic fluid volume.

- Increased volume will give a large-for-dates uterus that is smooth and rounded. The fetal parts may be almost impossible to palpate.
- Reduced volume may give a small-for-dates uterus. The fetus will be easily palpable giving an irregular, firm outline to the uterus.

Percussion

This is usually unhelpful unless you suspect polyhydramnios in which case, you may wish to attempt to elicit a fluid thrill.

Auscultation

Auscultation is used to listen to the fetal heart rate (FHR). This is usually performed using an electronic hand-held Doppler fetal heart rate monitor and can be used as early as 14 weeks.

Using Pinard's fetal stethoscope

A Pinard's fetal stethoscope is not useful until 28 weeks' gestation. It is a simple-looking device rather like an old-fashioned ear-trumpet.

- Place the bell of the instrument over the anterior fetal shoulder.
- Press your left ear against the stethoscope so as to hold it between your head and the mother's abdomen in a 'hands-free' position or hold the instrument lightly with one hand.
- Press against the opposite side of the mother's abdomen with your other hand so as to stabilize the uterus.
- It should sound like a distant ticking noise. The rate varies between 110 and 150/minute at term and should be regular.

Vaginal examination

Vaginal examination allows you to assess cervical status before induction of labour. You should attempt this only under adequate supervision if you are unsure of the procedure.

This examination allows you to assess the degree of cervical dilatation (in centimetres) using the examining fingers.

❗ Examination of the vagina and cervix should be performed under aseptic conditions in the presence of ruptured membranes or in cases with abnormal vaginal discharge.

Technique

The examination should be performed as described in ➲ Chapter 13. The findings take experience to recognize. The student should not shy away from this examination due to its intimate nature.

Findings

Assess:

- Degree of dilation.
  - Full dilation of the cervix is equivalent to 10cm
  - Most obstetric departments will have plastic models of cervices in various stages of dilatation which you can practise feeling.
- The length of the cervix.
  - Normal ~3cm but shortens as the cervix effaces secondary to uterine contraction.
- The consistency of the cervix which can be described as:
  - Firm
  - Mid-consistency
  - Soft (this consistency facilitates effacement and dilatation).
- Position.
  - As the cervix undergoes effacement and dilatation it tends to be pulled from a posterior to an anterior position.
- Station of the presenting part.
  - The level of the head above or below the ischial spines which may be estimated in centimetres.

The breast

Introduction

Anatomy of the breast

The two mammary glands are highly developed apocrine sweat glands. They develop embryologically along two lines extending from the axillae to the groin—the milk lines (see Fig. 15.1). In humans, only one gland develops on each side of the thorax although extra nipples with breast tissue may sometimes occur.

The breasts extend from the 2nd to the 6th ribs and transversely from the lateral border of the sternum to the midaxillary line.

For the purposes of examination, each breast may be divided into four quadrants by horizontal and vertical lines intersecting at the nipple. An additional lateral extension of breast tissue (the axillary tail of Spence) stretches from the upper outer quadrant towards the axilla (Fig. 15.2).

Each mammary gland consists of 15–20 lobes separated by loose adipose tissue and subdivided by collagenous septa. Strands of connective tissue called the suspensory ligaments of the breast (Cooper's ligaments) run between the skin and deep fascia to support the breast. Each lobe is further divided into a variable number of lobules composed of grape-like clusters of milk-secreting glands termed alveoli and is drained by a lactiferous duct that opens onto the nipple. Myo-epithelial cells surround the alveoli which contract and help propel the milk toward the nipples.

The nipple is surrounded by a circular pigmented area called the areola and is abundantly supplied with sensory nerve endings. The surface of this area also contains the 'sebaceous glands of Montgomery' which act to lubricate the nipple during lactation.

Lymphatic drainage

Lymphatic drainage from the medial portion of the breast is to the internal mammary nodes. The central and lateral portions drain to the axillary lymph nodes which are arranged into five groups (see Fig. 15.7).

Physiology—normal breast changes in women

- *Puberty:* during adolescence, oestrogen promotes the development of the mammary ducts and distribution of fatty tissue while progesterone induces alveolar growth.
- *The menstrual cycle:* towards the 2nd half of the menstrual cycle, after ovulation, the breasts often become tender and swollen. They return to their 'resting' state after menstruation.
- *Pregnancy:* high levels of placental oestrogen, progesterone, and prolactin promote mammary growth in preparation for milk production.
- *Postnatal:* the sharply declining levels of oestrogen and progesterone permit prolactin to stimulate the alveoli and milk is produced. Suckling stimulates secretion of prolactin as well as releasing oxytocin which stimulates myoepithelial cells to contract.
- *Menopause:* the breasts become softer, more homogeneous, and undergo involutional changes including a decrease in size, atrophy of the secretory portions, and some atrophy of the ducts.

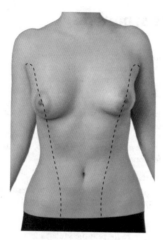

Fig. 15.1 Illustration of the two milk lines along which the nipples form—occasionally extra nipples can be found.

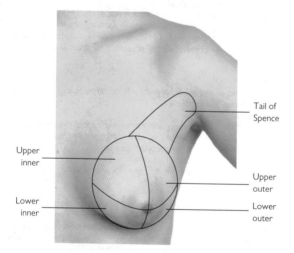

Fig. 15.2 Illustration showing the four quadrants of the breast with the axillary tail of Spence.

Important symptoms

First steps

You should begin by establishing a menstrual history (see ➔ Chapter 13). You should also determine the date of the last period of menstruation. It is important to note that pre-existing disease in the breast is likely to become more noticeable during the 2nd half of the menstrual cycle—lumps often get bigger or become more easily palpable.

▶ You should bear in mind that seeking medical attention for a breast lump or tenderness can produce extreme anxiety and embarrassment in patients. Men with gynaecomastia are also likely to feel anxious about their breast development. Ensure that you adopt an appropriately sensitive, sympathetic, and professional approach.

Breast pain (mastalgia)

As for pain at any other site, you should establish the site, radiation, character, duration, severity, exacerbating factors, relieving factors, and associated symptoms. Also ask:

- Is the pain unilateral or bilateral?
- Is there any heat or redness at the site?
- Are there any other visible skin changes?
- Is the pain cyclical or constant—and is it related to menstruation?
- Is there a history of any previous similar episodes?
- Is the patient breastfeeding?
- Is the patient on any hormonal therapy (especially HRT)?

The commonest cause of mastalgia in premenopausal women is hormone-dependent change. Other benign causes include mastitis and abscesses. 1 in 100 breast cancers present with mastalgia as the sole symptom.

Nipple discharge

Important causes of nipple discharge include ductal pathology such as ductal ectasia, papilloma, and carcinoma.

Ask about:

- Is the discharge true milk or some other substance? (See Box 15.1.)
- The colour of the discharge (e.g. clear, white, yellow, blood-stained).
- Spontaneous or non-spontaneous discharge?
- Is the discharge unilateral or bilateral?
- Any changes in the appearance of the nipple or areola.
- Mastalgia.
- Any breast lumps.
- Periareola abscesses or fistulae indicating periductal mastitis.
  - This is closely linked to smoking in young women. Periductal mastitis is also associated with hidradenitis suppurativa. Ask about abscesses elsewhere, e.g. axilla and groins. The symptoms are often recurrent.

> **Box 15.1 Galactorrhoea**
>
> Remember that after childbearing, some women continue to discharge a small secretion of milk (galactorrhoea). However, in rare instances this can be the 1st presenting symptom of a prolactin-secreting pituitary adenoma. You should, therefore, in the case of true bilateral galactorrhoea also ask about:
> - Headaches
> - Visual disturbance
> - Any other neurological symptoms.

Breast lumps

A very important presenting complaint with a number of causes—the most important of which is cancer. Establish:
- When the lump was first noticed.
- Whether the lump has remained the same size or enlarged.
- Whether the size of the lump changes according to the menstrual cycle.
- Is there any pain?
- Are there any local skin changes?
- Is there a history of breast lumps (ask about previous biopsies, the diagnoses, and operations)?
- A full systems enquiry should include any other symptoms which might be suggestive of a neoplastic disease (loss of weight, loss of appetite, fatigue, etc.) and metastatic spread to other organ systems (shortness of breath, bony pain, etc.).

Age

A good clue as to the likely diagnosis of a lump is the age of the patient:
- Fibroadenomas are common between 20–30 years.
- Cysts are common between 30–50 years.
- Cancer is very rare <30 years.

Gynaecomastia

This is enlargement of the male breast tissue which should not normally be palpable. There is an ↑ in the ductal and connective tissue.

A common occurrence in adolescents and the elderly. Gynaecomastia is seen in obese men due to increased adipose tissue.

In many patients, gynaecomastia is drug-related and the full causative list is long. Important drug causes include oestrogen receptor binders such as oestrogen, digoxin, and marijuana as well as anti-androgens such as spironolactone and cimetidine.

▶ In the history, ask about drug and hormone treatment (e.g. for prostate cancer).

▶ You should also make a full examination of the patient looking for signs of hypopituitarism, chronic liver disease, and thyrotoxicosis. Remember to make a careful examination of the genitalia.

Inspection of the breast

Before you start

- When examining the female breast, examiners should have a chaperone present. Ideally, the chaperone should be female.
- The patient should be fully undressed to the waist and sitting on the edge of a couch with her arms by her side.
- You should be able to see the neck, breasts, chest wall, and arms.

General inspection

Stand in front of the patient and observe both breasts, noting:

- Size.
- Symmetry.
- Contour.
- Colour.
- Scars.
- Venous pattern on the skin.
- Any dimpling or tethering of the skin.
- Ulceration (describe fully as in ➔ Chapter 4).
- Skin texture: e.g. any visible nodularity.
    - An unusual finding, but one that should not be missed, is the 'orange peel' appearance of *peau d'orange* caused by local oedema. Seen in breast carcinoma and following breast radiotherapy.

Nipples

Note whether the nipples are:

- Symmetrical.
- Everted, flat, or inverted.
- Scale (may indicate eczema or Paget's disease of the breast).
- Associated with any discharge.
    - Single duct discharge can indicate a papilloma or cancer
    - Multiple duct discharge at the nipple suggests duct ectasia
    - If abnormalities are present, make sure to ask if these are a recent or long-standing appearance.
- Make note of any additional nipples, which can occur anywhere along the mammary line.

Axillae

Ask the patient to place her hands on her head and repeat the inspection process. Pay particular attention to any asymmetry or dimpling that is now evident. Examine the axillae for masses or colour change.

Manoeuvres

Finally, dimpling or fixation can be further accentuated by asking the patient to perform the following manoeuvres (see Fig. 15.3):

- Lean forward whilst sitting.
- Rest her hands on her hips.
- Press her hands against her hips ('pectoral contraction manoeuvre').

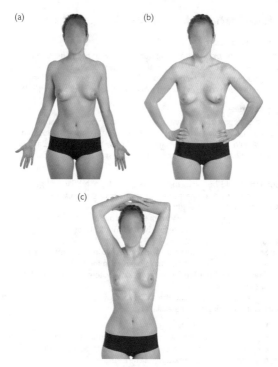

Fig. 15.3 Manoeuvres for breast inspection. (a) Anatomical position. (b) Hands on hips. (c) Arms crossed above the head.

Fig. 15.4 Correct position of the patient for palpation of the breast.

Palpation of the breast

Before you start

Palpation of the breast should be performed with the patient lying at about 45 degrees on the couch. Initially, the patient should have her hands by her sides. Examination of the upper-outer quadrant is best performed with the hand on the side to be examined placed behind her head (Fig. 15.4).

Palpation

Ask the patient if there is any pain or tenderness—and examine that area last. Also ask her to tell you if you cause any pain during the examination.

You should begin the examination on the asymptomatic side, allowing you to determine the texture of the normal breast first.

The breast

Palpation should be performed by keeping the hand flat and gently rolling the substance of the breast against the underlying chest wall.

🔔 Most breasts will feel 'lumpy' if pinched.

You should proceed in a systematic way to ensure that the whole breast is examined. There are two regularly used methods (see Fig. 15.5) of which the authors favour the 1st:

- Start below the areola and work outwards in a circumferential pattern ensuring that all quadrants have been examined.
- Examine the breast in 2 halves working systematically down from the upper border.

▶ Do not forget to examine the axillary tail of Spence stretching from the upper-outer quadrant to the axilla.

Lumps

- If you feel a lump, describe it thoroughly noting especially: position, colour, shape, size, surface, nature of the surrounding skin, tenderness, consistency, temperature, and mobility.
- Next ascertain its relations to the overlying skin and underlying muscle.
- You must decide whether you are feeling a lump or a lumpy area.

Skin tethering

A lump may be described as tethered to the skin if it can be moved independently of the skin for a limited distance but pulls on the skin if moved further.

Tethering implies that an underlying lesion has infiltrated Cooper's ligaments which pass from the skin through the subcutaneous fat.

On inspection at rest, there may be puckering of the skin surface (as if being pulled from within) or there may be no visible abnormality.

To demonstrate tethering:

- Move the lump from side to side and look for skin dimpling at the extremes of movement.
- Ask the patient to lean forwards whilst sitting.
- Ask the patient to raise her arms above the head as in Fig. 15.3c.

Skin fixation

This is caused by direct, continuous infiltration of the skin by the underlying disease. The lump and the skin overlying it cannot be moved independently. It is on a continuum with skin tethering. This may be associated with some changes of skin texture.

The relation of a lump to the muscle

The lump may be tethered or fixed to the underlying muscle (e.g. pectoralis major).

▶ Lumps that are attached to the underlying muscle can be moved to some degree if the muscle is relaxed but are less mobile if the muscle is tensed.

- Ask the patient to rest her hand on her hip with the arm relaxed.
- Hold the lump between your thumb and forefingers and estimate its mobility by moving it in two planes at right angles to each other (e.g. up/down and left/right).
- Ask the patient to press her hand against her hip causing contraction of the pectoralis major. Repeat the mobility exercise.

Immobile lumps

If a lump is immobile in all situations, it may have spread to involve the bony chest wall (e.g. in the upper half of the breast or axilla) or may be a lump arising from the chest wall.

The nipple

If the patient complains of nipple discharge, ask her to gently squeeze and express any discharge, noting colour, presence of blood and smell.

- Milky, serous, or green-brown discharges are almost always benign.
- A bloody discharge may indicate neoplasia (e.g. papilloma or cancer).

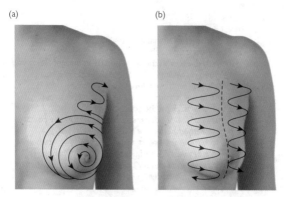

Fig. 15.5 Two methods for the systematic palpation of the breast. (a) Work circumferentially from the areola. (b) Examine each half at a time, working from top to bottom.

Examining beyond the breast

Lymph nodes

The technique is described in detail in ➲ Chapter 3.

Support the patient's arm. For example, when examining the right axilla, abduct the patient's right arm gently and support it at the wrist with your right hand whilst examining the axilla with your left hand.

Examine the main sets of axillary nodes including:

- Central.
- Lateral.
- Medial (pectoral).
- Infraclavicular.
- Supraclavicular (Fig. 15.6).
- Apical.

If you feel any lymph nodes, consider site, size, number, consistency, tenderness, fixation, and overlying skin changes.

Remember to also palpate for lymph nodes in the lower deep cervical lymph chain at the same time as the supraclavicular nodes.

The rest of the body

If cancer is suspected, it is worth performing a full general examination, keeping in mind the common sites of metastasis of breast cancer. Examine especially the lungs, liver, skin, skeleton, and central nervous system.

Skills station 15.1

Instruction

Examine this patient's breasts.

Model technique

- Clean your hands
- Introduce yourself
- Explain the purpose of examination, obtain informed consent
- Ask for any painful areas you should avoid
- Ask the patient to undress to the waist and to sit upright facing you
- Look for asymmetry, swellings, ulceration, skin changes, scars
- Repeat the inspection with the patient's arms crossed over her head and tensed at her hips (to tense the pectoral muscles)
- Ask the patient to lie back on the couch as in Fig. 15.4
- Using the palmar surface of your first three fingers, gently palpate the entire breast, remembering the axillary tail
  - Remember to elevate the breast and inspect and palpate below
- Palpate the nipple between index finger and thumb. Massage to express any discharge and carefully collect in a universal container
- Palpate the axillary lymph nodes
- Palpate the supraclavicular and cervical lymph nodes
- Examine the opposite side
- Thank the patient and ask them to re-dress.

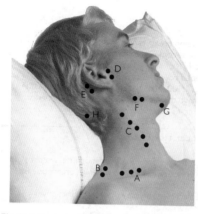

A = Supraclavicular
B = Posterior triangle
C = Jugular chain
D = Preauricular
E = Postauricular
F = Submandibular
G = Submental
H = Occipital

Fig. 15.6 Cervical and supraclavicular lymph nodes.

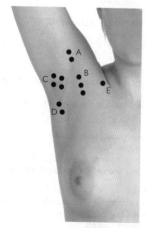

A = Lateral
B = Pectoral
C = Central
D = Subscapular
E = Infraclavicular

Fig. 15.7 Axillary lymph nodes.

Breast cancer

Background

- 1 in 9 women will develop breast cancer in their lifetime (most >50).
- Breast cancer is the most common cancer in women worldwide. It accounts for about 25% of all female malignancies, with a higher proportion in developed countries (see Box 15.2).
  - Male:female ratio is 1:100. Male patients present with the same physical signs and have the same prognosis as female patients.
- Over 1,000,000 new cases occur each year worldwide.

Box 15.2 Breast cancer risk factors

- Female
- Increasing age (80% of cases occur in postmenopausal women)
- Previous history of breast cancer, previous benign breast disease
- Not breastfeeding long term
- Use of hormone replacement therapy or oral contraceptives
- Family history of breast cancer
- No children or few children
- Having children late (especially over 30)
- Early puberty; late menopause
- Obesity (for postmenopausal women only)
- High consumption of alcohol
- Geographical (e.g. higher in Northern Europe, USA).

Symptoms

- 75% symptomatic, 25% present through screening.
  - Patients may present reporting a breast lump, nipple changes, skin changes, or symptoms of metastases
  - 1% of patients present with pain as the only symptom.

Triple assessment

All suspected breast cancer cases should have 'triple assessment':

- Clinical history and examination.
- Radiological examination (e.g. mammography, ultrasound).
- Pathological examination (e.g. fine needle aspiration/biopsy).

Inflammatory breast cancer

- Presents with oedematous, indurated, and inflamed skin. Skin may be red, hot, and itchy (easily misdiagnosed as mastitis).
- Accounts for 1–5% of all breast cancers.
- Prognosis is very poor (5-year survival 25–50%).
- Not usually associated with a lump and may be difficult to diagnose by mammography or ultrasound. MRI may be useful.

Examination findings

Inspection

- There may be no features visible on inspection.
  - Mass or dimpling
  - When there is lymphatic invasion the overlying skin has an oedematous look or *peau d'orange* (orange peel)
  - In late disease ulceration may be present
  - Nipples may be normal or show inversion, destruction, deviation, or be associated with a bloody discharge (see Box 15.3)
  - Paget's disease of the nipple/areola looks like eczema.

Palpation

- Hard, non-tender lump (may be impalpable).
  - 50% occur in the upper-outer quadrant.
- Indistinct surface with exact shape often difficult to define.
- The lump can be tethered or fixed to the skin, surrounding breast tissue, or chest wall.
- Look for axillary or supraclavicular lymphadenopathy.
  - May present with lymphoedema of the affected arm.

Further examination

- A full systems examination should be conducted, searching for evidence of metastasis.

Box 15.3 Nipple discharge

- 10% due to neoplasia (papilloma or cancer)
- ▶ Commonest symptom of cancer after 'lump'
- ❶ Beware of neoplasia if discharge is blood-stained, persistent, and from a single duct
- Multiple duct creamy discharge is often due to duct ectasia
- Bilateral galactorrhoea is usually medication-induced in the absence of pregnancy or beyond six months post-partum. The most common pathological cause is pituitary tumour.

Other important presentations

Fibroadenoma

Background and epidemiology

- Benign tumours that represent a hyperplastic or proliferative process in a single terminal ductal unit. The cause is unknown.
- Reducing incidence with increasing age; majority occur before the age of 30. Higher incidence in those taking the oral contraceptive pill.
  - May involute in postmenopausal women. May grow rapidly during pregnancy, hormone replacement therapy, or immunosuppression.
- Most stop growing after they reach 2–3cm.
  - Rule of thirds: 1/3 enlarge, 1/3 stay the same size, 1/3 get smaller.

Symptoms

- Often asymptomatic.

Examination findings

- Typically a smooth, mobile palpable lump.
- No fixation to skin or deep tissues.
- May occur in any area of breast.
  - Like other lumps, occurs especially in the upper-outer quadrant.
- Non-tender.
- Normally solitary but may be multiple.
- No lymphadenopathy.

Cysts

Background and epidemiology

- Can appear suddenly and cause pain.
- Commonest palpable lump in women aged 30–50 years.
  - Subareolar main duct cysts may occur in those aged 10–20 years.
- Related to oestrogen metabolism.
  - Can be perpetuated by hormone replacement therapy in women >50.
- Can coexist with cancer.

Symptoms

- Often asymptomatic and incidentally picked up on imaging.
- Patient may complain of a palpable, visible, or painful lump.

Examination findings

- Round, smooth, symmetrical, discrete lump.
- May be mobile or tender.
- May range from soft to hard.
- It is rare to be able to elicit fluctuance, fluid thrill, or transillumination.

Fat necrosis

This can occur after trauma and the physical signs can mimic cancer (e.g. a firm hard lump with skin tethering).

Abscesses

Mainly occur during childbearing years and are often associated with trauma to the nipple during breastfeeding.

Present with a painful, spherical lump with surrounding oedema. They often show additional signs of inflammation (hot, red). The patient may have constitutional symptoms such as malaise, night sweats, hot flushes, and rigors.

Most recurrent or chronic breast abscesses occur in association with duct ectasia or periductal mastitis. The associated periductal fibrosis can often lead to nipple retraction.

Abnormal nipple and areola

Diseases of the nipple are important because they must be differentiated from malignancy and cause concern to patients.

Unilateral retraction or distortion of a nipple is a common sign of breast carcinoma; as is blood-stained nipple discharge. The latter suggests an intra-ductal carcinoma or benign papilloma.

A unilateral red, crusted, and scaling areola suggests an underlying carcinoma (Paget's disease of the breast) or, more commonly, eczema. Ask the patient if she has eczema at other sites and examine appropriately.

Mastitis

Puerperal mastitis
- Most commonly seen in the first 6 weeks of breastfeeding.
- Caused by staphylococcal infection of ducts.

Periductal mastitis
- Mean age is 32 years and there is an increased incidence in smokers.
- Recurs in up to 50% due to persistence of underlying diseased duct.
- Mammary duct fistula:
  - Communication between the skin and a major subareolar breast duct
  - Develops in 1/3 of non-lactating periareolar abscesses.

Non-puerperal mastitis
- In many cases, starts as non-bacterial inflammation. Risk of recurrence, secondary infection, and abscess formation is high.
- Risk factors: smoking, diabetes, trauma, hyperprolactinaemia.

Symptoms
- Pain, tenderness, swelling (80%).
- Redness (80% cases).
- Lump or diffuse swelling of the breast.
- Systemic features of infection.

Examination findings
- Skin of affected area is red, hot, and tender.
- A cracked nipple may be evident.
- There may be a discrete tender lump or diffuse swelling.
- There may be ipsilateral tender axillary lymphadenopathy.
- If there is abscess formation, this may be evident as a firm, tender lump initially which may then develop into a fluctuant swelling.

The psychiatric assessment

Approach to the psychiatric assessment

In taking a psychiatric history and assessing mental state, it is crucial to communicate to the patient with empathy, respect, competence, and interest in a non-judgemental fashion. This approach will create an atmosphere of trust that encourages the patient to talk honestly about their innermost feelings and thoughts.

Central to the psychiatric interview is the art of active listening and an awareness of any unspoken feelings between patient and assessor.

Be prepared to spend anywhere from 30 minutes to an hour, depending on the circumstances, conducting an interview. This might seem a daunting task in the early stages, particularly as patients rarely find a narrative. However, staying on track is often made easier by remembering to write out the headings for parts of the assessment in advance. Use A4 paper and number the pages.

Preparation and preliminary considerations

The room

Before proceeding to questioning, adequate preparations should be made regarding the place where the assessment is to be carried out. An interview room should be a safe environment, especially when seeing a patient who is potentially violent.

- Inform your colleagues of your location.
- You should know where to locate, and how to use, the panic button.
- You should ideally be accompanied by a colleague if you are seeing a patient with a history of violence.
- Remove any objects that might pose a danger (i.e. those that can be used as a weapon).
- Know your nearest exit point and ensure that it is open or unblocked.
- Never allow the patient to come between you and the door.
- Ensure adequate privacy and lighting.
- Ideally, the patient should be sitting off-centre, so that all of their body may be seen but without the situation appearing too threatening.
- The height of your seats should be equal or similar.

Conduct of the interview

Begin by introducing yourself, explaining who you are and the purpose of your assessment. Use a handshake—a widespread sign of introduction and welcome. Establish whether or not the patient wishes a friend or relative to be present (and whether you feel it is appropriate).

The interview should generally start in an informal way to establish a friendly and concerned rapport, this might involve a short period of neutral conversation.

Try to avoid leading or direct questions. Remember to use relatively broad 'open' general questions and increase the level of specific 'closed' questions for further clarification. Allow breaks and digressions within reason, especially with sensitive individuals. At appropriate intervals, clarification of what the patient has said by repeating sentences and asking them to confirm is a useful strategy.

Examination

In psychiatry, you should be examining the patient's mental state and this is described in Box 16.1. However, don't overlook physical examination as this is often an important part of the assessment. Physical examination is described elsewhere in this book.

Box 16.1 Framework for the psychiatric assessment

History
- Name, age, marital status, occupation, ethnic origin, and religion
- Source, mode, and reason for referral
- Presenting complaint
- History of presenting complaint
- Risk assessment
- Past psychiatric history
- Past medical history
- Drug history
- Family history
- Personal history
  - Birth and early development
  - School
  - Occupational history
  - Psychosexual history
  - Marital history
  - Children
  - Forensic history.
- Premorbid personality
- Social history.

Mental state examination
- Appearance and behaviour
- Speech
- Mood
- Thought content
- Perception
- Cognitive functioning
- Insight.

Physical examination
- As appropriate—described elsewhere in the book.

The history (part 1)

The psychiatric history is very similar in structure to the standard medical history described in ➜ Chapter 2. Symptoms and issues should be dealt with in the same way (see Boxes 16.2 and 16.3).

Demographics

Start by making a note of the patient's name, age, marital status, occupation, ethnic origin, and religion.

Source, mode, and reason for referral

Record here all the information you have about the patient from other sources—relatives, carers, social workers, counsellors, primary care team, and police.

- Who has asked for the individual to be seen and why?
- What was the mode of referral—informal or formal (under section of the Mental Health Act?).

Presenting complaint

Obtain a brief description of the principal complaint(s) and the time frame of the problem in the individual's own words.

This can, of course, be difficult if the patient is psychotic and does not believe a problem exists. In these cases, try to comment on the presenting complaint as described by an informant.

History of presenting complaint

This is a detailed account of the presenting problems in chronological order (as for any other kind of symptom as in ➜ Chapter 2) including:

- Onset of illness (when was the patient last well?).
- How did the condition develop?
- The severity of the patient's symptoms.
- Precipitating factors (including any significant life events preceding the onset of the symptoms).
- Exacerbating factors (what makes the symptoms worse?).
- Relieving factors (what makes the symptoms better?).
- How has it affected his/her daily life, pattern, or routine (effect on interpersonal relationships, working capacity, etc.)?
- Treatment history.
  - Include treatment tried during the course of the present illness, previous drug treatments, electroconvulsive therapy, and psychosocial interventions.
- Associated symptoms.
- Systematic enquiry.
  - Similar to the standard medical history, run through other psychiatric symptoms and ask the patient if they have experienced them
  - Explore related symptoms—for example, if the patient admits to some depressive symptoms, ask about other symptoms of depression.

Box 16.2 (S)OC(R)ATES

Exactly as in ➜ Chapter 2, you should establish the factors relating to a psychiatric symptom just as you would a physical symptom (see Box 2.5). Obviously, 'site' and 'radiation' do not quite translate to a psychiatric history.

Remember that the patient may not regard their issue as a 'symptom' so tailor your language carefully.

- The exact nature of the symptom
- The onset:
  - The date it began
  - How it began (e.g. suddenly, gradually—over how long?)
  - If long-standing, why is the patient seeking help now?
- Periodicity and frequency:
  - Is the symptom constant or intermittent?
  - How long does it last each time?
  - What is the exact manner in which it comes and goes?
- Change over time:
  - Is it improving or deteriorating?
- Exacerbating factors:
  - What makes the symptom worse?
- Relieving factors:
  - What makes the symptom better?
- Associated symptoms.

Box 16.3 Tailoring the history

In the taking of a history in any specialty, you should mould your questions and the situation depending on what is said. Also, information may not be provided by the patient in the order you would like.

This is particularly true of psychiatry—if they are talking freely, you may find the patient providing information that comes under a number of different sub-headings in your history. You should be flexible, note the information in the appropriate places, and then 'fill in the gaps' with direct questions.

The history (part 2)

Past psychiatric history

Explore in detail previous contact with psychiatry and other services for mental health problems. Include as far as possible:

- Dates of illness, symptoms, diagnoses, treatments, hospitalizations, previous outpatient treatment, compulsory treatment under the Mental Health Act.

Past medical history

This should be evaluated in the same way as in the general medical history but remember to ask in particular about obstetric complications, epilepsy, head injuries, and thyroid disorders.

Drug and alcohol history

- Ask about all current drug intake including prescribed and over-the-counter medicines.
- Take a detailed history of substance abuse if relevant, recording type, quality, source, route of administration, and cost.
- Remember to ask about alcohol, tobacco, and any allergic reactions. If necessary, use the CAGE questionnaire (→ Chapter 2).

Family history

Explore family relationships in detail (parents, siblings, spouse, children).

It is useful to draw a family tree and record age, health, occupation, personality, quality of relationship, family history of mental illness including alcoholism, suicide, deliberate self-harm, as well as any other serious family illnesses.

Also record the details and times of certain important family events, such as death, separation, or divorce, and their impact on the patient.

Personal history

The personal history is a chronological account of the individual's life from birth up to the present. This section, which is often lengthy, should be tackled under the following subheadings:

Birth and early development

- The place and date of birth, gestation at delivery, and any obstetric complications or birth injuries.
- Enquire about developmental milestones.
- Ask about 'neurotic traits' in childhood (night terrors, sleep walking, bedwetting, temper-tantrums, stammer, feeding difficulties).
- Ask about relationships with peers, siblings, parents, and relatives.
- Record any adverse experiences (physical or emotional abuse).
- Note any significant life events such as separations and bereavement.

School

- Explore the school experiences: socially, academically, and athletically.
- Record the start and end of their education and qualifications.
- Ask about the type of school, relationships with peers, teachers, interest in games, and whether there was a history of truancy.

Occupational history
- Enquire about all previous jobs held, dates, and reason for change, level of satisfaction with employment and ambitions.
- Include present job and economic circumstances.

Psychosexual history

This can be a rather difficult section of the history to elicit and is often dependent on how willing the patient is to volunteer such intimate details. However, try not to avoid it. It may have to be excluded if judged inappropriate or likely to cause distress.
- Record the onset of puberty (and menarche if female).
- Sexual orientation (hetero-, homo-, or bisexual).
- First sexual encounter.
- Current sexual practices (including practice of safe sex?).
- Any sexual difficulties or sexual abuse.

Marital history

This includes a detailed account of number of marriages, duration, quality of relationships and personality, age, and occupations of spouses, and reason for break-up of relationship(s).

Children

Sex, age, mental, and physical health of all children.

Forensic history

This may or may not be volunteered by the patient. Begin by asking non-threatening questions. 'Have you ever been in trouble with the law?'
- Ask about criminal record and any previous episodes of violence or other acts of aggression.

Premorbid personality

This is the patient's personality before the onset of mental illness. An independent account is especially important for this part of the history.
- It may help to ask the patient how they would describe themselves and how they think others would describe them.
- Ask about social relationships and supports.
- Include interests, and recreational activities.
- Enquire specifically about temperament—what's their mood like on most occasions?
- Ask the patient to describe the nature of their emotional reactions, coping mechanisms, and character (e.g. shy, suspicious, irritable, impulsive, lacking in confidence, obsessional).
- What are their moral and religious beliefs?

Social history

Ask especially about finances, legal problems, occupation, dependants, and housing. If elderly, ask about social support such as home care, attendance at a day centre and how they cope with activities of daily living (hygiene, mobility, domestic activity).

Risk assessment

This includes not only an assessment of self-harm but also of the possibility of harm to others (Boxes 16.4–16.6). This should be broached in a serious and sensitive manner. Some useful questions in assessing suicide risk:

- How do you feel about the future?
- Does life seem worth living?
- Do you have thoughts of hurting or harming yourself?
- Have you ever thought of ending it all?

If suicidal thoughts are present, enquire as to how often they occur and if the patient has made a specific plan—and what the plan is.

- Ask about the means e.g. prescribed and over-the-counter drugs, guns, knives.
- Explore for feelings of excessive guilt and loss of self-esteem.

Previous history of self-harm

Ask about previous attempts—when, where, how, and why. Ask in detail about the most recent attempt:

- What events led up to the attempt?
- Were there any specific precipitating factors?
- Was there concurrent use of drugs and alcohol?
- What were the methods used?
- Was it planned?
- Was there a suicide note?
- Were there any active attempts made to avoid being discovered?
- What is the meaning of the action (wanted to die, share distress)?
- Also ask about the circumstances surrounding discovery and how they were brought to medical attention (if at all).
- Was this what he/she expected?

Protective factors for suicide

The factors that would stop a person attempting suicide. Record what social supports are available to the person (friends, CPN, church, GP, etc.).

Assessing homicidal intent

If faced with patient expressing homicidal intent, you should inform a senior colleague and/or the police immediately.

Some helpful questions to assess a homicidal/violent patient include:

- Are you upset with anyone?
- Do you have thoughts of hurting anyone?
- Have you made plans to harm someone?
- How would you harm them? (It is important to establish whether the patient has actually made plans for carrying out the action.)

Box 16.4 Protective factors for suicide

- Strong family and social connections
- Hopefulness, good skills in problem solving
- Cultural or religious beliefs discouraging suicide
- Responsibility for children.

Box 16.5 Factors that may precipitate suicide

The over-riding theme here is 'loss'. Loss of occupation, independency, family member, friend, social supports, or freedom.

- Death, separation, or divorce
- Imprisonment, or threat of
- Humiliating event
- Job loss
- A reminder of a past loss
- Unwanted pregnancy.

Box 16.6 Risk factors for suicide

Biological
- Age >40 years
- Male sex.

Medical and psychiatric history
- Previous suicide attempts
- Previous deliberate self-harm
- Psychiatric disorder (depression, substance misuse, schizophrenia, personality disorder, obsessive–compulsive disorder, panic disorder)
- Chronic physical illness
- History of trauma or abuse
- Substance misuse (including alcohol).

Personality
Impulsivity, poor problem-solving skills, aggression, perfectionism, low self-esteem.

Family history
Suicide or parasuicide, depression, substance misuse.

Social
- Lack of social support, isolation
  - Unemployment/retired
  - Single/unmarried/divorced/widowed.
- High-risk occupation: high rates in farmers, pharmacists, and doctors (especially psychiatrists and anaesthetists)
  - These occupations have lethal means available (farmers = guns, doctors and pharmacists = drugs).

Access to means
This may be through occupation or social activities.

▶ For more information, we recommend the factsheets produced by the British mental health charity 'Mind' which can be found at ♪ http://www.mind.org.uk/help

Mental state examination

The mental state examination is a vital part of the psychiatric assessment. It is your assessment of the patient's mental state based on your observations and interaction. It begins as soon as you see the patient. Mental state features prior to the interview, whether described by the patient or by other informants, are considered part of the history (Box 16.7).

Box 16.7 Framework for the mental state examination

- Appearance and behaviour
- Speech
- Mood and affect
- Thought content
  - Preoccupations
  - Abnormal beliefs
- Perception
  - Disorders of self-awareness
  - Illusions
  - Hallucinations
  - Sensory distortions
- Cognitive function
- Insight
- Summary.
  - Include a statement of diagnosis or differential diagnosis, aetiological factors, and a plan for further investigations and management.

Appearance and behaviour

This involves a brief descriptive note of your observations, both at first contact and through the interview process. It should include:

- Dress and grooming.
  - Evidence of self-neglect? (e.g. seen in depression or drug abuse)
  - Flamboyant clothes with clashing colours? (e.g. in mania)
  - Loose-fitting clothes (may indicate an underlying anorexia or other eating disorder).
- Facial appearance including eye contact.
- Degree of co-operation.
- Posture.
- Mannerisms.
- Motor activity.
  - Excessive movement indicating agitation?
  - Very little movement (retardation) suggesting depression?
- Abnormal movements.
  - e.g. tics, chorea, tremor, stereotypy—repetitive movements such as rocking or rubbing hands.
- Gait.

Speech

Describe in terms of:

- Rate.
- Quantity.
  - Increased = 'pressure of speech' and is often associated with flight of ideas (see Box 16.8)
  - Decreased = known as 'poverty of speech'.
- Fluency.
- Articulation.
  - Including stammering, stuttering, and dysarthria.
- Form.
  - This is the *way* in which a person speaks rather than actual content (Box 16.8).

Box 16.8 Some examples of abnormal speech/ thought form

The following are examples of abnormal speech—however, the speech is a manifestation of the underlying thought processes. One could argue, therefore, that the following are abnormalities of *thought form*.

- *Flight of ideas:* associated with mania. Ideas flow rapidly but remain connected although sometimes by unusual associations. The patient's train of thought tends to veer on wild tangents
- *Derailment:* loosening of association seen in formal thought disorders (e.g. schizophrenia) in which 'train' of thought slips off the 'track'. Things may be said in juxtaposition that lack a meaningful association or the patient may shift from one frame of reference to another
- *Perseveration:* mainly seen in dementia and frontal lobe damage. The patient finds moving to the next topic difficult, resulting in an inappropriate repetition of a response
- *Incoherence:* a pattern of speech that is essentially incomprehensible at times
- *Echolalia:* a feature of dementia. A repetitive pattern of speech in which a patient echoes words or phrases said by the interviewer
- *Neologisms:* found mainly in schizophrenia and structural brain disease. The invention of new words with no meaning. Sometimes this term is also used for an abnormal usage of an existing word, sometimes called a 'semantic extension'
- *Circumstantiality:* a long-winded pattern of speech loaded down with unnecessary detail and digression before finally getting to the point. The patient is, however, able to maintain the train of thought.

Mood and affect

'Mood' is a pervasive and sustained emotion that can colour the patient's perception of the world over long periods. 'Affect' is the patient's immediate emotional state, including the external expression.

Examining mood and affect involves consideration of the patient's subjective emotional state and your objective evaluation.

Abnormalities of mood include depression, elation, euphoria, anxiety, and anger. It should be noted whether mood is consistent with thought and action or 'incongruous'.

Abnormalities of affect include:

- *Blunting:* the coarsening of emotions and an insensitivity to social context. This is often used synonymously with 'affective flattening'.
- *'Flattening of affect':* this is a reduction in range and depth of outward emotion.
- *Lability:* superficially fluctuating and poorly controlled emotions. May be found in delirium, dementias, frontal lobe damage, and intoxication.

Thought content

Preoccupations

These include phenomena such as obsessional thoughts, or ruminations which are characterized by an intrusive preoccupation with a topic. The patient cannot stop thinking about it even though they may realize that it is irrational.

Phobias represent a fear or anxiety which is out of proportion to the situation, cannot be reasoned or explained away and leads to avoidance behaviour.

Other types of ruminations particularly important to establish here include suicidal or homicidal thoughts in addition to morbid ideation (e.g. ideas of guilt, unworthiness, burden, and blame).

Abnormal beliefs

Overvalued ideas

These are isolated beliefs which are not obsessional in nature and pre-occupy an individual to the extent of dominating their life. That is, the patient is able to stop thinking about them but they choose not to.

The core belief of anorexia nervosa—the belief that one is fat—is an example of an overvalued idea. Other examples include unusual sect or cult beliefs, forms of morbid jealousy, and hypochondriasis.

Delusions

These are fixed false beliefs which are based on an incorrect inference about reality, not consistent with a patient's intelligence and cultural background (Box 16.9). Importantly, these cannot be corrected by reasoning. They can sometimes be difficult to differentiate from overvalued ideas. The difference is that the patient firmly believes the delusion to be true.

Delusions may be 'primary' with no discernible connection with any previous experience or mood (characteristic of schizophrenia) or 'secondary' to an abnormal mood state or perception. In this way, the content of the delusions can give a clue to the nature of the mental illness.

Box 16.9 Some examples of delusions and associated terminology

- *Mood congruent delusion:* a delusion with content that has an association to mood. For example, a depressed person may believe that the world is ending
- *Mood incongruent delusion:* a delusion with content that has no association to mood. Seen in schizophrenia
- *Nihilistic delusion:* a false feeling that self, others, or the world is nonexistent or coming to an end
- *Paranoid delusion:* this is any delusion that is self-referent. In psychiatry, 'paranoid' does not carry the lay meaning of 'fearful/suspicious'
- *Delusions of reference:* a false belief that others are talking about you or that events are somehow connected with you. For example, the patient may believe that people on TV or radio are actually talking directly to them. The feelings and delusional messages received are usually negative in some way but the fact that the patient alone is being spoken to has a grandiose quality
- *Delusion of grandeur:* an exaggerated perception of importance, power, or identity. Usually, patients believe that they have made an important achievement that has not been suitably recognized
- *Delusions of control:* a false belief that a person's will, thoughts, or feeling are being controlled by external forces
- These include disorders of the possession of thought
  - *Thought broadcasting* is the false belief that the patient's thoughts can be heard by others
  - *Thought insertion* is the belief that an outside force, person, or persons are putting thoughts in the patient's mind; whilst thought withdrawal is the belief that thoughts are being removed
  - *Thought echo:* the belief that one can hear their thoughts being spoken aloud
  - *Thought blocking* is the experience of having your train of thought suddenly halted.
- *Passivity feelings:* these are delusions of control. They may include 'made acts and impulses' where the individual feels they are being made to do something by another, 'made movements' where patients believe their limbs are controlled by someone else, 'made emotions' where they are experiencing someone else's emotions
- *Erotomania:* a belief that another person is in love with the patient, often misinterpreting innocent glances
- *The Capgras delusion:* a belief that those around you (often loved ones) have been removed and replaced with exact replicas. They exist in a world of impersonators. The delusion may extend to include animals and objects—the feeling that they are in a duplicated world. The patient may even believe that he is his own double
- *Religious delusions:* these are any delusions with a religious or spiritual content. ❗ Careful here! Beliefs that would be considered normal for a person's religious or cultural background (e.g. a Christian believing that God has cured their illness) are not classed as delusions.

Perception

Alterations in normal perception consist of changes to our normal, familiar awareness or ordinary experiences. These include sensory distortions (heightened or dulled perception), sensory deceptions (illusions and hallucinations), and disorder of self-awareness (depersonalization, derealization).

Disorders of self-awareness

- Depersonalization is the feeling that the body is strange and unreal.
- Derealization is the perception of objects in the external world as being strange and unreal.

Both the above phenomena commonly occur in stressful situations, with drug intoxication, anxiety, depressive disorders, and schizophrenia. Many psychologically normal people can experience an element of derealization or depersonalization if sleep-deprived.

Illusions

An illusion is a misperception or misinterpretation of real sensory stimuli. It may affect any sensory modality. Enquire as to when they occur and what significance they have.

Illusions frequently arise from a sensory impairment such as partial sightedness or deafness and represent an understandable attempt at 'filling in the gap'. Most people have experienced some form of visual illusions—for example, mistaking a distant object for a person, particularly in poor lighting (e.g. at night).

Hallucinations

A hallucination is a false perception which is not based on a real external stimulus. It is experienced as true and coming from the outside world (Box 16.10).

They may occur in any sensory modality, although visual and auditory hallucinations are the commonest.

Importantly, hallucinations do not necessarily point to psychiatric disease. For example, some hallucinations occur in normal people, when falling asleep (hypnagogic) or on waking (hypnopompic) and, although the nature of dreams is heavily debated, it could be said that they are hallucinations. Note also the Charles Bonnet syndrome (Box 16.11).

Sensory distortions

This includes heightened perception with especially vivid sensations (e.g. hyperacusis), dulled perception, and 'changed perception'. For example, patients may experience objects as having a changed shape, size, or colour.

Box 16.10 Some examples of hallucinations
- *Auditory hallucinations:* false perception of sounds, usually voices but also other noises such as music. The hallucination of voices may be classed as 2nd person where the voice is speaking to the patient ('you should do this') or 3rd person where the voice or voices are talking about the patient ('he should do this')
- *Visual hallucinations:* false perceptions involving both formed (e.g. faces, people) and unformed (e.g. lights, shadows) images
- *Scenic or panoramic hallucinations:* a form of visual hallucination involving whole scenes such as battles
- *Olfactory hallucinations:* the false perception of odours
- *Gustatory hallucinations:* the false perception of taste
- *Tactile hallucinations:* the false perception of touch or surface sensation (e.g. phantom limb; crawling sensation in or under skin in delirium tremens—formication)
- *Somatic hallucination:* the false sensation of things occurring in or to the body, most often visceral in origin. Somatic hallucinations include haptic (touch, tickling, pricking), thermic (heat/cold), and kinaesthetic (movement and joint position)
- *Pseudohallucinations:* these are recognized as not being 'real' by the patient, acquiring an 'as if' quality, and have some degree of voluntary control.

Box 16.11 Charles Bonnet syndrome
We highlight this particular syndrome as it is a good example of hallucinations in a psychiatrically normal patient. In this syndrome, patients with some kind of visual impairment (usually older people) see visual hallucinations within the area of impaired vision.

The hallucinations are often cartoon-like characters or faces. For example, the authors once came across a patient with a visual scotoma due to retinal injury. The voice of our Irish consultant would trigger the hallucination of a leprechaun dancing and cavorting within their blind spot.

The syndrome is also an example of pseudohallucination as, often, the patient realizes that the visions are not real.

It was described by the Swiss philosopher Charles Bonnet in 1760, whose 87-year-old grandfather admitted seeing visions of buildings and people after developing severe cataracts in both eyes.

Charles Bonnet syndrome is likely much more common than most medical people realize. The elderly sufferers are often afraid to admit to it for fear of being diagnosed with a psychiatric disorder or being labelled 'mad'.

Cognitive function

Cognition can be described as the mental processes of appraisal, judgement, memory, and reasoning.

Notes on conducting the Mini-Mental State Examination (MMSE)

It is important to remember that there are no half marks in this test—be strict and rigorous. The maximum total score is 30 (Box 16.12).

- *Orientation:* rather than asking for each part of the date in turn, ask the patient for today's date and then ask specifically for those parts omitted. Do the same for place ('where are we now?').
- *Registration:* say the name of the objects clearly and slowly, allowing about 1 second to say each. The first repetition determines the patient's score ... but keep repeating the names of the objects until the patient has got all three to enable testing of recall later.
- *Attention and calculation:* if the patient can't perform this mathematical task, ask them to spell the word 'WORLD' backwards. The score is the number of letters in the correct order (e.g. dlrow = 5, dlorw = 3).
- *Repetition:* allow one trial. Score 1 only if the repetition is completely correct. Speak slowly and clearly so that the patient can hear.
- *Three-stage command:* say all three stages of the command before giving the piece of paper to the patient. Do not prompt the patient as you go. Score 1 point for each part conducted correctly.
- *Reading:* say 'read this sentence and do what it says'. Score 1 point if the patient closes their eyes. No points if they simply read the sentence out loud.
- *Writing:* be sure not to dictate a sentence or give any examples. The sentence must make sense and contain a subject and a verb. Correct grammar, punctuation, and spelling are not necessary.
- *Copying:* all 10 angles must be present and 2 lines must intersect. Ignore mistakes from tremor and ignore rotation of the diagram.

Interpreting the final score

The MMSE score will vary within the normal population by age and the number of years in education (decreasing with advancing age and increasing with advancing schooling). The median score is 29 for people with 9 years of education, 26 for 5–8 years of education, and 22 for 0–4 years.

Scores of <23 are taken to indicate mild, <17 moderate and <10 severe cognitive impairment. This is a non-linear scale, however.

Insight

This is how well the patient is able to understand or explain their condition. When assessing insight, ask:

- Does he/she recognize and accept that they are suffering from a mental or physical illness?
- Are they willing to accept treatment and agree to a management plan?

Note also whether an individual's attitudes are constructive or unconstructive, realistic or unrealistic.

If not accepting of a psychiatric diagnosis, to what does the patient attribute their difficulties or abnormal experiences?

Box 16.12 The Mini-Mental State Examination (MMSE)

Orientation (10)
(5) What is the (year), (season), (day), (date), (month)?
(5) Where are we: (country), (county), (town), (hospital), (floor/ward)?

Registration (3)
Name three unrelated objects. Allow one second to say each. Then ask the patient to repeat all three after you have said them. Give one point for each correct answer (e.g. ball, car, man).

Attention and calculation (5)
Ask the patient to take 7 from 100, and again ... total of 5 times. Give one point for each correct answer. Stop after five answers (93, 86, 79, 72, 65). Alternatively, spell WORLD *backwards* giving one mark for each letter in the correct order—see notes on p. 512.

Recall (3)
Ask patient to recall the three objects previously stated. Give one point for each correct answer.

Naming (2)
Show patient a watch and ask them what it is. Repeat for a pen/pencil.

Repetition (1)
Ask the patient to repeat the following: 'No ifs, ands, or buts.'

Three-stage command (3)
Ask the patient to follow these instructions: 'take this paper in your left hand, fold it in half, and put it on the floor'. Give the patient a piece of paper and score 1 for each stage completed correctly.

Reading (1)
Write 'CLOSE YOUR EYES' on a piece of paper, ask the patient to read and obey what it says.

Writing (1)
Ask the patient to write a sentence.

Copying (1)
Ask patient to copy the following design.

Maximum total score = 30

Folstein MF, Folstein SE, and McHugh PR (1975). Mini-mental State: a practical method for grading the state of patients for the clinician, *Journal of Psychiatric Research*, 12: 189–98.

Important presentations

Schizophrenia

The term schizophrenia* is often described as a single disease but the diagnostic category includes a group of disorders, probably with heterogeneous causes, but with somewhat similar behavioural symptoms and signs. It is a psychosis, characterized by 'splitting' of normal links between perception, mood, thinking, behaviour, and contact with reality.

The prevalence of schizophrenia is approximately 0.5% worldwide with equal incidence in both sexes. The onset is usually in adolescence or early adulthood. Symptoms tend to remit, although a return to baseline is unusual.

Clinical features

Schizophrenia is characterized by delusions and hallucinations with no insight. These symptoms are often followed by a decline in social functioning. Historically, several different diagnostic classifications have been developed (Box 16.13).

Bleuler's four As

In 1910, Bleuler coined the term 'schizophrenia'. He went on to characterize the key features, summarized as the 'four As'.

- Associative loosening (disconnected, incoherent thought process).
- Ambivalence (the ability to experience two opposing emotions at the same time—e.g. loving and hating a person).
- Affective incongruity (affect disassociated with thought).
- Autism (self-absorption and the withdrawal into a fantasy world).

Crow's positive and negative symptoms

In 1980, Crow[1] suggested that the symptoms of schizophrenia could be divided into two distinct groups—those that are 'positive' and those that are 'negative'. This remains a useful way to think of the symptoms.

Crow went on to suggest that schizophrenia could be split into two syndromes, comprising mostly positive or negative symptoms respectively.

Positive symptoms

- Delusions (including ideas of reference).
- Hallucinations.
- Thought disorder.

Negative symptoms

- Blunted affect.
- Anhedonia (lack of enjoyment).
- Avolition (lack of motivation).
- Alogia (poverty of speech).
- Social withdrawal.
- Self-neglect.

---

* Schizophrenia comes through Latin from the Greek *skhizein* 'to split' and *phren* 'mind'. The term 'phrenic', as readers will know, refers also to the diaphragm. This is because in ancient Greece, the mind was thought to lie in the diaphragm.

Schneider's first-rank symptoms

Kurt Schneider[2] listed his 'first-rank' symptoms of schizophrenia in 1959. One of these, Schneider said, is diagnostic of schizophrenia in the absence of organic brain disease or drug intoxication.

- Third-person auditory hallucinations (running commentary, arguments, or discussions about the patient).
- Thought echo or 'echo de la pensée'.
- Disorders of thought control (withdrawal, insertion, broadcast).
- Passivity phenomena.
- Delusional perception.
- Somatic passivity.

Schneider's criteria have been criticized for being 'too narrow', providing a snapshot of a patient at only one time and for not taking into account the long-term negative symptoms.

Box 16.13 Subtypes of schizophrenia

- *Simple:* negative symptoms tend to predominate
- *Paranoid:* delusions and hallucinations are prominent and tend to include religious, grandiose, and persecutory ideas
- *Hebephrenic:* affective incongruity predominates with shallow range of mood. Delusions and hallucinations tend to lack an organized theme
- *Catatonic:* anhedonia, avolition, alogia, and poverty of movement are the key features. This may lead to a 'waxy flexibility' where the patient's limbs can be moved into, and stay in, certain positions.

Obsessive–compulsive disorder

This is characterized by time-consuming obsessions ± compulsions which cause social impairment or mental distress.

- *Obsessions* are intrusive thoughts, feelings, ideas, or sensations. They are recognized by the patient as their own (compare with 'thought insertion')—the patient usually tries to ignore or suppress them.
- *Compulsions* are conscious, purposeful behaviours which attempt to neutralize or prevent a discomfort or dreaded event. Examples include repeated hand-washing, checking, and counting.

The key here is that the obsessions and compulsions are recognized as coming from within the patient, they feel powerless to stop, and are distressed by their presence.

Severe obsessions and compulsions can occur in depression, schizophrenia, generalized anxiety disorder, panic disorder, and others.

---

[1] Crow TJ (1980). Molecular pathology of schizophrenia: More than one disease process? *British Medical Journal*, 280: 66–8.

[2] Schneider K (1959). *Clinical Psychopathology*. New York: Grune and Stratton.

Anxiety disorders

Generalized anxiety disorder (GAD)

The main feature is excessive anxiety and worry about events or activities which the patient finds difficult to control—such as work or school performance. The symptoms must be present for more than 6 months and include three or more of:

- Restlessness or feeling 'on edge'.
- Easily fatigued.
- Difficulty concentrating or 'mind goes blank'.
- Irritability.
- Muscle tension.
- Sleep disturbance (insomnia and fatigue on waking).

Panic disorder

Spontaneous occurrence of severe panic attacks (periods of fear which peak within ~10 minutes).

These should be accompanied by four or more of tachycardia, sweating, trembling or shaking, shortness of breath, a feeling of choking, chest pain, dizziness, light-headedness or presyncope, paraesthesia, depersonalization or derealization, nausea, abdominal pain, fear of dying, fear of losing control, and hot flushes.

Phobic disorders

A phobia is an irrational fear that produces an avoidance of the subject of the fear (an object, person, activity, or situation). A phobia is perceived by the patient as excessive (i.e. they have insight).

Agoraphobia

Agoraphobia* is not fear of wide open spaces per se, as is commonly thought, but is anxiety caused by being in places or situations from which escape may be difficult or in which help might not be available in the event of a panic attack. These situations may include being outside, home alone, being in a crowded place, or travelling on a bus or a train.

Social phobia

This is a fear of social situations in which the person is exposed to unfamiliar people or to possible scrutiny by others. The fear is of the resulting humiliation caused by a poor performance.

Avoidance behaviour, anticipation, or distress at the time of the social encounter leads to impairment in functioning at work or in school and can have a significant impact on the patient's life.

Other specific phobias

These are marked and persistent fears cued by the presence or anticipation of specific objects or situations. The list is manifold. Our favourites, from which no medic can suffer, include bromidrosiphobia (the fear of body odour), spermophobia (the fear of germs), belonephobia (the fear of needles), phronemophobia (the fear of thinking), iatrophobia (the fear of doctors), and, of course, pinaciphobia (the fear of lists).

* The word actually means 'fear of the market place'.

Affective disorders

Bipolar disorder

It is important to note that patients presenting only with mania, and no evident depression, are also said to have bipolar disorder. There are three main patterns of disease:

- *Bipolar I disorder:* one or more episodes of major depression with episodes of mania.
- *Bipolar II disorder:* milder bipolar disorder consisting of recurrent periods of depression and hypomania but no manic episodes.
- *Cyclothymic disorder:* characterized by frequently occurring hypomanic and depressive symptoms that do not meet the diagnostic criteria of manic episodes or major depression.

Mania

Manic episodes are characterized by profound mood disturbance, consisting of an elevated, expansive, or irritable mood that causes impairment at work or danger to others. These patients may suffer delusions and hallucinations, the former usually involving power, prestige, position, self-worth, and glory. The key feature is 'disinhibition'.

There may be several of the following:

- Inflated self-esteem or grandiosity.
- Reduced need for sleep.
- Racing thoughts, flight of ideas, and distractibility.
- Excessive talking or pressured speech.
- ↑ level of goal-focused activity at home, at work or sexually.
- Psychomotor agitation.
- Excessive involvement in pleasurable activities, often with unfortunate consequences (especially sexual indiscretions, unrestrained spending).

Depression

Depressive disorders can be classified as bipolar or unipolar and as mild, moderate, or severe. They may include somatic symptoms and psychotic symptoms (delusions and hallucinations which are usually mood-congruent) in the case of severe depression.

In general terms, features of major depression include:

- Depressed mood with feelings of worthlessness.
- Diminished interest or pleasure (anhedonia).
- Significant weight loss or gain.
- Insomnia or hypersomnia.
- Psychomotor agitation or retardation.
- Fatigue or loss of energy.
- Diminished ability to think or concentrate; indecisiveness.
- Recurrent thoughts of death, suicide, suicide attempts, or suicide plans.

Hypomania

Hypomanic episodes are characterized by a persistently elevated, expansive, or irritable mood with similar features to mania. However, the episode is not severe enough to cause marked impairment in social or occupational functioning and delusions and hallucinations do not occur.

Dementia

Dementia is usually a disease of older people and refers to a global deterioration of higher mental functioning without impairment in consciousness that is progressive and usually irreversible.

Dementia usually presents with a history of chronic, steady decline in short- and long-term memory and is associated with difficulties in social relationships, work, and activities of daily living. Important manifestations include disruption of language and intelligence as well as changes in personality and behaviour. Apathy, depression, and anxiety are frequently found and psychotic phenomena may be seen in a third of patients. A diagnosis of dementia is based on MMSE and information from other sources such as the patient's family, friends, and employers.

Dementia may be 'primary' or 'secondary' to diseases such as:
- Chronic CNS infection: HIV, syphilis, meningitis, encephalitis.
- CNS trauma: anoxia, diffuse axonal injury, dementia pugilistica (repeated head injury—seen in boxers), chronic subdural haematoma.
- Raised intracranial pressure: neoplasia, hydrocephalus.
- Toxins: heavy metals, organic chemicals, chronic substance abuse.
- Vitamin deficiencies: B12, folate.
- Autoimmune disease: SLE, temporal arteritis, sarcoidosis.

Other possible causes include endocrinopathies, Wilson's disease, and lipid storage diseases.

Alzheimer's disease

The key pathological changes in Alzheimer's disease (AD) are reduced brain mass and ↑ size of the ventricles. There is neuronal loss and occurrence of amyloid plaques and neurofibrillary tangles. AD makes up 50% of all cases of dementia and 90% of all primary dementias. The main features are memory impairment and at least one of:
- Aphasia.
- Apraxia.
- Agnosia.
- Abnormal executive functioning (planning, organizing, abstracting, sequencing).

Vascular dementia/multi-infarct dementia

This makes up about 20–30% of all cases of dementia. Onset may be abrupt and/or with a step-wise decline. Vascular dementia is associated with more patchy cognitive impairment than AD, often with focal neurological signs and symptoms such as hyperreflexia, extensor plantar responses, pseudobulbar, bulbar, or other cranial nerve palsies, gait abnormalities, and focal weakness.

The primary pathology is multiple small areas of infarction (cortex and underlying white matter). It is important to note vascular risk factors such as previous stroke, hypertension, heart disease, diabetes, and smoking.

Lewy body dementia

Lewy body dementia accounts for up to 20% of all cases. Patients with this show features similar to AD but also often have recurrent visual hallucinations, fluctuating cognitive impairment, Parkinsonian features, and extra-pyramidal signs.

Fronto-temporal dementia

This accounts for 5% of all dementia. Pick's disease is a form of fronto-temporal dementia characterized by the presence of neuronal 'Pick's bodies' (masses of cytoskeletal elements). The predominance of frontal lobe involvement is evinced by profound personality changes, social impairment, and stereotyped behaviour. However, visuospatial skills are usually preserved. The patient may also show 'primitive reflexes'.

Huntington's disease

Huntington's is an autosomal dominant disease presenting as early as the third decade and is associated with a subcortical type of dementia. Apart from the movement disorder showing involuntary choreiform movements of the face, shoulders, upper limbs, and gait, the symptoms of the dementia include psychomotor slowing and personality alteration with apathy or depression.

Parkinson's disease

Patients with Parkinson's disease have cognitive slowing along with the signs described earlier. Dementia is seen in the later stages of the disease.

Creutzfeldt–Jakob disease (CJD)

Contrary to common perception, this is not a new disease or one that affects young people. The most frequently seen of this family of diseases is 'sporadic CJD' which has no known cause. Onset is usually between the fourth and sixth decades of life and is associated with a very rapid progression of dementia, in addition to signs such as myoclonus, seizures, and ataxia—the time to death is typically a few months.

Variant CJD (vCJD) is a disease mainly confined to the UK, first reported in 1996, and is thought to have resulted from transmission of infection from cattle suffering from bovine spongiform encephalopathy (BSE). The average age of onset is 27 years, presenting initially with behavioural symptoms.

Delirium

Delirium or acute confusional state is a transient global disorder of cognition which is characterized by an acute onset and a fluctuating course. It represents one of the most important and misdiagnosed problems in medicine and surgery. Delirium may occur in as many as 10–20% of hospital inpatients, with elderly patients being the most vulnerable. Approximately 60% of patients suffer delirium following hip fracture.

Below is a brief summary of the main features and causes. You should bear all the possible causes in mind and tailor your physical examination and investigations accordingly.

Predisposing factors (risk factors)

- Increasing age.
- Pre-existing cognitive defect.
- Psychiatric illness.
- Severe physical comorbidity.
- Previous episode of delirium.
- Deficits in hearing or vision.
- Anticholinergic drug use.
- New environment or stress.

Causes (precipitants)

Delirium is usually 'multifactorial' with a single cause difficult or impossible to identify. Some factors include:

Intracranial factors

- Trauma.
- Vascular disease (e.g. stroke).
- Epilepsy and post-ictal states.
- Tumour.
- Infection (meningitis, encephalitis, tuberculosis, neurosyphilis).

Extracranial factors

- Drugs—both prescribed and recreational, intoxication, and withdrawal.
- Electrolyte imbalances.
- Infection (e.g. urinary tract, chest, septicaemia).
- Endocrine (e.g. thyroid dysfunction, hypo- and hyperglycaemia).
- Organ failure (heart, lung, liver, kidney).
- Hypoxia.
- Acid/base disturbance.
- Nutritional deficiencies.
- Post-operative or post-anaesthetic states.
- Miscellaneous.
  - Sensory deprivation
  - Sleep deprivation
  - Faecal impaction
  - Change of environment.

Symptoms include
- Fluctuating level of consciousness.
- Difficulty maintaining, or frequently shifting, attention.
- Disorientation (often worse at night).
- Illusions.
- Hallucinations (often simple, visual).
- Apathy.
- Emotional lability.
- Depression.
- Disturbance of the normal sleep/wake cycle.

Medical conditions with psychiatric symptoms and signs

There are many medical conditions that can give psychiatric clinical features. This can sometimes lead to failure to recognize and treat the underlying medical condition appropriately. It is important in psychiatry to consider possible 'organic' causes for the symptoms and signs before starting psychiatric treatment. Further, many medical disorders are associated with psychiatric diagnoses.

The following is a sample of such situations, aimed at illustrating the above points, rather than providing an exhaustive list.

Neurological disorders

- *Seizure disorder:*
  - Ictal events, including status epilepticus, may mimic psychosis
  - Automatisms are seen in some temporal lobe seizures
  - The pre-ictal prodrome can involve changes in mood, particularly irritability, and auras (including auditory and olfactory hallucinations) can be seen in temporal lobe epilepsy. These may also include epigastric sensations, *déja vu*, or *jamais vu*
  - The post-ictal state often involves confusion and disorientation.
- *Parkinson's disease:* patients may suffer from major depression, anxiety syndromes, hallucinations, and delusions.
- *Brain tumours and cerebrovascular events:* (depend on location.)
  - Frontal: personality change, cognitive impairment, motor, and language disturbance
  - Dominant temporal lobe: memory and speech, Korsakoff psychosis in bilateral lesions
  - Occipital lesions: visual agnosis, visual hallucinations
  - Limbic and hypothalamic: affective symptoms, rage, mania.
- *MS:* cognitive deficits, dementia, bipolar disorder, major depression.

Infectious diseases

- *Neurosyphilis:* primarily affects the frontal lobe (irritability, poor self-care, mania, progressive dementia).
- *Meningitis:* especially with indwelling shunts, can cause acute confusion, memory impairment.
- *Herpes simplex encephalitis:* bizarre and inconsistent behaviour, seizures, anosmia, hallucinations (olfactory and gustatory), psychosis.
- *HIV encephalitis:* progressive subcortical dementia, major depression, suicidal behaviour, anxiety disorders, abnormal psychological reactions.

Endocrine disorders

- *Hyperparathyroidism:* delirium, sudden stupor, and coma. Visual hallucinations with associated hypomagnesaemia.
- *Hypoparathyroidism:* psychosis, depression, anxiety.
- *Hyperthyroidism:* depression, anxiety, hypomania, psychosis.
- *Hypothyroidism:* depression, apathy, psychomotor retardation, poor memory, delirium, and psychosis 'myxoedema madness'.

Rheumatological disorders

- *Systemic lupus erythematosus:* delirium, psychosis, severe depression.

Metabolic disorders

- *Hyponatraemia:* confusion, depression, delusions, hallucinations, seizures, stupor, coma.
- *Hypernatraemia:* acute changes of mental state.
- *Encephalopathy:* acute changes of mental state, confusion..
- *Uraemia encephalopathy:* memory impairment, depression, apathy, social withdrawal.

Vitamin deficiencies

- B_1 *(thiamine):* asthenia, fatigue, weakness, depression.
- B_{12} *(cyanocobalamin):* impaired cognitive function.

The paediatric assessment

History taking

Children and doctors

The specialty of paediatrics is very different to adult medicine. Children grow, change, and mature. Your style and approach to history taking and examination will very much depend on the child's age, independence, and understanding, so flexibility is essential. The most important thing to remember during your time as a student is that paediatrics should above all be pleasurable.

An approach to the child patient

The child needs to be put at ease and made to feel welcome.

- Make a complimentary remark about their clothes, or show them an interesting toy.
- Tell the child your name and ask theirs.
- Make friends with them by asking what their favourite lesson is at school or what they had for breakfast.
- Shake hands with children, even toddlers enjoy this formality.
- ▶ Let the child know what you are going to do. They may be dreading a needle when you have no intention of using one!

The history

A structured approach to history taking is important to avoid forgetting things, but this must not become too rigid, as it is sometimes necessary to pursue a different line of questioning to gain essential information. The list in Box 17.1 is a list of useful headings in paediatric history taking, and this should be memorized.

Talking to the child

Children should be asked to give their account of events with parental corroboration. Children under 5 years old will lack the vocabulary and communication skills to describe their symptoms, but will be able to point to parts that hurt.

Talking to the parents

Most of the history is likely to be gained from the parents or guardians.

- Ask if they have the infant medical record book—this contains information about height and weight centiles, immunizations, development, and illnesses in the first few years of life.
- Ask whether the parents have any views on what the cause of the child's trouble is. Listen carefully; parents are astute observers.
- Ensure that all terms used are appropriately defined—you should be gleaning information from the parents' observations and *not* their interpretation of the symptoms. For example, the word 'wheeze' is often used incorrectly and sometimes a demonstration can be helpful. Further, the parent may interpret a baby's cries as pain when, in fact, it is your task to establish the circumstances of the cries and, therefore, the cause.
- As children get older, the parents may have a hazy memory for early events. Establishing symptoms in relation to easily remembered events (e.g. first walked) may clarify the timeline.

Box 17.1 Outline paediatric history

- Presenting complaint and history of presenting complaint
- Birth history:
  - Place of birth
  - Gestation and pregnancy
  - Birth weight
  - Delivery
  - Perinatal events and SCBU admission.
- Feeding methods and weaning
  - If bottle fed, note how the bottle feed is mixed (how many scoops/number of ounces).
- PMH including hospital admissions, infections, injuries
- Developmental history
- School progress
- Immunizations
- Drugs
- Allergies
- Family tree with siblings' ages, including deaths, miscarriages, and stillbirths
  - Any consanguinity? ('Are you related to your husband by blood?')
- Parental age and occupation
- Family illnesses and allergies
- Housing
  - This should include a discussion about the child's bedroom as they may spend 12 hours of each day there.
- Travel
- Systems review.

Approaching the examination

Examination in children varies depending on the age and co-operation of the child. School-age children and babies may be examined on a couch with a parent nearby, whereas toddlers are best examined on the parent's lap. If the child is asleep on the parent's lap, much of the examination should be completed before waking them up.

Undressing

Unless your patient is a neonate, let the parent undress the child: and only expose the part of the body you will be examining.

Positioning

Some children may prefer to be examined standing up. Only lay the child down when you have to, as this can be very threatening.

Putting the child at ease

Slowly introduce yourself to the child's space during the examination by exchanging toys, for example.

Explain what you are going to do and be repeatedly reassuring, children can be embarrassed by silence after a doctor's question, but will be comforted by endless nattering. And remember—don't ask permission, as this will often be refused!

The examination

Firstly, use a hands-off approach. Allow the child to look at you, and let them play in your presence. Watch the child. How do they interact with their parents? Do they look well or ill? Do they look clean, well nourished, and well cared for?

▶ The vast majority of the examination can be done by inspection so spend most of your time doing this. A common error in formal examinations is that students rush to touch the child and don't spend enough time observing at the start of the examination.

Kneel on the floor so that you are at the child's level. Use a style and language appropriate to the age of the child—a toddler will understand the word 'tummy' better than the word 'abdomen'.

Be opportunistic

Do not adhere to a rigid examination schedule, e.g. you may have to listen to the heart first while the child is quiet, then look at the hands later. Never examine the presenting part only. Be thorough and train yourself to be a generalist.

Leave unpleasant procedures, such as examination of the tonsils, until last. See Boxes 17.2, 17.3, and 17.4 for other examination tips.

Presenting your findings

When presenting your findings, translate what you see into appropriate terminology. Informing a senior that a child 'looks funny' is not very helpful but saying that the child is dysmorphic, followed by a detailed description, is acceptable. Describe in simple terms the relevant features that make the child look unusual, e.g. low-set ears, wide-set eyes.

▶ There is no substitute for examining lots of normal children.

Box 17.2 Some distraction techniques to help with examination
- Playing peek-a-boo
- Letting toddlers play with your stethoscope
- Giving infants something to hold
- Asking mum or dad to wave a bright toy in front of them
- Constant chatter from yourself.

Box 17.3 The mother's knee

Be cautious about taking any baby or young child to a couch. It is often better to leave them on their mother's knee for the majority of the examination.

⚠ A baby should never be picked off their mother's knee if they are beyond 7–8 months of age—this will invariably result in screaming.

Box 17.4 'Pain'

Children may complain of 'pain' when they wish to indicate distress or discomfort that their vocabulary will not allow. Remember also that diseases may present differently in children than in adults.

For example, children may often describe 'chest pain' with chest tightness and asthma.

Pneumonia often gives abdominal pain in children.

The respiratory system

Key points from the history

- Is the child short of breath or wheezy (remember to define terms)?
- Is there stridor or croup?
- Is there a cough? Does it disturb sleep? (See Box 17.5.)
- Does anything trigger the symptoms—sport, cold weather, pets?
- Has the child expectorated or vomited any sputum?
- Is the infant short of breath during breast or bottle feeding?
- Is there a possibility the child could have inhaled a foreign body?
- Is there any FHx of respiratory problems such as asthma or cystic fibrosis?
- Does the child have a fever—suggestive of infection?
- Has anyone else been unwell? Any contacts with tuberculosis?
- Has the child travelled abroad recently?
- How does the respiratory problem limit the child's life—how much school is missed, can they play sport, how far can they run, is sleep disturbed?

Examination

Inspection

See Box 17.6. Look around for any clues—is the patient on oxygen? Are there inhalers or nebulizers at the bedside?

General inspection

- Are they comfortable or in respiratory distress? Look for:
  - Nasal flaring
  - Use of accessory muscles of respiration
  - Intercostal recessions (sucking in of the muscles between the ribs) and subcostal recessions (drawing in of the abdomen)
  - Grunting (a noise at the end of expiration which is the infant's attempt to maintain a positive end expiratory pressure).
- Is the child running around or just sitting on the parent's knee?
- Are they restless or drowsy?
- Count the respiratory rate (see Table 17.1).
- Listen for wheeze or stridor (a harsh inspiratory sound caused by upper airways obstruction).
- What type of cough does the child have?
  - If they don't cough spontaneously, ask them to cough for you.
- Has the child coughed up any sputum (children under 5 years will swallow sputum, which is often vomited after a bout of coughing).

Hands

- Clubbing (cystic fibrosis, bronchiectasis).
- Measure the radial pulse—pulsus paradoxus is an important feature of acute severe asthma in children.

Face

- Check the conjunctiva for anaemia and the tongue for central cyanosis.
- Look for petechiae (non-blanching spots from small burst blood vessels) around the eyes from a prolonged bout of coughing.

Chest
- Look for chest movement. Is it symmetrical? Is the child splinting (failing to move) one side of the chest?
  - Children who splint their chest as a consequence of pneumonia often also have a slight spinal scoliosis.
- Look at the chest shape. Is there any chest wall deformity?
  - Harrison's sulcus: permanent groove in the chest wall at the insertion of the diaphragm with splaying of the costal margin in chronic respiratory disease
  - Barrel chest (hyperventilation): air trapping in poorly controlled asthma
  - Pectus carinatum: 'pigeon chest' seen in long-standing asthma
  - Pectus excavatum: normal (and common) variant.

Table 17.1 Normal respiratory and heart rates by age

Age	Heart rate	Respiratory rate
<1 year	120–160	30–60
1–3 years	90–140	24–40
3–5 years	75–110	18–30
5–12 years	75–100	18–30
12–16 years	60–90	12–16

Box 17.5 Some childhood coughs

These factors may give important clues as to the origin of the cough.
- *Productive:* cystic fibrosis, bronchiectasis, pneumonia
- *Nocturnal:* asthma, cystic fibrosis
- *Worse on wakening:* cystic fibrosis
- *Brassy:* tracheitis
- *Barking:* croup (laryngotracheobronchitis)
- *Paroxysmal:* pertussis, foreign body
- *Worse during exercise:* asthma
- *Disappears when sleeping:* habitual cough
- *During/after feeds:* aspiration.

Box 17.6 The importance of inspection

▶ ↑ respiratory rate and work of breathing are the most important signs of a lower respiratory tract infection in infancy, as sometimes palpation, percussion, and auscultation will be normal.

Palpation
- Feel the neck for enlarged cervical lymph nodes.
- Palpate the trachea to ensure that it is central.
- Then move on to the chest:
  - Feel for the apex beat. This may be displaced in effusion, collapse, or tension pneumothorax. The apex may be on the right in dextrocardia with primary ciliary dyskinesia
  - Assess expansion, commenting on extent and symmetry
  - In young children, you may be able to feel crackles.

Percussion
Percussion is rarely useful in infants but is in children and toddlers. Remember to also percuss for the normal cardiac dullness as well as the upper and lower borders of the liver.
- Dull = consolidation.
- Hyperresonant = air-trapping or pneumothorax.
- Stony dull = pleural effusion.

Auscultation
 Before using a stethoscope on the child, pretend to auscultate the parent's chest or a less vulnerable part of the child's body (e.g. their leg).
▶ Remember to listen under the axillae as well as the anterior and posterior chest wall.
▶ Especially in young children, the upper airway noises may be transmitted to the chest, so if the child is old enough, ask them to cough to clear them.
Listen for:
- Breath sounds.
  - Are they vesicular (normal), absent, or bronchial?
- Added sounds (e.g. wheeze or crackles—see ➋ Chapter 6 for more details.
- Absent breath sounds in one area suggests a pleural effusion, pneumothorax, or dense consolidation.

Putting it all together
- See Table 17.2 for some common respiratory conditions.

Table 17.2 Some common respiratory conditions and signs

Condition	Age	Inspection	Auscultation
Bronchiolitis	<1 year	Pale, coryza, cough, recessions, tachypnoea	Wheeze and crackles throughout chest
Croup (laryngo-tracheobron-chitis)	1–2 years	Stridor, hoarse voice, barking cough	Clear
Asthma	>1 year	Tachypnoea, recessions ± audible wheeze and use of accessory muscles	Wheeze, variable air entry throughout chest. Crackles in young children
Pneumonia	Infant	Tachypnoea, recessions, flushing due to fever, grunting	May be clear, reduced breath sounds over affected area, crackles
Pneumonia	Child	Tachypnoea, recessions, flushed, generally unwell	Abdominal pain (may be the only symptom), crackles and bronchial breathing over affected area

Ear, nose, and throat

ENT conditions are a common reason for children to present to the doctor.
❗ Examination of this system should be left until last, as children find it unpleasant.

Key points from the history

- Does the child pull at their ears (suggests infection)?
- Does the child complain of earache or a sore throat?
- Are they coryzal (runny nose)?
- Does the child have a fever?
- Does the infant drool more than normal (suggests sore throat)?

Examination

Ears

- Sit the child on the parent's lap facing to the side.
- Ask the parent to hold the child's head against their chest with one hand, and to firmly hold the child's arms and upper body with the other hand (see Box 17.7).
- With an infant, gently pull the pinna back before inserting the auroscope. When examining an older child, pull the pinna upwards.
- Use the auroscope as in adults (⟳ Chapter 11). See Table 17.3.

Nose

- Examine the nose externally for discharge.
- The nose may be examined very gently using an auroscope.
  - Polyps are a common finding in asthma and cystic fibrosis
  - Pale, boggy nasal mucosa suggests allergic rhinitis.

Throat

- Sit the child upright on the parent's lap facing towards you.
- Ask the parent to hold the child's forehead with one hand, with the back of the child's head against their chest.
  - The parent should firmly hold the child's arms with their other hand.
- The difficulty now is encouraging the child to open their mouth!.
  - Ask the child to open their mouth 'as wide as a lion'
  - Tempt an infant to open their mouth with a dummy
  - Sometimes children will be more inclined to open their mouth if you promise not to use a spatula.
- When the child's mouth is open, gently depress the tongue with the spatula if it is obstructing the view of the tonsils.
- Decide whether the tonsils are:
  - Normal: pink and small
  - Acutely inflamed: red, enlarged, sometimes with pus spots
  - Chronically hypertrophied: enlarged and pitted, but not inflamed.

Lymph nodes

Always feel for cervical and supraclavicular lymphadenopathy.

Box 17.7 The importance of inspection

While asking the parent to hold the child's head during the ear examination is the usual taught method, this often leads to a struggle.

It is equally appropriate to allow the child free movement of the head providing you splint the hand holding the auroscope against the child's face so that your hand (and auroscope) will move as the child's head moves. This can lead to a less distressing examination.

⚠ In infancy, the pinna should be pulled forwards (not backwards) to straighten the auditory canal.

Table 17.3 Some common findings when examining the eardrums

Appearance of drum	Condition
Translucent, clear light reflex	Normal
Red, bulging, loss of light reflex	Acute otitis media
Retracted, loss of light reflex, dull	Glue ear (chronic otitis media with effusion)

The cardiovascular system

Key points from the history

- Does the child ever have blue spells (cyanosis)?
- Does the child ever become tired, pale, or sweaty (indicating heart failure)?
- If the patient is an infant, ask how long the child takes to feed from a bottle. Breathlessness may inhibit feeding.
- Is the child growing normally? Plot on a centile chart.
- Does the child suffer from recurrent chest infections?
- Does the child suffer from abdominal pain (caused by organomegaly)?
- Is there a history of fainting or collapse?
- Has the child ever complained of their heart racing (would imply an arrhythmia such as supraventricular tachycardia)?
- Is there a FHx of congenital heart disease or sudden death?

Examination

Inspection

Search for evidence of heart failure: pallor, cyanosis, sweating, respiratory distress, and tachypnoea.

Hands

- Clubbing—seen in cyanotic congenital heart disease.
- Search for signs of endocarditis, including splinter haemorrhages, Janeway lesions and Osler's nodes.

Face

- Anaemia in the conjunctiva.
- Central cyanosis ('stick your tongue out!').

Neck

The jugular venous pulse and pressure are difficult to appreciate in young children, due the relative shortness of the neck.

Blood pressure

Blood pressure recordings in children are not easy, but they are important, so remember to perform this test. The use of the correct cuff size is vital here to prevent inaccurate readings.

Anxiety and poor technique are the most common causes for raised blood pressure in children, so it should be measured several times.

Chest

Note the presence of:

- Precordial bulge: causes the sternum and ribs to bow forwards.
- Visible ventricular impulse: RV impulse may be visible under the xiphisternum. The LV impulse (apex beat) is often visible in thin children, and in children with true LV hypertrophy.
- Scars: indicative of previous heart surgery.

Palpation: chest and abdomen

Apex beat

- Feel the apex beat to determine its location and character. It is usually situated in the 4th intercostal space in the mid-clavicular line in infants or toddlers (often difficult to localize if they are plump), and in the 4th or 5th intercostal space in older children.
  - LV hypertrophy results in a diffuse, forceful, and displaced apex beat, felt as a 'heave'.
  - If the apex is impalpable, consider dextrocardia (inverted heart with apex pointing to the right) or pericardial effusion. 'Laevocardia' is the normal orientation of the heart to the left.

Right ventricular heave?

- Place your fingertips along the left sternal edge. If the child has right ventricular hypertrophy you will feel your fingers lift up with each impulse.

Four valve areas

- Palpate in the aortic, pulmonary, tricuspid, and mitral areas for thrills.

Abdomen

- Palpate for hepatomegaly, which suggests heart failure.
  - 🅘 Remember to percuss the upper border of the liver—a normal-sized liver may be displaced downwards by lung disease such as bronchiolitis
  - Raised JVP, pulmonary, and peripheral oedema is rarely seen in children.

Palpation: peripheral pulses

Palpate the radial, brachial, and femoral pulses.

🅘 The femoral pulse, although sometimes awkward to feel, must always be sought to ensure coarctation of the aorta is not missed. Assess:

- Volume: is it full or thready? (You will need to practise feeling lots of pulses to appreciate the difference.) A thready, weak, or small volume pulse is indicative of hypovolaemia. Look for pulsus paradoxus (➔ Chapter 5).
- Rate: heart rate varies with age, activity, distress, excitement, and fever (the pulse rate will ↑ by 10bpm with every temperature rise of 1°C).
- Rhythm:
  - Sinus arrhythmia: an ↑ in pulse rate on inspiration, with slowing on expiration. Very common in children
  - Occasional ventricular ectopic beats: normal in children.
- Character:
  - Collapsing pulse in children is most commonly due to a patent ductus arteriosus.
  - Slow rising pulse suggests ventricular outflow obstruction.

Auscultation

Listen to the four valve areas with the diaphragm and bell of the stethoscope (preferably paediatric size) for:

- Heart sounds.
- Added sounds.
- Murmurs (see Box 17.8 and Table 17.4).

First heart sound (S₁)

Best heard at the apex with the bell.

- Loud S_1 heard with high cardiac output states (e.g. anxiety, exercise, fever).
- Soft S_1 heard with emphysema and impaired left ventricular function.

Second heart sound (aortic = A₂ and pulmonary = P₂)

Best heard at the base with the diaphragm. It is normally split in children.

- Soft P_2 heard with stenotic pulmonary valve (e.g. tetralogy of Fallot).
- Loud P_2 heard with pulmonary hypertension.
- Wide fixed splitting caused by atrial septal defect.

Third heart sound

Due to rapid ventricular filling.

- Causes include ↑ LV stroke volume (aortic or mitral regurgitation) and restricted ventricular filling (constrictive pericarditis, restrictive cardiomyopathy). It may be normal in children.

Fourth heart sound

Due to forceful atrial contraction.

- Causes include hypertrophic cardiomyopathy and severe hypertension.

Box 17.8 Murmurs

Auscultate for murmurs over the four valve areas, and at the back. About 30% of children have innocent murmurs.

Innocent murmurs

Patient asymptomatic. Systolic (except venous hum). No radiation or thrill. Change with altering patient posture.

- *Venous hum:* due to turbulent flow in the head and neck veins. A continuous murmur in diastole and systole heard below the clavicles which disappears when child lies flat
- *Ejection murmur:* due to turbulent flow in the outflow tracts of the heart. Heard in the 2nd–4th left intercostal spaces.

Pathological murmurs

Systolic or diastolic. May radiate. May have a thrill. Patient may be symptomatic.

- *Atrial septal defect:* soft ejection systolic murmur at the upper LSE due to ↑ RV outflow. Fixed wide splitting of the 2nd heart sound may first be detected at school entry
- *Ventricular septal defect:* parasternal thrill. Loud pansystolic murmur at the lower LSE. Radiates throughout precordium. Signs of heart failure may be present
- *Coarctation of the aorta:* ejection systolic murmur heard between the shoulder blades. Femoral pulses weak or absent
- *Patent ductus arteriosus:* Collapsing pulse. Continuous 'machinery murmur' below the left clavicle.

Also see ➲ Chapter 5.

Table 17.4 Quick-spot guide to common paediatric murmurs

Signs	Cause
Cyanosis + murmur	Usually tetralogy of Fallot
Cyanosis + murmur + operation	Possibly tetralogy of Fallot or transposition of the great arteries
Pink + loud systolic murmur	Probable ventricular septal defect (commonest form of CHD)
Pink + murmur + impalpable femorals	Coarctation of the aorta
Continuous low-pitched murmur	Probable patent ductus arteriosus

The abdomen and external genitalia

Key points from the history

Determine whether the child takes in sufficient calories for growth and has a well-balanced diet. Ask about height and weight gain.

When taking a history, start at the head and work down.

- Does the child have a good appetite?
- Does the child vomit?
  - How much?
  - Are they hungry afterwards?
  - Is it forceful or effortless?
  - Is it related to feeds?
  - What does it contain? Ask about coffee-grounds or other appearances of the vomit. (Bile-stained vomiting in an infant must be considered as pathological.)
- Does the child suffer from abdominal pain?
- Does the child ever have a bloated abdomen?
- Are there any urinary symptoms?
- Ask about bowel habit—is the child constipated?
- Have there been any frequent or loose stools? Are the stools particularly offensive (suggests malabsorption)?
- Is there a relevant FHx (e.g. coeliac or inflammatory bowel disease)?

Examination

Inspection

Start with a general inspection of the patient, looking especially for:

- Does the abdomen move with respiration?
- Is the patient in pain?
- Jaundice.
- Observe for signs of liver disease (see ➲ Chapter 7), including spider naevi, xanthomata, and purpura.
- Oedema over the tibia and sacrum.
- Is the child under- or overweight?
- Wasted buttocks (suggesting weight loss—typical of coeliac disease).

Hands

- Clubbing, palmar erythema.

Face

- Check the conjunctivae for anaemia.
- Periorbital oedema (e.g. in nephrotic syndrome).

Abdomen

- Abdominal distension, visible liver edge, or spleen (see Box 17.9).
- Peristalsis (important in diagnosing pyloric stenosis during a test feed).
- Gross ascites may be evident—the umbilicus everted.
- Caput medusae (cutaneous collateral veins with blood flowing away from the umbilicus due to ↑ portal venous pressure).
- Check for peritonism as in Box 17.10.

Box 17.9 Causes of abdominal distension in a child

- Fat
- Fluid
- Flatus
- Faeces
- Organomegaly
- Muscle hypotonia.

Box 17.10 Detecting peritoneal inflammation

A further useful technique is to ask the patient to make their belly 'as fat as possible' and 'as thin as possible'. In the case of peritonitis, any of these manoeuvres may result in pain.

Also ask them to hop on each leg. If they can do this, they do not have peritonitis.

Palpation

⚠️ Young children may resist abdominal examination. First try distraction techniques. If these fail, use the child's hand to guide yours around the abdomen. If there is doubt as to the significance of tenderness in a child's abdomen, listen with your stethoscope and gently apply more pressure. Often quite firm pressure can be tolerated in this way where there was previously tenderness.

The aims of palpation are to:

- Determine the presence of normal abdominal organs.
- Detect enlargement of the abdominal organs.
- Detect the presence of abnormal masses or fluid.

Procedure

- Ensure the child is relaxed and that your hands are warm.
- Enquire about pain before you begin.
- Palpate for tenderness (light palpation first, then deep palpation).
  - Feel for guarding (tensing of the abdominal muscles which may indicate underlying tenderness)
  - ► ALWAYS watch the child's face (rather than your hand) to see if they are in pain whilst you palpate.
- Palpate the spleen. This is normally felt 1–2cm below the costal margin in infancy. It is soft and can be 'tipped' on inspiration. Begin palpation in the right iliac fossa and move towards the left upper quadrant to avoid missing a very large spleen. It may help to turn the child onto their right side.
- To palpate the liver, start in the right iliac fossa and move upwards in time with the child's respiratory movements until the liver edge meets your fingers. A liver edge 1–2cm below the costal margin is normal up to the age of 2 or 3 years. See Box 17.11.
  - Kidneys are not easy to palpate in children (they are easier to palpate in newborns), so if you can feel them they are probably enlarged. They are best palpated bimanually. The kidneys move with respiration, have a smooth outline, and one can get above them (unlike the liver and spleen).
- Palpate for other masses and check for constipation (usually felt as a hard, indentable, non-tender mass in the left iliac fossa).

Percussion

- Ascites. Percuss from the midline to the flanks. If you suspect ascites (dullness in the flanks), test for shifting dullness (⊃ Chapter 7).
- Gaseous distension.
- Percuss to determine the size of the liver and spleen.

Auscultation

- Bowel sounds.

Rectal examination

- This is rarely indicated in children. However, it is often useful to inspect the perianal region for fissures, tags, soiling, and threadworms.

Box 17.11 Confirming hepatomegaly

If in doubt, confirmation of liver enlargement can be made by:
- Placing the stethoscope over the xiphisternum
- Gently scratching the abdomen, progressing upwards from the right iliac fossa.
  - When the scratching hand is over the liver, the sound will be heard through the stethoscope.

Examining the external genitalia

Penis
- True micropenis is rare. If the penis looks small, it is probably because it is buried in suprapubic fat.
- Check the urethral orifice is at the tip of the glans.
  - If not, is there epispadias (dorsal opening, very rare), or hypospadias (ventral opening)?

Scrotum
The child should be standing up.
- Inspect for normal rugosity of the scrotum.
- Palpate for the testes.
  - If they are not present in the scrotum, feel at the inguinal canal and, if found, try to milk the testis down
  - Many undescended testes are subsequently found as retractile testes, so be gentle in your approach to avoid provoking a cremasteric reflex!

Female genitalia
- Inspect the female external genitalia if there are urinary symptoms.

The nervous system

Key points from the history

- Detailed birth and perinatal history including:
  - Maternal drugs/illness
  - Presence of polyhydramnios (neuromuscular disease)
  - Whether resuscitation was needed at delivery
  - Neonatal infections.
- Careful history of the developmental milestones (see Table 17.5).
  - At exactly what ages were they attained?
  - Is there any delay (common) or regression (rare)?
- Hearing or visual concerns. Did they pass the newborn hearing screen?
- Any change in school performance, personality, or behaviour (e.g. aggression)?
- Ask about symptoms of raised intracranial pressure (e.g. headache, vomiting).
- Any change in gait?
  - Are there increased falls or trips compared with other children?
  - Is there a change in coordination?
- Any evidence of weakness. Does the child have difficulty with:
  - Climbing stairs or brushing their hair (proximal weakness)?
  - Opening jars or writing (distal weakness)?
- Does the child have limited function—what can they do? What do they need help with?
- Relevant FHx of learning difficulties or genetic conditions.

Examination

Neurological examination of children and infants can be made largely by observation of their play and gait. Doing this provides a useful screening test, after which a more formal neurological assessment can be done to more specifically define an abnormality.

Neurological examination of children and infants is often dreaded by students and junior doctors alike, but if you learn a stereotyped examination sequence, it becomes easy.

The examinations of younger and older children are described separately.

Table 17.5 Developmental milestones

Age	Gross motor	Fine motor	Language	Social
3 months	Head control, pushes up with arms	Opens hand	Laughs	Smiles (6 weeks)
6 months	Sits	Palmar grasp, reaches, transfers	Babbles (monosyllabic— ba, ka, da)	Eats solid food
9 months	Crawls, pulls to stand	Pincer grip begins to develop	Double babble (dada, baba)	Stranger awareness, waves bye-bye
12 months	Walks	Developed pincer grip	Mummy, daddy— specifically	Peek-a-boo
18 months	Walks upstairs, jumps	Scribbles, 3 block tower	2-word phrases	Mimics
2 years	Kicks, runs	Draws straight line, 6–8 block tower	Beginning to use clauses (including verbs)	Uses spoon skilfully, undresses, symbolic play
3 years	Hops, walks upstairs adult-style	Draws a circle, builds a bridge with blocks	Says name, knows colours	Dresses, has a friend, dry nappies by day
4 years	Stands on one leg, hops	Draws a cross, makes 3 steps with blocks	Sentences of 5+ words	Does up buttons
5 years	Can ride a bicycle	Draws a triangle		Ties shoe laces, dry by night

Neurological examination: infant or small toddler

Start with the infant sitting on the mother's lap:

- Note how alert they are.
  - Do they interact with their mother and with you?
  - Any spontaneous vocalization or language?
- Observe range and symmetry of eye movements whilst tracking an interesting object (a ball, a torch, or your face).
  - If the baby can re-fix on an object moved from the central to peripheral vision, you can assume that their visual fields are intact
  - Note their facial symmetry when smiling (or crying)
  - You have now made a basic assessment of their cranial nerves!
- Opportunistically note the baby's arm and hand movements.
  - Do they grasp objects with each hand?
  - Can they transfer objects between each hand?
  - Do they mouth objects?
  - Can they scribble on paper?
  - Observe the upper-limb coordination, dexterity, and distal power.
- If the toddler can walk, watch them wander about the room.
  - What is the gait like?
  - Are they able to squat to pick objects up from the floor and then stand again (this requires good proximal muscle power)?

On the examination couch:

- Start with the baby lying supine, and note attempts to roll over or sit up (this will help you assess truncal and limb power).
- Also note their limb posture as an indication of tone:
  - Are they lying in a 'frogs-legs' position (hypotonia)?
  - Are their upper limbs held in flexion or extension (hypertonia)?
  - What are the spontaneous movements like?
- Using the baby's arms, pull them to sit.
  - Note the degree of head control.
- From sitting, note the need for support, and how curved the back is.
  - If the baby is sitting unsupported, gently tip to one side and note the righting reflex and its symmetry (if tipped to the left, the left arm should extend to prevent the baby from falling)
  - This will help you assess tone, power, and movement of the arms.
- If the baby is over about 6 months of age, lift to stand.
  - See if the legs 'scissor' (adduction is a sign of hypertonia in the lower limbs)
  - Does the baby seem to 'move as one piece' (hypertonia)?
- Now lift the baby onto their front whilst watching for parachute reflex (both arms should extend forwards. Is this equal?).
  - Observe their head control and upper limb strength when prone
  - Do they try to lift themselves up like doing a press-up?

Lift the baby back onto the mother's knee

- Fundoscopy. You will need an assistant to get the baby's attention behind you and plenty of patience!
- Examine the deep tendon reflexes.
- Take the head circumference and plot it on a centile chart.

Primitive reflexes

- These are reflexes (Box 17.12) seen in young babies which become 'extinct' at certain predictable ages (see Table 17.6).
- Preservation of primitive reflexes (or redevelopment) may be an indicator of neurological disease.

Box 17.12 Primitive reflexes

- *Palmar grasp:* fingers close to hold an object placed in the palm
- *Rooting:* when pressure is applied to the cheek, the head turns towards the pressure and mouth opens
- *Sucking:* when a finger is place in the mouth, the infant will suck vigorously
- *Stepping:* hold the infant with both hands and lower the feet onto a surface. The legs will move in a stepping fashion
- *Moro reflex:* lay the infant supine on your hand and forearm. When the head is dropped a few centimetres, the upper limbs abduct, extend, and flex in a symmetrical flowing movement. A unilateral response indicates damage (usually transient) to the 5th and 6th cervical roots producing Erb's palsy.

Table 17.6 Some primitive reflexes and age of extinction

Reflex	Age of extinction
Stepping reflex	2 months
Palmar grasp	3–4 months
Moro reflex	4–5 months
Asymmetric tonic neck reflex	6 months

Neurological examination: older child

- Whilst taking your history and performing the examination, you can make an informal assessment of the child's language and general understanding and participation in the consultation—is it age appropriate?
- Ask the child to stand up with their feet together, arms outstretched with palms facing upwards and eyes closed for 30 seconds. Watch for:
  - Pronator drift: a sensitive sign of UMN weakness of the upper limbs. The affected arm drifts downwards and pronates
  - Romberg's sign: standing with eyes closed is difficult due to impaired proprioception
  - Is the child able to stand straight? Hip or knee flexion causes a crouching stand.
- Ask the child to walk and then run over a good distance. Is the gait normal or abnormal? Some signs to watch to test for include:
  - Spastic hemiparesis: foot is kept in plantar flexion and catches the floor. There may be a swing of that leg, and the ipsilateral arm may be held flexed. Look for asymmetric toe wear on the soles of the shoes
  - Spastic diplegia: the child walks on their toes with both feet and has a crouched stance
  - Cerebellar ataxia: wide-based, staggering irregularly. Walking on a pretend tight-rope is very difficult
  - Proximal weakness: waddling gait. Throwing of hips to each side with each step. Patients often also have a lumbar lordosis.
- Move to the couch.
- Inspect the symmetry of the child's muscle bulk, and look at the soles of their shoes for unequal or abnormal wear.
- Tone. This may be easier to comment on through inspection of posture—children find it difficult to relax. Increased tone can be:
  - Spastic: feet held in equinus, legs extended and adducted (scissoring), arms either flexed or extended with wrists pronated
  - Dystonic: unusual postures, sometimes brought about by movement.
- Power. Demonstrate to the child what it is that you want them to do, and make it fun for them. Follow the adult sequence (➲ Chapter 8).
  - During your examination, try to distinguish between proximal and distal muscle weakness.
- Reflexes. Hold your thumb over the tendon and hit this with the hammer—this is less threatening to children.
  - Plantar reflex: run your thumb nail along the lateral aspect of their sole and then medial aspect of the ball of their foot (rather than the sharp end of a tendon hammer)
  - Look for the first movement of the big toe
  - The plantar reflex can be extensor until one year of age.
- Sensation: Generally only test if there is a specific indication to do so.
  - Isolated sensory losses without accompanying motor signs are extremely rare in childhood, so motor examination is generally enough unless there is a specific concern about sensation.

- Distinguish spinothalamic sensation (pain, temperature) from dorsal column sensation (light touch, two-point discrimination, proprioception).
- Coordination.
  - Lower limbs: you have already assessed this by getting the child to walk
  - Upper limbs: finger–nose test. Ask the child to move their finger from their nose to your finger and back again as accurately as possible. Do this with both hands. Are they able to reach their target without missing?

For examination of the cranial nerves of an older child, follow the same sequence as for an adult (➔ Chapter 8).

Additional optional tests

Gower's sign:
- A test for proximal muscle weakness.
  - Ask the child to lie supine on a mat, and then get them to stand
  - A child with a positive Gower's sign will turn prone, then use their hand to 'climb up' their legs to stand.

Fog's test
- Associated movement in the upper limbs (e.g. flexion due to spasticity) when the child is asked to walk on their heels or tip-toes.

Assessment of a squint

Any squint persisting beyond the age of 6 weeks needs specialist assessment, as an untreated squinting eye may lead to amblyopia (cortical blindness).
- Ask when the squint is most apparent—latent squints may only be present when the child is tired.

Examination

- *Corneal light reflection test:* shine a torch at a spot directly between the patient's eyes to produce a reflection in the cornea. The reflected light that you see should be at the same spot on each eye. If the reflection from the corneas is asymmetrical, a squint is probably present.
- *Eye movements:* to detect a paralytic squint (rare).
- *Cover test:* encourage the child to fix on a toy, and cover the normal eye with a piece of card. If the fixing eye is covered, the squinting eye moves to take up fixation.
- *Manifest (constant) squint:* on removal of the cover, the eyes move again as the fixing eye takes up fixation.

Developmental assessment

Development is a continuous process, the rate of which varies considerably between normal children. 'Development' describes the acquisition of learned skills and occurs in a cephalo-caudal direction (head to toe)—a child cannot sit before they develop head control, otherwise they would not be able to look around.

Development is divided into four areas (see also skills station 17.1):

- Gross motor.
- Fine motor and vision.
- Speech and hearing.
- Social.

Delay in all four areas is usually abnormal, but delay in one area may not be. For example, some children become expert at bottom shuffling and, having learned an effective means of travelling, the need to walk becomes less important to them and they do not bother to learn this until later.

Performing a developmental assessment

- Observation is key. Young children will often not cooperate. Take a history from the parents of which milestones the child has achieved.
- You will have to be opportunistic, and record (or present) your findings as you go along.
- Be systematic and evaluate each of the four developmental areas in turn.
- Learn a few essential milestones, as it is difficult to remember them all.
- ▶ If an infant was born prematurely, allow for this by calculating their 'corrected age' from their expected due date.
- Limit distractions and present one task at a time.

Developmental milestones

These are detailed in Table 17.5 and warning signs in Table 17.7.

Equipment for developmental assessment

- Wooden blocks.
- 'Hundreds and thousands'.
- Pencil and paper: for assessing fine motor skills.
- Different coloured card/colourful books.

Table 17.7 Developmental warning signs

Age	Warning sign
Any	Regression in previously acquired skills or a halt in developmental progress
8 weeks	No smiling
6 months	Persistent primitive reflexes. Hand preference (this should not appear until 18 months)
12 months	No sitting. No pincer grip. No double babble
18 months	Not walking. No words

Skills station 17.1 Developmental assessment

Gross motor

- Say what you see!
  - Are they sitting up? Cruising? Walking? Are they crouching down and standing again?
  - Roll a ball to them. Can they kick it? Can they catch a ball?

Fine motor

- Hand them a block.
  - Do they take it with a palmar grasp?
  - Do they transfer the block to the other hand?
  - Do they put it in their mouth?
  - How many blocks can they put on top of each other to make a tower?
  - Can they pick up a 'hundreds and thousands' from your hand?
  - How accurate is their pincer grip?
  - The child needs good vision to see the 'hundreds and thousands', so you are also making a crude assessment of their sight.
- Give them a pencil and paper.
  - Do they scribble?
  - Is it linear or circular?
  - Can they copy a line/circle/cross/square?

Speech

- Chat to them during the examination.
  - Are they babbling?
  - Do they say any words?
  - Are they putting one or more words together?
  - Can they name body parts or colours?

Social

- Examine the child's interactions with others.
  - Does the child smile and laugh?
  - Are they anxious about strangers (you!)?
  - Do they play peek-a-boo with you?
  - Play with them—what do they like to do?
  - Do they play symbolically?
- Do they have make-believe play?

The newborn

The vast majority of newborns have a normal intrauterine life, normal birth, and are physically normal. However, there is a wide variation in the spectrum of normal, and it is important to stress the value of examining a large number of neonates to appreciate the normal spectrum.

In the delivery room

All newborns should have a brief examination at birth to determine whether resuscitation is needed and to rule out any major abnormalities.

The APGAR score (Table 17.8) is used to gauge the need for resuscitation.

Table 17.8 APGAR score

Sign	0	1	2
Appearance	White/blue	Blue extremities, pink trunk	Pink
Pulse	Absent	<100bpm	>100bpm
Grimace on stimulation of foot	None	Frown/grimace	Cry
Activity, tone	Floppy	Some limb flexion	Active movement
Respiratory effort	Absent	Irregular, slow	Loud cry

On the postnatal ward

A more thorough examination is carried out prior to discharge. At this stage, the baby is unrecognizable from the one you met in the delivery room—they will be pink, vigorous, and feeding well.

Ask briefly about whether the baby has passed urine and meconium (the first, black sticky stool), and enquire as to the progress of feeding, as well as a FHx of congenital anomalies. Of particular importance is a FHx of dislocated hips, renal abnormalities, and deafness.

- Examination should start at the top and work down, to ensure nothing is missed.
- Undress the baby yourself as the examination proceeds, to get a feel for how the baby handles.

General observation

First observe the baby without disturbing him/her.

- *Colour:* pink, pale, cyanosed, or jaundiced? Acrocyanosis (cyanosis of the hands and feet) is normal provided the lips and tongue are pink.
- *Rash:* a blotchy erythematous rash occurs in about half of all neonates; this is usually harmless and is called erythema toxicum.
- Peeling of skin is common, especially in post-dates babies.

Hand and face

- *Shape of the head:* can vary widely in the first week.
- *Fontanelles:* they should be soft and flat. The size of the anterior fontanelle also varies widely, from 1–4cm in diameter. The posterior fontanelle may accept a little fingertip.
- *Cranial sutures:* are they fused?
- Look for trauma from the birth: such as caput succedaneum (oedema caused by pressure over the presenting part) and moulding (head changing shape as it passes through the birth canal), forceps marks, and subconjunctival haemorrhages. In general, these conditions will resolve within the first week.
  - A cephalhaematoma is a localized fluctuant swelling usually over the parietal bone, caused by subperiosteal bleeding. This will resolve over a few months.
- *Ears:* can be of different shape and size. Look for preauricular sinuses and ear tags, and observe their position.

Mouth

- *Palate:* look at it when the infant cries, then palpate it for a cleft with a clean finger.
  - 'Epstein's pearls' are small white cysts in the midline of the hard palate. They are normal and resolve spontaneously.
- *Jaw:* a small jaw (micrognathia) may be part of the Pierre Robin sequence (midline cleft, small jaw, posterior displacement of the tongue—can cause upper airway obstruction).
- *Tongue:* note the size. If it is large and protruding, this may indicate a number of syndromes (e.g. Down's syndrome).

Eyes

- Note position and size.
- Look for the red reflex with an ophthalmoscope to exclude a cataract, which would be seen as a white reflection.
  - To encourage the baby to open their eyes, wrap them in a blanket (a crying baby will not open their eyes) and sit them upright
  - If this fails, give the baby something to suck on, or startle with the Moro reflex.
- Sticky eyes can be the result of ophthalmia neonatorum (purulent conjunctivitis in the first 3 weeks of life). Usually due to accumulation of lacrimal fluid due to incomplete drainage of the nasolacrimal duct.

Respiratory system and chest

- *Observe:* this is best done in a quiet baby (preferably sleeping).
- *Chest:* comment on size, symmetry, and shape.
- *Respiratory rate:* should be <60/minute. Note the work of breathing. Are there any subcostal or intercostal recessions? Is the baby grunting?
  - Normal newborn respiration should be quiet, effortless, and predominantly diaphragmatic (abdomen moves more than the chest).
- *Auscultate:* the lung fields to ensure symmetrical air entry. Crepitations may be normal in the first few hours of life.
- *Breasts:* engorgement is common in male and female infants.

Cardiovascular system
- *Observe:* note colour, respiratory effort, and precordial heave.
- *Apex beat:* palpate and feel any thrills (not uncommon in neonates).
- *Femoral pulse:* this is extremely important; its absence may imply coarctation of the aorta. This requires a relaxed, still baby and lots of patience. ❶ Remember that too much pressure may obliterate it. A collapsing pulse suggest patent ductus arteriosus.
- *Heart rate:* should be between 100–160bpm.
- *Auscultate:* for the heart sounds and murmurs. Systolic murmurs are common, and usually best heard along the left sternal edge.

Abdomen
- *Observe:* distension could be bowel obstruction or an abdominal mass.
- *Umbilical stump:* count the three vessels. Note any signs of infection such as an unpleasant smell, discharge, or periumbilical erythema.
  - The cord will spontaneously separate around the 4th or 5th day.
- *Palpate:* gently feel the abdomen for the intra-abdominal organs and exclude organomegaly. Use warm hands and a soother if necessary.
  - ❶ The liver edge is soft and easily missed.
- *Kidneys:* determine presence and size by balloting.
  - It is possible to palpate the lower poles of the kidneys in normal neonates.
- *Bladder:* palpate suprapubically. If felt, suggests outlet obstruction.
- *Anus:* infants with an imperforate anus may still pass meconium via a fistula, so check the anus is patent and in the correct position.

Male genitalia
- *Urethra:* identify the urethral orifice and exclude hypospadias.
- *Testes:* palpate gently. If they cannot be found in the scrotum, commence in the inguinal area and palpate downwards.
  - If a testis appears larger than normal, transilluminate the scrotum to check for the common condition of hydrocoele.
- *Inguinal herniae:* these are more common in preterm infants.
- ❶ Put the nappy back on quickly for obvious reasons.

Female genitalia
- *Labia minora:* may not be fully covered, especially in preterm infants.
- *Vaginal tags:* are common and resolve spontaneously in the first week.
- *Vaginal discharge:* and occasionally bleeding can occur, and is normal.
- Note ↑ pigmentation and clitoromegaly.

Limbs
- Ensure all joints have full range of movement to exclude any congenital contractures.
- Examine fingers and toes for syndactyly (fused digits) or polydactyly (extra digits—surprisingly easy to miss!).

Examination of the hips
- This is to detect congenital dislocation and instability of the hips, and should be left until last as it will make the baby cry.
- Observe for unequal leg length and asymmetry of skin creases.

- Hip examination is in two parts. Lay the infant supine on a flat surface with hips and knees positioned at 90°. Stabilize the pelvis with one hand, and with the other grasp the knee between thumb and palm, with the fingertips over the greater trochanter.
  - Barlow test: assesses whether the hip *can be* dislocated. Pull the hip up and then push downwards and laterally
  - Ortolani test: assesses whether the hip *is* dislocated. Pull the hip upwards into the acetabulum (producing a 'clunk'), then the hip can be abducted. (Ortolani = out.)

Feet

- Talipes equino varus: primary club foot. Usually a fixed structural deformity requiring early manipulation and fixation.
- Calcaneo valgus: common. Dorsum of the foot is in a position close to the shin. Resolves after about 2 months with ↑ calf muscle tone.
- Positional talipes is extremely common and involves no bony deformity. It is easily corrected by movement and treated with physiotherapy.

Spine

- Lie the infant prone in one hand, and with the other palpate the spine, checking for spina bifida occulta or a dermal sinus.

Neurological examination

Because infants with little or no cerebral cortex can show normal reflexes and tone, you should observe the baby's state of consciousness throughout the examination. This should vary from quiet sleep to semi-wakefulness to an alert state. A normal infant will be consolable when they cry, whereas it is very difficult to settle a neurologically abnormal infant.

Inspection of the spine

- Any midline lesion over the spine requires investigation.

Posture

- Generally flexor, although abnormal intrauterine positions can distort this, such as extended breech position.

Movements

- Watch spontaneous limb movements, noting the presence of 'jitteriness'.

Tone

Assess and compare the flexor recoil of the limbs.
  Evaluate tone in response to gravity:
- Pull to sit test. Let the baby grasp your fingers and pull them up to sit. The head should flex and follow the traction to an upright position and hold momentarily. Also observe the tone in the baby's arms.
- Ventral suspension is assessed by grasping the infant under each axilla. A normal infant will support themselves in this position by extending their back and hips, lifting their head, and flexing their arms and legs.

Primitive reflexes (See Table 17.6)
- These are used to assess asymmetry of function, gestational age, and neurological function.

Vision
- Assessment of vision should be carried out with the infant in an alert state. The baby will fix on an interesting object 20cm away, and will follow the target.

Hearing
- This can be assessed by sounding a loud rattle outside of the infant's vision. The baby should still to the noise.

Head circumference and weight
- Finally, measurement and plotting of head circumference and birth-weight on a centile chart is of utmost importance.

Practical procedures

Using this chapter

- This chapter describes those practical procedures that the junior doctor or senior nurse may be expected to perform.
- Obviously, some of these are more complicated than others—and should only be performed once you have been trained specifically in the correct technique by a more senior colleague.

Rules are made to be broken

- Very many procedures and practical skills do not have a 'correct' method but have an 'accepted' method.
- These methods should, therefore, be abided by but deviation from the routine by a competent practitioner, when circumstances demand, is acceptable.

Infiltrating anaesthetic agents

A large number of procedures involve the infiltration of local anaesthetic agents. It is important that you deliver these safely—injection of a large amount of anaesthetic into a vein could lead to potentially fatal cardiac arrhythmias. It is also important, of course, to ensure that you do not damage any vessels.

Advance and pull back

- Whenever you inject anything, you should advance the needle and attempt to pull back the plunger at each step—if you do not aspirate blood, you may *then* go ahead and infiltrate the anaesthetic.

Making a surface bleb

- Take the syringe of anaesthetic (e.g. 1% lidocaine = 10mg/ml) and a small needle.
- Pinch a portion of skin, insert the needle horizontally into the surface.
- Withdraw, as above, and inject a small amount of the anaesthetic— you should see a wheal of fluid rise.
- The area of skin will now be sufficiently anaesthetized to allow you to infiltrate deeper.

Other notes on local anaesthetics

- The maximum does of lidocaine is 3mg/kg in an adult.
  - This can be increased to 7mg/kg if mixed with adrenaline (although never to be used in this way at end-arteries).
- Lidocaine is a weak base and only works in its non-ionized form. It is, therefore, relatively ineffectual in infected (acidic) tissue.
- Lidocaine and other local anaesthetics sting on initial infiltration so warn the patient.

Hand hygiene

When?

The WHO World Alliance for Patient Safety, in 2006, identified 'five moments' for hand hygiene. These are:

- Before patient contact.
- Before an aseptic task.
- After body fluid exposure risk.
- After patient contact.
- After contact with a patient's surroundings.

Soap or alcohol gel?

Repeated washing with soap and water can cause skin dryness and can be time consuming. For these reasons, alcohol gel has become commonplace in clinical settings. There are no hard and fast rules but:

- Alcohol gel should not substitute soap and water if your hands are visibly soiled or if you are undertaking an aseptic procedure.
- Remember that alcohol gel is not effective against *Clostridium difficile*.

Soap and water technique

- Adhere to the 'bare below elbow' rule.
- Wet hands with water.
- Apply soap (from a dispenser) to cover all hand surfaces.
- Ensure all seven parts of the hands are thoroughly cleaned:
  - Rub hands palm-to-palm
  - Rub back of each hand with the palm of the other, fingers interlaced
  - Rub hands palm-to-palm with fingers interlaced
  - Lock hands together and rub backs of fingers against opposite palm
  - Rub thumbs in rotational movement with opposite hand
  - Rub tips of fingers into opposite palms
  - Rub each wrist with opposite hand.
- Hold hands under running water, rub vigorously to remove all suds.
- Turn off taps using elbows.
- Dry thoroughly with paper towel.
- Dispose of paper towels in appropriate clinical bin (using foot pedal).
- DO NOT TOUCH any other objects until task is undertaken and completed.

Alcohol gel technique

Essentially the same technique as above but no need to rinse or dry with a paper towel.

- Squirt small amount of gel onto centre of palm.
- Ensure all seven parts of the hands are thoroughly cleaned as above.
- Allow 20–30 seconds for hands to dry, holding hands up.
- Following disinfection, DO NOT TOUCH any other objects prior to commencing procedure.

Consent

See the latest guidance at 🕭 http://www.gmc-uk.org

Introduction

Consent is permission granted by a person allowing you to subject them to something; anything from physical examination to surgical procedures. Performing an act on a competent adult without their consent constitutes a criminal offence. (See also Boxes 18.1 and 18.2.)

Capacity

The patient must be able to understand what a procedure involves, the possible consequences of a decision or of failure to make a decision. All adults are assumed to have capacity unless demonstrated otherwise.

Assessing capacity

The patient must be able to:
- Understand the information including any consequences.
- Retain the information.
- Weigh the information as part of decision making.
- Communicate their decision.

A patient lacking capacity

- Your reasons for believing a patient lacks capacity to make a certain decision should be clearly documented.
  - A patient may become temporarily incapacitated by, for example, acute confusion. Treatment may only be carried out in these circumstances if it cannot reasonably be delayed until incapacity is resolved. If this is the case, treatment must be decided according to the best interests of the patient.

Voluntary consent

- Consent is only valid if given voluntarily, without pressure from relatives, friends, or medical professionals.

Information

Patients must be provided with sufficient information to enable them to make an informed decision. Information must include:
- What the procedure entails and the rationale for doing it.
- Any alternatives available.
- Significant risks.
  - This includes any 'significant risk which would affect the judgement of a reasonable patient', not just those risks deemed significant by a responsible body of medical opinion (the Bolam test). Failure to disclose such risks may render you guilty of negligence.
- Additional procedures that may be necessary under the same anaesthetic should be discussed during initial consent.
- If patients refuse information about a procedure, this should be clearly documented and the patient provided with the opportunity to discuss later.

Consent forms

- Written consent is evidence that consent has been sought but does not confirm its validity.
- If consent is not voluntary, information is lacking, or the patient lacks capacity, then consent is not valid regardless of the presence of a consent form.
  - Certain procedures (included in the Mental Health Act and Human Fertilisation and Embryology Act) require written consent.
- ► Consent that is oral or non-verbal may also be valid.

Who should seek consent?

- Ideally, the professional providing the treatment or investigation in question, though this is not always possible.
- The professional seeking consent should at least have sufficient knowledge to understand and explain the procedure, its indication, and any risks involved.
  - If you are asked to seek consent for a procedure but lack this knowledge, it is your responsibility to seek advice from colleagues; failure to do so may result in invalid consent.

Refusal to consent

- If an adult with capacity refuses to give consent for a procedure, this **must** be respected (except in specific circumstances outlined in the Mental Health Act), even if refusal will lead to death of the patient or their unborn child.
- In these circumstances, rigorous examination of a patient's competence is necessary.
  - The same is true if a patient withdraws consent at any time, if they still have capacity.

Advanced refusal

- Advance refusal is valid if made at a time when a patient is competent and appropriately informed.
- Applicable when patient lacks capacity.
- Failure to respect the refusal may result in legal action.
- If doubt exists as to validity, the courts must be consulted.

Adults lacking capacity

- May be temporary, permanent, or fluctuating.
- ► No-one may give consent on behalf of an incompetent adult, unless a valid Lasting Power of Attorney exists.
- ► Patients must be treated in their best interests (not just medical interests) taking into account psychological, religious/spiritual, and financial well-being.
- Those close to the patient should be involved unless the patient has previously made clear that they should not be; independent patient advocacy services exist for consultation when the patient does not have anyone close.
- Where there is doubt as to best interests or capacity, the High Court may give a ruling.

Lasting powers of attorney (Mental Capacity Act 2005)

- A document created by someone (the 'donor') to confer authority to give consent for investigation or treatment (as well as other issues) to a named individual(s) ('donees').
- Must be registered.
- Only valid when the patient lacks capacity.
- Must specifically authorize the donee to make decisions regarding welfare or medical treatment.
  - ▶ Unless specifically stated, do not extend to decisions about life-sustaining treatment.

Patients under 18 years of age

16–17 years

- If competent, may consent to or refuse an intervention.
- If incompetent, an individual with parental responsibility may provide consent.

Under 16: Gillick competence

- A child under 16 may consent to treatment if they are able to fully understand what is involved in an intervention.
  - This may apply to some interventions and not others.
- If a child is Gillick competent, parental consent is not required, though it is good practice to encourage a child to inform their parents unless this is not in their best interests.

Overriding decisions: under 18 years

- Refusal may be overridden by an individual with parental responsibility or the courts.
- Should consider the person's welfare as a whole. May involve sharing information that the child does not wish divulged; necessary if refusal puts the child at serious risk.
- ▶ In dire emergency, where a person with parental responsibility is unreachable or refuses consent for life-saving treatment that appears to be in the best interests of the child, it is acceptable to preserve life.

Box 18.1 Pre-procedure ABCDE

Questions to ask yourself before any procedure:
- **A** = Allergies
- **B** = Bloods
- **C** = Consent
- **D** = Drug history
- **E** = Emergency cover in case of complication or failure of the procedure.

Box 18.2 WHO checklist

- The WHO pre-procedure checklist is a series of questions to ask of the patient and the person performing the procedure
- This is usually reserved for complex interventional procedures and surgery
  - Check your local guidance
- Questions cover introductions, patient details, allergies, details of the procedure and any other pre-procedure checks
  - You should familiarize yourself with the questions and perform these checks yourself before performing any procedure (even if not on a formal WHO checklist form)
- For more information, go to ⌘ http://www.who.int

Aseptic technique

▶ You should always consider the sterility of the items to be touched before you begin each procedure. If some or all items need to remain sterile, an aseptic technique should be used.

Aseptic non-touch technique

The highest level of asepsis, designed to minimize or completely remove the chance of contamination, is known as 'aseptic non-touch technique' (ANTT) (Boxes 18.3 and 18.4).

Before
- Wash hands with soap and water or alcohol gel.
- Put on disposable apron and any other protective items.
- Clean trolley/tray with wipes and dry with a paper towel.
- Gather equipment and put on the lower shelf of the trolley.
- Take trolley/tray to the patient.

During
- Wash hands with alcohol gel.
- Remove sterile pack outer packaging and slide the contents on to the top shelf of the trolley or onto the tray, taking care not to touch the sterile pack.
- Open the dressing pack using only the corners of the paper, taking care not to touch any of the sterile equipment.
- Place any other required items on the sterile field ensuring the outer packaging does not come into contact with the sterile field.
- Put a pair of non-sterile gloves on to remove any dressings on the patient and ensure that they are positioned appropriately.
- Discard gloves and wash hands.
- Put sterile gloves on.

After
- Dispose of contaminated equipment in the rubbish bag from the dressing pack. Dispose of all packaging.
- Dispose of aprons and gloves in the appropriate waste as per local policy.
- Wash hands.
- Clean the trolley with detergent wipes and dry with a paper towel.

Two-person technique

- An assistant can be very helpful in maintaining the position of the patient, opening packs, and decanting solutions for the person performing the procedure.
- The 'clean practitioner' must wear the sterile gloves and open the first pack to establish a sterile field.
- The second ('dirty') practitioner can then open all the other equipment and drop onto the sterile field.

Clean technique

- This is a modified aseptic technique, aiming to prevent the introduction or spread of micro-organisms and to prevent cross-infection to patients and staff. This is used when true asepsis is not required (e.g. when dealing with contaminated sites or when *removing* drains and catheters).
- Sterile equipment is not always used.
- 'Clean technique' allows the use of tap water, non-sterile gloves, multi-pack dressings, and multi-use containers of creams and ointments.

Box 18.3 ANTT or 'clean' technique?

When to use ANTT

- Insertion, repositioning, or dressing invasive devices such as catheters, drains, and intravenous lines
- Dressing wounds healing by primary intention
- Suturing
- When sterile body areas are to be entered
- If there is tracking to deeper areas or the patient is immunocompromised.

When to use clean technique

- Removing sutures, drains, urethral catheters
- Endotracheal suction, management of tracheostomy site
- Management of enteral feeding lines
- Care of stomas
- Instillation of eye drops.

Box 18.4 Interruptions

- If the sterile procedure is interrupted for more than 30 minutes, new sterile packs should be opened and the sterility process started from scratch.

Subcutaneous and intramuscular injections

Usual sites for subcutaneous injections are upper arms and the abdomen, particularly the periumbilical region.

Intramuscular injections can be administered at any site with adequate muscle mass. Usual sites are deltoids and the gluteal region (upper, outer quadrant of buttock).

Contraindications
- Contraindications regarding the drugs being injected will vary dependent upon the drugs being administered.
- Infection at the injection site.
- Oedema or lymphoedema at the injection site.

Risks
- Incorrect drug and/or dosage administered.
- Allergy to drug(s).
- Haemorrhage, haematoma.
- Infection.
- Injection into a blood vessel.
- Injection into a nerve.

Equipment
- Appropriate syringe.
- 25G (orange) needle (usually).
- Prescribed drug.
- Prescription chart.
- Antiseptic swab.
- Plaster.

Before you start
- Assess patient for drugs required (i.e. for pain relief, vomiting, etc.).
- Refer to prescription chart, double-checking the appropriate drugs and dosage to be given.
  - ▶ Always ensure you are fully aware of any possible side effects of any drugs you are due to administer.
- Double-check the prescription chart for date and appropriate route for administration.
- Check administration of previous dose—not too soon after last dose?
- Ensure that the drug to be given is within its use-by date.
- Check patient and chart for any evidence of allergies, or reactions.
- Once all above completed as per hospital policy, draw-up required drug and check appropriate needle size.
- Complete appropriate documentation.
- Once checked by suitably qualified staff, take drug and prescription chart to the patient.

Subcutaneous procedure

- Introduce yourself, confirm the patient's identity, explain the procedure and obtain informed consent.
- Check with patient: name and date of birth (if capable).
  - If incapable, check name band with another healthcare professional.
- Select appropriate site, and cleanse with the antiseptic wipe.
- Grasp skin firmly between thumb and forefinger of your left hand.
- Insert needle at 45° angle into the pinched skin, then release skin from your grip.
- Draw syringe plunger back, checking for any blood. If none, inject drug slowly.
  - ▶ If any blood is noted on pulling the plunger back, withdraw and stop procedure—provide reassurance and explanation to the patient.
- Once the procedure is completed without complication, withdraw needle and discard into a sharps bin.
- Monitor patient for any negative effects of the drug.

Intramuscular procedure

- Introduce yourself, confirm the patient's identity, explain the procedure, and obtain informed consent.
- Check with patient: name and date of birth (if capable).
  - If incapable, check name band with another healthcare professional
- Select appropriate site, and cleanse with the antiseptic wipe.
  - 🅘 If injecting into the buttock, mark a spot at the upper, outer quadrant to avoid the sciatic nerve
  - 🅘 If using the deltoid muscle, feel the muscle mass and ensure there is enough muscle to take the needle.
- Insert needle at 90° angle into the skin.
- Draw syringe plunger back, checking for any blood. If none, inject drug slowly.
  - ▶ If any blood is noted on pulling the plunger back, withdraw and stop procedure—provide reassurance and explanation to the patient.
- Once the procedure is completed without complication, withdraw needle and discard into a sharps bin.
- Monitor patient for any negative effects of the drug.

Documentation

- Drugs should always be signed for as per local policy.
- Signature and time should be clearly recorded.
- Site drug administered.
- Reason for drug administration, time given and any impact on the patient should be recorded.
- Immediate vital signs should be recorded in notes.
- Any causes for concern arising from administration of drugs should be clearly documented in the medical notes.
- Signature, printed name, contact details.

Intravenous injections

Intravenous injections can be administered by puncturing the vein with a needle and syringe and injecting directly. The procedure below describes injecting via an intravenous cannula. If no cannula is in place, cannulate first.

▶ Ensure that you comply with the local policy regarding drug administration. In hospital, two healthcare professionals should usually check and administer medication.

Contraindications

- Contraindications regarding the drugs being injected will vary dependent upon the drugs being administered.
- Infection at the cannula insertion site.
- Thrombosis within the vein to be injected.

Risks

- Incorrect drug and/or dosage administered.
- Allergy to drug(s).
- Injection of air embolus.

Equipment

- Appropriate syringe (dependent upon quantity of drug to be administered).
- Prescribed drug.
- Saline flush (10ml syringe with sterile saline).
- Prescription chart.
- Antiseptic swab.

Before you start

- Assess patient for drugs required (i.e. for pain relief, vomiting, etc.).
- ▶ Refer to prescription chart, double-checking the appropriate drugs and dosage to be given.
  - ▶ Always ensure you are fully aware of any possible side effects of any drugs you are due to administer.
- ▶ Double-check the prescription chart for date and appropriate route for administration.
- ▶ Check administration of previous dose—not too soon after last dose?
- ▶ Ensure that the drug to be given is within its use-by date.
- ▶ Check patient and chart for any evidence of allergies, or relevant drug reactions.
- Always comply with the local hand hygiene practices.
- Once all above completed as per hospital policy, draw-up required drug and check appropriate needle size.
- Complete appropriate documentation.
- Once checked by suitably qualified staff take drug and prescription chart to the patient.

Procedure

- Introduce yourself, confirm the patient's identity, explain the procedure and obtain informed consent.
- Check with patient: name and date of birth (if capable).
  - If incapable, check name band with another healthcare professional
  - 🛈 The patient may need to be assisted to change position, if unable to move themselves, and to enable access to an appropriate site.
- Cleanse the cannula port with the antiseptic wipe.
- Attach the saline flush to the syringe port and inject a few ml to check patency of the cannula.
  - ▶ Watch for a bleb forming as consequence of extravasation.
- If no problems are encountered, swap the flush for the drug-containing syringe and inject drug slowly.
- To finish, inject a few more ml of saline into the cannula port and re-attach the bung.
- Once the procedure is completed without complication, withdraw needle and discard into a sharps bin.
- Monitor patient for any negative effects of the drug.

Documentation

- Drugs should always be signed for as per local policy.
- Signature and time should be clearly recorded.
- Site drug administered.
- Reason for drug administration, time given, and any impact on the patient should be recorded in the notes.
- Immediate vital signs should be recorded in notes.
- Any causes for concern arising from administration of drugs should be clearly documented in the medical notes.
- Signature, printed name, contact details.

Venepuncture

Risks

- Bleeding, haematoma.
- Infection.
- Accidental arterial puncture.

Inappropriate sites

- Oedematous areas.
- Cellulitis.
- Haematomas.
- Phlebitis or thrombophlebitis.
- Scarred areas.
- Limb in which there is an infusion.
- Upper limb on the side of a previous mastectomy and axillary clearance.
- Limbs with arteriovenous (AV) fistulae or vascular grafts.

Equipment

- Gloves.
- Sterile wipe (e.g. chlorhexidine or isopropyl alcohol).
- Cotton wool balls or gauze.
- Tape.
- Tourniquet.
- Needle (try 12G first).
- Syringe (size depends on amount of blood required).
- Collection bottles.

Procedure: needle and syringe

- Introduce yourself, confirm the patient's identity, explain the procedure, and obtain verbal consent.
- Position the patient appropriately: sat comfortably with arm placed on a pillow.
- Wash hands, put on your gloves and apply the tourniquet proximally.
- Identify the vein; the best location is often at the antecubital fossa.
  - Palpable (not necessarily visible) veins are ideal.
- Clean the site with the wipe, beginning centrally and moving outwards in concentric circles/swirls.
- Whilst the sterilizing solution dries, remove the needle and syringe from packaging and connect together.
- Unsheathe the needle.
- Using your non-dominant thumb, pull the skin taut over the vein in order to anchor it.
- Warn the patient to expect a 'sharp scratch'.
- Insert the needle, bevel up, at an angle of 30 until a flashback is seen within the hub of the needle.
  - With experience you will feel a 'give' as the vein is entered.
- Hold the syringe steady and withdraw the plunger slowly until the required amount of blood is obtained.
- Release the tourniquet.

- Remove the needle, holding cotton wool or gauze to the puncture site.
- Secure the cotton wool or gauze in place or replace with a plaster.
- Vacuum collection bottles are filled by puncturing the rubber top with the needle and allowing the blood to enter the tube.
- Label the tubes at the patient's bedside and dispose of the sharps in a sharps bin.

Procedure: vacuum device

The procedure is much the same as with a syringe but:

- Vacutainer needles are double-ended, with one end a standard needle, the other covered by a rubber sheath. This end inserts into the holder and is screwed in place.
- On penetrating the vein no flashback is seen.
- Once the needle is in place, vacuum collection bottles are inserted into the holder over the sheathed needle in turn—the holder must be held firmly in place.
- Bottles are self-filling; some require filling to a pre-defined level or tests will be invalidated.
- Remove the tourniquet before removing the last bottle, then remove the needle from the skin.

Procedure tips

- If no veins are visible or palpable, don't limit yourself to the upper limb: any peripheral vein will suffice.
  - If veins are still not visible, try warming the limb.
- If several attempts have failed, seek help from a colleague.
- If the vacuum collection system is proving difficult, try using needle and syringe:
  - A 'flashback' will be seen on entering the vein
  - The flow of blood may be controlled
  - If this also proves unsuccessful, try using a butterfly needle (Box 18.5).

Documentation

- Detailed documentation of the procedure is usually not required—but you should record that blood was taken and what tests it has been sent for.
- Record any adverse incidents during the procedure or if multiple attempts were performed.
  - If a particularly good vein was found, you may wish to record this for the benefit of the person taking blood next time.
- Signature, printed name, contact details.

Box 18.5 Butterfly needles

A butterfly is a short needle with flexible 'wings' on either side, and a length of flexible tubing to connect to the syringe. It is easy to manoeuvre once the skin is penetrated, and can be easily fixed in place by the wing, pressed down by the non-dominant thumb. It carries a greater risk of needle-stick injury.

Sampling from a central venous catheter

▶ Central venous lines should only be used for blood sampling if it is not possible to obtain a sample via the peripheral route. Do not risk catheter sepsis or a clotted line unless there are no alternatives.

The following describes venous blood sampling from a line in the internal jugular vein. The principles are the same for a line at any site.

Risks
- Clot or infection in the line.
- Air embolus.
- Physical damage to the line: burst or torn port.

Equipment
- 3 x 10ml syringes.
- 0.9% isotonic or heparinized saline.
- Chlorhexidine spray or iodine solution.
- Sterile gauze.
- Sterile gloves and apron.
- Sterile drape.

Procedure
- Introduce yourself, confirm the identity of the patient, explain the procedure, and obtain verbal consent.
- Stop any infusions (if possible) for at least one minute before sampling.
- Place the patient in a supine position.
- Ask the patient to turn their head away from the line site during the procedure.
- Drape the site and put on a pair of sterile gloves and apron.
- Spray the line end with the chlorhexidine solution or wipe with gauze dipped in iodine.
- Clamp the line port and remove the cap, if present.
- Connect a 10ml syringe to the port and then unclamp.
- Withdraw 5–10ml of blood, clamp the line, and remove the syringe.
- Discard the blood.
- Repeat the procedure with a new syringe, withdrawing 10ml.
- Clamp the line, disconnect the syringe.
  - Keep this sample.
- Fill the final syringe with saline and attach it to the port.
- Unclamp the port and instil the saline.
- Clamp the port again before disconnecting the syringe.
- Replace the port cap.

Procedure tips

- Always be sure to clamp the port *before* removing the syringe and unclamp before withdrawing blood or instilling the saline.
- Most central lines have several ports: which should I use?
  - Blood should ideally be sampled from the port with its hole at the tip of the line—this is often the brown port
  - Check the ports: most will have the gauge printed on them, choose the largest gauge port available.
- Be sure to remove any bubbles from the saline before instilling.
- Infusions must be stopped: otherwise a significant portion of the sample obtained may be the solution that is entering via the other port giving inaccurate results at analysis!

Arterial blood gas sampling

Contraindications
- Negative modified Allen's test.
- Cutaneous or subcutaneous lesion at the puncture site (Box 18.6).
- Surgical shunt (e.g. in a dialysis patient) in the limb.
- Infection or known peripheral vascular disease at the puncture site.
- Coagulopathy.

Risks
- Bleeding.
- Haematoma.
- Arteriospasm.
- Infection.
- False aneurysm formation.
- Arterial occlusion.

Equipment
- Gloves.
- Sterile wipe (e.g. isopropyl alcohol).
- Cotton wool balls.
- Tape.
- Gauze.
- Heparinized self-filling syringe and needle.

Box 18.6 Choosing a site

The radial artery at the level of the radial styloid is the usual site of choice as it is both superficial and easily accessible.

If the vessel is not obviously palpable, it is also possible to sample arterial blood at the brachial artery in the antecubital fossa or femoral artery just distal to the inguinal ligament.

Procedure: radial artery
- Introduce yourself, confirm the patient's identity, explain the procedure, and obtain informed consent.
- Position the patient appropriately: sitting comfortably with arm placed on a pillow, forearm supinated, wrist passively dorsiflexed.
- ▶ Confirm ulnar arterial supply to the hand before starting (modified Allen's test):
  - Compress the radial and ulnar arteries with your thumbs
  - Ask the patient to make a fist and open it
  - The hand should appear blanched
  - Release pressure from the ulnar artery and watch the palm
  - The palm should flush to its normal colour
  - ▶ If not, there may be inadequate ulnar arterial supply and damage to the radial artery during blood taking may result in critical ischaemia.
- Put on your gloves.
- Identify the radial artery with index and middle fingers of your non-dominant hand.

- Clean the site, beginning centrally and spiralling outwards.
- Whilst the sterilizing solution dries, remove the needle and syringe from packaging and attach the needle to the end of the syringe.
- Eject excess heparin from the syringe through the needle.
  - ❗ Check local equipment. Some heparinized syringes contain a heparinized sponge and excess heparin/air should not be expelled
- Warn the patient to expect a 'sharp scratch'.
- Whilst palpating the artery (but not obliterating the pulsation), insert the needle just distal to your fingertips, bevel facing proximally, at an angle of 45–60° until a flashback is seen within the needle chamber.
- Hold the syringe steady and allow it to fill itself with 1–2ml blood.
- As you withdraw the needle, apply the gauze swab to the site, maintaining firm manual pressure over for at least 2 minutes
- Dispose of the needle and apply a vented cap, expelling any excess air.
  - (This may not be necessary depending on your equipment.)

Procedure: brachial artery

- Position the elbow in extension. Angle the needle 60°.

Procedure: femoral artery

- Position the patient with hip extended.
- The pulse is felt 2cm below the midpoint between pubic tubercle and anterior superior iliac spine.
- Angle the needle at 90° to the skin.
- Pressure must be applied for at least 5 minutes.

Procedure tips

- Before you start: know where the analyser is and how to use it!
- The key is carefully palpating the artery and lining the needle up to puncture it. Take your time!
- The majority of the pain comes from puncturing the skin. If no flashback is seen immediately, try repositioning the needle by withdrawing slightly without removing it from the skin.
- If there will be some delay in analysing the sample, store the blood-filled syringe on ice.
- Errors occur: if there is air in the syringe, if the sample is delayed in reaching the analyser (if this is anticipated, put the sample on ice), or if a venous sample is accidentally obtained.

Documentation

- Date, time, indication, consent obtained.
- Record how much (if any) supplemental oxygen the patient is on.
- Artery punctured.
- Modified Allen's test?
- How many passes?
- Any immediate complications.
- Signature, printed name, contact details.

Peripheral venous cannulation

Contraindications
- Cannulae should not be placed unless intravenous access is required.
- Caution in patients with a bleeding diathesis.

Risks
- Infection, which could be local or systemic.

Before you start
- Can the drug be given by another route?
- What is the smallest appropriate cannula? (Table 18.1)
- What is the most appropriate location for the cannula? (Box 18.7)

Box 18.7 Choosing a vein
- Avoid areas of skin damage, erythema, or an arm with an AV fistula
- Excessive hair should be cut with scissors before cleaning the skin
- It is best to avoid joint areas such as the antecubital fossa
  - This can cause kinking of the cannula and discomfort
  - A straight vein, in an area such as the forearm or dorsum of the hand where long bones are available to splint the cannula are usually best.
- Wide-bore access requires siting in large veins and often this is only practicable in the antecubital fossa
- In practice, especially in patients who have been cannulated many times before, it is often necessary to go wherever you find a vein.

Sizing cannulae
- Cannulae are colour-coded according to size. The 'gauge' is inversely proportional to the external diameter.
- The standard size cannula is 'green' or 18G but for most hospital patients, a 'pink' or 20G cannula will suffice. Even blue cannulae are adequate in most circumstances unless fast flows of fluid are required.

Table 18.1 Cannula sizes

Gauge	External diameter (mm)	Length (mm)	Approximate maximum flow rate (ml/min)	Colour
14G	2.1	45	290	Orange
16G	1.7	45	172	Grey
18G	1.3	45	76	Green
20G	1.0	33	54	Pink
22G	0.8	25	25	Blue

Equipment

- Gloves.
- Sterile wipe (e.g. chlorhexidine).
- Cannula of appropriate gauge.
- Sterile saline for injection ('flush') and a 5ml syringe.
- Cannula dressing.
- Cotton wool balls/gauze.
- Tourniquet.

Procedure

- Introduce yourself, confirm the patient's identity, explain the procedure, and obtain informed consent
- Put the gloves on.
- Apply the tourniquet proximally on the limb.
- Once the veins are distended, select an appropriate vein: it should be straight for the length of the cannula.
- Wipe with sterile wipe, beginning where you intend to insert the cannula and moving outwards in circles.
- Fill the syringe with saline and eject any air bubbles.
- Remove the dressing from its packaging.
- Unwrap the cannula and check that all parts disengage easily. Fold the wings down so that they will lie flat on the skin after insertion.
- Using your non-dominant hand, pull the skin taut over the vein in order to anchor it in place.
- Hold the cannula with index and middle fingers in front of the cannula wings, thumb behind the cap.
- Warn the patient to expect a 'sharp scratch'.
- Insert the needle, bevel up, at an angle of 30° to the skin, until a flashback of blood is visible within the chamber of the cannula.
- Advance the needle a small amount further, then advance the cannula into the vein over the needle, whilst keeping the needle stationary.
- Release the tourniquet.
- Place your non-dominant thumb over the tip of the cannula, compressing the vein.
- Flush the cannula with a little saline from the end and replace the cap.
- Write the date on the cannula dressing and secure in place.

Procedure tips

- Local anaesthetic cream may be of benefit if you have time.
- Reliable veins are located on the radial aspect of the wrist (cephalic vein), antecubital fossa, and anterior to the medial malleolus (long saphenous).
- If you fail initially with a large-bore cannula, try a smaller gauge.
- If no veins are visible/palpable at first, try warming the limb in warm water for a couple of minutes.
- It may be useful to get assistance to hold the patient's arm still if they are likely to move it during the procedure.
- If you are unable to cannulate after several attempts, try asking someone else. A pair of fresh eyes make a lot of difference!

Femoral venous catheter insertion

Contraindications

- Fem-fem bypass surgery, IVC filter, infected site, thrombosed vein.

Risks

- Arterial puncture, infection, haematoma, thrombosis, air embolism, arteriovenous fistula, peritoneal puncture.

Equipment

- Central line catheter pack.
  - Containing: central line (16–20cm length, multi-lumen if required), introducer needle, 10ml syringe, guidewire, dilator, blade.
- Large dressing pack including a large sterile drape and gauze.
- Normal saline.
- Local anaesthetic for skin (1% lidocaine).
- Sterile preparation solution (2% chlorhexidine).
- Securing device or stitch.
- Sterile gloves, sterile gown, surgical hat and mask.
- Suitable dressing.

Procedure

- Introduce yourself, confirm the patient's identity, explain the procedure, and obtain written consent if possible.
- Position the patient supine (1 pillow), abduct the leg and place a spill sheet under the patient's leg.
- Identify the entry point: 1–2 cm below the mid-inguinal point and 1cm medial to femoral artery.
- Wearing a surgical hat and mask, wash hands using a surgical scrub technique and put on the sterile gown and gloves.
- Set up a trolley using an aseptic technique:
  - Open the dressing pack onto the trolley creating a sterile field
  - Open the central line catheter pack and place onto the sterile field
  - Flush all lumens of the catheter with saline and clamp the ends
  - Ensure the guidewire is ready for insertion
  - Attach the introducer needle to a 10ml syringe.
- Clean the area with sterile solution and surround with a large drape.
- Inject local anaesthetic into the skin over the entry point.
- Identify the femoral artery with your non-dominant hand.
- Pierce the skin through the entry point with the introducer needle.
- Direct the needle at a 30–45° angle to the skin and aim for the ipsilateral nipple, aspirating as you advance the needle.
- ▶ On hitting the vein the syringe will fill with blood.
- Keeping the needle still, carefully remove the syringe—blood should ooze (and not pulsate) out through the hub of the needle.
- Insert the guidewire part-way through the hub of the needle.
  - Guidewires are over 50cm in length; do not insert more than 20cm.
- Remove the needle over the guidewire ensuring one hand is always holding either the proximal or distal end of the wire.

- Thread the dilator over the wire, firmly pushing it through the skin.
  - This may require a small stab incision in the skin with a blade
  - Aim to get 2–3cm of dilator into the vein, not its full length.
- Check the guidewire has not been kinked by ensuring it moves freely through the dilator.
- Remove the dilator and apply pressure over with gauze to stop oozing.
- Thread the catheter over the guidewire until it emerges through the end of the distal port (unclamp this lumen!).
- Holding the guidewire at its port exit site with one hand, push the catheter through the skin with the other.
- Remove the guidewire.
- Blood should flow out of the end of the catheter.
- Aspirate and flush all ports.
- Fix catheter to skin using either a securing device or stitches.
- Cover with transparent dressing.

Procedure tips

- Placing a sandbag underneath the patient's buttock may improve positioning (if a sandbag is not available, roll up a towel or wrap a 1-litre bag of fluid in a sheet as an alternative).
- Do not force the guidewire. If there is resistance to insertion:
  - Reduce the angle of the needle, attempt a shallower insertion
  - Check you are still within the vein by aspirating with a syringe
  - Rotate the needle: this moves the bevel away from any obstruction.
- ▶ Losing the guidewire can be disastrous—always have one hand holding either the proximal or distal end of it.
- Always consider the possibility of an inadvertent arterial puncture:
  - Signs include pulsatile blood flow, high-pressure blood flow or blood bright red in colour (in the absence of hypotension or hypoxaemia)
  - Do not dilate if in any doubt
  - The use of saline in the aspirating syringe may make flushing the needle easier but also makes it more difficult to differentiate between venous and arterial blood.

Documentation

- Time, date, indication, informed consent obtained.
- Site and side of successful insertion.
- Site, side, and complications of unsuccessful attempt(s).
- Aseptic technique: gloves, gown, hat, mask, sterile solution.
- Local anaesthetic: type and amount infiltrated.
- Technique used: e.g. landmark, ultrasound guidance.
- Catheter used: e.g. triple lumen.
- Length of catheter *in situ* (length at skin).
- Signature, printed name, and contact details.

Central venous access: internal jugular vein

❗ This is the 'landmark' technique for the internal jugular vein.

Contraindications
- Infected insertion site.
- Thrombosed vein.
- Coagulopathy.

Risks
- Pneumothorax.
- Arterial puncture.
- Haematoma.
- Air embolism.
- Arrhythmias.
- Thrombosis.
- Arteriovenous fistula.
- Infection.
- Malposition.

Equipment
- Central line catheter pack:
  - Central line (16cm length for right side, 20cm for left side), introducer needle and 10ml syringe, guidewire, dilator, blade.
- Large dressing pack including a large sterile drape and gauze.
- Normal saline.
- Local anaesthetic for skin (1% lidocaine) with suitable (22G) needle and syringe.
- Sterile preparation solution (2% chlorhexidine).
- Sterile gloves, sterile gown, surgical hat and mask.
- Trolley and ECG monitoring.

Procedure
- Introduce yourself, confirm the patient's identity, explain the procedure, and obtain written consent if possible.
- Position the patient supine (1 pillow), tilt the bed head down and place a spill sheet under the patient's head.
- Attach ECG monitoring to the patient.
- Turn the patient's head away from the side of insertion.
- Identify triangle formed by the sternal and clavicular heads of the sternocleidomastoid muscle and the clavicle.
- Identify the entry point at the apex of the triangle.
- Wash hands using a surgical scrub technique and put on the sterile gown and gloves.
- With assistance, set up a trolley using an aseptic technique:
  - Open the dressing pack onto the trolley creating a sterile field
  - Open the central line catheter pack and place onto the sterile field
  - Flush all lumens of the catheter with saline and clamp the ends
  - Attach the introducer needle to a 10ml syringe.

- Clean the area with sterile preparation solution and place a large drape around it.
- Inject local anaesthetic into the skin over the entry point.
- Identify the carotid artery with your non-dominant hand. Pierce the skin through the entry point with the introducer needle ensuring the needle is lateral to the artery.
- Direct the needle at a 30° angle to the skin and advance using continuous aspiration, aiming for the *ipsilateral* nipple.
- On hitting the vein, the syringe will fill with blood.
- Keeping the needle still, carefully remove the syringe.
  - Blood should ooze (not pulsate) through the hub of the needle.
- Insert the guidewire through the needle and watch the ECG.
  - ⓘ Guidewires tend to be over 50cm in length but do not introduce more than 20cm as this may lead to arrhythmias.
- Remove the needle over the guidewire ensuring one hand is always holding either the proximal or distal end of the wire.
- Thread the dilator over the wire, firmly pushing it through the skin.
  - This may require a small stab incision in the skin with a blade
  - Aim to get 2–3cm of dilator into the vein, not its full length
- Check the guidewire has not been kinked by ensuring it moves freely through the dilator.
- Remove the dilator over the guidewire and apply pressure over the site with gauze.
- Thread the catheter over the guidewire until it emerges through the end of the distal port (unclamp this lumen!).
  - This may require withdrawing some of the guidewire.
- Holding the guidewire at its port exit site with one hand, push the catheter through the skin with the other.
- ▶ Avoid handling the catheter, in particular its tip.
  - Insert 16cm for a right-sided line and 20cm for a left-sided line.
- Remove the guidewire.
  - Blood should flow out through the end of the catheter.
- Aspirate and flush all ports with normal saline.
- Fix catheter to skin with a fixing device or sutures.
- Cover with a transparent dressing.
- Request a chest radiograph to confirm position.

Documentation

- Time, date, indication, and informed consent obtained.
- Site and side of successful insertion.
- Site, side, and complications of unsuccessful attempt(s).
- Aseptic technique: gloves, gown, hat, mask, type of sterile solution.
- Local anaesthetic: type and amount infiltrated.
- Technique used: e.g. landmark, ultrasound guidance.
- Catheter used: length and number of lumens.
- Aspirated and flushed.
- Length of catheter *in situ* (length at skin).
- Chest radiograph: site of tip, absence/presence of pneumothorax.
- Signature, printed name, and contact details.

Procedure tips

- The right internal jugular vein is usually favoured due to its relatively straight course and the absence of the thoracic duct on this side (Fig. 18.1).
- Tilting the bed head down will minimize the risk of air embolism and help distend the veins of the neck.

Getting started

- Asking the patient to sniff or lift their head off the bed will help identify the sternocleidomastoid muscle.
- Asking the patient to perform the Valsalva manoeuvre will distend the veins of the neck and help identify the internal jugular vein.
- For added safety, you may wish to start by using a 21G ('green') hypodermic needle instead of the introducer needle to 'seek' out the vessel using the same technique.
- Check clotting prior to insertion. Aim for INR <1.5 and platelets >50x10^9/L.
- Minimize spillage.

During the procedure

- ▶ The internal jugular vein is relatively superficial and should be encountered within 2–3cm. Do not continue advancing the needle if the vein has not been hit by this point.
- ▶ Do not force the guidewire in. If there is resistance to guidewire insertion:
  - Try lowering the angle of the needle making it more in line with the long axis of the vessel
  - Check you are still within the vein by aspirating with a syringe
  - Try rotating the needle thereby moving the bevel away from any obstruction.
- ▶ Losing the guidewire can be disastrous. Always have one hand holding either the proximal or distal end of it.
- The use of saline in the aspirating syringe may make flushing the needle easier but also makes it more difficult to differentiate between venous and arterial blood.
- ❶ Always consider the possibility of an inadvertent arterial puncture (Box 18.8):
  - Signs include pulsatile blood flow, high-pressure blood flow, or blood bright red in colour (in the absence of hypotension or hypoxaemia)
  - Do not dilate if in any doubt
  - Consider sending blood for a blood gas to confirm venous placement.

Finishing off

- There is an increased incidence of vascular injuries and thrombosis with left-sided catheters mainly because of insufficient catheter depth leading to the tip abutting the lateral wall of the upper SVC. You must ensure left-sided lines are long enough so that their tip lies within the lower part of the SVC.

- On the chest radiograph, confirm catheter position and the absence of a pneumothorax.
- The tip of the catheter should lie at the junction of the superior vena cava and right atrium which is approximately at the level of the carina.

Alternative approaches

- Anterior approach: midpoint of sternal head of sternocleidomastoid aiming towards ipsilateral nipple.
- Posterior approach: posterior border sternocleidomastoid at the crossing of the external jugular vein aiming for the sternal notch.

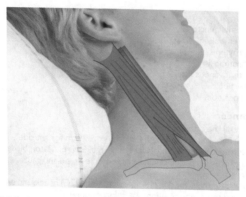

Fig. 18.1 Surface anatomy of the internal jugular vein.

Box 18.8 Structures your needle may hit

In front of the vein
- Internal carotid artery

Behind the vein
- Transverse process of the cervical vertebrae
- Sympathetic chain
- Phrenic nerve
- Dome of pleura
- Thoracic duct on left-hand side.

Medial to vein
- Internal carotid artery
- Cranial nerves IX–XII
- Common carotid and vagus nerve.

Central venous access: subclavian vein

This is the 'landmark' technique for the right subclavian vein (Fig. 18.2).

Contraindications

- Hyperinflated lungs (e.g. COPD patients).
- Coagulopathy.
- Infected insertion site.
- Thrombosed vein.

Risks

- Pneumothorax.
- Haemorrhage.
- Arterial puncture.
- Air embolism.
- Arrhythmias.
- Thrombosis.
- Arteriovenous fistula.
- Infection.
- Malposition.

Equipment

- Central line catheter pack:
  - Central line (16cm length for right side, 20cm for left side), introducer needle and 10ml syringe, guidewire, dilator, blade.
- Large dressing pack including a large sterile drape and gauze.
- Normal saline.
- Local anaesthetic for skin (1% lidocaine) with (22G) needle and syringe.
- Sterile preparation solution (2% chlorhexidine).
- Sterile gloves, sterile gown, surgical hat and mask.
- Trolley and ECG monitoring.

Procedure

- Introduce yourself, confirm the patient's identity, explain the procedure, and obtain written consent if possible.
- Position the patient supine (1 pillow), place a sandbag between shoulder blades and tilt the bed head down.
- Attach ECG leads onto the patient making sure they are not in the surgical field.
- Turn the patient's head away from the side of insertion.
- Identify the entry point, just inferior to the midpoint of the clavicle.
- Wash hands using a surgical scrub technique and put on the sterile gown and gloves.
- With assistance, set up a trolley using an aseptic technique:
  - Open the dressing pack onto the trolley creating a sterile field
  - Open the central line catheter pack and place onto the sterile field
  - Flush all lumens of the catheter with saline and clamp the ends
  - Ensure the guidewire is ready for insertion
  - Attach the introducer needle to a 10ml syringe.

- Clean the area with sterile preparation solution and place a large drape around it.
- Inject local anaesthetic into the skin over the entry point.
- Insert the introducer needle under the clavicle at a very shallow angle almost parallel to the floor.
- Advance the needle towards the sternal notch, aspirating as you advance.
- On hitting the vein the syringe will fill with blood.
- Keeping the needle still, carefully remove the syringe.
  - Blood should ooze (not pulsate) through the hub of the needle.
- Insert the guidewire through the needle and watch the ECG.
  - 🚨 Guidewires tend to be over 50cm in length but do not introduce more than 20cm as this may lead to arrhythmias.
- Remove the needle over the guidewire ensuring one hand is always holding either the proximal or distal end of the wire.
- Thread the dilator over the wire, firmly pushing it through the skin.
  - This may require a small stab incision in the skin with a blade
  - Aim to get 2–3cm of dilator into the vein, not its full length.
- Check the guidewire has not been kinked by ensuring it moves freely through the dilator.
- Remove the dilator over the guidewire and apply gauze to the site to mop up any spills.
- Thread the catheter over the guidewire until it emerges through the end of the distal port (unclamp this lumen!).
  - This may require withdrawing some of the guidewire.
- Holding the guidewire at its port exit site with one hand, push the catheter through the skin with the other.
- ▶ Avoid handling the catheter, in particular its tip.
  - Insert 16cm for a right-sided line and 20cm for a left-sided line
- Remove the guidewire.
  - Blood should flow out through the end of the catheter.
- Aspirate and flush all ports with normal saline.
- Fix catheter to skin with a fixing device or sutures.
- Cover with a transparent dressing.
- Request a chest radiograph to confirm catheter position and the absence of a pneumothorax.

Documentation

- Time, date, indication, and informed consent obtained.
- Site and side of successful insertion.
- Site, side, and complications of unsuccessful attempt(s).
- Aseptic technique: gloves, gown, hat, mask, type of sterile solution.
- Local anaesthetic: type and amount infiltrated.
- Technique used: e.g. landmark, ultrasound guidance.
- Catheter used: length and number of lumens.
- Aspirated and flushed.
- Length of catheter *in situ* (length at skin).
- CXR: site of tip, absence/presence of a pneumothorax.
- Signature, printed name, and contact details.

Procedure tips

Getting started

- Check clotting prior to insertion. Aim for INR <1.5, platelets >50x10⁹/L.
- 🚫 Direct pressure cannot be applied on the subclavian vessels so this route should be avoided in patients with a coagulopathy
- 🚫 There is a greater risk of pneumothorax than with internal jugular cannulation. A subclavian approach should, therefore, be avoided in patients with hyperinflated lungs.
- Minimize spillage.
- The underside of the clavicle can be reached by first directing the needle onto the clavicle and then carefully walking off it. The angle of the needle should however remain parallel to the floor.
- Asking an assistant to pull the ipsilateral arm caudally can improve access.
- If a sandbag is not available, roll up a towel or wrap a 1-litre bag of fluid in a spill sheet as an alternative.

During the procedure

- ▶ The subclavian vein should be encountered within 3–4cm. Do not continue advancing the needle if the vein has not been hit by this point.
- ▶ Do not force the guidewire in. If there is resistance to guidewire insertion:
  - Try lowering the angle of the needle making it more in line with the length of the vessel
  - Check you are still within the vein by aspirating with a syringe
  - Try rotating the needle thereby moving the bevel away from any obstruction.
- Catheter malposition, particularly into the ipsilateral internal jugular vein, is more common using the subclavian vein approach.
  - Many guidewires have a 'J' tip. Directing the 'J' tip caudally may help correct placement.
- ▶ Losing the guidewire can be disastrous. Always have one hand holding either the proximal or distal end of it.
- 🚫 Always consider the possibility of an inadvertent arterial puncture (Box 18.9):
  - Signs include pulsatile blood flow, high pressure blood flow or blood bright red in colour (in the absence of hypotension or hypoxaemia)
  - Do not dilate if in any doubt.
- The use of saline in the aspirating syringe may make flushing the needle easier but also makes it more difficult to differentiate between venous and arterial blood.

Finishing off

- The incidence of vascular injuries and thrombosis is increased with left-sided catheters mainly due to insufficient catheter depth leading to the tip abutting the lateral wall of the upper SVC.
  - You must ensure left-sided lines are long enough so that their tip lies within the lower part of the SVC.

- On the chest radiograph, confirm catheter position and the absence of a pneumothorax.
  - The tip of the catheter should lie at the junction of the superior vena cava and right atrium which is approximately at the level of the carina.

Alternative approaches
- Medial approach: junction of medial and middle thirds of the clavicle.
- Lateral approach: lateral to the mid-clavicular point. Often used with ultrasound guidance.

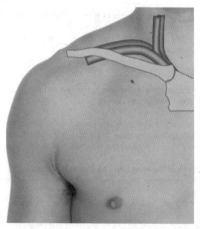

Fig. 18.2 Surface anatomy of the right subclavian vein.

Box 18.9 Structures your needle may hit

In front of the vein
- Clavicle
- Subclavius muscle.

Behind the vein
- Phrenic nerve
- Anterior scalene muscle
- Subclavian artery.

Below vein
- First rib
- Pleura.

Central venous access: ultrasound guidance

▶ Current recommendations in the UK are that ultrasound guidance should be considered when inserting any central venous catheter (NICE guidelines 2002).

Ultrasound basics

- 'Ultrasound' refers to sound waves of such a high frequency as to be inaudible to the human ear (>20 kHz).
- Medical ultrasound uses frequencies between 2 and 14 MHz.
- The 'linear' (straight) transducer is the probe of choice for imaging the vessels and other superficial structures.
- The frequency of the probe should be between 7.5–10 MHz for central venous access.

Basic controls

- Frequency.
  - Higher frequency may result in a better resolution but will not penetrate the tissues as deeply.
- Gain.
  - The gain control alters the amplification of the returned signals
  - This changes the grey scale of the image (can be thought of as increasing the brightness) but may not improve its quality.
- Depth.
  - The depth of the image on screen can be manually adjusted
  - It is wise to see the structures deep to the vessel to be cannulated.
- Focal length.
  - The focal point is usually displayed as an arrow at the side of the image
  - At this point, the image will be sharpest but resolution of the deeper structures will suffer
  - The focal point should be positioned in line with the vein to be cannulated.

Orientation

- By convention, the left of the screen should be that part of the patient to your left (i.e. the patient's right if you are facing the patient, the patient's left if you are scanning from behind them).
  - Touch edge of the probe and watch for the movement on screen to be sure you have the transducer the right way round.

Procedure: internal jugular vein catheterization

- With the patient positioned, squeeze sterile gel onto the patient's neck.
- Hold the probe cover open like a sock. Ask an assistant to squeeze ultrasound gel into the base and *carefully* lower the probe in after it. You can then unfurl the probe cover along the length of the wire using aseptic technique.
- Place probe over the surface markings of the vein (short axis of vessel).
- On the screen, look for two black circles side by side. These represent the vein and the artery.
- Identify the vessels by pressing down with the probe.
  - The vein will be compressible and the artery will not
  - The artery will be pulsatile. ❶ Note that the IJV may also be pulsatile with the patient head down (the JVP)
  - The artery is often circular in cross-section, the vein may be oval or a more complex ovoid shape.
- Follow the course of the vein up the patient's neck and identify a site where the artery sits relatively medial to the vein. At this point, centre the vein on to the screen holding the probe still with your non-dominant hand.
- ❶ Don't press too hard with the probe—you may compress the vein.
- Inject local anaesthetic into the skin around the midpoint of the probe using your dominant hand.
- Insert the introducer needle through the skin at the midpoint of the probe.
- Gently move the needle in and out to help locate the tip and its course on the screen.
  - ❶ The tip of the needle will only be visualized if it is advancing in the same plane as the ultrasound beam.
- Advance the needle (with continuous aspiration) towards the vein ensuring the tip is always in view.
- On hitting the vein, blood will be aspirated into the syringe. Flatten the needle ensuring blood can still be aspirated. At this point, the probe can be removed and the vein be catheterized using the Seldinger technique (see previous pages).
- The ultrasound can be used later in the procedure to ensure that the guidewire lies within the vein, if necessary.

Intravenous infusions

Equipment

- Gloves.
- An appropriate fluid bag.
- Giving set.
- Drip stand.
- 10ml syringe with saline flush.

Procedure

- ⓘ Intravenous infusions require intravenous access.
- Check the fluid in the bag and fluid prescription chart.
- Ask a colleague to double-check the prescription and the fluid and sign their name on the chart.
- ⓘ Flush the patient's cannula with a few millilitres of saline to ensure there is no obstruction. If there is evidence of a blockage, swelling at the cannula site, or if the patient experiences pain, you may need to replace the cannula.
- Open the fluid bag and giving set, which come in sterile packaging
- Unwind the giving set and close the adjustable valve.
- Remove the sterile cover from the bag outlet and from the sharp end of the giving set.
- Using quite a lot of force, push the giving set end into the bag outlet.
- Invert the bag and hang on a suitable drip-stand.
- Squeeze the drip chamber to half fill it with fluid.
- Partially open the valve to allow the drip to run, and watch fluid run through to the end (it might be best to hold the free end over a sink in case of spills).
- If bubbles appear, try tapping or flicking the tube.
- Once the giving set is filled with liquid, connect it to the cannula.
- Adjust the valve and watch the drips in the chamber.
- Adjust the drip rate according to the prescription (Box 18.10).

Documentation

- Ensure fluid and/or the drug is clearly timed and signed for as per local policy.
- Nursing and/or medical notes should be completed to include the reason for the infusion.
- Medical notes should be used to record any causes for concern arising from administration of the infusion.
- Cannula site (and cannula documentation) should be dated and signed on insertion.
- Ensure any fluid-monitoring chart is complete and updated as appropriate.
- Ensure that all entries in notes finish with your signature, printed name, and contact details.

Box 18.10 Drip rate

- Most infusions tend to be given with electronic devices which pump the fluid in at the prescribed rate. However, it is still important that healthcare professionals are able to set up a drip at the correct flow rate manually
- Using a standard giving set, clear fluids will form drips of about 0.05ml—that is, there will be approximately 20 drips/ml. You can then calculate the number of drips per minute for a given infusion rate as in Table 18.2.

Table 18.2 Drip rate

Prescription Number of hours per litre of fluid	Infusion rate (ml/hour)	Infusion rate (ml/minute)	Drip rate (drips/minute)
1	1000	16	320
2	500	8	160
4	250	4	80
6	166	3	60
8	125	2	40
10	100	1.6	32
12	83	1.4	28
24	42	0.7	14

Arterial line insertion

The following is the procedure for cannulating the radial artery.

Contraindications

- Infection at insertion site.
- Working arterio-venous fistula in the same limb.
- Traumatic injury proximal to the insertion site.
- Vascular insufficiency in the distribution of the artery to be cannulated.
- Significant clotting abnormalities.

Risks

- *Non-vascular:* superficial bleeding, infection, inadvertent arterial injection.
- *Vascular:* vasospasm, thrombosis, thromboembolism, air embolism, blood vessel injury, distal ischaemia.

Equipment

- Arterial catheter set:
  - Arterial catheter (20G), needle, guidewire
- Sterile gloves, sterile gown (+/– surgical hat and mask).
- Dressing pack including a sterile drape.
- Sterile preparation solution (e.g. 2% chlorhexidine).
- Local anaesthetic (e.g. 1% lidocaine), 22G needle, and 5ml syringe.
- (Optional) A three-way tap with a short extension (flushed with normal saline) connected to a 10ml syringe containing normal saline.
- Suture.
- Transducer set with pressurized bag of heparinized saline.

Procedure (modified Seldinger technique)

- Introduce yourself, confirm the patient's identity, explain the procedure, and obtain informed consent.
- Choose a site for arterial line insertion.
- Position the forearm so that it is supported from underneath and hyperextend the wrist.
- Set up a trolley keeping everything sterile:
  - Open the dressing pack onto the trolley creating a sterile field
  - Open the arterial catheter set and place onto the sterile field.
- Wash hands using a surgical scrub technique and put on the sterile gown and gloves.
- Clean the wrist, hand, and forearm with a sterile preparation solution and create a sterile field with the drape.
- Palpate the radial artery with your non-dominant hand and infiltrate the skin overlying the pulsation with some local anaesthetic.
- Insert the arterial needle, directing it towards the radial pulsation at a 30–45° angle. (Do not attach to a syringe.)
  - You can also use a syringe with the plunger removed. This allows identification of the arterial pulsation without excess spillage.
- On hitting the artery, blood will spurt out of the hub of the needle.

- Keeping the needle still, insert the guidewire through the hub of the needle. ❗ Don't force the guidewire.
- Remove the needle leaving the guidewire in place.
- Thread the arterial catheter over the guidewire making sure that the guidewire is seen at all times through the distal end of the catheter.
- Holding the distal end of the guidewire with one hand, push the arterial catheter through the skin with the other.
- Remove the guidewire.
  - Blood should spill out of the end of the catheter if it is within the artery.
- Connect to the short extension of the three-way tap, aspirate and flush with normal saline, and close off the tap.
  - Alternatively, connect immediately to a pressurized transducer set, aspirate and flush
  - ❗ Do not delay connection to transducer and flush-bag
  - ❗ Take extreme care not to allow any air bubbles to flush into the artery (risk of distal embolization).
- Suture in place.
- Label catheter as arterial and inform relevant staff.

Documentation

- Time, date, indication, and informed consent obtained.
- Site and side of successful insertion.
- Site, side, and complications of unsuccessful attempt(s).
- Aseptic technique: gloves, gown, hat, mask, sterile solution.
- Local anaesthetic: type and amount infiltrated.
- Technique used: modified Seldinger, cannula over needle.
- Catheter size used: 20G.
- Aspirated and flushed.
- Signature, printed name, and contact details.

Procedure tips

- ❗ Do not force the guidewire. If there is resistance, try lowering the needle to a shallower angle without removing it from the artery.
- ❗ Cover the floor with spill sheets as the procedure can be messy!
- ▶ The modified Allen's test should be used for assessment of the collateral supply to the hand before the radial artery is punctured but may not be completely reliable in predicting ischaemic injury.

Modified Allen's test

- Compress the radial and ulnar arteries at the wrist and ask the patient to clench their fist.
- Ask the patient to open the hand.
- Release pressure over the ulnar artery.
- Watch the palm for return of colour.
  - Return of colour should normally occur in 5–10 seconds.
- ▶ Return of colour taking over 15 seconds suggests an inadequate collateral supply by the ulnar artery and radial artery cannulation should not be performed.

Fine needle aspiration (FNA)

A method for obtaining a cytological sample of a mass lesion. This procedure should only be performed by, or under strict supervision of, an experienced practitioner.

▶ Fine needle aspiration usually takes place in the radiology department and is performed by an experienced radiologist under ultrasound or CT guidance. The following describes the older, 'blind' technique.

Contraindications

- Bleeding diathesis.
- Overlying infection.
- ⚠ Adjacent vital structures.
  - Image-guidance should always be used if available.

Risks

- Bleeding.
- Local infection.
- Damage to surrounding structures depending on site e.g. blood vessels, nerves.

Equipment

- Local anaesthetic (e.g. 1% lidocaine).
- Small-gauge (blue) needle and 10ml syringe.
- Sterile pack.
- Cleaning solution (e.g. chlorhexidine).
- Medium-gauge (green) needle.
- 10 or 20ml syringe for aspiration.
- Sterile gloves.

Procedure

- Introduce yourself, confirm the patient's identity, explain the procedure, and obtain informed consent.
- Position the patient according to the biopsy site, allowing easy palpation of the mass.
- Expose appropriately.
- Wash your hands and put on sterile gloves.
- Clean the area with the cleaning solution and apply drapes.
- Instil local anaesthetic to the skin and subcutaneous tissues, withdrawing the plunger prior to each injection to avoid intravenous injection and warning the patient to expect a 'sharp scratch'.
- Immobilize the mass with your non-dominant hand.
- Using your dominant hand, insert the needle through the skin into the lump, maintaining negative pressure on the plunger as you go.
- Once in the lump, the needle may be moved gently back and forth to obtain a greater volume of cells.
- It may be necessary to insert the needle several times to obtain a sufficient sample.
- Do not expect a large amount of material within the syringe! A tiny sample within the needle will usually suffice.

- Remove the needle and send the sample for cytology (you will need to gently expel the sample from the needle into a suitable container).
- Apply a sterile dressing to the site.

Alternative method

- There are two schools of thought in fine needle aspiration.
- Some practitioners use a small (blue) needle without a syringe attached.
  - This is moved in and out very quickly within the mass whilst also applying rotation
  - Capillary action deposits a cellular sample within the needle which can then be gently expelled using an empty syringe.
- This capillary action technique may result in a larger number of intact cells in the resultant sample as the negative pressure created when using a syringe can disrupt cell membranes.

Documentation

- Date and time.
- Indication, informed consent obtained.
- Type and amount of local anaesthetic used.
- Site of puncture.
- Aseptic technique used?
- How many passes?
- Volume and colour of sample obtained.
- Any immediate complications.
- Tests requested on resultant sample.
- Signature, printed name, and contact details.

Procedure tips

- 🛈 Radiological guidance should always be used if available.
- Contact the histopathology department in advance to ensure appropriate transport medium is used.
  - It may be possible to arrange immediate analysis, allowing diagnosis and repeat FNA if insufficient cells are obtained.

Lumbar puncture

Contraindications
- Infected skin or subcutis at the site of puncture.
- Coagulopathy or thrombocytopenia.
- Raised intracranial pressure with a differential pressure between the supra- and infra-tentorial compartments such as seen in space-occupying lesions. If in doubt, image first!

Risks
- Post-procedure headache.
- Infection.
- Haemorrhage (epidural, subdural, subarachnoid).
- Dysaesthesia of the lower limbs.
- Cerebral herniation (always check local procedures regarding contraindication to LP and whether to perform CT head first).

Equipment
- Sterile gloves.
- Sterile pack (containing drape, cotton balls, small bowl).
- Antiseptic solution (e.g. iodine).
- Sterile gauze dressing.
- 1 x 25G (orange) needle.
- 1 x 21G (green) needle.
- Spinal needle (usually 22G).
- Lumbar-puncture manometer.
- 3-way tap (may be included in a lumbar puncture 'kit').
- 5–10ml 1% lidocaine.
- 2 x 10ml syringes.
- 3 x sterile collection tubes and one biochemistry tube for glucose measurement.

Procedure
- Introduce yourself, confirm the identity of the patient, explain the procedure, and obtain verbal consent.
- Position the patient lying on their left-hand side with the neck, knees, and hips flexed as much as possible.
  - Ensure that the patient can hold this position comfortably.
- Place a pillow between the patient's knees to prevent the pelvis tilting.
- Label the collection tubes '1', '2', and '3'.
- Identify the iliac crest. The disc space vertically below this (as you are looking) will be ~L3/L4.
- Mark the space between the vertebral spines at this point with a pen.
- Wash hands and put on the sterile gloves.
- Unwrap all equipment and ensure it fits together correctly.
  - It is usually useful to give the 3-way tap a few twists as it can stick.
- Apply the drapes around the area and sterilize with the antiseptic solution and cotton balls in outward-spiral motions.
- Inject the lidocaine (using a 10ml syringe and the orange needle) at the marked site to raise a small wheal.

- Swap the orange needle for the green one and infiltrate the lidocaine deeper.
- Wait for ~1 minute for the anaesthetic to take effect.
- Introduce the spinal needle through the marked site at about 90° to the skin, heading slightly toward the umbilicus.
  • Keep the bevel facing cranially.
- Gently advance the needle to ~5 cm depth.
- A further slight push of the needle should produce a 'give' as the needle enters the subarachnoid space (this takes a little practice to feel).
- Withdraw the stilette from the needle. CSF should begin to drip out.
- Measure the CSF pressure: connect the manometer to the end of the needle via the 3-way tap (the CSF will rise up the manometer allowing you to read off the number).
- Turn the tap such that the CSF within the manometer pours out in a controlled manner and further CSF can drip freely.
- Collect about 5 or 6 drops into each collection tube *in the order in which they have been labelled*.
- Collect a few more drops into the biochemistry tube for glucose measurement.
- Close the tap so that the manometer will measure the pressure at the end of the collection ('closing pressure').
- Remove the needle, tap, and manometer in one action.
- Apply a sterile dressing.
- Send the fluid for analysis.
  • Cell count (bottles 1 and 3)
  • Microscopy, culture, and sensitivities (bottles 1 and 3)
  • Biochemistry: glucose (biochemistry tube), protein (bottle 2).
- Advise the patient to lie flat for ~1 hour and ask nursing staff to check CNS observations (see local guidelines).

Documentation

- Date, time, indication, and informed consent obtained.
- Vertebral level needle inserted.
- Number of passes before CSF obtained.
- Initial ('opening') pressure and final ('closing') pressure.
- Amount and appearance of CSF.
- Tests samples sent for.
- Any immediate complications.
- Signature, printed name, and contact details.

Procedure tips

- Always use the smallest gauge spinal needle available.
  • In some centres, 'pencil-point' needles are used which are associated with a much reduced incidence of post-procedure headache.
- If the needle strikes bone and cannot be advanced, withdraw slightly, re-angle, and advance in a stepwise fashion until the gap is found.
- Lumbar puncture can be performed with the patient sitting, leaning forwards. This is particularly useful if the patient is obese. However, pressure measurements will be erroneous if taken in this position.

Male urethral catheterization

Contraindications
- Urethral/prostatic injury.

Risks
- Urinary tract infection.
- Septicaemia.
- Pain.
- Haematuria.
- Creation of a 'false passage' through prostate.
- Urethral trauma.
- ⚠ Beware latex allergy.

Equipment
- Foley catheter (male) of appropriate French, usually 12–14 gauge.
- 10 ml syringe of sterile water.
- Syringe of lidocaine gel 1% (e.g. Instilligel®).
- Catheter bag.
- Sterile gloves.
- Catheter pack containing drape, kidney dish, swabs/cotton balls, and a small dish.
- Sterile water/chlorhexidine sachet.

Procedure
- Introduce yourself, confirm the patient's identity, explain the procedure, and obtain informed consent.
- Position the patient lying supine with the external genitalia uncovered.
  - Uncover from umbilicus to knees.
- Using aseptic technique, unwrap the equipment and pour the chlorhexidine or sterile water into the dish.
- Wash your hands and put on the sterile gloves.
- Tear a hole in the middle of the drape and place it over the genitals so as to allow access to the penis.
- Use your non-dominant hand to hold the penis upright.
- Withdraw the foreskin and clean around the urethral meatus using the water/chlorhexidine and a swab, moving from the centre outwards.
- Instil local anaesthetic via the urethral meatus, with the penis held vertically.
- Wait at least one minute for the anaesthetic to act.
- Place the kidney bowl between the patient's thighs.
- Remove the tip of the plastic sheath containing the catheter, being careful not to touch the catheter itself.
- Insert catheter into urethra, feeding it out of the plastic wrapper as it is advanced.
- Insert the catheter to the 'hilt'.
  - If the catheter will not advance fully, don't force it. Withdraw a little, extend the penis fully, and carefully try again.

- At this point, urine may begin to drain.
  - Let the hub end of the catheter rest in the kidney bowl to catch the inevitable spills.
- Inflate the balloon using sterile water inserted into the catheter side-arm according to the balloon's capacity (written on the cuff of the balloon lumen).
  - ▶ Watch the patient's face and ask them to warn you if they feel pain.
- Once the balloon is inflated, remove the syringe and attach the catheter bag.
- Gently pull the catheter until you feel resistance as the balloon rests against the bladder neck.
- Replace the foreskin (this is essential to prevent paraphimosis).
- Re-dress the patient appropriately.

Documentation

- Date and time.
- Indication, informed consent obtained.
- Size of catheter inserted.
- Aseptic technique used?
- Volume of water used to inflate the balloon.
- Residual volume of urine obtained.
- Foreskin replaced?
- Any immediate complications.
- Signature, printed name, and contact details.

Procedure tips

- Difficulty passing an enlarged prostate is a common problem. Tricks to try to ease the catheter past include:
  - Ensure the catheter is adequately lubricated
  - Try moving the penis to a horizontal position between the patient's legs as prostatic resistance is reached
  - Ask the patient to wiggle his toes
  - Rotate the catheter back and forth as it advances
  - If catheter fails to pass, consider using larger bore catheter (e.g. 16F instead of 14F) as this may prevent coiling in the urethra.
- If urine fails to drain despite the catheter being fully advanced:
  - Palpate the bladder: if palpable, the catheter is inappropriately placed
  - Manual pressure on the bladder may express enough urine from a near-empty bladder to show itself
  - Aspirate with a bladder syringe, or flush with a little sterile saline.
- ▶ If it is impossible to pass the catheter, ask for help.
  - If all else fails, it may be necessary to proceed to suprapubic catheterization.

Female urethral catheterization

Contraindications
- Urethral injury.

Risks
- Urinary tract infection.
- Septicaemia.
- Pain.
- Haematuria.
- Urethral trauma.
- 🕛 Beware latex allergy.

Equipment
- Foley catheter (female) of appropriate French, usually 12–14 gauge.
- 10 ml syringe of sterile water.
- Syringe of lidocaine gel 1% (e.g. Instilligel®).
- Catheter bag.
- Sterile gloves.
- Catheter pack: drape, kidney dish, swabs/cotton balls, and a small dish.
- Sterile water/chlorhexidine sachet.

Procedure
- Introduce yourself, confirm the patient's identity, explain the procedure, and obtain informed consent.
- Position the patient with hips externally rotated and knees flexed. Uncover from waist down.
- Using aseptic technique, unwrap the equipment and pour the chlorhexidine or sterile water into the dish.
- Wash your hands and put on the sterile gloves.
- Tear a hole in the middle of the drape and place it over the genitals so as to allow access.
- Use your non-dominant hand to part the labia.
- Clean around the urethral meatus using the water/chlorhexidine and a swab, moving from the centre outwards.
- Instil local anaesthetic via urethral meatus.
  - Wait at least one minute for the anaesthetic to act.
- Place the kidney bowl between the patient's thighs.
- Remove the tip of the plastic sheath containing the catheter, being careful not to touch the catheter itself.
- Insert catheter into urethra, feeding it out of the plastic wrapper as it is advanced.
- Insert the catheter to the 'hilt'.
- At this point, urine may begin to drain. Let the end of the catheter rest in the kidney bowl to catch any spills.
- Inflate the balloon using sterile water inserted into the catheter side-arm according to the balloon's capacity (written on the cuff of the balloon lumen).
- ▶ Watch the patient's face and ask them to warn you if they feel pain.

- Once the balloon is inflated, remove the syringe and attach the catheter bag.
- Gently pull the catheter until you feel resistance as the balloon rests against the bladder neck.
- Re-dress the patient appropriately.

Documentation

- Date and time.
- Indication, informed consent obtained.
- Size of catheter inserted.
- Aseptic technique used?
- Volume of water used to inflate the balloon.
- Residual volume of urine obtained.
- Any immediate complications.
- Signature, printed name, and contact details.

Procedure tips

- Difficulty passing the catheter may be alleviated by slowly rotating the catheter whilst inserting.
- Difficulty seeing the urethral meatus may be overcome by asking the patient to 'bear down'.
- If urine fails to drain despite the catheter being fully advanced:
  - Palpate the bladder: if palpable, the catheter is inappropriately placed
  - Manual pressure on the bladder may express enough urine from a near-empty bladder to show itself
  - Aspirate with a bladder syringe, or flush with a little sterile saline.
- ▶ If it is impossible to pass the catheter, ask for help
  - If all else fails, it may be necessary to proceed to suprapubic catheterization.

Basic airway management

Airway manoeuvres

The following manoeuvres are performed with the patient lying supine and the attender positioned above the head. The aim is to prevent the flaccid tongue from falling back and causing the epiglottis or tongue itself from occluding the airway (Box 18.11 and Fig.18.3). These can be performed with no equipment.

Before you start
- Get help!
  - A patient with an obstructed airway can rarely be adequately treated by one individual, even if appropriate kit is within reach.

Head tilt
- Place your hands on the forehead and tilt the head backwards, extending the neck.

Chin lift
- Place two fingertips below the mental protuberance of the mandible, with thumb in front.
- Draw the mandible anteriorly.

Box 18.11 The head tilt/chin lift
- Head tilt and chin lift are usually performed together
- ▶ Head tilt and chin lift are not suitable if there is any suspicion of cervical spinal injury
- Jaw thrust alone should be used in this situation.

Jaw thrust
- Place your fingertips behind the angle of the mandible.
- The base of the thenar eminence of each hand should be rested on the cheek bones.
- Use your fingers to pull the mandible anteriorly, whilst using your thumbs to open the mouth.
- If performed with a mask, the thenar eminence may be used to maintain a good seal.

Procedure tips
- After each manoeuvre, check for success.
- It is worth-while practising these skills on resuscitation dummies prior to having to do them in real life!
- Use the above manoeuvres in conjunction with face masks or bag–valve mask ventilation.

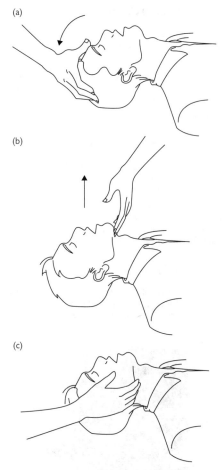

Fig. 18.3 Airway manoeuvres. (a) Head tilt. (b) Chin lift. (c) Jaw thrust.

Oropharyngeal (Guedel) airway

- A stiff tube with a fixed curvature is inserted through the mouth. A flange limits the depth of insertion.
- 🛈 Use when the patient is semi-conscious.

Indications

- Airway compromise in the patient with reduced conscious level.

Contraindications

- Active gag reflex.
- Conscious patient.

Procedure

- Insert the airway initially with the curvature upwards.
- Once inside the mouth, rotate 180°.
- Continue to insert, following the curvature of the tongue until the flange rests against the teeth or gums.
- Ensure there is no gagging, snoring, or vomiting and that air can move in and out freely.

Procedure tips

- May be used for suction (size 10, 12, or 14 catheters).
- Insertion can be guided with a tongue depressor.

Airway sizes

- Oropharyngeal airways come in many sizes and are colour-coded for convenience.
- ▶ Select the correct size of airway for the patient by measuring it against the side of the patient's face. The flange should sit at the corner of the patient's mouth and the tip at the angle of the jaw (Fig. 18.4).

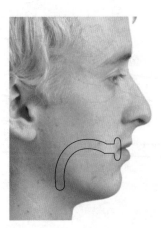

Fig. 18.4 Choose the correct size of oropharyngeal airway by measuring from the corner of the patient's mouth to the angle of the jaw.

Nasopharyngeal airway

- Tolerated better than a Guedel airway in semi-conscious patients.
- Consists of a soft plastic tube with flanged end.
- The pharyngeal end has a bevel and the body is curved to facilitate insertion.
  - Some designs have a small flange and a safety pin is often used to ensure the device does not migrate fully into the patient's nose.

Indications

- Patients with reduced conscious level and/or airway compromise who will not tolerate an oropharyngeal airway (intact gag reflex).

Contraindications

- Known basal skull fracture (relative contraindication).

Procedure

- Lubricate the device.
- Insert bevelled end into the wider nostril.
- Pass the tube along the floor of the nasal airway.
- Aim no higher than the back of the opposite eyeball.
- Use size 10 or 12 catheter for suction if required.
- Advance until the flange is flush against the nostril.

Procedure tips

- If insertion proves difficult, try the opposite nostril.

Airway sizes

- Nasopharyngeal airways come in several sizes, the size is usually stamped on the side.
- Determine the correct size by comparing those available with the pateint's little finger and the distance between the nostril and the tragus (Fig. 18.5).

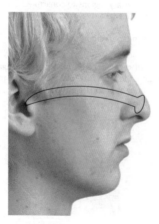

Fig. 18.5 Choose the correct size of nasopharyngeal airway by measuring from the nostril to the tragus.

Laryngeal mask airway (LMA)
- A tube with an inflatable cuff ('mask') around its base to create a seal around the laryngeal inlet.
- ▶ This does not prevent aspiration of stomach contents.

Indications
- Unconscious patient requiring ventilation.

Contraindications
- Conscious patient (absolute).
- Maxillofacial trauma.
- Risk of aspiration.
- >16 weeks' pregnant.

Procedure
- Ensure that the cuff inflates and deflates satisfactorily.
- For insertion, the mask should be completely deflated.
- Deflate the cuff with a 20ml syringe. Lubricate the outer cuff with aqueous gel.
- Gently extend the head and flex the neck (except in possible cervical trauma).
- Hold the LMA tubing near the cuff, like a pen.
- With the mask facing down, pass along the under-surface of the palate until it reaches the posterior pharynx.
- Guide the tube backwards and downwards (using an index finger if necessary) until resistance is felt.
- Remove your hand and fill the mask with the required amount of air (usually 20–30ml).
  - The tube should lift out of the mouth slightly and the larynx is pushed forward if it is in the correct position.
- Connect the bag-valve mask and ventilate.
- Auscultate in both axillary regions to confirm ventilation.
- Insert a bite block/Guedel airway next to the tube in case the patient bites down.
- Secure in place with tape/ribbon.

Procedure tips
- If inadequately deflated, lubricated, or not pressed against the hard palate on insertion, the LMA may fold back on itself making insertion difficult or preventing appropriate positioning of the mask (Fig. 18.6).

Fig. 18.6 Laryngeal mask airways. (a) Inflated. (b) Deflated.

Oxygen administration

▶ Oxygen is a drug with a correct dosage and side effects which when administered correctly may be life saving.

Oxygen prescribing

The primary responsibility for oxygen prescription at the time of writing lies with the hospital medical staff. It is good practice to record:

- Whether delivery is continuous or intermittent.
- Flow rate/percentage used.
- What SaO_2 should be.

Procedure

- Explain what is happening to the patient and ask their permission.
- Choose an appropriate oxygen delivery device.
- Choose an initial dose:
  - Cardiac or respiratory arrest: 100%
  - Hypoxaemia with $PaCO_2 < 5.3kPa$: 40–60%
  - Hypoxaemia with $PaCO_2 > 5.3kPa$: 24% initially.
- If possible, try to measure a PaO_2 in room air prior to giving supplementary oxygen.
- Apply the oxygen and monitor via oximetry (SaO_2) and/or repeat ABGs (PaO_2) in 30 minutes.
- If hypoxaemia continues, the patient may require respiratory support.

Oxygen administration equipment

- The method of delivery will depend on the type and severity of respiratory failure, breathing pattern, respiratory rate, risk of CO_2 retention, need for humidification, and patient compliance. (Fig.18.7).
- Each oxygen delivery device comprises an oxygen supply, flow rate, tubing, interface ± humidification.

Nasal cannulae

- These direct oxygen via two short prongs up the nasal passage.
  - Can be used for long periods of time
  - Prevent rebreathing
  - Can be used during eating and talking.
- Local irritation, dermatitis, and nose bleeding may occur and rates of above 4L/min should not be used routinely.

Low flow oxygen masks

- Deliver oxygen concentrations that vary depending on the patient's minute volume. At low flow rates there may be some rebreathing of exhaled gases (they are not sufficiently expelled from the mask).

Fixed performance masks

- A constant O_2 concentration independent of the minute volume.
- The masks contain 'Venturi' barrels where relatively low rates of oxygen are forced through a narrow orifice producing a greater flow rate which draws in a constant proportion of room air through several gaps.

Partial and non-rebreathe masks

- Masks such as this have a 'reservoir' bag that is filled with pure oxygen and depend on a system of valves which prevent mixing of exhaled gases with the incoming oxygen.
- The concentration of oxygen delivered is set by the oxygen flow rate.

High-flow oxygen

- Masks or nasal prongs that generate flows of 50–120L/min using a high flow regulator to entrain air and oxygen at specific concentrations.
- It is highly accurate as delivered flow rates will match a high respiratory rate in patients with respiratory distress. It should always be used with humidification.

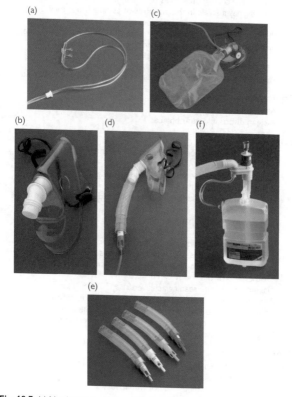

Fig. 18.7 (a) Nasal cannulae. (b) Low flow/variable concentration mask. (c) Non-rebreathe mask. (d) Mask with Venturi valve attached. (e) Selection of Venturi valves. (f) Humidification circuit.

Peak expiratory flow rate (PEFR) measurement

Background
- Normal values vary according to height, age, and gender (Fig.18.8).
- The value obtained may be compared against this and/or the patient's previous best PEFR.

Indications
- Asthma. Either in an acute attack to assess severity, or during the chronic phase to determine reversibility in response to treatment (>60L/min change defined as reversible).
  - PEFR may also aid in the diagnosis of asthma by examining the greatest variation over two weeks.
- PEFR may also be useful in assessment of COPD, particularly the degree of reversibility in response to inhaled bronchodilator.

Contraindications
- Any features of life-threatening asthma or severe respiratory distress.

Equipment
- A peak flow meter.
- A clean disposable mouthpiece.

Procedure
- Introduce yourself, confirm the patient's identity, explain the procedure, and obtain verbal consent.
- The patient should be standing or sitting upright.
- Ensure that the meter is set to '0'.
- Ask the patient to take a deep breath in, hold the mouthpiece in the mouth, and seal their lips tightly around it.
  - ▶ Ensure that the patient holds the device at the sides, avoiding obstructing the marker with a finger.
- The patient should blow out as *hard* and as *fast* as possible.
  - Patients sometimes have difficulty with this and a quick demonstration or advice to 'imagine blowing out a candle at the other end of the room' can help.
- Make a note of the reading achieved.
- Repeat the procedure and record the best of three efforts.
- If the patient is to keep a record, be sure to explain how to record the readings appropriately. (Sometimes a two-week diary is kept by the patient to assess for diurnal variation.)

Procedure tips
- If the patient is having difficulty performing correctly, a brief demonstration often proves very useful.
- If the highest two values are not within 40L/min, further values should be obtained.

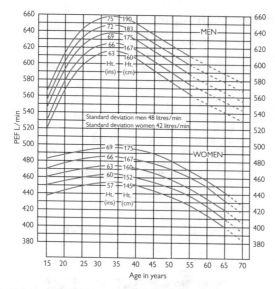

Fig. 18.8 Normal PEFR by age and gender. From BMJ 1989; 298: 1068–70.

Documentation

- Record the highest PEFR in L/min and as a percentage of the patient's best previous or predicted PEFR.
- Make a note of the time and whether the measurement was made before or after therapy.

Inhaler technique

Metered dose inhaler

- Requires coordination to use effectively and lacks a dose counter.
- May be unsuitable for the very young, elderly, or those with arthritis affecting the hands. (Fig.18.9.)

How to use

- Take only one dose at a time.
- Remove the cap and shake the inhaler several times.
- Sit upright, breathe out completely.
- Insert mouthpiece in mouth, sealing with lips.
- Take a deep breath in. Just after you begin to breathe in depress the canister whilst continuing to inhale.
  - The canister should be pressed *just after* the start of inhalation, not before.
- Inhale slowly and deeply.
- Remove inhaler and hold your breath for 10 seconds or as long as is comfortable.
- Recover before taking the next dose and repeat above as necessary.
- Replace cap.

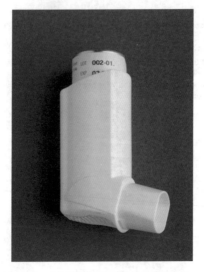

Fig. 18.9 A metered dose inhaler (MDI). A salbutamol inhaler is pictured.

Autohaler

- This is a 'breath-actuated' inhaler, releasing a dose automatically as a breath is taken (Fig.18.10).
- No hand coordination is required.
- The priming lever, however, can prove difficult to use and requires priming before each dose.

How to use

- Remove cap and shake inhaler several times.
- Prime by pushing the lever into the vertical position whilst keeping the inhaler upright.
- Sit upright, breathe out completely, and insert mouthpiece, sealing with lips.
- Inhale slowly and deeply.
  - Don't stop when the inhaler clicks.
- Remove inhaler and hold your breath for 10 seconds or as long as is comfortable.
- Push lever down and allow time to recover before taking the next dose.
- Once doses are taken, replace cap.

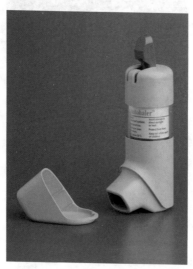

Fig. 18.10 A typical Autohaler.

Procedure tips

- Patients unable to operate the lever by hand may be able to use a hard surface such as the edge of a table for assistance.
- Use inhaler only for the number of doses written on the label.
- Patients should inhale slowly and steadily rather than hard and fast.

Easi-breathe

- Breath-actuated inhaler, as autohaler only primed by opening the cap hence this must be closed and opened again between successive doses (Fig.18.11).

How to use

- Shake the inhaler several times.
- Hold upright and prime by opening the cap.
- Sit upright, breathe out completely, and insert mouthpiece, sealing with lips.
  - Make sure that your fingers are not covering the air holes at the top.
- Inhale slowly and deeply.
  - 🚫 Don't stop when the inhaler puffs.
- Remove inhaler and hold your breath for 10 seconds or as long as is comfortable.
- Close the cap, with the inhaler upright.
- Recover before taking the next dose.

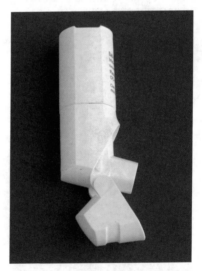

Fig. 18.11 A typical Easi-breathe inhaler.

Procedure tips

- It is essential to close and then open the cap between successive doses. This primes the inhaler.
- Advise the patient not to dismantle the inhaler. Patients used to using MDIs may be tempted to take the top off and attempt to depress the canister manually.

Accuhaler

- Dry powder device, superseding the Diskhaler and Rotahaler (Fig.18.12).
- Has a dose counter.
- The several step priming mechanism may be difficult for some to manage.

How to use

- Hold the outer casing in one hand whilst pushing the thumb grip away, exposing the mouthpiece, until you hear a click.
- With the mouthpiece towards you, slide the lever away from you until it clicks. The device is now primed.
- Sit upright, breathe out completely, and insert mouthpiece, sealing with lips.
- Inhale quickly and deeply.
  - (In contrast to breath-actuated devices).
- Remove inhaler and hold your breath for 10 seconds or as long as is comfortable.
- To close, pull the thumb grip towards you, hiding the mouthpiece in the cover, until you hear a click.
- Recover before taking the next dose.

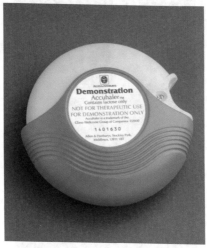

Fig. 18.12 A typical Accuhaler.

Procedure tips

- The Accuhaler must be closed and re-primed between successive doses.
- The dose counter indicates how many doses are left.

Turbohaler
- Dry-powder device with preloaded tasteless drug (Fig.18.13).
- There is no dose counter, but a window that turns red after 20 doses.
- The device is empty when there is red at the bottom of the window.
- Those with impaired dexterity may find the inhaler difficult to use.

How to use
- Unscrew and remove the white cover.
- Hold the inhaler upright and prime the device by twisting the grip clockwise and anticlockwise as far as it will go (until you hear a click).
- Sit upright, breathe out completely, and insert mouthpiece, sealing with lips.
- Inhale slowly and deeply.
- Remove inhaler and hold your breath for 10 seconds or as long as is comfortable.
- Recover before taking the next dose.
- The device must be primed again between successive doses.

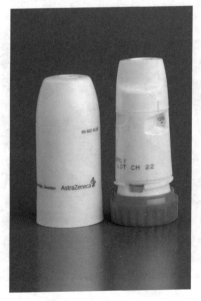

Fig. 18.13 A typical Turbohaler.

Procedure tips
- Advise the patient that they will not feel the dose hit the back of their throat.
- Patients used to an MDI may find this off-putting.

Clickhaler

- Disposable dry-powder inhaler with dose meter which turns red when only 10 doses are left to use.
- The inhaler locks when empty so patients can be sure that they have taken a dose.

How to use

- Take only one dose at a time.
- Remove the cap and shake.
- Whilst holding inhaler upright, depress the button firmly and release until you hear a click.
- Sit upright, breathe out completely, and insert mouthpiece, sealing with lips.
- Inhale deeply.
- Remove inhaler and hold your breath for 10 seconds or as long as is comfortable.
- Recover before taking the next dose and repeat above as necessary.
- Replace cap.

Handihaler

- A dry-powder device with an integrated cap.
- This requires a lower inspiratory flow rate than other devices.
- A dose needs to be inserted via a capsule at each use requiring some dexterity.
- Patients may also find the cap rather hard to open as it requires a moderate amount of strength.

How to use

- Open cap by pulling upwards exposing mouthpiece.
- Open the mouthpiece by pulling upwards exposing the dose chamber.
- Take a capsule from the blister-pack and insert it into the chamber.
- Replace the mouthpiece (it should click shut).
- Press the side button in a few times to pierce the capsule (you can watch through the small window).
- Sit upright, hold head up, and breathe out.
- Seal lips around mouthpiece.
- Breathe in deeply to a full breath.
- Remove inhaler and hold breath for as long as is comfortable.
- Remove the used capsule and replace the cap.

Non-invasive ventilation

▶ Non-invasive ventilation should only be set up by experienced operators. The following is a guide only.

Background

- CPAP = continuous positive airways pressure.
  - CPAP traditionally has its own equipment and 'set-up'
  - Recently more clinicians are delivering CPAP through the BiPAP Vision®. There is also a 'low flow' version used mainly for transport of CPAP dependent patients.
- BiPAP = bilevel positive airways pressure.

Contraindications/cautions

- ▶ Undrained pneumothorax. (Absolute contraindication).
- Facial fractures.
- Life-threatening epistaxis.
- Bullous pulmonary disease.
- Proximal lung tumours (air trapping).
- Active TB (spread).
- Acute head injury.
- Low blood pressure.
- Uncontrolled cardiac arrhythmias.
- Sinus/middle ear infection.

Risks

- Abdominal distension (secondary to 'swallowing' air).
- Decreased cardiac output (drop in BP).
- Pressure sores from mask.
- Aspiration of vomit.
- CO_2 retention if patient breathing small tidal volume against high PEEP.

Documentation

- Oxygen prescription charts.
- Ventilation prescription charts.
- Clear record of ABGs with evidence of time, inspired oxygen, and ventilation levels.
- Good practice to document the 'ceiling' of pressures and FiO_2 for the clinical environment.

CPAP equipment

- Mask (+/− T-piece), hood.
- Head strap (mask), shoulder straps (hood).
- Oxygen circuit and humidification.
- High flow generator (e.g. Whisper Flow®, Vital Signs®).
- PEEP valves (usually 5, 7.5, or 10cmH$_2$O).
- 'Blow off' safety valve (10cmH$_2$O above the PEEP used).

CPAP procedure

- Use available templates to assess appropriate sized interface and minimize air leaks (if using the BiPAP Vision®).
- Decide on level of PEEP to apply.
- Attach PEEP valve to mask (if using traditional set-up, may need T-piece).
- Attach oxygen circuit with humidification including 'blow-off' valve (for safety).
- Set inspired oxygen level.
- Set flow rate to ensure the PEEP valve opens a small distance and never closes.
- Titrate oxygen and PEEP in response to the patient's work of breathing, saturations, pH, PaO_2, and $PaCO_2$.
- If appropriate, set alarms on ventilator (if using BiPAP Vision®).
- Write a prescription chart of PEEP or ventilation settings and acceptable saturations, PaO_2, and $PaCO_2$, continuous or intermittent.

BiPAP equipment

- Interface (face mask, nasal pillows, nasal mask, etc.).
- Head straps.
- Ventilation circuit (exhalation port unless on mask).
- Humidification (if required).
- Ventilator (NIPPY 1/2/3/3+, BiPAP Vision®, etc.).
- Entrained oxygen (unless with ventilator, e.g. BiPAP Vision®).

BiPAP procedure

- Decide on which interface to use.
- Use available templates to assess appropriate sized interface and minimize air leaks.
- Start with low pressures (EPAP 4cmH$_2$O, IPAP 12cmH$_2$O).
  - Slowly increase pressures to levels agreed by MDT, for patient comfort and in response to pH, PaO_2, and $PaCO_2$.
  - The aim being to reduce RR and work of breathing, normalize ABGs (for the individual) using the minimal pressures possible.
- Set inspiratory and expiratory times to those of the patient.
- Continually reassess RR as this will change and therefore set times will have to change.
- Titrate oxygen and pressures in response to the patient's saturations, pH, PaO_2, and $PaCO_2$.
- If appropriate set alarms on ventilator.
- Write a prescription chart of ventilation settings and acceptable saturations, PaO_2, and $PaCO_2$.

Pleural fluid aspiration

This describes the procedure for aspirating as much pleural fluid as possible. If only a small sample is required for diagnostic purposes, use a green needle and 20ml syringe and follow a similar method to that described under 'ascitic fluid sampling'. (See Box 18.12 for alternative method.)

▶ Fluid should be aspirated from a position 1–2 intercostal spaces below the highest level at which dullness is percussed.

Contraindications

- Recurrent effusion (chest drain or pleurodesis should be considered).
- Empyema (requires intercostal drainage).
- Mesothelioma (tumour may spread down needle track).
- Bleeding diathesis.

Risks

- Pain.
- Cough.
- Failure to resolve.
- Re-expansion pulmonary oedema.
- Pneumothorax.

Equipment

- Sterile pack.
- Sterile gloves.
- Cleaning solution (e.g. chlorhexidine).
- Large-bore (green) cannula.
- 3-way tap.
- 50ml syringe.
- 5ml 1% lidocaine.
- 23G (blue) needle.
- 2 x 10ml syringe.
- Dressing/gauze.
- Selection of sterile containers and blood bottles.
- Heparinized (ABG) syringe.

Procedure

- Introduce yourself, confirm the patient's identity, explain the procedure, and obtain informed consent.
- Position the patient leaning forward with arms rested on a table or over the back of a chair.
- Percuss the effusion and choose a suitable spot for needle insertion.
- Clean the area with chlorhexidine.
- Using the blue needle and syringe, infiltrate local anaesthetic down to the pleura.
  - ❶ Insert needle *just above* a rib to avoid the neurovascular bundle
  - Be sure to pull back on the syringe each time before injecting to ensure you are not in a blood vessel
  - Once fluid is withdrawn, you have reached the pleura.

- Insert the cannula perpendicular to the chest wall, aspirating with another syringe as you advance until resistance reduces and pleural fluid is aspirated.
- Remove the needle and attach the 3-way tap.
- You may now aspirate fluid using the 50ml syringe.
- Once the syringe is full, close the tap, disconnect the syringe, and empty into a container. Re-attach the syringe, open the tap, and repeat.
  - ⏺ The pleural space should never be in continuity with the environment or pneumothorax will occur.
- Do not drain more than 2.5L at one time.
- Remove the cannula and apply the dressing.
- Send samples for:
  - Microbiology: microscopy, culture, Auramine stain, TB culture
  - Chemistry: protein, LDH, pH, glucose, amylase
  - Cytology
  - Immunology: ANA, rheumatoid factor, complement.
- Take simultaneous venous blood for glucose, protein, LDH.
- Request chest radiograph to confirm success and look for iatrogenic pneumothorax.

Procedure tips

- If unsuccessful, aspiration may be performed under ultrasound guidance: discuss with your radiology or respiratory department, depending on local policy.
- Passing a small fluid sample through a blood gas analyser may yield a rapid pH but should be avoided if the sample is purulent.

Documentation

- Date, time, indication, informed consent obtained.
- Aseptic technique used?
- Local anaesthetic used.
- Site needle inserted.
- Colour, consistency, and volume of fluid aspirated.
- Any immediate complications.
- Investigations requested.
- Signature, printed name, and contact details.

Box 18.12 An alternative method

- An alternative method is to attach a fluid-giving set to one port of the 3-way tap and the 50ml syringe to the other
- With this set-up, you can aspirate 50ml into the syringe, turn the tap and empty it down the tubing into a container before turning the tap back to the syringe port
- The syringe, therefore, never needs to be disconnected and the risk of pneumothorax or other complication is reduced.

Pneumothorax aspiration

Simple vs secondary pneumothorax

Simple pneumothorax
- Aspiration is indicated if the rim of pleural air visible on chest radiograph is larger than 2cm or the patient is breathless.
- If initial aspiration is unsuccessful, repeat aspiration may be successful in >30% of cases and may avoid intercostal drain insertion.
- The total volume aspirated should not exceed 2.5L.

Secondary pneumothorax
- That is, a pneumothorax in the presence of underlying lung disease.
- Aspiration is only indicated in minimally symptomatic patients with small pneumothoraces (<2cm) aged <50.

Contraindications
- Previous failed attempts at aspiration.
- Significant secondary pneumothorax.
- Traumatic pneumothorax.

Risks
- Pain.
- Cough.
- Failure to resolve/recurrence.
- Re-expansion pulmonary oedema may theoretically occur if large volumes (>2.5L) are aspirated.

Equipment
- Sterile pack.
- Sterile gloves.
- Cleaning solution (e.g. chlorhexidine).
- Large-bore (green) cannula.
- 3-way tap.
- 50ml syringe.
- 5ml 1% lidocaine.
- 23G (blue) needle.
- 2 x 10mL syringe.
- Dressing/gauze.

Procedure
▶ Pneumothorax is usually aspirated from either 2nd intercostal space at the midclavicular line or the 4th–6th intercostal spaces at the midaxillary line.
- Introduce yourself, confirm the patient's identity, explain the procedure, and obtain informed consent.
- Position the patient leaning back comfortably at about 45°.
- Identify the site for needle insertion and double-check the radiograph to be certain you have the correct side. Confirm with clinical examination.
- Clean the area with the chlorhexidine.

- Infiltrate local anaesthetic down to the pleura using the blue needle and a 10ml syringe.
- Attach the other 10ml syringe to the cannula and insert the cannula perpendicular to the chest wall, aspirating as you advance until resistance reduces.
  - ▶ Insert the cannula *just above* a rib to avoid the neurovascular bundle.
- Remove the needle and quickly attach the 3-way tap and 50ml syringe.
- Aspirate with the syringe; close the 3-way tap when the syringe is full, remove the syringe and eject the air; reattach and open the 3-way tap to continue aspiration.
  - 🛈 The pleural space should never be in continuity with the environment (i.e. tap open with syringe detached) or pneumothorax will reaccumulate.
- Aspirate until resistance is felt, or up to a maximum of 2.5L.
- Remove the cannula and apply the dressing.
- Request chest radiograph to re-assess.

Documentation

- Date, time, indication, informed consent obtained.
- Aseptic technique used?
- Local anaesthetic used.
- Site needle inserted.
- Volume of air aspirated.
- Any immediate complications.
- Investigations requested.
- Signature, printed name, and contact details.

Tension pneumothorax

In the case of tension pneumothorax, a wide-bore cannula should be inserted into the 2nd intercostal space, midclavicular line, *without delay* and left open to convert the tension pneumothorax to a simple pneumothorax.

Chest drain insertion (Seldinger)

- This describes the procedure for a Seldinger-type drain. Other drains are available.
- More and more trusts now recommend chest drain insertion under ultrasound guidance. Check your local policy and discuss with your radiology or respiratory departments as appropriate.

Contraindications

- ▶ The need for an emergency thoracotomy. This should not be delayed for the insertion of a chest drain.
- Coagulopathy.
- Large bullae.
- Thoracic/pleural adhesions.
- Skin infection over the insertion site.

Risks

- Inadequate placement.
- Bleeding (local or haemothorax).
- Liver or spleen injury +/− haemoperitoneum.
- Organ penetration (lung, liver, spleen, stomach, colon, heart).
- Infection.
- Iatrogenic pneumothorax.

Equipment

- 10ml 1% lidocaine.
- 10ml syringe.
- 25G (orange) needle.
- 21G (green) needle.
- Sterile gloves.
- Sterile pack (containing cotton balls, drape, container).
- Seldinger chest drain kit.
  - Chest drain, introducer, needle, syringe, scalpel, 3-way tap, wire.
- Suture (e.g. 1.0 Mersilk).
- Cleaning solution (e.g. chlorhexidine or iodine).
- Chest drain tubing and drainage bottle.
- 500ml sterile water.
- Suitable dressing (e.g. Hypofix® or drainfix®).

Procedure

- Introduce yourself, confirm the identity of the patient, explain the procedure, and obtain informed consent.
- ▶ Double-check radiograph and perform clinical examination to be sure of which side needs the drain.
- Position the patient sitting on a chair or the edge of their bed, arms raised and resting on bedside table with a pillow.
- ❶ The usual site for insertion is in the mid-axillary line, within a triangle formed by the diaphragm, the latissimus dorsi, and the pectoralis major ('triangle of safety').
- Mark your spot (just *above* a rib to avoid the neurovascular bundle).

- Wash hands and put on sterile gloves.
- Clean the area with antiseptic solution on cotton wool balls working in a spiral pattern outwards.
- Using the 10ml syringe and orange needle, anaesthetize the skin forming a subcutaneous bleb.
- With the green needle anaesthetize down to the pleura, withdrawing the plunger before injecting each time.
- Use the scalpel to make a small cut in the skin.
- Use the drain-kit needle with the curved tip and syringe (in some kits, this has a central stilette which needs to be removed first). With the curved tip facing downwards (upward for a pneumothorax), advance through the anaesthetized area until you aspirate either air or fluid.
- Remove the syringe and hold the needle steady.
- Thread the guidewire through the needle into the chest.
  • Once the wire is half in the chest, discard the covering.
- Withdraw the needle from the chest but be sure to not remove the guidewire, keeping hold of it at all times, and thread the needle right off the end of the guidewire.
- Thread the introducer over the guidewire and into the chest, twisting back and forth as you go to open up a tract for the drain's passage. Then slide the introducer back off the wire, being careful not to pull the wire out of the chest.
- With the central stiffener in place, thread the drain over the wire and into the chest, curving downwards.
  • Keep hold of the guidewire at all times and do NOT push it into the chest cavity!
- Once the drain is in place, remove the wire and stiffener.
- Attach the 3-way tap, making sure all the ports are closed.
- Stitch the drain in place (unless using a drainfix®).
- Apply a drainfix® or other suitable dressing.
- Attach the drain to the tubing and the tubing to the collection bottle which you have pre-filled with 500ml of sterile water.
- Open the 3-way tap.
  • You should either see the fluid start to flow or air start to bubble in the collection bottle. Ask the patient to take a few breaths and watch the water level in the tubing to see it rising and falling ('swinging').
- Request a post-insertion chest radiograph.

Documentation

- Date, time, indication, informed consent obtained.
- Aseptic technique used?
- Local anaesthetic used.
- Site drain inserted.
- Any immediate complications.
- Colour and consistency of fluid obtained.
- Investigations requested.
- Signature, printed name, and contact details.

Recording a 12-lead ECG

The term '12-lead' relates to the number of directions that the electrical activity is recorded from and is *not* the number of electrical wires attached to the patient!

Equipment

- An ECG machine capable of recording 12 leads.
- 10 ECG leads (4 limb leads, 6 chest leads).
  - These should be attached to the machine.
- Conducting sticky pads ('ECG stickers').

Procedure

- Introduce yourself, confirm the identity of the patient, explain the procedure, and obtain verbal consent.
- Position the patient so that they are sitting or lying comfortably with their upper body, wrists, and ankles exposed.
- Position the stickers on the patient's body (Fig.18.14).
- The chest leads:
  - V1: 4th intercostal space at the right sternal border
  - V2: 4th intercostal space at the left sternal border
  - V3: midway between V2 and V4
  - V4: 5th intercostal space in the midclavicular line on the left
  - V5: left anterior axillary line, level with V4
  - V6: left mid-axillary line, level with V4.
- The limb leads are often colour-coded:
  - Red: Right arm (**R**ed: **R**ight)
  - Yellow: Left arm (Ye**LL**ow: **L**eft)
  - Green: right leg
  - Black: left leg.
- Attach the leads to the appropriate stickers.
- Turn on the ECG machine.
- Ask the patient to lie still and not speak for approximately 10 seconds whilst the machine records.
- Press the button to record, usually marked 'analyse' or 'record'.
- Check the calibration and paper speed:
  - 1mV should cause a vertical deflection of 10mm
  - Paper speed should be 25mm/s (5 large squares per second).
- Ensure the patient's name, date of birth as well as the date and time of the recording are clearly recorded on the trace.
- Remove the leads, discard the sticky electrode pads.

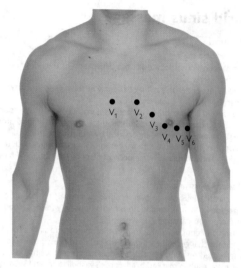

Fig. 18.14 Correct positioning of the chest electrodes for a standard 12-lead ECG.

Procedure tips

- Encourage the patient to relax otherwise muscle contraction will cause interference.
  - If unable to relax, or access to the peripheries is difficult, the 'arm' leads can be placed at the shoulders and the 'leg' leads at the groins.
- Breathing may cause a wandering baseline; breath holding for 6 seconds whilst recording may alleviate this.
- Ensure that you cleanse the area gently with an alcohol swab before attaching an electrode to ensure a good connection.
  - It may be necessary to cut chest hair to allow good contact and adhesion with the chest leads.
- The AC mains electricity may cause interference. If this is the case, try turning off nearby fluorescent lights.

Carotid sinus massage

Background

Anatomy and physiology

- The carotid sinus is located at the bifurcation of the common carotid artery.
  - It lies just under the angle of the jaw at the level of the thyroid cartilage.
- The carotid sinus contains numerous baroreceptors which coordinate homeostatic mechanisms responsible for maintaining blood pressure.
- These baroreceptors are innervated by a branch of the glossopharyngeal nerve (cranial nerve IX), which relays back to the medulla and modulates autonomic control of the heart and blood vessels.

Carotid sinus hypersensitivity

- The carotid sinus can be oversensitive to manual stimulation, a condition known as carotid sinus hypersensitivity (also 'carotid sinus syndrome' or 'carotid sinus syncope').
- In this condition, manual stimulation of the carotid sinus provokes significant changes in heart rate and/or blood pressure due to an exaggerated response to carotid sinus baroreceptor stimulation.
- This may result in marked bradycardia, vasodilation, and subsequent hypotension.
- The patient may complain of episodes of dizziness or syncope related to pressure on the neck (e.g. wearing a tight collar or turning the head quickly).
- The underlying mechanism behind this exaggerated response is not fully understood.

Carotid sinus massage

- Carotid sinus massage is a diagnostic technique used to confirm carotid sinus hypersensitivity and is sometimes useful for determining the underlying rhythm disturbance in supraventricular tachycardia (SVT).
- The procedure acts in a similar way to the Valsalva manoeuvre, increasing vagal tone and, therefore, reducing the heart rate.
- Carotid massage is less effective than pharmaceutical management of SVT (verapamil or adenosine) though is still the preferable choice in the young haemodynamically stable patient.
- ⓘ This procedure should be performed with caution in the elderly as it may cause disruption of atheromatous plaque disease in the carotid artery and result in stroke.

Before you start

- Explain the procedure in full to the patient and obtain written consent.
  - If the test is to confirm carotid sinus hypersensitivity, then warn the patient that they may feel like they are going to faint but reassure them it is a controlled procedure
  - If the test is to determine the underlying rhythm in SVT, explain that they may feel a bit peculiar as the heart rate slows down transiently.
- Auscultate over the carotids for any bruits.
  - ❶ If present the procedure will have to be abandoned as the risk of stroke is significant
- ▶ Document discussion of risks including failure, arrhythmias, stroke, faint, cardiac arrest.
- ▶ Secure intravenous access.
- ▶ Ensure that you have ECG monitoring with a recordable rhythm strip.
- ▶ Ensure access to full resuscitation equipment, including emergency drugs such as atropine and adrenaline.

Procedure

- Position the patient supine on a bed with the neck extended and head turned away from the side to be massaged.
- Whilst watching the ECG monitor (recording on a rhythm strip) gently massage the carotid sinus for 10 to 15 seconds using circular motions of your hand.
- If there is no response, switch to the opposite side.
- If successful (or 'positive' in the case of sinus hypersensitivity), the heart rate will slow.
  - This may allow you to determine the underlying rhythm in SVT.
- Ensure that the patient feels back to normal afterwards.

Documentation

- Date, time, indication, informed consent obtained.
- Intravenous access secured.
- ECG recording equipment operational.
- Emergency drugs on stand-by.
- Insert the rhythm strip into the patient's notes.
- Record details of what was seen on massage.
- Which carotid was used?
- Did the patient feel back to normal afterwards?
- Signature, printed name, and contact details.

Vagal manoeuvres

Background

The purpose

- Vagal manoeuvres can be used to determine the underlying rhythm or terminate supraventricular tachycardia (SVT) in haemodynamically stable patients.
- If the underlying rhythm is atrial flutter, slowing of the ventricular response by increasing vagal tone will reveal flutter waves.
- Vagal manoeuvres are part of the adult peri-arrest algorithm for management of narrow complex tachycardia. They can be performed in a controlled clinical situation (i.e. attached to an ECG machine), or taught to the patient to perform at home if the sensation of the arrhythmia recurs.

Physiology

- Vagal manoeuvres increase vagal tone by activation of the parasympathetic nervous system, conducted to the heart by the vagus nerve.
- Increasing vagal tone impedes the AV node and so slows transmission of the electrical impulse from the atria to the ventricle. In this way, any supraventricular tachycardia that relies upon the AV node will be modified by an increase in vagal tone.

The Valsalva manoeuvre

- This is forced expiration against a closed glottis. Increasing intra-thoracic pressure stimulates baroreceptors in the aortic arch and results in increased vagal stimulation.
- This can be successful in 25–50% of cases.

Procedure

- Ask the patient to take a deep breath in and then 'bear down' as if they are trying to open their bowels (or for women—as if they are in labour).

Some patients may struggle with this concept and so alternatively:

- Give them a 10ml syringe and ask them to blow into the tip, in an attempt to expel the plunger.

The diving reflex

- This involves either submerging the face in ice cold water (not very practical) or covering the face with a towel soaked in ice cold water.

Carotid sinus massage

- This is described separately (see previously).

Eyeball pressure

- 🚫 This is not recommended as a clinical procedure as it can be both painful and damaging. Do NOT perform.

Temporary external pacing

ℹ️ This describes temporary transcutaneous pacing as an emergency.

Before you start

- ► External pacing is usually performed in an emergency resuscitation situation following failure of response to initial management as per the bradycardia algorithm (see bradycardia algorithm from Resuscitation Council at 🖰 www.resus.org.uk).
- ► A senior doctor should be present and make the decision to proceed with external transcutaneous pacing.
- ► There should be a plan in place for an experienced clinician to insert a temporary pacing wire within the next few hours. External pacing should only be a short-term management of decompensated bradycardia.
- ► There should also be a bed available for the patient on a high-dependency unit or coronary care unit so that they can be closely monitored by experienced nursing staff whilst waiting for a temporary pacing wire. ℹ️ The patient should not be left on a general hospital ward.

Indications

- Symptomatic bradycardia unresponsive to treatment (see bradycardia algorithm from Resuscitation Council at end of this topic).
- Mobitz type II block.
- Complete heart block.
- Heart block secondary to myocardial infarction.
- Profound bradycardia secondary to drug overdose e.g. beta blockers, digoxin.
- Asystole or ventricular standstill.

Overdrive pacing

- External pacing can be used to terminate certain tachyarrhythmias that are unresponsive to initial treatment e.g. polymorphic ventricular tachycardia (torsades de pointes) or refractory ventricular tachycardia.

Risks

- Failure and progression to temporary pacing wire insertion.

Equipment

- Full resuscitation equipment: defibrillator with pacing setting.
- Defibrillator pads.
- Oxygen.
- ECG monitoring.
- Emergency drugs (including atropine and adrenaline).
- Intravenous fluids.
- Sedative drugs (e.g. midazolam or diazepam).
- Analgesia (e.g. morphine).
- Intubation equipment (in case indicated).
- Senior support.

Procedure

- The patient should already have:
  - Large-bore intravenous access
  - Intravenous fluids running (unless in heart failure)
  - Oxygen via a non-rebreathe mask at 15L/min
  - ECG monitor connected and running
  - Interval BP monitoring.
- Place the pacing pads from the defibrillation kit on the patient's chest: one anteriorly in the V3 position and one posteriorly below the left scapula.
- Sedation and analgesia may be required.
- Attach the leads from the defibrillator to the pads.
- Switch the defibrillator to its pacing mode.

Documentation

Temporary external pacing is usually an emergency procedure so documentation may be delayed until the patient is stable. It should outline the resuscitation and external pacing simultaneously:

- Date and time.
- Name and grade of persons present.
- Events leading up to the need for external pacing.
- Any drugs used e.g. atropine or adrenaline, volume/dose, and response.
- Indication for external pacing.
- If patient was conscious, document consent (usually verbal consent only).
- Any sedation used.
- When external pacing commenced.
- Details of plans for temporary pacing wire insertion.
- Sign and bleep/contact details.

DC cardioversion

Indications

- Elective cardioversion of atrial fibrillation.
- Emergency cardioversion in a peri-arrest situation where a tachyarrhythmia is associated with adverse signs.

Equipment

The 'crash trolley' should contain all the equipment required:

- Gloves, aprons, defibrillator, pads, leads, ECG electrodes.
- Oxygen, reservoir bag and mask with tubing, airways.
- Intubation equipment.
- Intravenous fluids, giving sets, selection of syringes, needles, intravenous cannulae, and fixation dressings.
- Access to emergency drugs (atropine, adrenaline, amiodarone).

Contraindications

- Elective: patients unsuitable for general anaesthetic, not anticoagulated or who have not signed a consent form.
- Emergency: only performed when a tachyarrhythmia is associated with adverse events in the presence of a pulse (pulseless rhythms require management as per the resuscitation guidelines).

Risks

- General anaesthetic risk, if performed electively.
- Embolic phenomenon, stroke, myocardial infarction.

Before you start

Elective procedure

- Obtain informed consent and save a copy of signed form.
- Ensure patient fasted >6hrs.
- Check serum potassium (>4.0mmol/L gives greater success).
- Confirm patient anticoagulated for previous 4 weeks (INR >2).
  - Warfarin is continued for 3 months post-procedure if successful.
- The procedure should be performed in an anaesthetic room, following short-acting induction by an anaesthetist.

Emergency procedure

- Ensure a senior doctor is involved in the decision.
- Ensure all other options have been tried or considered.
- If possible discuss with the patient or next of kin.

Energy selection

DC cardioversion usually uses biphasic energies. A reasonable guide is:

- 50 Joules synchronized shock. If fails ...
- 100 Joules synchronized shock. If fails ...
- 150 Joules synchronized shock. If fails ...
- 150 Joules synchronized anteroposterior shock. If fails ...
- ❶ Abandon procedure if elective, consult seniors if emergency (may need ICU input).

Procedure

- Ensure skin is dry, free of excess hair, jewellery is removed.
- Attach the ECG electrodes; red under right clavicle, yellow under left clavicle, green at the umbilicus.
- Switch on defibrillator and confirm the ECG rhythm.
- Place the defibrillator gel pads on the patient's chest; one under the right clavicle and the other inferolateral to the cardiac apex.
- ▶ Select the 'synchronous mode' on the defibrillator.
- ▶ Select the Joules required (see ❸ p.634).
- Place the paddles firmly on the chest on the gel pads.
- Press the charge button on the paddles to charge the defibrillator and shout 'Stand clear! Charging!'
- ▶ Check all persons are standing well clear of the patient and bed (including yourself) and that no-one is touching the patient or bed (including yourself).
- ▶ Ensure the oxygen has been disconnected and removed.
- ▶ Check the monitor again to ensure a shockable rhythm.
- Shout 'Stand clear! Shocking!'.
- Press both discharge buttons on the paddles to discharge the shock.
- Return the paddles to the defibrillator or keep them on the chest if another shock is required.

Documentation

General

- Date, time, and place. Name and grade of persons present.
- ECG rhythm, intravenous access secured.
- Number, volume, dose of any drugs used, and any response noted.
- Type of defibrillator machine used.
- Method of sedation/anaesthetic.
- Asynchronous or synchronous mode. Specify Joules of each shock.
- Confirm rhythm at end and 12-lead ECG findings.
- Sign and bleep/contact details.

Elective

- Indication for DC cardioversion.
- Informed consent obtained (retain copy of signed form).
- State time fasted from.
- Document anticoagulation type and duration.
- Serum potassium level.
- Any drug allergies.
- Name and grade of anaesthetist, type of anaesthetic used.

Emergency

- Events leading up to the peri-arrest situation.
- HR, BP, GCS on arrival and any deterioration.
- Time of decision to shock, name and grade of decision-maker.
- Verbal consent obtained? Type of sedation used.
- Next of kin have been informed or if they are present or en route?

Pericardiocentesis

Contraindications
- Cardiac tamponade secondary to cardiac trauma or aortic dissection (surgical intervention is preferable).
- Recurrent pericardial effusions (surgical pericardial window indicated).

Risks
- Pneumothorax.
- Myocardial perforation.
- Cardiac tamponade.
- Coronary artery laceration.
- Cardiac arrhythmias.
- Intra-abdominal trauma (especially to liver).
- Haemorrhage.
- Infection.
- Acute pulmonary oedema.
- Failure of procedure.
- Death.

Equipment
- Echocardiogram machine and sterile probe cover.
- Pericardial drain kit (14 gauge needle, syringe, guidewire, pigtail catheter, and drain).
- Sterile drape and towels.
- Iodine solution.
- Sterile gloves and gown.
- Local anaesthetic (1% lidocaine).
- 2 x 10ml syringe.
- Orange/blue/green needles.
- Sterile gauze.
- 50ml syringe.
- Three-way tap.
- Suture, scissors, sticky dressing (e.g. Tegaderm®).

You will also need:
- Intravenous access.
- ECG monitoring.
- Access to 'crash' trolley (defibrillator and emergency drugs).

Procedure
- Introduce yourself, explain procedure, and obtain informed written consent.
- Ensure IV access, ECG monitoring, normal clotting, and access to resuscitation equipment.
- (Consider light sedation).
- Position patient supine with 20–30° head tilt.
- Ensure all equipment is sterile and laid out on sterile trolley.
- Wash hands using surgical scrub technique and put on the sterile gown and gloves.

- Clean and drape site at the inferior border of the sternum.
  - Insertion point is below and to the left of the xiphisternum
- ▶ Confirm location of effusion using echocardiogram machine with sterile probe cover.
- Infiltrate overlying skin and subcutaneous tissue with 1% lidocaine. (Always aspirate before each injection.)
- Attach the 10ml syringe attached to the 14G needle.
- Insert the needle between the xiphisternum and left costal margin advancing slowly at 35° to the patient and aiming towards the patient's left shoulder. Aspirate continuously as the needle advances.
  - Pericardial fluid is usually aspirated at about 6–8cm depth
  - Depending on the size of the pericardial effusion and indication for the procedure, you may wish to attach the 50ml syringe and aspirate fluid to send for diagnostic purposes.
- A modified Seldinger technique should be used to insert the drain.
- Once pericardial fluid is aspirated, hold the needle in position, remove the syringe, and insert the guidewire slowly through the needle into the pericardial space.
- Remove the needle, holding the wire in place at all times.
- Pass the catheter over the wire into the pericardial space.
- Once the catheter position is confirmed on echo, remove the wire and attach the three-way tap and drain bag.
- Suture the drain in place and dress to maintain sterility.
- Request a chest radiograph to exclude iatrogenic pneumothorax.

Procedure tips

- ▶ Pericardiocentesis should be performed by a trained doctor (either cardiologist or thoracic surgeon usually) preferably in a sterile environment (theatre or the cardiac catheterization lab) and under echocardiographic guidance, with access to full resuscitation equipment.
  - ▶ The only exception is during cardiopulmonary resuscitation when pericardiocentesis is performed as an emergency to exclude cardiac tamponade as a reversible cause of cardiac arrest.
- ▶ Always check the patient's clotting beforehand.
- The clinician who performed the procedure should confirm the position of the drain using echo.
- Always request a post-procedure chest radiograph to exclude iatrogenic pneumothorax.

Documentation

- Date, time, and place.
- Name and grade of person who performed the procedure (and anyone who supervised).
- Consent obtained (enclose copy of consent form).
- Aseptic technique used and volume of anaesthetic used.
- Approach taken and anatomy confirmed by echocardiogram.
- Any difficulties i.e. 'first pass' or 'second attempt', etc.
- Appearance of pericardial fluid aspirated.
- Volume of pericardial fluid aspirated.

Nasogastric tube insertion

Indications
- Feeding in patients with poor swallow (e.g. post-cerebrovascular accident).
- Lavage of gastric contents in poisoning.
- Post-operative for stomach decompression.
- Bowel obstruction.

Contraindications
- Oesophageal stricture, obstructing tumour.
- Tracheo-oesophageal fistula.
- Achalasia cardia.
- Deviated nasal septum.
- Fractured base of skull.

Risks
- Malpositioning in a lung.
- Trauma to the nasal and/or pharyngeal cavities.
- Perforation of oesophagus.

Equipment
- Lubricant (e.g. Aquagel®).
- pH-testing strips.
- 50 ml syringe.
- Gallipots.
- Dressing pack.
- Nasogastric tube (12–18 French size).
- Hypoallergenic tape.
- Sterile gauze.
- Gloves.
- Disposable bowl.

Procedure
- Introduce yourself, confirm the patient's identity.
- Explain the procedure to the patient, stating that it may be uncomfortable and can cause gagging, which is transient.
- Make sure that the patient understands the procedure and agree a signal to be made if patient wants you to stop (e.g. raising hand).
- To estimate the length of the tube required, measure the distance from the bridge of the nose to the tip of the earlobe and then to the xiphoid process.
- Position the patient semi-upright.
  - If unconscious, place the patient on their side.
- Check the patency of the nostrils and select a suitable side.
- Wash hands and put on gloves.
- Unwrap the tube and lubricate the tip by wiping it through a blob of lubricating gel.
- Insert the tip of the tube in the nostril and advance the tube horizontally along the floor of the nasal cavity backward and downwards.

- As the tube passes into the nasopharynx, ask the patient to swallow if they are able to do so.
  - Using a cup of water and straw often helps here.
- If there is any obstruction felt during advancement, withdraw and try in the other nostril.
- ⚠ Watch for any signs of distress; namely cough or cyanosis and remove the tube immediately if any of the above occurs.
- Once the tube has reached the measured distance, secure it in place with the tape.
  - The GOJ is generally 38–42cm from the nostril so advancement of the tube 55–60cm from the nostril usually positions the NG tube tip within the stomach.
- Aspirate a sample of fluid using a syringe.
- Place the aspirate on a pH-testing strip.
  - A pH of 5.5 or less suggests that the tube is in the stomach.
- If no aspirate obtained, change position and try again. If still unsuccessful, perform chest radiography to confirm position.
  - Be sure to leave the internal wire in the tube if you are sending the patient to x-ray. The tube itself is not radio-opaque and will be invisible on the resultant image.
- Once satisfied that the tube lies within the stomach, remove the inner wire and secure the tube to the tip of the nose.
  - It is sometimes helpful to curve the remainder of the tube towards the ear and secure to the cheek also.

Procedure tips

- ⚠ Medications such as proton pump inhibitors and acid-suppressing drugs may elevate the pH of the aspirate giving a 'false-negative' result. If in doubt, request a chest radiograph before using.
- ⚠ Low-pH fluid may also be aspirated from the lung in cases of aspirated stomach contents. If in doubt, request a chest radiograph before using.
- Chest radiography should be performed routinely in high-risk patients (those that are unconscious, intubated, or have poor swallow).
- The absence of cough reflex does not rule out misplacement of the tube in the airways.
- Auscultation for gurgling in the stomach is not a recommended method for confirming position.

Documentation

- Date, time, indication, informed consent obtained.
- Size of tube inserted.
- Length of tube internally (there are markings on the tube).
- This is important to allow other staff to assess whether the tube has moved in or out since insertion.
- Method by which correct placement was confirmed.
- Any immediate complications.
- Signature, printed name, and contact details.

Ascitic fluid sampling (ascitic tap)

Indications
- Diagnosing nature of new-onset ascites (i.e. exudate or transudate).
- Diagnosis of spontaneous bacterial peritonitis (SBP).
- Cytology to diagnose malignant ascites.

Contraindications
- Acute abdomen that requires surgery.
- Pregnancy.
- Intestinal obstruction.
- Grossly distended urinary bladder.
- Superficial infection (cellulitis) at the potential puncture site.
- Hernia at the potential puncture site.

Risks
- Persistent leak of ascitic fluid.
  - This is more likely if there is a large amount of fluid under tension
- Perforation of hollow viscera (e.g. bowel and bladder). This is very rare.
- Peritonitis.
- Abdominal wall haematoma.
- Bleeding is very rare but may occur if there is injury to inferior epigastric artery (be careful to tap lateral abdominal wall as described).

Equipment
- Sterile gloves.
- Dressing pack.
- Antiseptic solution (e.g. iodine).
- 1% or 2% lidocaine.
- 1 x 20ml syringe.
- 2 x 5ml syringes.
- 21G (green) and 25G (orange) needles.
- Sterile containers.
- Culture bottles.
- Sterile dressing.

Procedure
- Introduce yourself, confirm the patient's identity, explain the procedure, and obtain informed consent.
- Examine the abdomen and select a site for aspiration, three finger-breadths cranial to the anterior superior iliac spine.
  - ▶ Beware of positioning too medial as this risks hitting the inferior epigastric vessels
  - ▶ Be sure to identify and avoid any organomegaly which might interfere with procedure (in patients with massive splenomegaly, for example, avoid left iliac fossa).
- Clean the area with disinfectant and apply sterile drape.
- Using the 25 gauge (orange) needle and the 5ml syringe, administer local anaesthetic to the skin and subcutis, raising a wheal.

- Using the 21 gauge (green) needle, infiltrate deeper tissues, intermittently applying suction until the peritoneal cavity is reached, confirmed by flow of ascitic fluid into the syringe.
- Note the depth needed to enter the peritoneal cavity.
- Discard the used needles and attach a clean 21G needle to the 20ml syringe.
- With the green needle perpendicular to the skin, insert carefully, aspirating continuously until you feel resistance give way.
- Aspirate as much fluid as needed (usually 20ml is plenty).
- Withdraw needle and syringe and apply dressing.
- Send sample for Gram stain and culture (in blood culture bottles), white cell count/neutrophils, biochemistry, cytology (if malignancy suspected).
  - White cell count can be calculated in haematology lab; send fluid in EDTA-containing bottle
  - ▶ Total white cell count >500/mm^3 or neutrophils >250/mm^3 suggests spontaneous bacterial peritonitis—SBP
  - Neutrophil count is usually a manual procedure via microbiology and may take longer
  - If malignancy is suspected, a large volume of ascites (e.g. 500ml) should be sent to cytology.

Procedure tips

- Check the patient's clotting and platelet count before the procedure and proceed with caution and senior advice if abnormal (correct if platelets <20x10^9/L, INR ≥2.5).
- Inform the laboratory especially during out of hours if cultures needed urgently and if SBP is suspected.
- ▶ If unable to obtain fluid despite correct technique, do not persist! Stop and seek senior advice.

Documentation

- Date, time, indication, informed consent obtained.
- Type and amount of local anaesthetic used.
- Site aspirated.
- Aseptic technique used?
- How many passes?
- Volume and colour of aspirate obtained.
- Tests requested on samples.
- Any immediate complications.
- Signature, printed name, and contact details.

Abdominal paracentesis (drainage)

The procedure below relates to a 'RocketMedical' non-locking drainage kit—the essence is the same for other catheter kits although minor details may differ. You should refer to the kit's instructions.

Contraindications

- Acute abdomen that requires surgery.
- Pregnancy.
- Intestinal obstruction.
- Grossly distended urinary bladder.
- Superficial infection (cellulitis) at the potential puncture site.
- Hernia at the potential puncture site.
- Caution is needed in the presence of omental or peritoneal metastatic disease. In these cases, drainage is often performed under imaging guidance by a radiologist.

Risks

- Haemodynamic instability, especially in cirrhotic patients; avoided by albumin replacement. (Usually 100ml 20% human albumin solution IV for every 2.5 litres fluid drained—check local protocols with the gastroenterology department).
- Renal dysfunction (in those with abnormal baseline renal function. May need to withhold diuretics and limit drain volume to 5L).
- Wound infection.
- Bleeding.
- Perforation of bowel and bladder.
- Abdominal wall haematoma.

Equipment

- Rocket abdominal catheter pack (catheter sleeve, puncture needle, and adaptor clamp).
- Catheter bag and stand.
- 1 x 25G (orange) needle.
- 1 x 21G (green) needle.
- 3 x 10ml syringes.
- 5ml 1% lidocaine.
- Iodine or antiseptic solution.
- Sterile pack (including gloves, cotton wool balls, and bowl).
- Suitable adhesive dressing.
- Scalpel/blade.

Procedure

- Introduce yourself, confirm the identity of the patient, explain the procedure, and obtain informed consent.
- Ensure that the patient has emptied their bladder.
- Position the patient lying supine or semi-recumbent.
- Percuss the extent of the ascitic dullness.
- Mark your spot in the left iliac fossa within the area of dullness.
  - Double-check clinical examination and imaging, if available. If splenomegaly is present, right-sided drainage is recommended.

- Wash hands and put the sterile gloves on.
- Clean the area thoroughly with antiseptic.
- Infiltrate the skin and subcutaneous tissues with lidocaine via the orange needle and 10ml syringe.
- Attach the green needle to another 10ml syringe and insert into the abdomen, perpendicular to the skin. Advance the needle as you aspirate until fluid is withdrawn.
- Prepare the catheter kit—straighten the curled catheter using the plastic covering sheath provided.
- Take the needle provided in the pack and pass through the sheath such that the needle bevel is directed along inside the curve of the catheter—continue until the needle protrudes from the catheter tip.
- Remove the plastic covering sheath.
- Attach a 10ml syringe to the end of the catheter.
- Make a small incision in the skin using the scalpel.
- Grasp the catheter needle ~10cm above the distal end and, with firm but controlled pressure, push the needle through the abdominal wall to ~3.5–4cm deep, aspirating with the syringe.
- Disengage needle from the catheter hub and advance catheter until the suture disc is flat against the skin, then withdraw the needle.
- Connect adaptor-clamp to the catheter hub and securely attach the rubber portion of the clamp into a standard drainage catheter bag.
- Secure the catheter to the abdomen using a suitable adhesive dressing.
- Ensure the clamp is open to allow fluid to drain.

Procedure tips

- Avoid any scars or engorged veins to minimize complications
- Low-grade coagulopathy is common in cirrhotic patients and fresh frozen plasma and platelets is not routinely recommended; seek advice.
- Fluid leak can be minimized by the z track technique, moving the skin and subcutaneous tissue during insertion of drain, creating a zigzag path.
- If no aspirate is obtained despite multiple attempts, liaise with radiology and request an ultrasound and marking of a suitable site for aspiration. Alternatively, ask the radiology department to insert the drain under ultrasound guidance.

Documentation

- Date, time, indication, informed consent obtained.
- Type and amount of local anaesthetic used.
- Site of drain.
- Aseptic technique used?
- How many passes?
- Volume and colour of fluid obtained.
- Any immediate complications.
- Document the required albumin replacement (if appropriate) and when the catheter should be clamped.
- Signature, printed name, and contact details.

Sengstaken–Blakemore tube insertion

⓵ This should be performed only by senior medical staff in close liaison with an anaesthetist and, ideally, with endotracheal intubation especially in agitated patients and those with hepatic encephalopathy.

▶ The threshold to perform endotracheal intubation should be low, as the risk of regurgitation and aspiration is extremely high. Perform nasogastric lavage and stomach evacuation prior to procedure.

Indications

- Life-threatening variceal bleeding where facilities for endoscopy are not available or pending endoscopic therapy.
- Life-threatening variceal bleeding where other modalities to control bleeding have failed.

Contraindications

- Variceal bleeding has ceased or significantly slowed.
- Recent surgery to the gastro-oesophageal junction.
- Known oesophageal stricture(s).

Risks

- Mucosal necrosis due to inadvertent traction.
- Oesophageal perforation. This may be due to a gastric balloon being inflated within the oesophagus or can occur secondary to over- or prolonged-inflation of the oesophageal balloon.
- Aspiration of fluid into the respiratory tract.
- Asphyxiation due to superior migration of the tube and balloons. See last 'procedure tip' below.

Equipment

- Gloves, gown, and goggles.
- Saline flush.
- 2 × 50ml syringe.
- Local anaesthetic spray.
- Sengstaken–Blakemore tube (usually kept in refrigerator to increase its stiffness).
- Lubricant jelly (e.g. Aquagel®).
- Basin with sterile water.
- Suction equipment.
- Sphygmomanometer for pressure monitoring.

Procedure

- Introduce yourself, confirm the patient's identity, explain the procedure to the patient, and obtain informed consent.
- Position the patient at 45 degrees.
- Administer anaesthetic throat spray to the oropharynx.
- Check the balloons in the tube for air leak by inflating them with an air-filled syringe and immersing in a basin of water. Air leak is indicated by air bubbles appearing.
- Deflate the balloons.

- Apply lubricant over the tip of the tube and advance it through the oral cavity slowly until it crosses the gastro-oesophageal junction.
  - The GOJ is generally 38–42cm from the nostril so advancement of the tube 55–60cm usually positions the tip within the stomach.
- Withdraw if the patient becomes breathless.
- Inflate the gastric (**not** oesophageal) balloon with 50ml air.
- At this stage an abdominal radiograph may be performed to confirm the position of the tube in the stomach.
- Once position is confirmed, inflate the gastric balloon to a total volume of 250ml air.
- Pull gently on the tube until resistance is felt.
- Secure with tape near the mouth with gauze pads, maintaining traction and tie the tube to a 500ml bag of saline. A pulley (e.g. a drip stand) is helpful in maintaining traction.
- Mark the tube near the mouth which will serve as an indicator to whether the tube has migrated later.
- Flush the gastric port with normal saline and aspirate at frequent intervals until it is clear, which indicates that bleeding has ceased.
- ❗ If bleeding continues, inflate the oesophageal balloon with 40ml air and monitor the pressures using the sphygmomanometer frequently.
- ▶ After 12 hours' traction, relax the tension and push the tube into the stomach. If there is evidence of further bleeding, the gastric balloon can be re-inflated and traction re-applied with a view to repeat therapeutic endoscopy.
- ▶ During extubation (usually after 10–12 hours depending on clinical condition), deflate the gastric balloon first then the oesophageal balloon and withdraw the tube slowly.

Procedure tips

- The tube can be used as a measure to control bleeding for about 12–18 hours. It should not be left in place for more than 24 hours.
- Frequent aspirations from the gastric port are needed to assess the status of bleeding.
- The tube has to remain in traction at the gastric balloon which will decompress the varices. However, direct pressure from the tube can cause mucosal ulceration. Examine frequently to ensure that excessive force is not being exerted.
- If the balloons migrate superiorly, airway obstruction may occur. In this instance, as an emergency measure, the tube can be quickly cut with a pair of scissors and removed. Keep a pair of scissors handy.

Documentation

- Date, time, indication, informed consent obtained.
- Those present, including anaesthetic support.
- How many passes?
- Volume balloon inflated to and level of tube insertion.
- Any immediate complications.
- Signature, printed name, and contact details.

Basic interrupted suturing

Many suturing techniques exist. The following is the most commonly used 'interrupted suture'.

Contraindications
- Bites.
- Contaminated wounds.

Risks
- Infection, bleeding, scar (including keloid scars).

Equipment
- Suture (use cutting 3/8 or 1/2 circle needle for skin).
- Needle holder.
- Forceps.
  - Toothed for handling skin; non-toothed for other tissues.
- Scissors.
- Antiseptic solutions, drapes, sterile gloves.
- Dressing.

Procedure: placing the suture
- Introduce yourself, confirm the identity of the patient, explain the procedure, and obtain verbal consent.
- Position the patient comfortably such that the wound is exposed. Clean and drape the area to be sutured.
- Mount the needle in the needle holder approximately 3/4 of the way from the point.
- Start suturing in the middle of the wound to ensure skin edges match up.
- Grasp the skin edge and support it with the forceps.
- Pass the suture through the skin at a 90° vertical angle and approximately 0.5cm from the skin edge.
- Rotate your wrist and follow the contour of the needle until the needle point is visible in the wound.
- Support the needle tip with the forceps and withdraw it from the wound.
- Remount the needle in the needle holder.
- Support the other edge of the wound with the forceps.
- Pass the needle horizontally into the skin edge. Aim to insert the needle at the same depth from the skin's surface as the needle emerged on the other side.
- Rotate your wrist until the needle is seen at the skin surface. Aim to pass the suture 0.5cm from the wound edge.
  - Ensure the entry and exit points are directly opposite each other to prevent distortion of the wound when the suture is tied.
- Support the needle with the forceps and withdraw it through the skin.
- Tie the suture (instructions follow).
- Cut suture ends with scissors leaving 0.5cm behind.
  - This allows it to be grasped when removing.

- Repeat the process proximal and distal to the first suture until the wound is closed.
- Cover with absorbable dressing.
- Give advice on signs of infection, wound care, and when sutures should be removed.

Procedure: tying the suture (instrument tie)

- Pull the suture through until a 2–3cm 'tail' remains.
- Place the needle down at a safe site.
- Grasp the exiting suture (attached to the needle) with your non-dominant hand.
- Hold the needle holders (closed) in your dominant hand.
- Loop the suture twice around the needle holder.
- Without letting the loops slip, open the needle holder and use the tip to grasp the end of the suture 'tail'.
- Move your hands in opposite directions such that the loops slip off the jaws and around the suture.
- Snug the knot down and tighten it.
- Repeat the knot but wrap a single loop around the jaws of the needle holder in the opposite direction to previously.
- Tighten the suture.
- Pull the suture through the wound so the knot lies to one side of wound.
- Repeat until 3 knots are tied.

Documentation

- Date, time, indication, informed consent obtained.
- Anaesthetic used?
- Suture used.
- Number of sutures.
- Dressing.
- Advice given on wound care and follow-up to patient.
- Signature, printed name, and contact details.

Cleaning an open wound

The treatment of open wounds depends on:

- Depth and area.
- Contamination.
- Tissue loss (e.g. vascular, tendon, or nerve damage).
- Other (open fractures or joints, compartment syndrome).

Contraindications

- Major injuries: vascular compromise, tendon rupture, nerve injury, open factures, or joints. These require senior and/or specialist advice.

Risks

- Infection, failure to decontaminate wound.
- Haemorrhage, scar, further surgery.

Equipment

- Anaesthetic (local or general).
- Gloves, mask and eye protection.
- 2 x kidney dish (1 for cleaning solutions, 1 to collect used wash).
- 50ml syringe.
- Swabs.
- Forceps, scalpel, scissors.
- Normal saline or antiseptic solution.
- Sterile drapes.

Procedure

Wound cleaning

- Swab for microbiology if visibly contaminated or history suggestive.
- Clean wound with copious amounts of normal saline and/or water-based antiseptics using syringe.
- Clean wound with swabs from the centre outwards.
  - ▶ Do not use high-pressure irrigation (can push debris deeper).

Inspection and removal of gross contamination

- Photograph wound with adjacent ruler to document size.
- Look for gross contamination and remove with forceps.

Deep palpation

- Methodically check each area visually and with deep palpation to avoid missing contaminants and tissue injuries.
- Use forceps and wound retraction to examine all areas.
- Look for any damage to blood vessel, nerves, and tendons.
- Move the joints above and below the injury whilst looking at the tendon as it moves. Tendon injuries are easily missed if the wound was incurred in a different position to the resting state (e.g. clenched fist).
- ▶ If deep tracts are palpated, the wound may need to be extended into the skin above it to allow adequate drainage.

Excision of dead tissue

- Cut away any dead tissue until healthy tissue is visible.

Maintaining drainage
- Any cavity must be adequately drained.
- Siting a drain:
  - Identify the most dependent part of the cavity
  - Use artery forceps to identify the depth of the tract
  - With scissors, taper and cut a corrugated drain to fit into the tract
  - Pass the tip of the forceps from the tract base so they can be seen at the skin surface
  - Make an incision over the forceps to allow the drain to be sited
  - Grasp the tip of the drain with the forceps and ease into the wound
  - To stop the drain dislodging, a loose suture can be placed into the skin and either around the drain or sutured through one of its corrugations. (This depends on the type of drain used.)
- Finally, wash the wound with antiseptic solution.
- A pack can be used to keep small tracts open and allow drainage.
- A loose suture can be placed to keep the pack in place.
- ▶ Contaminated wounds and bites should not be sutured closed.

Dressing
- A non-stick dressing should be placed over the wound and edges, followed by gauze and bandage or tape.
- Further wound inspection and debridement is required at 48–96 hrs.
  - Examine sooner in heavily contaminated wounds.

Procedure tips
- Instead of a syringe, a normal saline bag and giving set can be used.
- For finger lacerations, a digital nerve block provides good analgesia.
  - 🚫 Don't use adrenaline as this can infarct the digit!
- In an ATLS scenario, open wounds should be photographed and covered with an antiseptic-soaked dressing and bandage. The photograph will allow wound inspection by others, without the need to remove bandages and contaminate the wound further.
- ▶ Always x-ray glass and metal wounds.
- Small superficial wounds with no evidence of contamination on inspection can be closed with interrupted non-absorbable sutures.
  - Patients need to be given information on wound care, signs of infection and when the sutures should be removed.
- Superficial face and head wounds can be closed with skin glue.
- ▶ In some centres, facial wounds are only sutured by maxillo-facial specialists to improve cosmetic results. Check your local policy.

Documentation
- Time, date, mechanism of injury.
- Vaccination status.
- Sensation and pulses.
- Analgesia.
- Draw diagram of wound site and inspection findings.
- How much wash was used?
- If sutured, which suture and when should it be taken out?
- Printed name, signature, and contact details.

Applying a backslab

Plaster backslabs are used as immediate splints for fractures until definitive treatment is performed and are also used to protect the fracture fixation post-surgery.

Equipment
- Stockinette.
- Padding (10cm × 1 roll = above or below elbow backslab, 15cm × 2 rolls = below knee backslab).
- Plaster of Paris bandages.
- Bowl or bucket of water (lukewarm, 25–35°C).
- Crêpe bandage.
- Scissors.

Risks
- Circulatory and nerve impairment, compartment syndrome, pressure sores, joint stiffness.

Procedure tips
- Backslab application is a 2-person procedure.
- Ensure the plaster fits well. A loosely applied cast will not provide adequate splintage and can rub, causing soreness.
- Ensure the plaster does not cause constriction. In the early stages following fractures, the limb may swell, further restricting blood and nervous supply to the limb.
- Ensure bony prominences are adequately padded.

Documentation
- Date, time, indication, informed consent obtained.
- Neurovascular status of limb.
- Procedure performed.
- Plan of further management.
- Patient given instructions to contact staff if develops increasing pain, if extremities change colour (e.g. become blue), or develops 'pins and needles' or numbness.
- Signature, printed name, and contact details.

Procedure: below knee backslab

Used for fractures/dislocations at the ankle and fractures of the foot.

- Use a padded knee rest if available to hold the knee at an angle of 10–15°.
- Hold the ankle at 90° with the foot in a neutral position.
- Cut a length of the stockinette from just below the knee to the toes and apply onto the patient.
- Apply a layer of padding over the stockinette.
  - The padding should extend from just below the knee to the toes
  - Start the padding from one end, rolling it around the limb evenly, overlapping half of the previous turn each time.
- Measure a slab of 10 layers of 15cm plaster of Paris from just below the back of the knee down to the base of the toes.
- Fold the plaster slab and dip it into the water holding the ends.
- Remove the plaster from the water, squeeze gently, and straighten it out.
- Fan out the upper end of the slab to fit the calf area.
- Place from just below the knee along the posterior surface of the lower leg, underneath the heel, and down to the base of the toes.
- Mould and smooth the plaster to fit the contours of the leg with the palms of your hands.
- Cut two side slabs 10x20cm long (length dependent on size of patient) made from 6 layers of plaster.
- Dip these in water and apply either side of the ankle joint.
  - A U-slab may be used instead of the side slabs. A 10cm wide U-slab (made of 6 layers of plaster) should be applied down one side of the leg under the heel of the foot and up the other side. Great care must be taken not to let the slabs overlap anteriorly.
- Finally, turn the stockinette back over the top and bottom edges of the plaster.

Procedure: below elbow backslab

Used for fractures/dislocations at the forearm (including Colles-type injuries) and fractures of the hand.

- Cut a length of the stockinette from just below the elbow to the knuckles, cut a small hole for the thumb.
- Apply the stockinette to the patient.
- Apply a layer of padding over the stockinette.
  - The padding should extend from the elbow to the knuckles of the back of the hand and showing the palmar crease, allowing flexion of the fingers
  - The thumb should be completely free
  - Start the padding from one end, rolling it around the limb evenly and overlapping half of the previous turn each time.
- Cut a length of plaster from below the elbow to the knuckles from a plaster of Paris slab dispenser 15 or 20cm wide (dependent on size of patient), or by forming a slab from 15 or 20cm plaster of Paris bandage using 5 layers.
- Fold the plaster and dip it into the water holding the ends.
- Remove the plaster from the water, squeeze gently, and straighten it out.
- Carefully position the slab on the limb over the padding from just below the elbow, down the dorsal surface of the limb to the knuckles.
- Mould and smooth the plaster to fit the contours of the forearm with the palms of your hands.
- Turn the stockinette back over the edge of the plaster cast at either end.
- Finally, apply the roll of crêpe bandage over the plaster and the overturned stockinette to hold the plaster in place as it sets.

Procedure: above elbow backslab

Used for fractures/dislocations at the forearm and elbow, also supracondy-lar fractures of the humerus.

- Place the limb in a position of 90° flexion at the elbow.
- Cut a length of the stockinette from the axilla to the knuckles of the hand, cut a small hole for the thumb.
- Apply the stockinette to the patient.
- Apply a layer of padding over the stockinette.
  - The padding should extend from the axilla to the knuckles of the back of the hand and showing the palmar crease, allowing finger flexion
  - The thumb should be completely free
  - Start the padding from one end, rolling it around the limb evenly and overlapping half of the previous turn each time.
- Prepare a 10 or 15cm plaster of Paris slab (dependent on patient size), using 5 layers. The slab should be long enough to extend from the axilla to the knuckles of the hand.
- Fold the plaster and dip it into the water holding the ends.
- Remove the plaster from the water, squeeze gently, and straighten it out.
- Carefully position the slab on the limb over the padding running down the posterior surface of the limb over the back of the elbow.
- Mould and smooth the plaster to fit the contours of the forearm with the palms of your hands.
- Prepare two 10cm-wide slabs of five layers of 25cm length (adjust length according to size of patient). Place these on each side of the elbow joint to reinforce it.
- Turn the stockinette back over the edge of the plaster cast at either end.
- Finally, apply the roll of crêpe bandage over the plaster and the overturned stockinette to hold the plaster in place as it sets.

Manual handling

Assisting a patient to stand

Moderate assistance is required from the patient.

Procedure

- ▶ Before beginning the procedure, ensure the patient has been assessed as able to weight-bear.
- ▶ Ensure the immediate area is clutter free.
- Ensure the patient has full understanding of the manoeuvre, and what is expected of them.
- Encourage the patient to move forward in the chair.
- Stand at the side of the chair, slightly behind the patient.
- Ensure the patient, and any other staff, are aware of which command to respond to, e.g. 'ready, steady, stand'.
- With one hand, place your arm nearest the patient around the patient's lower back, reaching as long and as low as is comfortable.
- Place the other hand at the front of the patient's shoulder.
- On the 'stand' command, as the patient rises from the chair, move your position forward such that you are standing next to the patient when upright, to aid their balance.
- ▶ Get the patient to help as much as possible during the manoeuvre e.g. pushing down on the arms of the chair if available.
- ⓘ If the patient is unsteady and unable to complete the manoeuvre, gently lower the patient back into the chair and re-assess the situation.

Procedure tips

- ▶ This procedure is only possible with cooperative patients who are able to weight-bear, and are able to understand basic commands.
- This can be carried out with 1 or 2 people, dependent on the patient.
- Allow sufficient time, so that the patient understands the process.
- It is important to encourage the patient's independence; ask them how they would carry out this manoeuvre at home.
- Include the patient in all decision making about the procedure e.g. they may feel comfortable using a Zimmer frame or similar walking aid.
- Check bed area for any furniture/equipment that could be moved to allow more space to complete the manoeuvre.
- ▶ Always check that intravenous fluids, catheters, drains, and other devices are safe and not likely to be pulled out during the procedure.
- Check with staff whether the patient has any history of cognitive problems, violence, or aggression or has any health problems which may prevent or impact upon the manoeuvre.

Documentation

- All patients should have had a moving/handling assessment completed by a physiotherapist in the first 24 hours after admission.
- Any issues raised following the move should be documented in notes.
- Full assessment should be completed prior to each move if the patient's condition has changed.

Assisting a patient to roll whilst lying

Equipment
- 1 (or 2) members of staff.

Procedure
- Ensure the bed/trolley is at waist height and that the brakes are on, to avoid staff injuries.
- ▶ If the manoeuvre is being carried out with 1 member of staff, always roll the patient towards you.
  - ▶ If 2 members of staff are available, they should stand either side of the bed/trolley.
- Ensure adequate explanation is given to the patient.
- Ensure the patient's head is facing the way the patient will be moving.
- Place the patient's distant arm across their chest, and flex their distant hip and knee.
- Place an open-palmed hand on the patient's shoulder, and your other hand on the patient's hip or knee.
  - Staff may find it more comfortable to put one of their knees on the bed, to avoid stretching or bending.
- On the command 'ready, steady, roll', move back slightly, aiding the patient to roll towards you.
- Once the patient is on their side, they can be made comfortable with pillows.
- 🕐 It is also important to ensure the patient is secure, by making use of bedrails.

Procedure tips
- 🕐 Before carrying out the procedure ensure the area around the bed/trolley is clear of any obstacles.
- 🕐 Ensure there is adequate space on the bed/trolley for the patient to roll onto.
- It is important to have the correct number of staff available to carry out the manoeuvre.
- Do not rush and leave enough time to explain the procedure to the patient and other members of staff involved.
- It is important to have assessed the patient prior to carrying out this technique, to discover any contraindications to the patient lying on their side (e.g. problems with the patient's head and neck control, or any potential difficulties such as the patient's size).

Documentation
- All patients should have assessments carried out within 24 hours of admission. Care plan to be maintained/consulted as appropriate.
- Any issues or problems with manoeuvre should be documented in the notes.

Assisting a patient to change position in bed (using a glide sheet)

Equipment
- Single-patient use multi-directional slide sheet/glide sheet.
- Minimum of two staff.

Procedure
- Ensure patient is aware of the procedure and has given consent, if able.
- Patient should be lying flat in bed.
- ❗ Discuss desired end position of patient with the other handler(s).
- Move the bed to waist height to prevent staff injuries.
- Ensure the brakes on bed are secure.
- Staff should stand either side of the bed facing each other.
- To place glide sheet under patient, roll patient on bed sheet over to one side of the bed. Either:
  - One staff member leans over patient and pulls the bottom sheet to roll patient onto one side
  - Or, if possible, encourage the patient to roll themselves onto one side.
- The handler nearest the patient should hold sheet (and patient on their side) whilst the glide sheet is inserted by the other handler.
- Place the glide sheet between mattress and bottom sheet.
- The second handler should hold the glide sheet and push as far as possible under bottom sheet and the patient rolls back onto their back.
- Repeat from the other side until glide sheet is fully under the patient.
- Once the sheet is in place, agree which handler will give commands.
- Both handlers should grip the *bed* sheet, with both hands, as close to patient as possible. Place both feet firmly on the floor.
- On command of 'ready, steady, move', both handlers grip bottom sheet and gently move patient to previously agreed position.
- Place pillows appropriately for the patient's revised position.
- Reverse patient movement procedure to remove glide sheet.

Procedure tips
- Do not rush. Ensure sufficient time available to explain the manoeuvre to the patient and safely complete the manoeuvre.
- Check bed area for any furniture/equipment that could be moved to allow more space to complete the manoeuvre.
- ▶ Always check that intravenous fluids, catheters, drains, and other devices are safe and not likely to be pulled out during procedure.
- Check with staff whether the patient has any history of cognitive problems, violence, or aggression or has any health problems which may prevent or impact upon the manoeuvre.
- Ensure bedrails are put back into place following procedure.

Documentation
- All patients should have assessments carried out within 24 hours of admission and placed in their file.
- Any issues or concerns should be documented in the patient's notes to ensure other ward staff are aware of problems.

Transferring a patient laterally using a transfer board

Use to transfer patients who are unable to move themselves.

Equipment

- Patient transfer board or 'Patslide®'.

Procedure

- There should be at least three handlers.
- Open transfer board (if folded) and place on bed/trolley you plan to transfer patient to.
- Explain the manoeuvre to the patient.
- Place destination bed/trolley alongside origin bed/trolley.
  - Ensure there is only a minimal gap between the bed/trolley.
- Check bed is at waist height to prevent staff injuries.
- Staff stand either side of bed/trolley facing each other, two people on the 'destination' side and one on the other.
- ❶ Check brakes on bed and trolley secure.
- Staff at the patient's bedside to lean over patient and grip bed sheet as close to the patient's body as possible in both hands and roll the patient towards them.
- Staff at the bed/trolley onto which patient is to be transferred, put transfer board onto patient's bed/trolley.
- Staff at bedside allow patient to roll back onto board (which should be under the bed sheet).
- On command of 'ready, steady, move'....
- Handlers push and pull patient gently across on transfer board, dependent upon their position.
  - ❶ Staff should ensure their arms remain straight and they do not lean forward, bending at the waist.
- Once patient is transferred, ensure sheets/blankets are replaced.
- Bedrails should be put into place as appropriate.

Procedure tips

- Ensure time is available to safely complete the manoeuvre.
- Check bed area for any furniture/equipment that could be moved.
- Always check IV fluids, catheters, drains, etc. are safe and unlikely to be caught or pulled out during procedure.
- Move any attachments onto transferring bed/trolley prior to the move.
- Check with qualified staff/physiotherapists regarding any changes in the patient's condition prior to manoeuvre.
- Staff should wear suitable footwear and non-restrictive clothing.
- Check with ward staff that patient can be laid flat.
- If NG-fed, ensure it is switched off to prevent patient aspirating.
- ❶ Do not climb onto the bed/trolley.
- ❶ Ensure both surfaces are the same height, making the manoeuvre both easier and more comfortable for the patient.

Documentation

- Any issues or problems with equipment or manoeuvre should be conveyed to the nurse in charge, documented in the notes, and an appropriate incident form completed.

Transferring a patient using a hoist

Limited input from patient. Use this technique to transfer patients who are unable to weight-bear, sit patients up in the bed, or use a bedpan.

Equipment
- Hoist.
- Sling: single patient use (disposable).

Procedure
- ▶ There should be at least two handlers.
  - Check care plan regarding patient's suitability for hoist usage
  - Before getting equipment, ensure manoeuvre is explained to patient.
- Select appropriate sling: small, medium, or large.
- Ensure hoist and sling are compatible.
- Check hoist is able to take patient's weight: most are able to take up to 25 stones (170kg).
- Check bed is at waist height to prevent staff injuries.
- Staff stand either side of bed facing each other.
- ❗ Check brakes on bed secure.
- Patient should be rolled to one side of bed.
- Lay the hoist sling on the bed.
- Roll the patient to other side of the bed.
  - Sling should now be in a position from patient's head to thigh.
- Place the loops at shoulder end of sling on arm of hoist.
- Pass the thigh-end loops through each other, then place on hoist.
  - ▶ Ensure the loops are correctly positioned before moving.
- One handler should now manage the controls of the hoist.
- Second handler lowers patient's bed, then moves behind the patient/hoist, ready to guide them into the chair.
- Move patient back with hoist.
- Second handler gently guides patient into the chair.
- Once patient is in chair, disconnect loops from hoist.
- Remove sling from beneath lower legs of patient.

Procedure tips
- Ensure sufficient time available to safely complete the manoeuvre.
- Check bed area for any furniture/equipment that could be moved.
- Always check items such as IV fluids, catheters, and drains are safe and unlikely to be caught in hoist or pulled out during procedure.
- Check with qualified staff/physiotherapists regarding any changes in the patient's condition prior to manoeuvre. Transfer may be inadvisable.
- Staff should wear suitable footwear and non-restrictive clothing.
- Hoist should only be used to transfer patients short distances.
- Ensure hoist is fully charged before commencing manoeuvre.
- ❗ Ensure the brakes of the hoist are 'off'. This will allow the hoist to find its own centre of gravity.

Documentation
- Any issues with equipment or manoeuvre—advise nurse in charge and document in notes and complete an appropriate incident form.

Transferring a patient using a log roll

Use this technique to transfer patients in whom a cervical spine injury is suspected or confirmed. The following assumes that the patient's neck is immobilized in a brace or blocks.

Equipment
- ▶ Minimum five members of staff.
- Patient transfer board or 'Patslide®'.

Procedure
- ▶ The most senior member of the team should take charge of the patient's head and neck and initiate commands.
- Ensure adequate explanation is given to the patient, and to all members of staff involved.
- Place destination bed alongside origin bed at waist height.
- One member of staff should position themselves at the head end of the patient, the other three should be spread alongside the patient, at the origin side. The final member of staff should be at the destination.
- ❶ Check brakes on bed secure.
- ▶ The person responsible for the patient's head should have one hand either side of the patient's head, supporting the patient's shoulders.
- ▶ The person responsible for the patient's upper body should have one hand on the patient's distant shoulder, and the other on the lateral aspect of the patient's chest.
- ▶ The person responsible for the patient's pelvis should have one hand on the lateral aspect of the pelvis and the other under the thigh.
- ▶ The person responsible for the patient's lower legs should have both hands under the calves.
- On the command 'ready, steady, roll' the three members of staff at the side of the patient will slowly move backwards with straight arms, rolling the patient towards them.
- Staff at the bed/trolley onto which patient is to be transferred, put transfer board onto patient's bed/trolley.
- On the command 'ready, steady, roll' the four members of staff at the side of the patient roll the patient back flat, keeping the neck straight.
- One member of staff should now move around the bed such that there are two on each side and one at the head.
- On the command of 'ready, steady, move', handlers move the patient gently across keeping the head and neck immobilized.

Procedure tips
- Ensure sufficient time available to safely complete the manoeuvre.
- Check bed area for any furniture/equipment that could be moved.
- Staff should wear suitable footwear and non-restrictive clothing.
- ▶ It is essential that the patient's body be kept in alignment, and the manoeuvre is carried out in one smooth and controlled movement.

Documentation
- Any issues with equipment or manoeuvre, advise nurse in charge and document in notes and complete an appropriate incident form.

Aiding a falling patient

- ▶ It is essential that if a patient falls, the member of staff **must not** try to catch the patient, but must allow them to fall, as there is no safe method for this situation.
- ▶ Allowing the patient to fall may feel contrary to the staff's natural instincts to help but trying to catch a patient will only result in injury to staff.
- ❶ Instead, every attempt must be made to reduce injury to the patient (e.g. moving objects out of the patient's way if possible).

Falling in a forward direction

- If a member of staff is walking with a patient as they fall in a forward direction, the member of staff must allow the patient to fall.

Falling towards a member of staff

- If the fall is towards the member of staff, it may be possible to control the patient's movements safely to minimize injury to them.
- The member of staff should move close to the patient, standing directly behind them with their leg closest to the patient flexed. Then they should gently guide the patient's body down their flexed leg to the floor.

Procedure tips

- The risk of falling should be minimized by only performing tasks appropriate to the patient's ability (e.g. only allow patients to walk if they are fully mobile).
- Use equipment to reduce the risk of falls i.e. Zimmer frames or walking sticks.
- ❶ A patient falling is an unpredictable and sudden event. However, the member of staff should take every care to maintain a good posture at all times, avoiding twisting or stretching.
- ▶ If present when a patient falls, the member of staff should immediately call for assistance, to ensure an adequate number of staff are present if the situation turns into an emergency.

Documentation

- All patients should have assessments carried out within 24 hours of admission and placed in their file.
- Any fall or issues should be documented in the patient's notes to ensure other ward staff are aware of problems.

Aiding a fallen patient

- ▶ It is important to assess the fallen patient immediately, to establish the cause for the fall and any immediate consequences (e.g. fainting, fractures, or cardiac arrest) so that staff can respond to the situation accordingly.

Equipment

- Minimum of two members of staff.
- Other equipment dependent on circumstances:
  - Two chairs, trolley, slide sheets, hoist with appropriate sling.

Procedure: if patient is cooperative

- Instructions may be given to help the patient up from the floor. Ask the patient to follow this routine:
- Roll onto their side ...
- Push up on their hands until they are in a sitting position ...
- Bend their knees up and move onto all fours ...
- Place their hands onto the seat of a chair for balance ...
- Move one leg forward, so they are in a half-kneeling position ...
- At this point, the patient should be able to push with their hands to stand up, and sit on a chair placed behind them.
- If needed, the patient can now be hoisted onto a trolley for further assessment.

Procedure: if patient is uncooperative

- A hoist should be used.

Procedure: if fallen in a confined space

- Place a slide sheet under their body.
- With a minimum of two members of staff, the patient can then be slid on the floor a short distance to allow better access to assist the patient.
  - It is essential that the members of staff maintain a good posture at all times during this procedure.

Procedure tips

- ▶ It is essential to establish the cause of the fall and act accordingly.
- ▶ It is important that, as the patient is moving up from the floor, their condition is continuously monitored.
  - 🛈 If the patient has fainted, they may be at risk of falling again.
- It is important to allow the patient time to carry out the manoeuvre, as this will reduce the amount of manual assistance required from staff.
- ▶ It is extremely important that the patient is NEVER LIFTED.
  - Lifting a patient is hazardous and may result in staff injury.

Clinical data interpretation

Electrocardiography (ECG)

The first step in making sense of an electrocardiogram (ECG) printout is to understand the electrical conduction process in the normal heart.

Electrophysiology of the heart

Cardiac myocytes

In their resting state, the surface of cardiac myocytes (muscle cells) is polarized with a potential difference of 90mV across the cell membrane (negatively charged intracellularly and positively charged extracellularly).

Depolarization (reversal of this charge) results in movement of calcium ions across the cell membranes and subsequent cardiac muscle contraction. It is this change in potential difference that can be detected by the ECG electrodes and represented as deflections on a tracing.

The basics of the tracing

It is easiest to imagine an electrode 'looking' at the heart from where it is attached to the body.

Depolarization of the myocytes that spreads towards the electrode is seen as an upwards deflection, electrical activity moving away from the electrode is seen as a downwards deflection and activity moving to one side but neither towards nor away from the electrode is not seen at all (see Fig. 19.1).

Electrical conduction pathway

In the normal heart, pacemaker cells in the sinoatrial (SA) node initiate depolarization. The depolarization first spreads through the atria and this is seen as a small upward deflection (the 'P' wave) on the ECG.

The atria and the ventricles are electrically isolated from each other. The only way in which the impulse can progress from the atria to the ventricles normally is through the atrioventricular (AV) node. Passage through the AV node slows its progress slightly. This can be seen on ECG as the isoelectric interval between the P wave and QRS complex, the 'PR interval'.

Depolarization then continues down the rapidly conducting Purkinje fibres—bundle of His, then down left and right bundle branches to depolarize both ventricles (see Fig. 19.2). The left bundle has two divisions (fascicles). The narrow QRS complex on ECG shows this rapid ventricular depolarization.

Repolarization of the ventricles is seen as the T wave. Atrial repolarization causes only a very slight deflection which is hidden in the QRS complex and not seen.

▶ The P wave and QRS complex show the electrical depolarization of atrial and ventricular myocardium respectively, but the resultant mechanical muscle contraction—which usually follows—cannot be inferred from the ECG trace (e.g. in pulseless electrical activity (PEA)).

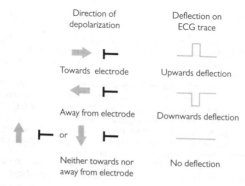

Fig. 19.1 Diagrammatic representation of how waves of depolarization are translated onto the ECG trace depending on the relationship to the electrodes.

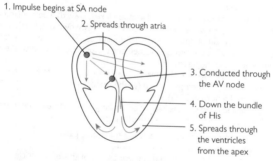

Fig. 19.2 Diagrammatic representation of the electrical conduction pathway in the normal heart.

The 12-lead ECG

Leads

Electrodes are placed on the limbs and chest for a '12-lead' recording. The term '12-lead' relates to the number of directions that the electrical activity is recorded from and is not the number of electrical wires attached to the patient.

The 6 chest leads (V_{1-6}) and 6 limb leads (I, II, III, aVR, aVL, aVF) comprise the 12-lead ECG. These 'look at' the electrical activity of the heart from various directions. The chest leads correspond directly to the 6 electrodes placed at various points on the anterior and lateral chest wall (see Fig. 19.3). However, the 6 limb leads represent the electrical activity as 'viewed' using a combination of the 4 electrodes placed on the patient's limbs—e.g. lead I is generated from the right and left arm electrodes.

▶ Remember there are 12 ECG leads—12 different views of the electrical activity of the heart—but only 10 actual electrodes placed on the patient's body.

🛈 Additional leads can be used (e.g. V_{7-9} extending laterally around the chest wall) to look at the heart from further angles such as in suspected posterior myocardial infarction.

ECG orientation

When a wave of myocardial depolarization flows towards a particular lead, the ECG tracing shows an upwards deflection. A downward deflection represents depolarization moving away from that lead. The key to interpreting the 12-lead ECG is therefore to remember the directions at which the different leads view the heart.

The 6 limb leads look at the heart in the coronal plane (see Fig. 19.4).

- aVR looking at the right atrium (all the vectors will be negative for this lead in the normal ECG).
- aVF, II, and III viewing the inferior or diaphragmatic surface of the heart.
- I and aVL examining the left lateral aspect.

The 6 chest leads examine the heart in a transverse plane ...

- V_1 and V_2 looking at the right ventricle.
- V_3 and V_4 at the septum and anterior aspect of the left ventricle.
- V_5 and V_6 at the anterior and lateral aspects of the left ventricle.

Although each of the 12 leads gives a different view of the electrical activity of the heart, for the sake of simplicity when considering the standard ECG trace, we can describe the basic shape common to all leads (see Fig. 19.5).

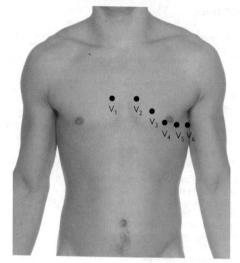

Fig. 19.3 Correct placement of the 6 chest leads.

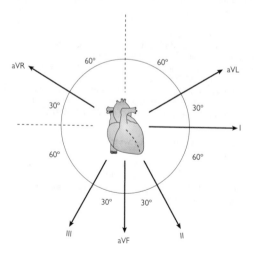

Fig. 19.4 The respective 'views' of the heart of the 6 limb leads. Note the angles between the direction of the limb leads – these become important when calculating the cardiac axis.

The ECG trace

Waves

- P wave represents atrial depolarization and is a positive (upwards) deflection—except in aVR.
- QRS complex represents ventricular depolarization and comprises:
  - Q wave: so called if the first QRS deflection is negative (downwards). Pathological Q waves are seen in myocardial infarction
  - R wave: the first positive (upwards) deflection—may or may not follow a Q wave
  - S wave: a negative (downwards) deflection following the R wave.
- T wave represents ventricular repolarization and is normally a positive (upwards) deflection, concordant with the QRS complex.

Rate

- The heart rate can be calculated by dividing 300 by the number of large squares between each R wave (with machine trace running at the standard speed of 25mm/sec and deflection of 1cm/10mV).
  - 3 large squares between R waves = rate 100
  - 5 large squares = rate 60.
- Normal rate 60–100 beats/minute.
  - Rate <60 = bradycardia
  - Rate >100 = tachycardia.

Intervals and timing

- PR interval: from the start of the P wave to the start of the QRS complex. This represents the inbuilt delay in electrical conduction at the atrioventricular (AV) node. Normally <0.20 seconds (5 small squares at standard recording speed).
- QRS complex: the width of the QRS complex. Normally <0.12 seconds (3 small squares at standard rate).
- R–R interval: from the peak of one R wave to the next. This is used in the calculation of heart rate.
- QT interval: from the start of the QRS complex to the end of the T wave. Varies with heart rate. Corrected QT = QT/square root of the R–R interval. Corrected QT interval should be 0.38–0.42 seconds.

Rhythm

- Is the rhythm (and the time between successive R waves) regular or irregular?
  - If irregular but in a clear pattern, then it is said to be 'regularly irregular' (e.g. types of heart block)
  - If irregular but no pattern, then it is said to be 'irregularly irregular' (e.g. atrial fibrillation).

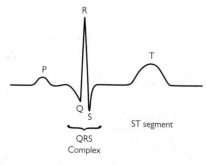

Fig. 19.5 The basic shape of a typical ECG trace.

ECG axis

Cardiac axis

The cardiac axis, or 'QRS axis', refers to the overall direction of depolarization through the ventricular myocardium in the coronal plane.

Zero degrees is taken as the horizontal line to the left of the heart (the right of your diagram).

The normal cardiac axis lies between −30 and +90 degrees (see Fig. 19.6). An axis outside of this range may suggest pathology, either congenital or acquired.

Note, however, that cardiac axis deviation may be seen in healthy individuals with distinctive body shapes. Right axis deviation if tall and thin; left axis deviation if short and stocky (Box 19.1).

Calculating the axis

Look at Fig. 19.7. Leads I, II, and III all lie in the coronal plane (along with aVR, aVL, and aVF). By calculating the relative depolarization in each of these directions, one can calculate the cardiac axis. To accurately determine the cardiac axis, you should use leads I, II, and III as described in Fig.19.7. There are less reliable short cuts, however.

- Draw a diagram like Fig.19.6 showing the 3 leads—be careful to use the correct angles.
- Look at the ECG lead I. Count the number of mm above the baseline that the QRS complex reaches.
- Subtract from this the number of mm below the baseline that the QRS complex reaches.
- Now measure this number of centimetres along line I on your diagram and make a mark (measure backward for negative numbers).
- Repeat this for leads II and III.
- Extend lines from your marks, perpendicular to the leads (see Fig. 19.6).
- The direction from the centre of the diagram to the point at which all these lines meet is the cardiac axis.

Calculating the axis—short cuts

There are many shorter ways of roughly calculating the cardiac axis. These are less accurate, however.

An easy method is to look at only leads I and aVF. These are perpendicular to each other and make a simpler diagram than the one described above.

An even easier method is to look at the print-out. Most computerized machines will now tell you the ECG axis (but you should still have an understanding of the theory behind it).

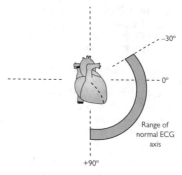

Fig. 19.6 The normal ECG axis.

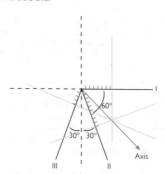

Fig. 19.7 Calculating the ECG axis using leads I, II, and III. See text.

Box 19.1 Some causes of axis deviation

Left axis deviation (<–30 degrees)
- Left ventricular hypertrophy
- Left bundle branch block (LBBB)
- Left anterior hemiblock (anterior fascicle of the left bundle)
- Inferior myocardial infarction
- Cardiomyopathies
- Tricuspid atresia.

Right axis deviation (>+90 degrees)
- Right ventricular hypertrophy
- Right bundle branch block (RBBB)
- Anterolateral myocardial infarction
- Right ventricular strain (e.g. pulmonary embolism)
- Cor pulmonale
- Fallot's tetralogy (pulmonary stenosis).

AV conduction abnormalities

In the normal ECG each P wave is followed by a QRS complex. The isoelectric gap between is the PR interval and represents slowing of the impulse at the AV junction. Disturbance of the normal conduction here, leads to 'heart block' (Fig.19.8).

Causes of heart block include ischaemic heart disease, idiopathic fibrosis of the conduction system, cardiomyopathies, inferior and anterior MI, drugs (digoxin, β-blockers, verapamil), and physiological (1st degree) in athletes.

First degree heart block

PR interval fixed but prolonged at >0.20 seconds (5 small squares at standard rate). See rhythm strip 1 (Fig. 19.8).

Second degree heart block

Not every P wave is followed by a QRS complex.

- Möbitz type I: PR interval becomes progressively longer after each P wave until an impulse fails to be conducted at all. The interval then returns to the normal length and the cycle is repeated (rhythm strip 2, Fig. 19.8). This is also known as the Wenckebach phenomenon.
- Möbitz type II: PR interval is fixed but not every P wave is followed by a QRS. The relationship between P waves and QRS complex may be 2:1 (2 P waves for every QRS), 3:1 (3 P waves per QRS), or random. See rhythm strip 3, Fig. 19.8.

Third degree heart block

Also called complete heart block. See rhythm strip 4 (Fig. 19.8). There is no conduction of the impulse through the AV junction. Atrial and ventricular depolarization occur independent of one another. Each has a separate pacemaker triggering electrical activity at different rates.

- The QRS complex is an abnormal shape as the electrical impulse does not travel through the ventricles via the normal routes (see ventricular escape).
- P waves may be seen 'merging' with QRS complexes if they coincide.

Notes

- If in doubt about the pattern of P waves and QRS complexes, mark out the P wave intervals and the R–R intervals separately, then compare.
- P waves are best seen in leads II and V_1.

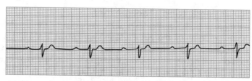

Rhythm strip 1—first degree heart block.

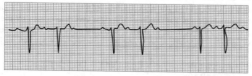

Rhythm strip 2—second degree heart block Möbitz type I.

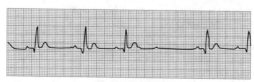

Rhythm strip 3—second degree heart block Möbitz type II.

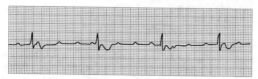

Rhythm strip 4—third degree (complete) heart block.

Fig. 19.8 Rhythm strips showing AV conduction abnormalities.

Ventricular conduction abnormalities

Depolarization of both ventricles usually occurs rapidly through left and right bundle branches of the His–Purkinje system (see Fig. 19.9). If this process is disrupted as a result of damage to the conducting system, depolarization will occur more slowly through non-specialized ventricular myocardium. The QRS complex—usually <0.12 seconds' duration—will become prolonged and is described as a 'broad' (Fig.19.9).

Right bundle branch block (RBBB)

Conduction through the AV node, bundle of His, and left bundle branch will be normal but depolarization of the right ventricle occurs by the slow spread of electrical current through myocardial cells. The result is delayed right ventricular depolarization giving a second R wave known as R' ('R prime').

RBBB suggests pathology in the right side of the heart but can be a normal variant (Fig.19.10).

ECG changes

(See Box 19.2 for bundle branch block mnemonic.)

- 'RSR' pattern seen in V_1.
- Cardiac axis usually remains normal unless left anterior fascicle is also blocked ('bifascicular block') which results in left axis deviation.
- T wave flattening or inversion in anterior chest leads (V_1–V_3).

Some causes of RBBB

- Hyperkalaemia.
- Congenital heart disease (e.g. Fallot's tetralogy).
- Pulmonary embolus.
- Cor pulmonale.
- Fibrosis of conduction system.

Left bundle branch block (LBBB)

Conduction through the AV node, bundle of His, and right bundle branch will be normal but depolarization of the left ventricle occurs by the slow spread of electrical current through myocardial cells. The result is delayed left ventricular depolarization (Fig.19.11).

LBBB should always be considered pathological.

ECG changes

- 'M' pattern seen in V_6.
- T wave flattening or inversion in lateral chest leads (V_5–V_6).

Some causes of LBBB

- Hypertension.
- Ischaemic heart disease.
- Acute myocardial infarction.
- Aortic stenosis.
- Cardiomyopathies.
- Fibrosis of conduction system.

🔴 LBBB on the ECG causes abnormalities of the ST segment and T wave. You should not comment any further on these parts of the trace.

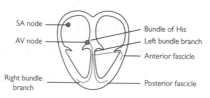

Fig. 19.9 Diagrammatic representation of the conducting system of the heart.

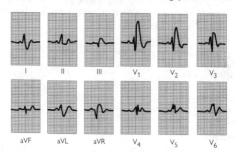

Fig. 19.10 Typical 12-lead ECG showing RBBB.

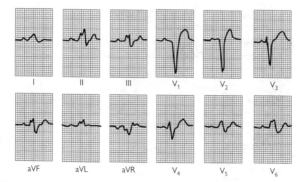

Fig. 19.11 Typical 12-lead ECG showing LBBB.

Box 19.2 Bundle branch block mnemonic
- LBBB, the QRS complex in V_1 looks like a 'W' and an 'M' in V_6. This can be remembered as 'WiLLiaM'. There is a W at the start, an M at the end and 'L' in the middle for 'left'
- Conversely, in the case of RBBB, the QRS complex in V_1 looks like an 'M' and a 'W' in V_6. Combined with an 'R' for right, you have the word 'MaRRoW'.

Sinus rhythms

Supraventricular rhythms arise in the atria. They may be physiological in the case of some causes of sinus brady- and tachycardia or may be caused by pathology within the SA node, the atria, or the first parts of the conducting system.

Normal conduction through the bundle of His into the ventricles will usually give narrow QRS complexes.

Sinus bradycardia

This is a bradycardia (rate <60 beats per minute) at the level of the SA node. The heart beats slowly but conduction of the impulse is normal. (Rhythm strip 1, Fig. 19.12.)

Some causes of sinus bradycardia

- Drugs (β-blockers, verapamil, amiodarone, digoxin).
- Sick sinus syndrome.
- Hypothyroidism.
- Inferior MI.
- Hypothermia.
- Raised intracranial pressure.
- Physiological (athletes).

Sinus tachycardia

This is a tachycardia at the level of the SA node—the heart is beating too quickly but conduction of the impulse is normal. (Rhythm strip 2, Fig. 19.12.)

ECG features

- Ventricular rate > 100 (usually 100–150 beats per minute).
- Normal P wave before each QRS.

Some causes of sinus tachycardia

- Drugs (epinephrine/adrenaline, caffeine, nicotine).
- Pain.
- Exertion.
- Anxiety.
- Anaemia.
- Thyrotoxicosis.
- Pulmonary embolus.
- Hepatic failure.
- Cardiac failure.
- Hypercapnia.
- Pregnancy.
- Constrictive pericarditis.

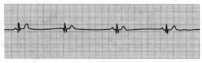

Rhythm strip 1—sinus bradycardia.

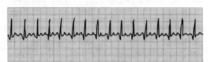

Rhythm strip 2—sinus tachycardia.

Fig. 19.12 Rhythm strips from lead II showing a sinus bradycardia (rhythm strip 1) and sinus tachycardia (rhythm strip 2).

Supraventricular tachycardias

These are tachycardias (rate >100bpm) arising in the atria or the AV node. As conduction through the bundle of His and ventricles will be normal (unless there is other pathology in the heart), the QRS complexes appear normal (Fig.19.13).

There are four main causes of a supraventricular tachycardia that you should be aware of: atrial fibrillation, atrial flutter, junctional tachycardia, and re-entry tachycardia.

Atrial fibrillation (AF)

This is disorganized contraction of the atria in the form of rapid, irregular twitching. There will, therefore, be no P waves on the ECG.

Electrical impulses from the twitches of the atria arrive at the AV node randomly, they are then conducted via the normal pathways to cause ventricular contraction. The result is a characteristic ventricular rhythm that is *irregularly irregular* with no discernible pattern.

ECG features
- No P waves. Rhythm is described as *irregularly irregular*.
- Irregular QRS complexes.
- Normal appearance of QRS.
- Ventricular rate may be increased ('fast AF')—typically 120–160 per minute.

Some causes of atrial fibrillation
- Idiopathic.
- Ischaemic heart disease.
- Thyroid disease.
- Hypertension.
- MI.
- Pulmonary embolus.
- Rheumatic mitral or tricuspid valve disease.

Atrial flutter

This is the abnormally rapid contraction of the atria. The contractions are not disorganized or random, unlike AF, but are fast and inadequate for the normal movement of blood. Instead of P waves, the baseline will have a typical 'saw-tooth' appearance (sometimes known as F waves).

The AV node is unable to conduct impulses faster than 200/min. Atrial contraction faster than that leads to impulses failing to be conducted. For example, an atrial rate of 300/min will lead to every other impulse being conducted giving a ventricular rate (and pulse) of 150/min. In this case, it is called '2:1 block'. Other ratios of atrial to ventricular contractions may occur.

A variable block at the AV node may lead to an irregularly irregular pulse indistinguishable from that of AF on clinical examination.

ECG features
- 'Saw-tooth' appearance of baseline.
- Normal appearance of QRS complexes.

Causes of atrial flutter
- Similar to AF.

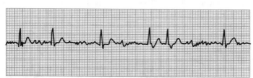

Rhythm strip 1—atrial fibrillation.

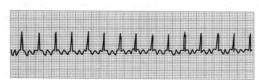

Rhythm strip 2—atrial flutter with 2:1 block.

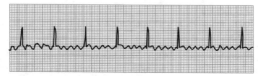

Rhythm strip 3—atrial flutter with 4:1 block.

Fig. 19.13 Rhythm strips from lead II showing some supraventricular tachycardias.

Junctional (nodal) tachycardia

The area in or around the AV node depolarizes spontaneously, the impulse will be immediately conducted to the ventricles. The QRS complex will be of a normal shape but no P waves will be seen.

ECG features

- No P waves.
- QRS complexes are regular and normal shape.
- Rate may be fast or may be of a normal rate.

Some causes of junctional tachycardia

- Sick sinus syndrome (including drug-induced).
- Digoxin toxicity.
- Ischaemia of the AV node, especially with acute inferior MI.
- Acutely after cardiac surgery.
- Acute inflammatory processes (e.g. acute rheumatic fever) which may involve the conduction system.
- Diphtheria.
- Other drugs (e.g. most anti-arrhythmic agents).

Wolff–Parkinson–White syndrome

In Wolff–Parkinson–White (WPW) syndrome, there is an extra conducting pathway between the atria and the ventricles (the bundle of Kent)—a break in the normal electrical insulation. This 'accessory' pathway is not special-ized for conducting electrical impulses so does not delay the impulse as the AV node does. However, it is not linked to the normal conduction pathways of the bundle of His.

Depolarization of the ventricles will occur partly via the AV node and partly by the bundle of Kent. During normal atrial contraction, electrical activity reaches the AV node and the accessory pathway at roughly the same time. Whilst it is held up temporarily at the AV node, the impulse passes through the accessory pathway and starts to depolarize the ventri-cles via non-specialized cells ('pre-excitation'), distorting the first part of the R wave and giving a short PR interval. Normal conduction via the bundle of His then supervenes. The result is a slurred upstroke of the QRS complex called a 'delta wave'.

This is an example of a 'fusion beat' in which normal and abnormal ven-tricular depolarization combine to give a distortion of the QRS complex (Fig. 19.14 and Box 19.3).

Re-entry tachycardia

The accessory pathway may allow electrical activity to be conducted from the ventricles back up to the atria.

For example, in a re-entry tachycardia, electrical activity may be con-ducted down the bundle of His, across the ventricles and up the acces-sory pathway into the atria causing them to contract again, and the cycle is repeated. This is called a 're-entry circuit' (Figs 19.15 and 19.16).

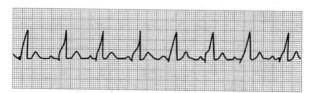

Fig. 19.14 Rhythm strip showing Wolff–Parkinson–White syndrome.

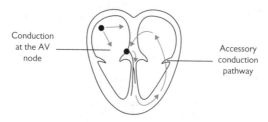

Fig. 19.15 Diagrammatic representation of re-entry tachycardia.

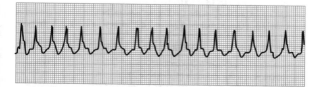

Fig. 19.16 Rhythm strip showing a re-entry tachycardia.

Box 19.3 Classification of Wolff–Parkinson–White syndrome

The bundle of Kent may connect the atria with either the right or the left ventricle. Thus, WPW is classically divided into two groups according to the resulting appearance of the QRS complex in the anterior chest leads. In practice, this classification is rather simplistic as 11% of patients may have more than one accessory pathway.

- *Type A:* upright delta wave and QRS in V_1
  - May be mistaken for RBBB or posterior MI.
- *Type B:* downward delta wave and QRS in V_1, positive elsewhere.

Ventricular rhythms

Most ventricular rhythms originate outside the usual conduction pathways meaning that excitation spreads by an abnormal path through the ventricular muscle to give broad or unusually shaped QRS complexes (Fig.19.17).

Ventricular tachycardia (VT)

Here, there is a focus of ventricular tissue depolarizing rapidly within the ventricular myocardium. VT is defined as 3 or more successive ventricular extrasystoles at a rate of >120/min. 'Sustained' VTs last for >30 secs.

VT may be 'stable' showing a repetitive QRS shape ('monomorphic') or unstable with varying patterns of the QRS complex ('polymorphic').

It may be impossible to distinguish VT from an SVT with bundle branch block on a 12-lead ECG (see also Box 19.5).

ECG features

- Wide QRS complexes which are irregular in rhythm and shape.
- A-V dissociation—independent atrial and ventricular contraction.
- May see fusion and capture beats on ECG as signs of atrial activity independent of the ventricular activity—said to be pathognomonic.
  - Fusion beats: depolarization from AV node meets depolarization from ventricular focus causing hybrid QRS complex.
  - Capture beats: atrial beat conducted to ventricles causing a normal QRS complex in amongst the VT trace.
- Rate can be up to 130–300/min.
- QRS concordance: all the QRS complexes in the chest leads are either mainly positive or mainly negative—this suggests a ventricular origin of the tachycardia.
- Extreme axis deviation (far negative or far positive).

Some causes of ventricular tachycardia

- Ischaemia (acute including MI or chronic).
- Electrolyte abnormalities (reduced K^+, reduced Mg^{2+}).
- Aggressive adrenergic stimulation (e.g. cocaine use).
- Drugs—especially anti-arrhythmics.

Ventricular fibrillation (VF)

This is disorganized, uncoordinated depolarization from multiple foci in the ventricular myocardium (Box 19.4).

ECG features

- No discernible QRS complexes.
- A completely disorganized ECG.

Some causes of ventricular fibrillation

- Coronary heart disease.
- Cardiac inflammatory diseases.
- Abnormal metabolic states.
- Pro-arrhythmic toxic exposures.
- Electrocution.
- Tension pneumothorax, trauma, and drowning.
- Large pulmonary embolism.
- Hypoxia or acidosis.

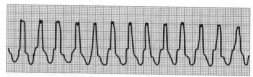

Rhythm strip 1—monomorphic ventricular tachycardia (VT).

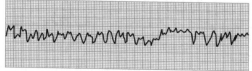

Rhythm strip 2—ventricular fibrillation (VF).

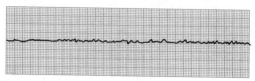

Rhythm strip 3—'fine' ventricular fibrillation.

Fig. 19.17 Rhythm strips showing ventricular rhythms.

Box 19.4 Fine VF

This is VF with a small amplitude waveform. It may resemble asystole on the ECG monitor (see Fig. 19.19), particularly in an emergency situation.

In a clinical situation, you should remember to increase the gain on the monitor to ensure what you think is asystole is not really fine VF as the management for each is very different.

Other ventricular rhythms

Ventricular extrasystoles (ectopics)

These are ventricular contractions originating from a focus of depolarization within the ventricle. As conduction is via abnormal pathways, the QRS complex will be unusually shaped (Fig.19.19).

Ventricular extrasystoles are common and harmless if there is no structural heart disease. If they occur at the same time as a T wave, the 'R-on-T' phenomenon, they can lead to VF.

Ventricular escape rhythm

This occurs as a 'back-up' when conduction between the atria and the ventricles is interrupted (as in complete heart block).

The intrinsic pacemaker in ventricular myocardium depolarizes at a slow rate (30–40/min).

The ventricular beats will be abnormal and wide with abnormal T waves following them. This rhythm can be stable but may suddenly fail.

Asystole

This is a complete absence of electrical activity and is not compatible with life.

There may be a slight wavering of the baseline which can be easily confused with fine VF in emergency situations.

Agonal rhythm

This is a slow, irregular rhythm with wide ventricular complexes which vary in shape. This is often seen in the later stages of unsuccessful resuscitation attempts as the heart dies. The complexes become progressively broader before all recognizable activity is lost (asystole).

Box 19.5 Torsades de pointes

Torsades de pointes, literally meaning 'twisting of points', is a form of polymorphic VT characterized by a gradual change in the amplitude and twisting of the QRS axis. In the US, it is known as 'cardiac ballet'.

Torsades usually terminates spontaneously but frequently recurs and may degenerate into sustained VT and ventricular fibrillation (Fig.19.18).

Torsades results from a prolonged QT interval. Causes include congenital long-QT syndromes and drugs (e.g. anti-arrhythmics). Patients may also have reduced K^+ and Mg^{2+}.

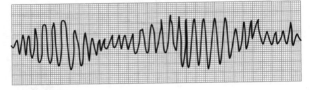

Fig. 19.18 Rhythm strip showing torsades.

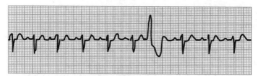

Rhythm strip 1—a single ventricular extrasystole.

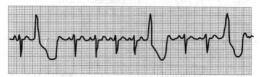

Rhythm strip 2—multiple, unifocal, ventricular extrasystole.

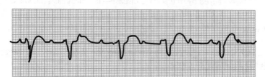

Rhythm strip 3—ventricular escape in the case of complete heart block.

Rhythm strip 4—agonal rhythm.

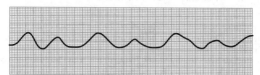

Rhythm strip 5—asystole.

Fig. 19.19 Rhythm strips showing ventricular rhythms.

P and T wave abnormalities

The P wave

Represents depolarization of the small muscle mass of the atria. The P wave is thus much smaller in amplitude than the QRS complex.

Normal

- In sinus rhythm each P wave is closely associated with a QRS complex.
- P waves are usually upright in most leads except aVR.
- P waves are <3 small squares wide and <3 small squares high.

Abnormal

- Right atrial hypertrophy will cause tall, peaked P waves.
  - Causes include pulmonary hypertension (in which case the wave is known as 'P pulmonale') and tricuspid valve stenosis.
- Left atrial hypertrophy will cause the P wave to become wider and twin-peaked or 'bifid'.
  - Usually caused by mitral valve disease—in which case the wave is known as 'P mitrale'.

The T wave

Represents repolarization of the ventricles. The T wave is most commonly affected by ischaemic changes. The most common abnormality is 'inversion' which has a number of causes.

Normal

- Commonly inverted in V_1 and aVR.
- May be inverted in V_1–V_3 as normal variant.

Abnormal

- Myocardial ischaemia or MI (e.g. non-Q wave MI) can cause T wave inversion. Changes need to be interpreted in light of clinical picture (Fig.19.20).
- Ventricular hypertrophy causes T inversion in those leads focused on the ventricle in question. For example, left ventricular hypertrophy will give T changes in leads V_5, V_6, II, and aVL.
- Bundle branch block causes abnormal QRS complexes due to abnormal pathways of ventricular depolarization. The corresponding abnormal repolarization gives unusually shaped T waves which have no significance in themselves.
- Digoxin causes a characteristic T wave inversion with a downsloping of the ST segment known as the 'reverse tick' sign. This occurs at therapeutic doses and is not a sign of digoxin toxicity.
- Electrolyte imbalances cause a number of T wave changes:
  - Raised K^+ can cause tall tented T waves
  - Low K^+ can cause small T waves and U waves (broad, flat waves occurring after the T waves)
  - Low Ca^{2+} can cause small T waves with a prolongation of the QT interval. (Raised Ca^{2+} has the reverse effect)
  - Other causes of T wave inversion include subarachnoid haemorrhage and lithium use.

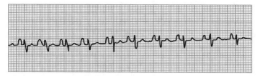

Rhythm strip 1—peaked P waves.

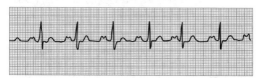

Rhythm strip 2—bifid P waves.

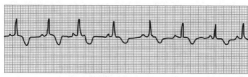

Rhythm strip 3—T wave inversion after myocardial infarction.

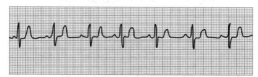

Rhythm strip 4—hyperkalaemia with peaked T waves.

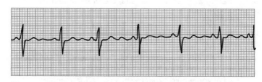

Rhythm strip 5—hyperkalaemia with small T waves and U waves.

Fig. 19.20 Rhythm strips showing some P and T wave abnormalities.

The ST segment

This is the portion of the ECG from the end of the QRS complex to the start of the T wave and is an isoelectric line in the normal ECG. Changes in the ST segment can represent myocardial ischaemia and, most importantly, acute MI (Fig.19.21).

ST elevation

The degree and extent of ST elevation is of crucial importance in ECG interpretation as it determines whether reperfusion therapy (thrombolysis or primary PCI) is considered in acute MI.

Causes of ST elevation

- Acute MI—convex ST elevation in affected leads (the 'tomb-stone' appearance), often with reciprocal ST depression in opposite leads.
- Pericarditis—widespread concave ST elevation ('saddle-shaped').
- Left ventricular aneurysm—ST elevation may persist over time.

ST depression

ST depression can be horizontal, upward sloping, or downward sloping.

Causes of ST depression

- Myocardial ischaemia—horizontal ST depression and an upright T wave. May be result of coronary artery disease or other causes (e.g. anaemia, aortic stenosis).
- Digoxin toxicity—downward sloping ('reverse tick').
- 'Non-specific' changes—ST segment depression which is often upward sloping may be a normal variant and is not thought to be associated with any underlying significant pathology.

Myocardial infarction

In the first hour following a MI, the ECG can remain normal. However, when changes occur, they usually develop in the following order:

- ST segment becomes elevated and T waves become peaked.
- Pathological Q waves develop.
- ST segment returns to baseline and T waves invert.

The leads in which these changes take place allow you to identify which part of the heart has been affected and, therefore, which coronary artery is likely to be occluded.

- *Anterior:* V_2–V_5.
- *Antero-lateral:* I, aVL, V_5, V_6.
- *Inferior:* III, aVF (sometimes II also).
- *Posterior:* the usual depolarization of the posterior of the left ventricle is lost, giving a dominant R wave in V_1. Imagine it as a mirror image of the Q wave you would expect with an anterior infarction.
- *Right ventricular:* often no changes on the 12-lead ECG. If suspected clinically, leads are placed on the right of the chest, mirroring the normal pattern and are labelled V_1R, V_2R, V_3R, and so on.

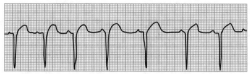

Rhythm strip 1—lead V_2 showing acute myocardial infarction.

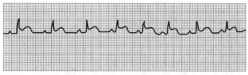

Rhythm strip 2—pericarditis. The ST elevation is usually described as 'saddle-shaped'.

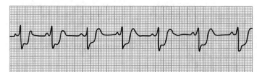

Rhythm strip 3—ischaemia.

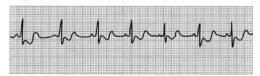

Rhythm strip 4—digoxin use showing the 'reverse tick'.

Fig. 19.21 Rhythm strips showing some ST segment abnormalities.

Hypertrophy

If the heart is faced with having to overcome pressure overload (e.g. left ventricular hypertrophy in hypertension or aortic stenosis) or higher systemic pressures (e.g. essential hypertension) then it will increase its muscle mass in response. This increased muscle mass can result in changes to the ECG.

Atrial hypertrophy

This can lead to changes to the P wave.

Ventricular hypertrophy

This can lead to changes to the cardiac axis, QRS complex height/depth, and the T wave.

Left ventricular hypertrophy (LVH)

- Tall R wave in V_6 and deep S wave in V_1.
- May also see left axis deviation.
- T wave inversion in V_5, V_6, I, aVL.
- Voltage criteria for LVH include:
  - R wave >25mm (5 large squares) in V_6
  - R wave in V_6 + S wave in V_1 >35mm (7 large squares).

Right ventricular hypertrophy

- 'Dominant' R wave in V_1 (i.e. R wave bigger than S wave).
- Deep S wave in V_6.
- May also see right axis deviation.
- T wave inversion in V_1–V_3.

Paced rhythms

Temporary or permanent cardiac pacing may be indicated for a number of conditions such as complete heart block or symptomatic bradycardia. These devices deliver a tiny electrical pulse to an area of the heart, initiating contraction. This can be seen on the ECG as a sharp spike (Fig.19.22).

Many different types of pacemaker exist, and can be categorized according to:

- The chamber paced (atria or ventricles or both).
- The chamber used to detect the heart's electrical activity (atria or ventricles or both).
- How the pacemaker responds—most are inhibited by the normal electrical activity of the heart.

On the ECG look for the pacing spikes which may appear before P waves if the atria are paced, before the QRS complexes if the ventricles are paced, or both.

🛈 Be careful not to mistake the vertical lines that separate the different leads on some ECG print-outs as pacing spikes!

▶ Paced complexes do not show the expected changes described elsewhere in this section. You are, therefore, unable to diagnose ischaemia in the presence of pacing.

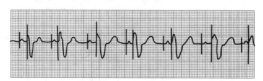

Fig. 19.22 Rhythm strip showing dual chamber pacing.

Peak expiratory flow rate (PEFR)

Peak expiratory flow rate (PEFR) is the maximum flow rate recorded during a forced expiration. Predicted readings vary depending on age, sex, height, and ethnicity (Fig.19.23).

See ➲ Chapter 18 for how to perform this test.

See Boxes 19.6 and 19.7 for other tests.

Interpreting PEFR

PEFR readings less than the patient's predicted, or usual best, demonstrate airflow obstruction in the large airways.

PEFR readings are useful in determining the severity, and therefore the most appropriate treatment algorithm, for asthma exacerbations:

- PEFR <75% best or predicted—moderate asthma attack.
- PEFR <50% best or predicted—acute severe asthma attack.
- PEFR <33% best or predicted—life-threatening asthma attack.

Reversibility testing

Improvement in PEFR or FEV$_1$ ≥15% following bronchodilator therapy (e.g. salbutamol) shows reversibility of airflow obstruction and can help to distinguish asthma from poorly reversible conditions such as COPD.

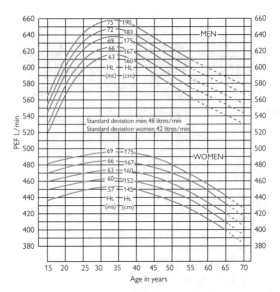

Fig. 19.23 Normal PEFR by age and gender. Image reproduced from the *Oxford Handbook of Clinical Medicine*, with permission.

Box 19.6 Gas transfer

- This test measures the capacity of a gas to diffuse across the alveolar–capillary membranes. This not only adds further clues to the nature of the lung disease but is also a measure of function which can give important prognostic information and help guide treatment
- DLCO (carbon monoxide diffusion capacity) measures the uptake from a single breath of 0.3% CO
- DLCO is reduced in interstitial lung disease (the fibrotic insterstitium limits gas diffusion) and emphysema (the total surface area available for gas transfer is reduced).

Box 19.7 Other lung function tests

Specialized lung function centres can calculate static lung volumes with a body plethysmograph or using helium rebreathe and dilutional techniques including:

- TLC—total lung capacity
- RV— residual volume.

Both can help when identifying patterns of lung disease and help assess patients prior to lung surgery.

Basic spirometry

Spirometry measures airflow and functional lung volumes; this can aid diagnosis of a number of conditions, but is primarily used to distinguish between restrictive and obstructive lung diseases.

Patients are asked to blow, as fast as possible, into a mouthpiece attached to a spirometer. This records the rate and volume of airflow.

Most spirometers are now hand-held computerized devices which will print a spirometry report for you and calculate normal values.

Two key values are:
- FEV_1: forced expiratory volume in the first second.
- FVC: forced vital capacity—the total lung volume from maximum inspiration to maximum expiration, in forced exhalation.

Flow volume loops can also be generated from spirometry data and show the flow at different lung volumes. These are useful in distinguishing intra- and extra-thoracic causes of obstruction as well as to assess for small airways obstruction (Figs 19.24 and 19.25).

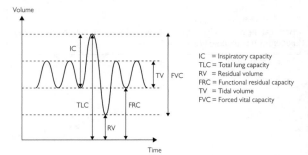

IC = Inspiratory capacity
TLC = Total lung capacity
RV = Residual volume
FRC = Functional residual capacity
TV = Tidal volume
FVC = Forced vital capacity

Fig. 19.24 Normal pattern of lung volumes.

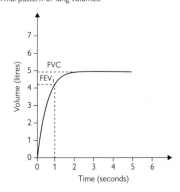

Fig. 19.25 Spirogram showing normal volume–time graph.

Common patterns of abnormality

Obstructive

When airflow is obstructed, although FVC may be reduced, FEV_1 is much more reduced, hence the FEV_1/FVC ratio falls. It can also take much longer to fully exhale. Note that FVC can be normal in mild/moderate obstructive conditions.

Conditions causing an obstructive defect include COPD, asthma, and bronchiectasis as well as foreign bodies, tumours, and stenosis following tracheotomy (all localized airflow obstruction).

Restrictive

The airway patency is not affected in restrictive lung conditions, so the PEFR can be normal. But the FEV_1 and FVC are reduced due to the restrictive picture.

Conditions causing a restrictive defect include fibrosing alveolitis of any cause, skeletal abnormalities (e.g. kyphoscoliosis), neuromuscular diseases (e.g. motor neuron disease), connective tissue diseases, late-stage sarcoidosis, pleural effusion, and pleural thickening (Table 19.1 and Fig. 19.26).

Table 19.1 Obstructive vs restrictive spirometry results

Pattern	FEV_1	FVC	FEV_1/FVC ratio	TLC	RV
Obstructive	↓	↔/↓	<75%	↑ (or ↔)	↑
Restrictive	↓	↓	>75%	↓	↓

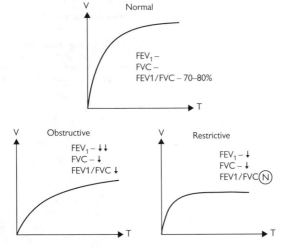

Fig. 19.26 Spirograms showing obstructive and restrictive volume/time curves.

Arterial blood gas analysis

A systematic approach

The printout from the ABG machine can have a bewildering number of results. Initially, just focus on the pH, $PaCO_2$, and HCO_3^- in that order (Box 19.8):

pH

- Is it low (acidosis) or high (alkalosis)?

$PaCO_2$

- If $PaCO_2$ is raised and there is acidosis (pH <7.35) you can deduce a respiratory acidosis.
- If $PaCO_2$ is low and there is alkalosis (pH >7.45) then the lack of acid gas has led to a respiratory alkalosis.
- If $PaCO_2$ is low and there is acidosis then the respiratory system will not be to blame and there is a metabolic acidosis.
  - Confirm this by looking at the HCO_3^-, it should be low.
- If $PaCO_2$ is high or normal and there is alkalosis, there must be a *metabolic alkalosis*.
  - Confirm this by looking at the HCO_3^-, it should be raised.

PaO_2

🕦 Note what FiO_2 the patient was breathing when the sample was taken.

Hypoxia is PaO_2 of <8.0kPa and can result from a ventilation–perfusion mismatch (e.g. pulmonary embolism) or from alveolar hypoventilation (e.g. COPD, pneumonia).

- Type I respiratory failure: hypoxia and $PaCO_2$ <6kPa.
- Type II respiratory failure: hypoxia and $PaCO_2$ >6kPa.

▶ If the PaO_2 is very low consider venous blood contamination.

Compensatory mechanisms

Mechanisms controlling pH are activated when acid–base imbalances threaten. Thus, renal control of H^+ and HCO_3^- ion excretion can result in compensatory metabolic changes. Similarly, 'blowing off' or retaining CO_2 via control of respiratory rate can lead to compensatory respiratory changes.

▶ A compensated picture suggests chronic disease.

Box 19.8 Reference ranges
- pH 7.35–7.45
- $PaCO_2$ 4.7–6.0kPa
- PaO_2 10–13kPa
- HCO_3^- 22–26mmol/L
- Base excess –2 to +2.

Table 19.2 Obstructive vs restrictive spirometry results

Pattern	pH	TLC	RV
Respiratory acidosis	↓	↑	↔ (↑ if compensated)
Metabolic acidosis	↓	↔ (↓ if compensated)	↓
Respiratory alkalosis	↑	↓	↔ (↓ if compensated)
Metabolic alkalosis	↑	↔ (↑ if compensated)	↑

Box 19.9 Anion gap
- $(Na^+ + K^+) - (HCO_3^- + Cl^-)$
- Normal range = 10–18 mmol/L.

Acidosis

A relative excess of cations (e.g. H^+), unless adequately compensated, will result in acidosis (more correctly acidaemia) (Table 19.2).

Respiratory acidosis
- pH ↓.
- $PaCO_2$ ↑.
- HCO_3^- may be ↑ if compensated.

Conditions which can lead to respiratory acidosis:
- COPD, asthma, pneumonia, pneumothorax, pulmonary fibrosis.
- Obstructive sleep apnoea.
- Opiate overdose (causing respiratory depression).
- Neuromuscular disorders (e.g. Guillain–Barré, motor neuron disease).
- Skeletal abnormalities (e.g. kyphoscoliosis).
- Congestive cardiac failure.

Metabolic acidosis
- pH ↓.
- HCO_3^- ↓.
- $PaCO_2$ may be ↓ if compensated.

It is useful to calculate the anion gap to help distinguish causes of metabolic acidosis (Box 19.9).

An increased anion gap points to increased production of immeasurable anions.

Conditions which can lead to metabolic acidosis:
- Raised anion gap.
  - Diabetic ketoacidosis
  - Renal failure (urate)
  - Lactic acidosis (tissue hypoxia or excessive exercise)
  - Salicylates, ethylene glycol, biguanides.
- Normal anion gap.
  - Chronic diarrhoea, ileostomy (loss of HCO_3^-)
  - Addison's disease
  - Pancreatic fistulae
  - Renal tubular acidosis
  - Acetazolamide treatment (loss of HCO_3^-).

Alkalosis

A relative excess of anions (e.g. HCO_3^-), unless adequately compensated, will result in alkalosis (more correctly alkalaemia). (See Box 19.10.)

Respiratory alkalosis

- pH ↑.
- $PaCO_2$ ↓.
- HCO_3^- may be ↓ if compensated.

Conditions which can lead to respiratory alkalosis:

- Hyperventilation, secondary to:
  - Panic attack (anxiety)
  - Pain.
- Meningitis.
- Stroke, subarachnoid haemorrhage.
- High altitude.

Metabolic alkalosis

- pH ↑.
- HCO_3^- ↑.
- $PaCO_2$ may be ↑ if compensated.

Conditions which can lead to metabolic alkalosis:

- Diuretic drugs (via loss of K^+).
- Prolonged vomiting (via acid replacement and release of HCO_3^-).
- Burns.
- Base ingestion.

Box 19.10 Mixed metabolic and respiratory disturbance

- In clinical practice patients can develop a mixed picture where acid–base imbalance is the result of both respiratory and metabolic factors
- For example, in critically ill patients, hypoventilation leads to low PaO_2, and O_2 depleted cells then produce lactic acid.

Cerebrospinal fluid (CSF)

CSF is produced by the choroid plexus lining the cerebral ventricles and helps cushion and support the brain. Samples are usually obtained by lumbar puncture (see Table 19.3).

Normal adult CSF

- Pressure 6–20cm H_2O.
- Red cells nil.
- Lymphocytes $\leq 5 \times 10^6$/L.
- Neutrophils nil.
- Protein <450 mg/L.
- Glucose 2.5–4.0mmol/L (2/3 of blood glucose).
- IgG 5–45mg/L.

▶ CSF glucose is abnormal if <50% of blood glucose level.

🌑 Premature babies, newborns, children, and adolescents have different normal ranges.

Table 19.3 Characteristics of CSF according to underlying pathology

Pathology	Appearance	Protein	Glucose (CSF:blood ratio)	Cells
Bacterial meningitis	Turbid	↑	↓	Neutrophils
Viral meningitis	Clear	↔/↑	↑/↔	Lymphocytes
Viral encephalitis	Clear	↔/↑	↓	Lymphocytes
TB meningitis	Fibrin webs		↓↓	Lymphocytes Neutrophils
Fungal meningitis	Clear/turbid		↓	Lymphocytes
Subarachnoid haemorrhage	Xanthochromia	↔/↑	↑	Red cells
Multiple sclerosis	Clear	↔/↑	↔/↑	Lymphocytes
Guillain–Barré syndrome	Clear	↑	↔/↑	
Cord compression	Clear	↑	↔	
Malignancy	Clear	↑	↓	Malignant

Urinalysis

Bedside dipstick urinalysis offers speedy and non-invasive testing that can help with the diagnosis of common conditions such as UTIs and diabetes mellitus. Samples can be sent to the laboratory for further analysis, including MCS.

Dipstick

Dipstick testing gives semi-quantitative analysis of:
- Protein (normally negative).
- Glucose (normally negative).
- Ketones (normally negative).
- Nitrites (normally negative).
- Blood (normally negative).
- Leukocytes (normally negative).
- Bilirubin (normally negative).
- pH (normally acidic with range 4.5–8.0).
- Specific gravity (normal range 1.000–1.030).

Notes on dipstick testing
- ▶ Test the urine within 15 minutes of obtaining the sample.
- ▶ Urine pregnancy testing is equally convenient and is indicated in females of child-bearing age who present with abdominal symptoms.
- ▶ Various foods (e.g. beetroot) and drugs (e.g. rifampicin, tetracyclines, levodopa, phenytoin, chloroquine, iron supplements) can change the colour of urine.

Microscopy, culture, and sensitivity (MCS)

Microscopy allows identification of bacteria and other microorganisms, urinary casts (formed in the tubules or collecting ducts from proteins or cells), crystals, and cells (including renal tubular, transitional epithelial, leukocytes, and red blood cells). Organism growth and antibiotic sensitivities and can also be determined.

▶ Asymptomatic bacteriuria is more common in pregnancy (up to 7%) and can lead to pyelonephritis and potential fetal complications.

Characteristic urinalysis findings
- UTIs: nitrites, leukocytes.
- Diabetes mellitus: glucose.
- Diabetic ketoacidosis: ketones.
- Cholestasis (obstructive jaundice): bilirubin.
- Pre-hepatic jaundice: urobilinogen.
- Glomerulonephritis: protein, blood.
- Renal stones: blood.
- Renal carcinoma: blood.
- Nephrotic syndrome: protein ++.
- Renal TB: leukocytes, no organisms grown (sterile pyuria).
- Sexually transmitted diseases (chlamydia, gonorrhoea): sterile pyuria.

Pleural fluid

Fluid in the pleural space can be classified as:
- Exudate (protein content >30g/L).
- Transudate (protein content <30g/L).

At borderline levels, if the pleural protein is >50% serum protein then the effusion is an exudate. Blood, pus, and chyle (lymph with fat) can also form an effusion. See ➲ Chapter 18.

See Box 19.11 for other tests.

Transudate causes

Transudates are largely cause by increased venous or reduced oncotic pressure.
- Heart failure.
- Hypoproteinaemia (liver failure, malabsorption, nephrotic syndrome).
- Hypothyroidism.
- Constrictive pericarditis.
- Meig's syndrome (ovarian fibroma and pleural effusion).

Exudate causes

Exudates are largely caused by increased capillary permeability.
- Pneumonia.
- Empyema.
- Malignancy (lung, pleura, lymph).
- Pulmonary infarction.
- TB.
- Systemic lupus erythematosus (SLE).
- Rheumatoid arthritis.
- Dressler's syndrome (post MI).

Box 19.11 Other pleural fluid tests

- Microscopy, culture (conventional and TB culture), and sensitivity (Gram stain, Ziehl–Nielsen stain)
- Cytology (malignant cells)
- Biochemistry.
  - Protein
  - Glucose (reduced if rheumatoid or pneumonia related)
  - Amylase (increased in pancreatitis)
  - LDH (lactate dehydrogenase—increased in empyema, malignancy, rheumatoid disease).

Ascitic fluid

Fluid in the peritoneal cavity can result in abdominal distension and breathlessness. As with pleural fluid, analysis of an aspirated sample can aid diagnosis. See ➲ Chapter 18 for ascitic tap guidance. See Box 19.12 for other tests.

Common causes of ascites
- Decompensated liver disease.
- Infection (bacterial peritonitis, TB).
- Malignancy (liver, ovary).
- Right-sided heart failure.
- Pancreatitis.
- Portal vein occlusion.
- Nephrotic syndrome.

Serum/ascites albumin gradient (SAAG)
- SAAG = [serum albumin] − [ascitic fluid albumin].

SAAG >11g/L
- Portal hypertension.
  - Cirrhosis
  - Alcoholic hepatitis
  - Cardiac ascites
  - Budd–Chiari syndrome
  - Portal vein thrombosis
  - Massive liver metastases
  - Acute fatty liver of pregnancy.

SAAG <11g/L
- Infection.
- Malignancy.
- Nephrotic syndrome.
- Pancreatitis.
- Biliary ascites.
- Serositis in connective tissue disease.
- Bowel perforation or infarction.

Box 19.12 Other ascitic fluid tests
- MCS (bacterial peritonitis, TB)
  - Spontaneous bacterial peritonitis = neutrophils >250/mm^3.
- Cytology (malignant cells, macrophages in inflammatory diseases)
- Biochemistry (protein, glucose, amylase).

Further tests you may consider for a patient with ascites include: liver function tests, clotting, urea and electrolytes (U&Es), hepatitis serology, auto-antibodies, ultrasound scan of liver/pelvis, OGD (varices).

Other investigations

Notes

The procedures detailed in this chapter are for information only—to enable the reader to discuss it with their patients, to prepare the patients correctly, and to identify those patients who may or may not be suitable.

▶ The reader is not expected to perform any of these investigations themselves and this chapter is not intended as a resource for those learning how to perform the investigations.

Computed tomography (CT)

Indications

- Indications are manifold and too numerous to list. See 'making best use of a department of clinical radiology' via ℛ http://www.rcr.ac.uk

Contraindications

- The standard radiation protection precautions apply.
- The patient must be able to lie flat and still.
- Examinations of the chest usually require the patient to hold their breath.

Technology

- The CT scanner (Fig. 20.1) houses an x-ray tube and rows of detectors which spin at 2–3 revolutions per second, creating a force of up to 25g.
- As the patient is moved slowly through the machine, spiral data is acquired which is then converted to 'slices' by the CT software and sent to PACS or a connected workstation for viewing.

Procedure

This depends on the part of the body examined and the indications for the examination.

- If indicated, the patient may be given oral contrast an hour or more before the examination.
- The patient lies (usually supine) on the scanner table.
  - Head-first for head and neck; feet-first for almost everything else.
- 'Scout' views are acquired which are brief swipes across the area of interest. The resultant images are then used by the radiographer to set the parameters for the scan.
- Most examinations involve intravenous iodinated contrast being given. Note that the contrast is not radioactive.
  - This is usually delivered via an intravenous cannula by an automatic pump-injection device, controlled remotely by the radiographer
  - Contrast may be hand-injected immediately before some scans.
- Depending on the part of the body examined, the patient may be asked to hold their breath via speakers in the machine. Microphones within the scanner allow the staff in the control room to hear the patient.
- The scan itself lasts no more than a couple of minutes.
- Time taken to transfer the patient onto the scanner and set up the intravenous injections will vary.

Risks

- Intravenous contrast reactions include anaphylaxis and nephrotoxicity.
  - Intravenous contrast should not be given to patients with renal impairment unless in special circumstances. Check local guidance.
- Extravasation of intravenous contrast (pain, swelling, erythema).

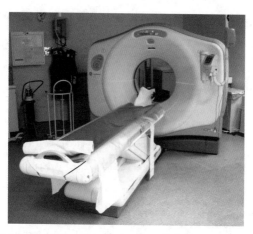

Fig. 20.1 A typical CT scanner. Note the presence of metal in the room (oxygen cylinder, etc.) indicating this is not an MRI scanner and the lead apron indicating that x-rays are being used. The CT scanner has a laser marker (shown) to help with patient positioning, an MRI scanner does not.

Patient preparation

- Fasting: not required for most examinations.

Magnetic resonance imaging (MRI)

Indications

- Indications are manifold and too numerous to list. See 'making best use of a department of clinical radiology' via ℅ http://www.rcr.ac.uk

Contraindications

- As there is no ionizing radiation, radiation precautions do not apply.
- ▶ All ferromagnetic materials will be strongly attracted to the scanner creating missiles which may prove extremely dangerous. MRI-safe trolleys, resuscitation equipment and wheelchairs must be employed.
- ▶ Implanted ferromagnetic devices, aneurysm clips, and retained foreign bodies (e.g. shrapnel or metallic fragments in the eyes) will also move towards the scanner potentially causing major injury.
- ▶ Although electronic pacemakers are not made of ferromagnetic material, they may be 'reset' or stop altogether. The next generation of very new pacemakers is 'MRI safe' – check with the manufacturer.
- A strict questionnaire is employed before anyone (staff or patient) is allowed near the magnet. If in doubt, access is denied.
- Magnetic tape and credit cards may be 'wiped' by the magnet.
- ▶ Many brands of mascara contain ferromagnetic filaments which may heat and cause burns to the eyelids.
- ▶ Caution should also be taken with tattoos; some contain iron.
- The patient must be able to lie flat and still for the duration of the scan.
- Most scanners are relatively tight; larger patients may not fit—check the size and weight limits with your local department.

Technology

- The MRI scanner (Fig. 20.2) houses a very large electromagnet which is always on.
- Radiowaves are produced by the machine which interact with hydrogen atoms in the patient. Radiowaves are, in turn, produced by the interaction with the hydrogen atoms and are detected by the machine which converts the data into images. The scanner has no internal moving parts.

Procedure

- This depends on indications and the part of the body examined.
- The patient lies on the scanner table. 'Coils' may be placed over the body part of interest.
- Most examinations do not involve intravenous contrast being given. If this is given, contrast containing gadolinium (Gd) is usually used.
  - This is usually hand-injected immediately before the scan.
- Depending on the part of the body examined, the patient may be asked to hold their breath via speakers in the machine.
- The scan itself can last up to 40–50 minutes for some body parts.

Risks

- ▶ *Nephrogenic systemic fibrosis (NSF):* linked to gadolinium exposure in 2006. Symptoms may begin up to 3 months from exposure and may include pain, swelling, erythema, fibrosis of internal organs, and death. Patients with renal impairment are at greatest risk (no cases recorded in those with GFR >60) and at least 9 hours of haemodialysis is required to remove it from the bloodstream. See latest guidance at 🖰 http://www.rcr.ac.uk.
- *Metallic artefacts:* twisting or movement of artefacts within the body.
- *Biological effects:* the magnetic fields employed may induce voltages within the body. The most common effect is 'magnetophosphenes' or visual flashes seen by the patient as the optic nerve is stimulated. Stimulation of other nerves and muscles may occur.
- *Tissue burns:* may occur if conducting loops (e.g. ECG leads) are in contact with skin.
- *Temperature:* the oscillating voltages create tissue heating. Overall body temperature may rise by 0.3°C.
- *Noise:* may reach up to 95dB. Headphones or earplugs are usually worn.
- *Claustrophobia:* experienced by up to 10% of patients.

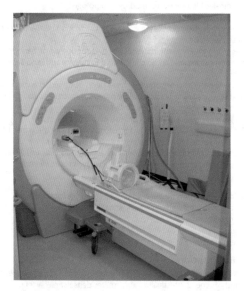

Fig. 20.2 A typical MRI scanner. Note the absence of metal in the room (oxygen cylinder, etc.). A 'coil' is shown within the scanner.

Barium swallow and meal

Barium swallows examine the oropharynx, oesophagus, and gastro-oesophageal junction; barium meals examine the stomach and first part of the duodenum. Swallows and meals are usually performed together as described here.

Indications

- Investigation of oesophageal and gastric pathology. Indications include dysphagia, odynophagia, dyspepsia, weight loss, anaemia, epigastric mass, partial obstruction.
- ▶ Always consider alternatives (e.g. OGD, MRI).

Contraindications

- *Absolute:* lack of informed consent, complete bowel obstruction, suspected perforation (a water-soluble contrast may be used instead).
- *Relative:* a large degree of patient cooperation is required so those unable to understand or follow instructions are unsuitable. Also, the patient must be able to stand for the duration of the examination and to lie supine if necessary.

Procedure

The patient drinks barium whilst the oesophagus and stomach are imaged fluoroscopically. Usually performed by a radiologist.

- The patient stands in the fluoroscopy machine (Fig. 20.3).
- A gas-producing agent is ingested (e.g. Carbex®) and the patient is asked not to belch.
- Images are taken as the patient swallows mouthfuls of barium. The patient must be able to hold the liquid in their mouth and swallow on command.
- Once views of the oesophagus have been obtained, the machine is tilted so the patient is supine. The patient is instructed to roll and tilt as images of the stomach are obtained from several angles.
  - ❶ This requires a certain degree of patient fitness.
- The time taken depends to a degree on how easily the patient follows the commands, although usually lasts 15–20 minutes.
- After the procedure, the patient may eat and drink as usual but is advised to open their bowel regularly to avoid barium impaction.

Risks

- Leakage of barium through an unsuspected perforation.
  - Intraperitoneal and intramediastinal barium has a significant mortality rate.
- Barium impaction (causing large bowel obstruction) or barium appendicitis.

Other information

- ▶ A barium study will prevent a CT examination of the same area for a period of time as intestinal barium creates dense streak artefact.

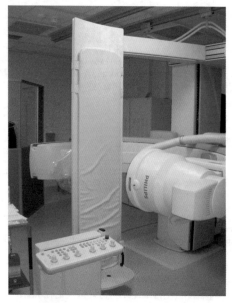

Fig. 20.3 A typical fluoroscopy room set up for an upper gastrointestinal barium examination.

Patient preparation

- *Fasting:* nil by mouth for 6 hours before the examination.
- *Bowel preparation:* none required.
- *Smoking:* patients are asked not to smoke for 6 hours before the procedure as this increases gastric motility.

Water-soluble contrast examinations

- In the case of recent surgery, suspected perforation, or investigation of a leak, water-based iodinated contrast is used instead of barium. Examples include Gastrograffin, Urograffin, Niopam, and Omnipaque.
- A single-contrast examination is performed (i.e. the gas-producing agent is not given) and many of the 'standard' views are not included.
- In contrast to the barium examinations, these studies can be carried out on patients who are frail and/or have recently had surgery.
- Intraperitoneal or intramediastinal water-soluble contrast does not carry the risks of barium but aspiration of the contrast can result in pulmonary oedema and lung fibrosis. Hypersensitivity is also a risk.

Barium follow-through

Indications

- Investigation of small bowel pathology, particularly suspected Crohn's disease and strictures. Indications include pain, diarrhoea, malabsorption, partial obstruction, and anaemia.
- ▶ Always consider alternatives (e.g. MRI, small bowel enema).

Contraindications

- Absolute: lack of informed consent, complete small bowel obstruction, suspected perforation (a water-soluble contrast may be used instead).

Procedure

The patient drinks barium and the small bowel is intermittently imaged until the barium has reached the caecum. Usually performed by a radiologist or senior radiographer.

- The patient is given a mixture of barium to drink.
- The exact mixture given to the patient varies between centres and between radiologists. Some add Gastrograffin to the barium, which has been shown to reduce transit time. Many add 20mg of metoclopramide to the mixture which enhances gastric emptying.
- Once the barium has been consumed, the patient is asked into the fluoroscopy room and images are taken of the small bowel with the patient lying supine (Fig. 20.4).
- Real-time fluoroscopy is employed to assess small bowel motility.
- Images are taken every 20–30 minutes until the barium has reached the colon.
- The radiologist may use a plastic 'spoon' or similar radio-lucent device to press on the patient's abdomen to separate loops of bowel.
- Additional images of the terminal ileum are usually obtained, often with the patient supine, and many radiologists also acquire an 'overcouch' plain abdominal radiograph with compression applied to the lower abdomen.
- The time taken depends on the small bowel transit time and, although usually an hour, patients are advised to allow up to 3 hours for the appointment.
- After the procedure, the patient may eat and drink as usual but is advised to keep their bowel moving to avoid barium impaction.

Risks

- Leakage of barium through an unsuspected perforation.
  - Intraperitoneal barium causes hypovolaemic shock and has a 50% mortality rate. Of those that survive, 30% have adhesions.
- Barium impaction (causing large bowel obstruction) or barium appendicitis.
- Medication effects (see 'other information').

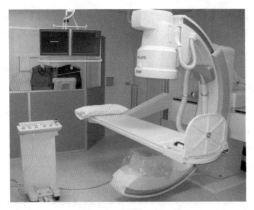

Fig. 20.4 A typical fluoroscopy room set up for an upper gastrointestinal barium examination.

Patient preparation

- Fasting: nil by mouth for 12 hours before the examination.
- Bowel preparation: laxative (usually Picolax® or similar) taken 12 hours before.

Other information

- Metoclopramide aids gastric emptying. Extra-pyramidal side effects may occur, especially in young women, and there is a risk of acute dystonic reactions such as an oculogyric crisis. Contraindicated in patients with Parkinsonism/Parkinson's disease.
- ▶ A barium study will prevent a CT examination of the same area for a period of time as intestinal barium creates dense streak artefact.

Barium enema

▶ The following refers to the standard 'double contrast' barium enema.

Indications

- Investigation of colonic pathology. Indications include pain, melaena, anaemia, palpable mass, change in bowel habit, failed colonoscopy, and investigation of remaining colon in the case of a known colonic tumour.
- ▶ Always consider alternatives (e.g. colonoscopy, CT colonography).

Contraindications

- Absolute: lack of informed consent, possible perforation, pseudomembranous colitis, toxic megacolon, biopsy via rigid sigmoidoscope within 5 days, biopsy via flexible endoscope within 1 day.
- Relative: barium meal within 7–14 days, patient frailty or immobility.
    - ▶ The procedure requires a large amount of patient cooperation. The patient must be able to lie flat and to turn over easily
    - ▶ The patient must be able to retain rectal barium and air.

Procedure

The colon is coated with barium, then inflated with air and images are taken from several different angles. Performed by a radiographer or radiologist.

- The patient lies in the left lateral position on the fluoroscopy table (Fig. 20.5).
- The operator may perform a digital rectal examination before starting.
- A rectal tube is placed, attached to a bag of barium sulphate. The barium is run into the colon under x-ray guidance until it reaches the right colon.
- The barium is drained.
- Intravenous buscopan or, if contraindicated, glucagon is given.
- The colon is inflated with air (or with CO_2 in some centres).
- The patient is instructed to roll and is tilted as images are acquired.
- Once the images are obtained, the colon is deflated and the patient can go to the bathroom to empty their bowel and shower if necessary.
- The examination may last 15–30 minutes.
- The patient should be kept in the department until any medication side effects (e.g. blurred vision) have worn off.

Risks

- Perforation (increased risk in elderly, ulcerating lesions, systemic steroids, hypothyroidism, large bowel obstruction).
    - Intraperitoneal barium causes hypovolaemic shock and has a 50% mortality rate. Of those that survive, 30% have adhesions.
- Cardiac arrhythmia (secondary to the large bowel distension).
- Medication effects (see 'other information').

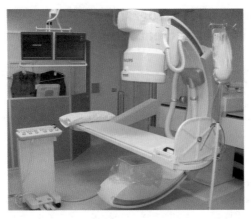

Fig. 20.5 A typical fluoroscopy room set up for a barium enema examination.

Patient preparation

- *Iron tablets:* stop 5 days before.
- *Constipating agents:* stop 2 days before.
- *Fasting:* low residue diet 2 days before, fluids only on the day before.
- *Bowel preparation:* laxative (usually Picolax®) taken at 08:00 and 18:00 on the day before.

Other information

- Buscopan is given to inhibit intestinal motility. Side effects include blurred vision, dry mouth, and tachycardia.
  - Contraindicated in angina, untreated closed angle glaucoma, prostatic hypertrophy, myasthenia gravis, paralytic ileus, pyloric stenosis
  - Glucagon is given if buscopan cannot be given. Risk of hypersensitivity and is contraindicated in phaeochromocytoma, insulinoma and glucagonoma.
- After the procedure, the patient may eat and drink as usual but is advised to keep their bowel moving to avoid barium impaction.
- ▶ A barium study will prevent a CT examination of the same area for a period of time as intestinal barium creates dense streak artefact.

Water-soluble contrast examinations

- In the case of recent surgery, suspected perforation, or investigation of a leak, water-based iodinated contrast is used instead of barium. Examples include Gastrograffin, Urograffin, Niopam, and Omnipaque.
- A single-contrast examination is performed (i.e. the colon is not inflated with air) and many of the 'standard' views are not included.
- No bowel preparation or fasting is needed.

Endoscopic retrograde cholangiopancreatography (ERCP)

Indications

- *Diagnostic:* largely superseded by safer modalities such as endoscopic ultrasound and MRI/MRCP. Diagnostic indications include sphincter of Oddi dysfunction and primary sclerosing cholangitis.
- *Therapeutic:* endoscopic sphincterotomy (biliary and pancreatic), removal of stones, dilation of strictures (e.g. PSC), stent placement.

Contraindications

- Lack of informed consent, uncooperative patient, recent attack of pancreatitis, recent MI, history of contrast dye anaphylaxis, severe cardiopulmonary disease, futility (anticipated short-term survival with no features of sepsis).

Procedure

An ERCP involves the passage of an endoscope into the duodenum. The endoscopist injects contrast medium through the ampulla of Vater via a catheter. Real-time fluoroscopy is used to visualize the pancreas and biliary tree. Selected images are taken.

- Dentures (if present) are removed.
- Patient is given anaesthetic throat spray (lidocaine) and sometimes intravenous sedation/analgesia (e.g. midazolam, pethidine).
- Patient lies on the couch in a modified left lateral ('swimmers') position with the left arm adducted and the right abducted. The endoscope is inserted as for OGD.
- Under x-ray guidance, a polyethylene catheter is inserted into the biliary tree and contrast instilled to outline the pancreatic duct as well as the common bile duct and its tributaries.
- Procedure time varies from 30–90 minutes.

Risks

- Pancreatitis (2–9% of procedures of which 10% of cases are mild–moderate). Serum amylase is temporarily raised in 70%.
- Infection (ascending cholangitis, acute cholecystitis, infected pancreatic pseudocyst, liver abscess, endocarditis).
- Bleeding, perforation of the oesophagus, duodenum, bile ducts.
- Failure of gallstone retrieval.
- Prolonged pancreatic stenting associated with stent occlusion, pancreatic duct obstruction, pseudocyst formation.
- Basket impaction around a large gallstone (may require surgery).

Patient preparation

- *Blood tests:* Liver enzymes, platelets, and clotting are checked prior to the procedure.
- *Fasting:* 4 hours except in the case of an emergency.
- *Antibiotic prophylaxis:* recommended for:
  - Patients in whom biliary decompression is unlikely to be achieved at a single procedure (e.g. dilatation of dominant stricture in multifocal sclerosing cholangitis or hilar cholangiocarcinoma)
  - Consider also in patients with severe neutropenia (<0.5 x 10^9/L) and/or profound immunocompromise.

Other information

- Intravenous sedation and analgesia is usually administered and the back of the throat is sprayed with local anaesthetic.
- Hilar biliary obstruction demonstrated on MR or CT imaging may be more successfully stented using percutaneous transhepatic cholangiography (PTC) than ERCP.
- Equipment allowing direct cholangioscopy (with the potential for sampling lesions) is becoming more widely available.

Ultrasound

Indications
- Indications are manifold and too numerous to list. See 'making best use of a department of clinical radiology' via ✎ http://www.rcr.ac.uk

Contraindications
- For some examinations, the patient must be able to cooperate with the operator and a degree of mobility is often required.
- Ultrasound becomes increasingly less diagnostic at greater depths. Images of deeper structures in large individuals are often unobtainable and this should be borne in mind when considering who to refer.

Technology
- The ultrasound probe houses a piezoelectric crystal which both projects and receives high-frequency sound waves. Much like radar, the 'echoes' are converted to images by the machine's software.
- Ultrasound cannot image through gas and requires a semi-liquid 'gel' between the probe and skin surface for optimum imaging.
- A typical ultrasound machine is shown in Fig. 20.6.

Procedure
- This depends on the part of the body examined and the indications.
- Time taken will vary depending on part of body examined, patient cooperation, and complexity of the findings. Most examinations last between 5–20 minutes.

Risks
- ▶ There is no published evidence that ultrasound has ever directly caused harm to a patient.
  - The acoustic output of modern machines, however, is much greater than previously used.
- *Heating:* some equipment can produce temperature rises of 4°C in bone. Most equipment in clinical use is unlikely to increase tissue temperature more than the 1.5°C which is considered 'safe'.
- *Non-thermal hazard:* ultrasound has been demonstrated to produce tiny gas pockets and bubbles in animal models. Neonatal lung is considered vulnerable to this but there is no evidence that diagnostic ultrasound can cause harm to other tissues.
  - Machines have a 'mechanical index' (MI) displayed on screen which acts as a guide to the operator.

Patient preparation
Depends on the indication and body part being examined.
- *Abdomen:* patients are usually asked to fast for 6 hours prior to the examination. This ensures distension of the gallbladder and prevents the epigastric structures being obscured by overlying bowel gas.
- *Renal tract/pelvis:* a full bladder is usually required. A full bladder creates an 'acoustic window', effectively pushing small bowel aside so that deeper structures (e.g. ovaries) may be seen.

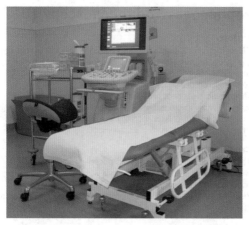

Fig. 20.6 A typical ultrasound room.

Oesophagogastroduodenoscopy (OGD)

Indications

- *Diagnostic:* haematemesis, dyspepsia (>55 years old), oesophageal and gastric biopsies (malignancy?), duodenal biopsies (coeliac?), surveillance (e.g. Barrett's oesophagus), persistent nausea and vomiting, iron-deficiency anaemia, dysphagia.
- *Therapeutic:* treatment of bleeding lesions, variceal banding and sclerotherapy, stricture dilatation, polypectomy, EMR, palliative intent (e.g. stent insertion, laser therapy), argon plasma coagulation for suspected vascular lesions.

Contraindications

- *Absolute:* lack of informed consent, possible perforation, haemodynamic instability, hypoxaemia with respiratory distress, uncooperative patient.
- *Relative:* pharyngeal diverticulum, recent myocardial infarction, or pulmonary embolus.

Procedure

- Endoscopic examination of the mucosa of the oesophagus, stomach, and proximal duodenum. Allows direct visualization, mucosal biopsies, and other therapeutic procedures.
- Dentures (if present) are removed.
- Patient is given anaesthetic throat spray (lidocaine) +/– intravenous sedation (e.g. midazolam).
- Patient lies on the couch in the left lateral position.
- Hollow mouthpiece is inserted to protect the patient's teeth and facilitate instrument passage.
- Endoscope (9.5–12.5mm diameter, max 120cm long) is slowly advanced and 'swallowed' by the patient (Fig. 20.7 shows a typical scope).
- Scope advanced and manipulated by the endoscopist to allow visualization of the target structures.
- Procedure time varies but averages 5–15 minutes.

Risks

- Minor throat and abdominal discomfort.
- Cardiorespiratory: arrhythmias, MI, respiratory arrest, shock, death.
- Infection (uncommon, e.g. aspiration pneumonia).
- Perforation (around 0.03% with a mortality of 0.001% during diagnostic procedures, higher with therapeutic procedures).
  - Overall 2–3% perforation with oesophageal dilatation; mortality 1%.
- Bleeding (caution with low platelet counts and high INR).
- Medication effects including anaphylactic reactions and over-sedation.
- Dental trauma.

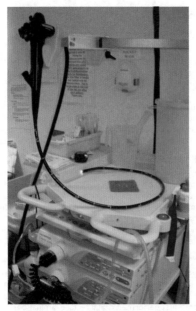

Fig. 20.7 A typical gastroscope.

Patient preparation

- *Fasting:* 4 hours prior to the procedure unless in an emergency situation.
- *Antibiotic prophylaxis:* none for OGD. See other topics for comparison.

Other information

- Dosages of benzodiazepines and opiates should be kept to a minimum to achieve sedation, with lower doses being prescribed in elderly patients.
- The pharynx is sprayed with local anaesthetic spray. There is some evidence that the combination use of local anaesthetic spray and intravenous sedation increases the risk of aspiration pneumonia.
- ⚠ Patients who have had intravenous sedation should not drive, operate heavy machinery, or drink alcohol for 24 hours afterwards.

Colonoscopy

Indications

- *Diagnostic:* gastrointestinal bleeding, iron-deficiency anaemia, chronic diarrhoea, lower abdominal symptoms (chronic constipation, lower abdominal pain, bloating), evaluation of known IBD, surveillance for cancer (in IBD patients/after colonic polypectomy/after curative intent resection of colorectal cancer), screening for colorectal cancer.
- *Therapeutic:* polypectomy (including endoscopic mucosal resection techniques: EMR), angiodysplasia treated with argon plasma coagulation (APC), decompression of volvulus or pseudo-obstruction, dilatation or stenting of strictures or malignant colonic obstruction.

Contraindications

- *Absolute:* lack of informed consent, toxic megacolon, fulminant colitis, colonic perforation.
- *Relative:* acute diverticulitis, symptomatic large abdominal aortic aneurysm, immediately post-op, recent myocardial infarction or pulmonary embolus, severe coagulopathies.
  - Colonoscopy can be performed safely in pregnancy but should be deferred in most instances unless requiring immediate resolution.

Procedure

Colonoscopy is an endoscopic examination of the mucosal surface from the anal canal to the terminal ileum.

- Patient lies on the couch in the left lateral position with knees bent.
- Endoscopist first performs a digital rectal examination.
- Sedation (e.g. midazolam) may be given with monitoring of oxygen saturation. Intravenous analgesia (e.g. pethidine) is also given.
  - Increasing use of either no sedation (with improved techniques such as 'Scopeguide®') or inhaled nitric oxide.
- Lubricated colonoscope (about 12mm wide and 185cm long) is passed rectally. Air is insufflated. Water-jet may also be used via the scope.
  - Figure 20.8 shows a typical scope.
- Aim is to pass to the terminal ileum.
- Duration varies but averages at about 20 minutes.

Risks

- Perforation (0.2–0.4% diagnostic; higher with therapeutic procedures).
- Bleeding (1 in 1000).
- Abdominal distension, medication effects (allergic reactions, nausea, vomiting hypotension, respiratory depression).
- Rarities: infection, post-polypectomy coagulation syndrome: pain, peritoneal irritation, leukocytosis and fever, splenic rupture, small bowel obstruction.

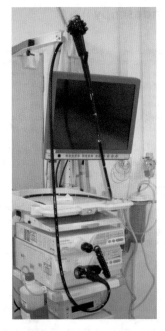

Fig. 20.8 A typical colonoscope.

Patient preparation

- *Iron and constipating agents:* discontinue iron tablets 7 days and constipating agents 4 days prior to the procedure.
- *Anticoagulant and antiplatelet therapy:* in the case of a planned polypectomy or other therapeutic procedure, refer to BSG guidelines on the management of anticoagulant and antiplatelet therapy: ✍ http://www.bsg.org.uk.
- *Antibiotic prophylaxis:* none for colonoscopy. See other topics for comparison.
- *Bowel preparation:* the colon must be empty. Protocols vary but usually include prescribing 1 sachet of sodium picosulphate (Picolax®) for the morning and afternoon of the day before procedure.

Other information

- The introduction of the bowel cancer screening programme has meant that endoscopists need to pass a 'driving test' to demonstrate high-level competency to perform safe screening colonoscopy.
- Endoscopic mucosal resection (EMR) is used for larger or difficult flat polyps. The lesion is lifted by submucosal injection of gelofusin, adrenaline, and dye followed by snare resection. Polyps can then be retrieved by 'Roth' baskets for histological assessment.

Capsule endoscopy

Indications

- Obscure gastrointestinal bleeding (in patients with negative gastroscopy and ileocolonoscopy), known or suspected small bowel Crohn's disease, assessment of coeliac disease, screening and surveillance for polyps in familial polyposis syndromes.

Contraindications

- Lack of informed consent, intestinal strictures, adhesions, obstruction.
- Diverticula or fistulae that may block the passage of capsule endoscope.
- Cardiac pacemakers or other implanted electronic devices.
- Difficulty in swallowing tablets or known swallowing disorders.
- Pregnancy (lack of available safety data).
- ► Patients with obstructive symptoms or known or suspected inflammatory bowel disease should have either a small bowel follow through or a patency capsule (dissolves after 36 hours), with an abdominal radiograph taken 24 hours post ingestion to identify whether capsule is retained within small bowel.
  - If retained, capsule endoscopy is not appropriate
  - ► Capsule retention can occur even in the absence of strictures on barium or MR-enteroclysis study.

Procedure

- The capsule (Fig. 20.9) consists of a disposable, wireless, miniature video camera which can be swallowed and passes through the intestine by peristalsis.
- Images taken by the capsule are transmitted, via sensors secured to the abdominal wall, to a battery-powered data recorder worn on a belt.
- The capsule leaves the stomach within 30 mins and the patient is allowed to drink after 2 hours and eat after 4 hours.
- The external equipment (Fig. 20.10) is removed after 8 hours (approximate battery life) by which time the capsule has reached the caecum in 85% of patients.
- The capsule is expelled naturally after 24–48 hours in the patient's stool and does not need to be collected.
- Data from the recorder is downloaded onto a computer workstation which allows approximately 50,000 images to be viewed as a video.

Risks

- Capsule retention (may cause partial or complete intestinal obstruction; highest risk in patients with extensive small bowel Crohn's disease, chronic usage of NSAIDs, abdominal radiation injury, previous major abdominal surgery, or small bowel resection).
- Capsule endoscopy may also fail in patients with dysphagia, gastroparesis, and anatomical abnormalities of the gastrointestinal tract.

(a) (b)

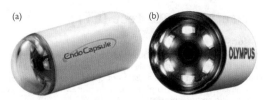

Fig. 20.9 Examples of a typical capsule endoscope. It is shaped to be easy to swallow and has its own light-source.

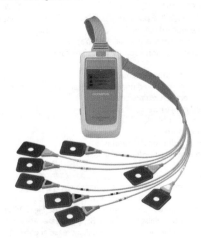

Fig. 20.10 The external equipment which the patient will wear, consisting of a data-recorder and electrodes.

Patient preparation

- *Iron supplements:* stop taking 1 week prior to procedure.
- *Constipating agents:* stop 4 days before the procedure.
- *Fasting:* patients are fasted for 8–12 hours prior to the procedure and may receive bowel prep (taken day before procedure).

Other information

- Incomplete examination in 10–25% of cases.
  - Presence of dark intestinal contents in distal small bowel may impair visualization of mucosa
  - Delayed gastric emptying and small bowel transit can lead to exhaustion of battery life before capsule reaches ileocaecal valve.
- Capsules are being developed to screen for oesophageal varices and may be more 'guided' in future as the technology develops.
- Positive findings on capsule endoscopy may be reachable using either single- or double-balloon enteroscopy or spiral enteroscopy.

Exercise tolerance test (ETT)

Indications

- Assessment of chest pain in those with known coronary artery disease (there is no longer a role for ETT in patients presenting with chest pain who do not have a history of coronary artery disease).
- Assessment of haemodynamic response in those with known valvular disease who are asymptomatic.
- Diagnosis of exertionally induced arrhythmias or syncope.

Contraindications

- Any undiagnosed or previously unknown murmur (patient should undergo echocardiogram first).
- Severe aortic stenosis (risk of syncope).
- Hypertrophic cardiomyopathy with significant outflow obstruction (risk of syncope).
- Severe hyper- or hypo-tension.
- Unstable angina (should undergo coronary angiography).
- Known severe left main stem disease.
- Untreated congestive cardiac failure.
- Complete heart block.
- Aortic aneurysm.
- Acute myocarditis or pericarditis.
- Any recent pyrexial or 'flu-like' illness.

Procedure

- ECG electrodes are put on the patient's chest and a sphygmomanometer cuff on an arm.
- The patient is asked to walk on a treadmill (see Fig. 20.11) connected to the computer whilst their ECG, BP, and heart rate are monitored. The speed and incline of the treadmill increase according to set protocols:
  - Bruce protocol: for assessment of physically fit and stable patients with suspected coronary artery disease. Seven stages starting at a 10% gradient at 1.7mph and increasing to 22% gradient and 6mph
  - Modified Bruce protocol: used in elderly patients or those who have been stabilized after a suspected episode of unstable angina. Starts at 1.7mph and 0% gradient and increases the gradient slowly to 10%.
- Termination of the test depends on the results seen.

Risks

- Risks are those associated with exercise and include:
  - Arrhythmia, cardiac ischaemia, myocardial infarction, syncope.

Patient preparation

- No specific preparation is required.
- Patients are asked not to eat or drink for 3 hours prior to the test.
- Comfortable clothing and shoes should be worn.

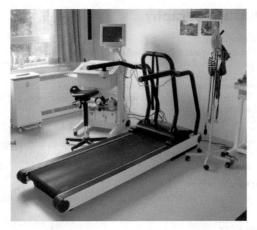

Fig. 20.11 A typical ETT room.

Indications for termination of procedure

- Patient requests to stop.
- *Symptoms:* fatigue, angina, dizziness, significant breathlessness.
- *Signs:* drop in oxygen saturations <94%, target heart rate achieved, hypotension during exercise (e.g. BP <100mmHg), significant hypertension (e.g. BP >200mmHg).
- *ECG:* any atrial or ventricular arrhythmia, frequent ventricular ectopics, new AV or bundle branch block, ST segment shift >1mm.

Causes of false positive results or low specificity

- Often due to difficulty interpreting results as result of resting ST segment abnormalities:
  - Wolff–Parkinson–White syndrome, LBBB, atrial fibrillation, left ventricular hypertrophy, digoxin therapy, hyperventilation, biochemical electrolyte abnormalities (e.g. hypo- or hyperkalaemia), cardiomyopathies, LV outflow obstruction.
- Beta-blocker therapy prevents the appropriate heart rate/blood pressure response during testing.

Echocardiography

Indications

- Myocardial infarction: assess wall motion and left ventricular function.
- Valvular heart disease: assess competency and examine prostheses.
- Embolic stroke: to exclude a cardiac embolic source.
- Infective endocarditis: look for valvular vegetations.
- Cardiomyopathy: assess ventricular dilatation/hypertrophy and function.
- Congenital heart disease.
- Pericardial disease.
- Pericardial effusion: distribution of fluid and suitability for drainage.
- Aortic disease: severity and site of aneurysm, dissection, or coarctation.

Contraindications

- The only contraindication is lack of patient consent or if the patient is unable to cooperate.

Technology

- Echocardiography is an ultrasound examination and uses the same technology (and machines) as general ultrasound (Fig. 20.12).
- Ultrasound becomes increasingly less diagnostic at greater depths and cannot see through lung. Images in large individuals are often suboptimal and the heart may not be seen at all in patients with hyperinflated lungs.
- See Box 20.1 for other types.

Procedure

- Time taken will vary depending on examinations performed and complexity of the findings.
- Most examinations last between 20–25 minutes.
- With the patient lying on their left side, the operator uses a hand-held probe coated with gel to examine the heart usually via the anterior chest and epigastrium.

Risks

- ▶ There is no published evidence that ultrasound has ever directly caused any harm to a patient.
- *Heating:* some equipment can produce temperature rises of 4°C in bone. Most equipment in clinical use is unlikely to increase tissue temperature more than the 1.5°C which is considered 'safe'.
- *Non-thermal hazard:* ultrasound has been demonstrated to produce tiny gas pockets and bubbles in animal models but there is no evidence that diagnostic ultrasound can cause harm to tissues other than neonatal lung.

Patient preparation

- No preparation is required.

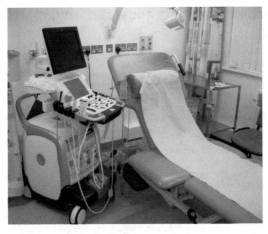

Fig. 20.12 A typical echocardiography room.

Box 20.1 Other types of echocardiography

Along with 2-dimensional trans-thoracic echocardiography, the following methods exist:

- *3D:* uses computer software to produce a 3-dimensional image. Useful in left-ventricular functional assessment especially post-infarction
- *4D:* 3D imaging with real-time movement captured
- *TOE:* trans-oesophageal echo is an invasive procedure. It requires written consent and is performed under sedation with local anaesthetic spray to the upper pharynx. The probe is covered, lubricated, and passed into the oesophagus behind the heart. It is used to visualize the posterior cardiac structures. The investigation of choice for infective endocarditis
- *Stress echo:* Used to assess myocardial ischaemia at 'rest' and during 'stress'. Stress is induced by exercise or (more commonly) by an intravenous infusion of dobutamine in a controlled environment
- *Bubble studies:* Used to assess for intra-cardiac shunts such as atrial or ventricular septal defects or patent foramen ovale. Air bubbles are agitated in a syringe and injected into a peripheral vein. The Valsalva manoeuvre is performed and, if a shunt exists, bubbles will be seen moving from the right side of the heart to the left.

Coronary angiography and angioplasty

Indications

- *Diagnostic:* unstable or refractory angina, acute coronary syndrome, positive or inconclusive stress testing.
- *Emergency therapeutic:* where possible, patients presenting with acute ST-elevation myocardial infarction should have primary coronary intervention rather than thrombolysis.
- *Elective therapeutic:* suitable 'target lesion' identified on diagnostic coronary angiogram.

Contraindications

- *Absolute:* refusal of patient consent.
- *Relative:* acute renal failure, pulmonary oedema, known radiographic contrast allergy, uncontrolled hypertension, active GI haemorrhage, acute stroke, and untreated coagulopathy.

Procedure

- A typical cardiac interventional suite is shown in Fig. 20.13.
- Percutaneous access via a guide needle into a peripheral artery (most commonly the radial artery).
- Guide catheter is introduced, the tip is placed at the coronary ostium, radio-opaque contrast is injected, and real-time x-ray is used to visualize the blood flow through the coronary arteries.
- The coronary guidewire is inserted through the catheter into the coronary artery using x-ray guidance.
- The guidewire tip is passed across the site of stenosis.
- The balloon catheter is passed over the guidewire until the deflated balloon lies across the target lesion.
- The balloon is then inflated and compresses the plaque and stretches the artery wall. A stent (wire mesh tube) can be inserted using a similar technique and be left in place maintaining the arterial lumen.
- The guidewire, catheter, and sheath are carefully removed.
- The patient should remain supine for 4 hours following the procedure unless an arterial closure device has been used.

Risks

- *Minor:* contrast allergy, vasovagal reaction, haemorrhage and haematoma at puncture site, thrombosis formation, false aneurysm, arteriovenous fistulation, pulmonary oedema, and renal failure due to contrast nephropathy.
- *Major:* limb ischaemia, coronary artery dissection, aortic dissection, ventricular perforation, air or atheroma embolism, ventricular arrhythmias, failure of procedure and need to proceed to CABG.
- Death (<1 in 1000).

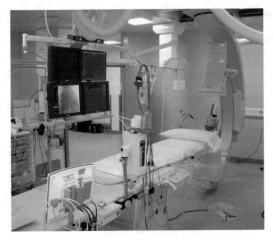

Fig. 20.13 A typical cardiac interventional suite.

Patient preparation

- Pre-procedure checklist: written consent, group and save, ECG, check FBC/clotting/urea and electrolytes.

Other information

- Coronary angioplasty is associated with increased thrombus formation (balloon inflation disrupts the intima, revealing pro-thrombotic cores of plaques), therefore antiplatelet therapy is necessary.
- Patients will need to have long-term antiplatelet therapy; usually lifelong aspirin 75mg od, but they will also need clopidogrel 75mg od (see local guidelines: usually 3 months for bare metal stents and 12 months for drug-eluting stents or angioplasty after acute coronary syndrome).
- Patients with renal failure should be carefully considered. Iodinated contrast can be nephrotoxic and renal decompensation may occur following coronary angiography/plasty. The risk can be minimized by hydration before and after the procedure. Renal function should be carefully monitored. Check local guidelines.

Bronchoscopy

Indications

- *Diagnostic:* histology/cytology in suspected lung malignancy, sample mediastinal lymphadenopathy, alveolar lavage (e.g. tuberculosis), transbronchial biopsy (e.g. diffuse lung disease).
- *Therapeutic:* placement of guidewire for local radiotherapy, direct treatment (e.g. diathermy to strictures).
  - Placement of endobronchial stents and the removal of foreign bodies are usually accomplished at rigid bronchoscopy under GA.

Contraindications

- *Absolute:* cardiovascular instability, life-threatening arrhythmia, severe hypoxaemia, respiratory failure with hypercapnia (unless intubated/ventilated).
  - *Rigid bronchoscopy contraindications:* unstable neck, severely ankylosed cervical spine, severely restricted temporomandibular joints.
- *Relative:* uncooperative patient, recent myocardial infarction, tracheal obstruction, un-correctable coagulopathy.
  - Transbronchial biopsy with caution in uraemia, SVCO, pulmonary hypertension (risk of bleeding).

Procedure

Bronchoscopy is an endoscopic examination of the bronchial tree.

- Patient sits on the couch, leaning back comfortably.
- Sedation (e.g. midazolam) may be given with monitoring of oxygen saturation. Atropine may also be given to decrease secretions.
- Pharynx is anaesthetized with aerosolized lidocaine.
- Lubricated bronchoscope (about 6mm wide and 60cm long) is passed nasally or orally with use of a bite-block (Fig. 20.14).
- Brushings, biopsy, or lavage (50–100ml saline) may be performed.
- Duration varies but averages about 20–30 minutes.

Risks

- Bleeding from a biopsy site and transient fever (10–15%).
- Medication effects: respiratory depression, hypotension, arrhythmias.
- Topical anaesthesia: laryngospasm, bronchospasm, seizures, arrhythmias.
- Minor laryngeal oedema or injury with hoarseness, hypoxaemia in patients with compromised gas exchange (1–10%).
- Mortality is 1–4 in 10,000 patients.
- Transbronchial biopsy: pneumothorax (2–5%), significant haemorrhage (1%); death (12 in 10,000).

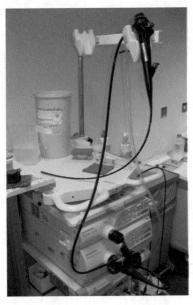

Fig. 20.14 A typical bronchoscope.

Patient preparation

- *Anticoagulant and antiplatelet therapy:* stop for 3 days. Clopidogrel should be stopped for 5 days.
- *Blood tests:* check clotting and full blood count.
- *Spirometry:* perform if underlying lung disease.
- *Fasting:* nil by mouth 2 hours before the procedure, no solids 4–6 hours before procedure.

Post-procedure

- *Oxygen:* supplemental oxygen for up to 1 hour.
- *Eating/drinking:* drink after 1 hour. If no problems, can eat.
- *Chest radiography:* only if dyspnoea or chest pain following biopsy (10% risk of pneumothorax).
- *Driving:* if had midazolam or similar, not to drive or operate heavy machinery for the rest of the day.

Index